A Secret at Windmill Cottage

BOOKS BY KRISTIN HARPER

DUNE ISLAND SERIES

Summer at Hope Haven
Aunt Ivy's Cottage
A Letter from Nana Rose
Lily's Secret Inheritance
My Grandmother's Inn
Aunt Violet's Locket
The Secret of Ruby's Lighthouse

A Secret at Windmill Cottage

Kristin Harper

Bookouture

Published by Bookouture in 2025

An imprint of Storyfire Ltd.
Carmelite House
50 Victoria Embankment
London EC4Y 0DZ

www.bookouture.com

The authorised representative in the EEA is Hachette Ireland
8 Castlecourt Centre
Dublin 15 D15 XTP3
Ireland
(email: info@hbgi.ie)

Copyright © Kristin Harper, 2025

Kristin Harper has asserted her right to be identified
as the author of this work.

All rights reserved. No part of this publication may be reproduced, stored in any retrieval system, or transmitted, in any form or by any means, electronic, mechanical, photocopying, recording or otherwise, without the prior written permission of the publishers.

ISBN: 978-1-83618-201-6
eBook ISBN: 978-1-83618-199-6

This book is a work of fiction. Names, characters, businesses, organizations, places and events other than those clearly in the public domain, are either the product of the author's imagination or are used fictitiously. Any resemblance to actual persons, living or dead, events or locales is entirely coincidental.

*Once more for my mother and my sisters—
in so many ways
you're always in the heart of these stories*

PROLOGUE

LATE AUGUST, TWENTY YEARS EARLIER

The teenager's bare feet skimmed the damp, velvety sand as she strode along the tidal flats, the sun warm on her face, the breeze lifting her hair from her shoulders.

This is my favorite place in the whole world, she thought, surveying the meandering network of rivulets and shallow pools, and the vast blue bay rippling gently in the distance to her right.

On her left, the golden dunes were crowned with aromatic wild roses. And up ahead, five or six spindle-legged little birds scuttled along the edge of the tidal river, which bisected the beach as it lazily wound its way inland.

Not only was the scenery magnificent, but the girl never felt as strong and special and carefree as when she was summering at the cottage with her aunt and uncle.

I wish August wasn't almost over already. The end of the season always seemed to come too fast, and this year leaving Dune Island until the following June felt unbearable.

I can't wait until Aunt Lydia and Uncle Albert retire and move here permanently. Then I'll be able to visit them at

Thanksgiving. I can still go beachcombing in the chilly weather, but afterward, instead of drinking lemonade on the porch with Aunt Lydia, we'll have hot chocolate in the windmill loft... she daydreamed wistfully, completely unaware that before the week ended, her life would change forever.

ONE

Caitlin Hines set her suitcase down on the tiled foyer floor and pulled the door shut behind her.

"Hello?" Melanie called, a note of alarm in her voice before she poked her head into the living room. "Caitlin! What are you doing back from the east coast already?"

"Sorry, didn't mean to startle you." She shrugged off her jacket. The autumn weather was much warmer here in Santa Fe than it had been in the mountains of New Hampshire. "I decided to catch a flight today instead of waiting till tomorrow morning."

"You should've let me know you changed your plans," Melanie scolded. "I would've picked you up."

Caitlin, who prided herself on being self-reliant, replied, "Thanks, but I'd never expect you to drive to the airport during rush hour. You're already doing me a big enough favor by letting me stay here."

Three weeks ago, a malfunctioning dishwasher in the apartment above Caitlin's had flooded her apartment and rendered it unlivable. Technically, Caitlin's landlord was responsible for providing alternative living arrangements. But since her landlord happened to be a friend of a friend, she didn't feel comfortable pushing the issue legally. The "alternative living arrangement" he suggested was that Caitlin stay with a family member until mid or late December, which was how long he estimated it would be before he could afford to hire a contractor to make repairs.

The landlord didn't know that moving in with her family wasn't practical. Her mom had died when Caitlin was six, and her father and stepmother lived in Florida, so Caitlin's stepbrother, Charlie, was the only family member living locally. She couldn't imagine staying with him, his wife, their three young children, two large dogs, and an untold number of bunny rabbits overnight, much less for two or three months. And as a nonprofit fundraising consultant, Caitlin didn't have any wiggle room in her budget to pay for temporary housing. So, when Melanie, whom Caitlin had once mentored at work, offered to let her stay in her two-bedroom apartment for a nominal fee, she'd gratefully but hesitantly accepted.

She appreciated Melanie's hospitality, but Caitlin hadn't lived with a roommate since college, and she considered herself to be a very private, independent person. Melanie, on the other hand, was an over-sharer. Which really wouldn't have bothered Caitlin that much, if only Melanie hadn't expected Caitlin to disclose almost every detail of *her* private life, too.

Caitlin tried to strike a healthy balance between maintaining her own personal boundaries and not offending her host by cutting their conversations short, but it wasn't always easy. Especially because she truly felt for Melanie, sensing that her constant chatter and nosy questions were actually the result of loneliness; her boyfriend had recently broken up with her, and Caitlin sometimes heard her sobbing in her bedroom after midnight.

Although Caitlin had gone through her own share of breakups over the years, she'd never been even a fraction as despondent as Melanie seemed to be. Maybe that was because Caitlin tried never to let down her guard. Or because she was usually the one who did the breaking up, instead of the guy ending it with her. It also might have been that her romantic relationships typically hadn't run long or deep enough to fragment her heart when they ended. But most likely, Caitlin had never been devastated by a breakup because she didn't really expect to find true love in the first place, so she wasn't crushed when it didn't happen.

Yet regardless of her personal experience, Caitlin still felt sorry for Melanie, and did her best to lend her a sympathetic ear. She also tried to provide a distraction by cooking with her after work or hanging out and watching movies, figuring that the food bank where she usually volunteered would manage for a few weeks, and that she could always catch up later on her pleasure reading. On the weekends, she even invited Melanie to join her and her boyfriend, Jonathan, when they went hiking, to art galleries, or out for dinner.

But after her long, three-stop cross-country flight, Caitlin was drained, and she hoped to take a shower and unwind alone in her room for the evening without engaging in a long conversation first.

"So, tell me all about it. How was your aunt's funeral?" Melanie's voice was unusually loud and animated, and when Caitlin turned from hanging her jacket in the closet, she noticed Melanie's cheeks were flushed. "I mean, I'm sure it was sad and everything, but was there a good turnout?"

A good turnout? It almost sounded as if she was asking about one of the fundraising presentations they helped their clients host, but Caitlin recognized the question was well-intentioned.

"Yes, it was sad, but Aunt Lydia had strong faith that she was going to a far better place, and I think she was ready, so the service was also very beautiful and hopeful. My aunt was almost eighty, and most of her friends and family members her age have already passed on, or they aren't in good health and couldn't attend, so it was a small group of us. But one of her nursing assistants came and she shared a few anecdotes about her, which was very touching. Her two nephews from her side of the family were there, too."

Caitlin thanked Melanie for asking about the funeral and then changed the subject. "There was so much turbulence on the way back that the flight attendants only came around with the beverage cart once. I'm dying for a glass of water."

She started toward the kitchen, but Melanie stepped in front of her. "I'll bring you one."

"That's okay, I can get it—you don't have to treat me like I'm a guest," Caitlin said with a chuckle.

Glancing anxiously over her shoulder toward the kitchen, Melanie insisted, "Trust me, you don't want to go in there. I've been cooking. It's a disaster zone." She practically pushed Caitlin to the sofa. "Have a seat."

I've been sitting all the way across the country, thought Caitlin, settling onto a cushion as Melanie disappeared into the kitchen. *But I suppose I can spend a few minutes catching up with her before I crash for the night.*

She pulled her phone from her purse and glanced at the time: 7:26. *I wonder why Jonathan hasn't checked in with me yet?* Usually, he called her at 6:00, during his evening commute, to chat or to invite her to dinner. At first, this habit had felt stifling to Caitlin, who'd thought he was coming on too strong for someone she'd only been casually dating, but lately, his persistence and reliability had begun to grow on her.

He really is a sweetheart, she reflected fondly. *Most men wouldn't want a chatterbox like Melanie tagging along on their dates and monopolizing the conversation or interrogating him about his life, but he's been so kind and patient. I should give him a call and let him know I came back early. Maybe I'll invite him out for dinner tomorrow night, just the two of us...*

Melanie bustled into the room again, handed Caitlin a glass of water, and plonked herself down on the sofa. "I'm dying to know what you found out at the meeting with the estate attorney." She bluntly asked, "Did you and your aunt's nephews inherit a fortune?"

Taken aback, Caitlin replied, "I-I don't feel comfortable disclosing the specifics of her Trust. But yes, her nephews received a nice sum of money." The two young men on Lydia's side of the family had been designated as the beneficiaries of her retirement accounts, and they'd also been awarded what was left of the proceeds from the sale of the home she'd owned before moving into an assisted living facility.

Melanie furrowed her brows. "What about you? Didn't she leave you any money?"

"Not exactly... but she did bequeath me her summer place in Hope Haven."

"*The* Hope Haven? On Dune Island, in Massachusetts? The place where presidents go on vacation?" Melanie slapped her thighs. "Who-hoo, lucky you!"

"Lucky" wasn't the word Caitlin would've used to describe how she felt when she'd learned she'd inherited Lydia's summer cottage. How she felt was utterly overwhelmed. Burdened. Maybe even a little resentful—which in turn, made her feel very ungrateful. But instead of confiding these emotions to Melanie, she agreed, "Yes, it's a very generous gift."

"It's *huge*. You never told me she had a summer place in Hope Haven," Melanie chided, as if Caitlin had neglected an obligation to disclose this information sooner. "I thought your aunt and uncle were schoolteachers. How did they ever afford to buy a vacation home on Dune Island?"

Refraining from rolling her eyes at Melanie's personal question about Lydia's finances, Caitlin figured it wouldn't hurt to share more about her aunt's home.

"The property was an investment, and they didn't exactly vacation there—they worked. Their place was the main house in a little colony of six cottages, which they also owned. They lived in New Hampshire, but they spent summers on the island, leasing out the cottages to guests. They planned to move there year-round after they retired. But then..." Caitlin paused as memories of one of the most difficult periods in her family's life came rolling back.

"But then... *what?*" questioned Melanie.

"My uncle got cancer and my aunt had to take an extended leave from work to care for him. They couldn't keep up with the mortgage on the summer property, so they sold off the surrounding cottages and they just kept the main one. They still planned to settle there, but ten years ago my uncle died and then my aunt started showing signs of dementia. So she had to move into an assisted living facility near her home in New Hampshire."

Even though she knew her aunt had received excellent care during the final decade of her life, it made Caitlin sad to visit Lydia during her rare trips back to New England—and those visits became even more heart-rending as her aunt's dementia progressed.

I kind of feel like I lost Aunt Lydia twice. The first time was when it became clear she no longer recognized me at all, and the second time was when she died... Caitlin reflected pensively, but Melanie was impatient to hear more details about her inheritance.

"Has the cottage sat unused the whole time your aunt was in an assisted living facility?"

"No. Her nephews had it renovated and then they hired a property management company to rent it out during the summertime."

The income generated by the rental had been used to cover the costs of Lydia's care. Apparently, Lydia's nephews had assumed that once she passed on, they'd inherit her summer property, and they'd been looking forward to collecting the rental income for themselves. So, as Caitlin discovered during the group meeting with the estate attorney after the funeral, they were more than a little disgruntled that Lydia had bequeathed the cottage to her, instead.

Considering the stipulation she put on my inheritance, I almost wish Aunt Lydia had left it to them, Caitlin brooded. She'd barely had time to think about what her aunt had asked her to do.

Melanie's question pulled her from her worrisome thoughts. "Did you ever get to go there on vacation?"

"Yes. When I was in high school, I spent a few summers helping my aunt clean the cottages in between guests and stuff. But then my family moved to the Southwest, so it wasn't convenient for me to go to the island anymore," claimed Caitlin. It was a flimsy excuse, but she couldn't admit the real reason why she'd never returned to Dune Island.

It was too dark. Too painful.

"What's the cottage like? Does it have an ocean view?"

"No. It's within walking distance of the bay, but it's only one story tall, so you can't see over the trees and shrubbery to the water." Describing it, Caitlin felt a swell of nostalgia for the cottage she used to love so much—before everything changed. "There's a windmill on the property, though, and—"

"A windmill?" interrupted Melanie. "For electricity?"

"Not a wind turbine. A wind*mill*, you know, like the kind you'd see in the Netherlands," explained Caitlin. "The original landowner was a Dutch miller, but over the years, the property switched hands several times. In the sixties, the owners who built the guest cottages removed almost all its functioning parts and installed electricity so they could use the first story as their rental office."

"That sounds cool! Do you have photos?"

Caitlin lifted her phone from where she'd set it on the coffee table and pulled up a photo from the internet. Angling it toward Melanie, she pointed to the weathered, silver-gray shingled house with an octagonal, conical-topped windmill right beside it, taller than the house but complementing it. Both the windmill and the house had cornflower-blue doors and trim.

"That's my aunt's house, and that's the windmill, obviously. And there are the cottages, which, as you can see, are just a little smaller than hers."

"Aww, how sweet," cooed Melanie. "All the cottages are identical."

"Yeah, except for the doors and trim. The colors were different so the guests could identify them. There's the yellow cottage, the turquoise cottage, the lavender cottage, and so on. The new owners had to agree not to change them or to alter their exteriors in any substantial way."

"Just look at those window flower boxes, and that picket fence around the yard. It's so charming." Melanie hinted, "I'd love to visit, especially in summertime."

"I'd say you have a standing invitation, but I plan to sell it before next summer."

"Sell it?" Melanie squawked. "Why would you want to sell it?"

"Do you really need to ask me that?" Caitlin retorted. "Nonprofit consulting may be rewarding in a lot of other ways, but it's hardly what anyone would call a lucrative career."

"That's true. It's more like we get stipends than salaries," said Melanie, rolling her eyes. "But are you sure you want to give up the house entirely? Couldn't you like, keep renting it out? That way, you could still vacation in Hope Haven whenever you wanted. I'm sure you have a lot of memories from the summers you spent there, right?"

It was primarily *because* of her memories that Caitlin had decided to sell the cottage, but she didn't want to talk about that with Melanie—or with anyone else, for that matter. "Dune Island's a gorgeous place, but I don't want the hassle associated with owning a rental. Besides, I need a new transmission for my car a lot more than I need a vacation home." *And the quicker I sell the property, the quicker I'll be able to put all thoughts of Dune Island out of my mind again.*

"Pfft, forget the transmission. With the money you'll get from selling the place in Hope Haven, you'll be able to buy a brand new *car*—or two." Melanie rubbed her hands together, feigning greed. "You're putting the house on the market right away?"

"Not *right* away." Caitlin inadvertently mumbled aloud, "First I need to remodel the windmill."

"Why?"

Caitlin wished she hadn't let it slip that Lydia was requiring her to remodel the windmill, but it was too late to take back her words now. "Because even though the downstairs space in there was used as a rental office, the windmill doesn't have finished rooms or anything. It has exposed beams and the wood is gorgeous, but you can't walk across the floor without shoes or you'll get splinters in your feet," she said. "The loft of the windmill is very bare bones, too, kind of like an attic, but my aunt used to talk about converting it into her own private sitting room. It's small—just one room on each floor—but I guess she thought it could be homey. She wanted to install a picture window upstairs so she could have a full-fledged ocean view while she knitted or read or just took some time alone for herself..."

Caitlin paused, feeling uncomfortable. She'd already shared more about her inheritance than she'd intended. "Anyway, a stipulation in the Trust is that before I sell the place—and even if I keep it—I have to go there to oversee the remodeling of the windmill."

"Aww, your aunt's sitting room must have meant an awful lot to her if she wanted you to carry out her wishes posthumously," remarked Melanie.

"Mm," Caitlin murmured noncommittally. She swallowed the last of her water and scooted to the edge of her seat, about to stand up, but Melanie prattled on.

"And I suppose if you have a quirky feature like a windmill next to your house, it should serve a practical purpose, otherwise it's just wasted space." She pressed, "So when are you going to get started on the remodel?"

"I don't know." Caitlin hadn't been to Dune Island since she was seventeen, and she loathed the idea of returning. "Probably in the spring, if I have enough time in between campaigns."

"You just finished a campaign before you left for the funeral," Melanie pointed out. "It's unlikely the agency will assign you another one right away, since most of our clients don't kick off their annual appeals in the fourth quarter. So you could go to Dune Island *now*, if you wanted."

Caitlin drew back in surprise. Was Melanie hinting she wanted her to leave sooner than they'd agreed? She'd repeatedly said how much she'd loved having Caitlin staying with her, but maybe she hadn't been as sincere as she'd seemed. Or else when Caitlin was in New Hampshire for a few days, Melanie had realized how much she preferred living alone to having a roommate.

Caitlin could hardly blame her for that, but there was still no way she was going to travel to Dune Island already. She'd barely begun to wrap her head around the fact that she'd inherited Lydia's summer place; she was going to need at least five or six months to prepare herself to visit it again.

"I doubt I could find a carpenter at such short notice," she countered. But that was illogical, since most carpenters were busier in the spring and summer than in the colder months. So she embellished, "Besides, converting the windmill was my aunt's dream, so I don't want to rush through the remodel. Waiting until spring will give me plenty of time to come up with a design I know she would have loved."

"Yeah, that's true," agreed Melanie. "It'll give you time to take out a loan to fund the remodel, too."

As a matter of fact, her aunt had left her money specifically designated for the remodel, but Caitlin didn't mention it. "Plus, the weather will be warmer in the spring, which is better for—"

She was interrupted mid-sentence by a distinct clinking sound coming from the kitchen. Melanie hopped up from the sofa. "Uh-oh. Sounds like the mountain of dishes I left stacked in the sink is shifting. I'd better go clean up in there before everything slides to the floor."

"You want a hand?" offered Caitlin, also rising to her feet.

"Nope, I've got it. You should go to bed. You look sapped." Melanie plucked the water glass from Caitlin's hand. "Sleep well."

Once again, Caitlin got the feeling Melanie didn't exactly want her around, so she obligingly said, "Thanks, you, too."

Melanie scurried into the kitchen, and as Caitlin headed toward the spare room, she caught a glimpse of herself in the hallway mirror. Melanie was right: she looked frazzled. Her blue-gray eyes, which usually appeared large and limpid, seemed clouded and squinty; the layers of her tawny, face-framing mane had gone lifeless and flat; and weariness had wilted her pert mouth into an unintentional frown.

I really need a shower and eight straight hours of sleep. She pressed Jonathan's name on her phone display. *I'll give him a quick call now, so he won't try to reach me after I've collapsed for the night.*

At the same moment Caitlin heard Jonathan's ringtone in

the earpiece of her phone, a muffled ringtone also sounded in the living room. Turning, she realized it was coming from the sofa. She backtracked, slid her hand into the space between the cushions and pulled out Jonathan's phone.

What's this doing here? He used it to call me yesterday evening at six, so he must have left it behind sometime after then. But why would he come here when I'm away? There was only one explanation. She glanced at the overhead light in the foyer; it was shining brightly. The bulb had burned out last week, but neither she nor Melanie had been able to unscrew the fixture to replace it. *He must have dropped by to change the bulb for us, just like he promised he would.*

Pleased that for once she was dating a man who was true to his word, Caitlin thought, *No wonder he hasn't called me yet—he couldn't. He's probably going out of his mind looking for his phone.*

As tired as she was from her long day of travel, Caitlin decided she'd swing by Jonathan's place to return it to him. *I'd better let Melanie know I'm leaving so I don't scare her again when she hears me coming in.*

She shuffled into the kitchen and abruptly came to a halt, barely able to process what she was seeing. A half-empty skillet of paella was cooling on a trivet beside the stovetop. Two place settings of dirty dishes littered the table in the dining nook. And, in the center of the room, Jonathan was touching the small of Melanie's back, and her hands were clasped behind his neck.

They were kissing so aggressively that for a second, Caitlin felt embarrassed, almost as if she were intruding on their privacy, and she momentarily had the impulse to tiptoe from the room. But then a bitter taste stung her mouth and when she cleared her throat, Jonathan and Melanie sprang apart.

"Caitlin!" he exclaimed. With Melanie's lipstick smeared around his mouth, he looked clownish, and he sounded ridiculous, too, as he uttered the biggest cliché of all time, "This... this isn't what it looks like."

"What it looks like is that you and Melanie were kissing." Caitlin retorted sarcastically, "But if you weren't, then I must be more jetlagged than I thought I was, and I'm hallucinating."

Melanie layered her hands over her heart, her forehead puckering into an expression of earnestness. "I'm genuinely, truly sorry, Caitlin. I didn't want you to find out this way, but I didn't expect you back until tomorrow," she said. Then, she iterated the *second* tritest cliché of all time. "We didn't mean for this to happen."

"Yeah, it's not as if I planned it," asserted Jonathan. "Yesterday on my way home from work, I stopped by to replace the lightbulb in the foyer and we—"

"Spare me the details," Caitlin snapped, but Jonathan continued.

"To be honest, we spent most of last evening talking about *you*," he said dolefully. "Melanie was consoling me because I was so disappointed that the minute you finished the campaign you've been working on all year, you took off for New Hampshire alone."

"I went to my aunt's *funeral*, Jonathan, not on a singles' cruise!" sputtered Caitlin.

"Yeah, but did it ever occur to you to ask me to come with you for moral support?"

"Did it ever occur to *you* I needed time to process my aunt's passing by myself?" Caitlin shot back.

"Can I just say something?" interjected Melanie, one finger pointed in the air.

Since when does she ask permission to speak? Caitlin resolutely replied, "No, you can't. I don't want to hear another word from you, Melanie, and there's no need for you to say anything anyway. If you and Jonathan want to get together, please, be my guests. I'm through with both of you."

"Wait a second, Cait—" Jonathan started to say but Caitlin didn't let him finish.

"You know something, Jonathan? You really should be more careful about where you leave your phone," she advised, holding it up and moving toward him. "It could get lost. Or ruined."

Shame-faced, he extended his hand to accept it but at the last second, she swung her arm sideways and dropped the phone into the skillet of leftover paella. Then she spun on her heel to go pack her other suitcases.

Whether she was ready or not, and no matter how much she dreaded it, for the first time in twenty years, Caitlin was going back to Dune Island.

TWO

Before Caitlin's flight to Massachusetts she wound up staying at her brother's house after all.

The air mattress was tolerable the first night, and when her young niece, Maya, and nephews, Logan and Archie, got up in the morning, they scampered into the room to snuggle in bed with her, which Caitlin thought was very sweet. She figured being their auntie was probably the closest she'd ever come to having children of her own, and even at 6:00 in the morning, she loved lavishing them with attention.

But the moment she rose to make coffee they began jumping on the air mattress as if it were a trampoline. Unsurprisingly, it must have developed a slow leak because it partially deflated the second night she used it. Caitlin woke during the wee hours with her right hip and shoulder pressed against the hard, cold floor, and a crick in her neck. At sunrise, the children came in to cuddle again, and for the rest of the day, their amusing antics kept her so busy that she barely had a chance to sit down or to even think about her trip until she reached the airport.

Now, after flying overnight from Albuquerque to Boston,

and then driving a rental car from Boston to Hyannis, Caitlin was exhausted. She boarded the Dune Island ferry, parked on the vehicle deck and went upstairs, hoping the fresh air would help her feel more awake and gather her thoughts.

During peak season, the seats would've been filled with cheerful travelers sunning themselves, sipping beverages, and chatting as the vessel crossed the scintillating aquamarine waters of Dune Island Sound. But on a cloudy, misty weekday in October, the weather deck was nearly empty except for Caitlin and a group of six people who appeared to be tourists. Although she didn't understand the language they were speaking, their excitement was obvious from the way they grinned as they stood at the railing and pointed to the greenish-gray oblong shape of the fog-enshrouded island barely visible in the distance.

Twenty years ago, Caitlin would have been on pins and needles with anticipation, too. She smiled, remembering how her uncle Albert would greet her inside the ferry terminal with a bear hug.

"Your aunt wanted to come, too, but she couldn't leave the guests on their own," he'd say. Then he'd hand her an insulated thermal bag and joke, "She thought you might be hungry after your long voyage at sea."

The food Lydia packed always included a note that said, "Welcome to your island home, Caitlin—I'm so glad you're here!" Nothing ever tasted as delicious as her first, simple lunch of the season; a tuna fish sandwich, chips, and a pickle, which she shared with her uncle as they inched toward the cottage in the slow-moving summer traffic.

Today, however, her stomach was knotted with apprehension about returning to Hope Haven. So instead of focusing on what lay ahead, she tried to concentrate on putting her feelings about Jonathan and Melanie behind her.

She was still more than a little ticked off at them. Oddly,

however, she found she wasn't nearly as angry about their betrayal as she was about their timing. *If they want to be together, that's fine with me. They're both so needy they make a perfect pair*, she thought. *I just wish they would've waited until after my ceiling was repaired to get involved with each other, so I wouldn't have to scramble to Massachusetts just because I need a place to stay...*

Yet as much as she regretted being forced to make the trip, Caitlin recognized how privileged she was to inherit the cottage just when she needed it most. Not only was the housing a godsend right now, but once she sold the property, she'd have enough money to move out of her crummy apartment for good and buy a place of her own. She hoped to help her brother and sister-in-law purchase a more suitable home for their growing family, as well. But while she was thankful deep down, Caitlin's gratitude was tinged with conflicting emotions and confusion.

It seems strange that Aunt Lydia bequeathed the cottage to me instead of to her nephews, she ruminated as she took a deep breath of the tangy, salty air. The two men were Lydia's blood relatives, whereas Caitlin was related only through Lydia's marriage to Caitlin's uncle Albert. Lydia had been his second wife, and she'd married him when they were in their late fifties, so while Caitlin had grown close to them in her teenage years, it wasn't as if Lydia had known her since she was a baby.

Furthermore, Lydia's nephews had always lived in New Hampshire, and they'd spent a lot more time with Lydia than Caitlin ever did. Yes, when Caitlin was in high school, she'd stayed on Dune Island to help manage the cottages, and she'd developed a close bond with her hard-working yet fun-loving aunt, who'd proudly introduce Caitlin to the guests as, "my right-hand woman" or "my all-around amazing niece."

But shortly after Caitlin's final summer there, her family relocated to New Mexico, and she and Lydia drifted apart, only crossing paths at an occasional wedding or funeral in New

Hampshire or catching up during a brief holiday phone call. So Caitlin couldn't help but feel guilty about receiving such a valuable inheritance from her aunt.

She also felt puzzled by why Lydia had required her to remodel the windmill after her death. Although the two of them used to chat about how much fun it would be to turn the loft into a sitting room, Caitlin had thought that was just a lovely but impractical daydream, not something her aunt truly had her heart set on.

I guess since Aunt Lydia put aside the funds for it when she drew up the Trust, the remodel must have meant more to her than I realized. She must have thought it meant that much to me, too, she reasoned after mulling it over. *So I suppose I can understand why she'd insist I convert the loft if I were keeping the cottage. But I don't get why she'd require me to convert it before I'm allowed to sell the property. What's the point of putting all that effort into designing a sitting room when neither of us will be there to use it?*

Most importantly, why had Lydia required her to be present to oversee the project? It would have been possible to handle the arrangements remotely.

Caitlin recognized that most people would consider supervising the remodel in person to be a very small price to pay for inheriting such a valuable piece of property. But that was because most people who didn't live on Dune Island had never heard about what had happened the last time Caitlin was there. They didn't know about *the incident with Nicole*, as Lydia used to call it.

And those who *did* know about it weren't aware of just how deeply it had affected Caitlin. Not even her aunt.

She couldn't blame Lydia for that; Caitlin had deliberately kept her feelings to herself. In the years following her final visit to Hope Haven, whenever Lydia had mentioned Nicole during one of their phone calls, Caitlin would downplay the effect that summer had on her.

"I'm only bringing it up because I'm concerned about you," her aunt would insist. "If you don't want to talk to me about it, I understand. But maybe you'd benefit from confiding in another adult, like a counselor? Someone who could help you process your emotions."

"I don't need a counselor and I don't want to talk about it, either. I mean, it was awful when it happened and I was... I was really upset, but I've come to accept it. I'm okay now," Caitlin would counter, and then she'd change the subject.

Eventually, she must have convinced Lydia that she was doing as well as she'd pretended to be doing, because the older woman stopped suggesting her niece would benefit from talking about it.

And in time, Caitlin really did work through most of her feelings about what had happened. Or at least, she'd learned to ignore them. In any case, it had been years and years since *the incident* had preoccupied her every waking thought, as well as most of her nighttime dreams. In fact, she rarely reflected on what happened anymore—which was exactly why she dreaded returning to Dune Island now.

Pushing her memories to the back of her mind had been manageable with time and distance, but what would happen once she returned to The Windmill Cottages, where she'd have to face reminders of that summer in person?

I'm an adult now, not a teenager, so I can handle this, she reminded herself. *Besides, it's autumn, not summer, and twenty years have passed, so I'm sure the island will seem a lot different from the last time I was there...*

Yet less than an hour later, when she disembarked the ferry in Port Newcomb, Caitlin noticed that the elegant village appeared almost the same as it had looked two decades ago. While a few shops had been added to the row of Main Street establishments, and some of the older brick buildings were renovated, she still recognized most of the upscale bakeries, cafés, and boutiques from her youth.

Their window displays included decorations in autumnal hues, and wreaths made of dried reeds, woven vines, dark berries, and colorful leaves hung from their doors. Almost every entryway was flanked by barrel planters bursting with mauve, white, and red mums, buttery marigolds, or purple-tinged ornamental cabbage. And up and down the one-sided waterfront street, wrought iron benches provided customers and passersby a place to rest and watch the island's tallest lighthouse guide the ferries, fishing boats, and other vessels of all sizes into port.

I'd almost forgotten how even on an overcast day, everything in Hope Haven seems postcard perfect—on the surface, anyway, she thought ruefully as she slowly drove along the crescent-shaped road.

Hope Haven was comprised of five towns, and while they were all stunningly beautiful, each possessed unique, distinguishing features. In addition to its appealing downtown shopping area, Port Newcomb was known for its tony yacht club and vibrant nightlife. Highland Hills, which faced the open Atlantic, hosted a vibrant artists' community. Rockfield had miles of scenic hiking trails through conservation land, as well as a picturesque, privately owned cranberry bog. Benjamin's Manor was renowned for its quaint harbor and historic captains' homes.

And then there was Lucinda's Hamlet, where Caitlin's aunt and uncle owned and managed The Windmill Cottages. The town sported a long bayside boardwalk with tourist traps galore, including a famed ice-cream parlor, an arcade, and souvenir shops and takeout eateries. Abbreviated as "Lucy's Ham" by the locals, the little village may not have enjoyed the prestigious reputations of the other four towns, but because of its wholesome entertainment and calm bay waters, vacationing families with young children were drawn to it in droves.

Caitlin smiled to herself, remembering how her aunt had once responded after reading a newspaper article about Lucinda's Hamlet. The reporter had written that the boardwalk was, "an embarrassment to Dune Island, but a beloved one, much like a favorite but loud and tacky relative."

Lydia had clucked her tongue at the backhanded compliment. "The honest, hardworking boardwalk business owners strive to provide a fun, safe environment, tasty food, and affordable shopping opportunities for vacationing families. There's no shame in that."

Caitlin sensed her aunt had also been defending the cottages from those who'd looked down their noses at the ornamental but now defunct windmill and the tiny abodes surrounding it. But such people were in the minority; many tourists considered the cottages and windmill to be so quaint that they'd visit the isolated side street—aptly named "Windswept Way"—for the sole purpose of taking their photos in front of the locally iconic landmark. And most guests appreciated staying in the cozy, well-maintained and reasonably priced cottages so much they returned year after year.

Recalling how her aunt and uncle had poured their time, money, and energy into their summertime business, Caitlin thought, *They were so hardworking and humble, and they never complained when they couldn't go fishing or beachcombing or take a swim because they were too busy meeting the guests' needs and maintaining the cottages and the grounds. That kind of physical labor couldn't have been easy, especially because Aunt Lydia had severe arthritis in her knee—and Uncle Albert was probably becoming sick with cancer, even though we didn't know it yet.*

But as industrious as her aunt and uncle were, Lydia always

insisted that once her niece's chores were finished, Caitlin had the rest of the afternoon free to read or go to the beach or the boardwalk or for a hike with her summer friends.

"You'll have the rest of your life to work," she'd say. "This is the time for you to enjoy your youth."

"But what about you and Uncle Albert? You should take a break, too."

"Don't worry about us. Your uncle will sneak a snooze in the hammock if he really needs one. And you know me—at the end of the day, I'll take time to stop and watch the sunset."

"Stop and watch the sunset" was Lydia's equivalent of "stop and smell the roses," which she also said—although because she was on Dune Island, she changed the saying to, "stop and smell the *wild* roses." A firm believer in appreciating life's simple pleasures, especially the beauty of the natural world, Lydia made it a habit to go view the sunset whenever the weather allowed.

Caitlin usually went with her, while Albert stayed behind, preferring to unwind by watching baseball on TV. The pair would cut across the back lawn, through the strip of pitch pines and scrub oaks, and past the fat juniper tree to the long, steep staircase leading down the dune. Because of Lydia's bad knee, they usually didn't descend it to the beach below. Instead, they sat side by side on the upper landing, a tight squeeze, with their bare, warm legs pressed against each other's.

No two sunsets were alike, and none of them ever disappointed. From blazing orange to silky pinks to vivid purples, the colors that imbued the bay and sky were breathtaking. Salty breezes and sea-spray roses perfumed the air, and when the tide was in, the water faintly rippled against the shore. "This is nothing short of glorious," Lydia had uttered on more than one occasion.

Caitlin loved the scenery, too, but what had made those

evenings even more special were the one-on-one discussions she had with her aunt. Rather, Caitlin mostly talked, and Lydia mostly listened. Unlike the teenager's parents, who worked long hours and rarely engaged in conversation with her, Caitlin's aunt always demonstrated an interest in whatever she was saying. It didn't matter whether Caitlin was confiding how she felt about a boy, describing a view she'd seen, or simply sharing a silly anecdote about a guest; Lydia genuinely seemed to care about her thoughts and feelings, and the details of her life. Often, the pair would linger on the stairs and chat until stars speckled the sky and Lydia's joints were so stiff from sitting in the same position that Caitlin would have to help her to her feet.

"Watching the sunset is worth the effort of trekking out to the dune, but the return trip is getting harder," she said one evening as she limped through the woods toward the cottage, leaning on Caitlin's shoulder for support. "I appreciate how fortunate we are to own property on Dune Island, and I try not to be greedy, but I admit, sometimes I envy those people who have a water view from their houses."

"Maybe Uncle Albert could cut down some of these trees, so you'd be able to see the bay from the porch."

"We can't—our property only extends from the cottages to the edge of the woods. The town owns the rest of the land. Besides, I wouldn't want to destroy the fragile dune environment, just for my convenience and pleasure."

"Well, since you and Uncle Albert are going to renovate the cottage before you retire here anyway, you should add a second story to it," suggested Caitlin. "Then you could watch the sun set from the upstairs window."

"Unfortunately, there are zoning regulations on this street that prohibit anyone from adding height to the existing buildings," Lydia started to explain, but then she abruptly stopped walking, and she pulled Caitlin to a halt, too. "But there's nothing to prohibit us from modifying the upper level of the *windmill!*"

That's how the idea of converting the loft into a sitting room was born. From then on, whenever Lydia discussed her vision for making the cottage a cozier, more inviting retirement residence, installing a big picture window in the windmill loft was at the top of her wish list.

"I'll be able to sit up there and knit or do my word puzzles and look out on the water to watch your uncle Albert fishing from his little skiff. We'll haul a love seat up there and a small coffee table, too, so when you visit us at Thanksgiving, we'll have a place to set our cookies and hot chocolate," she told her niece. "And we'll be able to see the sun setting without even leaving home... What could be more luxurious?"

Recalling Lydia's daydream now, Caitlin suddenly felt sad that it had never come to pass while her aunt and uncle were alive.

I really should have a better attitude about making it happen now, she scolded herself. *I should look at it as a privilege to honor Aunt Lydia's wishes, instead of focusing on how upsetting it is to return to the island.*

Yet the closer she came to Lucinda's Hamlet, the more anxious she felt. And when she pulled into the driveway and caught her first glimpse of the familiar cottages and windmill, Caitlin was so overwhelmed by memories about *the incident with Nicole* that it took all her willpower not to shift into reverse and drive straight back to the ferry dock.

THREE

MID-AUGUST, TWENTY YEARS EARLIER

On Saturday morning, Lydia and Caitlin rose before sunrise to bake windmill-shaped sugar cookies so they could give the departing guests a sweet sendoff, and the arriving guests a warm welcome.

"It's not seven o'clock and it's already as hot as blazes in here," Albert good-naturedly grumbled when he shuffled into the small kitchen, which retained the heat from the oven for hours. "Why do you need to serve homemade cookies?"

Lydia gave his shoulder a love tap and said, "You know why, Bertie. The previous owners did it, so it's become part of the tradition of staying at The Windmill Cottages. The guests expect it."

Then she handed him a warm cookie, and Caitlin fondly noticed how quickly he gobbled it down. Later, he enjoyed a second—or was it a third?—with his coffee, and when his wife and niece finally sat down for a quick breakfast, they both ate a cookie, too. Despite Albert complaining about the heat, and even though Lydia insisted she could handle the baking on her own, Caitlin wouldn't have missed this hectic Saturday morning ritual for the world.

. . .

"How adorable," remarked Pam McDougal, a newly arriving guest, when Lydia offered her and her daughter one of the signature treats at check-in shortly after 2:00 p.m. "Nicole and I don't eat carbs, but I'll take one for my husband. He's waiting in the driveway."

"*I* eat carbs. I *love* carbs," Pam's slender, dark-haired daughter emphatically contradicted, shooting her mother a defiant look and grabbing two cookies from the plate.

Her mother ignored her. "My husband and I are newlyweds, so we're here on a sort of honeymoon. A 'family-moon,' as he likes to call it, since Nicole's here with us, too," she explained, and Caitlin couldn't blame Nicole for rolling her eyes. "We had planned to spend two weeks in Benjamin's Manor—my husband's an avid golfer—but our reservation fell through and unfortunately, we couldn't find any other vacancies at short notice. That's how we wound up here."

It almost sounded as if the woman was embarrassed to be staying in Lucy's Ham instead of Benjamin's Manor, or as if she found it necessary to mention that The Windmill Cottages weren't her first choice. Caitlin wished her aunt would've pointed out how lucky Pam was that a long-standing guest suddenly had to cancel their reservation due to a work conflict; otherwise, there wouldn't have been a vacancy at The Windmill Cottages, either.

But Lydia just said, "Congratulations on your marriage. We're very glad you're staying with us. You'll find it's only a short drive to the golf club in Benjamin's Manor, and Lucinda's Hamlet has a popular course right up the road, too."

"Or Bob could just play mini-golf and afterward the three of us could stroll hand-in-hand down the boardwalk, eating cotton candy," Nicole suggested. "Although that's not carb-free, is it?"

Again ignoring her daughter's snarky comments, Pam remarked to Lydia, "I hope our cottage has a water view."

"Unfortunately, you can't quite see the water from any of the cottages here, including mine. The scrub oaks and pitch pines might be sparse and stubby, but there's just enough of them to block the view." Lydia pointed to the ceiling and added, "There's a peek-a-boo water view from the window in the storage loft. You're welcome to go up and take a look, but you'll have to navigate around the paper goods and cleaning supplies. It's easier to walk the short distance through the woods—there's a panoramic view from the stairs leading down to the beach."

Her remarks sufficiently appeased Pam, but Nicole's eyes lit up at the mention of the loft. "Ooh, *I'd* love to take a look from upstairs, please, Mrs. Walker," she politely requested.

"Sure," agreed Lydia. "Caitlin can take you up there. But you girls be careful, those stairs are steep."

"Don't worry. Nicole's very nimble," said Pam. "She attends LaRue Performing Arts High School. She's a dancer—she's been studying ballet since she was three."

"But now I'm studying *acting*," her daughter emphatically declared, and it was obvious that her preference was a point of contention between them.

As Nicole followed Caitlin to the loft, Lydia said to Pam, "Here are your keys and your welcome packet. The windmill's unlocked during the week, and we keep extra paper goods beside the filing cabinet. Feel free to take what you need. Either my husband or I are always on-site, so if you have questions or need anything else, please let us know. You can also ask Caitlin if you see her around—she's happy to help."

Pam replied at length, but she must have lowered her voice, because suddenly Caitlin couldn't distinctly hear what she was saying. Nicole apparently had noticed the drop in her volume, too.

"She's asking your aunt if you'll babysit me," she muttered

bitterly, nudging aside a bucket of rags with her toe; she seemed more interested in the floorboards beneath her feet than in the view beyond the window.

"Why does your mom think you need a babysitter?" Caitlin asked since the girl appeared only a year or two younger than she was. "You must be at least fifteen."

"I'll be *six*teen next month and I don't mean a literal babysitter. I was being sarcastic," sneered Nicole. She glided across the floor to the window. Resting her elbows on the wobbly board along the bottom, she peered into the distance, and slowly batted her thick, curved lashes. "She doesn't trust me enough to let me go anywhere or do anything by myself, but she doesn't want to have to spend time with me, either. It's a classic parenting dilemma."

A hurt look came across the girl's pretty profile, and Caitlin detected a note of vulnerability beneath Nicole's flippant veneer. Feeling sorry for her, she said, "I help my aunt and uncle until noon or one o'clock during the week, and for a little longer on Saturdays. But after that I usually go to the beach or hiking, and sometimes I meet up with my boyfriend and some other kids. You can come with me any time you want—it'll be fun."

"Oh, goody," said Nicole in a way that made Caitlin wonder whether she meant it or if she was being sarcastic again. She had a sinking feeling she was going to regret telling Nicole she could join her, but it was too late to take back the invitation now.

Oh well, she might not want to come with me very often anyway, and even if she does, it'll only be for a couple of weeks, she thought. *Besides, I want to help Aunt Lydia and Uncle Albert give the guests the best vacation they can have, and that includes Nicole and her family...*

. . .

Nearly two weeks later, Caitlin lugged a barrel of broken branches and twigs across the lawn. A recent tropical storm had fractured one of the windmill's arms, knocked down a large section of the picket fence near the driveway, and toppled a black locust tree, making a mess of the yard. Because Albert had been stricken with severe stomach pain, he was too weak to get out of bed, much less to make repairs to the property. So while Lydia was caring for him and managing the guests' needs, Caitlin was trying her best to clean up the grounds.

The air was heavy and humid, and she paused to wipe sweat from the back of her neck. *At least the electricity is on again and I can take a shower before the beach party tonight...*

The thought of seeing her boyfriend put a smile on her dirt-streaked face. Caitlin had met Donald while she was hiking through the conservation land. Like her, he was also entering his senior year in high school, and he'd come from Iowa to Dune Island to participate in a summer work-study program for students interested in pursuing higher education in ecology, environmental science, or wildlife management.

Tall and husky, Donald had fine blond hair like corn-silk, and his big blue eyes were magnified by thick-rimmed glasses. He'd been combing the trail near the marsh for litter and other debris—one of his responsibilities as a student ranger—when Caitlin first crossed paths with him. She'd excitedly described a turtle she'd seen with beige, brown, and black concentric markings on its shell, and asked if he knew what kind it was.

"It sounds like a diamondback terrapin. It gets its name because of the pattern on its scute," he confidently answered. "That kind of turtle only lives in brackish water, and it's on the 'threatened' list in Massachusetts, which means it's illegal to harass or move them. I need to make sure that's what it is so I can tell the sanctuary staff. Where exactly did you see it?"

Caitlin had led him to the shallows near the grass where she'd spotted it swimming. When they got there, it was gone, but they kept looking for it until another student ranger came to tell Donald that everyone else was waiting in the van to head back to the station. By that time, he and Caitlin had bonded over their mutual fascination with science and nature.

"Tomorrow I'll be working at Pilgrim's Park on the northern end of town. If you come by, I can show you the turtle nest protection boxes we've installed near the marsh there," he suggested before leaving. "The boxes are supposed to keep animals like raccoons and foxes and coyotes from digging up the turtles' eggs and eating them."

Even though it wasn't the most romantic proposal in the world, and even though he technically hadn't asked her out, Caitlin couldn't have been more thrilled by Donald's invitation. At seventeen, she'd never had a boyfriend; to her disappointment, she'd never even been on a real date, except for the time she'd gone to the junior prom with the boy next door, and even then, it was his mother, not the boy himself, who'd asked her to accompany him.

How could Caitlin develop a romantic relationship—or even socialize with her peers—when her father and stepmother expected her to earn top grades at school, as well as keep the house, make supper, and take care of her little stepbrother every evening and most weekends until they got home from work?

It was no wonder she could hardly wait until school ended each year, and her stepbrother was sent to his grandparents' house in Nova Scotia, and Caitlin got to go to Dune Island to help Lydia and Albert. The chores she helped with in the morning paled in comparison to the amount of freedom her aunt and uncle gave her in the afternoons to do whatever she pleased. Because she was so responsible, they trusted her to exercise good judgment, even allowing her to borrow their car if they didn't need it, which was something she rarely got to do at home.

So after she met Donald, Caitlin spent nearly all her free

time visiting the parks or beaches where he was scheduled to work. She'd sign up to participate in the guided tours he conducted, and they'd arrange to meet for a picnic during his lunch hour.

Because the program he was enrolled in was closely supervised, and the high schoolers were expected to participate in group recreational activities after hours, most of Caitlin and Donald's evening "dates" had been spent in the company of the student park rangers and other youth from the community. But once in a while, they'd manage to steal away to a secluded spot, and their conversations quickly progressed from discussions about plants and animals to more personal topics. They'd talk about things like their taste in food and music, their classmates and families, their secret struggles, and their hopes for the future—things Caitlin had never shared with anyone, except maybe her aunt.

In between all that talk, there'd been lots of sitting in silence, holding hands, lots of hugging, and lots and *lots* of kissing—Caitlin's favorite newfound activity. Donald's, too; like her, he was a bit of a late bloomer. Initially shy and reserved, after his first tentative, bumbling pecks on her cheeks, he'd grown increasingly zealous, and it was almost as if they were both making up for lost time.

Caitlin liked Donald so much, it nearly caused her physical pain to be apart even for a day. And now that summer was ending, the very thought of saying a permanent goodbye to him made her ache from the tips of her toes to the roots of her hair.

Tonight, I need to tell him how I feel, she decided as she stopped to pick up another broken branch. She cracked it in two over her knee before adding it to the barrel. *Maybe there's a way we can get together this winter...*

"Hey, Cinderella." Nicole's voice snapped Caitlin from her reverie. "What time are we leaving for the party tonight?"

"*We?*"

"*We?*" Nicole repeated, imitating Caitlin's incredulous tone. As an aspiring actor, she had developed some impressive but annoying impersonation skills. "Yeah, *we*. It's a pronoun. It means you and I."

Caitlin had barely seen Nicole since the storm struck three days ago, and she didn't recall telling her about the student rangers' end-of-summer get-together. "But I-I-I didn't know you wanted to go to the party."

"I-I-I *don't*," mocked Nicole. "But I want to go to dinner at the Club even less, and Pam and Bob won't let me stay at the cottage by myself."

She usually referred to her mother by her first name behind her back, but Caitlin noticed that Nicole always called her *Mom* to her face, which made her suspect that Nicole wasn't quite as irreverent as she often pretended to be.

"You know it won't be like, a real party, right?" Caitlin reminded her. The few times Nicole had hung out with Caitlin, Donald, and the other student rangers, she'd complained about how nerdy and boring they were. "We're just going to eat pizza on the beach and watch the sunset. Dave, the chaperone, will probably bring his guitar, so..."

"So it'll be really pathetic, I know. But I'll find a way to entertain myself... and all the dorky rangers." She threw back her head and laughed at herself.

During the short amount of time Caitlin had known her, she'd discovered that Nicole loved to make up "scenes" and then act them out. Usually, these theatrics involved flirting with young men who were instantly taken in by her charms. Once, Caitlin watched as the server at a bakery gave Nicole a coffee and pastry for free after she pretended to be a French tourist who'd lost her purse. Another time, she convinced a random guy on a hiking trail that she needed to use his bicycle to circle the park because her puppy had broken free of its leash, and she was desperate to find it.

Her charades supposedly were just in good fun. According to Nicole, she was "practicing her art," or "getting into character," and to her credit, she was a very talented actor. But it bothered Caitlin that she'd play on people's emotions, and she didn't want Nicole taking advantage of Donald and the other students' kindness toward her.

She bit her lip before tentatively suggesting, "You don't have to entertain anyone or put on an act, you know. You could just hang out and let people get to know the *real* you."

"The real me *is* an actor," countered Nicole. "But if you don't want me to come to the party, I guess I'll just have to go to the Club with Bob and Pam. I thought it would be special for them to spend their last evening on Dune Island alone, so they'd end our vacation at The Windmill Cottages on a happy note. It would kind of make up for the fact we didn't have electricity for a couple days, but whatever…"

She had struck a soft spot and she knew it: Caitlin would do whatever she could so Nicole's parents wouldn't badmouth the cottages. "I never said I didn't want you to hang out with me and my friends."

"Great, then what time are we leaving?"

"Quarter-to-six. The party runs till ten o'clock, and I want to stay till the very end," Caitlin informed her. "So don't expect me to leave early because you change your mind and want go to the Club with your mom and stepdad after all."

"As if," scoffed Nicole.

"I'm serious."

"So am I." Nicole raised her right hand and stated with exaggerated sincerity, "I, Nicole Dixon, do solemnly swear I won't change my mind and ask you, Caitlin Hines, to give me a ride to the Club or to leave the party early for any reason." Then she dropped her hand and said, "I promise, we'll stay as late as you want, and I won't complain or make fun of anyone or anything like that. You'll hardly even know I'm there."

I bet everyone will know you're there, because you always make yourself the center of attention, thought Caitlin resentfully. But she agreed, "Okay. I'll be waiting on our porch at five forty-five—don't be late."

"Got it," Nicole agreed. "Pam will drop by in a little while to confirm with Lydia that there really is a party, there won't be any drugs or alcohol, and you'll drive carefully, blah, blah, blah. You know the drill."

"Yeah, I know the drill," said Caitlin with a sigh.

True to her word, Nicole came traipsing across the green at 5:45. But instead of walking with Caitlin to the driveway, she veered toward the windmill. "I just wanna see if the waves have died down since the storm."

Ever since Lydia gave Nicole permission to go upstairs, the teenager made an excuse to visit the windmill loft almost every day. "I'm just taking a *peek-a-boo* of the water," she'd tell Caitlin, facetiously quoting Lydia. Or else she'd claim she was "grabbing extra TP for our cottage," even though there was a stack of spare rolls next to the filing cabinet downstairs.

Caitlin had quickly realized that Nicole was using the loft as a hiding place for her makeup, as well as for an assortment of skimpy halter tops and miniskirts, or anything else her mother prohibited her from wearing in public. Nicole would change into the forbidden clothing and then layer her regular outfit over it. Once she was out of sight, she'd take off her outer garments. Then, when she returned to Windswept Way, she'd sneak back into the windmill loft to wash her face and hide the other items again, confident that Caitlin would never tell anyone about her secret wardrobe.

Usually, Caitlin didn't care what Nicole wore; she figured if she was deceiving her mom, or if Pam was being too strict about her daughter's clothing, that was none of her business. But this evening, Caitlin could barely stand to wait another minute before reuniting with Donald.

"You're not interested in seeing the water. You're only going up there to put on a miniskirt or something," she grumbled. "You already look really nice the way you are. Why would you want to change?"

"You just answered your own question," Nicole said over her shoulder, before disappearing inside the windmill. "I don't want to look really *nice*. I want to look irresistible."

Oh brother, what "character" is she going to pretend to be tonight? And what poor guy is going to be her next victim? Caitlin wondered. She poked her head inside the windmill and threatened, "If you aren't down here in three minutes, I swear, I'll leave without you."

"No, you won't. You're the type who'd never leave someone behind," she called from the top of the stairs. "You'd feel too guilty."

Just try me, thought Caitlin, pacing angrily, but only a few minutes later, Nicole hopped through the door and accompanied her down the driveway.

"I didn't want to make you wait, so I brought my cosmetic bag with me. I can put on my makeup in the car," she said, as if she were doing Caitlin a big favor. "Are you sure you don't want me to do your eyes for you? They're such a pretty blue, but you could bring out the color even more."

"Thanks, but I'm good," said Caitlin, secretly flattered by Nicole's rare compliment.

They drove in silence as Nicole peeled off her T-shirt: beneath it, she wore a black, midriff-baring top. Next, she writhed out of her leggings to reveal a pair of very short denim cut-offs. Then she unclipped her barrette, allowing her dark, thick hair to fall in waves around her shoulders.

"My lipstick totally melted in the loft. Look, it's all soupy." She showed Caitlin the tube and then flipped down the visor to study her reflection in the mirror. Nicole pulled a kohl eyeliner pencil from her cosmetic bag and began applying the color to her upper eyelid. "We have to stop so I can buy another tube."

"No way!" exclaimed Caitlin. "I want to get to the beach."

"Relax. It's not like you're going to get a detention for being tardy," argued Nicole. "There's a pharmacy coming up soon. Turn right at that stop sign, and it's like, half a mile down the road. I'll run in and out before you can even find a parking space."

"No. You *promised* you wouldn't make me late."

"Actually, I only agreed I'd come to the windmill at five forty-five. What I promised was that I wouldn't make you leave the party *early* to take me anywhere," Nicole reminded her. "And I never said I wouldn't ask you to stop on the way for an emergency item I didn't even know I'd need."

"We're not stopping," Caitlin reiterated loudly. "This isn't an emergency. You don't *need* lipstick."

"I guess I shouldn't expect someone who doesn't ever wear makeup to understand why my appearance is important to me," Nicole retorted. "But fine. If you don't want to drive a couple more blocks or stop to let me out, then once we get to the beach, I'll walk to the pharmacy from there."

"That's two miles each way," said Caitlin, calling her bluff.

Nicole shrugged. "No problem. I'm sure I'll get back to the beach before dark—although wouldn't it be funny if Pam and Bob happened to drive by and see me walking down Main Street?"

Caitlin recognized the veiled threat; Nicole's mother would be very upset if Caitlin ditched her. Not that it would be unusual for Nicole to wander off on her own; whenever she went with Caitlin to the beach, Nicole would take a long walk by herself.

At the start of the girl's vacation, Caitlin had offered to go with her, but Nicole had been so snarly about needing her space that Caitlin had given up trying to accompany her. Since most of the other beach-goers were families with young children, she figured Nicole was fine on her own. Caitlin herself had walked countless times from the private beach in front of the cottages, past several town beaches, all the way to the boardwalk, and she always felt completely comfortable alone. The tidal flats in the opposite direction were far more isolated, but Nicole rarely headed that way because the walkable stretch of sand was cut off by a marshy inlet, and she didn't like its briny smell.

The only specific instruction Pam had ever given the girls was to watch out for each other if they went swimming, even though the waters were usually calm, and lifeguards were on duty seven days a week. But Nicole never took a dip with Caitlin; she claimed the sand felt too oozy and she didn't want any creepy crawlies touching her skin. Plus, the water would've ruined her makeup. So, there'd never been any reason to worry about Nicole's safety during the afternoon.

However, now that it was almost evening, Caitlin felt hesitant to let the young guest walk from the pharmacy to the beach. While Hope Haven had a very low crime rate, she wouldn't put it past Nicole to "act" as if she needed a ride from a stranger, which didn't seem like a good idea no matter how safe the island was.

"Fine, I'll stop at the pharmacy," she gave in. "But you'd better run right in and come right back out."

"I will." Yet Nicole didn't emerge from the store for twenty minutes. When she did, she showed Caitlin the inside of her wrists, which were dabbed with creamy red dots. "It took me forever in there because I couldn't find the lipstick I usually wear. I had to try, like, two dozen shades before I finally found one that complemented my skin tone."

Caitlin was too annoyed to speak. Gripping the steering

wheel so tightly her knuckles turned white, she stared straight ahead as they continued down the road.

After several blocks, Nicole asked, "What's up with the silent treatment? Is it because I didn't come out of the store right away?" When Caitlin remained silent, Nicole huffed. "You're being totally unfair. I *said* I was sorry."

"No, you didn't," snapped Caitlin. "You made an excuse. That's not the same thing as apologizing. But it doesn't matter if you say it, since you wouldn't mean it anyway."

"That's not true," Nicole objected in a plaintive voice. "I do, too, mean it. I'm truly very sorry I made you upset."

From the corner of her eye, she could see Nicole lift her hand to wipe her cheek, but Caitlin didn't believe she was genuinely tearful and she said nothing in reply.

After a few minutes of sniffling, Nicole tried again. "Listen, you've been so nice this whole time and I thought we were going to have fun together on one of my last nights in Hope Haven. But if you're sick of me, we can turn around and you can drop me off at the cottages."

"Yeah, right," snickered Caitlin. "That would make me even *later* to the party—and I'd also get in trouble with your mom for leaving you on your own."

"Not if I hang out at your aunt and uncle's place until Pam and Bob get back," suggested Nicole. "Maybe I could perform a little skit while we're waiting."

"I wouldn't wish *that* on them," uttered Caitlin under her breath, but she was softening.

"Sarcasm, nice. Sounds like something I'd say." Although Nicole chuckled, she seemed sad when she added, "But you'd better be careful or people won't want to be around you, either."

Caitlin exhaled heavily. "I didn't really mean it. I'm just crabby because..." She hesitated, unsure whether to confide in Nicole about how she was feeling. "Because I haven't seen Donald for three days. We've both been so busy cleaning up after the storm and there's still more work to do tomorrow. This is one of the last chances I'll get to be with him before he leaves the island, so every minute counts."

"Oh. I never thought of that. If you had told me, I would've hurried faster in the pharmacy."

"It's okay," Caitlin finally conceded. "I guess it doesn't matter if we're late. It's not like I'm going to be able to spend time alone with Donald anyway."

"Why not?"

"Because the chaperone, Dave, always wants the whole group to stick together."

"So, who cares what *he* wants? You should do what *you* want," advised Nicole. "Like I do."

Chuckling, Caitlin asked, "You mean wearing miniskirts and bikinis behind your mother's back?"

"Sort of, but that's mostly just for fun. I mean more important things, like auditioning for a role in a play instead of dancing as Clara in *The Nutcracker* for the fifth time like Pam thinks I should," she said, her tone a mix of resentment and determination. "If you're really passionate about doing something, and it's not going to hurt anyone else, then you owe it to yourself to go for it."

"I *can't*," Caitlin complained. "The only way I could be alone with Donald is if we sneak off down the beach, but Dave watches everyone like a hawk. We'd never get past him."

"Oh, brother, you're such a rule-follower," scoffed Nicole. She used the mirror as she applied her newly purchased, blood-red lipstick, rubbed her lips together, and then made an exaggerated smacking sound at her reflection, before flipping the visor upward again and shifting to look at Caitlin. "If you really want to be with Donald, then you can't let your doubts or fear stop you—you're going to have to take a risk. And just to prove how sorry I am for making us late, I'm going to help you out."

"How?"

"Once the chaperone starts playing his guitar, I'll get everybody singing and dancing. Dave won't even notice what you and Donald are doing. You can take off for as long as you want—I'll keep everyone distracted until you get back."

Caitlin chewed on her lower lip, hesitating. Nicole's plan gave her an uneasy feeling—more like bees than butterflies—in the pit of her stomach. She knew she should say that it wasn't necessary for Nicole to put on a show; that Caitlin didn't want to get in trouble, and that she and Donald would find another time to be alone. But what if they didn't get the chance before leaving the island? To Caitlin, that would be a lot worse than any consequence she could imagine from sneaking away from the group.

"Okay," she finally agreed, against her better judgment. "Let's go for it."

FOUR

PRESENT DAY

A tap on the car window startled Caitlin. She'd been so entranced in her thoughts that it took a second to get her bearings: she was parked in the driveway in front of her aunt's cottage and windmill, with the car's engine still running. She turned it off and twisted her head to find a round-faced, white-haired woman peering at her through silver-framed bifocals.

"Hello, there," the woman said loudly. "Are you okay?"

Caitlin nodded and answered just as loudly, "I'm fine, thanks."

The woman said something else, but Caitlin couldn't quite hear her, so she slowly opened the door, allowing the woman time to step back. That's when she noticed the leashed gray and white Havanese dog near the woman's feet. It vigorously wagged its tail and barked excitedly at her.

"Pepper, shush," the woman said sharply to quiet him, but Caitlin didn't mind.

She bent down to pet the friendly animal, stalling as she decided how to approach her conversation with the passerby. Caitlin had anticipated that she wouldn't be able to keep her presence on Dune Island a secret for very long, but she had hoped she'd at least be able to unpack before the locals discovered she was there.

"I don't mean to be intrusive," the woman said, as if she could read Caitlin's mind. "But if you're lost or looking for someone, maybe I can give you directions?"

As Caitlin straightened into a standing position and looked into the woman's eyes once again, she suddenly recognized her. Marion Graham, a widow and the only full-time resident on Windswept Way, had been what Lydia affectionately had called "my dearest Dune Island friend."

Apparently, at second glance, she recognized Caitlin, too. "Oh, look who it is—Lydia's niece," she exclaimed. "How wonderful to see you again, Caitlin."

"It's nice to see you, too, Mrs. Graham. How are you doing?"

"Please, call me Marion. I'm doing very well, thank you, just a little slower than I used to be." She puckered her forehead. "How about you—and how's your aunt?"

Although it made sense that Lydia's death wasn't announced in the local newspapers because she hadn't been a permanent Dune Island resident, Caitlin felt bad that Marion hadn't been informed. She tried to break the news gently. "I... I'm afraid she passed away a little over a week ago."

"Oh, dear." Marion mournfully shook her head. "I'm sorry to hear that."

"Thank you." Caitlin's eyes unexpectedly welled with tears, which she quickly blinked away. She'd been so composed at the funeral, but being back at her aunt's house was causing her to feel more emotional than usual.

"Even though Lydia and I didn't keep in close touch during the winter months, I always looked forward to spending time with her when she returned to the island each summer. I was very sad when she wrote me a note to say she had developed dementia and wouldn't be returning to Dune Island," Marion said. "I still try to keep an eye on her house. Not that there's ever been a problem with crime in Hope Haven, but on such a deserted road, during the off-season it doesn't hurt to know who's coming and going. That's why when I saw an unfamiliar car parked in the driveway, I came to find out what it was doing here—you must have thought I was a terrible busybody!"

"Not at all. I appreciate it that you've looked out for my aunt's home," said Caitlin. "And just so you know, the car's a rental and I'm returning it tomorrow. So after that, you won't see a vehicle parked in the driveway, but if you notice lights on in the cottage, please don't worry—it's just me, not an intruder."

"Ah, it'll be wonderful to have a neighbor on the street again. As you can see, once the vacationers go home, it's like a ghost town around here," said Marion. "Did you bring anyone with you? Your husband and children?"

"No, this is a solo trip," Caitlin answered evasively, without explaining that *all* her trips were solo these days, especially after breaking up with Jonathan.

"How long will you be staying?"

"I'm not sure. A few weeks, maybe." Caitlin felt self-conscious about arriving to sell the house so soon after her aunt's passing, almost as if she needed to justify her schedule. "I happened to have a long break from work, so I came here to... to make sure everything's in order in the cottage."

"I see." Marion glanced down at Pepper, who was standing on his hind legs and wiggling his backside as he pawed her shins. To Caitlin's relief, instead of asking more questions, the elderly woman said, "I hate to cut our conversation short, but it looks like Pepper's eager to get home to have his treat. I want to hear all about what you've been up to since I last saw you, so once you get settled in, please drop by for a visit."

Touched by the welcoming invitation, yet reluctant to commit to sharing "all about" her life, Caitlin smiled and simply replied, "Thank you—that's very kind."

As Pepper led Marion down the driveway, Caitlin reached into the car and retrieved her phone from the cupholder. She scrolled through the texts from the estate attorney until she found the code to the back door to Lydia's house. Caitlin tapped the number into the keypad, turned the handle, and braced herself for another wave of memories to wash over her.

Yet when she pushed open the door and saw how much the interior of the house had changed, the first emotion she felt was amazement. Gone were the dark cabinets, peeling linoleum flooring, and mismatched, oversized appliances; the kitchen now featured open shelves, ceramic tiles, and a sleek, energy-efficient fridge and oven.

In the living room and two small bedrooms, the décor was classic coastal chic. Simple, white-washed furniture and splashes of aquamarine and butter-yellow accents enhanced the neutral color palette of the walls and hardwood floors, creating a contemporary, airy feel.

Aunt Lydia and Uncle Albert would've loved how much brighter everything is in here, thought Caitlin, recalling that the room used to be so dim on rainy afternoons they'd need to turn on several lamps so they could see to do a jigsaw puzzle or play a board game together. Inevitably, Albert would bellyache about all the electricity they were wasting, and then Lydia would tease, "If you're that concerned about it, we can light candles instead."

The memory made Caitlin smile. Neither her aunt and uncle's playful quibbling, nor the cottage's minor flaws had ever really bothered her—in fact, their familiarity was kind of comforting. But she had to admit, the carpenter and designer Lydia's nephews hired had done a fantastic job renovating and redecorating the little house.

What impressed her most was that the screened-in porch adjacent to the living room had been transformed into a four-season sunroom, with casement windows overlooking the cluster of cottages in the backyard, and the large, crimson-tipped maple tree in the front. Light and warmth flooded the narrow room, and Caitlin imagined how comfy it would be to curl up on the thick-cushioned rattan sofa and bask in the autumn sunshine.

But for now, she was aching to stretch out for a proper nap, which meant she'd need to make up a bed. As she headed down the hall to the linen closet, someone knocked on the front door. *Are you kidding me? I've literally only been here two minutes!* She reluctantly went to see who her uninvited visitor was.

"Hi there," the courier greeted her. "Are you Caitlin Hines?"

"Yes, I am." *So much for keeping my presence here a secret.*

But he barely glanced up from his tablet as he handed her a cardboard envelope bearing the estate attorney's name and return address. "I'll need a signature, please."

She scrawled her name with the stylus, thanked him, and then circled back to the sunroom. *I wasn't expecting to receive any more documents from Lydia's lawyer*, she thought, dropping onto the sofa. *I wonder why he didn't just email them to me.*

Caitlin unsealed the outer packaging and slid out a sheet of letterhead clipped to a small, lavender envelope. "The attached is for you to receive upon your arrival at the cottage," read the short, informal memo from the attorney. "It should be self-explanatory, but don't hesitate to contact me with questions. Enjoy your stay and please be sure to let me know when the remodel is completed."

What could this be? Caitlin asked herself as she carefully ripped open the sealed flap. Her best guess was that it was a leftover amenity the property management company provided for all the guests, such as a beach parking pass or a modest gift card to a local restaurant.

But what she found inside was a letter. "*Dear Caitlin,*" it read in Lydia's flowery, unmistakable penmanship. *"Welcome to your island home—I'm so glad you're here!"*

Caitlin's eyes immediately smarted and she lowered the paper to her lap, shocked. Hadn't her arrival in Hope Haven been difficult enough, without receiving a personal, posthumous message from her departed aunt?

She took a deep breath, lifted the letter again and tentatively continued:

> *It feels strange writing to you in the present, knowing you won't read this letter until sometime in the future. I hope it doesn't upset you to hear from me like this, but I imagine you might have questions about why I've required you to return to Dune Island to supervise the windmill remodel. Instead of communicating my private intentions through an attorney, I'd like to personally elaborate.*

"That was thoughtful of her," murmured Caitlin, relaxing a little.

> *This week my doctor told me I'm experiencing mild cognitive impairment and she advised me to put my affairs in order while I'm still "of sound mind."*

Caitlin paused as it sunk in that her aunt had sat down to write this letter over ten years ago, just after she was diagnosed.

> *Right now, the dementia only affects my short-term memory, but if I live long enough, in time it will affect my long-term memory, too. It saddens me to think that one day, I might forget my loved ones, including you.*

A sob abruptly rose in Caitlin's throat. *Even though you*

eventually did forget me, I've never forgotten you, Aunt Lydia—and I never will, she silently replied.

Swallowing, she continued:

Over the years, we may have drifted apart—which is understandable, considering how far away you live and how busy we've both been—but I've always treasured the closeness we shared and especially our summers on Dune Island. I never stopped hoping one day you'd get the chance to visit us there again.

I used to love scheming with you about renovating the cottage, especially the windmill loft, so it would be cozier when Albert and I retired and lived in Hope Haven year-round. Remember how you used to plan to visit us there for Thanksgiving and Christmas, as well as in the summertime? I felt so honored that my teenage niece wanted to spend the holidays with her old auntie and uncle... Unfortunately, that's not how things turned out!

Despite her aunt's understanding acceptance of the change in their relationship, Caitlin felt a surge of remorse when she read how much Lydia had valued their connection and wished her niece would visit her at Hope Haven again.

As you know, for several years Albert was too ill to do any work on the cottage, then he passed on, and soon I'll need to move into an assisted living facility. To help offset the cost of my care, I'll task my nephews with arranging to update the cottage, at my expense, so they'll be able to rent it out at a competitive price during the summer months.

Between you and me, I anticipate they'll probably grumble when they find out I'm leaving the cottage to you. If they do, just ignore them.

Caitlin chuckled briefly, in spite of herself. Then, she picked up where she'd left off, reading quickly to the end:

They're already receiving a big enough inheritance, and Albert and I have always wanted <u>you</u> to have the property on Dune Island.

While I trust them to make good decisions about the basic renovations to the cottage, converting the windmill loft was <u>our</u> dream, yours and mine. They knew nothing about it, and if I didn't expressly prohibit it, they'd probably get rid of the windmill altogether. So that's why I'd like you to oversee the remodel whenever it suits your schedule.

This way, if you keep the cottage, you'll get to enjoy the living space we envisioned—and if you sell it, the remodel will drastically increase the appeal and value of the property. In either case, I'll have the satisfaction of knowing you'll benefit as much as possible from your inheritance. You deserve it.

With love from,

Aunt Lydia

Beneath the signature line was a brief postscript, which said, *"Don't forget to stop and watch the sunset!"*

Upon reading her aunt's familiar motto, Caitlin didn't know whether to smile or to weep. She lifted her head and absently stared out the window at the maple tree, her mind and heart whirling with conflicting thoughts and feelings.

On one hand, she was deeply moved to be reminded that their relationship had meant as much to Lydia as it had to Caitlin. She also appreciated her aunt explaining why she'd required her to return to the island to remodel the windmill. But on the other hand, the letter made her feel more guilty than ever.

The cottage was Aunt Lydia's most precious earthly possession, and remodeling the loft was her favorite dream, Caitlin lamented, rubbing her eyes. *She obviously wanted to give me the best of her best, but she was wrong—I* don't *deserve it.*

Suddenly too exhausted to make the bed in the other room and too overwhelmed to deal with her emotions, Caitlin folded the letter and slid it into the envelope. Then she reclined sideways on the sofa and went to sleep.

The following morning, Caitlin made a trip to the market to stock up on groceries and household items before dropping off the car at a satellite rental agency near the ferry dock. Then she caught a bus from Port Newcomb to Main Street in Lucinda's Hamlet.

The quickest way to get from the bus stop to the cottage was to head west a few blocks to the boardwalk and then amble a mile down the beach to the south. But walking along that sandy stretch literally would have been like strolling down memory lane—something Caitlin intended to avoid at all costs. So instead, she followed the sidewalks, weaving her way through the residential neighborhoods. It took over an hour, but she didn't mind: she enjoyed the exercise and the temperate weather.

The trees had barely begun to turn color; only a few pops of crimson, orange, or yellow leaves hinted at the changing season. It had been so long since she'd lived in New England that until she saw it again, Caitlin hadn't realized how much she'd enjoyed the contrast of the vibrant colors with the ubiquitous, gray-shingled Cape-style houses.

When she returned to Windswept Way, she unpacked the rest of her belongings, and then she vacuumed, dusted, and mopped the floors. The crew from the property management company had already given the cottage an extra-thorough cleaning at the end of the season, but scouring it again gave Caitlin an excuse to procrastinate going into the windmill.

For the next two days, she lingered in bed until 9:00 or even 10:00 a.m. Then, she'd rise, eat a leisurely breakfast, take a shower, and stroll to the market in town. She already had plenty of food in her cupboards, so she didn't even enter the store once she'd reached it, but having a destination gave her a sense of purpose.

When she came back, she'd research local carpenters online. Caitlin supposed she could have called Lydia's nephews and asked them who'd renovated the interior of the cottage, but it seemed like a touchy subject since the men had expressed resentment about Caitlin inheriting Lydia's summer place. So, she did her best to find a highly rated carpenter who was available on short notice for the project. She made at least half a dozen attempts to call her top choices, but no one answered directly, and she had to leave voice mail messages. Which in a way was kind of a relief, because she still wasn't ready to hear comments about what had happened at the cottage twenty years ago.

In the afternoons, she'd create photo galleries of her favorite designs and building materials. She also drew sketches and compiled a spreadsheet of comparative costs. Finally, she'd take a nap on the sofa in the sunroom and when she woke, she'd prepare and eat supper and then resume her research until bedtime.

By the third day of this regimen, Caitlin had caught up on her rest and she began to feel as if the walls were closing in. *I haven't spoken to anyone since I dropped the car off at the ferry dock*, she realized. *No wonder I've got cabin fever.*

Deep down, she recognized she was also on edge because she still hadn't gone inside the windmill. But she decided to put it off a little longer and drop in to see Marion instead. *Maybe she'll be able to recommend a good carpenter*, she thought as she headed toward the saltbox-style house at the end of the cul-de-sac.

Even before she raised her hand to ring the doorbell, Caitlin could hear Pepper barking. The door swung open and Marion kept the small, energetic dog from exiting by holding her foot in front of him.

"Pepper, shush. That's not how we greet our visitors," she scolded. "Hello, Caitlin. It's nice to see you again. Please come in if you can get past this little rascal."

Caitlin said hello to Marion and affectionately patted Pepper's head before following her host into the living room.

"You came at the perfect time. I was just about to have tea. Would you like a cup?"

"I'd love one, thanks," said Caitlin. While Marion and Pepper padded into the kitchen, Caitlin studied the photos of Marion's family on the mantlepiece. She vaguely recognized Darren, her only child, who was about eight years older than Caitlin. When Marion returned, she remarked, "These two with Darren must be his children?"

"Yes, that's Jordan and Natalie," said Marion, beaming. "It's an old photo—they're almost pre-teens now. And the woman standing beside him is Jeannine, his wife. She was pregnant in that photo with their third child, Finn, who's already seven years old."

"Three grandchildren, that's wonderful. Do you get to see them often?"

"Not as often as I'd like. They live in Pennsylvania, so it's a long trip—you know how that is." Marion's face brightened as she added, "But they're coming to visit at Thanksgiving."

Caitlin asked the older woman more questions about her family, and Marion seemed glad to talk about them as they sipped their tea and nibbled lemon pound cake, with Pepper taking up residence on the softa cushion between them. Even though Caitlin hadn't personally known Marion very well, she remembered how fond Lydia had been of her. Caitlin felt as if she were visiting an old family friend, and their conversation flowed easily.

After swallowing the last bite of her treat, Marion said, "Listen to me, rambling on about me and my own all this time. Now it's your turn. If I remember correctly, the last time I spoke to Lydia's nephews when they came to update the cottage, they said you and your family had moved to Arizona. Do you all still live there?"

"Close. I live in Santa Fe, New Mexico," Caitlin clarified. "My parents have retired to Florida, but my brother, Charlie, lives about an hour north of me. He's married, and has three children, two boys and a girl."

"Ah, so you're a doting auntie," said Marion with a smile. "But no children of your own?"

Caitlin set her empty teacup in its saucer. "No, no children of my own, and I'm not married," she stated neutrally, so Marion wouldn't think being single and childless saddened her, even if it did a little.

"How about a boyfriend?"

"I don't have one of those, either. Not right now, anyway." Then, Caitlin surprised herself by telling the older woman about what had happened with Jonathan and Melanie.

"Shame on them both!" Marion exclaimed. "You must have been devastated."

"I was very angry and hurt initially, but I wouldn't say I was devastated," Caitlin assured her. "To be honest, I'm kind of over it already."

"You're a lot more gracious than most people would be if someone betrayed them like that."

"I doubt that graciousness has much to do with it," Caitlin said with a chuckle, recalling what she'd done to Jonathan's phone. "I think it's easy to put it behind me because I hadn't been seeing Jonathan for very long, and Melanie and I weren't that close, either. So, it's not as if my soulmate ran off with my best friend or anything."

"But they still should have treated you better, especially Jonathan," Marion remarked. "I'd think the men in Santa Fe would be pounding down the doors to go out with such a lovely woman as yourself."

"Thank you for saying that, but even if they pounded down my door, I probably wouldn't be home," said Caitlin. "I travel a lot locally for work. It keeps me very busy."

"Don't tell me what it is you do, let me try to guess," Marion suggested, tapping her chin. "Let's see, Lydia always used to say how well you did in school and how fascinated you were with nature. So I imagine you work in the natural science field, or maybe in medicine?"

Her comments made Caitlin shrink inside. It had been so long since she'd put away her aspiration of becoming a health care professional that she'd almost forgotten all about it. "No," she answered. "I'm a capital campaign manager. I coach nonprofits on how to conduct their annual appeals and secure funding over an extended period of time."

Marion's surprise was apparent in her expression, but her response was a diplomatic, "That sounds very interesting."

"It is," Caitlin blandly agreed. *Or at least it used to be, when I first started twelve years ago.* Lately, she'd been itching for a change. A challenge.

"Helping nonprofit organizations must be rewarding," prompted Marion. "Is that why you chose that field?"

"Yes," said Caitlin, even though she hadn't exactly *chosen* her career; it was more like she'd stumbled into it. Teaching other people how to ask for money was an unlikely employment position for someone who preferred to be as self-sufficient as Caitlin was. So at first, she'd struggled to develop the skills required to succeed in the role. Now, however, she had the opposite problem, in that she felt like she could conduct the campaigns blindfolded. But because she was motivated by such a strong commitment—or was it an obligation?—to "make a positive difference" in the local communities, she remained in the position.

She quickly changed the subject, telling Marion about volunteering at her local food bank. She also mentioned she liked to hike, and she described how different the Santa Fe terrain was from the mountains in New Hampshire or the coast in Massachusetts.

"It sounds beautiful," said Marion. "Hopefully the warm weather will hold for a while, and you'll be able to enjoy some nice walks here, too. How long did you say you were staying?"

"I'll be here for several weeks." Since Caitlin needed to ask Marion for a recommendation for a carpenter anyway, she figured it was time to tell her about the windmill remodel. "I mentioned that I'd come to Dune Island to check up on the cottage, but I'm also here to oversee a project that my aunt wanted me to complete."

When Caitlin was done explaining about Lydia's requirement that she convert the windmill loft into a living area, Marion exclaimed, "Oh, that sounds just like Lydia! She worked so hard all summer that our visits were usually quite brief. We'd barely sit down for a cool drink and she'd jump up and say, 'I'm sorry, I've got to run. But one day when I'm retired, I'm going to install a big picture window in the windmill loft, and I'll have Albert haul a love seat and a few comfy chairs and ottomans up there so I can put my feet up and watch the tide roll in and out all day if I want.' She said I was welcome to join her any time." Marion quickly clarified, "Don't worry, I'm not hinting for an invitation."

Caitlin hadn't realized that Lydia told Marion her dream to one day convert the loft, and after hearing her aunt's friend reminisce about their conversations, she felt even guiltier confessing that she intended to sell the house.

"You're very welcome to visit me at the cottage any time, and I'll be glad to show you the windmill loft after it's been converted to a living space," she said. "But I, um, I should let you know that I intend to sell the house once the remodel is complete."

Marion's eyes widened with surprise, but her only comment was, "I see."

"I know it probably seems really greedy of me, but I've had some financial challenges lately and—"

"No need to explain," Marion interrupted, holding up her hand. "Lydia left the house to you, so your reasons for selling it are your business, not mine—or anyone else's."

Caitlin nodded and relaxed her shoulders. "I admit, I do feel kind of protective about my privacy and my plans for the house. You're the only person on Dune Island I've told."

"I won't say a word to anyone."

"Thank you." Caitlin smiled. "Although there is at least one other person I need to tell—I need to find a carpenter to take on the project. Unfortunately, I can't seem to get anyone to return my calls."

"Ah, that's because most of them have joined the crew for the resort that's being constructed about a mile south of the harbor in Benjamin's Manor. Hard to believe that such a quaint little town is going to be home to a monstrosity like that. But at least it's providing job opportunities for the islanders." Marion shook her head in dismay. "Anyway, I'd highly recommend the carpenter who worked on my deck last spring. He refuses to be involved with the construction of the resort on principle—he prefers to remain completely independent. He's an all-around great guy and he does excellent work, but he's only lived on the island a couple of years, so he hasn't built up a big client base yet."

I like the sound of that. Even if she was being overly sensitive, Caitlin preferred to hire someone who wasn't a die-hard

Dune Islander. Or at least, someone who hadn't lived on the island when she used to visit. Someone who didn't know her or what had happened, and wouldn't want to discuss it. "Terrific. If you tell me his name, I'll look him up."

"It's Shane Adams and I'll give you his number, too." Marion enthused, "Trust me, you're going to love him."

It took Caitlin until almost 5:00 to work up the courage to call Shane. Although she'd grown comfortable enough to confide in Marion about the project, she still felt hesitant about sharing her plans with anyone else, even a carpenter.

Marion may not be judgmental about me selling the house immediately after Aunt Lydia's death, but that's probably because they were friends, she thought. *I know how gossip spreads on Dune Island, and once the residents find out about my plans, everyone will have an opinion... Even worse, they'll start gabbing about what happened the last time I was here.*

Caitlin decided to ask for Shane's discretion before she provided any details about the project. *If he's as wonderful as Marion says he is, then he'll honor my request not to tell anyone about the remodel,* she thought as she tapped his number into her phone.

"Hello?" he answered, his voice barely audible over the sound of running water in the background.

"Hi. Is this Shane Adams?"

"Yup, sure is," he said. "Who's this?"

Thrown off by his unprofessional tone, Caitlin was suddenly reluctant to tell him her name and she stuttered, "You-you don't know me. I got your number from a mutual acquaintance—she spoke very highly of you."

"Oh, did she now?" He chuckled, as if she'd made a joke.

"Yes." *Although I'm starting to question her judgment.* "She suggested you might be available this fall?"

"Available for...?"

Caitlin paused, uncertain how to describe the project without giving away too much information, just in case she decided not to hire him after all. "I need to have a room refinished."

"Oh! Could you hold on a sec?" He must have turned off a faucet, because suddenly Caitlin didn't hear the water running any longer. "Sorry, I didn't realize this was a professional call. I thought you were calling to ask if I'd be interested in going out. You know, on a date."

"No. That's the last thing I want!" Caitlin blurted out. Okay, maybe that was overkill. But did he always assume his female clients were interested in going out with him? "I'm looking for a carpenter, not a date."

He apologized again. "My mistake—I'm very sorry and completely embarrassed. It's just that my cousin is constantly trying to set me up. So when you said a mutual acquaintance gave you my name, and then you asked if I was available, I thought, well, you know..." He sounded very contrite and Caitlin decided to give him the benefit of the doubt.

"I guess I can see how you might make that assumption."

"Yeah, especially since no one calls my landline for business purposes."

"This is your personal landline?" *I guess that explains his unprofessional greeting. Marion must not have realized she'd given me the wrong number.*

"Yes. My cell phone connection is iffy, so I have a landline at home for backup. My parents are getting up there in age, and my mom's had some health problems lately. So I want to be sure they can reach me at any time of day or night," he said. "Not that I could help if there was an emergency—they live in South Carolina now—but at least I could be on the first flight out to see them."

Shane had shared a lot, virtually all at once, and she got the sense he was flustered. It was charming, though. And touched by his concern for his family, Caitlin said, "I didn't realize the number my friend gave me was for your home phone. If you give me your cell phone number, I can call back during business hours."

"Sure, I'll give it to you for the future, but this is fine for now. I'd like to hear more about your project."

"Well..." She stalled a moment, unsure how to describe it without mentioning the windmill.

"If you're having second thoughts about hiring me, I understand. But I promise I'm a lot more professional than I came across just now."

"No, no, it's not that," she said. "But before I go into detail, I should confirm that you're actually available—for the project, I mean. Ideally, I'd love it if you could get started right away and finish it before the holidays."

"Yeah, I've got some openings in my schedule. But before I can commit to a timeline for the project, I need to hear more about it. And I'll need to come take a look at the space, give you an estimate and all that. What's the address? I could stop by tomorrow afternoon and we can chat about it then."

"That would be great, but there's just one more thing," hedged Caitlin. "I, um, I have a kind of unusual request. I'd appreciate it if you didn't tell anyone about the project, or even that I'm here visiting the island..."

"That's not such an unusual request." Shane assured her, "Discretion's the name of the game in this business, especially with so many celebrities and politicians buying property and building or renovating homes on the island. You have my word, I won't mention any specifics about you or your project to anyone else."

"Thanks." Caitlin gave him the address.

"Hey, I know that location—that's where the windmill house is," he said, which was how people often referred to

Lydia's place. "No wonder you don't want anyone to know you're on the island or what your remodeling plans are. The locals would really give you an earful."

Caitlin's heart sank. He knew about her history? "Wh-what?"

"That place is an iconic landmark. If the residents find out you're going to alter it, even if it's just painting the doors a different color, they'll start spouting off their opinions..."

Relieved, Caitlin said, "Right, exactly."

"Like I said, mum's the word," he promised. "But if you're not too worried I'll blow your cover, can you at least tell me your first name?"

She giggled at his light-hearted teasing. "Sure, of course. I'm Caitlin. Caitlin Hines."

"I'll stop by around two o'clock, Caitlin—if that's okay with you?"

"Sounds good," she said. "I'm looking forward to it."

The next morning, Caitlin decided that there was no putting it off any longer: she needed to go inside the windmill before Shane arrived. For one thing, the maintenance crew stored lawn equipment for the property there, and Caitlin wanted to be sure it wasn't blocking access to the loft stairs. More importantly, she was concerned about how she'd react to being back in the windmill, and she didn't want to risk becoming emotional in front of a stranger.

It's better if I'm by myself the first time I go inside, she thought as she unlocked the padlock. *Although I'm probably worried for nothing.*

But when she pushed open the door and entered the dim interior, the familiar earthy scent of wood filled her nostrils and she felt as if she'd just stepped back in time.

FIVE

LATE AUGUST, TWENTY YEARS EARLIER

Nicole's plan to help Caitlin and Donald slink away from the beach party went off without a hitch.

After ravenously consuming three party-sized pizzas, the group of teenagers played volleyball in the fine, cool sand until the sun hovered just above the horizon. Then they stopped to watch it tint the sky pink and purple before it vanished.

Dave, the chaperone, supervised as the student rangers lit a small campfire, and when everyone had circled around it, he began strumming his guitar. Almost immediately, Nicole burst into song, and she encouraged the pudgy, smiling boy on her left and the tall girl with braces on her right to sing along, too. Dressed in a revealing halter top and high-cut shorts, Nicole appeared out of place sandwiched between the two student rangers, who were still wearing their uniforms. But the trio sounded surprisingly harmonious, and by the second song, most of the other youth had joined in, as well. Encouraged by their enthusiastic response, Dave smiled and closed his eyes as he played, and Caitlin and Donald slipped away unnoticed.

In the lilac haze of dusk, they stole down the beach, ducked into the slope between two dunes, and dropped onto the sand.

The pair kissed until they were sweaty and breathless, and their lips went numb.

"I've missed you so much," Caitlin said when they paused to cool down. She propped herself on her elbows, watching Donald wipe his steamed-up glasses with the hem of his shirt. "The past three days without you have been torture."

"I felt that way, too. And it's going to be a thousand times worse after we leave Dune Island." He groaned. "For the first time in my life, I wish I didn't have to go back to school."

Caitlin smiled to herself; she didn't enjoy school quite as much as he did. "I'm always sad when summer ends, but this year, I really wish it would last forever."

"So do I." Donald leaned over. Touching her cheek, he studied her face with almost scientific concentration. Finally, he cleared his throat and parted his lips to speak, but no words came out.

"What is it?" she prompted. "What are you thinking?"

"That I..." His voice was raspy. "That I love you, Caitlin."

She traced his jaw with her finger and whispered back, "I love you, too, Donald."

As they kissed again, Caitlin's heart thrummed so intensely it seemed to shake the dune beneath her. Donald abruptly pulled back and cocked his head. Was it happening to him, too? Before she could ask, the chh-chh-chh-chh-chh sensation inside her chest filled her ears, and a bright light illuminated the shoreline. She sat up and blinked, confused.

"A search and rescue 'copter!" Donald exclaimed, pointing to the sky.

Still trying to understand what was happening, Caitlin marveled, "Dave sent someone to look for us?"

She'd been serious, but Donald laughed as he stood up. "No, it's not for us, but someone else must be lost. Student rangers are required to be available to assist in the search, so we'd better get going. If I'm not in the van when everyone's ready to leave, I'm going to be in a lot of trouble with Dave—just like the first time you and I met."

"You got in trouble that day?" she asked, scrambling to her feet.

"Yeah," he said with a shrug. "But it was worth it."

Caitlin felt as if she were floating on air as they raced down the beach. By the time they reached the group, most of the other kids had left and the campfire had been extinguished.

"Where have you been?" Dave growled at Donald, but Caitlin counteracted with a question of her own.

"Where's Nicole?" she asked.

"Who?"

"You know, the girl with the dark hair, the one who has a really good voice. She's wearing short-shorts and a halter top." *You couldn't miss her.*

"Oh, her. She got bored and went home a while ago," said Dave.

"Someone gave her a ride?"

"No. She said the cottages are just a little way down the beach, so she walked. I assigned two female student rangers to escort her, but she wanted to go alone. She even said if they followed her, she'd report me for harassment." Dave shook his head in disgust.

"She wanted me to give you a message," the tall girl who'd been singing with Nicole chimed in. "She said not to worry, she'd meet you at the windmill, and to bring the clothes she left in your car."

Caitlin understood: Nicole had meant that she didn't have to worry about Pam finding out. Nicole would hide in the windmill until Caitlin returned, and then she'd change back into her baggy T-shirt and leggings.

I should've known she'd never stay for the entire party, thought Caitlin. But she was too concerned about Donald's fate to be upset at Nicole for breaking her promise. Heading home, she fretted, *I hope he doesn't get in so much trouble with Dave that he isn't allowed to meet up with me tomorrow night.* And she spent the rest of the drive planning how she and Donald could see each other that fall.

When Caitlin reached the cottages and parked at the far end of the shared driveway, she was relieved that she didn't see Pam and Bob's car in any of the spaces reserved for guests. Avoiding the outdoor lighting, she tiptoed to the windmill and creaked open the door. "Nicole?" she whispered into the dark. "Nicole? Are you in here?"

Not wanting to turn on the single, overhead lightbulb, Caitlin felt along the floor near the entrance until her fingers clasped the flashlight her uncle kept there. She switched it on and crept up the stairs to the loft. Nicole wasn't there, either, so Caitlin set the teen's T-shirt and leggings on top of a large package of paper towels, where she could easily find them. She went downstairs and put the flashlight back where it belonged and then hurried across the green to Nicole's cottage.

It was dark and no one answered when she rapped the door, so she cut through the small stretch of woods leading to the bay. Fat clouds galloped across the moon, intermittently obscuring its light, and twice she stumbled on thick roots before she reached the stairs to the beach. She squinted into the distance but she didn't see anyone approaching.

"Nicole?" she called softly. Her question was answered only by the *shh-shh-shh* of waves lapping the shore.

She'd better hurry before the tide comes all the way in. Caitlin sat down on the top step, figuring she'd wait there until Nicole returned. But then it occurred to her that she should move the car down the street. *That way, if my aunt and uncle peek outside, they won't see it and wonder where we are, since we're supposed to hang out at the cottage together until Pam and Bob get back around eleven or twelve.*

She dashed through the woods, and stopped to check Nicole's cottage and the windmill again, but both were dark and empty. Caitlin had just reached the driveway, when Bob and Pam returned, much earlier than expected. Caitlin momentarily froze in the glare of their headlights. She shoved the car keys into her pocket and forced a smile as the couple got out of their vehicle.

"Hi, there, Caitlin. How was the party?" slurred Pam, clearly tipsy. "Did you girls have fun?"

"Um, yes, we did." Caitlin peeked over her shoulder, hoping that somehow Nicole had materialized behind her. Instead, she saw her aunt coming out of the front door to the house.

"Good, I'm glad. Nicole seemed so happy to be spending the evening with you and your friends," Mrs. McDougal gushed as Lydia reached them.

"Hello, Pam. Hi, Bob." She turned to her niece. "Donald just called, but I didn't think you were home yet. He said he'd try again in a few minutes, so you might want to come inside so the phone doesn't wake your uncle."

Uh-oh. If Donald's calling this late, he must be really upset. I bet Dave chewed him out all the way back to the station, Caitlin surmised.

"Okay, I'll be right in. I was just telling Mrs. and Mr. McDougal how much fun Nicole and I had at the party," she said, stalling. She'd hoped to buy a few minutes before Bob and Pam headed to their cottage, but her plan didn't work.

"Where is my daughter, anyway?" asked Pam.

"Uh, I'm not sure."

"What do you mean?"

There was no way around it, so Caitlin confessed, "She, um, she decided to walk to the cottages by herself, on the beach. And she's not here yet."

"She walked back *alone*? Why didn't you stop her?" exclaimed Mrs. McDougal.

"I-I-I didn't know she'd left the party. She promised me she'd stay till the end."

"What do you mean you didn't know?" Pam's volume grew louder with each question she asked. "Weren't you with her?"

"No. I-I went for a walk with my boyfriend and when I got back, everyone said Nicole was bored so she left. The chaperone tried to send two rangers to go with her, but Nicole wouldn't let them." Caitlin didn't add, *She even threatened to report Dave for harassment.*

"Then he should've tried harder—and *you* shouldn't have left her alone in the first place!" Pam shouted accusingly. "If I had known you were so irresponsible, I never would've let her go to the party with you."

Caitlin was shaking and speechless, but her aunt calmly and firmly replied, "I can appreciate that you're upset, Pam. And I assure you that Caitlin and I will do everything we can to help you look for Nicole. But I will not allow you to speak to my niece that way. It isn't Caitlin's or the chaperone's fault that Nicole walked away from the party. You've said it yourself—Nicole's a very strong-willed girl."

"How dare you criticize my daughter? Your niece's behavior isn't any better," Pam screeched. "She might have you fooled into believing she's a straight-A, straight-laced, goody-two-shoes prude, but obviously she's not. Otherwise, she wouldn't have abandoned Nicole to go do who-knows-what with her boyfriend!"

Tears sprang to Caitlin's eyes and Lydia started to say something, but Bob stepped forward and touched his wife's elbow. "That's enough, Pam."

She jerked her arm away so forcefully she nearly lost her balance, and as her husband steadied her, Albert came out of the house, dressed in pajamas and carrying a cordless phone.

Donald must have called again and woken him from a deep slumber, because he was walking crooked.

Yet when he reached the group, instead of handing his niece the cordless phone, Albert grimly said, "Pam and Bob, I'm afraid we need to call the police."

Pam clearly thought he meant because she was creating a disturbance, and she pointed a finger at him and drunkenly shrieked, "Don't you dare threaten me! I have every right to express how upset I am when my daughter's missing!"

"Of course you do, and I want to help you find her," Albert quietly replied. Catching Bob's eye, he explained, "There's been a... an incident with a young swimmer near the marsh. I think we need to tell the police that Nicole's missing. I can make the call, if you'd like."

"The marsh? Nicole wouldn't go within five hundred yards of that smelly marsh—she hates it there. Besides, it's way past the cottages," her mother scoffed, expressing exactly what Caitlin was thinking. "That's not her. It couldn't be Nicole."

"No, probably not, but it's still a good idea to let the police know she hasn't come back yet, so they can keep an eye out for her," her husband said, and Albert handed him the phone.

Marion, the neighbor next to the cottages, must have heard the commotion or seen the gathering, because as Bob placed the call, she came walking up the driveway. "Hello. Is everything okay?"

"No, it isn't. My daughter's missing," sniffed Pam, her voice suddenly small. "My husband's on the phone with the police."

"Aww, that's so upsetting," Marion said sympathetically.

As Pam started to weep, Bob paced back and forth, describing his stepdaughter into the phone. "Fifteen years old. Long dark hair, very fair skin. Slim, but muscular, she's a dancer..." He paused to ask his wife, "What was Nicole wearing when she went out tonight?"

"I don't know. Jeans, I think? Maybe leggings. And a white T-shirt that said 'LaRue Performing Arts High School' on it."

Caitlin swallowed hard; she had to tell them. "Nicole changed her clothes before we got to the party. She was wearing a black halter top and denim shorts."

Mrs. McDougal narrowed her eyes at Caitlin. "Why would she be wearing something like that? Where else did you girls go?"

"Nowhere," Caitlin insisted. "She just likes to dress... *different* sometimes for fun. She says it's like a costume."

Bob repeated her description of Nicole's clothes into the phone. Then he said, "Yep. Okay. That's in Port Newcomb, right?" He handed the phone to Albert and turned to his wife. "Pam, we need to go. A teenager matching Nicole's description fell into the water tonight. She's been airlifted to the hospital."

"Noo! No-oo!" Pam cried, sinking to her knees. "It's not my daughter. It's not Nicole. It can't be."

Bob crouched down and put his arm around her shoulder. "Honey, we need to get to the hospital quickly."

"We'll take you," offered Albert, even though he was in no condition to drive.

"Yes, we will," agreed Lydia. "Caitlin, run inside and get my purse and keys."

"No!" barked Pam, waving her arm. "I don't want you people anywhere near me."

She allowed her husband and Marion to help her to her feet, and as they assisted her into the car, Marion volunteered to wait at their cottage, in case their daughter wasn't the same girl who'd been taken to the hospital, and Nicole returned while they were gone.

Everything that happened after that seemed surreal, almost as if it were a dream and Caitlin and her aunt and uncle were sleepwalking.

"I'll make tea," Lydia told Albert when the trio went inside their little house, but he was too nauseated to drink anything and too weak to sit up. So Lydia went to help him into bed as Caitlin filled a kettle for her aunt and put it on the stove. She could hear her aunt and uncle talking softly on the other side of the wall, but she couldn't make out what they were saying.

When Lydia came into the kitchen, her niece asked, "How did Uncle Albert know about the swimmer near the marsh?"

"Donald told him the second time he called," answered Lydia. "Apparently, he'd heard a rumor at the ranger station about someone calling 9-1-1 because a teenager got swept up in the current. So he'd called you to check whether Nicole had gotten back to the cottages yet. By the way, he told your uncle that he couldn't call again this evening, but he'll talk to you in the morning."

"Did he say anything else about the girl? Like if she's going to be okay?" asked Caitlin.

"No, all he knew was that she was airlifted to the hospital."

"That could just be a precaution though. They could be giving her an X-ray or something, to be sure she didn't get water in her lungs, or whatever, right?"

"Yes, I suppose," said Lydia, but her tone lacked conviction, so Caitlin repeated what Pam had said about her daughter hating the marsh.

"I feel really bad for whoever it is who fell into the current and I hope she's going to be all right, but Nicole doesn't even like to wade through the tidal pools in the daytime, because she's afraid of the little critters. So I don't think she'd go near the marsh at night, when she can't even see what's in the water," she reasoned. "Besides, the inlet is, like, a quarter mile past the stairs to the cottages. Why would she have kept walking down the beach? That doesn't make any sense."

"No, it doesn't," Lydia agreed, frowning.

"She probably turned off at one of the beaches closer to the party and went into town or something, and that's why it's taking her so long to get back."

"Maybe..."

In the quiet spell that followed, Caitlin was struck by another possibility. Even though she felt disloyal, she confided, "I think I know what else may have happened, Aunt Lydia. See, Nicole does this thing where she makes up a scene and then she acts it out to see how convincing she can be. She says it helps her grow as an actor. I bet that's what she's doing now—she's playing the role of a girl who goes missing and falls into the water. She can be very dramatic like that."

"Hmm," her aunt murmured. "I suppose it's possible that's what's going on. But if it really was Nicole who fell into the current and she's getting checked out at the ER, it'll probably take several hours before she gets the all-clear. So you should go to bed. I'll wake you up if I hear anything from Pam or Bob."

"No, I want to stay up and wait with you," insisted Caitlin. "I'll be right back—I'm just going to check at Nicole's cottage to see if she came home yet."

But Marion was still holding vigil for the teen. She promised she'd let Caitlin and her aunt and uncle know if Nicole returned.

This is probably just an act that went too far, but I'm sure Nicole's fine, Caitlin told herself as she came home again and took a seat beside her aunt, who'd moved to the sofa in the living room to work on the merino wool cardigan she was knitting. Usually, Caitlin found the clicking of her needles to be a comforting background noise, but this evening, the disquieting sound reminded her of a ticking clock; it reminded her that time was passing. And with each minute that went by without any word from Pam or Bob, Caitlin became more anxious.

She tried to console herself with the thought, *If she's in the hospital, it means she's not missing. And Aunt Lydia always says*

Hope Haven Hospital has an excellent reputation, so Nicole must be getting very good care.

But she was riddled with worry and guilt, and finally she burst out, "If it was Nicole who fell into the current, and if she did get hurt, then it's all my fault! And even if she isn't the same girl as the one who's at the hospital, it's still my fault she's missing!"

"Nonsense!" Lydia hissed and stopped knitting. "Put that idea out of your head this instant, do you hear me?"

"But I-I-I warned her that I wasn't going to leave the party early to take her home or to meet up with her parents. She said she was okay with that, and it seemed like she really meant it. But then Donald and I went for a walk and when we got back, she was gone."

Lydia furrowed her brow, as if she couldn't understand Caitlin's logic. "So how is that your fault?"

"Don't you see? If I hadn't been so mean about saying I didn't want to leave the party early, she wouldn't have felt like she had to walk back by herself and she wouldn't have fallen into the water."

"She *didn't* have to walk back to the cottages by herself. You said a couple student rangers offered to go with her and she refused to let them," Lydia pointed out. She set aside her knitting and put her arm around her niece. "Listen, darling, I hope with all my heart that Nicole's okay. But no matter what happens, it's very important that you understand it's *not* your fault. It's not the other kids' fault, or the chaperone's fault, either. Nicole knew full well she shouldn't have left that party by herself. She knew her mother wouldn't have wanted her to do that, she knew the chaperone was concerned about her safety, and she knew it wasn't a fair thing to do to you, especially after she said she wouldn't. But she did it anyway because it was what *she* wanted to do. It was selfish."

But deep down, Caitlin knew that *she* was the selfish one.

She realized Mrs. McDougal was right: *she* was the one who'd snuck off with her boyfriend, when she should've been looking out for Nicole. Suddenly, as she thought of saying, *I love you*, and kissing Donald, a bilious taste filled Caitlin's mouth and her eyes brimmed with tears.

When she squeezed her lids shut, Lydia must have seen her and thought she was tired because she left the room and returned a moment later with a pillow. "You're welcome to stay out here with me," she said. "But I think you should put your head down for a while and try to get some rest."

Caitlin didn't know what time it was when she drifted off to sleep, but it was after daybreak when she woke to the sound of the phone ringing. At first, she couldn't figure out where she was, but then she heard her aunt's voice from the kitchen saying, "Oh, no. Oh, no. That's horrible, Bob. I'm terribly, *terribly* sorry."

Caitlin bolted upright on the couch and noticed her uncle leaning against the door frame across the room. The phone call must have jarred him awake, too. Their eyes met but they remained frozen, speechless. It was as if time were suspended while they waited for Lydia to say something else.

"Mm-hmm. Mm-hmm. I see." Her murmuring was barely audible. There was another extended pause before she spoke again. "How can we help? We'll do anything, anything at all."

Caitlin could hardly hear over the commotion of her heart. She leaned forward, cocking an ear toward the kitchen.

"No, of course not. That's fine, I completely understand," Lydia said, coming into the living room, the phone pressed against her ear. Her skin looked ashen as her eyes darted from Albert to Caitlin. She nodded and said, "We'll be sure it's ready… Thank you for calling, Bob. Please take good care."

The second she ended the call, Caitlin pounced toward her.

"That was about Nicole, wasn't it?" she asked, even though the answer was obvious.

"Come, sit with me. You, too, Albert," Lydia said, plunking onto the middle sofa cushion. Albert shuffled across the room and took a seat, wrapping an arm around his wife, but Caitlin was too anxious to sit still.

Shifting from foot to foot in front of them, she asked, "What did Mr. McDougal say? What happened?"

"I'm afraid it's very bad news." Lydia took both of her niece's hands, forcing Caitlin to stop fidgeting. "According to two witnesses—a married couple who were night fishing nearby —Nicole must have completely lost her bearings. Or else she thought she was crossing a tidal pool instead of the tidal river, and she didn't realize how wide and deep the water was. In either case, she fell in and screamed for help, but the current was so strong, it pulled her inland, to the marsh. She must have panicked or she got tired and couldn't keep her head above water. By the time they found her, she was unconscious and she wasn't breathing."

"But-but-but someone did CPR, right? They revived her and she's going to be okay, isn't she?"

"No, I'm afraid she's not." As Albert moaned and covered his eyes, Lydia squeezed her niece's hands tighter. "Nicole passed away, Caitlin. She died."

"No, she didn't, Aunt Lydia," Caitlin immediately argued, yanking her hands free. "She was airlifted to the *hospital*, remember? She's been there for hours and hours. That means they're treating her."

Suddenly, Lydia looked exhausted, her face lined with wrinkles, her shoulders sagging. "It's Pam who's been getting treatment, Caitlin. When she found out that Nicole died—" Her voice caught mid-sentence. "She was very upset and the doctors thought it was best to give her some medication and keep her there overnight, so she could rest. Her relatives are flying in to help with... with everything. Someone will stop by the cottages for their luggage, so Bob wanted us to ask Marion to pack their things for them."

"I'll go talk to her," said Albert, his voice somber and low. He slowly rose to his feet. "When she's done packing, I can bring the bags around front so they'll be ready for Pam's family."

"Why won't either of you listen to me?" cried Caitlin. "Nicole's not dead! This is just an act. You've never seen her perform, but once she gets into character, she's super convincing. She does this kind of thing all the time. It's her way of getting attention. But she probably snuck out of the hospital by now and I bet I know right where she's hiding."

"Caitlin, I understand that this is a huge, horrible shock, and it's very difficult to accept, but Pam and Bob confirmed that—"

Before her aunt could finish her sentence, Caitlin bolted from the house, allowing the door on the screened-in porch to slam behind her, and charged into the windmill. Calling Nicole's name, she clambered up the stairs to the loft, but even before she reached the top step, she saw that the room was empty and Nicole's T-shirt and leggings were balled up on top of the package of paper towels, just where Caitlin had left them for her to find.

She snatched up the clothes and shook them hard in front of her face, asking, "How could you do this? You promised you wouldn't leave the party. You promised, Nicole! How could you go off by yourself and *die*?"

She kicked the pack of paper towels, spilling the rolls across the floor. She kicked those, too, and they bounced against the walls and knocked over a mop and broom. Caitlin kept kicking and stomping until she was exhausted, and the loft was strewn with paper products, dented cardboard boxes, and upended buckets.

Then she dropped to the floor, buried her face in Nicole's T-shirt, and sobbed.

SIX
PRESENT DAY

Caitlin wiped a tear from the corner of her eye. *Crying now won't change what happened in the past*, she told herself. *It'll only keep me from making progress today.*

Even so, she couldn't bring herself to go up into the loft of the windmill. So she cleared a path for Shane through the neatly arranged gardening and lawn tools. Then she turned around, went outside, and locked the door behind her.

After she'd washed her face and lingered over a second cup of coffee, Caitlin felt composed enough to take her daily stroll into town. Inspired by the crisp, autumn air, when she reached the market, she went inside and purchased the ingredients for making apple cinnamon muffins.

Baking will be a good distraction from dwelling on the past, she reasoned. *And if the muffins turn out, maybe I'll bring a few to Marion as a thank-you for recommending Shane.*

The prospect of baking made her recall her uncle's exaggerated complaints about how hot the kitchen became when Lydia baked cookies for the guests on Saturday mornings. *It's too bad Uncle Albert never made it to the island in the fall, when the weather was cooler. On a day like today, he would've been glad to warm up near the oven, reading his paper while Aunt Lydia baked dessert...*

The scenario was bittersweet to imagine. It also hurt to think about how pleased Lydia had been that their niece had wanted to spend Thanksgiving with them on Dune Island. But what could Caitlin do about it now that her aunt and uncle had passed away? Shaking her head, she pushed the recollection from her mind, just as she'd done with the other plans she and Lydia had made before Nicole drowned, and everything changed.

Converting the loft into a sitting room is the only dream from the past that I can still fulfill for Aunt Lydia, she realized. *So instead of acting like such a baby about being here, I need to muscle through it and do whatever it takes to make sure the results are amazing.*

Caitlin had just set the muffins on the cooling rack when her phone rang.

"Hi, Caitlin," her sister-in-law whispered.

"Suzanne? Is everything okay?" replied Caitlin, baffled by her low voice.

"Yes. I'm just being quiet so the children won't hear me. I don't want to get their hopes up in case you're busy, but is there any chance you have time for a quick video chat with them today? I've been trying to stall until you were more settled in, but they're dying to see 'Auntie's Auntie's windmill.'"

Caitlin had to laugh at the reference. Although she'd told her brother and sister-in-law about the stipulation for her inheritance, all she'd said to the children was that she was fixing up her aunt's old windmill so someone would want to buy it. Because they'd never met Lydia, and Charlie had barely known her, either, Caitlin had omitted the details about her aunt dying and leaving the property to her. So the children thought it still belonged to Lydia, and they'd been calling it "Auntie's Auntie's windmill," as if that were its proper name.

"Sure, I'd love to chat with them," agreed Caitlin. "Just give me half an hour to clean up a mess I made in the kitchen."

When Suzanne called back and Caitlin showed the children the cottage through her phone screen, they thought it was cute—but when she showed them the view from outside, they were utterly fascinated by the windmill.

"Can you press the button?" Logan, her older nephew asked.

"What button?"

"The one that makes that big fan on the roof spin around."

Caitlin smiled and explained the function of the windmill's arms, adding, "They're locked in place now, so they don't turn. But that's okay because the windmill isn't used for grinding grain anymore—it's mostly just for decoration."

"We have a 'coration, too. It's for Halloween," Caitlin's younger nephew, Archie, piped up. "We made it out of leaves and Daddy's clothes. 'Cept I forgot what it's called."

"A scarecrow," his brother wisely informed him. "It has a jack-o-lantern for its head and a LED candle inside so his eyes light up. Show her, Mom."

Caitlin's sister-in-law directed the camera toward the front step, so Caitlin could see it. "He looks so real that if it wasn't for his orange noggin, I'd think it was your daddy sitting there," she raved.

"Can you show us what the windmill looks like on the inside?" interjected Caitlin's niece, Maya, keeping them on topic.

"Okay, I'll give you a quick peek, but then I have to go—I have a meeting with the carpenter who's going to fix it up."

The children oohed and ahhed when they saw the rustic, rough-hewn, eight-walled interior of the windmill.

"It's like a fort," Logan said.

"No, it's like a log cabin," countered Maya. "What's that ladder for?"

"That's a staircase. It leads to the loft on the second story."

"Cool. Can you show us what's up there?"

"Mm, maybe another time." Despite resolving to be braver, Caitlin still felt apprehensive about being on the phone with the children the first time she went into the loft. "Right now, I have to hop into the shower before the carpenter comes."

"Okay, you guys, let's say goodbye to Auntie Caitlin," her sister-in-law instructed, and the children chorused their farewells.

"Bye-bye, everyone. I love you," Caitlin echoed.

After going outside and locking the door behind her, she lingered next to the windmill for a moment, smiling at her niece and nephews' childish excitement about its old, skeletal and somewhat drab interior. Funny, how seeing it through their eyes had made being inside "Auntie's Auntie's windmill" feel a little less daunting. *Now, my next challenge is to get over my hangup about going into the loft...*

When Shane showed up at 2:00 on the dot, Caitlin's first thought was, *Why on earth would his cousin think he needs help finding a date? I bet women hit on him all the time—he's the epitome of tall, dark, and handsome!* He was also incredibly muscular, neatly dressed, and he had a cleft in his clean-shaven chin.

"Hi, Caitlin," he said, extending his hand. Little surprise that his skin was smooth and warm, and his grip was firm.

"Hello, Shane," she replied, hoping she hadn't squeaked. Usually, Caitlin wasn't flustered like this by a man's appearance. Maybe it was because after he'd made such a poor impression on the phone, she wasn't expecting him to look so pulled-together in person. "Should I show you the space, first, or do you want to hear what I envision for the remodel?"

"We can do both at the same time." He gave her a friendly grin, and Caitlin felt oddly relieved to notice his teeth were a little crowded.

"Okay, sure." She moved toward the windmill. Patting the gray shingled exterior, she said, "So, the project is to convert *this* into a living area. It has a loft, which will need to be remodeled, too."

"This is my lucky day." His grin broadened. "When you told me your address, I was hoping the project would include the windmill."

"You might not feel so lucky when you see the interior," warned Caitlin, although she was pleased by his enthusiasm. "The windmill was built in the mid-1800s, so obviously it has been structurally restored a couple of times since then and it's had some minor repairs, too. Sadly, the previous owners gutted it in the 1960s so they could use the space as their rental office. If you ask me, it was a shame to destroy all that history, especially since they only needed room for a desk, a chair, and a filing cabinet, which they could've squeezed in if they'd really tried. At least, that's what my uncle said when he and my aunt bought the property twenty-some years ago."

"So the previous owners didn't leave *any* of the functioning machinery?"

"Only the gear shaft mechanism near the ceiling, and this." Caitlin tapped her foot against the millstone that had been repurposed into a step in front of the windmill door. She'd always loved that feature. "And wait till you see the beams and rafters. Some of the wood is original—or nearly original—and I have a feeling that beneath the grime, it's gorgeous."

She unlocked the door and pushed it open. Shane followed her inside and almost immediately gave a low, appreciative whistle. "Wow, you weren't kidding. This wood is amazing. Please tell me you don't want to cover it up with drywall?"

"No way—I want to keep as much of it exposed as possible."

"Phew, that's good. 'Cause if you wanted to cover it up, it would be such a travesty I'd have to turn down the job on principle."

Caitlin laughed, something she wouldn't have pictured herself doing inside the windmill. "I do think the stairs will need to be completely replaced though."

"Agreed." He sidestepped the lawn equipment to examine the staircase. "We'll have to get creative because of the shape of the walls, but I'll put in something much safer. Although this is sturdy enough for now. Can we go up and take a look around?"

"Sure."

"Great. After you." He stepped back and gestured for her to go first.

I can do this. I can do this, she thought but she couldn't seem to move.

Her hesitation was so prolonged that Shane suggested, "I can go alone if you're uncomfortable with heights? Or with... bats?"

"No, I don't mind the height, and as far as I know, there's no evidence of bats getting in."

"Good, 'cause if I saw a colony of them up there, I'd probably scream."

Caitlin chuckled. His good-natured banter quieted her anxiety and she crossed in front of him and climbed the stairs. To her relief, the empty room didn't evoke any strong emotional response, although the dusty floor elicited a sneeze.

"Gesundheit." As he crested the landing, Shane tipped his head back so far to study the gear shaft near the ceiling that Caitlin was concerned he'd topple over. "That is really something," he marveled. Then he crossed the room and gazed out the back window. "Yep, I figured there'd be an awesome view from here."

Caitlin moved closer to take a look, too. She peered over the slanted rooftops of the little cottages in the back yard, and beyond the shaggy brown scrub oaks, the scraggly, yellowing pitch pines, and the glossy, reddish-orange wild black cherry trees, to the water. At this time of day, the sterling, sun-illumined bay glittered so radiantly it made her squint.

"It's incredible. That's why I'd like to replace this window with a much bigger one."

"Why limit the window to just one wall? Why not two or three? Taking advantage of the octagonal structure would give you more of a panoramic view of the bay."

"You're right," Caitlin agreed. "I just don't want *too* many windows, so it feels like a fishbowl up here."

"It wouldn't." Shane turned and pointed. "Not if we left the four walls on this side as they are, with just one small window, so you'd have privacy from people passing by on the main road."

Caitlin loved that plan. They also discussed her ideas for flooring and lighting, as well as his suggestion to add a large picture window on the lower level, overlooking the rectangular green where the other cottages were located.

"Since you don't plan to cover up the original wood, I'll use an insulation technology that's applied in coats, almost like painting, throughout the windmill. It'll help a lot with thermal regulation. But what did you have in mind for a heating source?" he asked.

"I thought we could install an electric fireplace on each level for the cooler months. But I figured the windmill will be more like a three-season porch—it wouldn't be used very often in the winter."

"Hmm." Shane rubbed his chin. "I agree that an electric fireplace seems like the most reasonable option for heating, although I realize electricity can be expensive. Is that why you don't want to use the windmill in the winter?"

"It's more that it would be inconvenient to go outside to access it, especially if there's snow on the ground." Caitlin appreciated the way he asked about her preferences before making suggestions, and she was eager to hear his ideas, too. The project already felt like a collaboration. "Do you have any input about that?"

He nodded, his eyes shining. "I noticed the windmill nearly abuts the end of your sunroom. If you opened up those adjacent walls, and connected the two buildings, you wouldn't have to go outside to enter the windmill. There'd be a nice sense of flow between the windmill and the house, and it would make the sunroom seem larger, too."

Caitlin was intrigued by this option. "I hadn't really considered anything like that. I mean, I like the idea a lot, but whenever my aunt and I talked about remodeling the loft, I got the sense she wanted a private space for herself, so having direct access from the house wasn't a priority."

"I could put in a trap door of sorts in the loft that you could close for privacy, as well as a door between the windmill and the sunroom. That way, you could have the best of both worlds—continuity *and* seclusion. But I don't want to push. You can talk it over with your aunt and get back to me about it."

The notion of discussing the remodel with Lydia again made Caitlin unexpectedly sentimental. "Unfortunately, I can't talk it over with her," she said, a quaver in her voice. "My aunt recently passed away."

When Shane leaned toward her, she caught a faint hint of woodsy aftershave. "Oh. I'm sorry to hear that."

"Thank you." Caitlin cleared her throat and explained, "I inherited the property from her, and she requested that I convert the windmill loft into a sitting room. So we spoke a lot about her dream for the loft, but she didn't really mention what she wanted done on the ground level."

Shane's forehead was furrowed in a thoughtful expression and he hesitantly replied, "Well, like I said, connecting the buildings would provide easier access and more continuity. But if it's total seclusion that you want, then it makes sense to leave the windmill as a separate space. I guess it all depends on what you find most appealing."

"Actually, it depends on what *buyers* find most appealing. I plan to sell the property after the remodel is completed." Caitlin felt compelled to elaborate, "I live in Santa Fe, New Mexico, so it's not practical for me to keep a summer place in Massachusetts."

Shane nodded slowly, as if processing this information. "Okay, then, if your priority is increasing the market value of the house, I'd strongly advise connecting the buildings. Most buyers would want conjoined living spaces."

"I think you're right about that," she agreed. "I just wish I had talked to you sooner. Now, I'll have to redesign my floorplan."

"You made a floorplan?" He raised an eyebrow, appearing impressed. "Are you a designer by profession?"

"Not even close," admitted Caitlin. "I'm a capital campaign consultant, and a lot of my clients raise funding to build or renovate their facilities. So I've learned to read blueprints and floorplans in order to present them to donors."

"That's cool," said Shane. His imperfect smile was perfectly charming. "Can you show me what you'd drawn up before I threw a monkey wrench in your plans with my suggestions?"

"Sure." So they went downstairs, and after Caitlin had locked the door behind them, Shane followed her into the cottage. Because it was only polite to offer her first invited guest a refreshment, she asked him if he wanted an apple cinnamon muffin. "I can make coffee or hot chocolate to go with it."

"Hot chocolate would hit the spot, thanks." He took off his jacket and hung it on the back of his chair, making himself comfortable. She found his confidence attractive. *Like almost everything else about him so far.* "Are you staying on the island for the duration of the remodel, or will you be traveling back and forth?"

"I'm here for the duration." Caitlin wondered if he was concerned that she'd be breathing down his neck while he worked, or if there was another reason he'd asked that question. "I've got some time off before my next campaign, so I figured it was the perfect time to tackle this project."

"That's great, I'm glad you're sticking around." He grinned and nodded, but then he abruptly broke eye contact and reached to take a muffin from the basket in front of him. "I-I mean I'm glad the timing works out for you to stay because it would be an awfully long haul if you were traveling back and forth between Santa Fe and Hope Haven... Have you always lived in the Southwest?"

"No. I grew up in New Hampshire." As she carefully unpeeled the paper liner from her muffin, Caitlin was pleased to notice he was devouring his. *I guess that means it tastes all right.*

"So did you get to vacation here at your aunt's place every summer?"

"Not really. I only visited a few times when I was in high school." Feeling jittery about the topic, and interested in learning more about Shane, she quickly redirected the conversation. "What about you? Where did you grow up?"

"Maine—near the Belgrade Lakes. Lived there most of my life. I just moved to Hope Haven a few years ago."

"I've been to the Belgrades—they're beautiful! Was it difficult to leave them behind?"

"It sure was, although I loved Dune Island the minute I set foot on it. I came here because my cousin's husband was in poor health and he needed a hand with his business. I was only going to stay for the season, but then he passed away, and two years later, I'm still here," he explained. "I'm teaching their only child, Sammy, the trade. He's just about to graduate from high school and he's my apprentice. I mostly work alone, but if you hire me for this project, I'll need his help from time to time."

Uneasy, Caitlin twisted her mouth to one side. "He's a teenager?"

"Yeah, but don't worry, he's only assisting me. I supervise everything he does—he's not allowed to lift a hammer without my permission. And I triple check all his work."

"I'm sure you do. It's just that..." Caitlin didn't want to offend him. "I remember when I was that age, kids liked to talk about, you know, stuff they're working on, or stuff they know and as I said, I want to keep this project quiet. It's important no one finds out I'm selling until I'm ready to put the cottage on the market."

"Don't worry about that. I'll tell him not to mention you or the remodel to anyone. He knows if he doesn't do what I say, I'll sic his mother on his case," said Shane with a laugh. "He'll never hear the end of it."

Caitlin felt comfortable enough with him to ask, "Is this the same cousin who tries to set you up?"

"Yeah. That's how I know she can be relentless." He chuckled again. "But honestly, Sammy's such a good kid. He never gives either of us any grief."

Relieved, she smiled. "I look forward to meeting him."

As they drank hot chocolate and finished eating their muffins, Caitlin showed Shane her drawings, and the photo galleries on her laptop. They also discussed a schedule, her budget, and his fee for labor.

Finally, he excused himself, saying he had an appointment in town. "I'll come back tomorrow to take measurements so I can write up an estimate for the materials I'll need to order. What time works for you?"

"I don't have a car, so unless I go for a walk, I should be around the house most of the day. But in case I'm not, let me give you a spare key to the windmill. Feel free to stop by whenever it fits your schedule. We can always catch up by phone if we miss each other in person."

Shane texted her so she'd have his cell phone number, in addition to his home phone. "I'm really looking forward to this project," he said, standing to leave. As he stretched his arms to put on his jacket, his shirt rode up, exposing his toned abdomen and causing Caitlin's face and neck to flush with warmth.

What's going on with me anyway? she asked herself later as she cleared the dishes from the table. It wasn't like her to feel such a strong pull of attraction to someone at first sight, especially considering it had only been a matter of days since she'd dumped Jonathan. Yet now she found herself wondering how Shane would've answered last night if she actually *had* been calling to ask if he was available for a date, instead of for a carpentry project.

Almost immediately, Caitlin censored the thought. *Asking a guy out isn't my style, even if I weren't employing him. Besides, Shane might be attractive on the surface, but I don't know anything about him. And he knows even less about me—which is exactly how I want to keep it*, she told herself. *I'm just glad that we've gotten the ball rolling on the remodel. The sooner he gets started, the sooner he'll finish, and the sooner I can put the cottage on the market.*

SEVEN

"I noticed Shane's truck parked at your house yesterday," said Marion the following morning. Caitlin had brought her half a dozen apple cinnamon muffins, and while Pepper gnawed on a rope toy, the two women sat on the sofa, enjoying the treat. "What did you think of him?"

"He seems to really know what he's doing," said Caitlin. "I like it that he gave me a few suggestions, but he's not too pushy."

"Yes, he's a very talented craftsman. But what I meant was what do you think of *him*? He's very kind, smart, and quite the looker, isn't he?"

"Well, I only just met him but he seems to be all those things, yes," she admitted.

"He's single, just like you are. Maybe the two of you could go out sometime."

Caitlin chuckled at her boldness. "I'm not interested in him in that way."

"No? Why not?" Marion seemed offended, as if Caitlin had indicated something was wrong with him. "You said there wasn't anyone special in your life."

"It's nothing personal. It just wouldn't be appropriate, since he's going to be working for me," she explained. "And I'm sure Shane wouldn't consider it professional to get involved with a client, either."

"Ack, you kids these days are too worried about what's *professional* or *appropriate*. It takes the fun out of being young and single," said Marion.

Caitlin chuckled. "You might be right about that. But I'm only here for a short amount of time anyway, so there's no sense in dating anyone from the island."

"I'm not suggesting you commit to him for the rest of your life. I'm just saying you seem lonely and he seems lonely." She turned her hands up in a half-shrug. "What's the harm in having dinner together?"

"It's not that there's necessarily any harm, but I'm not lonely," said Caitlin. "I'm independent, and I need my space. Most of the time, I prefer being alone."

"Hmpf, I guess that's where we differ. I'm alone by circumstance, not choice. Even at this age, I wish I had a man in my life. A husband. Not only to be my friend and companion, but to love and cherish me for the rest of our days, and vice versa." Marion seemed genuinely perplexed as she tipped her head at Caitlin. "I know it may seem old-fashioned, but don't you want to find that special someone, too?"

"Mm, not especially," Caitlin said.

A more truthful answer would've been, "Not anymore." Or, "Not since Nicole drowned."

Her thoughts drifted to that terrible morning after she'd found out what had happened and she'd trashed the windmill loft.

Caitlin must have lain on the floor and cried for over an hour, stopping only when she heard her aunt talking to another woman in the driveway. As their voices carried through the small upstairs window, Caitlin figured out the woman was Nicole's grandmother, who'd come to collect the family's luggage. After expressing her deepest condolences, Lydia inquired about how Pam was doing.

"She's devastated, of course—we all are," Nicole's grandmother tearfully answered. "But the doctors have sedated her, so I don't think the reality has hit her yet. Right now, she's still numb."

Although she couldn't make out the words of her aunt's response, Caitlin recognized the sympathy in Lydia's tone. Nicole's grandmother responded by weeping openly.

"I just can't believe my beautiful granddaughter is gone. Nicole isn't—she *wasn't*—even sixteen," she cried. "She had so much talent, so many dreams. It's unfathomable that she'll never go to college or travel or have a career. She'll never fall in love and get married. She'll never give birth. She won't even get her driver's license or her voter's registration card. I can't believe it. I just can't believe that Nicole is gone. Her life is over."

Whatever else the two women said, Caitlin wasn't listening. *Nicole is gone. Her life is over*, she silently repeated, vacantly staring up at the windmill's gear shaft until she felt dizzy.

It was possible she passed out briefly from heat and dehydration. Or more likely, she fell asleep. But the next thing she knew, her aunt was wiggling her shoulder. "Caitlin, Caitlin, wake up. We've been looking everywhere for you. It's time for lunch. Come and have something to eat."

Her mouth was so parched she had to lick her lips before speaking. "I'm not hungry."

"Come downstairs anyway," her aunt urged her. "We're worried about you, sweetheart."

Please don't call me that, thought Caitlin, because she knew there was nothing sweet or lovable about her. Nicole's mother was right; Caitlin was a phony. Her behavior hadn't been any better than Nicole's. Both girls had strayed from the party, even though they'd known they shouldn't. The only difference was that one of them was dead now, while the other one was living. It wasn't fair.

Caitlin unwillingly rose to her feet and followed her aunt down from the loft and into the cottage. But then she went straight to her room. And even though Donald called five times, she wouldn't—she *couldn't*—speak to him. When he biked twelve miles to see her in person, she wouldn't come to the door, either.

For weeks after they both left the island, she refused to read his email messages and handwritten letters, and she turned off the phone, too. It hurt her heart to do it and part of her was desperate to reach out to him. But how could she? She didn't deserve Donald, and it would be better for him to be without her, even if it tore them to pieces.

After a while, her stepmother essentially made her talk to him. Yet even then, and even though he was crying—he was audibly *bawling*—she forced herself to swallow her own sobs. All she said was, "I'm sorry, but I don't want you to contact me again. Summer's over and my feelings have changed."

Everything had changed.

Nicole's grandmother's words played over and over in Caitlin's mind. *My beautiful granddaughter is gone.*

The memory of what she'd overheard that morning—and the awful way she'd ghosted Donald—was so painful that for a moment Caitlin had lost the thread of the conversation with her neighbor. She bit her cheek and tried to refocus.

"Of course, I've got Pepper here to keep me company," Marion was saying. "I'm also in a bimonthly book club. And three or four times a week, I go to the community center."

"Sounds like you've got a very active social life."

"Yes, I suppose I do, although it would be nice if I didn't

have to drive into town to interact with people," she remarked. "That's one of the reasons why I once was looking forward to Lydia retiring here. Not only would I have gained a year-round neighbor, but I think we would've developed an even closer friendship than we already shared. It was so sad she became unwell."

"I know Aunt Lydia would've liked to develop your friendship, too," said Caitlin. "Even though I'll only be here for a couple of months, and I'm no substitute for her, I hope you'll enjoy being neighbors with *me*."

"I already do—and not just because you brought me muffins," replied Marion with a wink. "But I won't complain if you keep 'em coming."

Chuckling, Caitlin promised, "Don't worry, I will. I plan to do a lot of baking while I'm here."

Then she steered their conversation to recipes, a topic she was much more comfortable discussing than subjects like loneliness or love.

Half an hour later, Caitlin stepped outside and caught a whiff of woodsmoke as she scuffed through a scattering of greenish-brown oak and golden elm tree leaves in Marion's driveway.

Pretty soon, I'll need to rake up the leaves on the back lawn by the cottage and beneath the maple tree in the front yard, too. She didn't mind: she'd always enjoyed helping her uncle Albert maintain the grounds. Working together had made her feel closer to him, and even though he wasn't here now, maybe caring for the lawn was a way to recapture that feeling.

Caitlin's phone buzzed and she took it out of her pocket and shielded the screen so she could see who was calling. "Hi, Shane," she said brightly. "How are you?"

"Great, thanks. Beautiful morning—did I catch you during your daily walk?"

"Not really. I was just on my way back to the cottage after visiting my neighbor at the end of the cul-de-sac, Marion Graham."

"I know Marion. She's a gem."

"She thinks the same about you. She was the one who gave me your name after I confided in her about the remodel."

"That was nice. I'll have to thank her at our next book club meeting."

"You're—you're in her book club?"

"Yes. Does it surprise you that I like to read?"

"Not at all." Caitlin hadn't meant to be insulting, but there was a smile in Shane's voice. "It's just that... I assumed most of the people in Marion's book club are women in their seventies and above."

He chuckled. "You assumed right. Most of them are, although we've got a couple guys in the group, too," he said. "I'm the youngest one by far, but I don't mind and neither does anybody else. It's all about the books."

"As it should be," said Caitlin.

"Right! So, listen, I was calling to say I stopped by and took the measurements I needed."

"Already?" Caitlin felt a twinge of disappointment that she'd missed seeing him in person.

"Yeah. The early bird and all that," he said. "I can write up the estimate for materials and go over each line item with you before I order anything. But I wanted to mention that while I was poking around in the loft, the window stool popped off the back window."

"The window stool?"

"Yeah, some people refer to it as the windowsill, but technically the stool is the horizontal board across the bottom of the window. It makes a little ledge, if you can picture that? Anyway, it came right off in my hand."

"I'm not surprised. That old thing was already starting to

give way when I was in high school," she said. "And you'd have to replace it when you install a new window anyway, right?"

"Right, but what I wanted to tell you was that when it came off, I could look down into the wall. See, there's a... a sort of hollow pocket beneath the window, right between the stud and the plywood. It would be a lot easier to show you in person, but my point is, I found something inside that space."

"A sac of spider eggs?" guessed Caitlin with a shudder.

"No, no, nothing like that," laughed Shane. "It's a small plastic pouch. Or maybe you'd call it a bag."

"Like what you'd discard trash in?"

"No, it has a zipper on it. Reminds me of something a kid would use for storing pencils. Or for bringing a sandwich to school."

"Oh, gross—that's not what you found inside, was it?" asked Caitlin, aware it had been well over a month since the last guests had stayed at the cottage. If someone had hidden food in the loft, it would be rotten by now.

"I didn't open it. I figured it belongs to you, so it's none of my business. But it didn't smell, so I doubt it contains food." Shane lowered his voice. "I left it on the floor near the entrance to the windmill, and then I made sure to lock the door, just in case it's valuable."

Caitlin figured it was more likely something inconsequential that a child had left behind, although she was surprised the guests had access to the windmill. Maybe the housekeeping crew had forgotten to lock the door?

"Okay, I'll grab it before I go inside the house. Thanks for letting me know about it."

After arranging to meet the following morning at 10:00 to discuss the estimate for the materials, they said goodbye. Curious to find out what Shane had found stuffed in the wall, Caitlin hurried up the driveway and retrieved the faded blue bag from the windmill. About the size of a paperback book, it was softer and lighter than she'd expected. It was cleaner, too—Shane must have dusted it off for her. *That was nice of him.*

She carried the pouch into the sunroom to examine its contents. To her frustration, the zipper was rusted shut, but after several minutes of fiddling, she finally got it open. "Ta-da!" Caitlin gleefully exclaimed, feeling pleased with herself.

But when she peeked inside the bag and recognized the familiar snakeskin print material, her vision blurred with tears. Even though the fabric was balled into a compact wad, Caitlin realized it could only be one thing: Nicole's string bikini, the one her mother wouldn't let her wear.

Caitlin knew the teenager had hidden other wardrobe items and makeup behind the stacks of paper products in the loft, but she hadn't been aware that Nicole had stashed anything in a bag in the wall. *She must have really been concerned about getting in trouble if her mom found out she was wearing the bikini, so she had to find a better hiding place in case Aunt Lydia stumbled upon it while she was restocking paper supplies*, she reasoned.

The location had been a smart choice. If it weren't for the remodel, the swimsuit might have remained hidden indefinitely—or at least until the windows needed to be replaced. *Seems like every time I start to feel a little calmer about being on Dune Island, I get hit with another reminder of what happened the last time I was here*, Caitlin thought mournfully, wiping her eyes on her sleeve.

As she gingerly lifted the skimpy material from the bag, a square of folded paper dropped onto the table. She began to unfold it and saw the words, Pirate's ARR-Cade across the top of the page, along with a cartoon image of a parrot wearing a tricorn hat. Caitlin instantly recognized that she was holding a paper placemat from a popular arcade on the boardwalk. She continued to unfold it, and a smaller, rectangular piece of thick paper fluttered to the floor.

Reaching for it, Caitlin noticed it wasn't a piece of paper

after all; it was a strip of snapshots, the old-fashioned kind that were dispensed from a photo booth like the one at the arcade. There were four photos in all, and Nicole was pictured front and center in each of them. Dressed in the same snakeskin print bikini that Caitlin had just pulled from the bag, the teen was wearing bright red lipstick and heavy eye makeup.

Three other people were squeezed into the booth with her: a brunette girl in a blue tank top and sunglasses, and two guys dressed in orange lifeguard T-shirts. The guy to Nicole's right was blond-haired and broad-chested. To her left was a slimmer, very tanned, dark-haired boy. Standing on the other side of him, the brunette girl was partially edged out of the frame.

The teenagers were all making silly faces and gestures in the first snapshot. In the second, they were smiling naturally at the camera. The third photo showed Nicole had swiveled sideways to kiss the cheek of the grinning blond boy. In the final picture, she was turned toward the dark-haired guy, her puckered lips near his ear, her arms around his neck, pulling him closer.

Typical Nicole behavior, Caitlin thought, amused.

Strangely, seeing her face again wasn't nearly as disturbing as accidentally coming across her swimsuit. Maybe that was because Nicole looked so happy in the photos. Or maybe it was that Caitlin's sadness was overshadowed by her curiosity about the other teenagers. She couldn't stop staring at the snapshots and wondering who they were.

Nicole probably met up with them at the beach near the arcade—maybe that's why she never wanted me to come with her when she took a walk? I wonder if the four of them were sort of on a double date. Although if that was the case, Caitlin imagined the brunette girl would've been annoyed that Nicole had kissed *both* boys in the photos.

Maybe she was only mugging it up for the camera? Caitlin surmised. *Or else she was acting out one of her "scenes," or playing a game to see which boy would give her the most attention? Or maybe Nicole and the other girl had picked out two cute, random guys at the arcade and they were just flirting with them for fun?*

But Caitlin sensed there was more going on between them than that—otherwise, why would Nicole have kept the strip of photos hidden in the wall? She turned it over, looking for a clue, but the other side was blank. Caitlin glanced at the paper placemat. Inscribed with a maze leading from the parrot on the top of the page to a treasure chest on the bottom, it was designed to keep children occupied while waiting for their food to arrive at their tables. There were no markings on the front of the placement, and only a reddish-pink stain on the back.

Nicole must have blotted her lipstick on this, Caitlin guessed. But as she started to turn the paper to the front again, she noticed that there was faded writing beneath the pink smudge.

She squinted at the barely legible print and read, "N♥ R". Beneath the initials was a drawing of three cubes in a row. The middle one had a large X on it. Above the cubes was a series of straight lines; below the cubes were several squiggles.

N obviously stands for Nicole, and R must be the first initial of one of the guys in the photos, Caitlin deduced. It surprised her that Nicole, who'd always acted as if she were more sophisticated than her peers, had scribbled such a cutesy note on the placemat—and then, apparently, she'd kissed it. Was she being serious or was it some kind of ploy, part of an act?

And what about the drawing? Was the picture a random doodle, or was it supposed to depict something specific?

Caitlin got up and turned on a lamp. Holding the placemat an inch above the bulb, she scrutinized the sketch. Only then did she see there was a fainter inscription below the squiggly lines. "Thurs Aug 29," it read.

A chill turned her skin to gooseflesh and she dropped onto

the sofa. Thursday, August 29, was the day Nicole drowned. So why was that date written on the placemat? Was it the date she'd taken the photos?

No, that can't be right. The arcade and all the other shops on the boardwalk were still closed because the tropical storm knocked out their electricity and it hadn't been restored yet, she remembered. *Maybe Thursday, August 29, was just the day Nicole was doodling on the placemat?*

Caitlin shook herself. There was no use wondering any further. Focusing on the past only made her miserable, and even if she figured out the significance of the scribblings, it wouldn't change what had happened.

Not that I'm blaming Shane, but I wish he hadn't given me this bag—or that he'd never found it in the first place. Caitlin was already plagued by enough guilt and sad memories about that summer, without receiving tangible reminders of Nicole's youth. Of her death day.

She quickly refolded the placemat and the bikini and tucked them back into the plastic pouch, along with the photo strip. She had no reason to keep Nicole's belongings, but it didn't seem right to discard them, either.

I'll decide what to do with these things some other time, she thought, and buried the bag beneath her clothes in her bottom dresser drawer, where it at least would be out of sight, even if it wasn't completely out of mind.

EIGHT

Once Caitlin finalized the project details with Shane, she knew she needed to think about her career back home.

In Santa Fe, she usually spent her spare time between campaigns catching up on the paperwork, household chores, and medical appointments she'd let lapse while she was working. She also liked exploring new hiking trails with friends, taking pottery-making classes, and hanging out with her brother's family. But in Hope Haven, she wanted to keep to herself to avoid the gossips. Letting herself ruminate on Nicole—on the clothing and photos she'd found and on the scribblings with the date Nicole had died—wasn't helping anyone, either. So she decided to call her consulting agency and inquire about upcoming campaigns.

Maybe I can get a head start on the preliminary analysis, she thought as she tapped the director's name, Tobias, in her contacts list.

"You know I can't officially offer you a campaign until the client signs a contract with us," he told her. "But off the record, we're about to close the deal with a parochial school that needs funding to build a new gymnasium. You'd be perfect for that one, since you've done so many similar campaigns."

That's exactly why I wouldn't *want to do it*, thought Caitlin, but she tried to be more diplomatic in her reply. "I enjoy working with private and parochial schools, but there are lots of consultants qualified to conduct a campaign like that one. I'd love to take on something a little more challenging."

"Hmm." There was a quiet pause, followed by what sounded like a door closing. Then he said in a low voice, "There *is* another organization I've been courting. A local major hospital plans to add a children's wing to its facility. Of course, they'd need to conduct a feasibility study, first..."

Tobias discreetly filled her in on the details, and the more Caitlin heard, the more she wanted to manage the campaign. Emphasizing her experience, she told him she thought she'd be effective in helping the hospital meet or even surpass its campaign goals.

"I agree," he said. "But for a project of this scope, *if* the hospital signs with our agency, they'd want to interview consultants and decide for themselves who'd be the best fit. I can put you at the top of the list, if you're sure you're up for it?"

"I'm sure," confirmed Caitlin, figuring she could do an online interview or else fly back for an in-person if that's what they preferred.

"Great. I expect to hear from them in a few weeks and I'll be in touch when I do."

Buoyed by the hope of a more challenging campaign that aligned with her interests, Caitlin threw herself into researching the hospital, potential grants, and prospective major donors, in preparation for her upcoming interview. When she needed a break, she'd read, visit Marion, or take a walk into town to enjoy the fall foliage.

Although not as overtly spectacular as what she'd witnessed growing up in New Hampshire, the autumn hues in Hope

Haven were still undeniably beautiful—and one of the most striking trees she'd seen was the red maple directly in front of the cottage. During the late afternoons, Caitlin frequently nestled on the sofa in the sunroom and stared at its fiery leaves, which reminded her of watching the sunset.

In the evenings, Caitlin sometimes called one of her friends from Santa Fe, or else she read for hours, or took a long, hot soak in the bath, which felt like a luxury at first. Yet despite telling Marion that she preferred to be alone and needed her own space, Caitlin quickly discovered the amount of solitude she had on Dune Island felt like too much of a good thing.

By morning time, she'd feel desperate to talk to someone in person, instead of just on the phone. So she began a habit of stopping by the windmill to ask if Shane wanted coffee, which he usually did. He'd show her the progress he was making, and explain what he intended to do next. But their conversations always moved on to other topics.

It was during these exchanges that he mentioned what he liked and didn't like about the book he was reading for his book club. And she shared how excited her nephews and niece had been when she'd shown them the windmill during a video call. Caitlin also learned about Shane's newfound passion for kiteboarding, and she told him about her work at the food bank.

Even though their conversations weren't deeply personal, Caitlin usually walked away feeling as if she'd gleaned another small insight into Shane's personality, and she'd given him a glimpse of hers, too. She appreciated that he seemed to respect her need for privacy—he never even asked what was inside the bag he'd discovered—and because of that, she found it easier to let down her guard and enjoy being in his presence. Of course, it didn't hurt that he was incredibly handsome and strong... but his looks weren't all that had caught her attention; she was also drawn to his warmth, humor, and thoughtfulness.

She didn't realize how much she looked forward to their

little chats until the first time he brought Sammy to work with him. Although Caitlin instantly liked the polite, slightly gawky teenager, she regretted that her small talk with Shane was suddenly reduced to a couple of bland comments about the weather. Then, he got right down to business.

"Sammy's going to be helping me out a lot this week, and into next week, too. His classes have been canceled because a water main busted in the school's cafeteria," he explained. "Usually, he's only available in the afternoons or on the weekends, so this timing works out perfectly, since I just received delivery of the rest of the materials I need to start the framework, which is a two-person job."

"By 'framework,' do you mean putting in the windows?" Caitlin asked.

"Yes, if we have time. But first we'll work on restructuring the wall and roof between the windmill and the sunroom," he clarified. "So we'll need to move the furniture out of the way. We'd also better shut the interior door between the sunroom and the living room, otherwise, it might get drafty in there. Not to mention, loud."

"No problem, I'll be wearing earbuds and listening to music," said Caitlin agreeably.

But she wasn't quite prepared for just *how* loud the demolition would be, nor how jarring. No matter how high the volume of her music, or which room she was in, she could hear every sledgehammer blow. The noise and reverberations set her teeth on edge and made her head throb, so she'd escape it by taking two long walks in the morning. After lunch, she'd go to the library in Benjamin's Manor, which was larger than the tiny one in Lucinda's Hamlet, to do her research for a couple hours.

However, being in the public setting made her anxious. Because there were few visitors on the island at this time of year, she was concerned that a librarian or a patron would recognize she wasn't a resident, and that they'd try to strike up a friendly conversation about what had brought her to Hope Haven. Although not as distracting as the noise at the cottage, Caitlin's anxiety kept her from being as productive as she'd hoped to be, and on Friday afternoon, she decided that instead of going to the library, she'd visit Marion.

I haven't seen her and Pepper out walking in a couple days. I wonder if the weather is too chilly for them, she thought as she rang her neighbor's doorbell.

It seemed to take an unusually long time for Marion to open the door, and when she did, she was dressed in a bathrobe, her skin was pale, and it appeared she hadn't combed her hair.

"Are you all right?" Caitlin asked over Pepper's boisterous barking.

"I'm afraid I've had better days," she began to say. But when Pepper hopped up and pawed Caitlin's leg, Marion snapped in an uncharacteristically stern voice, "Pepper, stop that! Get down!"

The scolded animal immediately stopped barking, turned, and slunk down the hall. Marion opened the door wider to let Caitlin in. As she led her to the living room, her neighbor apologized for her pet's behavior. "Sorry about that. He's been misbehaving all morning—not that I blame him. He's a creature of habit and I've completely disrupted his schedule."

"Why, what happened?"

"I had dental work for an infected tooth a few days ago, and I'm on pain relievers which make me a little dizzy. I haven't felt quite up to taking a walk, so poor little Pepper's been cooped up inside, too. And let's just say when he doesn't get exercise, it affects both our temperaments."

Caitlin immediately empathized, "I'm so sorry you've been under the weather. I'd be happy to take Pepper for a walk if you want me to."

"You would?"

"Absolutely. I wish you would've asked me sooner."

"I considered it, but I didn't want to impose, especially since you mentioned that you need your space."

"It's not an imposition at all," insisted Caitlin, feeling bad that she'd come across as unapproachable to Marion. "When I said I need my space, I mostly meant in the context of a romantic relationship. I'm not the type of person who has to be around her significant other 24/7, that's all. But I love visiting with you, and I hope in the future you won't hesitate to call me for any reason, and especially if there's something you need. Okay?"

"Okay—and the same goes for you calling on me whenever I can be helpful, too," she said, and Caitlin agreed.

A jangle of Pepper's leash was all it took to lure him from wherever he'd gone to sulk. He trotted back into the living room, wagging his tail.

"How long do you usually walk with him?" Caitlin asked.

"The entire loop takes about thirty or thirty-five minutes. Pepper will show you the way," Marion answered, stooping to give her darling pet a pat on the head. "Be a good boy for Caitlin and I'll have a treat waiting for you when you get home."

The frisky little dog led Caitlin down the street at a brisk pace, and as they passed the windmill, she could hear Shane and Sammy hammering away. "Slow down, Pepper," she said, in no hurry to return to the racket at the cottage.

When they reached the end of Windswept Way, Pepper turned north, keeping to the edge of the main road for a hundred yards until turning onto a side street named Seashell Drive. He expertly navigated the deserted neighborhood, which appeared to contain more summer homes than year-round residences. A few new streets had been added, and a myriad of houses had been constructed since Caitlin had ridden a bike through these blocks as a teenager. She wouldn't have known which direction to go without Pepper guiding her.

After several more turns, the dog led her down a long, straight street. As the pavement gave way to a sandy stretch of road, Caitlin realized they were headed for the beach. Pepper made a beeline for the staircase that descended the dune toward the water.

"No, no, Pepper. We don't want to go down there. Come on boy, come on," she coaxed him. He turned and looked at her, but then he darted forward, straining on his leash. Knowing that if she refused to budge, he'd hurt his neck, Caitlin reluctantly followed him down the steps. When he got to the bottom, he turned south, looping back toward Windswept Way.

"Okay, we can walk on the beach for a while, but we're not going to the end," she warned, referring to where the dunes dwindled to a flat expanse and the beach was interrupted by the tidal river and marshland. On the other side of this inlet, the beach and dunes picked up again in Benjamin's Manor, which could be reached on foot during extreme low tides. But Albert and Lydia had always referred to the inlet as "the end," so that's what Caitlin called it, too.

As a teenager, she'd loved strolling along the remote, pristine stretch of shoreline that lay south of The Windmill Cottages. She could spend hours combing the tidal pools for the prettiest periwinkle, scallop, moon snail, and jingle shells she could find, or studying the behaviors of horseshoe, hermit and fiddler crabs, as well as piping plovers, egrets, and oystercatchers.

But after Nicole drowned, Caitlin felt betrayed by her beloved seascape. She developed such an intense disdain for the land near the inlet that even now she could barely raise her eyes to glance at it in the distance.

Instead, she focused on Pepper as he happily padded over the shallow pockets of soft, golden sand. They passed several wooden dune staircases until they came to the one leading to The Windmill Cottages.

"Okay, Pepper, this is our stop," Caitlin announced. "We're going up, even if I have to carry you."

But her threat was unnecessary because Pepper was already several paces ahead of her. The small animal impressively hoisted himself up the tall stairs so quickly she could hardly keep up with him. When they reached the top, they hurried through the woods, cut across the lawn near the cottages, and headed down Windswept Way toward Marion's house.

"Back so soon? Did you have a good walk?" she asked when she opened the door.

Caitlin wasn't sure if she was addressing her or Pepper, but she joked, "It was very pleasant, but I don't know who was walking whom. If it weren't for Pepper leading the way, I'd probably still be wandering around that network of new streets over in the Seashell Drive area."

Marion smiled like a proud parent and unhooked the animal's leash. "Sounds like you deserve *two* treats," she said to Pepper, and he raced down the hall to the kitchen, where his goodies apparently were set out for him. "While you were gone, one of my book club members dropped off a meal of butternut soup, with bread pudding for dessert. Would you like to join me for an early supper?"

Caitlin appreciated the offer, but when she and Pepper had passed the cottage, she noticed Sammy's car was gone, but Shane's truck was still parked in the driveway. She hoped to say goodbye to him before the weekend.

I'd better not tell Marion that, or she'll think I lied about not being interested in going out with him—which I'm not, she thought. *But it's always fun to chat with him, and I've missed doing that while Sammy's been here.*

"Thanks, but I bought fish that I need to make while it's fresh," Caitlin said. After promising to come back the next afternoon to walk Pepper again, she hurried down the street toward the cottage.

"Hi, there," Shane called when she came up the driveway where he was removing a stack of folded tarps from his truck bed.

"Hello," she replied, a little breathless.

"You're looking very rosy this afternoon," Shane said, and she was sure his comment made her cheeks burn an even deeper shade of pink.

"Must be this fresh Dune Island air."

"Yeah, that'll do it," he said with a grin. Was he perpetually in a smiling mood? "You'll be happy to know that we're done knocking holes in your walls for now, so next week you won't feel the whole house shaking."

"*You* were the ones causing that?" teased Caitlin. "I thought Hope Haven had been hit by a series of earthquakes."

"I'm sure you did," he acknowledged with a chuckle. "Even though you shouldn't notice any more seismic activity, don't put away your earbuds just yet—you'll need them for when I start to reconstruct what we just demolished."

Caitlin wished she could come up with a witty response to keep the banter going, but she drew a blank. "Thanks for the heads-up."

"I also wanted to let you know that Sammy's going back to school on Monday, which is sooner than expected."

"Oh, that's good!" she said a little too enthusiastically. "I-I mean it's good they got the water pumped out and the damage repaired so quickly, although I'm a little envious. The apartment above mine in Santa Fe flooded last month, and I won't be able to move back into my place until almost Christmas."

"What happened, dripping ceiling?"

"It was more like a waterfall."

Shane made a face. "Aw, man, that's rough."

"Not as rough as going to stay with a coworker and discovering she'd started seeing my boyfriend behind my back," Caitlin blurted out.

The situation suddenly seemed more amusing than maddening to her, but Shane sounded appalled when he said, "You've got to be kidding."

"I know, it sounds like a bad joke, right?" she replied with a breezy laugh. "Unfortunately, it wasn't. But it's okay—I'm over it and I've got a dry place to stay now."

"I'll make doubly sure of that," he said, shifting the stack of tarps in his arms. "I'm covering the openings in the walls with these until I install the windows. If it's okay with you, I'll put one over the door from the living room to the sunroom, to seal it off, nice and tight. Which means you can't use the sunroom for a while, but at least it won't let cold air into the house. After what you've been through, I want to keep you toasty warm."

The innuendo of his words was probably unintentional, but Caitlin was already growing toasty warm at the thought of his arms around her. She tried to ignore how she was feeling, and casually replied, "Sounds good, thanks. I'll try not to open that door by accident."

"Hmm, maybe I shouldn't use a translucent tarp. Otherwise, if you forget it's there and try to step through it, you'll be like a bird flying into a glass window." Shane did an imitation that was a little morbid but just goofy enough to make them both laugh.

"You joke, but I could see myself doing that—especially in the morning before I've had coffee," she admitted.

"In that case, I'll definitely use a blue tarp," he said. "I'm not going to let you get hurt on my watch, Caitlin."

Maybe it was the timbre of his voice or the way he held her gaze, but Shane's promise made her feel a little heady. "Thanks. My body and I appreciate that very much."

She'd been trying to make a joke, suggesting her body would appreciate not getting hurt if she inadvertently stumbled into the tarp. But it came out all wrong and there was no way to explain herself without sounding even more inane, so she abruptly strode toward the house, calling over her shoulder, "See you tomorrow."

It wasn't until she went inside that Caitlin realized tomorrow was Saturday, so she wouldn't see Shane after all. "Real smooth, Hines," she muttered, giggling about the undeniable effect he had on her.

I can think of half a dozen reasons why we can't get involved, so I should probably stop flirting with him, she begrudgingly acknowledged to herself. *But on the other hand, what's the harm, since I know it isn't going anywhere anyway?*

That evening, Caitlin enjoyed a thick, succulent cod fillet and scrumptious roasted acorn squash, Brussels sprouts, and cauliflower florets for dinner. Then, with a new appreciation for her peace and quiet, she took a bubble bath before stretching out in bed to finish the eighth book she'd read since arriving on Dune Island. But she was drowsy from her vigorous outdoor exercise, so she set aside her e-reader and snuggled beneath the covers.

Closing her eyes, Caitlin reflected on her excursion with Pepper. Walking along the beach again reminded her of seeing an ex for the first time after a very painful breakup: it was uncomfortable, but it was also empowering. She still couldn't imagine ever going all the way to the marsh, but she felt as if she'd overcome a major hurdle just by taking the short jaunt from the beach at Seashell Drive to the staircase near the cottages.

Now that I've faced it once, going back tomorrow won't be as difficult, she reflected with a sleepy yawn. In fact, she felt like everything was a little more manageable now. *I've got a promising career opportunity, a new friendship with my neighbor, a hunky, capable carpenter handling the remodel, and a homey place to stay.*

Dune Island was the last place she would have chosen to visit, but all things considered, Caitlin supposed her time there was going better than she'd expected.

"This is so delicious it almost makes me glad I can only eat soft foods for now," Marion raved about the homemade mac 'n' cheese Caitlin had brought to her house so they could have lunch together before she took Pepper for a walk. "What's your secret for making it so creamy?"

"It's all in the cheese—gruyere, fontina, and cheddar. The combo is extra melty," she answered. "I'm very glad you like it."

As they ate, Caitlin told Marion about the progress Shane and Sammy were making in the windmill. She also mentioned how excited she was about the potential hospital campaign. "It's not a sure thing yet, but I'm trying to prepare as well as I can for the interview."

"They'd be lucky to have someone as smart and dedicated as you working with them," remarked Marion. "Did I mention that I'm on the fundraising committee for Hope Haven's community center?"

"No, you didn't, but good for you!"

"Well, the money we raise is small potatoes compared to the campaigns you conduct, but we all try to do our part—and we have a lot of fun doing it. We've got a big event coming up at the end of the month, a Halloween costume party. It's being held at the cranberry farm in Rockfield, and there will be a hay bale maze, dancing, and refreshments, of course. You should come."

"Thanks, but I, um, I..." hemmed Caitlin. "I don't really know anyone on the island."

"That's the point of socializing—to meet new people," she exclaimed. "Besides, you know *me*. And you know Shane. He'll be there, if I can convince him to go."

Oh, no, is this a setup? It was one thing for Caitlin to drink coffee and chat with Shane at the cottage, but it was quite another for her to meet up with him at a party. *The whole reason I feel so free to joke around and flirt with Shane is because I know it won't go any further. But it's clear Marion is trying to push us together, and I don't want to do anything that would make it seem like I'm agreeing to date him.*

But since she knew her neighbor wouldn't take no for an answer, she gave her a *maybe* instead. "I'll think about it," Caitlin said, even though she'd already made up her mind.

Marion looked disappointed, but she let the topic drop. They finished their meal and then Caitlin set out with Pepper for another walk. Just as she'd expected, she felt much more relaxed when the energetic animal bounded toward the beach stairs at the end of Seashell Drive, and this afternoon she raised her eyes to take in the scenery.

Although the beachgrass was a subtler shade of green than its chartreuse summer hue, and the bay's cerulean blue was also subdued in the autumn light, the seascape struck Caitlin as beautiful as ever, just in a quieter way.

As she glimpsed the water, gentle memories came floating back. She recalled riding in Albert's skiff to the bait and tackle shop at the nearby harbor in Benjamin's Manor. The way her aunt always squealed when her toes touched the water, no matter how warm it was. Roasting marshmallows over an open fire or playing volleyball with the guests. Sloshing through the tidal pools toward the horizon...

Caitlin was so lost in thought that she might have kept walking right past the cottages if Pepper hadn't veered toward the staircase.

It's amazing that he can see where he's going with all that long hair in his eyes, she observed, wondering if it was time for a trim. *Although I suppose he relies more on his sense of smell than on his vision. I bet he could find his way home even in the pitch dark...*

Out of nowhere, the observation made Caitlin think of Nicole walking along this stretch of sand the evening she died. But instead of reliving the shock and sadness of her death like she usually did, Caitlin puzzled over a logistical issue that she'd once put aside: why had Nicole continued walking past the staircase leading to The Windmill Cottages and ended up in the water, rather than just coming home?

It was after dusk when she left the party, so I suppose it's possible that she didn't see our stairs. But there were additional sets of staircases belonging to each of the four houses farther down the beach. If Nicole had missed turning off at The Windmill Cottages, wouldn't she have gone up one of the other sets of steps, recognized her mistake, and then reversed direction?

Furthermore, just beyond the final house, the dunes began to dwindle, until the sandy slopes diminished completely. *Nicole had seen the terrain near the marsh in the daytime, so she knew how flat it was. Even in the dark, she must have noticed that there weren't any dunes beside her.* Then why had she continued walking? It didn't make any sense, considering how squeamish Nicole was about the little sea creatures that inhabited the tidal pools.

Caitlin suddenly felt so bothered by the incongruity that she could feel the muscles in her shoulders and neck tighten into knots. Just as she'd done after discovering the photos and the placemat with the date of Nicole's death written on it, she told herself, *Obsessing over this isn't going to do me any good, and it won't change the past.*

Yet no matter how hard she tried, for the rest of the weekend Caitlin couldn't shake the sneaking suspicion that she didn't know what *really* happened the evening Nicole drowned.

NINE

The last Friday in October, just after Caitlin slid a tray of muffins from the oven, Shane knocked on the back door. Still wearing her oven mitt, she held the door open and gestured for him to come in.

"I'd better not. My boots are covered in sawdust." He inhaled deeply. "I thought I smelled something tasty while I was working."

"They're pumpkin spice muffins. I don't usually bake so often, but I've got extra time on my hands lately, so I've sort of turned my kitchen into a muffin factory. You know how it is when you're single—it's impractical to make an entire pie or cake for yourself. But muffins freeze well, so I can thaw a single serving whenever I want a yummy homemade treat," she rambled before she realized that Shane probably wasn't interested in her latest culinary practices. "Anyway, they're still too hot to eat right now but if you want, I can bring a couple to you with a cup of cocoa in a few minutes."

"Thanks, but I was coming to tell you I need to take off for the day." He explained, "I wouldn't usually interrupt one client's scheduled project to go work on someone else's, especially not at short notice. But unfortunately, this client urgently needs his wheelchair ramp repaired, so I have to make an exception."

"Of course," said Caitlin. "And if you need to work on the ramp next week, too, please feel free. The windmill can wait."

"Nah, the ramp should only take a couple hours. I just need to finish it before his family brings him home from the hospital around six o'clock."

As they were chatting, Marion and Pepper came up the walkway behind Shane. "Oh, good, you're both here," Marion said in a singsong voice.

They greeted her and Shane kissed the elderly woman's cheek, which Caitlin thought was quite sweet of him.

"It's good to see you. I take it you're feeling better?" he asked Marion as Caitlin stepped outside and bent down to gently scratch Pepper behind his ears.

"I feel fantastic—and just in time. Tonight's the Halloween costume party at the cranberry farm, and I'm hosting the refreshment table. As I've mentioned to both of you, all the proceeds from the party benefit the community center," she said in a rush. "Even though I'm on the committee I've been a bit derelict in my fundraising duties. So I thought I'd better pop over to remind both of you to show your support for a very good cause. There's a suggested donation of ten dollars to attend, and another five to go through the hay bale maze, which you won't want to miss."

Caitlin stopped petting Pepper and straightened into a standing position. She was about to tell Marion that she'd be happy to make a donation to the community center, but she'd decided not to attend the party.

However, Marion didn't give her a chance. "Shane, you'll have to give Caitlin a ride since she doesn't have a car and I have to be there early to set up," she directed him, as if the matter of their attendance had already been decided.

Mortified by her neighbor's obvious matchmaking attempt, and aware that Shane resented being set up by his cousin, Caitlin objected, "I can't go. I don't have a costume."

"Neither do I," said Shane. "Although I'm sure I could put something together after work. What time does the party start?"

"The festivities for children and their parents or caretakers run from six thirty to eight o'clock, but the adults-only party doesn't start until eight thirty," Marion countered. "So, you two bright, creative individuals will have plenty of time to make costumes by then. Just wait till you see mine—it's inspired by Pepper."

Hearing his name, the little dog barked and sprang to his feet. He gazed up at Marion as if to say, "it's time to go now." She bid them goodbye, waved her hand, and allowed Pepper to lead her toward the driveway.

Shane turned back to Caitlin. "What do you think? You want to go?"

"It sounds like a lot of fun and I'm tempted, but, you know, I..." Caitlin let her sentence dangle. She didn't know how to express her reservations about going to the party. It wasn't as if she could say she didn't think it was a good idea to date someone who worked for her, since he hadn't exactly asked her out—Marion had been the one to suggest it. And of course, she couldn't explain how mortifying it would be if someone recognized her or remembered her name and started talking about the accident, especially in front of him. So she offered a minor excuse, instead.

"I'm kind of keeping a low profile while I'm on the island, remember?" Even as she said it, Caitlin felt ridiculous; it wasn't as if she were a celebrity dodging paparazzi. "I mean, I still don't want people to find out that I'm here to remodel the cottage before I put it up for sale, but I also wouldn't want to be rude if someone asked an innocent, friendly question about who I am or why I'm on the island or whatever."

Shane's face fell. "Yeah, I can see your dilemma." Suddenly his expression brightened again. "But with the right costume, you could go completely incognito!"

"You mean, like if I wore a bedsheet over my head and went as a ghost?" Caitlin laughed, amused at the idea of dressing up as a ghost so she wouldn't be seen.

But Shane was being earnest. "Yeah, although you could do something a little more involved than that—like wrapping your head and body with strips of a cut-up sheet and going as a mummy," he said enthusiastically. "Or, you could be an old-time Wild West outlaw and wear a kerchief over your face. Or if you want to be more respectable, you could go as a surgeon and wear a mask."

His suggestions were fun and doable, but Caitlin hesitated, weighing the pros and cons of going to the party. On one hand, completely disguising herself to go to a party seemed to defeat the purpose of socializing. On the other hand, it *would* allow her to get out of the cottage for the evening, and she'd get to spend time with Shane, who really seemed to want her to go. But wasn't that potentially a red flag, too? *He might only consider this a platonic night out together, but just in case he doesn't, I don't want to give him the wrong impression—I think I'd better just say no.*

"Those are excellent costume ideas," she began. "But—"

He didn't give her a chance to continue. "Before you say you still don't want to go, can I just emphasize that the party's for a very good cause? And I get the feeling Marion's counting on us to be there?"

He's really putting the squeeze on me, Caitlin realized, and his eagerness to take her to the party was so disarming that she decided to throw caution to the wind.

"You didn't let me finish." she replied. "I was going to say, those are excellent costume ideas, but I've got something else in mind, since I have everything I need for it already."

Shane's eyes widened. "So you'll come with me?"

"Yes, thanks. Count me in."

"Great, I'll pick you up at eight fifteen. Not sure what I'll be dressed as yet, so don't be frightened when you see me."

She laughed. "I'll try not to scream."

When Shane showed up at precisely 8:15, Caitlin was dressed from head to toe in black; black leggings, black turtleneck, and black socks and shoes. She used mascara to draw thin whiskers beneath her black-tipped nose, stretching toward her cheeks.

But as she opened the door and saw Shane, her heart sank: he was wearing overalls and work boots. He had a hammer hanging from one of the loops and the pockets on his bib were filled with an assortment of small tools, and he was nervously fiddling with a couple of long, black wires.

"Hi, Shane," she said cheerfully, trying to contain her disappointment. Apparently, he still hadn't finished repairing his client's ramp. "Don't tell me—you didn't finish the job, so you can't go to the party after all?"

"No, I finished a couple hours ago. But I was sort of hurting for ideas, so this is my costume."

"You're going to the party as a carpenter?"

"Not quite..." He affixed the pair of black wires atop his head, so they bent forward at an angle. "I'm going as a carpenter *ant*."

Caitlin cracked up. "I see. And those must be your antennae, right?"

"You got it. Originally, I'd planned to wear sunglasses, too, for a more ant-like appearance, but since we'll be outside in the dark, that idea didn't pan out." He cocked his head at her. "So you must be going as something feline... a panther?"

"Close." She donned a black balaclava over her head and

adjusted it over her face until only her eyes, nose and whiskers were showing. "I'm a *cat* burglar. Get it?"

It was Shane's turn to laugh. "I hope they give out prizes for the cleverest couple, because you and I will win." The tips of his ears turned pink as he said, "Not that I'm trying to imply we're a couple..."

"You shouldn't even imply we're clever," teased Caitlin, taking his slip-up in stride. "Although if they award prizes for the cringiest, punniest costumes, we'll be shoo-ins."

"Hey, now." Shane feigned offense. "It took me upward of three whole minutes to make my antennae."

Caitlin giggled. "That's two minutes more than I spent on my costume. Like I said, I'd brought this entire outfit with me, so it was easy and inexpensive." She pulled the door shut behind her, and started down the driveway with Shane, activating the outdoor light sensors along the way. "Best of all, I'm completely unidentifiable. I figure if I don't talk, no one will even know if I'm a man or woman."

"Mm, I think they'll know you're a woman," mumbled Shane, giving her a sidelong glance that made her face flush with warmth. "Speaking of being unrecognizable, how do you want me to introduce you when people ask who you are?"

"I figured we'd just say I'm Caitlin, and leave it at that," she answered. "I was sort of joking about being completely unidentifiable. I'd rather not be bombarded with questions about my aunt's property, but it's not as if I want to be invisible, either."

"Who said that? Who's speaking? I heard a voice, but I don't see anyone." Shane exaggeratedly turned his head from side to side, looking around.

"Stop it!" Caitlin protested through her laughter. "Your antennae are moving and it's creeping me out."

They'd reached the truck and Shane opened the passenger door for her. "I know cat burglars are notoriously agile, but it's a big step up. Let me give you a hand."

"Thanks." Allowing him to take her arm and boost her into the cab of his truck, Caitlin thought, *This evening has already been a lot of fun, and we haven't even left the driveway yet.*

As they drove to Rockfield, Shane asked if she'd ever been to the Lindgren Cranberry Farm.

"No, although I drove by it lots of times when I was a teenager because I used to go hiking on the trails in the conservation area." Caitlin remembered how beautiful the cranberry vines looked in the summertime when they blossomed with blush-pink flowers.

She also remembered hearing rumors from her local acquaintances about an arsonist who lived in the old farmhouse on the property. Caitlin doubted the accuracy of those accounts, just like she couldn't quite believe the stories she'd heard about the eccentric old lighthouse keeper, or the mad woman who used to howl from the widow's walk of a historic captain's house in Benjamin's Manor. Unfortunately, it didn't seem to matter how preposterous the tales were; once the gossip started, the landmarks became forever synonymous with scandal.

I hate to imagine what the islanders have said about The Windmill Cottages ever since Nicole drowned... Caitlin made a concerted effort to dismiss the thought and focus on listening as Shane told her the cranberry farm now included a gift shop and an education center, as well as a kitchen that offered cooking classes to the public.

"The owners, Lily and her husband, Jake, are a very generous couple, very community-minded. This isn't the first time they've hosted a fundraiser on their property. They always help put on terrific events—although that's just my opinion. I'm not a professional fundraiser, like you are."

"The kind of fundraising I do is a little different." Caitlin explained her role as a consultant, and she also shared that she wanted to stretch her wings a little by landing the hospital campaign.

"I hope you get it," he said. "Did you always know you wanted to work in philanthropy?"

"No. When I was in high school, I had my heart set on taking pre-med coursework in college. I wanted to become a doctor, or maybe a medical researcher."

"What made you change your mind?"

"I guess I sort of... lost interest," she answered vaguely. "And during my senior year, my grades slipped quite a bit, so enrolling in a pre-med program wasn't really an option anymore."

"Yeah, well, that happens. When I was a high school senior, I was a total slacker. I cut classes so many times, I almost didn't graduate," Shane admitted, which surprised Caitlin because he seemed so disciplined, reliable, and punctual now. "For someone who thought he knew it all, I was pretty stupid—oh, look, here's our turn."

They pulled off the main road and slowly crept up the long driveway to the parking area, which was illuminated by an orange floodlight. The split-rail fence surrounding the lot was draped in artificial spider webs with oversized spiders, and on top of every post sat a hand-carved jack-o-lantern or a fake black cat.

Nice decorations. Not too scary for the children who were here earlier, but not too silly for the adults, either, thought Caitlin, feeling a pang of loneliness for her young niece and nephews. She snapped a few photos to text to them later.

"How about if we go through the maze first, and then we can head to the barn for refreshments?" Shane asked when they got out of his truck. "Kind of a work-before-pleasure strategy."

Caitlin agreed, and they followed the signs to the hay bale maze, where they took their place in line behind a clown, a cowboy, and a gorilla. After putting money into the donation box guarded by a man costumed as a security officer, they entered the dimly lit maze and quickly discovered it was larger and much more complex than they'd expected.

The pair kept coming to dead ends, and then they'd pretend to bicker about which way to go next. Occasionally, someone would recognize Shane or he'd recognize them, and they'd give each other a friendly greeting in passing. But the aisles were narrow, and most people were so preoccupied in navigating their way through them that they didn't stop and chat.

Just when Shane and Caitlin were so frustrated and lost that they were ready to split up and go their separate ways— "survival of the fittest," Shane said—they stumbled onto the exit.

"Finally! You'd think that someone with antennae would have a better sense of direction," she joked. "I was starting to worry we'd be trapped in there all winter."

"Trapped? What kind of cat burglar doesn't know how to scale a wall?"

Caitlin rolled her eyes in mock derision, but she was enjoying their kidding. They sauntered along the lighted path to the barn and made another donation before entering.

"This looks great," exclaimed Caitlin. The interior was aglow with purple, orange, and white fairy lights and hanging lanterns. Topped with black tablecloths and autumn harvest centerpieces, picnic tables of various shapes and sizes were arranged to face the DJ in the far corner of the barn. The 80s-themed music was loud but not deafening, and at least fifteen costumed revelers were already on the dance floor. Closer to the entrance, a few daring souls bobbed for apples in galvanized tubs.

Shane glanced at them and then caught Caitlin's eye. They both simultaneously shook their heads, and kept walking toward the food and beverage tables, respectively labeled, "Treats" and "Boos."

The refreshment table was laden with trays of candied apples, popcorn balls, chocolates, and a wide array of other tasty snacks. Marion was standing beside it, wearing a blue-and-white gingham pinafore, a white top, and blue ribbons in her hair, which was styled into two short braids. Caitlin immediately recognized her as the character Dorothy from *The Wizard of Oz* movie, even though Marion's feet were shod in sensible red gardening boots instead of ruby slippers.

"Hi, Marion. Fabulous costume," she said, at the same moment Shane also greeted her.

"Hi, Shane—and Caitlin, is that really you?" Marion asked, delighted. "I'm so pleased you both came, but I'm afraid I don't quite understand what you're supposed to be dressed as."

After explaining their punny outfits, Shane teased, "Where's your little dog Toto tonight? Did he run into bad weather?"

"I wanted to bring him, but I knew he'd get overly excited about seeing people in costumes. It wouldn't be good for anyone," Marion said.

They chatted for a few more minutes until they needed to move on to make room for a group of people dressed as a professional bowling team. After selecting their drinks—spiced cider for Shane and cranberry juice made on the premises for Caitlin—they found a vacant picnic table off to the side of the barn. As they hungrily devoured their food, they barely spoke except to make admiring remarks about the creative costumes worn by the other attendees.

They'd almost finished eating when a woman dressed as a mermaid slid onto the bench beside Shane and gave him an affectionate nudge with her shoulder.

"Hi, stranger. I never expected to see you here," she said. "What are you supposed to be?"

"Isn't it obvious?" He wiggled his head, pointing to his antennae. "I'm a carpenter ant."

"Wow, that's just... wow." She smiled at Caitlin. "Hi, I'm Joyce—Shane's cousin."

"Hi. I'm Caitlin," she said, shaking Joyce's hand.

"I don't think I've ever seen you around Hope Haven. Are you—" Joyce started to say, but Shane interrupted with a laugh.

"Most of her face is covered, so how would you know whether you've ever seen her in Hope Haven?"

Joyce ignored him. "Are you new in town, Caitlin?"

"No... I live off-island," she hedged. "What town do *you* live in?"

"Right here in Rockfield, a couple streets over from Shane," she answered. "So if you live off-island, how do you two know each other?"

"We have friends in common." Shane abruptly jumped to his feet and tugged Caitlin's hand. "I *love* this song. C'mon, let's dance."

"Excuse us—it was very nice meeting you," Caitlin said to Joyce before Shane led her across the room.

When they reached the dance area, he said something, but the music was too loud for her to hear it. He leaned over and repeated himself into her ear. "Sorry, I sensed an interrogation coming on. For both our sakes, I needed a reason to escape from my cousin, but we don't really have to dance. We can just hang out here for a while."

"You're not getting out of dancing that easily," exclaimed Caitlin. "C'mon, show me your moves, bug man."

"Technically, ants are insects, not bugs," he corrected her, before breaking into a dance that set his antennae in motion.

Caitlin joined him and she couldn't stop smiling. There was something wonderfully frivolous about dancing with a bunch of adults in costumes. She felt freer and younger than she'd felt in years. In *decades*.

When the song ended and Shane started to walk off the dance floor, she objected, "You're leaving already? We were barely warming up!"

"I'm coming back. I just need to unload this hammer and these screwdrivers," he explained, referring to the tools in his bib. "Otherwise, I'm going to hurt someone—namely, me."

"Here, you can wrap them in my balaclava, it's making me too hot," she suggested, pulling it over her head and handing it to him. Since she was no longer incognito, she figured she might as well take the elastic out of her hair, too. As her locks cascaded to her shoulders, Shane stared at her with a quizzical expression on his face. She shrugged and explained, "Anonymity is overrated. Besides, as long as we keep moving, no one will have a chance to ask us any questions—including your cousin."

"If we're going to be dancing that long, I'd better get rid of my work boots, too," he said. "Otherwise they'll give me blisters."

Aww, that's so sweet that he'd take off his boots—most guys I know would just refuse to dance any longer, thought Caitlin, thoroughly charmed.

After six or seven more songs, the DJ played a quieter number. As much fun as Caitlin was having—and even though deep down she may have wanted to feel Shane's arms around her waist—common sense dictated that it crossed a line to slow dance with a man who was also her hired contractor.

Shane seemed to come to the same conclusion, because he announced, "I'm thirsty. Can I get you a drink? Cider? Beer? More cranberry juice?"

"Just water, please," said Caitlin. "I'd like to use the restroom. Do you know where it is?"

"It's over at the education center—just follow the signs with the skeletons on them. They're pointing the way. I'll meet you back at the table where I left my tools."

Heading toward the building, Caitlin thought, *I'd love to*

visit the education center when it's open. It's too far to walk here from the cottage, but I think it's on the bus line...

After using the bathroom, she hurried toward the exit, eager to get back to the barn and dance with Shane again. A tall man wearing a firefighter's costume was coming in, but he backed up and held the door for her. There were two more firefighters behind him, and they also moved aside to let her pass.

"Hey, I know you!" the first one said to her.

"Y-you do?" There was something familiar about him, too, and Caitlin's shoulders tensed.

"Yeah. Didn't we rescue you from a tree last week?" He gave her a cocky smirk.

It took a second for Caitlin to realize he was making a joke in reference to their respective costumes. "Nope, wasn't me. I'm an indoor cat," she said with a cheeky smile, making all three men laugh.

As she walked away, she heard one of the guys ribbing the man who'd spoken to her. "You gotta work on your pickup lines—that was embarrassing."

"Yeah, Chief," agreed the third guy. "You just got *burned*!"

Caitlin was halfway down the path when it struck her why the jokester looked familiar: he bore a slight resemblance to one of the lifeguards in the photo with Nicole. He was much older, of course, and he was wearing a fire helmet, so it was difficult to see his hair, but Caitlin could've sworn he had the same wide, puckish grin as the blond kid in the photo.

She was tempted to go back into the education center for a second look. But it would be weird if she hung out by the bathrooms, waiting for him. Besides, even if she confirmed that he was the same guy as the one in the photo with Nicole, then what would Caitlin do with that information? It wasn't as if she was going to question him about how they'd known each other.

Shane's waiting for me, and I'd much rather dance with him than chase down some stranger to satisfy my curiosity, she thought, and continued toward the barn.

It was close to 11:00 when Shane and Caitlin left the party. Fortunately, the people she'd met throughout the rest of the evening didn't question how they knew each other or ask where Caitlin was from, the way Joyce had done. They simply exchanged warm greetings, commented about each other's costumes, or expressed enthusiasm for the fundraiser, and then they resumed eating, drinking, or dancing.

As they pulled into the driveway to Lydia's house, Caitlin started to say, "I'm glad Marion encouraged us to go tonight. That was the most—"

"You've got to be kidding me!" interrupted Shane.

It took a second for Caitlin to understand what had caught his attention: the arms of the windmill were shrouded in long, thick toilet paper streamers, and so was the sunroom roof. There were also several rolls of toilet paper unfurled across the lawn.

Shane rapidly parked his truck, jumped out, and strode up the walkway, leaving Caitlin to lower herself from the high cab seat.

"Who would do something like that?" he fumed, tilting his head back as he surveyed the windmill.

"Probably teenagers." Caitlin was surprised he seemed so mad about it. TP-ing houses and smashing jack-o-lanterns had been a fairly common Halloween prank when she was young. Trying to lighten the mood, she said, "They've made a mess, but on the plus side, this is the closest the windmill has come to having sails on its arms in centuries."

Shane looked at her. "I don't see how you can joke about it."

"It's just a little harmless fun. No big deal."

"Trespassing and defacing someone else's property *isn't* just a little harmless fun! Whoever did this was being completely disrespectful," Shane said. "I only wish I'd been here to catch the stupid little punks in action. They should be held accountable."

She didn't know why he was getting so bent out of shape, but Caitlin pointed out, "They didn't *deface* anything. It's biodegradable toilet paper. I can clean it up in the morning."

"How? I hope you don't intend to climb up there on a ladder."

"No, but if I lean out the loft window and use a really long broom, I bet I could sweep most of it away."

"Don't even *think* of trying that," warned Shane. "It's dangerous. *I'll* clean everything up in the morning."

"But tomorrow's Saturday, your day off. You shouldn't have to spend part of it working here."

"Unfortunately, that's what happens when someone does something so irresponsible—other people usually end up paying the consequences."

"Okay, I'd appreciate your help," Caitlin conceded, sensing that it was futile to insist she'd deal with the mess by herself. "I should go in now. Thank you for taking me to the party."

"You're welcome," said Shane, but he was surveying the sunroom roof instead of looking her way. "I'll see you tomorrow. Is nine o'clock all right?"

"Sure," agreed Caitlin. Yet as she retreated into the cottage, she thought, *I hope there's a big windstorm overnight and it blows everything away, so he doesn't have to come back in the morning.*

After having such a pleasant time dancing and literally letting her hair down, she was utterly disappointed that the evening had ended on a sour note. *Everything had been going so well, and our chemistry was fantastic,* Caitlin thought dejectedly. *I mean, he works for me, so it's not as if I thought he was going to kiss me good night or ask me out on a real date. But I at* least expected him to say he was glad I went to the party or that he had a good time, too—instead of obsessing over what somebody did to the windmill.

She didn't entirely blame him for being upset about the toilet paper mess: it showed that he believed in being a good neighbor and he valued personal accountability. Yet his response to the prank seemed a little over-the-top, bordering on self-righteousness. *Didn't he say he always triple-checked Sammy's work? Maybe he has unrealistic standards for how teenagers should behave...*

If Shane is this upset about kids TP-ing the cottage, how would he feel if he knew how irresponsible I was when I was a teenager? she wondered as she went into the bathroom and began washing the mascara whiskers off her cheeks, and the black dot from her nose. *What would he think of me if he knew my actions led to Nicole's death?*

Despite Lydia insisting it wasn't her niece's fault Nicole had drowned, Caitlin had always felt her aunt was wrong about her, and Mrs. McDougal was right. *Instead of making out with Donald in the dunes, I should have stayed at the party with Nicole. If I hadn't abandoned her, she never would have gotten bored and walked back to the cottages by herself...*

Usually, the memory of Pam screaming at her filled Caitlin with so much shame she could barely stand the sight of her own reflection. But tonight, she caught her eye in the mirror and questioned the narrative she'd believed for twenty years. Was it true that Nicole left the party because she was bored? And did she really pass the staircase to the cottages by mistake? Or was there more to the story than that?

Caitlin also wondered whether the blond lifeguard in the photo was the same guy dressed as a firefighter tonight. And if he was, did he know why the date of Nicole's death was written on the placemat?

She splashed water on her cheeks and then scowled at her

reflection. "Stop it," she said aloud. *Stop looking for a way to rewrite the past. The fact is that Nicole died and it was my fault, so I can forget about someone like Shane ever liking me.*

Her muscles aching from dancing, and her guilt closer to the surface than ever, she wearily changed into her pajamas and collapsed into bed.

Caitlin woke at dawn to a hard rain battering the roof. She rose, shuffled to the living room, and opened the front door. Peeking out, she noticed the heavy precipitation had washed virtually all the toilet paper off the windmill. White fist-sized blobs littered the lawn beneath its arms, like snowballs. The sunroom roof was clean, as well, and she assumed the toilet paper had been washed into the gutter, where it would soon dissolve.

She went back to her room and texted Shane: *The rain cleared the TP off the windmill and roof, so no need for you to come by this morning. Thanks anyway.*

She hit the send arrow and set down her phone. *I should've trusted my intuition that going to the party with him was a bad idea*, she thought regretfully. *But I won't make that mistake again. From now on, I'm keeping our relationship strictly professional.*

TEN

Caitlin decided to spend as much time as possible away from the cottage—and away from Shane. Rather than drinking coffee with him each morning, she took off on her daily walk to the market before he even arrived. When she returned, she'd either briefly visit Marion, or else she'd pack her lunch and then leave again, heading to Benjamin's Manor.

Once or twice, she saw Shane in passing, but instead of stopping to chat, she smiled and called hello and then hurried on her way. She'd eat on a bench by the harbor on Main Street, and then head into the library to work on her research until around 4:00, when she figured Shane was winding down his work for the afternoon.

However, by the end of the week, she was restless from doing so much campaign research and even her pleasure reading didn't seem very pleasurable anymore. Recognizing she needed a change of scenery, Caitlin caught a bus to the conservation land in Rockfield, adjacent to the cranberry farm.

Hiking a trail along the periphery of the marsh, she noticed the yellowish-green inflorescent cordgrass was accented by seaside goldenrod, claret-colored pickleweed, and a smattering of sea lavender. Caitlin veered onto a side path through the woods, and just when she started to wonder if she'd gone the wrong way, she happened upon a clearing and spotted the red-speckled bogs beside the rambling white farmhouse.

To her surprise, there was no admission fee to enter the education center, and she relished learning about the Lindgren farm, as well as about cranberry harvesting in general. She snapped a few photos to send to her niece and nephews, who couldn't have been more fascinated by everything she did or saw on Dune Island than if she'd been staying on the moon.

Christmas is just around the corner, she thought, heading down the hall to the gift shop. *Maybe I can find an entertaining, educational present for them, or at least a few souvenirs.*

There was no one in the shop but the door was open, so Caitlin went in and began to browse. A few minutes later, a woman about her age appeared, carrying a stack of boxes, which she set behind the front counter. "Hi, I'm Lily. How are you?"

"Fine, thanks. I hope it's okay that I came in here—the door was open."

"I'm glad you did. Usually, someone's here to assist customers, but we're short-staffed today, so I'm filling in wherever I'm needed. Is this your first time in the shop?"

"Yes, but not my first time on the farm. I attended the Halloween party. It was such a great event. Very festive but not overdone."

"I'm glad you enjoyed it. I wish we could take credit, but it was the community center who put that on. We just provided the venue."

"The farm is what made it feel so authentic," Caitlin said. "I was intrigued by the education center so I came back. Now I'm browsing for gifts for my niece and nephews. I'd also like to purchase a bag of cranberries."

"We usually keep them on the roadside stand, but I haven't replenished it yet, so I'll get a bag for you from the kitchen while you're browsing," said Lily. "There's a children's section in that corner over there, and the rest of the displays are self-explanatory. All our merchandise is locally sourced or created by Hope Haven residents. And of course, the cranberry items are fresh from the farm. If you have any questions, just let me know—I'll be right down that hall."

As Caitlin was perusing a rack of notecards painted by a Highland Hills artist, she heard the bells jingle on the door, and vaguely registered that someone else had entered the shop. Caitlin moved on to examine several handblown Christmas tree ornaments, thinking, *These are so pretty and they're reasonably priced. Maybe I should bring one home for my brother's family—or would it just end up getting broken?*

As she was dithering, she noticed movement in the corner of her eye. Turning her head, she saw a woman obviously giving her the once-over.

"Sorry for staring," she said loudly. "But I recognize you from somewhere. I'm Claire Griffin. What's your name?"

Flustered, Caitlin nearly dropped the ornament she was holding. Instead of telling the woman her name, she rambled, "You might have seen me here at the Halloween party the other night. I was dressed in all black, and I had whiskers on my face. I was supposed to be a cat burglar, but I don't think the pun translated well." She chuckled, hoping to distract Claire by making light of her costume.

"I didn't go to the Halloween party, so that's not why I recognize you." She repeated, "What's your name?"

"It's Caitlin, but I don't think we've ever met. Maybe we've crossed paths in town." She quickly rehung the delicate bulb on the display and started inching down the aisle, but the woman snapped her fingers and stepped closer.

"Wait, I know who you are! Your grandparents owned The Windmill Cottages where that Nicole girl drowned like, twenty years ago."

Stunned by her insensitivity about Nicole, Caitlin could only mumble, "Those weren't my grandparents."

Claire narrowed her eyes. "Okay, so it was your aunt and uncle, or whoever, but I'm sure it was you because I was at the party the night she drowned, too—my cousin Dave was the chaperone. I remember how mad he got because one of the student rangers took off with you instead of staying with the group. He was a tall boy from Kansas or somewhere in the Midwest. I think his name was Derrick. Or was it Drew?"

She was getting the names wrong, but Claire recalled the gist of what had happened, and Caitlin knew there was no sense denying it. "His name was Donald," she said flatly.

"Really?" Claire wrinkled her nose. "Are you sure?"

Was she sure she knew the name of her first love? Of the boy whose heart she'd broken? Caitlin was so ashamed of how deeply she'd hurt him that she would've liked to pretend she could barely recall anything about him. But he was indelible in her memory, and she felt she owed it to him to assert, "Yes, I'm sure. He was my boyfriend and his name was Donald."

"Hmm, that's weird. Usually I get my facts straight," Claire claimed, without any sense of self-awareness. "But I distinctly recall seeing both of you at that party. I also remember seeing your aunt and uncle on the news."

Two days after Nicole died, a Boston TV station had sent a crew to cover the story, and they'd shown up unannounced at The Windmill Cottages. As ill as Albert had been—in retrospect, Caitlin realized he must have had cancer already, although they hadn't known it at the time—he'd gone outside to ask them to leave.

"This is a tragic situation for all concerned. Please, respect the privacy of our guests," he'd pleaded, but the reporter carried on with the coverage anyway.

Albert had been so wan and weak that Lydia had stood beside him to prop him up. Caitlin could still picture their shell-shocked expressions on the TV screen. In the background, the windmill's broken arm and the fallen black locust tree added to the sense of devastation captured by the camera. Just thinking about it made Caitlin queasy and her forehead and the back of her neck broke out in a sweat, but Claire blithely continued rambling.

"Isn't it amazing that all those details from twenty years ago are still so vivid in my mind?" she boasted. Then she made a pitying, tsk-ing sound. "I'll never forget how worried I felt when I heard you'd locked yourself in your family's windmill for three days because you were so freaked out about what happened to Nicole."

"I never locked myself in the windmill," Caitlin objected weakly. "I fell asleep in the loft for a couple hours, and no one knew I was up there."

"A few days, a few hours, either way, it's totally understandable why you hid. If I were you, I probably would've been a mess, too. I'm just glad everything apparently turned out okay for you." Claire barely took a breath before asking, "So what are you doing here now?"

"Just browsing." Caitlin looked at the clock on the wall. "But it's almost lunchtime, so—"

Claire cut her off. "I meant what are you doing here on Dune Island?"

"I-I..." Caitlin licked her lips. She needed fresh air, but her legs felt too wooden and heavy to carry her to the door. "I'm visiting."

"You can't mean you're visiting your relatives? Because I heard that they went bankrupt and had to sell the cottages after the drowning because no one wanted to rent from them anymore."

"That's not what happened," said Caitlin, refusing to dignify Claire's gossip with an account of her uncle's illness.

Lily suddenly appeared in the doorway. "I have those cranberries you wanted in the kitchen, if you'd like to follow me," she said to Caitlin. Then Lily addressed Claire. "It's really nice to see you but I'm afraid I'm closing shop for the lunch hour. After this customer collects her produce, I've got to run to the bank before it closes. So, unless you have your purchases ready for me to ring up, would you mind coming back another time?"

"I'm not buying anything from the shop," said Claire. "I just popped in to place an order for a cranberry cheesecake for Thanksgiving."

"Terrific, I'll have it ready for you on the Wednesday before the holiday," said Lily, ushering her to the door, which she then opened. "You can pick it up any time between nine a.m. and five p.m. Talk soon—bye-bye."

"Bye, Lily. Bye, Caitlin. I hope to see you around town—"

Lily closed the door before Claire could complete her sentence. She turned and smiled at Caitlin. "Now, let's go get those berries."

She led her to the instructional kitchen and pulled out a chair, saying, "Have a seat. You seem a little shaky. Can I get you a glass of juice? Or water?"

"That's okay. I don't want to make you late for your bank errand."

Retrieving a pitcher of crimson juice from the fridge, Lily confessed, "You caught me in a fib. I only said that because I wanted to get rid of Claire. I was appalled when I overheard her interrogating you like that. She's such a blabbermouth, even by Dune Island standards. She isn't necessarily ill-intentioned, but she has absolutely no filter."

"I was so caught off guard by her bluntness that I couldn't think of a way to shut down the conversation," Caitlin admitted, sinking into the chair and accepting the beverage Lily handed her. "Thanks for ending it for me. My name's Caitlin, by the way."

"You're welcome, Caitlin." Lily filled a second glass for

herself and then sat down on the opposite side of the table. "I know what it feels like to be put on the spot by the local gossips."

"You do?" Caitlin was surprised; from what Shane had said about Lily and her husband, they were the darlings of the island.

She nodded. "When I was in high school, one of my family members was burning debris in the yard and they accidentally started part of the conservation land on fire next door," she said, and Caitlin recalled the rumors she'd heard when she was a teenager about an arsonist living at the farmhouse. "No one was hurt, and we made restitution for the property, but some of the islanders were understandably upset. A few of them even signed a petition to boycott our cranberry farm."

Caitlin frowned. "That must have felt so demeaning."

"Yes, in fact, it was one of the reasons I decided to leave Dune Island as soon as I graduated high school. I didn't come back for almost twenty years—and the only reason I returned was because I inherited my family's farm," she said. "I intended to sell it, but obviously, I didn't, and wild horses couldn't drag me away from Hope Haven now."

"May I ask why you changed your mind and decided to stay?"

"Love, mostly. My son adored Dune Island and the farm, and I fell in love with it again, too. I also fell hard for Jake, my husband, and vice versa." A pretty smile creased Lily's face with lines. "I'm not saying it was easy to get past... the past. Especially not when there were people here telling my son their distorted version of events. But they were in the minority and I'm glad I didn't allow their gossip—or my shame and resentment—to keep me from enjoying living on Dune Island again. My only regret is that I stayed away so long."

Caitlin slowly nodded, letting Lily's words sink in. The two women sipped their juice in silence, and after a few minutes,

Caitlin's nausea subsided. She stood to leave. "Thank you for the juice," she said. "And for what you told me. I feel much better now."

"You're very welcome. Don't forget your cranberries." Lily crossed the room to bring her the small sack. "No charge. Consider them a welcome-back-to-Hope-Haven gift from a kindred spirit."

As Caitlin walked the short distance to the bus stop, she thought about how humiliating it must have been for Lily when the locals boycotted her family's farm. Her courage to return to her hometown after twenty years away and reside there again was inspiring.

I wonder how she learned to let people's criticism and ignorant comments roll off her back. It was a skill Caitlin sensed she'd soon need to practice, too. Because although she trusted Lily not to mention anything about her, she had a feeling Claire was already spreading the word that Caitlin had returned to Dune Island.

It rained all weekend, a blowy, drenching downpour that buffeted the roof and windows and stripped the remaining leaves from the maple tree in the front yard. Initially, Caitlin welcomed the excuse to stay tucked away in the cottage. Her interaction with Claire had left her feeling even more anxious about bumping into residents who might recognize her.

It had been both painful and appalling to hear her casual, misinformed rendition of how "that Nicole girl's" death had affected Caitlin and her family. *If Lily hadn't interrupted the conversation, I might have broken down in tears,* she thought. *And no matter how sympathetic she pretends to be, I'm sure Claire would've loved sharing the juicy little tidbit that I'm still a mess after all...*

Which Caitlin supposed was true, in a way, but it still

wasn't anyone else's business, and she'd do whatever was necessary to avoid another public conversation about it. So she was content to spend Saturday morning making cranberry-pumpkin scones, the afternoon cleaning, and the evening curling up with her e-reader.

On Sunday she began feeling antsy, especially because none of the friends she called in New Mexico answered their phones. And by Monday morning she was so eager to speak to someone face-to-face that if Melanie had shown up on her doorstep, Caitlin would've welcomed her in and listened with rapt attention while she overshared details about her relationship with Jonathan.

However, it was actually Shane who knocked on the kitchen door. When he flashed his friendly smile, she nearly forgot how temperamental he'd been the last time she'd seen him. "Hi, Caitlin. How are you doing?"

"Fine, thanks. How about you?" she asked without inviting him in.

"I'm good." He tilted his head and questioned, "You sure everything's okay? You haven't stopped by to check out my progress for a while."

Feeling a little foolish that it was so obvious she'd been avoiding him, Caitlin said, "Now that you've done the framework, I figured it would be more fun to wait till the rest of the remodel is finished before I see it." It wasn't a complete lie; Caitlin *did* appreciate an element of suspense, but that wasn't the main reason she hadn't dropped in on Shane.

"That's understandable," he said. "But I've missed chatting with you. I, um, I've wanted to apologize for how loud and obnoxious I was the other week. I didn't mean to drive you from your home."

"No problem. Drilling and hammering are part of the equation. It's not as if I expect things to be quiet when you're remodeling."

"I wasn't referring to the drills and hammers. I meant my big mouth," he said sheepishly. "I really went off about whoever TP-ed the windmill and your roof."

Touched by how candid he was being, Caitlin gently admitted, "Yeah, I was a little surprised by how upset you were about it, considering it was only a silly prank."

"I know. I overreacted and I'm sorry. See, the thing is... when I was in high school, I made some poor choices. They started out small, and relatively harmless, kind of like the trick someone played on you. But my first trespass was a slippery slope, and after that, I kept crossing lines I shouldn't have crossed. Nothing illegal or violent, but I did things that were reckless and irresponsible, without any regard for other people—or for myself, for that matter. Eventually, I got caught, which was the best thing that could've happened to me. Otherwise, who knows what else I might've ended up doing."

He shook his head and jammed his hands into his pocket before continuing. "Anyway, when I saw what someone had done to your property, I wished I could've caught them in the act and lit into them, so maybe it would prevent them from going down a path like the one I went down."

Relieved to learn the real reason Shane had seemed so sanctimonious about the windmill mischief, Caitlin gave him a saucy half-smile. "So what you're saying is all that ranting was your way of expressing concern for their future?"

"Nah. All that ranting was because I lost my temper," he said self-deprecatingly. "But beneath my anger, yeah, I do feel concerned for them."

"The stupid little punks," kidded Caitlin, quoting Shane.

"I really said that, didn't I?" He grimaced.

"Yes, but it completely makes sense now. Thank you for explaining what was going on in your head." Caitlin still wondered what Shane had done in high school, but she didn't press him for details. He already seemed embarrassed enough and it wasn't any of her business anyway.

"You're welcome. Like I said, I'm sorry if my outburst made you uncomfortable—especially after we had such a great time together at the party."

"It *was* fun, wasn't it?" exclaimed Caitlin, glad to hear he'd felt the same way. She excitedly told him about her second visit to the cranberry farm, and about meeting Lily.

"You're really getting around the island for someone who doesn't have a bike or car," he remarked.

She shrugged. "I like to walk whenever I can and the public transportation system here isn't bad, considering how small the island is. So if I'm going beyond Lucy's Ham, I just catch the bus. It's kind of liberating not to have a car."

"You might not feel that way when the cold weather sets in," he warned. "Any time you want a lift, just say the word."

"Thanks," she said. "So, what have you been up to this past week... other than working here, I mean."

"Nothing too exciting. Usually, I spend Monday or Thursday night catching a football game at Ahab's."

"Is he a friend of yours?"

Shane chuckled. "No, Ahab's is a pub off Main Street in Benjamin's Manor. In my opinion, they serve the best clam chowder on the island. No kidding, I could eat it morning, noon, and night."

"I've never heard of Ahab's. When I used to visit Dune Island, my aunt and uncle always took me to the Clam Shack, right up the road."

"Yeah, their chowder's delicious, too. So is Captain Clarke's. But Ahab's has them both beat, and unlike the Shack, it's open year-round. I also like going there because it's quieter during the week than most sports bars, and I can watch the game with other people, but sort of on my own, if you get what I mean."

"I'm the same way," she acknowledged. "I like my independence, but too much time alone makes me crawl the walls."

"Yup. It's a delicate balance." Shane nodded extra slowly, as if there was something else on his mind. Finally, he said, "I should get to work, but, uh, just to confirm... it's all good between us again, no hard feelings, right?"

"It's all good—no hard feelings," she repeated, and gave him a smile, which he returned.

I'm glad I don't feel like I need to avoid him any longer, she thought as he pivoted toward the windmill. But their little rift—coupled with her recent encounter with Claire—had left Caitlin feeling shaken and vulnerable, as if she might be exposed at any moment.

I've got to be more careful about not letting my defenses down—which means being friendly with Shane is fine, but no more flirting, she resolved and firmly shut the door.

ELEVEN

By mid-November, when Caitlin still hadn't heard anything from the agency director, Tobias, about an interview date, she decided to reach out and ask if the hospital had signed a contract yet. She also hoped to impress him with the prospective donor research she'd done. But when she called his work cell phone, his assistant, Max, picked up and told her Tobias was out of town.

"His mother's been very ill. She just got out of the intensive care unit, so he won't be back for at least a couple weeks."

"Oh, no, I'm very sorry to hear about his mother," Caitlin sympathized. "That must be so distressing."

"Yes, I'm sure it is." Max sounded rushed. "Is there something I can help you with while he's gone?"

Because Tobias wasn't supposed to tell her about the campaign before the potential client signed the contract, Caitlin couldn't let on that she already knew about the possibility. So she said, "That's all right. It's nothing urgent. I'll try again when he's back."

After hanging up, Caitlin paced from the kitchen to the living room, wondering if the hospital was still deliberating about whether to sign on as a client yet, or if they'd chosen a different agency. Or could it be that they'd already signed, but Tobias had neglected to contact Caitlin about an interview?

Although she recognized there was little she could do except wait and try to reach Tobias in another week or two, Caitlin felt so apprehensive that she repeatedly paced from her tiny kitchen to her living room until she'd literally worked up a sweat.

I wish I could tell Shane about this, she thought. But since it wouldn't be appropriate to interrupt his work to complain about her personal situation, she decided to walk to town instead. *I'm bored with my usual route—this time, I'm hiking down the beach. When I get to the boardwalk, I'll circle back to the cottage on the side streets.*

The weather was so unseasonably warm—it must have been at least 65 degrees—and the tide was in, so as soon as she reached the sand, Caitlin took off her shoes and socks and rolled up her pant legs so she could tread along the water's edge. Turning her back on the inlet, she headed north and didn't break her stride until she reached the boardwalk.

Then she paused to take in the slightly weatherbeaten yet colorful facades of the eateries, shops, and recreation venues lining the waterfront. She immediately recognized her youthful favorites: Lucy's Tees, Bleecker's Ice Cream Parlor, The Donut Shanty, Sandy's Souvenirs, and, of course, Pirate's ARR-Cade.

Recalling that Albert used to treat her and Lydia to ice cream cones at Bleecker's on the last day of each month, Caitlin was overcome with nostalgia—and with hunger. *A double scoop of caramel sea salt and chocoloate-cranberry would really hit the spot right now*, she thought, her mouth watering.

But Bleecker's Ice Cream Parlor was boarded up until next summer, and so were most of the other establishments, except for a few cafes and coffee houses that she guessed remained open on weekends through the shoulder season. Although a handful of people were strolling the beach, and an elderly couple was resting on a nearby bench, the waterfront was virtually deserted.

There aren't even very many seagulls here today, thought Caitlin, stamping the sand from her feet on the wooden promenade.

Just then, she remembered she'd left her socks and shoes beside the staircase by the cottages. Because it would hurt to walk barefoot on the streets, she went back the same way she came. Her anxiety had significantly diminished, and she sauntered along at a leisurely pace, scouring the sand for beach glass.

By the time she neared the stairs to The Windmill Cottages, she was fatigued, as well as hot. *Who can believe it's November?* she thought, sloshing shin-deep into the water. She stopped and stood still as the tiny swells nudged her legs, such a familiar, refreshing sensation. When she was a teenager, the first thing she'd do after finishing her morning chores was to hustle down to the beach and wade into the bay to feel the little waves lick her skin with salty kisses.

Since leaving Dune Island, Caitlin had waded and swum in freshwater lakes, rivers, hot springs, and waterfalls. But this was the first time in twenty years that she'd so much as dipped her toes in the ocean, and suddenly, her desire to immerse herself was irresistible.

She jogged up the incline to the dry sand, wiggled out of her jeans, and peeled off her hoodie. Then, wearing nothing but her T-shirt and underclothes, she ran into the water. When she was thigh-deep, Caitlin flung herself forward in a movement that was a cross between a dive and a belly-flop, with her abdomen absorbing most of the impact.

The water felt bitingly cold as it sprayed her hair and shoulders, but she forced herself to duck her face and head entirely beneath the surface. A few seconds later, she came up gasping, but after taking a deep gulp of air, she plunged in again and paddled toward the horizon.

By the time she ran out of breath, her body had already acclimated to the temperature, and she felt warmer submerged in the bay than when she surfaced and the air hit her body. She paddled until she couldn't touch the seabed with her toes, and then she treaded water, slowly rotating her body to view the placid blue expanse, the boardwalk in the distance, the closer, golden dunes, and finally, without thinking about it, the marsh. Coming full circle, she treaded water for a few more minutes, and then she slowly rotated in the other direction, taking it all in until her teeth chattered and her fingers were prune-y.

One more time, she thought, and twisted in a final slow-motion pirouette before returning to shore.

Shivering, she pulled on her jeans and grabbed her shoes, socks, and hoodie, and took the stairs by twos. Caitlin reached the cottage just as Shane was exiting the windmill.

"November 14, good for you," he said and it took a moment for her to realize he meant because she'd gone swimming so late in the year. Had he seen her from the window in the loft, or had he made a logical assumption because she was wet?

"Thank you." She took an exaggerated bow, her dripping hair sliding across her shoulders.

"Yeah, way to go, but you haven't beat my personal best," he chided.

"Oh, really? What's the latest date you've gone swimming?"

"November 24 in the oceanside, December 8 in the bay."

She shrugged and acted unimpressed. "It's early. There's still time for me to break your record."

Shane gave her a hearty laugh. "I look forward to congratulating you on that."

She smiled, but as she scampered inside, she already felt triumphant for a different reason: for the first time since she'd arrived, she hadn't thought about Nicole's death the entire time she'd been at the beach.

Caitlin was freezing. *How is it possible that just the other day I went swimming, and today I wish I'd worn my balaclava?* she silently grumbled, ducking her head against the raw wind.

She wouldn't have ventured outside the cottage at all this morning, since she didn't like going into town on Saturdays, but she'd accidentally left her phone charger at the library in Benjamin's Manor yesterday. She figured she'd pick it up and then stop for groceries in Lucy's Ham on her way back.

But she got so cold walking the short distance from the bus stop to the library that after she collected the charger from the volunteer at the reception desk, Caitlin decided to sit near the gas fireplace to warm herself. She'd barely had time to settle into an oversized leather chair when a blaring sound and flashing lights filled the room.

A recorded voice came on the loudspeaker: "Everyone must evacuate the building immediately. Please leave your belongings where they are and calmly proceed to the nearest exit," it said, and then repeated the warning.

Caitlin pulled on her coat, shoved her phone charger into her pocket, and then she followed the other patrons outside. *Forget this, I'm going to a café for a maple pecan latte or a hazelnut hot chocolate.*

She started down Main Street when she realized in her haste to evacuate the library, she'd left her purse behind. So she rejoined the other patrons who were hugging their chests and stamping their feet, trying to keep warm as they waited on the front sidewalk for the all-clear signal.

"This is the second time the alarm has gone off this week," one of them complained loudly. "I betcha anything a staff member burned something in the toaster oven again. The library really needs to invest in a higher-quality smoke detector."

"Or they should take the toaster oven out of the breakroom," someone else chimed in. "And replace it with a microwave."

"What good would that do? They'd just be burning popcorn instead of toast, which would still set off the alarms," a third person said, and a spirited discussion ensued about the pros and cons of updating the breakroom's appliances and smoke detectors.

Even though their comments seemed tongue-in-cheek, Caitlin noticed how freely the islanders expressed their opinions before they had all the facts about what had happened. *If they're this passionate about a smoke detector going off, I can only imagine the rumors that circled the island when Lily's family member set the conservation land on fire,* she thought. Hearing the locals talk made Caitlin even more eager to collect her purse and continue on her way.

A few minutes later, a fire truck pulled up in front of the library with its lights flashing, but no siren on. When the driver hopped down from the cab, Caitlin did a double take. *That's the guy from the Halloween party, the one who made the joke about rescuing me from a tree,* she realized. *Which means he wasn't dressed in a costume after all—he was wearing his uniform.*

The head librarian circled around from the other side of the building just as he was coming up the walkway. "Hi, Miriam. Are you burning books again?" he joked.

She gave him an apologetic look and shook her head. "Sorry to make you come out here a second time for a false alarm."

"Better a false alarm than a fire." When he smiled and his cheeks dimpled, Caitlin had no doubt he was the blond guy pictured in Nicole's old photos from the arcade. "We'll reset the detector in a jiff so everybody can get back inside where it's warm."

"That would be great, Craig."

Craig? Caitlin silently questioned, as he and a second firefighter jogged up the front steps and disappeared into the building. *If that's his name, it means he wasn't the boy Nicole meant when she wrote N. hearts R. So R. must have been the other guy in the photo—the one with dark hair and a tan.*

Then again, perhaps Caitlin hadn't heard the firefighter's name correctly; maybe the librarian had called him *Ray*, not *Craig?*

A flicker of yellow in her peripheral vision caught her eye, pulling Caitlin from her thoughts: the firefighters were hustling down the front stairs. She tried not to gawk as they headed to the truck.

"All clear," the driver called, waving to the waiting crowd.

"You guys are the best. Bye, Jose. See you later, Craig," the librarian replied, putting to rest Caitlin's doubt that she'd misheard his name.

She filed into the library behind the other patrons and retrieved her purse from where she'd left it. But now Caitlin was too cold to walk to the bus stop, or even to hurry a couple doors down to a café to get a hot beverage. Yet she was too agitated to sit idly by the fire. Despite her best attempts to put what happened to Nicole out of her mind, now that she was positive that Craig was the same guy she'd seen in the photo, it was all Caitlin could think about.

Using her phone, she did a quick internet search for the local fire department. Sure enough, she found his name: Craig Thompson. *He's not just a firefighter, he's the fire chief,* she realized, a little impressed. *I wonder if rescuing swimmers as a teenage lifeguard influenced his professional aspirations?*

But now she was far more curious about the other lifeguard in the photos she'd found, the guy Nicole apparently had liked. Who was he, and did he still live on Dune Island? *If I could find out more about him—about what he was like twenty years ago—it might give me a better picture of what else Nicole was doing that summer. It might even shed some light on why she'd written "August 29" on the placemat from the arcade. But how can I research R., when I only know his first initial and what he looked like as a teenager?*

It occurred to her that as a lifelong islander, Marion undoubtedly had known Craig and R.—as well as the brunette girl in the photo—when they were young, or at least she'd been acquainted with their families. Caitlin supposed she could question her about them, but then her neighbor would want to know why she was asking. And so far, Marion hadn't uttered a word about Nicole's drowning, which was one of the reasons Caitlin felt so at ease in her presence. It was as if they had an unspoken agreement that they wouldn't talk about what had happened, and that was the way Caitlin wanted to keep it.

She was suddenly struck by an idea. *I can search the library's online copies of Hope Haven High School yearbooks! I'm sure I'll recognize R.'s photo, and he'll be identified by his full name. Most senior yearbooks also list the graduating students' interests and activities, which will give me a lot more information about him.*

Yet within a few minutes of logging onto the library's system, Caitlin discovered the digital copies of the yearbook only dated back fifteen years. So, even though it made her feel conspicuous, she approached the reference librarian's desk and inquired, "Does this library have print copies of Hope Haven High School yearbooks?"

"We certainly do. They're kept in an archival storage room, to protect them from heat, moisture, and light, and they're available for in-house use only." She pulled a big ring of keys from her desk and stood up. "Which year would you like to peruse?"

"I... I'm not sure," Caitlin faltered, since she didn't know when R. had graduated. He looked a little older than Nicole, who'd been about to enter her junior year, so she took her best guess and asked, "Could I see the copies for twenty to twenty-three years ago?"

The librarian frowned. "Yes, but only one at a time. I'll bring you the copy from twenty years ago, and if you don't find who you're looking for, let me know, and I'll bring you the one from the next year." Then, in a whisper, she added, "You wouldn't believe how many visitors return to the island in search of locals they had summer flings with when they were teenagers."

Caitlin protested, "That's not what I'm doing!" Her voice carried throughout the quiet room, causing several patrons to glance her way.

"No, of course it isn't," the librarian said, winking.

As the woman scurried from the room, Caitlin felt so mortified she was tempted to flee the library completely. *If I had known I was going to draw so much attention to myself, I never would have asked to see the yearbooks*, she thought ruefully.

Once she was seated at a desk with the book in hand, Caitlin kept her head down as she flipped it open. Dune Island's regional high school was home to students from all five towns in Hope Haven, but because the year-round population was small, it didn't take Caitlin long to scrutinize the seniors' formal photos.

As she expected, beneath each picture, the student's name was listed, along with their hobbies, club and sport participation, aspirations, and favorite quote. There were only a handful of boys whose first names began with the letter *R*; none of them even slightly resembled the boy in the photo with Nicole. She examined the swim team members' faces, too, but didn't see R. among those boys, either. Caitlin also kept an eye out for the brunette girl from the arcade, but since she'd been wearing sunglasses and was on the periphery of the frame, she would've been difficult to identify.

Reluctantly, she closed the cover and asked the reference

librarian if she could see the yearbook from twenty-one years ago. Caitlin repeated the process, with similar results. By then, her fingers and toes had sufficiently warmed and she was getting hungry. Caitlin's burning curiosity had faded to a dim flicker, and she decided she'd rather eat lunch than continue her wild goose chase.

I think the pub Shane told me he likes is just around the corner. I should go there for chowder, she thought.

"Any luck with that one?" the librarian asked when Caitlin handed her the yearbook.

Skirting the heart of her question, Caitlin answered, "I'm all set, thanks."

"Okay, but if there's anything else I can do to help, just ask. I know everyone on the island, so if you were to describe the student to me, I could tell you who he is, where he lives now, and what he does for a living."

I'm sure you could, which is why I'd never ask you, thought Caitlin, but she just smiled. "Thanks, I'll keep that in mind."

"No problem. I'm a sucker for a good reunion romance," she said with another wink.

Lesson learned, thought Caitlin as she hurried down the sidewalk. *That's the last time I'll ask for help with personal research.*

Caitlin wasn't expecting Ahab's to be so crowded, but she supposed it made sense; because it was a weekend, residents had more time to eat lunch out than they did on weekdays. Still flabbergasted from her interaction with the nosy librarian, Caitlin had hoped to linger over a quiet meal, but she could hardly hear her own thoughts above the rowdy conversations and background thump of music. *I think I'll take my chowder to go.*

"Hello," the host greeted her. "Table for one or are you meeting your party here?"

"Neither, thanks," she answered. "I'd just like to get a bowl of chowder to go, please."

"No problem. You can tell the bartender, and he'll put that order through for you," he replied, gesturing toward a jam-packed area to the left of the entrance.

Caitlin twisted this way and that, squeezing through the customers who were milling around the bar, drinks in hand. Finally, she reached an opening near a single vacant stool. Leaning forward over the soiled dishes, she focused her gaze on the bartender until she caught his eye.

"What can I get you?" he asked.

"A bowl of chowder to go. I don't need crackers or utensils, thanks."

"That'll be out in two minutes."

After paying him, Caitlin decided to sit down. When she turned to ask the customer next to her if he knew whether the seat was still occupied, her mouth dropped open. *"Shane?"*

He'd been angled in the opposite direction so he could watch the game on the screen at the other end of the bar, but when he swiveled to face her, he looked as surprised as she was. "Ca-Caitlin. What are you doing here?"

"Getting chowder, same as you." She smiled as she pointed to his empty bowl and then she perched on the stool. She'd only ever seen him wearing plaid flannel shirts over dark-colored tees; he was so handsome in his forest green Aran sweater. Touching his sleeve, she said, "This is a nice look on you."

The words were barely out of her mouth when she felt a tap on her shoulder. "Excuse me. That's my seat."

Caitlin turned to apologize to the customer, a tall, blond woman. "Sorry. I didn't realize it was still taken." She quickly slid off the stool and stood beside Shane, speaking into his ear so she wouldn't have to shout, "Are you planning to hang out here a while longer?"

She figured if he had ordered something else, she'd stay to eat her chowder here while it was piping hot and freshly served. But if he was done, she could avoid a bone-chilling wait at the bus stop by taking him up on his offer to give her a ride any time. She pulled back to meet his eyes, but before he could answer, the woman poked Caitlin in the shoulder again.

"Do you *mind?*" she asked loudly when Caitlin wiggled a semi-turn to face her. "We're on a date here and you're in the way."

"Oh!" gasped Caitlin, utterly chagrined. Shane had told her this was one of his favorite places to eat alone, or to catch a game on TV, and she just assumed that's what he was doing. "I'm sorry. I didn't know."

"Now that you do, you might want to back off a little."

"Of course." Caitlin didn't know whether the woman meant figuratively or literally, but she shimmied backward, and bumped into the customer behind her, nearly causing him to spill his beer.

"Hey!" he exclaimed. "Use your rearview mirror before you throw yourself into reverse like that."

"Sorry, sorry," she repeated, and then she dashed out the door and down the street to the bus stop.

Caitlin's face was so flaming hot she could've walked all the way back to the cottage with her coat unzipped and she still would have felt her skin burning when she got there. She couldn't believe she hadn't realized Shane and that woman were on a date.

Why didn't he clue me in from the beginning, or introduce her, or even utter a single syllable? she wondered. *Instead he just let me stand there, yammering away, until his date told me to get lost. Not that I blame her—she probably thought I was some random stranger hitting on him.*

Not only did Caitlin feel embarrassed about her faux pas, but she couldn't help being disappointed to learn that Shane had been on a date—and her disappointment, in turn, made her feel even more foolish. *Why am I so annoyed? I promised myself that I wasn't going to flirt or socialize with him anymore, since a romantic relationship isn't an option for us. So it's not as if I can get mad at him for dating someone else. That would be completely unreasonable, not to mention, immature.*

And yet, Caitlin couldn't seem to shake her disappointment. *What's going on with me, anyway? I didn't even feel this upset after I caught Jonathan kissing Melanie—and I'd been seeing him for half a year!*

She stewed about it all the way home, for the rest of the afternoon, and well into the evening. Finally, she went to bed at 8:30, just so she wouldn't have to think about it any longer.

By morning, Caitlin's embarrassment had faded, and in its place was a gnawing homesickness. The way Shane's date had spoken to her, making it clear she was *in the way*, had left Caitlin longing to be with someone who treated her as if she were special.

She'd often wished she were closer to her parents; her relationship with her father and stepmother was cordial, but distant. However, Caitlin's connection to her stepbrother was almost maternal, since he was ten years younger than she was and she'd spent so much time babysitting him. She was close to his wife, too, and of course, Caitlin cherished their three children and they thought the world of her.

Since nothing in Lydia's Trust indicated she couldn't leave the island for a short break, Caitlin impulsively decided to go back to Santa Fe for Thanksgiving. After her morning walk, she sat down to book a flight, but the holiday airfares were astronomical, and every flight included multiple stops.

I guess it's just not worth it, she decided.

Crestfallen, she stood and stretched and then she went into the kitchen to make lunch. She'd barely had a chance to open the fridge when someone rapped on the door: it was Shane, hugging a brown paper bag to his chest. His pink-tipped ears were sticking out on both sides of his wool hat, and when he said hello, the word made a vapor puff in the air.

"Hi, Shane." Despite the cold, she didn't invite him in. "It's Sunday, you know. Your day off."

"I'm not here to work. I'd like to talk. Can I come in?"

She opened the door wider and he stepped inside and wiped his boots on the small rug. She supposed she should've offered him tea or asked if he wanted to take a seat, but she wasn't feeling especially courteous. She folded her arms across her chest and waited for him to explain his presence.

"I, um, I'm sorry about what happened at the pub yesterday. It was an awkward situation, and I didn't handle it very well."

That's an understatement, thought Caitlin. *You didn't handle it at all—you just sat there like a bump on a log.*

"It's just that I was really surprised to see you." Shane shifted the bag he was holding to his other arm. "And it was so loud in the pub that I could hardly think straight. The next thing I knew, you were sitting down, and Darcy was coming back from the ladies' room, and it kind of felt like two worlds were colliding." He gave a little nervous laugh, but Caitlin wasn't amused.

"I can understand how uncomfortable that must have been for you," she said stiffly, only half-meaning it. "After all, I disrupted your lunch, and I upset your date by unintentionally taking her seat and chatting with you. I'm very sorry. It won't happen again. From now on, if I see you in public, I'll pretend we don't know each other."

"That's exactly what *I* was trying to do!" exclaimed Shane. Did he have to rub it in?

"Right, I get that now, but I didn't realize it at the time," she replied as patiently as she could. "I said I'm sorry, so I don't know what else you want—"

"I want you to *listen* for two minutes, please," he interrupted, looking her squarely in the eyes. "The reason I was acting as if I didn't know you was because Darcy's one of my cousin's off-island acquaintances—Joyce set us up. I didn't want word getting back to her that you're still on the island, because then she might somehow put two and two together and figure out what you're doing here. And I know how important it is to keep the remodel and your plans to sell the cottage under wraps. So I figured the less said, the better."

"Oh." Caitlin felt completely humbled by his explanation, even though she was still a little disappointed that Shane had agreed to go out with Darcy. "It didn't occur to me you were protecting my privacy. I mean, you introduced me to people at the Halloween party."

"Yeah, but ever since then, Joyce has been grilling me about you. She got it in her head that I'm seeing you or something. I told her I wasn't, but she doesn't believe me. To be honest..." He paused and Caitlin waited with bated breath for what he'd say next. "The whole reason I went out on a blind date in the first place was to throw Joyce off. You know, to make her think I'm interested in getting out there on the dating scene again."

"But you're not?"

"Not with anyone as rude and insecure as Darcy." His assessment made Caitlin smile to herself, since that was how Darcy had struck her, too. "Worst hour I've had in a long time."

Secretly pleased their date had only lasted an hour, Caitlin said, "At least the chowder was good, right?"

"Yes. But I noticed you left without yours." He extended the bag he'd been holding.

"You saved it for me?"

"No. This is freshly made. There's a bowl in here for me,

too. I figured we'd have lunch together, if you haven't already eaten."

Aww, he's really gone out of his way for me. First by agreeing to a setup, just to protect my privacy, and then by making a special trip to the pub so he could bring me fresh chowder. Even if I vowed I wouldn't socialize with him any longer, after all he's done, it would be rude to say no to having lunch together now. More importantly, Caitlin didn't *want* to say no.

"You don't mind eating chowder for a second time in a row?"

"Actually, it's my third time in a row—when the server brought out your order, I took it so I could deliver it to you, but I had a splitting headache, so I went home and crashed. When I woke up, I ate your chowder for supper," he admitted, making Caitlin laugh for the first of many times during their afternoon together.

"How is Shane doing?" asked Marion as she served Caitlin a mug of mulled cider a few days later.

"Great," she answered, scratching Pepper's head, which he rested on her lap. "Although he's disappointed because it's unlikely his football team will make the playoffs this season."

Marion gave her an amused look. "That's too bad, but what I meant was how is he doing with the remodel?"

Embarrassed that it was obvious she'd been thinking about Shane in a personal way, Caitlin took a slow sip of cider before answering. "I haven't been inside the windmill for ages, because I want to be surprised by how the remodel looks when it's finished. But from what I've seen on the outside—especially the picture windows—Shane's doing a fantastic job."

"When does he plan to finish the project?"

"Around the middle of December. It all depends on when he can get the floorboards. He's using reclaimed wood from an old sea captain's house in Benjamin's Manor. Apparently, one of his colleagues is renovating the home for a client who wants a more modern look. Shane says the wood is beautiful and in excellent condition, and I trust him completely, so—" Realizing she was rambling about Shane, Caitlin stopped mid-sentence and took another sip from her mug.

"It sounds lovely," said Marion. Letting her off the hook, she switched topics. "Will you be going back to Santa Fe for Thanksgiving?"

"No. The flights are very expensive and it's such a hectic time to travel. It doesn't seem worth the expense and inconvenience for such a short visit," Caitlin said. "My niece and nephews are sad about it, but I'm returning to Santa Fe on December 21, so I'll be there to celebrate Christmas with them."

"It's understandable that you'd decide to stay put," agreed Marion. "Have you made plans with anyone locally for the holiday?"

Since Shane and Marion were the only two people Caitlin really knew on the island, she wondered if what her neighbor was indirectly asking was whether she'd made plans to spend Thanksgiving with him. Which she hadn't; Caitlin didn't even know what Shane was doing for the holiday, but she imagined he was either getting together with Joyce and Sammy, or else he was going to Maine for a few days.

"No, I haven't made plans with anyone. But that's okay—I intend to buy a small, premade turkey pot pie for myself, which means the preparations and cleanup will be a cinch." Caitlin chuckled, but Marion seemed stunned.

"You can't spend Thanksgiving alone," she said. "You must join my family and me. You won't be disappointed. I don't do all the cooking anymore, but between Darren, Jeannine, and me, we put on a good spread."

"I'm sure you do, and I appreciate the invitation, but you've been looking forward to your grandchildren's visit for ages. I don't want to disrupt your family time together."

"Pfft, you won't be disrupting anything," she said with a wave of her hand. "I *want* to have you there, and I won't take no for an answer, so there's no sense in arguing."

Caitlin smiled. "Then I'd love to come, thank you. What can I bring?"

"You're such a good baker. Would it be too much of an imposition for you to make pie?"

"I'd love to!" exclaimed Caitlin. "Does your family have a preference for pumpkin or apple?"

"We'd happily devour either—or both," hinted Marion.

"I'll make one of each. Is it okay if I also bring the cranberry sauce? The berries I bought from Lindgren farm were so fresh and tangy the last time I got them that I can't wait to make more."

"That sounds wonderful." Marion lowered her voice, as if someone might overhear. "Just between you and me, my daughter-in-law usually serves cranberry sauce from a can. It's enough to make the Pilgrims roll over in their graves!" she said, causing Caitlin to crack up.

This is going to be a lot of fun, she thought later, as she tramped back to the cottage. If she couldn't celebrate the holiday with her brother and his family in Santa Fe, celebrating it with Marion and hers seemed like the next best thing. And although her aunt and uncle weren't there with her, Caitlin liked to believe they would be pleased to know she was finally spending Thanksgiving on Dune Island.

TWELVE

Caitlin was crouched down, examining the children's display of cranberry-themed puzzles, books, and toys in the gift shop at the farm when a young boy came up beside her.

"Hi. Do you need a basket?" he asked, extending one to her.

Noticing he was wearing a cap that had the farm's name and logo printed on it, Caitlin deduced the helpful child was probably Lily's son. She was only holding two small items—a recipe book and a bag of cranberries—but she accepted the basket and said, "Thanks. This will come in handy once I decide what to buy for my niece and nephews. Do you have any ideas about what they might like?"

He cocked his head and wrinkled his freckled nose. "How old are they?"

"The boys are four and seven, and my niece is almost six. I'm looking for something small that I can mail to them."

"That harvesting game is small." He pointed to a deck of cards. "You have to try to match all the same cards with the same number of berries, and the person with the most pairs wins."

"Hmm, that *is* small enough to fit in an envelope, and it's educational, too," said Caitlin. "The only problem is my four-year-old nephew can't count very high yet, and he'd probably bend the cards. Is there anything easier and more durable you think they'd like?"

The boy nodded enthusiastically and pulled a large box from the lower shelf. "This is called Frog in a Bog. It's a jumping game."

"Now *that* sounds like fun."

"Yeah, and it's good for all ages. Even my stepdad, Jake, likes to play it," he said. "'Cept it's probably too big to send in the mail."

"Well, then, I guess I'll just have to bring it to them in my suitcase, instead," she said. "Thanks for your help."

"You're welcome. You want me to carry it for you? It won't fit in that basket."

Caitlin chuckled. "That would be awesome."

A burly blond man with a ready smile was standing at the cash register. He took the box from the boy, who darted away as quickly as he'd appeared. "Ah, I see Ryan gave you the hard sell on Frog in a Bog," he said to Caitlin.

"He was very convincing," she answered, handing him the recipe book and cranberries, as well. "He told me even grown-ups like to play it."

"Guilty," Jake acknowledged with a laugh. "Although fair warning, the game can get rambunctious. My wife doesn't allow Ryan and me to play it indoors."

Caitlin smiled; she could see why Lily had fallen hard for this good-natured, good-looking man, who clearly loved her son. "Speaking of your wife, is Lily here today?"

"She's in the kitchen, teaching a class. I think she'll be done in about ten or fifteen minutes, if you want to wait to talk to her," he said. "Or maybe I can help you?"

"No, thanks, I'm all set. I just wanted to say hello to her."

She extended her hand. "My name's Caitlin Hines, by the way."

"Nice to meet you, Caitlin. I'm Jake Benson," he replied. "I'll be sure to pass along your greetings to Lily."

A few moments later, as she tramped back to the bus stop carrying her purchases, Caitlin reflected on how much had changed over the course of a few weeks. *The first time I visited the farm, I was dressed incognito because I was so worried someone would recognize me and bring up Nicole's drowning. The second time I came here, that's exactly what happened—and I practically passed out when I was confronted by Claire. But just now, I made a point of telling Jake my first and my last name.*

To her, that was a sign of huge progress. Granted, she was favorably biased toward Jake because she liked his wife, Lily, so much, but Caitlin had still surprised herself by proactively introducing herself to him. *It's not as if I'll be giving windmill tours and dinner parties at the cottage any time soon,* she thought, tongue-in-cheek. *But it's a relief to feel a little more comfortable about going out in public on Dune Island again.*

On the Monday morning before Thanksgiving, Caitlin tried again to reach Tobias, but the call went straight to voice mail. Unsure whether his assistant still had access to his cell phone, she hesitated to leave a specific message. So she expressed concern about his mother, wished him a happy Thanksgiving, and said, "I look forward to talking when it's convenient for you."

It's not December yet, she tried to console herself after hanging up. *Even if the hospital intends to start the feasibility study at the beginning of the New Year, there's still plenty of time for them to interview consultants before the holidays.*

She popped out for a walk, just as Shane was coming

around the corner. "Good morning." he said, his smile causing her to forget her worries. "Nice weather for a walk."

"Yeah, it's a little warmer than last week."

"Enjoy it while you can. Supposedly, we're in for a harsh winter, with record-breaking cold temperatures this December," he reported. "Although I don't think we'll get any snow until after the new year, so you'll be gone by then."

To Caitlin's surprise, she felt a twinge of sadness at the thought of leaving. "Unless it's so cold before Christmas that the ocean freezes and I'm stranded here till spring."

"That wouldn't be so bad, would it?" He looked her in the eyes so intently she felt as if he seriously wanted to know what she thought about that possibility.

"No, it wouldn't be so bad," she said. "Although it's not very realistic."

"The ocean freezing or you staying till spring?"

She chuckled. "Both."

"Yeah, I guess not." He rubbed his hands together and then blew on his bare fingers. "So, I hear you're going to Marion's for Thanksgiving, too."

"*Too?*" She echoed. Was there no end to her neighbor's attempts to push them together? Not that Caitlin really minded. "Marion invited you for Thanksgiving?"

"You sound shocked."

"That's not it. I just assumed you'd be spending the holiday with Joyce and Sammy. Or visiting your parents in South Carolina."

"No. Joyce takes Sammy to see his paternal grandparents in Maine. Since my parents live so far away, my sister and I take turns visiting them for the holidays. She's got Thanksgiving this year, and I'll get to see them at Christmas," he explained. "Marion knew I'd be alone, so she was kind enough to invite me to join her family for a what she promised will be a delicious feast—including two kinds of pie made by my favorite baker, apparently. How could I say no to that?"

He gave her a huge grin and Caitlin wondered what part of Marion's invitation he'd found so appealing, the food or the company?

"Well, I'm very glad you'll be there, too," she said. *In fact, I'm a lot happier about it than I probably should be...*

Caitlin was heading up Marion's walkway when Shane's truck came down the street, so she waited for him to park and join her.

"Happy Thanksgiving," they greeted each other at the same time.

"What have you got there?" he asked, referring to the covered glass bowl she was carrying.

"Homemade cranberry sauce."

"What, no pies?" He looked despondent.

"Don't worry, I dropped them off yesterday," she answered and they continued to the front steps.

"Risky move. Someone might have dug into them already."

"That's fine—as long as it wasn't Pepper." She motioned to the platter in Shane's arms. "What did you bring?"

"Appetizers. Shrimp cocktail and crabcakes with lemon garlic aioli. It's sort of a Dune Island Thanksgiving tradition."

"Wow. I'm impressed you know how to make crabcakes."

"Don't be." He leaned closer and whispered, "These are from Captain Clarke's."

"Not Ahab's?"

"Nope. Ahab's makes the best chowder, but Captain Clarke's is my go-to for crabcakes." He joked, "I don't like to brag, but as a single guy who rarely cooks for himself, I dine out a lot and I consider myself to be something of a seafood restaurant connoisseur."

"Oh, really? Then in your opinion, where would you suggest I go for the best lobster?"

"To Maine," he deadpanned.

"You're just biased because you grew up there," she ribbed him.

"Nope, I'm telling it like it is. You can't find better lobster anywhere than in Maine."

"I've heard that Captain Clarke's makes an awesome lobster roll," argued Caitlin.

"If that's true, it's only because they serve lobsters that swam here from Maine."

Caitlin could've stood on the doorstep kidding around with Shane for the entire holiday, but he rang the bell and immediately Pepper started barking. A moment later, Marion opened the door and a delectable aroma wafted out.

"Hello, hello," she said cheerily. "We're so glad you're here."

As soon as the pair stepped inside, Marion's son, Darren, and his wife, Jeannine, introduced themselves, offering to hang their coats and carry Caitlin's bowl and Shane's platter to the kitchen. Caitlin instantly felt at ease among them, and the conversation flowed freely as the adults put the finishing touches on the meal and the children set the table. When there was nothing left to do except wait for the turkey to finish roasting, the children took Pepper for a walk, while the adults indulged in drinks and appetizers.

The crabcakes were as delicious as Shane had indicated they'd be, and Caitlin found it difficult to exercise self-restraint and limit herself to two. In between bites of the tender seafood, she nibbled on the crudités that Jeannine had prepared.

Shortly after the adults finished snacking, the children returned, bright-cheeked and smelling of salty air. "Are you going to put lights on your windmill?" Finn, the youngest, asked Caitlin. "You could get the most votes."

"The most votes?" she repeated.

Jordan, the middle child chimed in, "Yeah, for the Shine-Your-Light contest."

"What's that?"

"It's a contest to see who has the best lights. And people come to your house and sing and you give them candy and cookies, or rugelach and hot chocolate."

"You've got the details mostly right, but I'm not sure you're quite capturing the spirit of the contest," Marion told her grandson with a chuckle. She explained to Caitlin that the event was an opportunity for community members to socialize with fellow Dune Islanders during the busy holiday season, without the pressure of hosting people in their homes. "Serving treats is optional and it's a contest in name only. There's no prize, just bragging rights, and all the participants' displays are photographed for the online newspaper, *The Dune Islander*."

"What a wonderful way to celebrate with each other," Caitlin acknowledged.

"So are you gonna do it?" Finn asked, his voice hopeful. "It would look so cool if you put a bazillion lights on those big twirly parts."

His enthusiasm about decorating the windmill's arms reminded Caitlin so much of her niece and nephews that she hated letting him down. But she couldn't imagine allowing the local media to publish a photo of the windmill, especially now that its windows made it appear so different. *The last thing I want to do is advertise to the entire island that I've remodeled the windmill in preparation of selling it. That would be like extending an open invitation for everyone on the island to comment about my plans—and about my past.*

At a loss to explain, she stammered, "Well, I... I would, but..."

Shane piped up, "Shine-Your-Light isn't held until December 22 and 23. You won't be on the island then, will you, Caitlin?"

"No. I'm flying back to New Mexico on December 21. Sadly, that means I can't enter the contest," she said, even though she was relieved she had a valid excuse not to participate.

"That's too bad," Finn said. "Cause you'd totally win."

"Maybe next year," his mother innocently remarked. Clearly, Marion hadn't told her son or daughter-in-law about Caitlin's plans to sell the property, which Caitlin appreciated.

As everyone else debated who they thought would put on the most impressive light display this season, Caitlin turned to give Shane a grateful smile for coming to her rescue. Apparently, he recognized her relief because he nodded and winked, and she was sure Marion noticed, but Caitlin was too happy to care.

An hour later, when everyone was gathered around the table, Marion asked them to hold hands while she said grace. Darren's daughter, Natalie, was sitting to Caitlin's left, and Shane was to her right, and when she slid her palm against his, she was so aware of the softness of his touch that she could hardly concentrate on what her hostess was saying until Marion ended, "Amen."

When everyone lifted their heads, the hospitable matriarch announced, "Shane and Caitlin, we have a family tradition. In lieu of making a toast, before eating we each say one thing we're especially thankful for this year. We'll start on this side of the table and go counter-clockwise, so you'll have a chance to think about it before your turn."

Jordan began by expressing thanks that his arm, which he'd broken, had healed well enough for him to play basketball this season. Next, Jeannine said she was grateful that Darren had found a full-time position again after being laid off, and he, in turn, kissed her cheek and said how fortunate he felt that she'd been so supportive of him.

Finn announced, "I'm really super glad that on Thanksgiving Mom doesn't make me eat any vegetables."

"You're going to eat corn," his brother pointed out. "Corn's a vegetable and you love it."

"Yeah, but it's yellow. I mean I don't have to eat the *green* kind," he clarified, and everyone laughed.

"I'm thankful I have a nice tutor to help me with my math homework," Natalie sweetly stated.

Caitlin was the next person to offer thanks. It had been such a difficult autumn, but in the warmth of the moment, her answer came easily. "I'm very thankful that I get to spend Thanksgiving with all of you, instead of all alone."

Then it was Shane's turn. As he squared his shoulders and sat up straighter, Caitlin realized he was wearing the forest green Aran sweater he'd had on the day she'd run into him in the pub. She shifted slightly to see him better but tried not to stare. "It's difficult to choose just one thing I'm especially grateful for this year, but I'd say I'm most thankful that business is picking up and I'm able to spend my time doing work that's meaningful to me and to my clients," he said, and Caitlin couldn't help but feel he was including her and the windmill remodel in his comment.

"Caitlin sort of stole my answer," Marion teased. "I was going to say I especially appreciate being able to spend Thanksgiving with all of you. But now I guess I should come up with something else..." She bit her bottom lip, contemplating.

"Duplication's okay, Mom," Darren prompted.

"Especially when it's heartfelt," Jeanine agreed.

"What you really mean is especially when the food is getting cold—I can take a hint." Marion laughed good-naturedly. "All right, enough said. Let's eat!"

. . .

After enjoying second and third helpings of their veritable Thanksgiving feast, everyone pitched in to clear the table, store the leftovers, and wash, dry, and put away all the pots, pans, and other dishes that couldn't fit into the dishwasher. Tidying the dining room and kitchen took well over an hour, but even then, everyone still felt too full to eat dessert.

"Let's take Pepper for a walk on the beach," Natalie suggested. But Marion pointed out that the little animal was too tuckered from his earlier excursion.

"To be honest, I'm a little tired, too. I could use a nap," she admitted. "Why don't you all go without us, and when we reconvene, we'll have pie?"

"The guys probably want to watch the game. I'll take the children to the beach," said Jeannine. "Do you want to come with us or are you a football fan, Caitlin?"

"I'd love to go with you."

"Me, too," said Shane.

"Really?" objected Darren. "You know you're making me look bad for staying behind, don't you?"

"Sorry, man," he replied. "But if my team's not playing, I'm not watching."

So Jeannine, Caitlin, Shane, and the three children set off down the street and through the woods behind the cottages. They descended the staircase and at the bottom, Jordan urged his siblings, "Let's go this way this time!"

As they headed south, toward the inlet, a surge of panic filled Caitlin's heart. She hadn't been to that part of the beach—where Nicole had drowned—in twenty years. Could she really go there now? But then she decided she'd be too distracted by watching the kids and conversing with Jeannine and Shane to dwell on what happened to Nicole there.

The tide was out, so the children wove their way through the maze of long, narrow tidal pools while the adult slowly strolled along the drier sand, chatting about Jeannine's work as a part-time nurse. She was interrupted by her daughter's screams; the boys seemed to be ganging up to throw seaweed at their sister. Jeannine cupped her hands around her mouth and shouted at them to stop, but when they continued, she said, "Excuse me, I need to put an end to this before it escalates."

She broke into a sprint and soon she was a hundred yards away. Shane and Caitlin continued to hug the shoreline. As they approached the "end" of the beach where the river would divide Lucy's Ham from Benjamin's Manor when the tide came in, Caitlin spotted a bench overlooking the inlet.

"Hey, look, that was never there when I was a teenager. I'll race you to it."

Shane groaned. "Let me save you the effort. You win, I concede. I'm so stuffed I can hardly move."

"That's exactly why you need to pick up your pace," Caitlin called over her shoulder, as she began to jog. "It's good for digestion."

"Show-off!" he shouted, making no attempt to catch up with her.

When she neared the bench, she noticed what looked like a slanted, waist-high table in front of it. *Oh, cool, it's a plaque of some sort*, she realized.

But when Caitlin drew closer, she gasped to see the plaque was superimposed with a large photo of a ballerina. Her dark hair was pulled into a sleek bun. Wearing a white, gauzy dress that looked more like a nightgown, the young dancer was striking an Arabesque pose. Although her face was only shown in profile, Caitlin immediately recognized the girl was Nicole, even before she read her name and the dates of her birth and death beneath the photo.

Her breath was coming in quick puffs and Caitlin gripped a corner of the plaque as she read the inscription:

The tidal river you see 25 yards in front of you during high tide may appear shallow and gentle, but the current is unpredictable. It can turn swift and strong without warning, knocking waders off their feet. When the tide is ebbing, the current has the potential to pull a child or small adult out to sea. When the tide is coming in, it can push them toward the marsh.

Even the most experienced swimmers may have difficulty keeping their heads above water, which is what happened to Nicole Dixon, a young, beautiful ballerina visiting Dune Island on a family vacation. Unfortunately, despite the heroic efforts of two bystanders, they couldn't rescue Nicole and she died.

Nicole's family and the Dune Island community urge you to exercise caution. If you must enter the tidal river, please only go in ankle-deep, and use the buddy system. Taking extra care could save your life and spare your loved ones the grief of losing you.

Caitlin clutched her sides and staggered backward. Reading the plaque was like hearing Nicole's grandmother all over again, and she was overcome with grief and sadness. *Nicole had so much talent, so many dreams. It's unfathomable that she'll never go to college or travel or have a career...*

"Hey, there," Shane said softly, touching her arm. "You okay?"

She'll never fall in love and get married... Nicole is gone. Her life is over.

"I-I-I have a stomach ache."

"Maybe you should sit down?"

"No. I need to go to my cottage."

"Sure. We'll take it slow."

"I want to go alone—I need to be by myself. Please don't follow me," she pleaded. "And tell Marion I'm sorry I can't come back for..." Too nauseated to say the word *pie*, Caitlin didn't finish the sentence.

Her eyes smarted with tears as she hurried to the cottage, where she rinsed her mouth, peeled off her clothes, and stepped into the shower. She stood under the hot spray for nearly twenty minutes, wishing she could wash away her shame and guilt.

What made me hope I could ever be at peace on Dune Island, even for a little while? Reminders of what happened to poor Nicole are everywhere—in the walls, on the beach, in conversations with strangers. They're such a part of this place— like the salty air—and there's no escaping them.

It wasn't as if Caitlin ever expected to forget the accident, but neither had she anticipated that the account of Nicole's drowning—and her loved ones' suffering—would be captured on a plaque as a public reminder.

Maybe Lily is a stronger person than I am, or maybe she didn't feel as ashamed as I do because no one died in the fire her family member started, she thought. *But clearly, I'm not very well-adjusted if I can't even read about Nicole's drowning twenty years later without falling to pieces.*

Adding to her humiliation was the fact that Shane had been there to witness her breakdown. *I hope he didn't read the plaque and figure out I was upset because of what it says*, she fretted. *Because if he questions me about it, I can't bear to explain how I was involved in Nicole's drowning. What would he think of me then?*

Caitlin's only consolation was that it was more likely that Shane assumed she'd suddenly retreated because she felt ill from jogging after such a big meal. She turned off the water, dried her skin and hair, and put on her warmest pajamas. Then she crawled into bed, thinking, *If there's anything I'm especially grateful for this Thanksgiving, it's that I'm one day closer to leaving Dune Island.*

THIRTEEN

Marion's brows were knit with concern. "How are you feeling this morning, dear?" she asked Caitlin.

"Much better, thanks," she answered, holding open the door so her neighbor could come inside. "I had such a wonderful time with you and your family yesterday. I'm sorry I didn't return for dessert."

"Shane told me your stomach was upset. He said it was because you went for a jog so soon after dinner. But I've been worried all night that my stuffing might have been too rich for you. Or perhaps it was the gravy..." Marion fretted.

She looked so worried that Caitlin pulled out a chair for her to sit. Joining her at the table, she confessed, "It wasn't the food that upset my stomach, Marion. It was seeing the plaque by the inlet. You know, the one by the bench with Nicole's photo on it."

Recognition dawned on her face. "Oh, dear, I'd forgotten about that. I haven't walked down there in years. If I had remembered, I would've told Jeannine not to take the children that way. I'm so sorry."

"It's not your fault. I don't know why I had such a visceral reaction."

"It's completely understandable," said Marion kindly. "It must have been a shock to see that image of Nicole after all these years."

Caitlin nodded. Even though she'd already seen snapshots of Nicole at the arcade, stumbling upon the photo of the teenager at the marsh had left her reeling. It was also what was written beneath the photo, not just the image of Nicole herself, that had intensified how upset she felt.

Marion continued, "There was a town meeting before that plaque was installed, so I know the group who installed it on behalf of Nicole's family had good intentions. They wanted to make sure something positive came out of the tragedy, and they thought the plaque was a way to provide a public service announcement about the tidal river, as well as to honor Nicole's memory. I understand why that's important, but personally, I think their plan was misguided."

Caitlin was surprised that Marion had such a strong opinion about the plaque. "Why do you think that?"

"For one thing, only a handful of people ever walk to that end of the beach, and those who do are mostly old-timers who live in the immediate area. I used to hike out to the inlet almost every day because I found its unspoiled beauty to be so soothing and peaceful. But the plaque is a constant reminder of the tragedy."

She elaborated, "Don't get me wrong—I'm not saying we should forget about Nicole because her death makes us sad. I'm saying only a few people will ever see the plaque, and most of us don't need a reminder because we know what happened, and we already carry that sadness with us. So I wish the people who installed it would have found a more uplifting way to commemorate Nicole's life—like creating a scholarship for aspiring actors or something along those lines."

"That would've been a good way to honor her," Caitlin agreed. "But like you said, the plaque was also a way of warning other people—visitors to the area, perhaps—about the tidal river."

"That's the *other* reason I was never in favor of the plaque," declared Marion. "What's written on it isn't accurate. When the stream is low enough to wade in it, I doubt very much it could knock an adult off their feet. Darren and his friends used to float in that current all the time when they were young, and yes, when the tide was coming in, it would carry them toward the marsh, but it was usually quite gentle. Furthermore, it was virtually *impossible* for the outgoing tide to pull them out to sea —there are too many sandbars in the way. Of course, in any body of water, it's imperative to exercise caution, which is why..." Marion suddenly pressed her lips together, as if she'd thought better of completing her thought.

"Which is why *what*?" prompted Caitlin.

Marion remorsefully shook her head. "It's why I can't understand what Nicole was doing anywhere near the marsh that night," she admitted. "Especially since it was only a few days after a tropical storm, and the surf was still unusually choppy. Not to mention, there was an astronomically high tide that evening."

Caitlin was confused; hadn't Lydia told Marion why Nicole had wandered to the end of the beach? Or hadn't Marion heard about it from the other islanders? Trying to keep the emotion from her voice—and hiding the fact it was a question she'd asked herself, privately, too—she summarized, "Nicole got bored and walked home alone from a beach party we went to, and she missed the turn-off for the cottages by mistake."

"Yes, I realize that was the common consensus, and it's what the police concluded, too," acknowledged Marion. "What I mean is that the story doesn't add up to me. I only met Nicole briefly a couple times in passing, but from what I could tell, she was an exceptionally bright, observant girl. I find it difficult to believe she didn't notice that she'd not only walked farther than the staircase to the cottages, but she'd passed by all the dunes, too."

A shiver rippled up Caitlin's spine. She asked Marion the question that had been playing at the back of her mind ever since the day she'd taken Pepper for a walk. "But-but why would Nicole deliberately keep walking down the beach?"

Marion glanced down at the table. "I shouldn't speculate. I hardly knew her."

Caitlin pressed her, "But just between you and me, if you had to guess...?"

"Well, from what I noticed and from what Lydia shared with me, it seemed that Nicole was at odds with her mother. Not that I'm one to judge. Most parents and their teenage children don't get along at some point—just ask my son, Darren, about the arguments we had when he was that age!" Marion admitted. "So I speak from experience when I say that it seemed like there was a power struggle going on between Pam and her daughter. And I wouldn't be surprised if Nicole went to the marsh as a way of deliberately scaring her mother."

"By swimming alone in the current?" Caitlin shuddered.

"Goodness, no. I doubt she intended to go in the current at all—as the couple who tried to save her attested, they heard her scream when she fell in," Marion reminded Caitlin. "But I've often wondered if she planned to hide out at the end of the beach until her mother and stepfather became worried that something had happened to her."

"I can't really picture her doing that," said Caitlin. "Nicole told me she wished her mom would back off and stop smothering her. She already felt like her mother didn't trust her, and that she treated her like a baby. So why would she do something to make her mother worry about her even more than usual?"

"Perhaps she craved her mother's attention, but she didn't

want to admit it? Or it could've been a way of rebelling against her mother's control, testing her limits. Maybe Nicole intended to manipulate her mother's emotions to get something she wanted," suggested Marion. "Who knows? My point is, unless Nicole was drinking or taking drugs—and by all accounts, she wasn't—then it defies belief that she didn't realize how far she'd walked beyond the cottages. Whatever her motivation was, it was foolish of her to go anywhere near the current that evening. And unfortunately, she paid dearly for her foolishness, as you're well aware."

"Yes, I am," said Caitlin soberly, tears springing to her eyes. She quickly blinked them away, but not before Marion noticed.

"Oh, dear, how insensitive I've been, blathering on about my theories when Nicole's relationship with her mom was completely none of my business," she chastised herself. "I should've simply said how sorry I am that you stumbled across that plaque. It's such a heartbreaking visual reminder of Nicole's drowning, which is why I stopped walking to the end of the beach... Now it's my ample thighs and tummy that prevent me from going that far."

Caitlin feebly smiled at Marion's attempt to lighten the mood. Knowing her neighbor had been disturbed by the plaque, she felt comfortable enough to confide, "As least you've only been avoiding a little section of the beach—I've been avoiding the entire island for twenty years! And even before I saw the plaque, I've been struggling with memories of what happened that summer." She sniffed. "I hate to admit this because I've really enjoyed seeing you again and getting to know you better... but most of the time I wish my aunt hadn't insisted that I come back here to Dune Island for the remodel. It sort of feels like torment."

"*Torment?*" echoed Marion, misunderstanding her. "You yourself have a young niece, so I think you know that *tormenting* you was the furthest thing from your aunt's mind."

"Oh, no, that's not what I'm saying," Caitlin protested, regretting her phrasing. "I know that my aunt always had my best intentions at heart. What I meant was that—as beautiful as Dune Island is, and as grateful as I am to receive such a valuable inheritance—being here has triggered so many agonizing memories about Nicole, that at times it feels... unbearable."

"I'm sure it does." Marion sympathetically patted Caitlin's arm. After a thoughtful pause, she suggested, "But maybe Lydia wanted you to return so you'd relive memories about *her*. Or about your uncle. Happier times, when you loved being together at the cottage."

"Mm, maybe," murmured Caitlin.

"Maybe she also wanted you to make a few new memories while you were here—some very pleasant ones. So that when you say goodbye to Dune Island this time, you'll be able to give it a fond farewell."

Brightening, Caitlin chuckled. "Fond farewells were very important to my aunt."

"They certainly were. Do you remember those windmill cookies she used to make for the guests?" she asked and Caitlin nodded. Marion abruptly reached into her coat pocket and instructed, "Close your eyes and hold out your hand."

Caitlin did as she was told, and when Marion placed a cold object on her palm, she knew what it was before she opened her eyes again. "Aunt Lydia's windmill cookie cutter! Where did you get this?"

"When her nephews were updating the cottage, they asked if I wanted any of Lydia's kitchen items. So, I took it, as well as her favorite mug, because it reminded me of drinking coffee with her."

"You mean the cup with scallops and starfish that says, 'Seas the Day' inside, on the bottom?" Caitlin asked, remembering it well. Her uncle had a special mug he always used, too, which read, "Hooked on fishing."

"Yes, that's the one. Unfortunately, it broke years ago, but I'd stored the windmill cookie cutter in a box of Christmas decorations, along with my gingerbread house supplies," she explained. "This morning, Darren took the box out of the attic for me so I could start decorating and baking for the holidays in a couple weeks. When I saw the little windmill, I couldn't wait to show it to you."

"I can't believe it," said Caitlin, tracing the steel outline with her finger. "Can I borrow it?"

Marion nodded as she stood to leave. "You can *keep* it—on one condition."

Caitlin didn't need to ask what that condition was. "Yes, I'll bring you windmill sugar cookies when I bake them," she promised.

Shortly after Marion's visit, Caitlin received a text from Shane. It said:

Good morning. How are you feeling today?

She wrote back:

Better, thanks.

Then, so Shane wouldn't suspect she'd felt sick because of the plaque—Caitlin didn't want him to question her about why it had triggered such an extreme reaction—she added:

That's the last time I ever go running after Thanksgiving dinner.

He texted again:

Is there anything I can bring you?

Caitlin appreciated Shane's thoughtfulness, but after what happened yesterday at the marsh, and in light of what Marion had said she realized she just needed time alone to think. She replied:

Thanks, but I'm all set.

A moment later, he responded:

You sure? It's no problem. I was planning to work for a couple hours in the windmill anyway.

Now Caitlin felt a little panicked, a little crowded, the way she used to feel when Jonathan called her at 6:00, just to check in. She dictated:

I don't need anything except more rest. If it won't mess up your schedule too much, it would be helpful if you didn't come back to work until Monday.

His reply was immediate:

Sure thing. I'll see you then. Hope you keep feeling better and better, Caitlin!

Shane's response was so sweet and understanding that she almost regretted turning down his offer to pay her a visit. But because she truly did need solitude and rest, she shuffled into her room and burrowed beneath the covers on her bed.

I wonder if Marion could be right about Nicole going to the end of the beach to scare her mom and stepdad for some reason, she ruminated. Then, she was struck by a possibility. *If that's what she did, does that mean she didn't leave the party early because she was bored...? Did she plan to leave early all along?*

Now that she thought about it, Nicole *had* been insistent that Caitlin and Donald go for a walk alone. She'd even volunteered to distract the chaperone, Dave. Had Nicole been trying to get rid of them, because she herself had intended to take off in the other direction?

But if she wanted to scare her mom into thinking she'd gone missing, why would she have told the student ranger that she'd meet me in the windmill? Caitlin asked herself. Contrary to Marion's theory, it seemed to Caitlin that Nicole had fully intended to return to the cottages before her mother and stepfather did. Yet Caitlin couldn't completely dismiss the possibility that Nicole had walked all the way to the marsh on purpose.

She got up and removed the blue plastic pouch of Nicole's belongings from the bottom dresser drawer. Pushing aside the bikini, she reached in and pulled out the photo and the paper placemat, hoping to discover a clue she'd overlooked that would explain why Nicole might have deliberately walked to the inlet the evening she died.

Assuming she'd gone that far on purpose, I wonder if her reason had anything to do with R., Caitlin thought, studying the snapshots.

She supposed that now that they'd broached the subject of Nicole's drowning, she could ask Marion what she knew about any of the teenagers in the photo. But Caitlin would need to speak to her in private and she didn't want to take up any more of her time while her family was visiting. Besides, even if Marion knew R. or the other kids, it was unlikely she'd be able to shed light on their relationship with Nicole when they were teenagers.

Caitlin set the snapshots aside and examined the back of the placemat. *N ♥ R*. The sentiment was easy enough to understand, but what did all the doodles mean? And why was the date written beneath them?

As she was examining the faded red lipstick smudges to see if they were obscuring any additional information she may have missed earlier, Caitlin was struck by a memory of the last time she'd seen Nicole applying makeup. *We were in the car, on the way to the party. I remember how angry I was that she made me stop at the pharmacy so she could buy a new tube, because she wanted to look "irresistible."*

Almost instantly, another perplexing question occurred to her. Why had Nicole wanted to look irresistible to go to a party with kids she considered dorks? It wasn't as if she cared whether they found her attractive. On other occasions when Nicole had joined Caitlin and her friends, she hadn't made quite as much of an effort with her makeup.

I always assumed she was wearing a skimpy outfit and so much makeup because she was "getting into character" for whoever she was going to pretend to be. But now I wonder if R. was the guy she was planning to impress, she thought. *The student rangers' events were always open to the public, so maybe Nicole heard about the party and jotted down the date on the placemat.*

Hanging out with a bunch of nerdy kids would've been the perfect ruse to keep Nicole's mom from suspecting she was meeting up with a guy. Yet even if Caitlin's theory was true, it still didn't explain why Nicole had wandered so far beyond the staircase in front of the cottages.

Dave and the student rangers said she was alone when she left. Caitlin reasoned, *So assuming I'm right about Nicole inviting R. to the party, he obviously was a no-show.*

Was it possible she'd felt so hurt about being stood up that she needed time alone to cry? *If she'd been super upset, she might not have been paying attention to her surroundings, and that's why she accidentally passed the staircase,* thought Caitlin.

But she couldn't imagine Nicole being that torn up about a guy she'd just met; it seemed like she was usually the heartbreaker, and not the other way around.

She racked her memory for anything else that stood out about Nicole's behavior that evening. *Dave said she was adamant that no one follow her*, she recalled. *What if that was because instead of meeting R. at the party, she was on her way to meet him farther down the beach? Maybe they walked together for a while, and then they had an argument or something, and she stormed off past the cottages? Which is why the couple fishing said she was alone when she fell into the current...*

Aware that this scenario was pure conjecture, Caitlin set down the placemat and massaged her temples. *The only way I'm going to find out whether R. knows anything about what happened that evening is to talk to him directly. But first, I need to figure out who he is, and I think the best person to ask about that is Craig.*

She was aware that she might be opening a can of worms by drawing attention to herself and inviting comments about the past. But Caitlin figured that ever since Claire had seen her, it was only a matter of time before other islanders realized she was back on the island, anyway.

So what have I got to lose by talking to Craig? she thought.

The answers wouldn't change the heartbreaking facts: Nicole had died, and her family had been shattered. But the questions still niggled at Caitlin in a way that was becoming harder and harder to ignore.

FOURTEEN

"I'd like to speak to the fire chief, if he's in," Caitlin requested, feeling intimidated when she entered the fire station lobby the following Monday morning, and hoping that the firefighter wouldn't inquire what she wanted to discuss.

"We don't usually get drop-ins, but let's see if he's available." He motioned for Caitlin to follow him down a short hall. He stopped and rapped on an office door, and then stuck his head in. "Hi, Chief. Someone's here to see you. Have you got a second?"

He must have said yes because the firefighter stepped aside to let Caitlin enter, and then he left. Craig came around from behind his desk and amiably shook her hand. "Craig Thompson, nice to meet you."

"I'm Caitlin Hines." She didn't mention they'd nearly met in passing at the Halloween party. "I-I'm just visiting the island, but I have something to discuss that's kind of a sensitive issue..."

"Would you like me to close the door?" he asked, and she nodded, so he did. "Have a seat."

"Thank you," Caitlin said nervously as he settled into his chair behind the desk. She licked her lips, wishing she had rehearsed what she wanted to say. "I, um, I know this might seem like a strange question, but I-I'm trying to make sense of an accident that happened in Lucinda's Hamlet twenty years ago and I wondered if you might be able to give me information that would be helpful."

He rubbed his jaw. "That depends on the type of accident, and whether the fire department responded to the call. We keep records of fires, but the department of motor vehicles or the police department is your best bet for information about vehicular collisions and crashes."

"It wasn't that kind of accident. It was a drowning," said Caitlin. "I should've been clearer. I'm not asking you for information because you're the fire chief. I'm asking because I think you may have been friends with the girl who drowned. She was visiting Dune Island on a family vacation, and staying at The Windmill Cottages, which my aunt and uncle owned at the time. Her name was Nicole Dixon."

Craig's expression and posture didn't change, but Caitlin noticed a tiny flicker of recognition pass across his eyes. "I'm familiar with the details of the drowning, but I wasn't friends with the victim," he stated.

"Are you sure?" Caitlin gently prodded. She pulled the photos and paper placemat from her pocket. "I think you're in these snapshots with her and two other kids from that summer. I'm sorry if this is upsetting, but if you could take a look, it might jog your memory." She handed him the strip of photos, which he glanced at briefly and handed back to her.

"Yeah, I guess that looks like me," he said, as if he kind of doubted it.

Caitlin was incredulous. She held the photo so it was facing him. "You really don't remember hanging out with Nicole?"

He shrugged. "Back then, lifeguards were very popular. Girls came up to us all the time on the beach and asked to take photos with us."

"But this wasn't taken at the beach—it was taken at the arcade."

"Same difference. That's where I went on my lunch break, and there were lots of girls hanging out in there, too."

"But in this photo, the two of you were kissing, so—"

"Look again. *I* wasn't kissing her. *She* was kissing *me*. On the cheek." He seemed to be splitting hairs for some reason, and it reminded Caitlin of when Jonathan implied she wasn't really seeing what she thought she was seeing.

"Okay, but it seems strange you wouldn't remember hanging out with Nicole, considering she drowned shortly after this photo was taken. Everyone on the island was talking about it. The accident was even covered on the Boston news."

Instead of refuting her point, Craig said, "You seem to know a lot more about her and the accident than I do, so I'm not sure how I can be helpful to you."

Feeling stonewalled, Caitlin tried not to let her frustration show. "Could you please look at this again and tell me if you know the names of the other kids?" she asked politely.

He took the strip of photos from her extended hand and squinted at it. "I can't even see this girl's face. I don't know who the guy is, either."

"Didn't you work with him?"

"It's possible, but he could've worked at any of the beaches in the area. He doesn't look like anyone I grew up with from around here, so he was probably one of the summer people who landed a seasonal job as a lifeguard."

He handed the photo back to Caitlin a second time and shuffled his feet beneath his desk as if he was getting impatient. But she couldn't leave without asking what she'd come to find out.

"Is it possible his name began with the letter *R*?" She quickly unfolded the paper placemat from the Pirate's ARR-Cade, laid it flat on his desk, and pointed to the faded inscription. "I'm asking because Nicole apparently had a crush on someone whose first initial was R. She wrote it here, right above this doodle, see?"

Craig narrowed his eyes, leaned forward, and examined the placemat. Then he drew back and crossed his arms against his chest. "Like I said, I don't remember the other lifeguard in the photo, so knowing his initial doesn't ring any bells. But frankly, I don't understand why you think it matters now whether Nicole had a crush on someone twenty years ago."

"It's just that she never mentioned liking any boy while she was here, so I was curious about him..."

"Listen, there are plenty of people on this island who'd be willing to speculate about the love lives of people they hardly know, but I'm not one of them. Professionally and personally, I mind my own business," he said emphatically, and stood up. "Excuse me, but I've got work to do."

"Wait, please." Caitlin sensed Craig was hiding something, and she didn't budge from her seat. She lifted the placemat from the desk and hurriedly explained, "I'm not just trying to satisfy my curiosity. It's kind of hard to see in this lighting, but beneath the little drawing of these cubes and squiggly lines, Nicole wrote, "Thursday, August 29," which was the date she died. It was also the date of a beach party we went to together. My theory is she jotted it down so she'd remember to meet R. there—or to meet him nearby. Anyway, I was worried she'd want to leave the party early, but she promised me she wouldn't. Then, for some reason, while I was on a walk, she changed her mind, and she decided to head home alone. Except instead of turning off the beach at The Windmill Cottages, she wandered all the way to the inlet. Which doesn't make any sense to me, because she hated the marsh. But I have a hunch something must have happened between her and R., and that's why she ended up down by the current."

She was rambling—although... did she imagine it, or did

Craig's face just blanch? "You don't think there was foul play, do you?" he asked in a gruff voice. "Because I believe the police and medical examiner ruled the drowning accidental. But you're welcome to confirm that with them."

"Oh, no, I'm not suggesting anything like that," Caitlin insisted. The thought had never occurred to her, but she could understand why the suggestion might put Craig on the defensive, especially if he was photographed hanging out with R., whether or not he remembered him. "I just meant I suspect R. was supposed to show up at the party, and when he didn't, she got upset and stormed too far down the beach or something like that."

Craig shook his head. "Like I said, I barely remember her and I have zero recollection of the other two kids in that picture." Then, not unkindly, he added, "Twenty years is a long time. You should let this go."

He opened the door and waited beside it until Caitlin got up, thanked him for his time, and left. Then he shut the door behind her.

*He's hiding something, I'm sure of it, because I've been evasive like that, too, especially when someone mentions Nicole's drow*ning. But Caitlin recognized that if her favorite aunt had never been able to persuade *her* to talk about the accident, then it was unlikely she herself could convince Craig, a virtual stranger, to open up about his memories of that summer, either.

Looks like I'm somehow going to have to locate R. by myself to ask if he knows whether Nicole really walked past the cottages by accident, or if she had some other reason for continuing all the way to the end of the beach...

For several days, Caitlin puzzled over how to figure out who R. was, and she kept circling back to the option of asking Marion for help. *She seems to have an excellent memory. I could show her the photo of Nicole with Craig and the other kids to see if she can identify them. Or she might remember someone else whose name starts with the letter R and who would've been a teenager that summer.*

But Caitlin's conscience held her back. It wasn't as if she could casually mention that she'd found a photo of Nicole and she was curious to learn more about the teenager's summer acquaintances. An easy-going approach wouldn't be credible—not when Marion had witnessed how troubled Caitlin was after stumbling across the plaque. Her neighbor would want to know the reason behind her inquisitiveness. And having been the object of hurtful gossip and speculation, Caitlin hesitated to plant any seeds of doubt in Marion's mind about her fellow Dune Islanders—and especially not about Hope Haven's highly esteemed fire chief.

Maybe I should just leave well enough alone, she thought one morning following a particularly restless night of stewing about it. *I've only got a couple weeks left in Hope Haven. Rather than chasing shadows, my time might be better spent preparing for my interview with the hospital or even doing something relaxing, like going Christmas shopping.*

Just as she took her first sip of coffee, her phone rang.

"Hello, Caitlin."

"Tobias, it's wonderful to hear from you." They chatted about his mother's improving health for a few moments, and then Caitlin said. "I was hesitant to leave explicit messages but the reason I called a few times was to ask whether the hospital signed with the agency yet?"

"Yesss..." He drew out the word as if he was confused by her question. "They finalized the contract while I was away."

"Oh." Caitlin wondered why he hadn't told Max to mention that to her, but she imagined Tobias must have been too distracted by his mother's health crisis. "I'm glad to hear that because I've done a ton of research. When do they intend to start interviewing consultants?"

"Interviewing? The interviewing phase is over. They've already chosen someone."

"What?" Caitlin practically wailed into the phone, "But-but you said I was on the top of your list! I've been looking forward to the opportunity to speak with them."

"I-I'm sorry Caitlin, but there's been a misunderstanding," Tobias said, groaning. "I asked Max to reach out to you for an interview, but he told me you were out of town indefinitely on bereavement leave."

"Where did he get that idea?" Caitlin asked, even though she had a hunch.

"Melanie Boyd told him. She said you'd left for the east coast because your aunt had died and you were involved with putting her estate up for sale. Isn't that true?"

"Yes, it is, but I could've done a video interview. Or I would've been on the next flight back to Santa Fe if the hospital wanted to meet with me in person," said Caitlin, barely able to control her volume.

"Ugh. Like I said, it was a miscommunication. I'm sorry," Tobias reiterated.

"I understand how it happened, and I don't blame you, Tobias." *I blame Melanie.* "But I've done a lot of research and I'd still like a chance to interview. I honestly believe I'm the best consultant for this campaign."

"I think you would've been great, too, but I can't ask the hospital to reconsider now. They've already made up their minds. They're crazy about the consultant they chose."

"Who is it?"

"Melanie," he said, and Caitlin audibly snorted.

I should've known. Seems like everyone's falling in love with her lately, she thought.

Tobias continued, "The good news is that the parochial school campaign is still available if you want it." He chuckled. "That is, if you're still willing to accept an assignment from my agency?"

What other choice do I have? I need an income, thought Caitlin. But she didn't want to admit defeat so easily. "I really was looking forward to more of a challenge. Maybe the hospital would benefit from a two-consultant team?" she asked, even though the idea of working with Melanie turned her stomach.

"They don't have the budget for two consultants." Tobias paused, as if waiting for Caitlin to respond, but she was too angry to say anything. "Listen, you don't have to commit to the school campaign yet. I'll hold it for you—you have my word on that—and we'll see if anything more interesting comes up in the next few weeks. Sometimes, things start happening right after the new year."

Caitlin begrudgingly agreed to touch base when she returned to Santa Fe later in the month. As soon as she said goodbye, she put on her coat, hat, and gloves, and stormed outside for a vigorous walk down the beach.

When she returned an hour later, Caitlin's burning anger had cooled to a smoldering resentment about Melanie betraying her a second time. And because she'd set aside her coffee when Tobias called, she was desperate for caffeine. She shot through the woods and across the lawn, arriving at the cottage just as Shane stepped out of the windmill.

"Hi, Caitlin." He started to give her his usual high-beam smile, but she must have been wearing her emotions on her face because his forehead abruptly creased and he asked, "Is something wrong?"

She bitterly recounted her conversation with Tobias, and Shane's response was so animatedly supportive it immediately made her feel better.

"That blows!" he exclaimed. "Don't you have any form of recourse? Can't you, like, sue Melanie or something for starting a rumor that cost you an employment opportunity?"

"If I tried, she'd probably steal my lawyer, too," Caitlin muttered sardonically.

"Then at least hold her feet to the fire in some other way—and the assistant's, too," he urged her. "It seems to me that the agency director should be making more of an effort to reconcile their mistake. He should be bending over backward to demonstrate how valuable you are to his agency. Are you sure you want to keep working for him?"

"No, I'm not sure, but what other option do I have?" Caitlin sighed.

"You could strike out on your own!" Shane exclaimed enthusiastically. "I realize it can be tough to build a client list, but in my experience, the benefits of being totally independent far outweigh the cons of working for someone else."

"I've often considered starting my own business. The problem is, when I accepted consulting assignments through the agency, I signed a non-compete clause," Caitlin explained. "Even if I worked independently, I couldn't manage campaigns from any nonprofit organizations in New Mexico. Not in Texas or Arizona, either, because they're in the agency's territory. Which means my hands are tied, so to speak."

"Yeah, I guess they are." Shane wrinkled his nose in disgust. "But it stinks that you have to get your work through an agency whose director is so unethical."

"Oh, I don't think he's unethical," countered Caitlin. "Tobias had so much going on in his personal life that I think he miscommunicated with his assistant, who made an honest mistake."

Shane shook his head. "You're a lot more easy-going than I could ever be."

"I might be cutting *Tobias* some slack, but believe me, I'm furious at Melanie," said Caitlin. "I just spent the past hour fantasizing that she'd contract some sort of itchy rash her first day of working at the hospital and she'd bring it home to Jonathan. I wouldn't necessarily want the rash to be painful, but it would have to be infectious enough that they'd need to be quarantined together for five or six months. That seems like a suitable amount of suffering for them both."

Shane laughed. "And you'd accept the hospital campaign in Melanie's place?"

"How could I say no, if Tobias begged me to take it and sent me a dozen long-stemmed roses every day until I agreed?" she joked.

"Skip the roses. As long as you're dreaming, make him double your salary," suggested Shane. "That should be a non-negotiable. You're worth it."

"I'm glad *you* think so, but I'm not sure that's how Tobias sees me," she replied facetiously.

"If he doesn't, its only because he's got his eyes closed," he solemnly asserted.

"Th-thank you," she stammered. But in her mind, she downplayed Shane's compliment, thinking, *He wouldn't say that if he really knew me. If he knew what happened the summer I was seventeen...*

As her departure date drew closer, Caitlin discovered she wasn't nearly as eager to leave Hope Haven as she thought she'd be. Although she missed her brother's family and could hardly wait to see the children, once she lost the hospital campaign, she also lost her drive to return to work in Santa Fe.

I've conducted so many school campaigns I can do them in my sleep, she thought. *So I'm not especially looking forward to talking to Tobias about accepting another one, and I definitely don't want to cross paths with Melanie at the office.*

Caitlin also felt reluctant about leaving Dune Island because she hadn't figured out who R. was, or what information Craig was possibly hiding. The fire chief had been so cagey that she reconsidered going back to the station and confronting him again. But she doubted he'd be any more helpful than the first time she'd dropped by, and she was concerned he might feel as if she were harassing him.

Instead, she returned to the library in Benjamin's Manor to do more research. *I realize Craig suggested the other lifeguard wasn't a year-round resident, but I'm not sure I believe him.* Caitlin got the distinct feeling the fire chief was protecting R.—whoever he was—for some unknown reason.

Shrugging off whatever assumptions the librarian might make about her motives, Caitlin requested to see print copies of the high school yearbooks again. Although she went through four more years' worth, and found dozens of boys whose names began with the letter R, they weren't matches with the lifeguard from the arcade. *Maybe Craig was telling the truth about him being an off-island resident after all*, she thought. Or maybe the lifeguard and the guy named R. were two different people. It was entirely possible that Nicole had stashed the photo and the placemat together, but they weren't related to each other at all...

I guess it's time to give up and accept the fact that I may never know for certain why Nicole wound up near the inlet the night she drowned, Caitlin reluctantly concluded. Considering that she'd spent two decades pushing the accident from her mind, she was surprised it was such a struggle to dismiss her doubts about it now.

Likewise, she was startled by how nostalgic she felt about leaving the cottage for a final time even though she'd been so reluctant to return to it in the first place. But when those feelings popped up, she rationalized, *I'm probably just being sentimental because the cottage is one of my last tangible reminders of Aunt Lydia and Uncle Albert. Or maybe it's that I'm subcon-*

sciously remembering how sad I used to feel about leaving Hope Haven when I was a teenager.

Regardless, the more she wished time would slow down, the faster the minutes flew by—especially during her morning coffee chats with Shane in the kitchen.

"Great news," he announced one morning shortly after Tobias's phone call. "Looks like I can finish up a few days early, so you'll get to enjoy your last week at the cottage in peace and quiet."

Caitlin caught herself thinking, *What's so great about that? I like your company.* But she said, "No need to rush on my account."

"I'm not—it's just that everything's coming together beautifully." Shane beamed at her, and their eyes met. "I'm excited to show you the finished product."

"I'm excited to see it." Wondering if she was blushing, Caitlin tipped her cup and took a sip of coffee. "So, when will you fly out to spend Christmas with your parents?"

"Not until December 23, which is a busy time to travel, but it works out well because it gives me a chance to squeeze in a small, last-minute project for a new client before I leave," he explained. "It she's pleased with the results, it may lead to a major gig, which would be great, since winter's usually a downtime for business."

"I'm sure she'll love your work so much she'll hire you on the spot," Caitlin said with a big smile.

She was truly happy for him, yet for the rest of the morning, she felt glum, and she didn't know why. *Am I disappointed because I have fewer mornings to chat with Shane than I expected?* she asked herself. *Or is it that I suddenly feel like I'm just another client, and he's moving on?*

She acknowledged that would have been illogical, since she *was* his client, and they did have a professional relationship. But there was more to their connection than that. Whether it was friendship, flirtation, or a little of both, Caitlin liked to think what they shared was special—and she was sorry it was almost over.

Maybe it doesn't have to end. Maybe we could stay in touch, she thought. But what would be the point? She didn't want a pen pal—she didn't want another *pal* at all. But she didn't want a romantic relationship with Shane, either... did she?

Almost as soon as she asked herself the question, she decided the answer didn't matter. Even if she wanted a romantic relationship with him, and even if they didn't live 2,000 miles apart, she knew she couldn't have one: because she hadn't opened up to him about Nicole. And she was afraid if she told him what happened, he'd judge her for it. But if she didn't tell him, they'd never have a very deep relationship anyway.

Enough moping and ruminating, she scolded herself. *I came here to accomplish a specific goal. Now that the remodel is almost finished, I need to focus on researching real estate agencies so I can put the cottage on the market as soon as possible, just like I planned from the beginning.*

"Are you ready for the grand unveiling?" asked Shane the following Tuesday afternoon.

Caitlin had just returned from walking to the market and she hadn't had a chance to put away her perishable groceries, but Shane seemed so exuberant she immediately declared, "Absolutely!"

He grinned. "I know you wanted to be surprised by the final results, so close your eyes and I'll take you to the sunroom. That way, you'll get the full effect of seeing the windmill as you enter it from inside." His hands were warm on Caitlin's shoulders as he guided her through the living room, stopping when they reached the entrance to the sunroom. "Okay, on the count of three you can—"

But she was too impatient to wait another second. Her eyes flew open, and she exclaimed, "Wow, you were sure right about taking down that wall!" The sunroom appeared much bigger now, and the flow between it and the windmill was fantastic; the rooms seemed connected, yet separate, and the transition from one space to another felt seamless.

"I love being able to see all the other cottages on the green," said Caitlin, entering the windmill and peering out the oversized picture window. "And I can't believe how bright it is in here."

"Yeah, the new window lets in a lot of natural light. Otherwise, the flooring might have seemed too dark."

"It doesn't, though, not at all. The reclaimed wood looks perfect, as if it's always been here—except it's so smooth," she said, recalling that she never would've crossed the old floor without wearing shoes, for fear of snagging her socks or getting a splinter in her foot. Caitlin kept circling the room, uttering how beautiful everything was until Shane told her she was making him dizzy.

"Let's take a look at the loft," he suggested. "I'll go first to block your view until you're at the top step, so you can be surprised."

Holding on to the sturdy, polished wooden handrail, Caitlin followed him up the semi-spiral staircase, which curved gently as it followed the windmill's rounded shape. When she crested the top landing, Shane stepped out of her way and she was greeted by the sight of the gleaming walls and floor, and the warmth of the electric fireplace. Even without furniture, the remodeled loft was stunning, but it was outshone by the sweeping view provided by the triple windows.

From this angle, the bay appeared to be a neat, navy-blue ribbon of water not more than two inches wide, while the sky was a boundless disarray of billowy white clouds. Astonished, Caitlin opened her mouth but she couldn't say a word.

"What's wrong?" asked Shane. "It didn't turn out like you expected?"

"N-no," she uttered. "It's even *better!*"

Deep lines fanned out from the corner of his eyes when he smiled. "Phew! You had me worried. For a second I thought you were going to cry."

"I still might," she said. "But only tears of joy. My aunt Lydia would've... she would've..." Overcome by emotion and not trusting herself to speak, Caitlin could only gesture toward the windows.

Shane seemed to understand what she meant. "I wish she could be here to see it, but I'm happy you're pleased with it, too."

"I'm not just pleased, Shane. I *love* it." Caitlin added something she never anticipated she'd feel. "I could stay up here all day."

He laughed. "In that case, you'll need something to sit on. I'll carry up a couple of chairs if you want me to?"

"That would be great, especially since I want to invite Marion over to see the remodel," she said. "How about the chairs from the sunroom?"

"Sure. It'll be a tight squeeze up the staircase, but I'll make it work."

"You need a hand?" Caitlin asked, but she was planted in front of the windows and made no motion to move; she barely even blinked as she gazed at the view.

"Nope, I got it," he answered, chuckling. "You stay where you are."

He managed to angle the chairs through the narrow opening. But instead of bringing up the long, heavy, glass-topped coffee table, he brought in a wooden storage crate from the shed, carried it up to the loft and flipped it over. "It kinda spoils the atmosphere, but at least you'll have a flat surface to put your cups on."

"That's a great idea. Would you like tea and a peppermint mocha muffin?" she offered.

"Wish I could, but I told my cousin I'd pick her up from the ferry in about twenty minutes, so after I gather my tools and the tarps, I've got to run."

"Aw, too bad," said Caitlin. "I really hoped you'd get a chance to enjoy the view."

He grinned. "I've been looking out that window for weeks."

But that's not the same as enjoying it with me, she thought. Without him there, the completion of the remodel suddenly seemed anticlimactic. "Oh, okay, I understand... but I was going to give you a speech about how much I appreciate your hard work—and Sammy's, too. It was going to be epic."

Shane chuckled. "No speech necessary. It was my pleasure."

She knew he'd have to hurry to pick up Joyce, so she said, "Well, at least let me fold the tarps while you're gathering your tools."

So Shane went outside to load his truck, and a few minutes later, she brought him the tarps, which he stacked on the passenger seat. Then he shut the door and gazed back toward the cottage.

"Is something on your mind?" she asked, noticing the expression on his face. She hoped he'd say he'd enjoyed getting to know her, or that he was going to miss having her on the island, or something else that acknowledged the connection they'd shared.

To her disappointment, he answered, "I was just thinking about a riddle." He paused and cleared his throat. "What has four arms but never embraces?"

"That's easy. A windmill."

"Good guess, but not the answer I had in mind."

Playing along, she said, "Okay, I give up. What has four arms and never embraces?"

"You and I."

Caitlin giggled at Shane's cheesy, winsome way of asking for a hug. *That is what he's suggesting, isn't it?* She couldn't be sure.

"So, um, do you think we should change that by embracing now?"

"Seems like an appropriate way for two friends to say goodbye, doesn't it?" He spread his arms and when she stepped closer, he drew her to his chest.

I don't want to just be friends and I don't want to say goodbye, either, she admitted to herself. But then Shane released her and a moment later, he was gone.

FIFTEEN

Marion set her teacup on the overturned crate that was serving as a coffee table, and she picked up a windmill sugar cookie. Seated in the rattan chairs, she and Caitlin absently nibbled their snacks and sipped their drinks, but they were too mesmerized by the view to speak.

Yesterday, the wind-battered bay had pushed slushy waves onto shore; today, the receding tide was logjammed with irregular nuggets of ice.

"From up here, the water looks like a gigantic jigsaw puzzle," Caitlin finally remarked. "Have you ever seen anything like this?"

"It happens every ten or twelve years—but never until late January or February." Marion contentedly dabbed her lips with a napkin before commenting, "Sitting here, I can hardly believe how cold it is outside. That fireplace generates quite a bit of heat, doesn't it?"

"Mm," Caitlin murmured. "It keeps the room comfy-cozy, as my aunt Lydia used to say."

Marion smiled. "She would've been absolutely thrilled with

how the remodel turned out. You've done a beautiful job of fulfilling her dream."

"Shane deserves the credit, not me," said Caitlin. "But I'm glad you think she would've been thrilled with it. I do, too—except she always envisioned sitting in a big fat love seat up here, not in wicker chairs. And she wouldn't have used a crate for a coffee table."

"I can't imagine how you'd maneuver a love seat up those narrow stairs, even if you had one," Marion remarked, and took a sip of tea. "Remind me again, when will you be headed back to Santa Fe?"

"My flight leaves on December 21."

"Will you be seeing Shane again before you go?"

"Noo..." Caitlin stretched out her arms, palms up. "There's nothing left for him to do here. It's perfect."

"I wasn't asking if he was coming back to work," Marion said in a tone that implied it should've been obvious. "I meant are you going to see him socially before you leave?"

She's shameless, thought Caitlin, inwardly groaning. "No, I don't have any plans to see him again."

"Why not? He isn't working for you anymore, so it wouldn't be, what was that word you used?" She answered her own question. "*Inappropriate.* It wouldn't be *inappropriate* for you to invite him to dinner. The two of you could eat up here, and watch the sun set..."

Caitlin couldn't help herself; she burst out laughing at her neighbor's blatant last-ditch attempt to set up her and Shane.

Marion seemed offended. "What's so funny about that? I think dining in the loft is a wonderful idea. It's what I'd do every night if I lived here."

"You're right, and as a matter of fact, I ate my supper up here last night," Caitlin said, trying to wipe the smile off her face. "I was only laughing because I think it's a little... amusing that you seemed to be determined to matchmake Shane and me, right up until the end."

Marion clapped her hands to her cheeks in genuine embarrassment. "Have I been that obvious?"

Caitlin giggled. "Yes, but it's okay, I don't mind. I appreciate your good intentions, but I'm afraid it's not going to work out the way you hoped it would. Shane and I have said our goodbyes."

Marion's face fell. "That's too bad. He must be so disappointed... you're the first woman he's allowed me to try to set him up with in the two years I've known him."

Caitlin nearly spat out her tea. "Shane *knew* you've been trying to get us together?"

"Yes, of course. I'd never try to set him up without his permission—he hates it when his cousin does that to him," answered Marion, to Caitlin's astonishment. "When you mentioned you were single, I thought you'd make a terrific couple, but you resisted my suggestions about hanging out with him. And he was too concerned about jeopardizing your professional relationship to outright ask you on a date, so I came up with a subtler plan."

"The Halloween party?" Caitlin asked, feeling both shocked and flattered that Shane allowed Marion to mastermind their night out.

"Yes. But I suppose it wasn't that subtle after all, if you figured out it was a setup." She shook her head. "I just don't understand where I went wrong. Usually, I'm quite perceptive about who might make a good couple. And you seemed to be hitting it off so well at Thanksgiving, but I guess my instincts aren't as accurate as they used to be."

Her friend seemed so dejected that Caitlin confessed, "Your instincts were right on target, Marion. Shane and I *did* get along very well, and I think very highly of him. In fact, I like him more than any guy I've met in... well, in a long, long time."

"Then what's the problem?"

"I'm leaving Dune Island in a week," said Caitlin, instead of telling Marion the *real* problem. "So it wouldn't make any sense to become romantically involved with him."

"The way I see it, since you like him more than any guy you've met in a long time, it doesn't make any sense *not* to become romantically involved with him," countered Marion.

"What about the fact that I live two thousand miles away?"

Marion waved her hand dismissively. "Distance makes the heart grow fonder." She wheedled Caitlin, "He's probably pining away for you right now. I'm sure he'd jump at the chance to see you again."

"If that's true, then why didn't *he* mention he'd like to get together?" she argued.

"Because he isn't sure you'd be interested," suggested Marion.

She might be right about that. Caitlin recognized that despite her attraction to Shane, she'd been holding back, so it may have seemed she was sending mixed messages. Ever since the other day when he'd said goodbye, she'd wondered if his awkward joke about embracing each other had been an attempt to clarify how she really felt about him, now that he wasn't working for her.

"Why not at least invite him over for dinner before you leave?' her neighbor prodded.

"I'll think about it." The idea of seeing Shane again was certainly appealing, but it also would postpone the inevitable. Having already said goodbye to him once, Caitlin wasn't sure she was willing to face those sad, wistful feelings a second time. "But please don't mention it to him."

"I won't say a word. I may not be subtle, but I know how to keep a secret." She made a motion as if she were locking her lips closed.

"Oh, that reminds me," exclaimed Caitlin. "Even though

the remodel's completed, I still need to finalize a few details with the attorney before I can put the house on the market. I'll be working remotely from Santa Fe with a local real estate agent, but I haven't chosen one yet. Would you mind holding on to a housekey to give to them once everything's official?"

"I'd be glad to," she agreed.

"There's something else I almost forgot." Caitlin leaned over and pulled a gift bag from where she'd stashed it beneath her chair and handed it to Marion.

"A present? Should I wait till Christmas to open it?"

"No, it's not for Christmas. It's a very small token of my appreciation for how helpful and kind you've been to me," said Caitlin. "Please, open it."

When Marion pulled out the delicate turquoise coffee mug, with sand-colored scallop shells and starfish embossed on it, she exclaimed, "It's just like the one Lydia used to have! Look, it even says, 'Seas the Day' inside it on the bottom! Where did you find it?"

"When you told me my aunt's nephews had given you her favorite mug but it broke, I searched online for a replacement," said Caitlin. "It just arrived yesterday. I was going to serve you tea in it, but I wanted to be sure you liked it, first."

"I love it! Receiving a mug like Lydia's and eating windmill cookies is the perfect way to commemorate the completion of the remodel." Marion sighed. "How your aunt would've loved to be sitting here with us now."

"Yes, she would've," said Caitlin, choking up a little. It was bittersweet to realize that even though she'd fulfilled her aunt's dream, Lydia would never get to enjoy it. *And soon, I won't be able to enjoy it, either.*

After they'd finished their tea and Marion went back home to Pepper, Caitlin called her niece and nephews to share a video of the inside of the remodeled windmill with them. She wasn't entirely surprised that the boys liked the pre-renovated version better.

"It doesn't look all dark like a fort anymore," said Logan. "It's kind of boring."

"It is *not*. It's beautiful," argued Maya. "Auntie Caitlin, aren't you going to put a bed in the loft?"

"No, it's supposed to be a sitting room, which isn't for sleeping in. It's for... well, for sitting and admiring the ocean view while someone reads or knits or listens to music."

"When I come to visit, can we bring sleeping bags up there and have a slumber party?"

Her question caught Caitlin completely off guard, but the little girl's mother answered, "Honey, you know Auntie Caitlin isn't staying on Dune Island. She told you she was fixing up the cottage and windmill so someone else would want to buy it."

"But won't I get to visit it first?" Her niece looked at the camera, her eyes filling. "Please, Auntie Caitlin? Just once?"

"If she gets to go, I want to go, too," whined Archie.

Apparently, Logan had a change of mind about the "boring" windmill and he chimed in, "Yeah, we've never been to Massachusetts. We could visit you when we have Christmas break from school."

"No, we can't," Suzanne said. Referring to her parents, she reminded him, "Grandma Joan and Grandpa Barney would be heartbroken if they had to spend Christmas all alone here while we were in Hope Haven."

"They could come, too," suggested Archie.

"Auntie Caitlin doesn't have enough beds for everybody in that little cottage," Suzanne pointed out.

"That's okay. I'll sleep with you and Daddy and we can bring extra sleeping bags for Grandma and Grandpa."

"You'd make your grandma and grandpa sleep on the cold hard floor while you were cuddled up in a nice warm bed with

Daddy and me?" his mother teased lightheartedly, obviously trying to indicate how impractical Archie was being without hurting his feelings. "I don't think they'd be very comfortable."

"Then *they* can cuddle up in a nice warm bed with you and Daddy, and *I'll* sleep on the cold hard floor," he volunteered.

His mother used a firmer voice. "I'm afraid the answer is no. Please stop talking about it or you'll make Auntie Caitlin feel bad that she can't invite us to the cottage."

Too late, I already feel terrible, she thought. "I miss you all so much and I can't wait to come back and visit you at *your* house for Christmas." She told her niece and nephews about Lydia's special cookie cutter, and then she suggested, "When I get back to Santa Fe, maybe you can come to my apartment for a sleepover. It's been renovated, too, and we can make windmill cookies. How does that sound?"

"Good," they duly answered, although Caitlin knew her offer was a poor substitute for what they truly wanted to do.

And she couldn't blame them; Caitlin felt like she'd rather spend the holidays on Dune Island than in Santa Fe, too. Long after their phone call ended, she imagined how much the children would enjoy exploring the woods and running down the beach. She could also picture herself reading to them in the loft and helping them make colorful drawings of the ocean view.

Maybe if the cottage doesn't sell right away, we could all make a trip here during the children's spring break from school, she daydreamed. *I'm sure I could work remotely for a week...*

Deep down, she knew it was unlikely that the cottage wouldn't be snapped up as soon as she put it on the market. *I suppose I could wait to list it...* But Caitlin recognized that if the children came to Dune Island once, they'd love it so much they'd want to return every year.

Then I'd have to tell them no, and they'd be crushed, she thought. *And this place already has more than enough heartache associated with it.*

. . .

That night, the temperature dropped to 8 degrees Fahrenheit, but the wind chill factor made it feel as if it was ten below, according to the weather forecaster Caitlin heard on the news the following morning.

"Winds will pick up throughout the day, driving the temperatures down even further. The weather service has issued an extreme cold warning for the entire state, and residents are urged to stay indoors. Under these conditions, there is a high risk of frostbite or hypothermia, so if you must go out, dress in dry, warm inner layers, and wear a tightly-woven coat or jacket, as well as a hat, scarf, and—"

Caitlin clicked off the TV. *I guess that explains why I had to turn up the heat in the middle of the night,* she thought. Intended for summer use, the duvets in the cottage were made of lightweight material, and even though she'd used three of them on her bed, she'd woken up so cold she would've taken a bath just to get warm if she hadn't been so tired.

Curling her fingers around her coffee mug, she hurried upstairs to the loft to sit in front of the fireplace. *I'm glad I'm in here and not out there,* she thought as she watched large shards of white ice bumping against each other in the undulating waters. *Thanks to Shane's expertise about thermal regulation, I think it's warmer in the windmill than it is in the rest of the cottage.*

Caitlin contemplated Marion's tempting suggestion that she invite him to dinner. *Making a special, homecooked meal seems like a pleasant, personal way to thank him for all the work he poured into the remodel.*

Yet the next instant, she questioned whether prolonging her time with Shane would only remind her of how much she liked him—and how much she wished they *could* have a romantic relationship.

But that would mean telling him about what happened the summer Nicole drowned. And even though he himself had confided that he'd made a lot of stupid mistakes as a teenager, Caitlin was sure they weren't as consequential as what she had done. No, she couldn't risk opening up to him about that.

Still, just because our relationship can't go any further than a flirtation, it doesn't mean we can't spend a fun evening together, does it?

Caitlin vacillated for over an hour about whether or not to extend a supper invitation to him, and when she still couldn't make up her mind, she turned her attention to calling the estate attorney to tell him the remodel had been completed.

"I can text you photos if you need proof," she offered.

"That won't be necessary," he said with a chuckle. "I believe you, and I'm sure your aunt trusted you to honor her request."

"I'll text a photo anyway," Caitlin insisted, and sent it to him, proud to show off Shane's handiwork. "I'm very pleased with the way it turned out. Shane—the carpenter—did a fantastic job."

The attorney seemed impressed, too. "If I could afford it, *I'd* buy the cottage and windmill from you. Although, once my wife got there, she'd probably never want to come back home with me again," he joked. Or maybe he was serious. "Are you sure you want to sell it?"

"Sometimes, I have my doubts," she answered with a sigh. "But yes, I'm going to move forward with the sale."

The attorney told her that his paralegal would send her e-copies and the original paperwork she'd need related to the deed of the cottage, as well as other legal documents and correspondence. "After you review everything, if you have questions or concerns, don't hesitate to reach out. I'll be out of the country for the holidays, starting tomorrow through the New Year, but my paralegal will be covering for me."

I wonder if his paralegal would mind if I called just because

I wanted to chat with someone, Caitlin thought drolly after thanking him and hanging up. For someone who supposedly treasured solitude, she was bothered by how much quieter the cottage was now that Shane had finished the remodel. *If it weren't for the wind howling outside, the silence in here would be deafening.*

Since it was too cold to hike into town—it was even too cold to walk to the bus stop—she spent most of the day cleaning and packing, in preparation for her departure. *This makes me feel like I've come full circle,* she thought, because even though so much had changed, she was fundamentally alone again, just like when she'd first arrived.

Caitlin woke in the middle of the night again. It wasn't that she was too cold—she'd left the heat turned up when she went to bed, and she'd worn a sweater over her pajamas. It was that she heard a dull, rhythmic knocking coming from the back of the house.

Puzzled, she padded into the kitchen, flicked on the outdoor lights and peered through the window. No one was there, but the thumping noise persisted. She opened the door and was met by a blast of arctic air that took her breath away.

No wonder there are frostbite warnings on TV! she thought, as she leaned halfway out the door and scanned the backyard and the windmill for the source of the noise. Relieved that she didn't see any damage, she looked the other way and immediately noticed that the gutter above the kitchen window had come loose at one end and was thumping against the cottage. *It's too high for me to reach and even if I had a ladder, I wouldn't know how to secure it in place again.*

The banging noise kept her awake for hours, but she was too excited to sleep anyway, knowing that she'd *have* to ask Shane back one more time before she left Dune Island.

SIXTEEN

Because she was eager to hear Shane's voice again, instead of texting, Caitlin phoned him first thing in the morning.

After exchanging greetings, she said, "I thought you should know that Marion loved the loft. She gave me a smug I-told-you-so about hiring you."

"Glad she liked it, but I hope Pepper's toenails didn't scratch the floor."

"No. She didn't bring him because she was worried about that happening, too," replied Caitlin with a chuckle. "So the floors are still in flawless condition, but there's a small problem on the roof. I wondered if you'd be available to take care of it for me?"

"What kind of problem? Did someone TP it again?" he joked, making her smile.

"No, the gutter came detached. It banged against the house all night. It's been quieter now that the wind is dying down, so there's no rush to do it this week—as long as it's fixed before the cottage goes on the market." Swallowing, she screwed up the courage to add, "But if you have the time, it would be great to see you again before I leave. And if you come at the end of the day, when you're finished, I'll make dinner and we can eat in the loft. It's so cozy I practically live up there now."

Shane's answer was swift and enthusiastic. "Sounds great. I'll have to bring Sammy with me in case I need his help, but we'll drive separately, and I'll send him away as soon as we're done rehanging the gutter."

Feeling guilty, Caitlin haltingly offered, "He's—he's welcome to stay for supper, too."

"No way!" Shane exclaimed. In a quieter voice, he said, "He might be on the skinny side, but believe me, that boy eats a ton. He'd clean you out. Let's keep supper to just us."

Caitlin was only too happy to agree. "Okay. Do you have any food preferences or aversions?"

There was a momentary pause before he answered. "Never thought I'd say this, but no clam chowder, please. I discovered this week that I can't eat it for every meal after all. Anything else would be terrific. Thursday at three thirty okay?

Grinning from ear to ear, Caitlin said, "It's perfect. See you then."

As she hurriedly got dressed, she mentally planned the menu: steak, twice-baked potatoes, sauteed asparagus, and—just to try to dispel Shane's bias—lobster stuffed mushrooms as an appetizer. For dessert, she'd make cranberry cheesecake using the recipe book she'd purchased from the farm.

It suddenly occurred to Caitlin that she'd have to brave the harsh wintry elements to get to the grocery store and the fish market. She supposed she could've asked to borrow Marion's car, but she figured, *If I can go outside my emotional comfort zone and invite Shane here for a pseudo date, then I can go outside my physical comfort zone, too...*

Ironically, it was while she was waiting in line at the store, instead of while walking on the beach, that Caitlin discovered the harbor and a large section of the bay had frozen solid during the night.

"Supposedly, a couple of icebreaker ships are on their way, but until they get here, ferry service has been suspended," the elderly gentleman in front of Caitlin told the cashier.

"Who needs ferry service?" the woman replied. "I just had a customer in here who said the ice is so thick on the beach near him that he could drive a car straight across Hope Haven Sound to Hyannis if he wanted to."

That's obviously an exaggeration, thought Caitlin. But she was fascinated by this innocuous Dune Island rumor and she could hardly wait to find out to what extent it was accurate. As soon as she returned to the cottage, she set her groceries on the kitchen table and dashed up to the loft.

Caitlin was awestruck by the otherworldly view: beyond the bare-branched scrub oaks and the gnarled pitch pines on the cliff, the bay was an unbroken plain of white. How could anything so stark be so beautiful?

When I made a joke to Shane about the bay freezing over, I didn't realize it could happen, especially not at this time of year, Caitlin thought, remembering her crack about being stranded on Dune Island until spring. *Like he said, it wouldn't be the worst thing that could happen, would it?*

On Wednesday afternoon, Caitlin had just slid the springform pan of cheesecake batter into the oven when her phone rang. Recognizing the New Hampshire area code on her screen, she assumed it was one of her relatives calling with early holiday greetings.

"Hello?" she answered in a cheery tone.

"Caitlin Hines?" The man's voice was so grim her first thought was that he was calling to tell her someone had died.

"Yes, this is Caitlin," she confirmed.

"Attorney Bruce Wegford here," he stated. "I'm calling on behalf of my clients, who are contesting your right to inherit Lydia Walker's estate."

His call was so unexpected and he spoke so quickly that at first, Caitlin could hardly absorb what he was saying. But by the end of his monologue, she'd caught the gist: Lydia's nephews were claiming that her Trust was invalid because she'd already been diagnosed with dementia when she'd drawn it up.

"Of course, I'll be in touch again when I formally file the complaint in probate court after the holidays. But my clients asked me to forewarn you, as a courtesy."

"How thoughtful." Unable to hold her tongue, Caitlin decided to kill them with kindness. "Please, wish them both a very Merry Christmas for me—and happy holidays to you, as well."

She hung up without another word and burst into tears. How could they do this? And how could they do it now? *If they were going to contest the Trust, why didn't they do it from the beginning?* she fumed. *It's as if they were just waiting until the remodel was completed! After all the thought I put into designing it, and all the work Shane did to make it perfect—not to mention all the emotional turmoil I went through by coming back to Dune Island—and now they're just going to steal the cottage out from under me?*

Caitlin was so upset she didn't even try to gather her composure before phoning Lydia's estate attorney to speak to the paralegal. He didn't answer, so she left an urgent voice mail message and then did an online search for "contesting the will of someone with dementia." She'd hoped to read something that would put her mind at ease, but the more she researched the topic, the more convinced she became that Lydia's nephews had a strong case against her.

Even if their claim is shaky, I can't afford to hire an attorney to represent me, she fretted. *And they know that full well—I can't believe they'd be so merciless. And greedy. And...* Caitlin paced circles through the tiny cottage, adding to her list of unflattering adjectives to describe their behavior until she got her anger out of her system.

As obnoxious as they're being, I can't let them get the best of me, she told herself. *Especially because I haven't even spoken to the estate attorney's office yet. For all I know, they'll tell me Lydia's nephews don't have a legal leg to stand on...*

Unfortunately, when the paralegal returned Caitlin's call at the end of the day, his response was more exasperating than consoling.

"I'm not as familiar with your aunt's Trust as the attorney is, but off the top of my head, I can confirm that if she lacked the capacity to create the Trust, then your aunt's nephews might have a valid case."

"Right, I'm aware of the *general* grounds for contesting a Trust," said Caitlin through clenched teeth. *I already figured out that much from the internet.* "But the reason I called was to ask about my *specific* situation, and to confirm whether my aunt's nephews actually *do* have a strong case to prevent me from inheriting her property."

"I can't confirm that yet—like I said, I'd need to familiarize myself with the Trust, which I can do and get back to you. But while I have you on the phone, let me get a little more information about your aunt's health."

After telling him as much as she could remember, Caitlin asked the paralegal for an estimate of the legal fees for defending her inheritance. The range of figures he quoted seemed astronomical to her, and she hung up feeling completely discouraged.

That evening, as she lay in bed, her anger began creeping up on her again. How could Lydia's nephews do something so underhanded? Not just to Caitlan, but to their aunt's memory? How could they be so unconscionable, and violate Lydia's final wishes after she'd been so generous to them their entire lives?

I've got to fight this. Caitlin schemed, *Maybe I could withdraw money from my retirement account to hire a lawyer. If I win the case, I'll be able to replenish my savings after I sell the cottage.*

On the other hand, if she lost the case, she would have wasted a lot of money, and she'd have to pay early withdrawal fees and taxes, on top of it. Not to mention, a legal battle would be extremely stressful.

If the estate attorney ultimately advises me I don't have a good chance of winning, I guess I should just concede instead of going through all that, she thought dolefully. *After all, I won't be any worse off than I was two months ago. And isn't the most important thing that I fulfilled Aunt Lydia's dream, like she requested?*

But no matter what she told herself, the injustice of Lydia's nephews taking ownership of the cottage was so maddening that Caitlin couldn't sleep. She got up and turned on the TV for a distraction from her thoughts.

"The bad news is that our cold snap continues. Temperatures should hover right around ten degrees Fahrenheit tomorrow," the Boston forecaster announced. "But the good news is that the winds will be calm and the skies will be sunny. However, if you're going outside, you'll still need to protect yourself from the extreme cold."

Maybe I should suggest that Shane and Sammy postpone repairing the gutter until the weather is warmer? thought Caitlin. *Or maybe they should just leave it as it is. If Lydia's nephews end up taking the cottage, they should be the ones to hire a contractor to fix it!*

She switched the TV to a local news channel, where a prerecorded daytime segment was playing. "Today Fire Chief

Craig Thompson returned to his post after an unpaid three-day suspension," a reporter said. Shocked, Caitlin turned up the volume and leaned forward.

The reporter continued, "The suspension was a disciplinary action taken after Thompson punched a bartender in the face, breaking his nose. Thompson was off-duty at the time, and the bartender, who wishes to remain anonymous, declined to press charges. Earlier this week, we asked local residents whether they thought a three-day suspension was too lenient. Here's what they had to say."

The camera cut to a woman who appeared to be in her late sixties standing in front of a café on Main Street. "Too lenient? No. If anything, it's too harsh. Chief Thompson has never done anything like this before and I'm sure he'll never do anything like it again. He's a pillar of the Hope Haven community."

"Yeah," agreed the younger man beside her. "I've known him since high school and I've never seen him raise his hand to anyone, ever. Don't get me wrong. I have no idea what happened the other night, and I feel bad for the bartender, getting his nose busted up. All I'm saying is that ordinarily, Craig wouldn't hurt a flea. He's dedicated his entire career to helping people, and keeping the island safe—and many times he's risked his life to do it. If you ask me, Rip is a hero."

"*Rip?*" asked the reporter at the same moment Caitlin repeated the name, too.

"It's short for *riptide*," explained the bystander. "In high school, our swim team coach called him Rip because he was so fast and strong."

A photo of Craig dressed in his uniform appeared on the screen, as the reporter concluded, "Before resuming his post, Chief Thompson issued a formal apology to the unnamed bartender, the entire Dune Island community, and his colleagues at the fire station."

Caitlin jumped to her feet and pointed an accusing finger at

Craig's image on TV. "You *lied* to me! You said you didn't know who R. was—but you did. It was *you*, wasn't it? *You* were the boy Nicole liked!"

After learning this morning that Lydia's nephews were trying to swindle her out of her inheritance, Caitlin couldn't let Craig's deception go. She called the non-emergency number for the fire department and followed the prompts until she reached his voice mail.

As directed, she stated her name and number, adding, "I spoke to you a few weeks ago about Nicole Dixon and I have additional questions." She didn't want to go into detail, just in case someone else was checking his messages for him. Yet Caitlin also needed him to appreciate the urgency and nature of her call, so she said, "I'm leaving the island soon, so if I don't hear from you by Saturday morning, I'll drop in at the fire station to speak in person. Looking forward to talking, *Riptide*."

There. That should get his attention. *I've had it with deceptive people!* thought Caitlin as she turned off the TV and went back to bed. But she was still too wound up to sleep.

Why wouldn't Craig have mentioned the fact his nickname began with an R*, unless he was trying to cover up something about his connection to Nicole?* she wondered, recalling how defensive he had seemed when she'd suggested that something might have happened between R. and Nicole that had led to her wandering to the inlet the night she'd died. *He was awfully quick to point out that the police ruled the drowning an accident.*

Caitin's skin tingled as a disturbing possibility occurred to her: was it possible that the "pillar of the community" was somehow involved in Nicole's drowning?

But no, she was getting carried away by her imagination. As angry as she was that Craig hadn't been forthcoming about his nickname, Caitlin recognized it was unfair to speculate he'd had sinister reasons for withholding that information.

I'll have to wait to hear what he says, she concluded,

burrowing deeper under her covers. *Just like I'll have to wait to hear what the estate attorney or the paralegal says about Lydia's nephews contesting her Trust. But in the meantime, I'm not going to talk to Shane about it because it'll just bring me down and I want our last evening together to be very special.*

When Caitlin texted Shane the following morning, he insisted that he didn't want to postpone rehanging the gutter, despite the formidable weather.

Sammy and I will have it fixed so quickly, we won't have time to get cold, he wrote.

True to his word, they re-secured the gutter within twenty minutes of arriving at the cottage.

"Thanks so much, it looks as good as new," said Caitlin, sticking her head out the door to peek at it. Although she'd agreed not to invite Sammy to stay for dinner, she figured the least she could do was serve him a snack.

But when she asked him in, he said, "I wanna go check out the bay, first. I've never seen it when it's been completely frozen over."

"Neither have I," said Shane. "I think I'll go take a look, too. You want to come with us?"

"Sure." Caitlin hadn't been down to the beach since it froze, although she'd been admiring the view from the loft. "The three of us can have hot chocolate when we get back, and then I'll begin making dinner."

So Sammy started off on his own, and Shane came inside and waited while Caitlin bundled herself in layers. He must have noticed her puffy eyelids, because as they tromped through the woods, he remarked, "You seem kind of... pensive. Is everything okay?"

"I'm not sure yet," she answered. Even though she hadn't been planning to mention the attorney's call so it wouldn't spoil their evening, it was still weighing heavily on her mind. And because Shane could sense something was wrong, she figured she should answer honestly. "Unfortunately, yesterday I found out my aunt's nephews are contesting my right to inherit the cottage."

"What?" Shane momentarily stopped dead in his tracks. "They don't have any grounds to do that, do they?"

"I don't know. They're claiming that since she'd already begun experiencing symptoms of dementia when she created her Trust, it isn't valid," she explained, and they continued walking. "Unfortunately, my aunt's estate attorney is out of the country for the holidays, so I haven't been able to discuss the situation with him directly."

They'd reached the clearing and Caitlin gasped at the sight of the white, craggy field of ice stretching hundreds of yards out from the shore. "I've seen the bay from the loft, but it's even more beautiful up close! I feel like we're at the Arctic Circle!"

But Shane seemed too intent on their conversation to admire the sight. "Isn't there anyone else who can give you legal advice while your lawyer is away?"

"His paralegal is covering for urgent matters. And believe me, even though my aunt's nephews' attorney isn't filing the complaint in probate court until after the holidays, I felt like my anxiety qualified as an *urgency*," said Caitlin, trying unsuccessfully to laugh at herself. "The paralegal isn't as familiar with the Trust as the attorney is, so he couldn't give me a definitive answer and to be honest, I don't trust his opinion as much as I trust the estate attorney's anyway. But the paralegal said it's possible my aunt's nephews have a valid argument."

"Ugh. I'm so sorry you have to go through that kind of legal battle with them."

"Well, if my aunt's estate attorney thinks they can build a very strong case, I'm not sure I *will* go through a legal battle." Standing at the top of the staircase, she pointed at Sammy who'd walked a hundred yards or so onto the frozen bay. "Is it safe for him to be out that far?"

"Yeah. The ice is at least a foot thick," said Shane. "What do you mean you might not go through a legal battle? You're not going to give in without a fight, are you?"

Starting down the steps, she said over her shoulder, "Yes. I've been considering that option."

"You *have?*" He sounded appalled. "I know it's not really my business, but why would you be open to surrendering your inheritance so easily?"

She waited to respond until they were standing side by side on the sand. "Because I might not want the stress or expense of trying to hold on to something if I'm probably going to lose it anyway. And because I've fulfilled my aunt's dream by converting the loft. To me, that's what was most important."

"Wow. I'm—I'm floored," he muttered. "I never saw this coming."

"Neither did I. But I probably should have read the signs—my aunt's nephews were pretty ticked off when they found out I'd inherited the cottage. I should've known they were going to try to claim it for themselves."

"I didn't mean I'm floored by *them*, and what *they're* doing," Shane emphatically clarified. "I meant I'm surprised by *you*, and what you're *not* going to do."

What difference does it make to him how I resolve this family dispute? Although she felt stung by his comment, Caitlin guessed that Shane's feelings were hurt because he'd put so much work into the remodel.

Touching his arm, she gently told him, "Even if I choose to forfeit the estate to my aunt's nephews, it won't change how much I appreciate all you did to transform the windmill. As I've said, it's even more wonderful than what my aunt and I had envisioned, especially the loft, and I can't thank you enough for all the talent and effort you poured into it."

"It isn't necessary to thank me again—I was well compensated for my work." His words may have been polite, but his tone was so flinty that Caitlin dropped her hand and stepped back. Why was he acting like this?

She reasoned aloud, saying, "You knew all along I was going to sell the cottage, and it was always going to end up being owned by someone else. If my aunt's nephews win their case, they'll probably sell the cottage, too. So I don't understand why you sound so... so disgusted or something."

Before he could answer, she was distracted by movement in her peripheral vision; Sammy was kicking the heel of his work boot against the ice in a chopping motion. *That doesn't seem like a good idea*, she thought, and then turned her attention back to Shane. Was he red-faced from emotion or from the bitterly cold air?

"I'm not disgusted. I'm *surprised*," he claimed. "Although I guess I shouldn't be. Like you said about your aunt's nephews, the signs were all there from the beginning. Giving up the cottage is consistent with your character."

Losing patience, Caitlin retorted, "What's *that* supposed to mean?"

"Well, when your apartment was flooded, or your boyfriend cheated on you, or your coworker took your job, you rolled over and played dead," Shane answered, almost accusingly. "So why should this time be any different?"

For a moment, she was speechless. *I can't believe I confided in him about all those private, humiliating situations, and he acted so sympathetic, but the whole time he was judging me for how I responded! Who does he think he is? It's not as if he handled the Halloween prank perfectly, either!*

"Well, excuse me if I don't get up in arms at every offense or every time something doesn't go my way, like *some* people do," she said curtly.

"Maybe *some* people think things like their property and

careers and relationships are worth fighting for," he shot back. "Maybe they try to protect the things they care about. The things that matter."

Caitlin would've responded but at that moment, Sammy began jumping up and down, clearly trying to break through the ice. "Stop it!" she shouted. When he didn't, she remarked to Shane, "What's wrong with him? That water's frigid. If he falls in, he'll get hypothermia—or drown!"

Without waiting for his reply, she jogged beyond the sand and started climbing over the bay's jagged, frozen crust, waving her arms and yelling at Sammy. But either he didn't hear or he was ignoring her, because he continued jumping in place, his heavy boots making a dull thumping sound.

Caitlin raised her voice and shouted louder, just as Sammy broke through. The lower half of his body disappeared beneath the ice, but she could still see his shoulders and head.

"Sammy! Hold on, I'm coming!" she screamed and rushed across the pointy, uneven surface. He must have been in shock because he slowly turned his head and stared at her, as if she were speaking a language he couldn't understand.

"Caitlin, wait! What are you doing?" called Shane from behind her. Hadn't he seen what had happened?

"Sammy fell through!" she shouted over her shoulder. Still moving forward, she tripped on a chunk of ice and landed hard on her right hip and knee, her cheek and ear striking the cold, uneven surface. The sensation was like an electric shock, followed by a rush of warmth.

"Caitlin!" Shane was suddenly crouched beside her, touching her left shoulder. "Are you okay?"

"Sammy's going to drown!" Ignoring her pain, she scrambled to her knees, unwound her scarf from her neck, and pressed it into his hand. "Use this to pull him out but don't get too close to—"

"He's fine," interrupted Shane. "Look." He pointed to

Sammy, who gave them a friendly wave from the hole in the ice and then he adjusted his cap over his ears.

"But-but-but he's..." stuttered Caitlin, her teeth chattering. She couldn't comprehend what had happened.

"He's standing on dry sand," explained Shane. "It's low tide, so there's no water beneath the ice. See, it kind of makes a shelf that's suspended about four feet above the seabed. The space will fill in with water again at high tide. But right now, it's just air."

It took Caitlin's brain another moment to readjust to what she was seeing, and when she realized Sammy wasn't in danger, she turned toward Shane and cried out, "That was a mean joke to play on me! It was really, really cruel."

"It wasn't a joke. I don't think he meant to scare you, Caitlin," he said softly, concern filling his eyes as he caught sight of her right cheek. He quickly rolled her scarf into a thick pad and lifted it toward her. "You cut your face and it's bleeding—a *lot*. Here, let me apply pressure to it."

She snatched the scarf from his hand, pressed it against her cheek, and stood up. "I can take care of it myself."

As she picked her way back across the ice toward the dunes, she could hear Shane yelling, "Get out of there, Samuel. I'm driving Caitlin to the ER, so you need to move your car. RIGHT NOW!"

But Caitlin was so angry at Shane for what he'd said, and even angrier at Sammy for scaring her that she didn't want either of them near her right now. She hurried to the stairs and by the time she reached the upper landing, her scarf was saturated with blood. Aware she didn't have bandages in the cottage, she headed straight for Marion's house.

"I'm bleeding. Do you have any butterfly strips?" she asked as soon as her neighbor opened the door, with Pepper at her feet.

"No. But let me grab my car keys. I'll bring you to the hospital."

Because she was bleeding when she arrived at the emergency department, Caitlin was able to see a physician right away. As the doctor sutured and dressed her wound, he assured her that it was superficial, and he expected her skin to heal nicely within a few weeks or so.

"Would you like to spend the night at my house?" asked Marion as they drove home. "I'll make soup for supper, and you can sleep in the guest room. I promise not to crowd you, but sometimes when you've suffered an injury like yours, it's comforting to know someone else is nearby to chat or to bring you whatever you need."

"Thank you, that's very thoughtful, but I'll be fine," insisted Caitlin. "I'm too exhausted to even pack an overnight bag. After a hot bath, I'm going straight to bed."

"On an empty stomach?" Marion looked worried.

"All that blood made me queasy. But if I get hungry, I've got plenty of food in my fridge." Not that she could imagine eating lobster-stuffed mushrooms, or even glancing at a raw steak, for at least a week.

"All right, but promise you'll call if you change your mind—it doesn't matter what time it is," Marion said as she pulled into the driveway.

"I will, thanks—and thank you for bringing me to the hospital. Going there was a much better idea than trying to bandage my face by myself."

Just before Caitlin got out of the car, Marion told her, "Oh, I almost forgot—while I was in the waiting room, Shane called me to ask how you were. He also said he'd be happy to bring you anything you need."

"That was nice of him," Caitlin responded politely, even

though he'd already texted the same message to her and she'd deleted it without replying. *The only thing I need from Shane is distance*, she thought.

That night, for the first time in at least a decade, Caitlan dreamed of Nicole. The two teenagers were in the car, on the way to a party, and Nicole was rummaging through the blue pouch, which she held on her lap. After pulling out several miniskirts, her snakeskin print bikini, and a dozen tubes of melted lipstick, she finally removed a small bottle of concealer.

Handing it to Caitlin, she said, "After I drown, you're going to be scarred for life, but if you cover it up, maybe no one will notice."

Caitlin woke with a start, and for the rest of the night, she couldn't stop shivering.

SEVENTEEN

Even though the sky was clear, the sunshine was brilliant, and she imagined the bay view was dazzling, Caitlin couldn't bring herself to drink her morning coffee upstairs. Being in the loft would remind her too much of Shane.

My cheek is already causing me enough pain—I don't want to think about the hurtful things he said. And I don't want to think about Lydia's nephews trying to take away my inheritance, either.

As she rose from the kitchen table to make a second cup of coffee, there was a knock at the back door.

Maybe because he had a scrape across his forehead and a yellow half-ring of a bruise beneath his eye, or maybe it was because he was wearing casual clothing and a wool cap instead of a uniform, but when she saw the man standing on her doorstep, Caitlin didn't immediately recognize him.

She cracked open the door. "Hello. Can I help you?"

"I'm here to answer your questions."

It dawned on her who he was, and she stepped back. "Oh, of course! Come in, Craig."

"I'd rather talk outside," he said gravely, eyeballing the

bandage on her face. "There's a path through the trees to the beach, right? I'll meet you there."

He turned and left before she answered, heading toward the woods. As Caitlin put on her coat, hat, and gloves, she felt a little surge of discomfort. *He wouldn't lure me from the house to hurt me, would he?*

But while Craig's tone had been grave, he'd sounded more somber than angry. And despite the recent bar fight, as the fire chief, he had to be an upstanding person, didn't he? Besides, he was here to give her more information and Caitlin felt she owed it to Nicole's memory to find out as much as she could from him.

And despite what Shane thinks of me, I'm not just going to roll over and play dead, she resolved.

Before leaving the cottage, Caitlin retrieved the strip of photos, as well as the placemat, and tucked them into her coat pocket, just in case she needed them for reference. Then she hurried through the woods to the beach.

Craig was sitting on the upper staircase landing, scanning the horizon. He scooted to the side to make room for her. Caitlin sat down and waited in silence until he said, "I'm sorry I lied to you at the station, but I'll answer honestly this time. So go ahead, ask whatever it is you want to know."

His candor surprised her, but since he was being straightforward, she didn't beat around the bush, either. She took the photos and the placemat from her pocket, her gloved fingers fumbling to unfold it. "Why did you pretend you didn't know who R. was?" she asked, pointing to the phrase, N♥ R, scribbled on the bottom of the paper. "And that you hardly remembered Nicole—or the other two kids in these photos?"

He glanced sideways to look at the paper and the pictures, and then back at the horizon. "I swear, I don't remember anything about that guy or the other girl, except that they weren't locals. But I lied about remembering Nicole because I was worried you'd somehow figure out... what happened between her and me."

Even though she hadn't moved a muscle, Caitlin's heartrate quickened, and her mouth went dry. She licked her lips, but her voice was still barely a whisper. "What happened?"

Craig blew the air from his cheeks in a heavy sigh before answering, "We had a huge fight a few days before she died, and it got really ugly."

"So you and Nicole *were* seeing each other?"

"Not really. I mean, she'd come to the beach while I was on my lunch break and sometimes we'd go to the arcade or the ice cream shop on the boardwalk. We were just flirting. Nothing physical happened, except that kiss you saw in the photo," he said. "But yeah, initially, I was interested. I even invited her to a party after hours at the lifeguard station, but she was a no-show."

That's because Pam wouldn't have allowed her to go out in the evening without me. "So you had a fight because she stood you up?"

"No, we had a fight because I found out from a friend who worked at the club where her stepfather golfed that she was only fifteen, not eighteen, like she told me."

Caitlin didn't see what the big deal was, although of course older high schoolers sometimes looked down on going out with younger students. "How old were you? Sixteen? Seventeen?"

"I was twenty," he said, shocking Caitlin. Even now, his baby face made him appear much younger than his age. "Obviously, I was way too old to be interested in Nicole. When I found out how young she was, I felt completely humiliated, completely played. I was scared of losing face in front of my peers and getting in trouble with our parents—or even with the law. So I told her off, big time."

"How did she react?"

"She said something about how I shouldn't be embarrassed

because plenty of older men have fallen for *ingenues*—I didn't even know what that word meant! I told her she was lucky I was one of the good guys, because one day her twisted little act was going to get her into a world of trouble. But no matter what I said or how explicit I was, I couldn't get through to her. Every day, she kept showing up at the beach and doing things to try to get my attention or make me jealous."

"Like what?"

"You know, doing ballet poses on her towel right in front of my lifeguard chair, or asking my coworkers to put sunscreen on her shoulders. I tried to ignore her, but I was also scared if I was too mean, she'd make up some lie about me and show that photo of us to her parents or something."

As he was speaking, Caitlin noticed Craig's features were contorted with disgust. While it was possible he was lying again, she knew enough about Nicole's behavior to believe his account of their relationship. *Oh, Nicole*, she thought sadly. *You just didn't know when to give up, did you?*

"One afternoon—it was the day before the tropical storm—she showed up just as the guards were getting ready to head home. It was drizzling, so there were hardly any other people on the beach. But Nicole decided to go swimming, and since I was the head guard, and my shift technically hadn't ended yet, I was required to stay and keep an eye out for her. So she waded into the water, maybe up to her chest, and then she dove in and kept swimming the backstroke parallel to shore, back and forth, for about a hundred yards at a stretch. She knew she had my attention, she knew I couldn't leave. It was like she was toying with me."

Craig stared out at the frozen bay, as if he were still watching her, and his resentment was almost palpable. "She was swimming real slow and easy, but out of the blue, she stopped. At first it looked like she was treading water, and I thought maybe she was taking a break, or she'd gotten a cramp.

But then she tipped her head back and started pushing down on the surface with her arms, like this." He made the motions. "It's called 'instinctive drowning response.'"

Caitlin gasped. "She was actually in danger?"

"That's what I thought, yeah, so I charged in to get her. She seemed very weak when I was carrying her to shore, like she had muscle fatigue," he said. "But when I laid her down in the sand, she held onto my neck really tight and made some crack about not letting go until I gave her mouth-to-mouth."

"Pff." Caitlin didn't realize she'd been holding her breath until she let it out in a huff. "That must've been infuriating. What did you do?"

"I completely lost it. I pushed her off me—and I wasn't gentle about it. I yelled at her, too. I said if she really *did* get into trouble in the water one day, she'd better hope someone else was there to rescue her. I told her I'd let her sink like a stone before I'd even extend a finger to pull her out." He covered his face with his hands and shook his head. "Can you believe those were the last words I spoke to her?"

Caitlin could hear the anguish in his voice and she knew exactly how he felt. But—unlike in her case—Craig hadn't done anything wrong in his account so far. "You had every right to be furious at Nicole for pretending to be drowning and for lying about her age. What you said was... unfortunate, considering how she died, but it was just a coincidence."

"No, it was an inexcusable thing to say. I was a *lifeguard*," he protested emphatically. "As a public servant, I had a duty to—"

She cut him off. "You performed your duty by rescuing her, even though she was faking it. And I bet if she repeated the same stunt the next day, you would've been just as quick to pull her out again, because you couldn't have lived with yourself if you didn't, right?"

"Yeah, probably," he acknowledged.

"So don't beat yourself up over something you said in anger."

"I probably shouldn't beat up *other* people over it, either," he said with another heavy sigh.

"Excuse me?"

"Sorry, poor attempt at humor." He pointed to his eye. "You must have heard that I started a fight in a bar last week?"

"Yes. It was on the news. That's how I found out your nickname," admitted Caitlin. "Was the bar fight related to what happened between you and Nicole?"

"Indirectly." Craig explained, "I took a swing at the bartender, John, because I was drunk and he cut me off. But my excuse for getting drunk in the first place was because I was so upset after…"

When he didn't finish his sentence, Caitlin guessed, "After I came to the fire station and questioned you about your relationship with Nicole?"

"Yeah—not that it's your fault. *I'm* responsible for my sobriety," he quickly asserted. "See, it was such a shock when Nicole died and I felt guilty about getting so angry at her. *Really* guilty. I mean, on my worst days—even though I knew it wasn't true—I used to wonder if she drowned on purpose, to get back at me for what I said. And then I'd think if that's what she did, it served me right because I shouldn't have been such a jerk."

The brutal honesty of his confession struck a chord with Caitlin. On *her* worst days following the accident, she used to wish she'd wake up with amnesia, figuring she'd gladly forget every single thing about the first eighteen years of her life if it also meant she didn't have any recollection of what happened the night of Nicole's death. So she understood how guilt—as well as the trauma of the accident—had made Craig feel the way he'd felt, even if those emotions were extreme. But she was surprised he was being so open with her, and she held her breath, silently waiting for him to continue.

"For obvious reasons, I couldn't talk to anyone about what I was going through," he said. "So I started drinking to numb my emotions. It wasn't that much at first, just whatever I could steal from my parents' liquor cabinet. But it got worse and worse until I was binge-drinking three or four nights a week. There were other contributing factors, but essentially it became a lifestyle for about six years until I'd totaled my car, destroyed my relationships, and drained my bank account. Finally, I went to a recovery center and I got sober."

"Good for you," Caitlin murmured. Even though she was aware that people in recovery programs often shared personal stories about their addiction struggles, once again she was struck by how vulnerable Craig was being, since they barely knew each other. It was almost as if they shared an affinity, an unspoken trust, because of their history with Nicole.

"In the process, my sponsor helped me work through my issues, and I thought I'd made peace with what happened that summer. For fourteen years, I was happy, healthy, successful, never drank a drop. For fourteen years, I left the past in the past. Even when someone mentioned you were back on the island and people started rehashing the drowning again, I held it together."

I wonder if Claire was the one who fanned those flames, thought Caitlin.

"But when you came to the station and showed me the map—"

She interrupted, "What map?"

He tapped the faded sketch on the placemat she was holding. "This is a map of where I used to live. I never gave Nicole my address, but she must have tracked it down." He snickered. "The little stalker."

"Ohh. So this cube with the X on it is supposed to be your house?"

"Yep, and all these straight lines above it are streets. The squiggly lines below it are waves." Craig stretched his arm in front of her, pointing to the south. "See those dunes on the other side of the inlet?"

Caitlin squinted. "Just barely."

"That's Bayview Circle, where I grew up in Benjamin's Manor."

"I can't see any houses from here."

"There were only three of them on our street, and they were all condemned and demolished after they were damaged by Storm Brody in 2018. Ever since then, the land's been too fragile for anyone to rebuild in that area," he said.

"Now that you mention it, I kind of remember passing those houses when I went to the harbor in my uncle's boat." She empathized, "That's very sad your childhood home was destroyed,"

He grimaced. "What's even sadder is Nicole drowned trying to get to it."

Caitlin gasped. "Wh-wh-what makes you think that's what she was doing?"

"I don't just *think* it anymore—I *know* it now. The date on the placemat proves it." He swallowed twice before explaining, "My parents were supposed to be out of town on August 29, so I'd secretly planned to throw a little party at our house while they were gone. I never invited Nicole, of course, but one of the other lifeguards must have told her about it. I figure that's why she sketched the map and jotted down the date—or who knows, maybe whoever told her about the party wrote the info on the placemat for her. Anyway, it turned out my parents had to cancel their travel plans because of the tropical storm, so I had to cancel the party, too. But apparently, no one told Nicole it had been called off. She must have tried to take a shortcut down the beach... and, well, it all adds up. She died on her way to my house." When Craig blinked, moisture dripped from his eye and rolled down his cheek.

Caitlin realized with a start that maybe some small part of her thought if she could prove that Nicole had always intended to leave the party—that it wasn't her fault for sneaking off with Donald—then she'd finally feel exonerated. But that was a selfish way to think; Nicole was still gone, and nothing would bring her back. And Caitlin was still filled with self-recrimination. *If I had stayed at the party and kept an eye on Nicole, she wouldn't have been able to slip away to Craig's house.*

In addition to guilt, Caitlin felt shame and regret about how her search for answers had affected him. "I'm so, so sorry I stirred up the past," she said.

He held up a hand to silence her. "No apology necessary. On some level, I think I always suspected she was on her way to see me that night. I mean, she died awfully close to where I lived, and it was kind of unbelievable she didn't realize she'd passed the dunes," he reasoned. "But like I said, after I saw that map with the date written beneath it, I knew for sure, and I couldn't seem to stop agonizing over it again. Couldn't stop wondering if I had handled things differently—like if I'd given her the attention she craved, instead of telling her off and ignoring her—would Nicole still have tried to come to my house? Would she still be alive today?"

"It wasn't your fault she died," rasped Caitlin, trying not to cry. "You can't blame yourself for *her* choices. *Her* actions."

"Are you talking to yourself or to me?"

"What?"

He turned sideways to look directly at her. "I don't know the particulars of your story or your relationship with Nicole, but I do know guilt when I see it, and it was written all over your face the day you visited the station... which is one of the reasons I decided to come clean with you. I figured if I told you the truth, maybe I could prevent you from being triggered to pick a bar fight, too." His eyes darted to her bandage. "Looks like I might have been too late though."

Caitlin absently lifted her hand to touch her cheek. "I didn't get this injury in a bar fight, but I suppose in a way, it is a result of what happened that summer with Nicole..."

After a quiet pause, Craig prompted, "Do you want to talk about it? Any of it, I mean, not just how you hurt your face?"

Caitlin's head throbbed when she shook it. "No, thanks. I think I need time to process all the things you just told me."

"Makes sense, but if you change your mind, I'm a good listener and my gut tells me I'd probably understand how you feel better than a lot of people would," he suggested, and judging from what he'd shared about himself, Caitlin figured he was right. "You've got my number, so you can call any time."

"I appreciate it. And thank you for being so honest with me."

"Like I said, I wanted to spare you more grief if I could. But it was also a matter of self-preservation," he admitted. "My sponsor helped me see that unless I made amends for lying to you, and unless I acknowledged how broken up I was when I realized Nicole was trying to track me down and dealt with those feelings, I'd be on the path to self-destruction again."

"Well, it was still very brave. And rest assured our discussion will stay between the two of us. I won't tell a soul."

"That's too bad," he said, and she thought he was joking. But then he placed his hand on her shoulder and gently added, "Because confiding in someone trustworthy about this stuff might help you a lot, Caitlin."

Her eyes filled with tears, but she gave him a weak smile and nodded. Then she extended the photos and the placemat. "I think these belong to you."

He shook his head. "They belong to the past. I don't want them." But to her relief, he took them from her hand anyway. "I'll destroy them before they do any more damage to *us*, okay?"

. . .

After Craig left, Caitlin stayed on the staircase, contemplating their conversation. It was so easy to recognize he was bearing the burden of false guilt, but until she'd spoken to him, she hadn't fully realized the same had been true for her.

Looking at him was like seeing my reflection in a mirror, she thought. Not just his wounded face, and his hurt, angry, and ashamed expression, but the way he felt responsible for Nicole drowning. *It wasn't his fault, and it wasn't mine. And even if Nicole shouldn't have been on her way to see him, I can't blame her, either. She never intended to fall in the current. It was an accident, a foolish, tragic teenage accident...*

For the past twenty years, Caitlin had trained herself not to think or talk about what had happened that summer. She was convinced that putting it out of her mind was the only way she could cope. But now she saw that the deeper she'd pushed down her grief and guilt, the more they'd become a part of her, shaping her perspective.

It suddenly struck her that even though Shane had been unkind, he'd also been right. *I've literally been "playing dead" about so many aspects of my life—my career, my housing situation, my relationships... And it's all linked to Nicole's drowning and how I responded to it emotionally.*

As the realization sank in, Caitlin felt like weeping, but she was sure that if she did, her tears would freeze on her face. As it was, the stairs she was sitting on were so cold her bottom was going numb, so she stood up.

Maybe now I can finally start to make peace with what happened, instead of just suppressing my emotions and trying to avoid everything that reminds me of that summer—including Dune Island, she thought as she tromped through the woods. *Not that I'll have a cottage anymore, but maybe I can rent a place and bring the children here sometime in the future...*

. . .

Shortly after returning to the cottage, Caitlin heard another knock on the door. *Marion?* she wondered, but it was the mail carrier with a large, certified envelope—the paperwork from the estate attorney. She signed for confirmation of receipt and tore open the packet as soon as she shut the door. *Maybe something in here will also help me defend my right to the cottage*, she thought.

As she sat down and began flipping through the imposing legal documents, a lavender envelope slipped from the stack of paperwork. Caitlin turned it over to see her name written in familiar cursive.

"Aunt Lydia!" she exclaimed aloud and tore it open.

As quickly as she could, she devoured the letter, which read:

Hello again, Caitlin,

Congratulations on completing the windmill remodel! Thank you for all the time, thought, and energy you poured into converting the loft. I'm sure the sitting room is every bit as charming and the view is just as magnificent as I always pictured they'd be.

However, now that the project's finished, I have to make a confession: as much as I appreciate you fulfilling my dream, overseeing the remodel wasn't the only reason I wanted you to return to Dune Island. The truth is, I believed being there would give you the clarity you'd need to make the best decision about whether to sell or keep the property.

I'm sorry if that seems like a cruel trick, but I promise I only have your best interest in mind. Please, let me explain.

In the years following Nicole's death, I longed for you to visit us at the cottage again, but I understood why you couldn't. Even though you denied it, I recognized the accident had a devastating and far-reaching effect on you. I tried my best, but I couldn't seem to break through your resilient façade and help you heal.

Unfortunately, when I told your father and stepmother how worried I was about you, my concerns fell on deaf ears. As you got older—and when I became increasingly consumed by Albert's care—I backed off. But deep down I always hoped if I didn't push too hard, you might eventually change your mind and talk to me or to someone else about it.

As far as I know, that still hasn't happened—and I still wouldn't want to force the issue. But neither would I want you to make a decision about the cottage based on unaddressed feelings from your past. So, that's why I drew you back to Hope Haven, and I deliberately left the timeline open-ended, so you wouldn't feel pressured to undertake the project until you were ready to return.

Even so, I recognize how courageous you were to go back there again, and I hope your visit hasn't been too painful or stirred up troubling memories that outweigh the good ones. My deepest desire is that staying in the cottage has somehow freed you from the emotional burdens you've been carrying. At the very least, my wish is that being there again has given you true clarity about what to do next.

Life can be so hard, Caitlin, so grievous. But it also can be filled with wonderful things if our hearts are open to receiving them. Whatever you decide to do with your inheritance, as long as it brings you joy, you have my blessing.

Love,

Aunt Lydia

Caitlin dabbed her eyes and then she reread the poignant letter a second time, lingering over her aunt's words. Lydia shouldn't have worried that her niece would feel as if she'd played a "cruel trick" on her, because all Caitlin felt was gratitude for her aunt's concern and sensitivity.

I can see now that no matter what I claimed, Aunt Lydia always knew that Nicole's death affected me deeply, she realized. *It must have been so frustrating when I denied it and when my parents and I rejected her attempts to help me.*

Caitlin also acknowledged, *Aunt Lydia and I didn't really drift apart—I* pushed *her away.* Which wasn't because she'd ever intended to hurt her aunt or that she'd stopped loving her; it was because Caitlin was trying to cope with her feelings by shutting down, rather than by opening up.

Aunt Lydia was so gracious that she let me go, and she never held a grudge. But she also never gave up on trying to help me— she was just waiting until I was ready. And she was right about the cottage. I did *need to come to Dune Island to have clarity about whether to sell or keep it.*

Before she'd arrived, Caitlin had been so certain of what the right decision was that she didn't even question it. But in the past few weeks, so much had changed. *She* had changed.

I'm fed up. I'm not going to allow Lydia's nephews to steal the inheritance she intended for me. And I'm not going to allow the past to steal my joy, either, she silently declared, as a smile crept over her face. *But Melanie can keep Jonathan, and she can keep the hospital campaign.*

EIGHTEEN

Although the weather seemed warmer the following morning, Caitlin dressed in several inside layers, in addition to her outer winter garments, including her balaclava beneath a winter hat. Then she trekked down to the marsh and sat on the bench. In the distance, silvery puddles seeped through the white blanket of ice; the frozen bay was breaking up, and Caitlin felt as if something inside her was thawing, too.

Snow lightly fluttered onto the plaque, melting as soon as it landed. Watching it dissolve on Nicole's photo, Caitlin could picture the teenager dancing the part of Clara in *The Nutcracker*, and she had to smile. *Nicole would've hated it that the photo commemorating her life was of her dancing instead of acting in a play... but at least she's wearing her trademark bright red lipstick.* Caitlin was quiet for a few minutes, and then she cleared her throat and began as if she were speaking on the phone, "Hey, Nicole. It's me, Caitlin."

Feeling a little foolish, she started again. "I just want to say how sorry I am that you died when you were only fifteen."

Gripped with emotion, Caitlin paused, took a few calming breaths, and continued, "I was devastated when you drowned. I was also angry and hurt because I trusted you and you tricked me into believing you were going to stay at the party. It wasn't fair of you to do that. And it wasn't fair of me to blame myself for your death all these years. Not that I'm blaming *you* for dying, either—I know that was an accident. But I *do* blame you for leaving the party after you promised you wouldn't."

She sighed. "I also forgive you and I'm going to try to forgive myself, even though it wasn't my fault. That's my New Year's resolution—to go to therapy and get some help. Anyway, I'll never, ever forget you, Nicole." Caitlin brushed away a tear. "But I can't dwell on the past anymore. It's time for me to start living my best life. Just like I wish you could still be here, living yours."

She got to her feet and started to walk back to the cottage, but then she paused and swiveled to look at the plaque again. "By the way, I threw out your snakeskin print bikini. Your mom was right—you were probably too young to wear something like that." She half laughed, half sobbed. "But I always thought you looked great in that lipstick."

Caitlin had barely begun to warm up after her hike to the marsh when she heard someone pull into the driveway. Peeking outside, she saw Shane's truck, and behind it was Sammy's car. *Good, I'm glad they're here*, she thought, eager to talk to each of them again.

Exchanging greetings at the door, Shane remarked, "Wow, that's a big bandage. Does it hurt a lot?"

"No, it looks worse than it feels," she assured him, and invited them in.

But Shane told her, "Sammy wants to speak to you alone, so I'll hang out in the yard until he's done."

"Uh-oh, you better talk quickly, or Shane will turn into an icicle," Caitlin joked to put the teenager at ease as he came into the cottage. He was holding a rectangular pan wrapped in tin foil.

"I, uh, I just wanted to say I'm sorry I scared you the other day," Sammy said, his eyes downcast. "I didn't mean to. And I'm sorry you slipped and cut your face."

"I know you didn't intend to scare me. It's not your fault I got hurt." Caitlin had already decided that as one of her first steps toward openly acknowledging the past, she was going to level with him, so she explained, "When I was your age, I had a friend who drowned in the bay, so when I saw you out there on the ice, I overreacted."

"Yeah, but if I hadn't—"

"Sammy, take it from me, you can't go down that road," she interrupted. "You didn't intend to scare me, and you said you were sorry. That's all you can do. Besides, I'm fine. You're fine. We're good. And hey, thanks for helping Shane fix the gutter."

"You're welcome." He gave her a sheepish smile and handed her the pan. "This is from my mom. She said to tell you it's a soft noodle dish, in case your injury makes it difficult for you to chew."

"Thank you. That's very sweet... but I'm surprised you told her what happened."

"I didn't—Shane did."

"I hope you're not in trouble?"

He mumbled, "Not too much."

"When I call to thank her for the meal, I'll let her know it wasn't your fault," she said.

"Okay, but she won't know who you are. Shane and I never told her whose cottage we were working on, even though I think she got suspicious after she met you at the Halloween party."

Caitlin laughed and she could've hugged the sweet teenager but she didn't want to embarrass the poor kid. "Thanks for being discreet, and thanks for all your good work on the windmill. I think you're going to be very successful in your field."

"Mm-hmm," he mumbled, ducking his head. Then he pushed open the door to let Shane in as he went out.

As usual, Shane took care to wipe his feet on the rug—it was one of the small, considerate things Caitlin liked about him—and then he removed his hat. "It's my turn to apologize now."

"I have something to tell you, too."

"Me, first," he insisted, nervously running a hand through his hair. "I'm very sorry I made those obnoxious comments. I was completely out of line. Whatever you do with the cottage is *your* business and I had no right to say anything about it. I think I was just frustrated because I felt so personally invested in it. I mean, I felt privileged to help you fulfill your aunt's dream. It was sort of like we were... like we were partnering together in a really meaningful way."

He paused, his eyes searching Caitlin's face, as if to read her reaction. Moved by his openness, she nodded. "I felt like we had a strong connection, too."

He continued. "And even though you were going to sell the property, I knew the remodel would add to the value of the house, which would ultimately benefit you. And that made me happy because you'd been through a rough time recently and I liked knowing something good was coming your way. So that's why I was hoping you'd fight for it instead of..."

"Rolling over and playing dead?" she prompted, recalling his words.

His ears went scarlet. "No. I was going to say instead of letting those swindlers rip it out of your hands, but I didn't want to be too derisive toward your aunt's relatives," he clarified with a wry smile. "I never should've said you rolled over and played dead about any of the circumstances you shared with me. I truly do admire you for how easily you can let some offenses slide and get on with life."

"Hmm, it might seem that way, but I'm afraid that's not accurate." Figuring it would be easier to be vulnerable if they weren't standing face-to-face, she said, "I'd like to explain, but it might take a while. Can we chat up in the loft?"

So she made coffee for him and tea for herself, and they carried their mugs to the loft, where Caitlin turned up the electric fireplace. For a few minutes, they sat in silence, staring out the window as the sun bathed the icy water with soft light. When Caitlin began speaking, she asked if Shane had ever heard any stories about Nicole drowning.

"Yes," he acknowledged. "I've heard a few different accounts."

"I guess I shouldn't be surprised, since it's a small island," she said. "But how come you didn't let on that you knew?"

"Why would I? It didn't have anything to do with you and me, or with remodeling the loft. Besides, I'm sure it's a painful topic, and it was clear you were very guarded about your privacy," he said. "I didn't want to bring up something that would hurt you or something you obviously didn't want to talk about. I can't even imagine how traumatizing that was for you when you were a teenager."

"That's what everyone thinks. And it's true, I was completely broken up about Nicole dying. But there's more to it than that." Without mentioning anything about Craig, Caitlin recounted what had happened that evening, and she confided how guilty she'd felt for sneaking off with Donald. "I always felt like if I had only stayed at the party, then Nicole wouldn't have walked down the beach alone."

"That's a boatload of guilt for a kid," he said. "It wasn't your fault."

"My aunt tried to say that from the very beginning, but..." Her voice drifted off as she thought about how ferociously Lydia had defended her when Pam blamed Caitlin for Nicole's disappearance.

"Your aunt was right." Shane's tone was unequivocal. "Trust me. I was a lot like Nicole when I was in high school.

Strong-willed. Bent on doing my own thing, my own way. I'm telling you, even if you had stuck to Nicole like glue, if she wanted to ditch the party early, she would've found a way."

"Yeah, I know that intellectually, but emotionally... it's hard to internalize. Now I've lived with the guilt for so long, it almost seems wrong to let go of it," she admitted. "But I'm going to try."

"Good," he said emphatically.

"Anyway, I know you're sorry that you asked me why I roll over and play dead, but honestly, it was a valid question, and it made me realize something about myself." Then she told him what she'd never told anyone else. "See, after Nicole died, I came up here to the loft, and I cried. You may have heard rumors about how I freaked out and locked myself up here, or whatever, but that's not what happened. I'd been awake most of the night, so I was really tired and I cried myself to sleep."

He shifted a little, waiting for her to continue. After she told him what she'd heard Nicole's grandmother saying, Shane squeezed her shoulder. "That must have been unbearable for her—and so sad for you to hear it."

"Yes, it was. And in a way... I think on some level, I stopped living a little that day, too. I mean, after that, I felt like it wasn't fair that I should get to go to college or travel or have a career." Her voice wobbled as she continued, "And I especially didn't feel like it was fair for me to fall in love, or to have anyone truly love me, since I was... I was off making out with my boyfriend while Nicole was drowning..."

Shane's voice was like a moan. "Oh, Caitlin."

"So when something unfair happens and I don't fight back, it's not because I'm passive by nature. And it's not because I'm particularly generous, or forgiving, either—although I try my best to take extenuating circumstances into consideration," she said. "It's that deep down, I feel like, well, like at least I'm alive, so who am I to complain? Or maybe that I don't deserve any better."

"That's so untrue."

She nodded. "I'm starting to see that now... which is why I've decided I'm going to fight to keep the cottage, no matter what it takes. Even if I have to drain my retirement account to hire an attorney."

"Yes!" Shane shouted, punching both fists into the air. "I'm sure you'll win and when you do, you can replenish your savings from the money you'll get from the sale of the cottage."

"No, I won't." She clarified, "When I say I'm going to fight to keep the cottage, I mean keep it for *myself*—I'm not going to put it on the market."

His jaw dropped. "So does that mean you're going to...?" He looked so bewildered that Caitlin connected the dots for him.

"If I win the case, I'm going to move here, and start my own consulting business. I figure if I win, I'll have a place to live rent-free while I'm building my client list. And if I need to, I can always work at a bakery or something," she said. "And if I lose—"

Shane cut in. "You *won't*."

"But if I do, then at least it won't be because I gave up."

Shane's eyes were gleaming. "That's the spirit!"

Caitlin smiled and slapped her hands on her knees. "You know what? I still have the steaks I was going to make for dinner the other day. Are you hungry?"

"I'm *starving*."

"Starving enough to try Dune Island lobster-stuffed mushrooms?" she asked as they both stood up.

He rubbed his hands together. "By the potful."

"Don't make me laugh—it hurts my face," complained Caitlin, even though she didn't mind at all.

The sun had long set by the time they'd made dinner, so they ate in the kitchen, but after they'd finished their meal and washed and dried the dishes, they brought slices of cheesecake upstairs to the loft to savor in front of the fireplace.

As Shane set the tray on the upturned crate, Caitlin dimmed the lights so they could see the sky. "No stars, but it's flurrying," she announced, and he joined her at the triple window.

"Beautiful," he murmured.

"Yes, it is, even at night."

"No, I meant *you*." He gently took her by the shoulders and guided her to face him. "I think you're beautiful, Caitlin, inside and out."

Self-consciously touching her bandage, she asked, "Even with this?"

He tenderly lowered her fingers from her face. "Even if you were wrapped in gauze from head to toe," he said, with a fetching smile. "I was attracted to you the moment we met and the more I've gotten to know you, the more infatuated I've become."

"I... I feel the same way about you, Shane," she whispered.

It was a different season and a different decade, but as they embraced and Shane tentatively brushed his soft lips against her cheek, Caitlin felt as blissful and carefree as the first time she fell in love on Dune Island.

EPILOGUE

THANKSGIVING, THE FOLLOWING YEAR

After a boisterous but cheerful Thanksgiving dinner, Caitlin and her sister-in-law washed and dried the dishes and put away the leftovers while the men went outside to hang lights on the windmill and cottage, and the children played in the yard.

"That's the last one," Caitlin announced, placing a large, clean pot on the bottom shelf.

"Good. I hope the guys are almost done, too, so we can all go for a walk on the beach before the sun sets. The children need to burn off some energy, and I'd like to burn off a few calories before I have dessert," said Suzanne. "I've never tasted cranberry cheesecake. I can't wait to try it."

"I hope you like it. I got the recipe from a cookbook I bought at my friend Lily's cranberry farm," Caitlin said. "Unfortunately, when I made it last month to bring to a dinner party for volunteers at the Center, it sank in the middle. But this time I didn't beat the ingredients as long, so I think it turned out better."

Suzanne gave her a once-over and broke into a smile. "You seem to be fitting right in here and you're positively glowing. Island life really agrees with you."

"*Married* life agrees with me, too," said Caitlin. "And so does my new job."

The previous January, the estate attorney had informed Lydia's nephews that her medical records, as well as her handwritten letters to Caitlin, would prove that Lydia had been mentally capable of drawing up a Trust and designating beneficiaries. He'd also warned them that Caitlin was prepared to tenaciously defend her right to the cottage. The two men quickly recognized it would have been futile to engage in a prolonged, expensive legal battle they had little chance of winning, and they'd decided not to contest Lydia's Trust after all.

So, after celebrating Christmas with her brother's family in New Mexico, Caitlin had moved into the cottage for good. It had taken her until June to land the role of Director of Development at Hope Haven's Marine Life Center. While it was nerve-racking to be unemployed for so many months, Caitlin believed it was worth it—*she* was worth it—to wait until she found a professional position that was both challenging and meaningful to her.

Besides, Shane had proposed in April, so she'd used her time off work to plan their July wedding, which was held on a lake near the New Hampshire-Maine border, halfway between where they'd both grown up and where many of their extended family members still lived.

Reflecting on how much had changed during the past year, Caitlin gave a contented sigh. "The only downside to living in Lucy's Ham is that I'm so far away from you and Charlie and the children," she said as she and Suzanne put on their coats and hats. "I miss you all a lot. That's why I'm so glad you came out here for a visit."

"Are you kidding me? We couldn't wait. I just hope you and Shane don't feel too cramped sharing your space with us."

"No way. The cottage feels cozy, not crowded," said Caitlin. *Just like Aunt Lydia hoped it would.*

The women exited through the kitchen door and came around to the front of the house to see Shane retracting the ladder from the roof. Charlie helped him lay it on the ground and then they strode over to the women.

"Perfect timing," Charlie said. "We just finished."

"What do you think, do we have enough lights?" Caitlin fretted. "Because there's still plenty of time to buy more before the Shine-Your-Light contest starts."

"Not *too* competitive, are you?" Charlie teased his sister.

"I don't care about winning," she protested. "I'm just excited about participating and I want to give our visitors a spectacular experience—which means we need tons of lights."

Shane wrapped his arm around Caitlin's waist. "Sweetheart, if I add even one more bulb, the entire windmill's going to tip over," he teased. "Trust me, our visitors will be thrilled—especially when they taste your windmill cookies."

Before she could reply, the children came tearing across the lawn toward the adults. "Can you plug the lights in, Uncle Shane?" asked Logan.

"Not yet," his mother interjected. "It's not dark enough. Besides, we need to be polite and wait until Mrs. Graham and her family drop by for dessert, so they can see the lights when we turn them on, too. Her grandchildren were the ones who gave Auntie Caitlin the idea of entering the contest in the first place."

"Couldn't we have a little peek?" Archie pleaded. "Just for a minute?"

"Sorry, but your mom's right—we need to wait," said Caitlin. "I tell you what though, once we plug them in, we can leave the lights on all night. So we'll be able to see them on the windmill's arms right outside our window."

"Does this mean you're sleeping in the loft with the kids

again?" Shane quietly groaned into his wife's ear. "I miss you downstairs in *our* bed."

"I miss you, too," Caitlin whispered longingly, even though they'd only been apart for a couple nights.

Suzanne abruptly motioned to her husband and children. "C'mon, you guys, let's go for a walk."

"I'll race you," Logan challenged his siblings. "First one to the staircase wins."

The boys took off toward the woods, but Maya announced, "I don't want to race. I'm going to walk with Auntie Caitlin and Uncle Shane."

"The newlyweds might want to walk by themselves, honey," her mother hinted.

"That's okay. She's welcome to stay with us," Caitlin insisted.

So the little girl took her aunt's and uncle's hands and skipped between them, chatting nonstop as they made their way to the beach. By the time they reached the bottom step of the staircase, Charlie, Suzanne, and the boys had already wandered onto the damp tidal flats and were heading toward the southwest horizon. But Maya wanted to stay on the soft, dry sand, so instead of following the others, the trio skirted the dunes, their heads ducked against the brisk, onshore breeze.

When they neared the "end" of the beach, Maya exclaimed, "Look, a bench! We can sit there to watch the sunset."

"Don't you want to watch it with everyone else, out near the water?" her aunt suggested.

"Nah, it's too cold." She dropped their hands and scampered across the sand.

Even though Caitlin wasn't concerned that she herself would become emotional about seeing the plaque, she was worried that her inquisitive niece might ask questions about Nicole's photo. Last spring, Caitlin had confided in her brother and sister-in-law about the accident, and how deeply it had affected her, but she hardly thought it was an appropriate subject to discuss with a child Maya's age.

Caitlin pivoted toward the flats, hoping to signal Charlie or Suzanne to come and facilitate the discussion if necessary, but their backs were turned as they crouched near the sand, examining something. So she glanced at Shane and shrugged, and they trudged up the slight incline to the bench.

Sure enough, the child, who could barely read, was studying the photo when Caitlin and Shane reached her. "Who's this?" Maya asked, patting the image with her mittened hand.

"Her name is Nicole."

"Is she a princess?"

"She looks like one in that costume, doesn't she?" Caitlin replied, stalling a little as she tried to come up with a lighthearted, yet honest answer that would satisfy Maya's curiosity. "But no, she's not a princess. She was wearing that pretty white dress because when she was young, she was a ballerina. She liked to dance, but she *loved* to act in plays."

"And now she's famous?"

"Noo... not exactly." Caitlin felt Shane place his hand on her back, a gesture of support, although he remained silent.

"Then how come her picture is on the beach?"

Caitlin hesitated before settling on an uplifting version of the truth. "So people will remember her."

"Because she died?"

She was startled by her niece's perceptiveness. Or had the child been able to read some of the words on the plaque after all? Instead of answering, Caitlin asked, "What makes you think she died?"

"Because there's a picture like this near the park at home, too, 'cept it's a boy, not a girl. He got hit by a car and he died and Mommy says his picture is supposed to remind grown-ups not to drive fast and little kids not to go near the street," she explained in a longwinded sentence. Then she took a breath and asked, "So did this girl die, too?"

Figuring that since Suzanne had already spoken to her about a similar situation, she should answer truthfully, Caitlin admitted, "Yes, she died."

Maya tipped her head and squinted up at her aunt. "Did she get hit by a car? Or a boat?"

"No. Cars aren't allowed on this beach, and this water is too shallow for speed boats, so we don't have to worry about them here," Caitlin reassured her, thinking of what to say next. She didn't want to scare the child, who was just learning how to swim, but she also didn't want to dodge the truth. So she matter-of-factly stated, "She was walking alone at night and she fell into the water."

"Oh. That's sad."

"Yes, it is," agreed Caitlin. "It's very, very sad."

Maya was silent a moment and as she traced her hand over Nicole's gracefully extended arm to her fingertips, Caitlin worried she'd said too much. Or maybe she'd said too little? She'd thought it was best to keep her answers short and simple. But maybe she should've elaborated or been more comforting?

Suddenly, Maya jerked her head up. "Hey, they found something—maybe it's a buried treasure!" She pointed across the flats, where her brothers and dad were on their hands and knees in a semi-circle, frantically digging. "You guys wait for me! I want to see it, too!"

Suzanne turned and waved Maya toward them. Caitlin and Shane watched the little girl circumventing the tidal pools on her way to join her family. When she safely reached them, they simultaneously sat down on the bench, their thighs and hips touching as Shane wrapped his arm around Caitlin.

For a moment, they were silent as they watched the sun reemerge below a low, purple band of clouds, spraying golden light across the water and illuminating their faces. Then Shane remarked, "You handled your niece's questions really well."

"Thanks," she said. "I wasn't sure how much to say. I'll tell Suzanne and Charlie about our conversation later, so they can follow up with Maya if they need to. But it doesn't seem like she was too upset by what we discussed, did it?"

"No." He stroked a lock of hair off her cheek. "Was it upsetting for *you*?"

"Not in the same way it used to be. Counseling has helped a lot with that." She turned to him and met his eyes. "Now whenever I remember Nicole or come down here and see her photo, instead of focusing on how tragic her death was, I try to focus on how inspiring her life was, or I think about the helpful things she said to me."

"Like what?" he softly questioned.

"Well, once she told me that if I was really passionate about doing something, I shouldn't let anything or anyone stop me from going for it," explained Caitlin. "I mean, obviously she was too young or immature to recognize that some risks aren't worth taking. But I admire it that she was pursuing her dream to do what she loved and study acting, even though it wasn't what her mother wanted her to do. It's funny, because when I was a teenager, I didn't realize how much courage she had. But last year, when I thought back on it, her example was one of the things that helped me decide to fight to keep the cottage, and to move to Dune Island."

Shane nodded thoughtfully, and his gaze briefly shifted toward the plaque. "In that case, I'm very grateful to Nicole."

"You should be," Caitlin teased, lightening the mood. "Because her advice to *go for it* also inspired me to say *yes* when you proposed even though we'd only known each other for six months."

"*Only* six months?" Shane sounded indignant. "I thought I was showing a lot of patience and restraint waiting for half a year. I wanted to propose in January, after I'd known you for *three* months."

Caitlin threw back her head and laughed at her handsome husband. "It's too bad you didn't, because I would've said *yes* then, too."

"Because you realized marrying me was a risk worth taking?" Shane hinted, fishing for a compliment.

"Yes." Caitlin wriggled even closer and warmed his ear with a kiss. "And because I realized I deserve to be this happy."

A LETTER FROM KRISTIN

Dear reader,

Thank you for choosing to read *A Secret at Windmill Cottage*! I hope you felt transported to Dune Island and that you were gripped by Caitlin's story.

If you did enjoy the book, and want to keep up to date with all my latest releases, just sign up at the following link. Your email address will never be shared and you can unsubscribe at any time.

www.bookouture.com/kristin-harper

Receiving reader feedback is one of the highlights of writing, and I would absolutely love it if you'd post a short review about your favorite parts of *A Secret at Windmill Cottage*. Sharing your opinions is also a very effective way to encourage readers to pick up one of my novels for the first time.

In addition to sharing a review, you can also get in touch through my website, where you'll find my email address. I can honestly say I'm *delighted* when readers reach out to me directly, and I always try to reply as soon as possible.

I truly appreciate your feedback and reviews. And thanks again for reading *A Secret at Windmill Cottage*!

Best wishes,

Kristin

                www.kristinharperauthor.com

ACKNOWLEDGMENTS

As always, the deepest thanks to my mom and sisters for inspiration, laughter, and encouragement—and especially to Sue for joyfully jumping in with research, as well as when my words failed me. Thank you to my dad for tech support, among other kinds, and to my brother for remodeling input.

Thank you to Ellen, my editor, for optimism and guidance at every stage, and to the Bookouture team listed on the next page, for expertise and devotion.

And extra special thanks to my extra special readers, for interest in this series!

PUBLISHING TEAM

Turning a manuscript into a book requires the efforts of many people. The publishing team at Bookouture would like to acknowledge everyone who contributed to this publication.

Commercial
Lauren Morrissette
Hannah Richmond
Imogen Allport

Data and analysis
Mark Alder
Mohamed Bussuri

Cover design
Emma Graves

Editorial
Ellen Gleeson
Nadia Michael

Copyeditor
Sally Partington

Proofreader
Elaini Caruso

Marketing
Alex Crow
Melanie Price
Occy Carr
Ciara Rosney
Martyna Młynarska

Operations and distribution
Marina Valles
Stephanie Straub
Joe Morris

Production
Hannah Snetsinger
Mandy Kullar

Publicity
Kim Nash
Noelle Holten
Jess Readett
Sarah Hardy

Rights and contracts
Peta Nightingale
Richard King
Saidah Graham

Made in United States
North Haven, CT
13 September 2025

Compliance Norms in Financia

Tomasz Braun

Compliance Norms in Financial Institutions

Measures, Case Studies and Best Practices

palgrave
macmillan

Tomasz Braun
Lazarski University
Warsaw, Poland

ISBN 978-3-030-24968-7   ISBN 978-3-030-24966-3 (eBook)
https://doi.org/10.1007/978-3-030-24966-3

© The Editor(s) (if applicable) and The Author(s), under exclusive license to Springer Nature Switzerland AG 2019
This work is subject to copyright. All rights are solely and exclusively licensed by the Publisher, whether the whole or part of the material is concerned, specifically the rights of translation, reprinting, reuse of illustrations, recitation, broadcasting, reproduction on microfilms or in any other physical way, and transmission or information storage and retrieval, electronic adaptation, computer software, or by similar or dissimilar methodology now known or hereafter developed.
The use of general descriptive names, registered names, trademarks, service marks, etc. in this publication does not imply, even in the absence of a specific statement, that such names are exempt from the relevant protective laws and regulations and therefore free for general use.
The publisher, the authors and the editors are safe to assume that the advice and information in this book are believed to be true and accurate at the date of publication. Neither the publisher nor the authors or the editors give a warranty, expressed or implied, with respect to the material contained herein or for any errors or omissions that may have been made. The publisher remains neutral with regard to jurisdictional claims in published maps and institutional affiliations.

This Palgrave Macmillan imprint is published by the registered company Springer Nature Switzerland AG
The registered company address is: Gewerbestrasse 11, 6330 Cham, Switzerland

Contents

1. **Introduction** — 1
   1. *Aim of the Book* — 1
   2. *Methodology* — 7
   3. *Assumptions* — 9
   4. *The Problem Significance* — 13
   5. *The Current State of Research* — 22
   6. *The Structure of the Book* — 25

2. **Compliance Norms and Legal Coherence** — 29
   1. *Introduction* — 29
   2. *Legal Consistency* — 30
   3. *Parallel Non-legal Regulations and the Legal System* — 34
   4. *Norms Developed by Corporations* — 39
   5. *The Collision of Legal and Corporate Norms* — 45
   6. *Resolving Conflicts of Legal and Corporate Compliance Norms* — 49

3. **Compliance in Financial Institutions: Tasks, Functions and Structure** — 53
   1. *Introduction* — 53
   2. *Financial Institutions' Compliance—Specificity of the Regulated Industry* — 55
   3. *The Tasks of Compliance Services in Financial Institutions* — 63

4	The Advisory Function of Compliance Services in Financial Institutions	77
5	Compliance Assurance—Example of IP Risks	84
6	Reputational Risks Management	92
7	Sovereign Risks Management	100
8	The Compliance as Control Function in the Three Lines of Defence Model	115
9	The Compliance Function Responsibilities in External Relations	125
10	Compliance Function and Corporate Governance	144
11	Compliance Risk Management and Legal Risk Management	158

4 The Scope of Compliance Norms in Financial Institutions — 163

1	Introduction	163
2	Extraterritorial Normative Systems as the Reference Points for Compliance Norms	164
3	Compliance Norms and Other Normative Systems	177
4	Compliance Norms and Irregularities in Financial Institutions	186
5	Norms Ensuring Compliance with the Law	218
6	Norms Ensuring Compliance with Corporate Guidelines	231
7	Types of Internal Corporate Acts Containing Compliance Norms	246

5 The Impact of Cultural Differences on Compliance Norms — 257

1	Introduction	257
2	The Influence of Cultural Legal Differences on the Methods of Regulation	258
3	Difficulties in the Application of Compliance Norms Due to Cultural Differences	272
4	Differences in the Interpretation of Compliance Norms	278

6	Organising Postulates—A Proposal for a Model Approach	285
	1 Introduction	285
	2 Hierarchy of Norms—*Conclusions* de lege ferenda	286
	3 The Interdependence of Compliance Norms Due to Their Content	294
	4 Flexible Norm-Setting Approach to Assure Compliance Adjustment to Changing Environment	300

Summary	313
Legal Acts	315
Other Documents	323
Bibliography	325
Index	347

CHAPTER 1

Introduction

1   Aim of the Book

The aim of this book is to present a theoretical legal analysis of the nature and function of contemporary compliance norms in corporations from the perspective of a general theory of norms based on the example of financial institutions. The term 'Compliance norms' is understood as a set of interrelated norms introduced in corporations, which impose on their addressees the obligation of specific ways of behaving, whose aim is to ensure the operation of these corporations in accordance with binding laws, the administrative regulations of supervisory authorities, and other rules of conduct specified in internal normative acts of these corporations.[1] Compliance norms are, therefore, all those norms created within the framework of global business institutions, addressed to their employees, statutory authorities and shareholders, as well as to entities entering into economic relations with them. The purpose of these compliance norms are to ensure

---

[1] Accordingly, the concept of "compliance" is a state of conformity, a manner of conducting business in which the corporation complies with all applicable laws, regulations and other applicable norms. The development of the concept of compliance and its adoption by business practice is, above all, the result of historically observed irregularities in the functioning of international corporations when they acted contrary to the binding normative environment. In view of the fact that this concept, developed in the Anglo-Saxon legal culture, goes beyond the narrower meaning of compliance with the law. The international practice adopted the use of the English expression "compliance" interchangeably with their relevant equivalents in the national languages in this Anglo-Saxon broader meaning, regardless the particular specificities of a given language. According to M. Romanowski's definition,

---

© The Author(s) 2019
T. Braun, *Compliance Norms in Financial Institutions*,
https://doi.org/10.1007/978-3-030-24966-3_1

that they act in conformity with the norms binding in the territories in which these financial institutions operate, as well as with other normative recommendations, which, due to their administrative, social, economic, ethical or cultural nature, have been included by these organisations to a catalogue of binding obligations, prohibitions and empowerments.[2]

This book also aims to analyse the conceptual apparatus used by corporations and in particular by the financial institutions, relating to compliance norms from the point of view of the theory of norms.[3] The aim of the study is also to characterise the specific properties of particular types of compliance norms. The book describes the scope of these norms together with examples and practical complications resulting from their global reach.[4] What is also important is the real impact that these norms have on financial institutions activity today, and indirectly also on much broader global economic relations.[5]

The research described in this book covers the phenomenon of norm-setting by financial institutions corporations.[6] As a result of it,

---

compliance is "a set of rules of conduct determining the way in which the employees of a company comply with the law, good practices in a given industry and internal regulations of the company. Compliance is therefore an internal corporate law". M. Romanowski, Wpływ compliance na skuteczność prawa gospodarczego [in] T. Giaro [ed.] *Skuteczność prawa*, Konferencje naukowe WPiA UW, Warsaw 2010, p. 82.

[2] For that purpose, the compliance norms form part of the 'financial architecture' defined as '[...] the layout of the institutions and the laws and principles on which the financial relations existing between public and private operators in different States are based.' This definition covers both institutions or markets and activities (practices) undertaken at State level by authorities and private entities in the economic and financial spheres. See A. Jurkowska-Zeidler, Nowa Globalna Architektura Finansowa, *Gdańskie Studia Prawnicze* XXV/2011, p. 535.

[3] The conceptual apparatus proposed in the paper refers both to the terms used in practice related to particular types of compliance norms, as well as to the features defining the scope of their subject matter that defines these norms.

[4] This paper assumes that "global coverage" is one of the features of the compliance norms that require the addressees of these norms to comply with them in all jurisdictions in which these corporations operate.

[5] See W. Heyderbrand, Globalization and the Rule of Law at the End of the 20th Century [in] A. Febbraio, D. Nelken, V. Olgiati [ed.] *Social Process and Patterns of Legal Control*, European Yearbook of Sociology of Law 25/2000(2001), p. 72 et seq.

[6] See L. C. Backer, Global Panopticism: Surveillance Lawmaking by Corporations, States, and Other Entities, *Global Legal Studies* 101/2008 and the same author: Multinational Corporations as Objects and Sources of Transnational Regulation, *International Law and Compliance* 14(2)/2008, p. 499 et seq.

entire sets of norms are created for entities, who have different degrees of connection with these corporations.[7] Such activities also take place in non-financial institutions corporations, i.e. large international business institutions, that carry out other types of activities.[8] Their common feature is that these institutions issue different types of internal regulations, the scope of which varies depending on many factors, such as the type of economic activity conducted by them, the jurisdictions in which corporates' activities are conducted, and the various legal cultures resulting from these differences, as well as because of the place of particular norms in the internal hierarchy of those organisations.[9]

One of the reasons why all corporations, including financial institutions, create their own global norms is the need to ensure consistency across their activities, despite the differences that characterise individual markets.[10] All corporations, including large financial institutions, strive to create conditions for the uniform and therefore coherent development for their operations, among others, in the area of corporate governance and compliance.[11] The latter area is especially worthy of attention due to its growing importance and dynamic development, and it is the subject of analyses carried out in this book.

---

[7] U. C. V. Haley, *Multinational Corporations in Political Environments: Ethics, Values and Strategies*, Knoxville 2001, p. 42.

[8] See W. Twining, Diffusion of Law: A Global Perspective, *The Journal of Legal Pluralism and Unofficial Law* 36/49/2004, p. 12.

[9] For this reason, the study's observations on compliance norms, their material scope, hierarchical relationships, addressees, and even the tasks, functions and modes of operation of compliance services relate both to financial institutions and, more generally, to their groups linked by ownership and capital structure, and in extenso to all corporations engaged in non-financial activities.

[10] Therefore, 'scope' refers to the geographical criterion as one of the main characteristics distinguishing multinational corporations, which are large economic organizations, operating simultaneously in many countries, from other enterprises in this sense that they are not corporations. In this meaning, the term is used later in this book. About the attempts of corporations to regulate in a uniform way the way they conduct their activities despite local differences see np. D. A. Krueger, D. W. Shriver Jr., L. L. Nash, M. Stackhouse, *The Business Corporation & Productive Justice*, Abingdon Press Studies in Christian Ethics and Economic Life, Nashville 1997, p. 75 et seq. Also: R. C. Wolf, *Trade, Aid and Arbitrate: The Globalization of Western Law*, Oxford 2004, p. 30.

[11] S. Conway, M. E. Conway, *Essentials of Enterprise Compliance*, New Jersey 2008, p. 15 et seq.

Compliance risk management is understood as the management of risk, due to a corporation not entirety conforming its activities to the binding norms in their environment.[12] It has developed mostly in companies operating in the regulated sectors (finance, financial institutions, insurance, pharmaceuticals, energy). It is noteworthy that the development of compliance in other areas (automotive industry, biotechnology, passenger transport, environmental industries) has also become more and more noticeable in recent years. Each of these areas is characterised by the need to take action to ensure compliance of their operations with the requirements resulting from their respective normative environment.[13] Legislators have a duty to take this new dynamic phenomenon into account and the theory of law, including the theory of norms, to examine it and their impact on the effectiveness of the law.

The normative environment of financial institutions consists both of legal regulations resulting from the law-making activity of states, and the international organisations empowered to issue the regulations, which define the formal framework of their activity, as well as non-legal norms, including in particular the regulations of administrative supervisory authorities. The normative environment of financial institutions, as understood in this book, are also administrative decisions resulting from the proceedings against them, self-regulations issued by the industry organisations of which they are members, and other norms resulting from self-regulatory activity of financial institutions.[14]

The complexity resulting from their legal and regulatory environment, as well as from the different weight of issues in the area of compliance, and from different scopes of regulations concerning the activity of financial institutions, results in the creation of their own meta-norms. The nature of them differs from each other. These differences, taken together with the place these norms occupy in the hierarchy, and the objectives

---

[12] See R. Markfort, Verantwortung der Gschaeftsleitung fuer Compliance, *Risk, Fraud and Compliance. Praevention und Aufdeckung durch Compliance-Organisationen* 4/2004, p. 180.

[13] The process of creating a compliance culture in an enterprise as a result of developing relations between regulators and regulated entities as a form of preventing more than just legal sanctions see H. Elffers, P. Verboon, *Managing and Maintaining Compliance*, The Hague 2006, p. 80.

[14] R. W. Kaszubski, *Funkcjonalne źródła prawa bankowego publicznego*, Warsawa 2006, p. 266.

they are intended to serve, constitute the basic criteria for distinguishing the different types of norms.[15]

According to these criteria, four basic types of compliance norms can be distinguished, with the proviso that their nature may differ from one financial institution to another and that, apart from the basic types listed here, there are also other types of norms, more broadly characterised in the following part of this book. It should be noted here that the division listed below concern the types of compliance norms and not normative acts that may contain such norms. Apart from specifying individual types of compliance norms, the same notions are also used to designate internal normative acts, which may include both compliance norms and other types of statements, including statements that are not of a directive nature.[16] These four types of compliance norms are principles, rules, recommendations and guidelines.

- a. Principles are understood as binding internal norms within the compliance system of a given corporation, which in this system occupy an overriding, directional position in relation to other norms, and play a role of setting the framework for all actions that should be taken.
- b. Rules, on the other hand, set out the desired behaviour in such a way that the addressees can only either fulfil the obligation imposed on them or breach it if a situation other than that indicated takes place.
- c. Recommendations are the compliance norms, most often formulated as a result of controls, reviews or audits, which require actions to be taken, as a result of which the state of compliance with the applicable law or supervisory regulations is restored.
- d. Guidelines indicate the desired pattern of conduct, determined as a result of the way in which corporations interpret and apply applicable laws or supervisory regulations.

---

[15] On compliance tasks in the area of adjusting the corporate business activity to the regulatory requirements see C. Parker, V. L. Nielsen, *Explaining Compliance: Business Responses to Regulations*, Northhampton 2011, p. 10 et seq. Also, about the role of lawyers in building communication with business representatives see J. Jabłońska-Bonca, O partnerskiej komunikacji prawników i biznesmenów, *Studia Iuridica* 40/2002, p. 27 et seq.

[16] More on the types of normative acts created in financial institutions containing compliance norms and compliance norms supplemented by other types of statements see Chapter III. 5.

There are eleven basic ways of grouping compliance norms, which can be distinguished based on the criterion of weight and object matter regulated. These are: norms, principles, rules, policies, strategies, codes of conduct, manuals, instructions, recommendations, guidelines and regulations for direct application. As a result, the extent that they act as a binding force on the entities to which they are addressed also varies. The creation of compliance norms takes place in a dynamic legal, regulatory and economic environment and in areas of very different jurisdictions, i.e. the legal cultures in which international financial institutions corporations operate.[17] What is more, the expectations of financial institutions expressed by their own stakeholders other than legislators and regulators, such as shareholders, employees, customers, the general public, non-governmental interest groups, etc., are also different.

Compliance norms created in such complex circumstances, which at the same time take into account the dynamics of changes in the environment and the expectations formulated towards the financial institution, are characterised by three common features. First of all, they create their own autarkic systems.[18] Secondly, the feature that characterises compliance norms is that the process of creating parts of them often takes place spontaneously.[19] Thirdly, as a result of the spontaneous creation of parts of the compliance norms, the non-unified terminology used in them is largely the result of this methodological disorder. The description and analysis of these norms in terms of a general theory, as well as the links between them, the interaction between them, and the effects of the wider and dynamically changing legal and regulatory environment

---

[17] See Z. Ofiarski, Źródła prawa finansowego i problemy legislacji finansowej [in] C. Kosikowski [ed.] *System Prawa Finansowego* vol. I, Warsaw 2010, p. 175.

[18] The "autarky" of normative systems created by corporations is understood here as a characteristic that results from the fact that they are exclusive for each of these corporations. They are created by every corporation in relation to its only proper scale and character of activity, the set strategy, the will of its own stakeholders, its current problems and its only proper organizational structure.

[19] The "spontaneity" of the process of creating compliance norms is understood here as an immediate reaction to the requirements formulated by entities external to the corporation in relation to the manner of its operation. One group of such circumstances are changes in the legal and regulatory environment, and another group are the expectations formulated by corporate stakeholders. In this sense, the development of compliance norms takes place spontaneously, i.e. according to the needs identified on an ongoing basis and in a loose connection with the general business strategy formulated by the corporation.

of financial institutions, including cultural differences characteristic for a diverse area of their operations, is therefore the aim of this book.[20]

2 Methodology

The book examines the relation between compliance norms and the wider legal, social, economic, cultural and axiological environment within which they are located. The theses of this work emerged from observations concerning the interrelation between the regularity environment and compliance norms and was derived from detailed research into the operation of financial institutions, and observations concerning the wider economic space, in which they operate.[21] This allows for a richer illustration of the phenomena and relations occurring within financial institutions, and to check the hypotheses put forward in this book.

The compliance normative regulations of financial institutions, and their practical application also vary due to differences in the legal cultures typical of different geographical areas. This was also the subject of research described in this book. The book describes of what financial institutions do and what in the ideal situations they should do in order to assure the coherent system of compliance norms. The text provides the analysis which is led from the point of view which repeatedly is called as a 'legal theory perspective' or 'general theory of norms' perspective. There is a variety of methods of analysis that could have been proposed here. This in particular refers to this part of the business law which relates to compliance norms.

Often, in the common law academic tradition it is expected the researchers ask about interdependencies between the letter of the laws (including the soft laws and internal companies' norms) and its spirit, primary intentions of the law-makers, the goals the norms are intended to achieve. They also analyse the impact of these norms on the business activities and how they influence the corporate practice. There is a multitude of questions that could be asked solely to this last problem. Starting

---

[20] About the reconstructive pursuit of the essence of norms through the study of their theory see S. Kaźmierczyk, O tożsamości prawa w związku z jego jakością, *Acta Universitatis Lodziensis. Folia Iuridica*, 74/2015, p. 208.

[21] E. Huepkes, Compliance, Compensation, Corporate Governance [in] M. Roth [ed.] *Close-up on Compliance Recht, Moral und Risken – Nahaufnahmen zu Compliance Management und Governance – Fragen*, Zürich 2009, p. 121.

from the governance practices, conduct towards the markets and the clients, internal employees' relations, attitude to discovered irregularities, etc. The book in various ways addresses these questions and to various degrees provides examples of how these norms function in practice. The book refers to different problems—starting from norm-setting, through their implementing and interpreting, looking at the complexities deriving from the internationality of financial institutions, regulatory pressures up to the impact these norms do have on individuals, markets, societies and the companies themselves. The book only to a limited extend focuses on explaining why norms took their form and whether their shape is a result of a particular interest groups lobbying. But it does refer in relevant places across the text to the norm-setting processes.

The practice of norm-setting activities carried out by multinational corporations, including financial institutions in particular, has been developing for some time. It is also the subject of working arrangements between entities of a similar nature. This phenomenon has been noticed by market regulators, NGOs representing the interests of customers and opinion-forming think-tanks. Despite this, and undoubtedly contrary to the juridical character of the compliance norms, it is still relatively under researched area.

The emergence in the international arena of compliance norms relating to the complex system of economic and financial dependence is a sustained trend that is becoming more and more widespread. This phenomenon should be permanently included into research concerning legal theory. Furthermore, it also illustrates the problem when law and other disciplines, including economics, management, political science and other social sciences, as well as descriptive ethics, intersect with each other.

Due to the internal nature of compliance norms, and the fact that these studies covered specific institutions with robust confidentiality regimes,financial institutions, information on the process of creating these norms, but also on the guidelines relating to the scope of their application, are often available only to a very limited extent. This was an important element that had to be taken into account, when the research hypotheses of the work presented in the book were formulated, as it imposed limitations on the study.[22]

---

[22] The confidential nature of most of the internal norms is almost the rule in the majority of global corporations. Access to these documents for people from outside the circle of eligible recipients is difficult and disclosure of these documents in breach of the

The practice of corporations' norms-setting activities described in the book was narrowed down to one particular type of business actor: the financial institution, for during the period from the end of the twentieth to the beginning of the twenty-first century. The scope of the book is also limited to law-making activities informed by the West's legal culture, in the sense that it is not limited to one country but multiple jurisdictions.[23]

3 Assumptions

The analysis undertaken in this book is based on the statement that regardless of the sources of universally and internally binding law described in legal doctrine, the phenomenon of conducting quasi-law-making activities by corporations—international business institutions—is becoming more and more obvious. The first and main hypothesis for this book is therefore the statement that within the activities of modern corporations, including financial institutions, new types of abstract norms are being created, namely compliance norms which, although they are similar to legal norms, they have so far been insufficiently described by the theory of law. Consequently, the second hypothesis is that as a result of these activities there are whole sets of norms with different degrees of interconnections, which regulate the activities of entities and behaviours of persons linked or not linked with these corporate norm-makers. In the case of this book, the hypotheses are put

---

confidentiality requirement is usually treated as a violation of basic employee obligations in the field of information security risk (ISR). See e.g. A. Kolk, Sustainability, Accountability and Corporate Governance: Exploring Multinationals reporting Practices, *Business Strategy and the Environment* 17/2008, p. 5; R. D. Russel, C. J. Russel, An Examination of the Effects of Organizational Norms, Organizational Structure and Environment Uncertainty on Entrepreneurial Strategy, *Journal of Management* 18/1992, p. 645; M. Gibbins, A. Richardson, J. Waterhouse, The Management of Corporate Financial Disclosure: Opportunism, Ritualism, Polices and Processes, *Journal of Accounting Research* 1/1990, p. 123 et seq.

[23]The assumption concerning the western legal culture refers to the indication of the sources of creation and development of concepts relating to compliance norms. Corporations operate worldwide, including jurisdictions with completely different legal cultures than Western ones. However, due to the fact that the companies operating in these culturally different areas belong to larger capital groups, compliance norms are also adopted there.

forward ex post, as they constitute generalised conclusions drawn from the facts observed from the practice of functioning of international financial corporations.

The above-mentioned hypotheses are answers to the primary and secondary questions, detailed problematic questions, which relate to causal relations and other relations that are examined below. The working hypotheses that appear in the course of research correspond to the issues related to the research topic of the book and take the form of answers to the research questions listed below. They were formulated in order to examine the research gathered for this book. In the following part of the book, however, they are general statements that are illustrated by examples. Some of these working questions arose directly from the main research hypotheses presented above, and others are indirectly related to them. They represent aspects of the issues analysed in this book, and illustrate the complexities resulting from the analysis of the data. These questions are divided into five groups that are presented below.

These questions relate to the origins of self-regulation by corporations, including financial institutions, whose aim is to ensure that they operate in accordance with the normative systems applicable to them, understood more broadly than just legal regulations. Although the book does not focus on the reasons for the development of compliance norms, the answer given indirectly in the book to the questions concerning the reasons for why such a phenomenon occurred is important for research aimed at what the compliance norms created by financial institutions today are. These answers, explaining the source, but also the manner of the implementation and the content of compliance regulations, indicate, on the one hand, the social expectations (expressed in legal and supervisory norms) towards financial institutions, and on the other hand, the numerous irregularities detected in the functioning of these institutions. Among the questions that arise during the analysis of contemporary phenomena that are the sources of compliance norms, four basic questions come to the fore:

a. Why are compliance norms being created at all?
b. Does the development of compliance norms result from specific needs relating to social expectations and, at the same time, arise from the need to fill gaps in the existing legislation?

c. Is the phenomenon of creating compliance norms really so new, or can one observe its origins in medieval trade guilds that persist still in today's corporations?[24]
d. Can this phenomenon to be traced back to the expansion of the regulatory sphere and the emergence of new spheres of society in which legislators do not yet have a strong enough presence to prevent the emergence of irregularities in the functioning of financial institutions?[25]

Compliance norms do not only play the role of ensuring that operations measured by financial institutions conform correctly with the law. But they also relate to social expectations, by imposing certain behaviours and prohibiting others, and as such they constitute a form of self-restriction imposed by financial corporations on themselves in areas where the law and supervisory regulations are silent. This is particularly the case with regard to those issues where legislators are lagging behind in responding to changing economic circumstances, and the complex types of global transactions. This raises three questions about compliance norms:

a. What is the role of the current compliance norms?[26]
b. If compliance norms are created because of the need to fill gaps in existing legislation, what are these gaps and what needs are covered by the creation of such norms?
c. Do regulatory and supervisory deficiencies need to be addressed by compliance norms because legislators are not keeping pace with the pace of change today?

These are key questions from the point of view of the research described in this book. They refer to the scope of norms, i.e. to those issues which, in various aspects, are the subject of the analysis presented here. Below are four questions belonging to this group:

---

[24] See W. T. Singleton, *Compliance and Excellence*, Baltimore 1979, p. 55.

[25] About this J. E. Murphy, G. J. Wallance, *Corporate Compliance: How to be a Good Citizen Corporation Through Self-Policing*, New York 1996, p. 340 and a little later the same authors: C. L. Basri, J. E. Murphy, G. J. Wallance, *Corporate Compliance: Caremark and the Globalization of Good Corporate Conduct*, New York 1998, p. 803 et seq.

[26] More on the same and similar issues in the collective work of S. Dinah [ed.], *Commitment and Compliance: The Role of Non-Binding Norms in the International Legal System*, Oxford 2000 *passim*.

a. Which areas are regulated by financial institutions compliance norms, and which entities are subject to such regulations?
b. Do they form unified systems of norms, or a loosely bound system, or are they unrelated and do not form part of the larger regulatory elements for financial institutions?[27]
c. What sets of norms do compliance norms comprise of and what sets of compliance norms should be created by financial institutions issuing such regulations (deontological codes of conduct, gatherings of rules of ethics, prudential norms, etc.)?[28]
d. Is the scope of the provisions of these norms being extended to cover new business areas of financial institutions and other corporations over time?

The primary reason for creating compliance norms is to ensure that financial institutions operate in compliance with legal norms. In practice, however, one can get the impression that the scope of compliance norms is becoming wider and wider. and corporations are creating their own norms, which relate to new issues that are not necessarily already regulated by the law. The book contains examples that relate to the following six questions:

a. Do compliance norms supersede fixed, publicly established elements of legal systems, occupying ever wider fields, or merely supplement existing legal provisions without replacing them at all?
b. Can a conflict be observed in this connection: legal versus non-legal norms, although it is similar to them, are legal norms compatible with corporate norms?
c. If such a conflict exists, how is it settled in practice?

---

[27] The question of whether or not intra-corporate standards create standards systems refers to the existence of such strong structural and functional links between norms within the same corporation that they result in a system of mutually dependent, terminologically and purposefully coherent norms and, possibly, whether they are based on a unified and catalogued set of values common to the whole corporation. All elements of this understanding of the normative system related to the tested compliance norms are analyzed in specific sections of this paper.

[28] Similar questions can be found in the extensive work on the relationship between compliance norms and the law, morality and risk.—M. Roth, *Close up on Compliance: Recht, Moral und Risken: Nahaufnahmen zu Compliance Management und Governance Fragen*, Zürich 2009, p. 42.

d. What attitude do financial institutions adopt, and what attitude should be adopted by publicly empowered lawmakers towards this phenomenon?
e. Is there a conflict between public lawmakers and quasi-lawmakers? And, if so, is it manifested in the discrepancies between the public and private regulations?
f. Do the addressees of compliance norms, including in particular consumers but also entire communities, benefit, or perhaps lose out, from the fact that the norms affecting their rights and obligations are set by entities which are not public law-makers?[29]

One of the justifications for the creation of compliance norms is that while there is not a global legislator, economic corporations, with their geographical reach, and their mutual economic interdependencies, together with the related social and economic processes that occur—are all global. However, although these phenomena are subject to globalisation, the understanding of norms, and so the way they are interpreted remain culturally determined. This book seeks to consider these issues through research aimed at answering the following two questions:

a. What is the impact on the interpretation and application of compliance norms of the different legal cultures in which corporations operate?
b. Is there a conflict in the way in which the same rules are applied, due to a different understanding of the same rules depending on cultural legal differences, and how are such conflicts possibly resolved?

4 THE PROBLEM SIGNIFICANCE

In order to illustrate how many serious problems of both a theoretical and practical nature appear in the financial industry contemporarily in relation to compliance norms, five examples were selected. They demonstrate the difficulties that arise from the expectation that intra-corporate compliance norms will be applied regardless of the legal norms governing the same issues in different jurisdictions. Such expectations are

---

[29] On the impact of corporate norms on consumer rights and obligations see N. D. Lewis, *Law and Governance*, London 2001, p. 159 et seq.

formulated both in relation to international financial institutions structures, but it is also similar in other types of international corporations. In order to facilitate comparison, the same organisational structure has been employed for all of the examples, by first by presenting the circumstances (reasons) that gave rise to the need for compliance norms, then the resulting complications, in order to finally show the possible solutions for their resolution.

The first very typical situation in which there are often problems consist of discrepancies between the compliance norms that were established by corporations, and the domestic norms of law is the so-called matrix organisational structure. This is where a separate system that runs in parallel to the official one, which is different from the structures regulated by the local commercial companies' laws, internal company statutes and organisational regulations.[30] This results in the imposing of certain additional reporting lines, that are binding within the corporation, on top of the established business dependencies, whose task is to ensure the direct subordination of employees of one organisation to persons from outside the organisation, most often employed in the headquarter. As a result of the introduction of such informal organisational subordination, day-to-day decisions concerning the activities of a given institution are de facto taken in centres located outside the formal bodies responsible for financial institution management.[31] Such situations are the not the exception, but are rather the rule in international financial institutions, in which it is these informal structures, and not the hierarchical arrangements in accordance with national legal norms, that are decisive for making the most important decisions.

However, these corporate decision-making power structures can cause practical complications. These issues have different dimensions—from the employee's legal status (for example, this concerns decisions relating to the way of providing work, evaluation of its results, principles of remuneration and bonuses, etc.), through to the organisational (for example, issues of mutual settlements of costs that are borne by individual entities, prioritisation of individual tasks, etc.), to the fundamental

---

[30] See M. Fairfax, Rhetoric of Corporate Law: The Impact of Stakeholder Rhetoric on Corporate Norms, *Journal of Corporate Law* 675/2005–2006, p. 30.

[31] J. E. Stiglitz, Multinational Corporations: Balancing Rights and Responsibilities, *Proceedings of the American Society of International Law* 101/2007, pp. 3–60.

one concerning giving appropriate attention to the individual interests of a given company (an example may be the situation where decisions concerning the operation of a given financial institution do not take into account what serves its best interests). However, it is of fundamental importance that such problematic corporate governance is contrary to both legal norms and the guidelines of regulators responsible for ensuring that the operation of their subordinate institutions are controlled correctly.[32]

In this type of situation, there is in principle no solution, which, on the one hand, would make it possible to reconcile the interests of the entire corporation as formulated by various compliance norms, whose task in this case is precisely to ensure the consistency of the entire capital group, and, on the other hand, would guarantee that the financial institution would operate in accordance with the legal and regulatory norms in force in a given area. The most common solution to this issue is based on the use of double reporting lines. These consist of an informal obligation for financial institution employees to accept the principle that, regardless of the formal hierarchy of an entity, there is for them a parallel informal subordination of the senior positions in the corporate hierarchy, which performs the role of superiors for them. These so-called 'functional' or 'dotted reporting lines' exist alongside the formal reporting lines resulting from norms interpreted by local law ('solid' or 'entity-based reporting lines'). Such a solution has many drawbacks, all of which are of a similar nature, since they presuppose the introduction of a solution that is clearly at odds with the overall legal and regulatory environment in force in a given jurisdiction. Among the uncertainties that arise from such a solution is, for example, that of a situation where risk management issues are transferred to a centre outside the financial institution, or where high-risk business decisions, or decisions in general, are made outside it. They can be classified as management decisions for the whole entire institution, which are strictly reserved for the competence of its management body.

Another, completely different, situation described in this book, which raises just as many legal doubts and therefore deserves detailed studies, is the frequently occurring practice that there is an expectation that

---

[32] I. Love, Corporate Governance and Performance Around the World, What Do We Know and What We Don't, *The World Bank Observer* 2010, pp. 1–29.

information will be transferred between entities within the corporation, regardless of the secrecy regimes in force in particular jurisdictions. These secrecy regimes also apply to other financial institutions, which are formally third parties despite being part of the same group.[33] The nature of this information may, of course, vary and may have completely different purposes. Starting from the need to collect the transaction data of clients, which would be necessary for making business decisions outside the structure of the financial institution, through to the personal data of these clients, but also of employees, to data on the final beneficiaries of individual entities involved in cooperation with this institution.[34] It should be noted that, depending on the perspective of the problem, there are, of course, important arguments, particularly clearly visible from the perspective of the interests of the whole corporation, which argue in favour of recognising such expectations as legitimate.[35] This is precisely the advantage that large financial institutions have over the smaller ones, that they have among their capabilities, apart from other things, access to a multi-source extensive database of information. However, this does not change the fact that local laws do not usually allow for the freedom of such movements involving information legally protected by qualified forms of confidentiality.

This issue can be examined from a range of perspectives. It can be considered that the dissemination of information in the case of a large international financial organisation is not only useful, economically advantageous for making knowledge-based decisions, but also necessary to ensure its proper functioning, as it may reduce various types of risks

---

[33] S. Bottomley, *The Constitutional Corporation: Rethinking Corporate Governance*, Applied Legal Philosophy, London 2007, p. 111.

[34] More on the flow of information within international corporations, with particular emphasis on the analysis of contemporary trends in this area, writes L. Moerel, emphasizing the unprecedented practice of data transfer between corporations and their service providers. One of the methods adopted by corporations in this respect is the adoption of binding corporate rules (BCRs) which are designed to ensure compliance with legislation on personal data protection. The author of this article also refers to scientific debates on transnational private-law, including the rights of corporations to control the use of data held by them. L. Moerel, *Binding Corporate Rules: Corporate Self-Regulation of Global Data Transfers*, London 2012, p. 32 et seq.

[35] On the same regularities with regard to government-owned corporations see M. J. Whincop, *Corporate Governance in Government Corporations, Law Ethics and Governance*, Berlington 2005, p. 25.

(including, for example, the risk of external and internal fraud, the risk of infiltration by people involved in money laundering, etc.). In this context, compliance activities consisting of launching processes and creating uniform intra-corporate norms aimed at ensuring the sharing of this type of information should be considered understandable and justified. On the other hand, however, there are no valid legal arguments that would prove inapplicable to corporations' norms that define the obligations to ensure the security of data held by financial institutions.[36]

As in the previous example, it is very difficult to unequivocally determine how to eliminate the conflict between corporate compliance norms and the local norms of law. In practice, any solutions used in similar situations usually consist of accepting compromise solutions, usually related to making certain concessions in order to take into account the requirements of the whole corporation, with a partial limitation of the scope of the data provided in relation to the originally formulated expectations in this respect. However, depending on the type of data concerned, there are also sometimes steps which, albeit in part, sanction the financial institution's non-compliance with legal norms, such as the collection of stakeholder approvals (although in many situations, obtaining consent alone does still not mean restoring compliance, since such consent may not necessarily have to be taken under conditions of full freedom, etc.). The long list of outstanding legal issues arising in connection with issues relating to the flow of protected information between theoretically third parties within a corporation proves the complexity of this type of subject matter.[37]

Yet another situation that gives rise to legal dilemmas which are difficult to resolve is the fact that there are compliance norms which require financial institutions to comply with the principle of full tax transparency, including in particular the prohibition of tax avoidance. The following factors may be taken into account when deciding whether a financial institution should comply with the principle of full tax transparency. Investors clearly expect that the tax efficiency and appropriate organisational structuring of the whole corporation will ensure the highest return

---

[36] See I. Seidl-Hohenveldern, *Corporations in and Under International Law*, Cambridge 1987, p. 59.

[37] Criticism regarding the abuse of the strong position of corporations vis-à-vis their dependent companies: J. Bakan, *The Corporation: The Pathological Pursuit of Profit and Power*, New York 2004, p. 111.

on their investments. This can result in an understandable collision between the demand for tax transparency and the expectation of maximum economic efficiency.

Complications have arisen in such a situation when a corporation declares publicly that it is transparent, to avoid taking any action that might give rise to the suspicion that their purpose or nature may be related to an evasion of their obligations related to a fair settlement and payment of any public law contributions. Moreover, the obligations declared by financial institutions, not only towards tax authorities, but also towards investors, public opinion of employees, etc., impose obligations on the organisation undertaking such activities, but also on its clients, correspondent financial institutions and other cooperating entities. It is therefore a desirable effect of compliance norms, that its scope extends far beyond the circle of entities directly related to internal financial institutions regulations.

However, there is other side to this issue, that causes further complications in the area of tax obligations. This concerns the clear expectations of markets and investors in this regard. These expectations are based on the use of all legally available solutions labelled as the optimisation of tax liabilities. In a simplified way, the aim is to take advantage of the opportunities offered by the simultaneous presence on many international markets, where tax obligations are often shaped differently, and thus by skilfully constructing organisational structures and the interdependencies between them, so that the total final amount and method of settling tax liabilities are more advantageous than their total amount would have had such opportunities not been taken into account.

An imperfect, but often employed solution is the preparation, by financial institutions of special documentation, the content of which assumes an absolute obligation to comply with the tax transparency declared by a given corporation, which are offered to clients and associates to sign. In specific situations where the refusal by third parties to undertake such obligations could result in financial losses, expose the financial institution to the risk of penalties or other sanctions, or there would be a risk of reputation damages, it is not uncommon practice to terminate relations with such clients.

Similar in nature to those above, are those issues regarding the operation of compliance regulations within the corporation, which require the exit from the existing business relations, as well as not concluding certain types of transactions with certain types of entities, which could carry risks, other than market or credit risks, at a level unacceptable to the corporation. Situations of this kind are special in that such expectations are often formulated in relation to entities for which the risk may be quite subtle and difficult to measure objectively, while for subjective reasons it is defined as being contrary to the interests of the financial institution.[38] Some of these reasons are, of course clear (for example, transactions such as arms trade, financing trade with embargoed countries, etc.), which make it possible intuitively assume the validity of such regulations. However, there are other transactions which financial compliance norms may prohibit, even though their conclusion would not incur a reputation risk at all. In this book the notion of reputation risk will be defined as an action that will have an adverse effect on the institution's public image.[39] An example is the prohibition of accounts for diplomatic missions and the financing of US dollar transactions in which one of the parties has its registered office or residence in sanctioned countries.

Naturally, such an approach is difficult to justify on the basis of objective criteria. I may also give rise to significant doubts on the part of investors and employees expecting financial institutions to take action to grow. It is clear that a selective and, at the same time, unclear approach to customers and transactions can lead to a loss of competitive advantage and, over time, of market share and expected profits, even though, in principle, the institution is predisposed to finance such transactions, which it avoids in this case, given the global scope of its activities. What is more, especially in the case of these vague criteria, which are the basis for creating compliance regulations that are to be imposed no specific transactions, there may even be accusations based on the suspicion of discriminatory practices by financial institutions due to the lack of such prohibitions in legal norms.[40]

---

[38] T. A. Smith, The Efficient Norm for Corporate Law: A Neotraditional Interpretation of Fiduciary Duty, *Michigan Law Review* 98(1)/1999, pp. 214–268.

[39] Each corporation may define in a slightly different way for its own use what reputation risk is to it, what situations create it, how to measure it and how to prevent it. According to the Financial Times lexicon, the definition of reputation risk is even simpler and means "likely loss of reputation capital". See http://lexicon.ft.com/Term?term=reputational-risk (download 15 April 2019).

[40] One possible defense strategy against such allegations is to apply arguments relating to the potential insolvency of the entities with which the corporation resolves the relationship. See T. C. Halliday, B. G. Carruthers, The Recursivity of Law: Global Norm Making

In this type of situation, there are generally no compromise solutions that would allow for the reconciliation of compliance guidelines requiring an institution from refraining from specific actions, and the norms of law in force locally, which do not formulate such prohibitions. Of course, from the practical point of view, this problem can be considered relatively easy to solve by simply recognising that since a given financial institution can make autonomous decision to act on special compliance regulations that obligate it not to establish certain economic relations, the lack of such a ban in legal norms resulting from mandatory legal regulations does not exclude the possibility of freely shaping the business model conducted by the financial institution precisely by establishing such internally binding bans. However, this is not such a one-dimensional situation in the sense that the theoretical absence of contradictions between certain prohibitions and the absence of such prohibitions, and thus the very absence of exclusion of these regulations means that they do not contradict each other only in so far as, as they do not belong to the same normative order, as they are different in nature. On the one hand, these are 'only' norms of compliance, and on the other hand, 'as much as' norms of law.[41] However, the observation of economic reality most often leads to the conclusion that stakeholders do not necessarily perceive this difference as a non-contradiction.

An example that can be classified as a kind of complications described here, between internal regulations created by corporations and norms of law binding locally, is a situation in which the source of these corporate norms are guidelines issued by regulators of some countries requiring certain actions in foreign jurisdictions other than those expected by domestic regulators in that jurisdiction.[42]

and National Lawmaking in the Globalization of Corporate Insolvency Regimes, *American Journal of Sociology* 112(4)/2007, p. 1150.

[41] See D. A. Wirth, Commentary: Compliance with Non-Binding Norms of Trade and Finance [in] D. Shelton [ed.] *Commitment and Compliance: The Role of Non-Binding Norms in the International Legal System*, Oxford 2003, p. 330 et seq.

[42] More on the role of corporate internal norms in the transfer of regulations between jurisdictions and more generally on corporate norms in international law and the role of corporations in the international legal order in general see P. Muchlinski, *Corporations in International Law*, Oxford 2009, http://opil.ouplaw.com/view/10.1093/law:epil/9780199231690/law-9780199231690-e1513?rskey=35hRr8&result=1&prd=EPIL (downloaded 5 April 2019) and also of this author: P. Muchlinski, *Multinational Enterprises and the Law*, Oxford 2007, p. 91 et seq.

This kind of cross-border activity by some regulators is even accompanied by an omission to inform the regulators from a given country about it. Such situations frequently occur in the operating conditions of international corporations, especially those which have their main decision-making centres in jurisdictions where regulators are particularly active. This is often the case when they are headquartered in the main financial centres, where many corporations are based, that regulators are generally very much involved in activities aimed at ensuring control of financial institutions.[43] This control often takes the form of requirements which are not known in other, less advanced markets. At the same time, these regulators reserve the privilege of controlling all corporate activity, including those which takes place in its structures present in other jurisdictions. In order to ensure compliance with these regulatory requirements, corporations impose obligations on their subsidiaries in other countries that are unknown in these markets.

The complications resulting from this state of affairs relate primarily to the fact that, without a valid authorisation, the power of some regulators in relation to others, where regulators from jurisdictions with more advanced methods of control and regulation of multinational corporations operate, is widening. This is usually done by means of intra-corporate norms created by the compliance function, which in this case performs the function transmitting regulatory obligations from the home markets where the financial institutions' headquarters are located. These compliance norms from parent companies are passed on to subordinate companies, but also to companies that do not belong to the ownership structure, but to companies, which cooperate with the corporation or its subordinate companies. These obligations may range from capital requirements, through to business continuity obligations in the event of unforeseen events, orders to provide the regulator with information relating both to the financial institutions themselves and to the entities they serve, etc. The obligations in question may range from capital requirements to the obligation to ensure business continuity in the event of unforeseen events. Their distinguishing feature in the context of the problem described here is the source of their origin located in another

---

[43] On the specificity of financial institutions, including international financial institutions see A. Drwiłło, D. Maśniak, *Leksykon prawa finansowego*, Warsaw 2015, p. 168.

jurisdiction and, at the same time, the lack of a similar obligation in the country in which the corporations recommend their use.[44]

Looking at how such a problem is being addressed, it should be noted that the practical approach is to comply with the recommendations of compliance norms, recognising that such recommendations do not adversely affect the day-to-day operations of the financial institution. However, the specific scope of such additional obligations is usually not communicated to the local regulator, except when explicitly requested to do so. The interpretation of whether additional obligations imposed on local financial institutions by foreign regulators may adversely affect their operations is difficult to determine as it depends on how broadly defined the categories of what is and what is not disadvantageous. Outside the scope of these considerations, remain obligations that would require operating contrary to local law. However, it is worth pointing out that even such norms, in which a financial institution would face tasks requiring additional resources in order to achieve compliance with conditions which would not exist if it were not for the requirements of a foreign regulator, could be considered unfavourable for the local financial institution.

These issues, like the other problems mentioned above, create legal and ethical dilemmas, that can be considered from a practical point of view. These examples show that the sources of these problems are often the globalisation of economic processes and the associated cross-border scope of intra-corporate regulation. On the other hand, if we analyse these problems from the theoretical-legal position, it opens interesting areas of research that are worthy of exploring.

5 The Current State of Research

Particular attention was paid in the research to the analysis of the relevant literature, and more specifically to findings relating to comparative issues. This applies in particular to those norms that arise in relation to financial issues. These more theoretical studies have been enriched with

---

[44] Among the many possible issues arising in connection with the occurrence of the phenomenon consisting in the actual obligation to take into account in the practical implementation the norms coming from other jurisdictions is, amongst others, the question of legal certainty as one of the postulates of stability and transparency of the normative environment see M. Wojciechowski, *Pewność prawa*, Gdańsk 2014, p. 57.

conclusions derived from detailed studies of several hundred reliable primary sources of information.[45] These materials include:

a. a set of published internal regulations, including financial institutions' compliance regulations;
b. classified documents constituting internal sets of compliance norms and accompanying interpretative guidelines;
c. working documents of international business associations;
d. guidelines of financial market regulators; and
e. thematic analyses, reports, white and green papers.

Writing this book in this manner, i.e. with references to practical examples taken from modern legal transactions and an attempt to classify them in relation to normative theoretical and legal issues, would not have been possible without the accumulated knowledge and experience gained in the course of work in a corporate legal practice. The theses presented in this book were also possible thanks to the observations made for many years as the person responsible for the management of the legal as well as compliance areas, and co-participating in the management of entire financial institutions. This experience also included participation in numerous intra-corporate and industry forum discussions on compliance issues.

The research was based on my own observations as well as on information collected from other people working in similar structures in various jurisdictions, as well as from legal professionals working for international law firms.

The description of the evidence and regulations contained in this book has been made possible as a result of prior practical observations that illustrate theoretical issues to which this study relates. In the result, these observations, construct the analysis of phenomena, a description of their properties, and further course of their development, have been provided in this book. To a large extent, therefore, they complement the research, which consisted of a critical analysis of the literature. The description of the studies included is also enriched by the review of cases, which constitute a representative basis for general conclusions. In those places where examples are cited in the content of the book without a clear indication

---

[45] See the list of documents on page 286.

of the source, they are derived from their own experiences as a result of this participatory observation.

To a large extent, the research described in the book focuses on the issue of corporation's normative practice through the prism of theoretical and legal reflection. The limited amount of law research related to the subject of compliance norms was a complication. The specificity of the theoretical and legal issues related to compliance norms in the financial industry has resulted in the fact that this phenomenon has not been widely enough analysed in research literature.[46] The existing literature required an obvious openness to pluralistic legal theories.[47]

It is worth noting that there is more and more economic literature on compliance issues. In view of the growing importance of this topic, there are also books written by researchers specialising in the theory of management. Unfortunately, so far only a limited amount of useful legal literature, especially of a theoretical nature, on compliance norms has been produced. This may be the result of a relatively limited number of academic researchers, who wish to engage with practical problems, such as creating a broader framework for the characteristics of compliance norms. In addition, some areas of research are also lagging behind because of the pace of change in the business world, and this is currently the biggest practical challenges in this area. On the other hand, practitioners writing about these topics usually discuss them in an impressionistic way, which lacks a deeper reflection on wider research. This may be due to the fact that their professional activity in relation to these norms is actually often reduced simply to ensure their application.[48]

---

[46] This does not mean, of course, that there are no good positions in literature, such as J. N. Drabek [ed.], *Norms and the Law*, Cambridge 2006, or D. Sciulli, *Corporate Power in Civil Society: An Application of Societal Constitutionalism*, New York 2001.

[47] This includes, for example, multi-source and pluralistic concepts of sources of law. See e.g. W. Twining, *Globalization and Legal Theory*, Cambridge 2000, p. 79; S. Ehrlich, *Oblicza pluralizmów*, Warsaw 1985, p. 32 et seq.; S. Ehrlich, *Wiążące wzory zachowań. Rzecz o wielości systemów i norm*, Warsaw 1995, p. 17 et seq.; J. Winczorek, Pluralizm prawny wczoraj i dziś [in] K. Dobrzeniecki, D. Bunikowski [ed.] *Pluralizm prawny. Tradycje, transformacje, wyzwania*, Toruń 2010, p. 12.

[48] Cf. article on the standardization of compliance norms in relation to the Directive 2004/39/EC of the European Parliament and Council of 21 April 2004 on *Markets in Financial Instruments* amending the Council Directive 85/611/EEC and 93/6/EEC and Directive 2000/12/EC of the European Parliament and the Council on Council Directive 93/22/EEC (O. J. L 145 of 30.4.2004—*Markets in Financial Instruments*

An important reason for discussing this subject is also the lack of descriptions systematising theoretical and legal issues that arise in connection with the existence of norms, whose task is to ensure the effective management of compliance risk in financial institutions.[49] Despite the growing importance of financial institutions as sui generis norm-setters, which operate in an increasingly complex and dynamic changing legal, regulatory and economic environment, and despite the overlapping of factors related to the internationalisation of their activities in different legal systems, there limited interest in broader theoretical research concerning the norms issued by these financial institutions.[50] As emphasised above, attempts to systematise the role, structure, tasks and scope of regulation of compliance norms have been predominantly produced either by researchers from the disciplines of Economic and Management, or alternatively by legal practitioners employing legal analysis of specific examples. This book aims to propose a model approach to compliance norms from the point of view of the theory of law.

6 THE STRUCTURE OF THE BOOK

This book consists of an introduction and five chapters. The second chapter is devoted to issues of particular importance for further research found in the following chapters. These are considerations concerning the relation between the postulate of legal consistency and corporate compliance norms. In this chapter, its individual parts refer to reflections on the coherence of law and its function in the legal system, both as a principle of legislative technique, and as a value system on which the whole normative order is based and with which it should be consistent. The next

---

Directive—MiFID) useful to practitioners working in the field of financial investment products. G. Włodarczyk, *Norma ISO 19600 – próba standaryzacji zarządzania ryzykiem braku zgodności (compliance) – zagadnienia wstępne*, Warsaw 11 June 2014, http://compliance-mifid.wordpress.com/ (download 9 October 2018).

[49] For instance, emerging studies on such important issues as those already covered by advanced regulatory practices in the area of ensuring compliance of corporate activities with criminal law regulations may serve as an example. Especially in the context of the increasingly common practice of introducing subsidiary criminal liability of companies for crimes committed by their employees. See B. Dennis, *Criminal Compliance*, Baden-Baden 2011 passim.

[50] One of the exceptions is the work: P. A. Schott, G. T. Schwartz, *Bank Compliance*, Washington 1989.

part of this chapter directly refers to regulations functioning parallel to legal norms and their relation to the legal system. In the following part, considers the norms created by corporations, and considers the conflicts between the norms created by corporations with the binding legal norms that occur in practice in the functioning of corporations. The chapter ends with a reflection on how conflicts between corporate and legal norms could be resolved.

Chapter 3 discusses the compliance found financial industry at present, with examples illustrated in a descriptive way referring to both the tasks of compliance services and their role in the management of financial institutions. This chapter describes compliance from the point of view of the challenges posed to financial institutions by regulated markets. The groups of tasks currently performed by compliance services in financial institutions are listed, along with an approximation of their specificity and importance for ensuring the correct operation of financial institutions. In this chapter, there is also a description of recently observed trends in the way of arranging the organisational structure of financial institutions and the place that compliance occupies in them. In practice, what emerges is the multitude of tasks and the complexity of the functions assigned to compliance.

Chapter 4 discusses the scope of the regulation of compliance normative acts, indicates those normative systems which are a reference for compliance norms and issues covered by compliance norms in the subject matter. The chapter ends with a list of types and presentation of types of compliance norms currently being developed in financial institutions. This chapter, which is an attempt to systematically describe the factors that influence the creation of compliance norms and their specificity and presents the differences in the norms created by financial institutions in order to ensure compliance status.

Chapter 5 of the book discusses the practical differences in assessing how compliance is understood, and in particular the scope of the regulation of compliance norms, and also the results of the cultural differences between financial institutions operating in different jurisdictions. In this chapter, the impact of cultural differences depending on the place of business on the application of compliance norms is analysed. These cultural differences are understood relatively broadly here and do not only concern different legal cultures, but also other cultural manifestations reflected in the types of social behaviour characteristic for a given area. The examples contained in this chapter refer in particular to the differences observed between the countries from Anglo-Saxon common law jurisdictions and continental legal cultures. The influence of cultural legal differences relates both to the different way in which similar issues are regulated in different countries, and to different way the same norms are interpreted. This chapter also describes the difficulties in the practical application of some of the compliance norms precisely because of cultural differences between different jurisdictions.

The last, Chapter 6 of the book contains conclusions and proposals for a model systemisation of compliance norms depending on the subject they regulate. This chapter also presents *de lege ferenda* conclusions relating to a proposed hierarchy of norms, including ordering postulates, presented taking into account the principles of the general theory of norms, due to their mutual result in a static approach. Further, there is also a reference to the subject interdependence of compliance norms in a dynamic perspective due to the regulatory area, as well as proposals for the application of appropriate legislative practices in order to ensure flexible formulation of compliance norms depending on changing environmental conditions. The last part of this chapter, provides a summary of the considerations included in this book, and discusses the issue of whether it is possible to unify compliance norms from different legal cultures, as well as how such possible unification could be carried out, and how the model approach to compliance norms should look like.

CHAPTER 2

Compliance Norms and Legal Coherence

1 Introduction

The relation of compliance norms to legal norms is important, among other things, because it may influence the assessment of one of the basic demands addressed to legal systems, which is their consistency. The effect of compliance norms is not only to ensure compliance with the law, i.e. the effectiveness of the law, but also to regulate issues previously reserved for the competence of lawmakers. The question therefore arises as to whether this does not jeopardise the coherence of entire legal systems. The purpose of this chapter is to examine this issue.

The starting point of the analysis is a description of the issue of legal coherence from the theoretical and legal point of view, including the postulate of nonconflicting of legal norms. Then, the relation between legal norms and non-legal norms that create the normative environment of international corporations and constituting a reference for further consideration of compliance norms is presented. In subsection three reference is made to compliance norms, presenting their distinguishing criteria, and indicating their role in the conditions of today's complex business environment of international ownership and transactional relations. Subsection four describes examples of conflicts between corporate norms and legal norms on the basis of practical examples of data transfer, matrix management and the selection by financial institutions of legal systems that provide the most favourable regulatory environment for them. Finally, the fifth subchapter refers to the need to resolve these conflicts as a prerequisite for the coherence of the legal system.

The main hypothesis in this chapter is that the normal activities of financial industry corporations are not without effect on the coherence of the legal systems in which they operate. It is therefore necessary to indicate how to remove possible conflicts between the norms of compliance and the law. Consistency of the law, regardless of whether it is treated as a legislative principle or as a value determining the quality of the legal system, should be protected as it is the foundation of the rule of law.[1]

2 Legal Consistency

The cohesion of the legal system, as well as the lack of conflicting legal norms within this system, may, on the one hand, be considered as requirements of the legislative technique, but they may, and should also be perceived, as one of the guiding principles in the rule of law, which, for the addressees of norms, guarantees that the legal system is constructed with respect for their legitimate expectations as to its quality. From this perspective, and thus mainly as referring to legal norms, the principles of legal technology and, at the same time, the principles of the rule of law are considered later in this chapter.[2] For the sake of order, it should only be pointed out that both cohesion and noncontradiction can also be analysed from the point of view of the values considered in legal axiology.[3] In doing so, these considerations apply both to the legal

---

[1] Both the description and the verification of the assumptions contained in this section are based on the analysis of compliance regulations relating to selected examples, the further development of which is included in the following sections of the book. Research on the transfer of commercial data and other data held by corporations, matrix management issues affecting the assessment of corporate governance and legislative and regulatory arbitrage, which is the choice of a place of conducting business activity made by corporations, which is more advantageous from the point of view of the normative environment, were conducted on the basis of analyses carried out in a number of international corporations. The data used for the analyses are also derived from information from international industry associations.

[2] More on consistency, see W. Lang, J. Wróblewski, *Współczesna filozofia i teoria prawaw USA*, Warsaw 1986, pp. 74–89; G. Skąpska, J. Stelmach, Współczesne problemy i modele legitymizacji prawa, *Colloquia Communia* 41/1988–1989, pp. 5–18; S. Wronkowska, *Podstawowe pojęcia prawa i prawoznawstwa*, Poznań 2005, p. 120; K. Pałecki, *Prawoznawstwo zarys wykładu*, Warsaw 2003, p. 126.

[3] Z. Ziembiński, *Wstęp do aksjologii dla prawników*, Warsaw 1990, p. 176.

norms themselves, as well as to the legal provisions from which they are derived.[4]

The rules of legislative technique may differ not only in their function, but also in the importance of the issues to which they relate. They can therefore be classified according to different criteria. According to one of these classifications, there are recommendations to legislative techniques of significant importance in relation to the model of the entire legal system, and those which are of an ordering nature.[5] In the case of recommendations for non-conflict and consistency, it should be assumed that they belong to the first group, as the quality of the entire legal system is affected by the action of the lawmakers in compliance with them.[6] Norm-setters who follow these recommendations construct a legal system, for which one of the leading assumptions is to ensure that there are proper logical relations between particular norms (coherence), and that the quality of individual elements of this system manifests itself in the absence of mutual exclusion (not contradiction).

Irrespective of the fact that non-conflict and coherence belong to the group of technical legislative recommendations addressed to lawmakers, they also have other, no less important, systemic importance. They are the result of rules, the application of which in the legal system affects the legal situation of all entities operating within this system.[7] Hence the assumption that in this sense these are concepts defining recommendations addressed not only to the legislators themselves, but to all persons (citizens) to whom they communicate a solemn declaration that the law

---

[4] For the purposes of this text, the term norm shall be understood as the smallest reasonable form of provision, formulated as a demand or authorization to conduct a particular type of general abstractive behavior derived from the law applicable in the system. See T. Stawecki, P. Winczorek, *Wstęp do prawoznawstwa*, Warsaw 2003, p. 63.

[5] The first example is the directive on the clarity of the text, the second one is the directive which establishes that laws are divided into articles and regulations into paragraphs. So M. Błachut, W. Gromski, J. Kaczor, *Technika prawodawcza*, Warsaw 2008, p. 6. Also S. Wronkowska, M. Zieliński, *Komentarz do zasad techniki prawodawczej z dnia 20 czerwca 2002 r.*, Warsaw 2012, p. 20.

[6] About the quality of law see, e.g., S. Kaźmierczyk, O trzech aspektach jakości prawa, *Studia z Polityki Publicznej* 1(5)/2015, p. 83 et seq.

[7] See footnote 62 on the rules that prescribe the realization of a specific value that is essential for the law. In this context, this important value for the law is the coherence of the whole system and the non-contradiction of the norms that constitute it.

should be created in a coherent manner and that its individual norms should not be mutually exclusive. Any entity operating within a given legal system may therefore have a legitimate expectation towards a legislator guided by the principles of coherence and non-contradiction that the system will be characterised by these features.

Non-contradiction is a principle referring to norms, in relation to which it is demanded that the recommendations formulated for them should not give rise to fears of a different reading of the situations regulated in them.[8] This refers to the case in which a person reading its normative disposition from two different provisions within the same system could not derive from each of those provisions a disposition to behave in a specific way excluding the possibility of different behaviour. In the case of prohibitions, those which, by reference to a particular factual situation in which the addressee is located, do not make recommendations to the addressee to refrain from actions, which it would not be possible to implement at the same time will not be contradictory. On the other hand, as far as the norms conferring powers are concerned, the principle of no conflict will be to ensure that their application does not imply an infringement of other prohibitive rules. In this case, the relation between any non-conflicting norms of duty is similar.

The noncontradiction of norms understood in this way consists of three elements that characterise it:

a. The first of these is the condition that rules binding under the same normative system should not contradict each other. This means that the normative content of some provisions cannot give one legal meaning to certain factual situations, whereas the content of other provisions would give the same situations a different normative meaning.
b. Secondly, the non-conflicting nature of the dispositive element of the norm also means that the norms are not mutually exclusive, that is to say, that they do not create an obligation on the part of the addressee of the norm to behave in a particular way which would at the same time be an infringement of another norm.

---

[8] More about the principles of law in the political order of the state, including the principle of non-contradiction: J. Kuciński, W. J. Wołpiuk, *Zasady ustroju politycznego państwa w konstytucji Rzeczypospolitej Polskiej z 1997 roku*, Warsaw 2012, p. 92.

c. Thirdly, non-conflict must also be read through their axiological references and must therefore be understood as a state in which the norms refer to a set of statements that are jointly true, but also refer to other values that are not in conflict with each other.[9]

The consistency feature postulated for the normative system as a whole defines the expectations that each of its related elements remains in a justifiable logical relation by taking into account any of the following justifications: axiological, teleological, functional or systemic.[10] Therefore, in order to determine the concept of coherence in relation to the legal system, it would be advisable to point out first of all the relation between norms, manifested by the different nature of the links—purposeful, functional and systemic. A system in which normative recommendations flow from each other in a meaningful way, carrying out tasks for which the reference is wider than the content contained in each of the individual norms, will be coherent. The notion of cohesion also includes the assumption that the connections within the system are compact, that they have no gaps, or at least the aim to eliminate them. Moreover, the feature worth mentioning when describing the concept of cohesion refers to the strength of the interrelations described here. There will not be a coherent system in which norms are not very strongly bound together or are even loosely or even poorly connected together. In this case, we are talking about the logical relation between norms, which can be derived from their content, but these might not be not obvious, or they may be ambiguous, allowing for different

---

[9] It is precisely the axiological references, which are the basic element legitimizing good law or, more precisely, the rule of good law, that have become the main axis on which the theses formulated by Fuller and developed by the continuators of his concepts are based. One of these theses concerns the principle of the need for the law to avoid conflicting rules. See L. L. Fuller, *Moralność prawa*, Warsaw 1978, p. 68 et seq.; K. Pałecki, Uwagi o dobrym prawie – wprowadzenie do dyskusji [in] P. Mochnarzewski, A. Kociołek-Pęksa [ed.] *Dobre prawo, złe prawo – w kręgu myśli Gustawa Radbrucha*, Warsaw 2009, p. 91.

[10] The situation in which no element of the group violates the accepted formal and substantive rules (natural), the order of internal relations in this group means the feature of coherence. So e.g. A. Sulikowski, *W poszukiwaniu zasad prawa*, Wrocław 2006, p. 65 et seq. Also e.g. A. Aarnio, R. Alexy, A. Pecznik, W. Rabinowicz, J. Woleński, *On Coherence Theory of Law*, Lund 1998, p. 7 et seq. and newer relations to these positions: A. Amaya, Justification, Coherence, and Epistemic Responsibility in Legal Fact-Finding, *Journal of Social Epistemology* 5/2008, p. 306.

interpretations, or they may require additional connections to be made. It is only when there are strong logical interconnections between norms that the legal system is characterised as having cohesion attributes.[11]

Both the principle of cohesion, which characterises the legal system, as well as the non-conflicting nature of its regulations, whose importance of ordering from the point of view of legislative technique is difficult to overestimate, and guarantee from the point of view of the expectations formulated from the perspective of citizens, are of particular importance in the situation when new phenomena of a legal nature appear in the normative space.[12] These phenomena refer to normative regulations parallel to the legal system, that overlap with the area of relations between entities, which has been adopted so far as the natural domain of the state.

3 Parallel Non-legal Regulations and the Legal System

Whether one considers that the system of law is a natural or an artificial conceptual system, which as a whole is composed of interconnected norms, according to accepted principles, articulated in a given period of time, in a given area, it is important for any analysis that is conducted,

---

[11] Cf. B. Brożek, *Legal Interpretation and Coherence* [in] M. Araszkiewicz, J. Savelka [ed.] *Coherence: Insights from Philosophy, Jurisprudence and Artificial Intelligence*, Law and Philosophy Library 107, Springer 2013, p. 113 et seq.

[12] When trying to decide whether the cohesion of the normative system is a principle or a value, it is worth noting the view that the principles of law, including the principle of cohesion, are the kind of norms that form the order of realization of a certain value. They differ from the rules, i.e. ordinary norms, by the subject of the obligation formulated in them, which in their case is not a specific course of action. Therefore, the principles do not refer to the sphere of obligation to act (refrain from acting) in relation to a specific deed but order the realization of a specific value important for the law. See M. Kordela, *Zasady prawa studium teoretycznoprawne*, Poznań 2012, p. 150 et seq. In contrast to the principles of law, it distinguishes between directive and descriptive principles, among which directive principles are those which aim at influencing the behavior of certain entities in the direction of their behavior. In this sense, these are legally binding norms, but in a sense superior to other norms of the system. Descriptive principles, in turn, refer to the patterns of specific subjects of the norm and indicate the way of resolving a given issue, distinguished from a specific point of view, or the pattern of shaping a legal institution. See S. Wronkowska, Z. Ziembiński, *Zarys teorii prawa*, Poznań 2001, p. 187. More on the consistency resulting from the linguistic clarity of normative expressions, see M. Zieliński, *Wykładnia Prawa. Zasady, reguły, wskazówki*, Warsaw 2012, p. 150.

especially for the description of new, intrusive phenomena appearing in this system, to look at the relations between the elements of this system.[13] Therefore, within this system it should be possible to distinguish content links, including logical, linguistic, axiological, etc., as well as hierarchical and formal ones. The latter two types of elements are particularly important for the analysis of non-legal norm-setting processes generated by entities outside the recognised circle of legislators.

The established and hierarchically order of the sources of law is more and more often not only enriched and supplemented, but also torn apart and chaotic as a result of the activities of entities performing de facto law-making functions (corporations, regulatory authorities, industry associations) undertaken independently of the activities of traditional legislators.[14]

In addition to the existing legal systems that organise the political, social, economic, cultural aspects, etc., there is an increasing number of new types of regulation in each of these areas.[15] The distinguishing factor is the type of entities that issue these norms. The clearest (and assessed) element characterising these entities is that, unlike recognised legislators, such as public authorities with legislative powers, these

---

[13] When dividing the systems of law, its theorists, depending on the concept they pursue, will point to an independent genesis, free from human creative interference, either as legal naturalists or, on the contrary, as anthropogenic, being the product of human activity, as positivist schools. From the point of view of the incidence of these disputes on the subject-matter of these considerations and given that the genesis of the legal system is much more complex in nature, the most useful here seems to be to ignore these differences. See T. Stawecki, P. Winczorek, op. cit., p. 114 et seq.

[14] Although such a situation may seem to be worrying for a long time now, there is a belief that it is not an unnatural phenomenon at all. J. Rawls argues that it seems natural to suppose that the distinct character and autonomy of the various elements of society require that in certain spheres they operate on the basis of their own rules, designed to suit their specific nature. J. Rawls, *Liberalizm polityczny*, Warsaw 1998, p. 356.

[15] This applies in particular to internal regulations issued by corporations—international business organizations with global reach. These regulations take the form of internal normative acts (e.g. of different rank of internal regulations of very different scope and detail of regulations), but also regulations statued in a much less unambiguous form (e.g. in all kinds of "standards", "policies" or "manuals"). Importantly, those regulations contain rules imposing a certain type of behavior not only applicable to employees or other entities in direct relations with those corporations, but also much more broadly. More on this subject is included further in this book.

entities are not democratically empowered.[16] It is impossible to interpret their power out of the existing chain of competence. However, they do introduce regulations that apply not only to themselves or, possibly, to those who have a direct relation with them. The scope of these regulations is sometimes much broader, but in many cases, it goes beyond the area of a specific legal system and becomes universal and global in nature.[17] Consideration of the mechanisms contributing to the effectiveness of these regulations is a separate and equally interesting issue.[18]

It is worth mentioning here that when pointing to extra-legal regulations resulting from the normative activity of entities other than public lawmakers, we are not talking here about moral, ethical, moral, cultural norms or other normative systems of this type, which have a clearly autonomous relation to the law.[19] These are norms whose structure, content, scope of impact and importance indicate their similarity to legal norms. As it has been indicated, the source of such norms may be regulations, flowing from very different entities, for which the only common feature is the lack of legitimacy to act as lawmakers.[20] Despite this,

---

[16] It is primarily international corporations that create their own normative systems. In practice, however, at least some of these norms also affect the outside world. Similarly, regulations resulting from mutual agreements between corporations may have a broad impact. These are not only simple agreements relating to their dominant or monopolistic position, but also much more complex agreements such as those relating to the fixing of interest rates on certain interbank markets, for example LIBOR or EURIBOR, agreements concerning the level of fees and the clearing method between payment institutions such as Visa and MasterCard and banks, etc.

[17] Cf. A. Bator, Integracja i globalizacja z perspektywy filozofii prawa [in] J. Stelmach [ed.] *Filozofia prawa wobec globalizmu*, Kraków 2003, pp. 9–26.

[18] About the pressure groups as one of the forms of intermediary bodies see, e.g., D. T. Ostas, The Law and Ethics of K Street: Lobbying, the First Amendment and the Duty to Create Just Laws, *Business Ethics Quarterly* 17(1)/2007, p. 33.

[19] More on the autonomous relationship between some normative systems and law—a monographic study W. Gromski, *Autonomia i instrumentalny charakter prawa*, Wrocław 2000 *passim*.

[20] An example of such norms is the corporate compliance norms described in this text, but not only these. Other similar norms shaping the normative situation of broad groups of actors are created by agreements between corporations, by various types of trade unions, as well as by private international organizations and associations, e.g. *lex sportiva* or *lex internet*.

they undoubtedly form, at least similar to legal norms, directives of an abstract nature functioning in parallel to legal norms.[21]

While it is difficult to identify the characteristics common to these norms, other than the source of their origin that are located outside the established system of democratically legitimised legislators, despite their abstract nature and the wide scope of application, it is possible to try to describe them by identifying the differentiated features that constitute their distinctiveness.[22] Over time, as the process of creating such parallel normative systems becomes entrenched in the social space, it will certainly be possible to develop a coherent conceptual apparatus, which will be imposed on such phenomena. However, at best, at this stage it is possible to attempt to describe their characteristics that are similar to legal norms, which are the subject of this book's considerations.

If one omits the issue of the lack of power to legislate for the entities creating these norms, which would result from a chain of competence binding them with the body representing the sovereign will to legislate in a given jurisdiction, then perhaps the most important common connecting factor that characterises these norms is the subject matter of regulation. To be more precise, certain dominant *link* resembles the matter, which is essentially different in nature, and which these norms regulate. It is the need to define and parameterise the behaviour towards completely new phenomena occurring on the border of social, economic and cultural spaces.

The internationalisation of certain communication processes, such as social networking sites, instant messaging, trading platforms, etc. built

---

[21] Examples can be commonly used guidelines such as ISDA—International Swaps and Derivatives Association Inc., which are renewed every few years, as economic relations become more complicated. It is currently difficult to find such practices in relations between financial institutions and entities concluding derivative agreements with them that would not be based on ISDA templates detailing the scope of powers of financial institutions and the responsibilities of their clients. The generally abstract nature of these norms, their widespread application and the actual impossibility of any different shaping of relations between the parties speaks in favor of looking at these acts as normative rules rather than typical contractual patterns.

[22] The broad reach of these norms is due, inter alia, to the fact that these organizations often operate simultaneously in several jurisdictions, with hundreds of thousands of employees and hundreds of millions of customers. Cf. B. Roach, *Corporate Power in Global Economy*, Medford 2007, p. 28. Also C. Derber, *Corporation Nation: How Corporations Are Taking Over Our Lives and What We Can Do About It*, New York 1998; I. Hobson, Jr., *The Unseen World of Transnational Corporations' Powers*, New York 2004, p. 26.

on universal, remote and mobile access to the Internet, has given rise to completely new models of economic exchange. Based on these direct communication tools, hitherto unknown, innovative or distant patterns became available at first, and then over time the dominate medium of communication. Hence there is the need to propose solutions that would make it possible to normalise behaviour. Here, however, there is a significant mismatch—formally legitimised legislative structures of states and international organisations, if they decide to take steps to regulate these phenomena at all, it is only when these phenomena are already of a permanent nature, and not when they first appear.[23]

It is certainly a natural process for these structures. Usually economic and social processes, etc., at the point of their creation are so new and unrecognised that they are not accompanied by certain or precisely formulated social reflection or political demands. However, this delay results in the occupation of these spaces by more efficient and flexible entities, which fill them with the normative matter that they create. For corporations, the ability to adapt efficiently to these phenomena is at the same time an existential necessity, in which they have developed unique competences. It is the corporations that react the fastest to emerging economic needs, taking advantage of new technological possibilities, and at the same time regulating these areas much earlier than they will be in the sphere of interest of state legislators.[24] States prefer not to leave these areas beyond the scope of their interest for too long.

Without in-depth research that would help to verify certain hypotheses from a historical perspective, it is not possible to state unequivocally why the monopoly of recognised public norm-setters, which has been present in the Western world for two hundred years, has been broken. It would be especially interesting to discovery whether this process is not so new, and whether one can observe the behaviour of this phenomenon from medieval trade guilds, until today's corporations. It is a fact,

---

[23] Examples include information security standards, how corporations consent to their use of data, methods of settling international transactions, and even the conditions required for the performance of specified benefits. The beginnings of this process and its evolution, see E. M. Dodd, R. J. Baker, *Cases and Materials on Corporations*, New York 2000, p. 99.

[24] High-frequency transactions and their impact on the macroeconomic situation in global markets can be one of many examples. Cf. E. T. Swanson, *Let's Twist Again: A High-Frequency Event-Study Analysis of Operation Twist and Its Implications for Quantitative Easing*, San Francisco 2011, p. 20 et seq.

however, that one of the leading, but also particularly interesting roles in this field are played by corporations and in particular by large international financial institutions.

4 Norms Developed by Corporations

Regulations of this kind, i.e. norms created by corporations, are therefore issued by entities, which traditionally do not belong to the group of lawmakers, and which are most identified as operating in the economic sphere.[25] These are in particular those large global economic organisations, whose scope of activity and influence make it possible to flexibly adapt how they function to the changing conditions of the social environment. One of the ways the corporations adjust in this way is to try to regulate the behaviour of entities entering into various types of relations with them.

One particularly interesting observation for concerning this problem is that although it does not result from a well-established system, norms issued by these entities may be classified as norms of a nature similar to

---

[25] There are many attempts to establish a legal definition of a corporation under different legal systems. The descriptive definition adopted in the US legal doctrine is based on its jurisprudence and specifies that a corporation is: "a legal person created under State law in rare cases by a natural person and his successors, albeit usually by a group of natural persons who, acting jointly and under the law, collectively, have a legal personality distinct from the legal personality of the individual persons, having the capacity conferred upon it to maintain continuity notwithstanding any change which may occur in its composition, for a specified or indefinite period of time, and capable of acting as one body for matters relating to a common purpose, within the limits laid down for legal persons". The derivation of this definition is based on the case-law of the courts and the literature relating to it: Sutton's Hospital, 10 Coke. 32; Dartmouth College vs. Woodward, 4 Wheat. 518, 636, 657. 4 L. Ed. 629; the United States vs. Trinidad Coal Co., 137 U.S. 160, 11 Sup. Ct. 57. 34 L. Ed. 640; Andrews Bros. Co. vs. Youngstown Coke Co., 86 Fed. 585, 30 C. C. A. 293; Porter vs. Railroad Co., 76 111. 573; State vs. Payne, 129 Mo. 468, 31 S. W. 797. 33 L. R. A. 576; Farmers' L. & T. Co. vs. New York, 7 Hill (NY) 283. *State Business Law Dictionary*, Washington 2013. It reflects the essence of how the concept of corporation is understood today in legal practice and in many other languages. For the purpose of this analysis, a definition can be proposed, according to which it is assumed that this is a specific type of entrepreneur, conducting business on an international scale, usually in the form of a complex ownership structure consisting of interconnected entities with common management at the highest level of consolidation.

the legal ones.[26] This is due to the fact that they are often of a general abstract nature, and the scope of the obligation extends far beyond the circle of recipients, as it is not only limited to entities within the direct range of their impact.[27] For it is not only the employees of corporations, but entities cooperating with them and providing them services, and also their customers, and in the case of companies that are conducting global activities on a mass scale—a wide range of entities also become addressees of these regulations.[28] What is more, these corporate norm-setters introduce regulations, the subject matter of which also extends beyond this area of activity, to which the corporation's activity seems to be limited. Such regulations are codes of conduct which are considered by these entities to be in line with their ethical conduct procedures, or so-called norms of conduct, but which, contrary to their name, are binding.[29] In such cases there are complications. This is because there are norms, whose aim is to indicate a specific behaviour (a directive element), that is shaped by a certain axiologically motivated concept of equity (an evaluative element, related to the ethos understood as a model of proper behaviour desired by a given organisation). These norms are equipped with a relatively strong attribute of binding force, which may

---

[26] Even the doctrine of formal sources of law, complemented by the distinction between autonomous and dependent sources of law, indicates that norms arising from dependent sources of law cannot be an independent source of rights and obligations. *A contrario*, only those rules and principles that can constitute an independent basis for a judicial decision or other act of law application can be considered an autonomous source of rights and obligations. Cf. L. Morawski, *Główne problemy współczesnej filozofii prawa. Prawo w toku przemian*, Warsaw 2005, p. 244.

[27] D. Shelton [ed.] *Commitment and Compliance: The Role of Non-binding Norms in the International Legal System*, New York 2000, p. 9 et seq.

[28] The fact that still too little attention is paid to the norms created by group norms and private law systems, which influence both the whole society and the behavior of its individual members, is noticeable, L. E. Mitchell, *Understanding Norms*, Toronto 1999, p. 200.

[29] An example is the inclusion of any form of non-contractual gratuity for services rendered in a relationship between a corporation and its customers as prohibited conduct, because it is considered to be corrupt in such situations. We are talking here about such a tightening of standards that, in a given jurisdiction, a certain action remains both fully compliant with the law and not only does not violate good manners but is even advisable in accordance with these customs. It is precisely this global application of uniform standards, which are absolutely binding on the entities cooperating with a given corporation, without taking into account local legal and customary specificities, that in practice raises a number of doubts about the nature of these regulations.

belie their seemingly soft character.[30] Therefore, it would be a mistake to analyse them simply from the point of view of one of the many types of soft laws.[31] In addition, other norms with similar characteristics, the so-called regulatory, prudential or directional norms issued by public authorities acting as regulators of individual markets, which are not the subject of these considerations, are comparable.[32]

When examining the phenomenon of corporate norm-setting activity, and trying to separate it from other groups of norms, it is worth pointing out that there are three additional criteria, apart from those listed above, relating to the characteristics that distinguish these norms—the criterion of interest, the criterion of value and the criterion of recipients.

The first criterion of this type is the criterion of interest, which reflects the common feature that characterises all activities, including the norm-setting activities of a corporation. By definition, a corporation is established to conduct business on a large scale, and function within a framework of complex international ownership and organisational structures. In addition, they have their own long-term market strategies that include both their economic objectives that are aimed at development, and organisational objectives aimed at optimisation or, in extreme conditions, at survival. The task of norms created by corporations is therefore to ensure the achievement of these goals. Since the activity of the corporation takes place within the environment of economic competition, these norms must always, although not necessarily directly, pursue the interests of a given organisation, often different or contrary to the

---

[30] On axiological justifications for the existence of standards, see A. Bator, W. Gromski, A. Kozak, S. Kaźmierczyk, Z. Pulka, *Wprowadzenie do nauk prawnych. Leksykon tematyczny*, Warsaw 2015, p. 114 et seq.

[31] More on *soft laws*, see J. Jabłońska-Bonca, Soft justice w "państwie sieciowym" [in] S. L. Stadniczenko, H. Duszka-Jakimko [ed.] *Alternatywne formy rozwiązywania sporów w teorii i w praktyce. Wybrane zagadnienia*, Opole 2008, p. 65 et seq.; A. T. Guzman, T. Meyer, International Soft Law, *The Journal of Legal Analysis* 2(1)/2011; G. C. Shaffer, Mark A. Pollack, Hard vs. Soft Law: Alternatives, Complements and Antagonists in International Governance, *Minnesota Law Review* 94/2010, p. 712.

[32] These administrative bodies and regulators have powers to undertake regulatory actions in relation to particular sectors of the economy, but these powers do not necessarily mean the authority to undertake legal actions. In relation to regulatory and supervisory powers in the area of banking law, see M. Bączyk, E. Fojcik-Mastalska, L. Góral, J. Pisuliński, W. Pyzioł, *Prawo bankowe. Komentarz*, Warsaw 2003, p. 509.

interests of other entities operating in the same area.[33] At this point it can be seen that a potential conflict may appear as a result of a collision between norms created by corporations for pursuing their interests, with norms derived from the law in force in a given jurisdiction that regulates the same area, which is particularly interesting.

The second distinguishing feature relating to the characteristics of norms created by corporations is the value criterion.[34] We are talking here about axiologically justified references, which are always at the basis of the normative process within a corporation.[35] As a rule, the larger and more heteronomous an institution from the point of view of the nature of its activities or cultural differences in the different jurisdictions in which it operates, the greater the need to develop a uniform set of patterns of desired behaviour, and to base them on ethical or cultural foundations, usually created especially for the needs of a given corporation.[36] A separate question worth examining is whether what is proclaimed by a corporation as a its values are values at all, or whether it would be more correct to return to the reflection on the criterion of interest, assuming that it is the interest and not the values that determine the shape of a given normative system in this case.

The third criterion distinguishing norms created by corporations is the criterion of recipients. This is a broadly defined circle of the

---

[33] At the same time, since the purpose of these standards is to ensure compliance, they must take into account the entire legal system constituting the normative environment of financial institutions. On financial law standards, see C. Kosikowski, J. Matuszewski, Geneza i ewolucja oraz stan obecny i przewidywana przyszłaość prawa finansowego [in] C. Kosikowski [ed.] *System Prawa Finansowego*, vol. I, Warsaw 2010, p. 15 et seq. And also C. Kosikowski, *Samodzielny byt prawa finansowego jako działu prawa i problem jego autonomiczności*, Warsaw 2010, p. 419.

[34] About the importance of the value criterion in the process of establishing and interpreting legal norms in general: M. Safjan, *Wyzwania dla państwa prawa*, Warsaw 2007, p. 25 et seq.

[35] Cf. G. R. Weaver, L. K. Trevino, Compliance and Values Oriented Ethics Programs: Influences on Employees' Attitudes and Behavior, *Business Ethics Quarterly* 9(2)/1999, p. 315.

[36] More about cultural conditions of international corporations: J. Galli, *Plemienna korporacja*, Warsaw 2013, p. 33 et seq. See also about creating desired patterns of corporate behavior based on values and culture: M. Baczewska-Ciupak, *Przywództwo organizacyjne w kontekście aksjologicznych i moralnych wyzwań przyszłości*, Lublin 2013, p. 65 et seq.; W. Gasparski [ed.] *Etyka biznesu w zastosowaniach praktycznych: inicjatywy, programy, kodeksy*, Warsaw 2002, p. 32.

addressees of norms, although it is usually rather abstract nature, it always refers to those entities, which in any way enter into relations with a given corporation. These are first and foremost employees and customers, but may also include shareholders, service providers, other cooperating entities, including advisors, funding providers, etc., as well as shareholders. For each of these groups, the prescribed behaviour may be shaped differently, but it is these entities, and not any other or indefinite ones, that are affected by these rules.

As a result of the analysis of the nature of norms created by corporations due to the criteria of interest, values and addressees described above, it is possible to distinguish the nature of compliance norms, which correspond to the nominal definition quoted at the beginning of the Introduction to this book, which is of key importance for this book.[37]

Reflections on what compliance norms are, how they are built, what areas they cover are in fact reflections on the dynamics of norm-setting and the regulatory processes taking place in the social space of today.[38]

This reflection should not avoid such fundamental questions as whether the structures of corporations that are so able to adapt to changing trends that we discussed previously, is a sufficient explanation of the process of undertaking regulatory tasks by these organisations. The question of the reason for this phenomenon can be addressed by means of a detailed inquiry to determine whether there is a gap in traditional regulation, which is thus filled. Whether this is due to the fact that traditional legislators simply do not keep up with the pace of change in the modern world.[39] Perhaps this is also because the sphere requiring regulation is expanding into new spaces of social activities, which traditional legislators

---

[37] See B. Makowicz, *Compliance w przedsiębiorstwie*, Warsaw 2011, p. 37.

[38] Cf. A. G. Scherer, G. Palazzo, Toward a Political Conception of Corporate Responsibility: Business and Society Seen from a Habermasian Perspecive, *Academic Management Review* 32(4)/2007, p. 1100 et seq.; M. S. Ausslaender, J. Curbach, Corporate or Government Duties? Corporate Citizenship from a Governmental Perspective, *Business and Society* 5/2015, p. 90.

[39] An example is the self-regulation of financial institutions aimed at creating binding standards for prudent risk management in response to emerging cyclical crises. Legal regulations are often the consequence of sanctioning earlier industry self-regulations. The most significant example, in terms of the scope of impact and scope of regulation, are the recommendations of the Basel Committee, which have been mentioned several times in the paper, and discussed in more detail in Chapter 3.

have not been before.[40] Perhaps international corporations and not public legislators take on the role of a cross-border norm-setter, because there is no single global legislator, while a world based on the exchange of information and goods consists of global relations. The following phenomena have a direct impact on the global nature of social and economic relations in the contemporary world:

a. the ease of mobility;
b. the range of activities of global businesses;
c. the increasing interdependence of financial markets worldwide;
d. the internationalisation of interests and the ease with which transactions are implemented, irrespective of the place of supply or the domicile of the entities;
e. the convergence of behavioural patterns that superseded traditional cultural differences;
f. the similarity in lifestyle aspirations.[41]

Questions about the impact of these phenomena on the norm-setting processes conducted by large multinational corporations remains open, and therefore are worthy of further investigation, perhaps especially by the theory of law.

Legal research on what are the norms created by corporations, concern, among other things, what they manifest themselves in, i.e. how their content is expressed and whether and what written forms they adopt (deontological codes, sets of ethics, prudential policies, etc.), as well as what kind of interpretative rules are adopted to extract their content and remove any uncertainties that may appear during reading. Equally interesting is the question of whether they merge into more extensive systems of norms or whether they remain merely scattered

---

[40] There are many examples of areas that are largely outside the scope of legal regulations and where the need to regulate has been reflected in corporate norms. These include, for example, matters related to managing the security of confidential information, resolving conflicts of interest, ways of protecting resources contained in IT clouds, etc.

[41] Extensively on the globalization of law and its consequences for the science of law resulting from globalization phenomena, see B. De Sousa Santos, *Towards a New Legal Common Sense: Law, Globalization, and Emancipation*, London 2002.

fragments of systems or lose particular norms that do not make up larger elements regulating certain areas of economic relations or more broadly social relations.[42]

5   The Collision of Legal and Corporate Norms

Leaving aside the internal coherence of each of these sets of norms, it can be assumed that they have their own characteristics, and that each of these sets has been created as a result of completely different norm-setting practice, using typical instruments.[43] However, it can be indicated that these sets of norms show at least two common features described earlier. Firstly, they consist of the unobvious empowerment of corporations to norm-setting.[44] Secondly, the scope of application of these norms, that cover both its own employees or entities directly cooperating with them, as well as whole groups of entities, who indirectly interact with these corporations.

---

[42] On the subject of the separation of branches of law through its differentiation, see A. Bator, *Dyferencjacja* [in] A. Bator, W. Gadomski, A. Kozak, S. Kaźmierczyk, Z. Pulka [ed], *Wprowadzenie do nauk prawnych. Leksykon tematyczny*, Warsaw 2012, p. 148.

[43] These differences result from many factors, beginning with differences resulting from the sphere of a business in which each of these corporations operates (because the normative systems of banks will look different, and insurance companies, energy companies, consulting companies, and yet also multi-sector industrial corporations such as GE, Siemens, or some Korean chebols). Another feature that significantly influences the shape of the normative system within a corporation is the age-related tradition of regulation in a given company (differently these regulations will look like in old enterprises like Mercedes-Benz or ThyssenKrupp, and differently in young Google and Facebook. The factor that cannot be overestimated is the cultural tradition of the corporation's home country (the internal normative systems in the Japanese bank Namura are different, in the British bank Lloyds, and in the American Citigroup). See B. Scholtens, Cultural Values and International Differences in Business Ethics, *Journal of Business Ethics* 75(3)/2007, p. 273 et seq., as well as G. Hofstede, B. Neuijen, D. Ohayv, G. Sanders, Measuring Organizational Cultures: A Qualitative and Quantitative Study Across Twenty Cases, *Administrative Science Quarterly* 35(2)/1990, p. 290.

[44] An unobvious empowerment in the understanding proposed in this text is any situation in which corporations regulate the sphere of duties of entities entering into relations with them regardless of, and especially to a greater extent than it results from, the provisions of law. Numerous examples include the obligation for customers and business partners to provide additional information concerning them, the collection of which is not related to the transaction in which the information was requested. See N. Hsieh, Does Global Business Have Responsibility to Promote Just Institutions? *Business Ethics Quarterly* 19/2009, p. 260 et seq.; J. M. Kline, TNC Codes and National Sovereignty: Deciding When TNCs Should Engage in Political Activity, *Transnational Corporations* 14(3)/2005, p. 30.

Due to the fact that corporations create norms similar in design and content to legal norms, and they regulate the rights and obligations of numerous groups of entities, it happens that they enter the area regulated or partially regulated by legal norms. In such situations, collisions between the two types of norms inevitably occur. The most common examples concern areas where corporate regulations directly relate to the protection of their economic interests.[45] We present below in more detail the three types of issues, previously mentioned in the Introduction, to illustrate the complications associated with the application of compliance norms in corporate practice.

One of the issues in which there is a conflict between the norms contained in intra-corporate norms and the norms of law is the issue of providing data on corporate matters. This, of course, applies not only to the access itself, but even more so to the scope of rights related to the disposal of this data, including its processing, storage, disposal or use for purposes deemed justified by the corporation. The type of data determines the protection regime that is required. The personal data of employees to whom the corporation wishes to have access, not only for statistical purposes or related to the management of its personnel, but also in connection with specific requirements relating to prescribed behaviours or personal and professional qualifications of employees, are subject to various protection regimes. Another use of data is the personal data of customers of the corporation, or its potential customers, to whom, depending on the features held by them, specific products and services may be offered. Still another protection will be granted to data covered by financial institutions, insurance secrecy, etc. The data will be subject to the same protection as the data subject to financial institutions, insurance secrecy, etc. Moreover, conflicts of compliance norms issued by the corporation with other norms in relation to data protection relate not only to the type of data, but also to the way they are used.

Other examples of data use are the expectations of corporations with regard to the use of data to determine the economic profile of clients using mathematical scoring models or historical-behavioural comparisons, or the use of the personal data of employees, which are needed to determine, for example, the quality of their work or career advancement

---

[45] More about the law as an element that defines the whole social and economic life and at the same time unites this life—R. Stammler, Gospodarka i prawo [in] M. Szyszkowska [ed.] *Europejska filozofia prawa*, Warsaw 1995, p. 80.

plans. Depending on the scope and manner of use, the scope of their protection may vary according to the law applicable in a given jurisdiction, and the way in which corporations interfere with the confidentiality of such data in those jurisdictions may vary considerably. A separate issue, which is an example of the collision of intra-corporate norms with generally binding ones, and which relates to the data sphere, is their reporting. This is due to the fact that, based on the need to preserve the integrity of the financial system or the wider economy, the legislator usually establishes rules for which commercial, financial, etc. data transfers cannot take place. At the same time, however, international economic organisations set their own, usually very different rules in this area, and they expect these to be strictly applied.

Now that we have identified the importance of norm clashes, it is possible to point to much more serious examples that arise from conflicts of competence between corporate representatives and its organisational units, regardless of the structures resulting from the principles of corporate governance and ensuring proper ownership supervision. We are talking here about the previously mentioned matrix management, which is popular in corporations characterised by a wide range of activities, which consists of giving corporations the power to directly control the way in which subsidiaries conduct their business, and even to take individual management decisions by persons outside these structures, regardless of the division of competences applicable within their framework.[46] The consequence of this type of situation is that the limits of acceptable corporate governance are exceeded. As a result, it leads to the direct management of economic decisions of companies, i.e. from the fact that a given corporation remains in a state of non-compliance with the applicable law. In fact, it is a de facto presentation of norms set internally by corporations above legal norms.[47]

---

[46] More on matrix management e.g. J. Wieland, Corporate Governance, Values Management, and Standards: A European Perspective, *Business Society* 1/2005, p. 74 et seq.; C. A. Barlett, S. Ghoshal, Matrix Management: Not a Structure, a Frame of Mind, *Harvard Business Review* 60(4)/1990, p. 138; E. W. Larson, D. H. Gobeli, Matrix Management: Contradictions and Insights, *California Management Review* 29/1987, p. 126; D. I. Clelant, W. R. King, *The Cultural Ambience of Matrix Organization*, Wiley 2008 (download 6 March 2019); M. R. Gottlieb, *The Matrix Management Organization Reloaded*, London 2006, p. 26 et seq.

[47] A major problem of admissibility of non-compliance with selected legal norms occurred in the situation of prior criticism of them from the position of their place and tasks in the hierarchy of norms—R. Dworkin, *Biorąc prawa poważnie*, Warsaw 1998, p. 68.

The willingness of corporations to remain in compliance with the law while being determined to implement business decisions in accordance with their own norms results in the use of the instrument of legislative or regulatory arbitrage.[48] It consists of choosing the applicable law governing the contractual provisions or determining the place of business in such a way, so that it may be more advantageous from the point of view of the regulatory environment. An interesting example of which, is the marginalisation of the role of private international law regulations, the rules of which, were designed to remove collisions resulting from different regulations being in force in different territories, but are not applied in this case, because it is the corporations which decide which regulation is more advantageous for them. Acting in accordance with this identification, they take steps to choose the applicable law. However, of course, such instruments are only available to very large business institutions with appropriate legal and organisational instruments.

The issue that is arising here is whether norms and even entire normative systems created by corporations supersede traditional, public legal orders, and so occupy ever wider fields, or whether they merely supplement the existing regulations without superseding them. In the absence of extensive cross-cutting research in this area, it can now only be said that it regulates those areas in which states, through public authorities, have so far remained absent and thus fill gap in the existing normative structures.

In practice, however, this does not mean the two normative systems are fully autonomous, since there are numerous conflicts between the various regulations, as there are between the divergent interests of the legislative bodies representing the sovereign will of the individual states, and the interests of the slightly less powerful economic organisations.

---

[48] According to the definition of the Financial Times Lexicon, regulatory arbitrage occurs when companies take advantage of loopholes in their regulatory systems by avoiding compliance with certain regulations. It takes place through conducting business activities, creating products and services in locations outside the area appropriate for selected regulators. Example: there are concerns about the possibility for UK banks to relocate to other countries to avoid disclosure of salaries and bonuses of their employees. More on regulatory arbitrage, see B. Minton, A. Sanders, P. E. Strahan, *Securitization by Banks and Finance Companies: Efficient Financial Contracting or Regulatory Arbitrage?* Ohio State University Papers, 2004, p. 19 et seq.; J. F. Houston, C. Lin, Y. Ma, *Regulatory Arbitrage and International Bank Flows*, Hong Kong 2012; A. K. Shah, *Regulatory Arbitrage Through Financial Innovation*, Colchester 2007, p. 85.

At the general theoretical and legal considerations level, examples of these conflicts take the form of a fundamental conflict between corporate norms of a general and broad, cross-border scope, and the norms of law established as a result of legislative processes. Therefore, since such a conflict is taking place, a reflection on how it should be resolved should be undertaken with a view to eliminating it. It should be determined whether the conflict between politically legitimate legislators, and corporate norm-setters, manifests itself as a disagreement over the regulation of particular spheres of the functioning of societies and individuals by others, or whether there is no such tension, because the attitude adopted so far by publicly empowered lawmakers towards this phenomenon remains passive, or unconscious.

6 Resolving Conflicts of Legal and Corporate Compliance Norms

If the dynamics of social and especially economic change will consolidate the influence of large economic institutions operating across the borders, the result will be the continuation of the existing conflict of corporate and legal norms, and the emergence of new areas of conflict. It is already becoming important to look at the possible ways to resolve such conflicts that arise from differences in the way some areas are regulated, and to recognise that their importance depends to a large extent on the regulated matter, on how it is relevant, vital and, above all, on what it concerns.

Conflicts between the norms created by corporations and the legal norms in force in a given jurisdiction, are observed by practitioners, are numerous in number, and at the same time heterogeneous. Depending on the nature of these collisions, the methods of solving them may be different, and may be achieved with the use of interpretative instruments, although not necessarily interpretation techniques—an example here may be deconstructive reading.[49] Another way of solving these collisions is to use implementation techniques, where concepts are built on the basis of assumptions referring to the thesis of non-determination present both

---

[49] More on deconstructivism where the reading of the normative language happens through the contact with the text, from which the privileged meanings are derived with the use of the valuating notions that reverse the the existing relations. See J. Derrida cited by: M. Zirk-Sadowski, *Wprowadzenie do filozofii prawa*, Warsaw 2011, p. 163.

in realism and in legal postmodernism.[50] Conflicts between these norms must be resolved by conducting a detailed analysis regarding the scope of their application, i.e. by analysing the subject matter of the regulation of the specific content of the norm under examination. Only as a result of such an examination may it be determined whether the norm is in conflict with the rules of law in force in a given jurisdiction.

Another opportunity to remove potential conflicts between corporate norms and the norms of law in various jurisdictions, takes place at the level of interpretation. Of the by Practitioners of law can employ established rules of interpretation, in particular linguistic, teleological and functional ones, and to a lesser extent, systemic ones to determine meaning. Of these methods, systemic interpretation is usually considered the least useful source of an explanation as it does not establish what should be the order and hierarchy in the system of norms of those among them, and also which are determined by corporations in relation to other norms resulting from the provisions of law.[51]

In resolving these conflicts, the rules of interpretation are, of course, helpful. Regardless of this, the practitioner can rediscover the role of legal intuition in solving problems related to the validity of norms. However, resolving conflicts between norms, and more broadly of reaching conclusions concerning the scope and power of their validity, that are solved with the use of legal intuition may reach different conclusions depending on which philosophical starting positions represented by different legal schools are considered.[52]

---

[50] See, e.g., *Critical Legal Studies* and also K. Llewellyn, *The Common Law Tradition: Deciding Appeals*, Boston 1960, pp. 135 and 228.

[51] This complication is also due to the fact that, in the case of corporations operating worldwide, such conflicts of corporate norms occur at the same time when they clash with the legal norms of many countries with different legal traditions and cultures. Lawyers from continental European countries that are members of the European Union have a different approach to this type of collision than those from the United States, Brazil or China. The methods of interpretation and legal conclusions, especially from the perspective of the role and function of evaluation: S. O. Hansson, *The Structure of Values and Norms*, Cambridge 2004, p. 30 et seq.; A. Marmor, *Interpretation and Legal Theory*, Oxford 2005, p. 74 et seq.; M. Safjan, The Universalization of Legal Interpretation [in] J. Jemielniak, P. Mikłaszewicz [ed.] *Interpretation of Law in the Global World: From Particularism to a Universal Approach*, Berlin 2010, p. 107.

[52] More on the subject of the lawyers' intuition by various legal theories T. Pietrzykowski, *Intuicja prawnicza*, Warsaw 2012, p. 162.

However, both the use of interpretative rules and legal intuition presuppose the existence of a certain ideal situation, consisting of leaving the lawyers themselves the power to make decisions on what norms should be applied in the face of conflicts between norms or systems of norms. Business reality, with its multidimensional complexity, the need to guarantee the optimal use of the capital employed; the need to ensure the expected returns on investments; scientific knowledge about risk management; the possibility to immediate verify the truthfulness of the data provided; discrepancies in local interests; matrix management; dispersed stakeholder communities and, last but not least, haste, often makes decisions in this respect less based on legal instruments.[53] On the other hand, the mechanism for reconciling conflicting norms with other problems that result from the day-to-day management of a corporation is much more frequent, so the solution is its escalation to higher management structures, who are authorised to make binding decisions as to the will of the corporation in this respect.[54]

Such solutions allow corporations to operate, in a state of non-compliance with local legal norms, as long as they are not in conflict with the recommendations resulting from their internal axiological normative system. Such a situation, although it satisfies the current interests of the corporation, could rarely be considered satisfactory to supporters of the need for non-legislative regulations to be non-contradicting and consistent with legal regulations.[55]

For those who analyse the changes taking place in law, and who recognise the fact that supranational economic organisations play a norm-forming role, there will be a question whether the fact that entities with both a *dominium* and an *imperium* in relation to large populations

---

[53] The reflections undertaken as part of the economic analysis of the law are useful here. See J. Stelmach, Law and economics jako teoria polityki prawa [in] M. Soniewicka [ed.] *Analiza ekonomiczna w zastosowaniach prawniczych*, Warsaw 2007, pp. 45–66.

[54] Cognitive science calls it a framing phenomenon, which is based on the difference in perception of the situation depending on the perspective of profit or loss. Cf. J. N. Druckman, The Implications of Framing Effects for Citizen Competence, *Political Behavior* 23(3)/2001, p. 225.

[55] About the contemporary school of economic law analysis and its influence on the contemporary interpretation of the interdependence of legal norms and economic processes: J. Stelmach, R. Sarkowicz, *Filozofia prawa XIX i XX wieku*, Cracow 1999, p. 184 et seq. and also A. Bator, W. Gromski, A. Kozak, S. Kaźmierczyk, Z. Pulka, *Wprowadzenie do nauk prawnych. Leksykon tematyczny*, Warsaw 2012, p. 34.

does not, however, constitute a final basis for recognising their right to issue norms regulating the social and economic spheres in which they operate.[56] Therefore, is not the most effective way of removing possible conflicts of corporate and legal norms. Does such a view not allow for a significant approximation to the situation of the desired cohesion of the currently inconsistent legal systems?

---

[56] Recognition of the existence of 'sovereignty outside the legislature', as the legislature outside the sovereignty, see H. L. A. Hart, *Pojęcie prawa*, Warsaw 1998, p. 104 et seq.

CHAPTER 3

Compliance in Financial Institutions: Tasks, Functions and Structure

1 Introduction

When examining compliance norms in financial institutions, it is first of all necessary to present the tasks and the functions performed by the services appointed to manage non-compliance risk in these institutions, and to describe their position in the organisational structures of financial institutions. The complexity of relations within financial institutions, the complications of transactions, the extensive decision-making structures equipped with different powers of competence, and the heterogeneity of solutions adopted in the financial institutions, make such a presentation aimed at facilitating an examination at what compliance is in financial institutions today complicated. An exacting description of the practice of compliance services depends on a correct analysis of issues related to the norms created by financial institutions to ensure compliance. Therefore, it is necessary to present the tasks and the functions performed by compliance services in financial institutions, and their place in the organisational structures of financial institutions. It is from them, in effect, that the content of compliance norms emerges from.

The further analysis is divided into seven subchapters, the first two of which relate to tasks performed by compliance services in financial institutions, with the first subchapter describing the characteristics of these tasks in international institutions, such as financial institutions subject to different regulations in force in many markets at the same time, while the second subchapter analyses particular types of tasks common to all

© The Author(s) 2019
T. Braun, *Compliance Norms in Financial Institutions*,
https://doi.org/10.1007/978-3-030-24966-3_3

financial institutions regardless the geographical scope of their operation. The following three subsections deal with the role of compliance services in financial institutions. Distinguishing the tasks from the functions performed by compliance in financial institutions is not only the key to the conceptual apparatus used in this chapter, but it is also helpful in further analysis of compliance norms.

The functions performed by compliance in financial institutions are understood as the role of ensuring compliance that includes elements that make up their whole management system. Unlike the tasks entrusted to a financial institution, which vary according to the characteristics of the financial institution's activities, the functions performed by the compliance services relate to the categories of purposes for which they were set up, as opposed to other functions performed by other services supporting the management of financial institutions. The advisory function is therefore described in subsection 3, the compliance risk management function in subsection 4 and the compliance control function in subsection 5. The subject described in subchapter 6 are the duties performed by financial institutions compliance services in relation to entities inside and outside financial institutions, such as their employees, shareholders, customers and public entities, including market regulators. Subchapter 7, on the other hand, refers to the position of compliance in the organisational structures of financial institutions, not only taking into account their location, but above all their powers, guarantees of independence, access to management centres and the role they play in relation to other services with similar functions, for example those responsible for managing legal risks.

This chapter reflections on the question whether, in order to determine the content and importance of compliance norms, it is necessary to analyse the tasks and functions performed by compliance services and the place they occupy in the organisational structures of financial institutions. The conclusions were based on the results of research conducted at several international institutions, where the location of compliance in the structures and the tasks imposed on them are reflected in internal documents containing compliance norms created by them. In these studies, access to internal documents defining organisational structures and areas of competence of individual organisational units in the financial institutions were used. Any sections of these documents that contained sensitive commercial information were anonymised.[1]

2   Financial Institutions' Compliance—Specificity of the Regulated Industry

When describing the tasks performed by compliance services of financial institutions, and analysing the scope of regulations created by them, one should first of all pay attention to the characteristic feature of modern financial institutions, which is a high degree of regulation of financial institutions activity. This applies not only to legal regulations relating to financial institutions, but also to regulations issued by administrative supervisory authorities, referred to as market regulators.[2] The tendency to directly influence the activity of financial institutions through both casuistically formulated laws and detailed supervisory regulations has been maintained for many years.[3]

An intensive regime of regulation poses a number of challenges for financial institutions, for which compliance with the law and supervisory recommendations is a prerequisite for conducting business. Some of them are highlighted further in this book. These challenges relate in particular to international financial institutions, operating in a complex legal, regulatory, social, political, etc., reality. Among these challenges there are the following, the list of which will be helpful for further analysing of the scope of compliance norms in corporations. These challenges relate to three groups of problems identified below.

[1] Among the non-confidential documents there are most often documents which are declarations on corporate social responsibility, which are at the same time recommendations of compliance by employees with the principles set out therein, as well as various codes of ethics, which at the same time are a marketing instrument for shaping a positive image of a corporation. Other non-classified documents also include corporate governance rules and the procurement rules provided to cooperating companies.

[2] On the modern role of market regulators in relation to companies see K. K. Reed, A Look at Firm—Regulator Exchanges: Friendly Enough or Too Friendly, *Business and Society* 48(2)/2009, p. 150.

[3] Criticizing the tendency for market regulators to take too casuistic a stance and the counter-effectiveness of such a method see W. D. Loppit, The Neoliberal Era and the Financial Crisis in the Light of Social Structure Accumulation Theory, *Review of Radical Political Economics* 46(2)/2014, p. 142.

The first set of challenges is precisely to ensure that financial institutions adapt their activities to all the legal and regulatory norms that apply to them. The difficulty here lies in the multi-source origin of these obligations arising simultaneously from different types of norms issued (and subject to constant change) in different places. It is in this context of constant changes that business planning is difficult to accomplish. These difficulties result from at least the following four groups of factors.

a. The supervisory authorities of the countries in which the major international financial institutions have their registered offices, which are obliged to apply, and which have been recognised as being of systemic importance for the whole world economic order issue particularly restrictive regulations.
b. The norms of compliance, especially for international financial institutions, also apply to ensure there are compliance with recommendations of foreign regulators in so far as they relate to the activities of such financial institutions.[4]
c. In case of the simultaneous cross-border effectiveness of norms originating from different jurisdictions, compliance norms in financial institutions also provide for binding interpretations allowing financial institutions to act in accordance with them. Issues related to the application of interpretation rules, which respond to the volatility and complexity of the global legal and regulatory environment, while taking into account the economic interests of financial institutions, constitute one of the most interesting and at the same time complex issues being the subject of regulation of compliance norms in financial institutions operating simultaneously in many markets.
d. Due to the specific, global and de facto binding nature of the Basel Committee on Financial institutions Supervision recommendations, a practical problem within the scope of compliance regulation is also the control of the mechanisms in place within financial

---

[4] Interestingly about the dynamics of regulatory intervention in the activity of banks in global markets, especially in the context of ensuring control over the management of different types of risk in banks. por. *Evolving Banking Regulation: Is the End in Sight*, KPMG 2014 EMA Edition, p. 6 et seq.

institutions to ensure that the activities of financial institutions comply in particular with these recommendations.[5]

When analysing the content of the regulations imposed on financial institutions, compliance obligations can be divided into four types, as follows.[6]

a. Regulations containing recommendations relating to the market structure, the purpose of which is to ensure that the activities of financial institutions take place within entities separated by their risk profile (financial wholesale regulations).[7]
b. Regulations containing prudential norms relating to the way prudential regulations should be managed within financial institutions (prudential regulations).[8]

---

[5] The difficulty here is largely due to the Basel Committee's introduction of new solutions imposing so-called prudential obligations on banks, particularly with a view to increasingly stringent control of the processes involved in various types of risk. This was also followed by European Union regulations, including in particular Directive of the Directive 2013/36/EU of the European Parliament and of the Council of 26 June 2013 on access to the activity of credit institutions and the prudential supervision of credit institutions and investment firms, amending Directive 2002/87/EC and repealing Directives 2006/48/EC and 2006/49/EC Text with EEA relevance, *OJ L 176, 27.6.2013, pp. 338–436* and Regulation of the European Parliament and of the Council (EU) No. 575/2013 of 26 June 2013 Regulation (EU) No. 575/2013 of the European Parliament and of the Council of 26 June 2013 on prudential requirements for credit institutions and investment firms and amending Regulation (EU) No. 648/2012 Text with EEA relevance, *OJ L 176, 27.6.2013, pp. 1–337*.

[6] It should be noted that these are groups of regulations that can be described as systemic in the sense that they apply to all banks because of the role that they play in the entire financial system by virtue of the nature of their activities. For regulation in relation to the exercise of oversight of systemic risk in the European Union, including inter alia the structure, objectives and tasks of the European Systemic Risk Board, see more M. Fedorowicz, *Nadzór nad rynkiem finansowym w Unii Europejskiej*, Warsaw 2013, p. 130 et seq.

[7] See the report prepared by a team chaired by Erkki Liikanen on 2 October 2012 under the auspices of the European Commission containing a proposal for structural reform in banking "Final Report High-Level Expert Group on Reforming the Structure of the EU Banking Sector," http://ec.europa.eu/internal_market/bank/docs/high-level_expert_group/report_en.pdf (download 10 November 2018).

[8] See Directive 2013/36/EU of the European Parliament and of the Council of 26 June 2013 on access to the activity of credit institutions and the prudential supervision of credit institutions and investment firms, amending Directive 2002/87/EC and repealing Directives 2006/48/EC and 2006/49/EC Text with EEA relevance, *OJ L 176, 27.6.2013, pp. 338–436*.

c. Regulations concerning the way financial institutions act in relation to customers when offering them products (conduct regulations).[9]
d. Regulations on preventing the circulation of money related to criminal activity (protection of the financial system by preventing money laundering and corruption—financial crime regulations).[10]

The primary challenge for financial institutions operating simultaneously in many markets is to build organisational structures in line with the applicable corporate governance requirements. Differences in local legal solutions in this respect, that are usually related to the need to maintain the autonomy of decisions taken in individual markets, complicates the simultaneous need to maintain control over the activities carried out in individual countries. This complexity is reflected in the two problems indicated below.

a. The expectations of the regulators specify that the corporate governance model adopted by financial institutions should be a factor guaranteeing compliance with the entire normative order constituting its environment. However, this usually only applies to the legal and regulatory environment in a given jurisdiction, and therefore these expectations may not take into account the degree of complexity resulting from operating simultaneously in different jurisdictions.[11]

---

[9] See Directive 2004/39/EC of the European Parliament and of the Council of 21 April 2004 on markets in financial instruments amending Council Directives 85/611/EEC and 93/6/EEC and Directive 2000/12/EC of the European Parliament and of the Council and repealing Council Directive 93/22/EEC (MiFID), *OJ L 145, 30.4.2004, pp. 1–44* and also Commission Delegated Regulation (EU) No. 148/2013 of 19 December 2012 supplementing Regulation (EU) No. 648/2012 of the European Parliament and of the Council on OTC derivatives, central counterparties and trade repositories with regard to regulatory technical standards on the minimum details of the data to be reported to trade repositories Text with EEA relevance, *OJ L 52, 23.2.2013, pp. 1–10* (EMIR).

[10] *The United Kingdom Bribery Act (An Act to make provisions about offences relating to bribery and for connected purposes, 2010 Chapter 23 of 4 April 2010); The United States Foreign Corrupt Practices Act (Public Law No. 95-213, S. 305 of 19 December 1977); The Hong Kong Prevention of Bribery Ordinance (An Act to make further and better provision for the prevention of bribery and for purposes necessary thereto or connected therewith, HK Law 1997 Chapter 201 of 30 June 1997); The USA Patriot Act: Preserving Life and Liberty (Uniting and Strengthening America by Providing Appropriate Tools Required to Intercept and Obstruct Terrorism, Public Law No. 98-1 and 357-66 of 25 October 2001).*

[11] B. M. Hutter, *Compliance: Regulation and Environment*, Oxford 1997, p. 196.

b. Proportionately to the systemic importance, size, complexity of the financial products offered and the scope of activity, recommendations concerning strengthening and independence of the internal departments responsible for ensuring compliance in financial institutions are formulated with respect to financial institutions, which are of interest from the point of view of this study.

A specific group of challenges for global institutions is to build appropriate mechanisms to ensure uniformity of action despite, and sometimes even against, local differences. These challenges, which are divided into three groups below, are all the greater as they should take place while ensuring that the normative obligations arising from the law and supervisory regulations are not violated.

a. Apart from the above mentioned legal and supervisory regulations, among the norms defining the way financial institutions operate, there are also guidelines, which are international or even global norms of conduct.[12]
b. The challenge of needing to ensure a lawful and well-managed flow of information within the framework of international activities conducted by financial institutions.
c. The challenge of ensuring that account is taken of the fact that financial institutions activities are carried out in different, often very different, legal cultures.

It is important to consider the complexity of the tasks performed by compliance services in financial institutions at present, to pay attention to those financial institutions whose activities are of an international nature.[13] These institutions carry on such a complex business activity that, depending on the nature and complexity of the services offered, the products, the type of customers to which they are addressed and, in particular, the scale of their operations, some of these institutions have

---

[12] See, e.g., W. C. Frederick, *Values, Nature, and Culture in the American Corporation*, Oxford 1995, p. 30 et seq.

[13] Cf. W. Twining, *General Jurisprudence: Understanding Law from a Global Perspective*, Cambridge 2008, p. 116.

a systemic importance.[14] Those systemically important financial institutions are those whose proper functioning is vital for the smooth running of the entire global financial system and, conversely, the emergence of irregularities in the activities of those institutions may have serious consequences for the safe functioning of that system.[15] These systemically important institutions are therefore usually referred to as the group of the largest financial institutions mentioned by name. However, most financial institutions, regardless of whether or not they are included in this group, may have a systemic importance not by themselves, but by the very fact that they participate in financial trading on global markets.

In general, therefore, the proper functioning of financial institutions, especially, but not exclusively, the most important ones, is of vital importance for the smooth operation of the entire international financial system.

Successive cyclical crises on the financial markets, resulting from the malfunctioning of individual, systemically important financial institutions, reveal the need for constant identification of all potential threats that could negatively affect the correctness of their operations. In practice, there are two main mechanisms, which are key to pre-emptively identifying these risks, and which have tools at their disposal to help preventing possible irregularities. One of them is the supervisory tools of market regulators, and the other is internal self-control procedures, which include the possibility for these financial institutions to create internal compliance norms.[16] This is why the regulatory role of the administrative supervisory authorities, which control and ensure the safety of the financial systems and use tools to ensure that financial institutions operate prudently, as well as the similar self-regulatory role of internal compliance by the financial institutions themselves, is so important.[17]

---

[14] These are the Systemicly Important Financial Institutions (SIFIS).

[15] R. P. Buckley, *International Financial System: Policy and Regulation*, Alphen am den Rijn 2008, p. 28.

[16] A. Baker, The New Political Economy of the Macroprudential Ideational Shift, *New Political Economy* 1(18)/2013, p. 114.

[17] Apart from the subject of this discussion, the description of the phenomenon of accepting, also by non-financial and even non-commercial global organizations, the obligation to develop compliance norms remains beyond the scope of this discussion. About this: A. J. Meese, N. B. Oman, Hobby Lobby, Corporate Law, and the Theory of the Firm, *Harvard Law Review* 5/2014, p. 275.

The last crises and turmoil in the financial markets resulted in the spectacular financial institutional bankruptcy, and subsequent rehabilitation of several large financial institutions. Although each was the result of slightly different direct causes, it was subsequently shown that deficiencies in the functioning of compliance processes played a significant role.[18] The obvious and expected response to this state of affairs has been an unprecedented and accelerated intensification of regulatory efforts to ensure the functioning of an independent, strong compliance services within financial institutions, the task of which should be to guarantee even more prudent financial institutions operations and, consequently, a more secure financial system. As a result of these activities, we have created legal norms, but also issued supervisory regulations imposing many new obligations on financial institutions.[19] Due to the characteristics of financial institutions activity, in particular due to the scale and scope of operations of financial institutions considered to be systemically important, i.e. the fact that they take place simultaneously in many different markets, and thus in many different jurisdictions and different legal cultures, the density of the regulatory space surrounding financial institutions is characterised by an even greater casuistry than before. It is not very elegant, but it is an effective method of determining duties, the content of which remains legible despite local cultural and legal differences. A significant part of these regulations relates to the provision by financial institutions of appropriate self-regulation and self-control processes, the ways of identifying risks and methods of their prevention. It also includes instruments to ensure that compliance services are empowered to participate in the identification and management of these risks.

When discussing the challenges faced by compliance services in financial institutions, attention should be paid to the tasks, and the

---

[18] R. M. Steinberg, *Governance, Risks Management, and Compliance: It Can't Happen to Us Avoiding Corporate Disaster While Driving Success*, New Jersey 2011, p. 30. About the controversies on financial crises see R. Gwiazdowski, *A nie mówiłem? Dlaczego nastąpił kryzys i jak naszybciej z niego wyjść*, Prohibita 2012, p. 363.

[19] Cf. T. Stawecki, *Prawo i zaufanie. Refleksja czasu kryzysu* [in] J. Oniszczuk [ed.] *Normalność i kryzys – jedność czy różnorodność. Refleksje filozoficzno-prawne i ekonomiczno-społeczne w ujęciu aksjologicznym*, Warsaw 2010, p. 115.

importance attached to compliance norms in these institutions. These tasks and their importance are not only the result of the legal and regulatory environment directly related to how financial institutions' compliance mechanisms should work. They are also the result of the will expressed by various forms of other entities, external to financial institutions, who are interested in the fact that the compliance activity is conducted in a suitably robust manner by compliance services.[20] This is because there is a widely accepted belief that a robust compliance service that is equipped with the appropriate control instruments is necessary for the safe operation of financial institutions.[21] Not only do they wish to comply with the applicable laws, but they also expect compliance with other norms. What other norms are involved depends on the nature of the stakeholders.[22] These may be entities directly involved in how these financial institutions operate—shareholders, employees, customers, but also other entities that are completely external to financial institutions, such as the media, non-governmental industry and customer organisations, etc.[23]

---

[20] About other entities influencing how corporations operate, including their impact on compliance see F. den Hond, F. G. A. de Bakker, Ideologically Motivated Activism: How Activists Groups Influence Corporate Social Change Activities, *Academy of Management* 32(3)/2007, p. 901 et seq. as well as H. Cronqvist, R. Fahlenbrach, Large Shareholders and Corporate Policies, *The Review of Financial Studies* 22(10)/2009, p. 394.

[21] On the tasks of control functions in banks and the impact of the control function of compliance on business decisions see J. Heckman, S. Navarro-Losano, Usining Matching, Instrumental Variables, and Control Functions to Estimate Economic Choice Models, *The Review of Economics and Statistics* 86(1)/2004, p. 30.

[22] On the cascading of unpopular norms within the organization in response to external social expectations, and consequently also political and further, regulatory expectations see C. Bicchieri, *The Grammar of Society: The Nature and Dynamics of the Social Norms*, Cambridge 2006, p. 176.

[23] About the influence of opinion leaders and the methods they use to influence internal compliance regulations in international corporations see G. Hilary, *Regulations Through Social Norms*, London 2014, p. 11.

3 The Tasks of Compliance Services in Financial Institutions

Depending on the type of these expectations, the profile of the activity conducted by a given financial institution, the industries and markets in which it operates, or even its history, the tasks of compliance services are different. They are determined both by the internally formulated profile of activity of a given financial institution, and by entities external to the financial institution, as referred to above. As a result, various spheres of financial institutions activity remain within the sphere of reference of compliance.[24] In the following subsections, we will examine the ten groups of tasks imposed on compliance services, and the areas to which the compliance norms relate, with particular emphasis on the specificities resulting from the characteristics of the complex regulated market, which is the international financial industry today. For the purpose of this book, it has been assumed that a task is a concept which refers to the issues related to compliance activities in response to the challenges posed to financial institutions by regulators.

The first task is the expectation, formulated by entities external to financial institutions, that they should ensure the involvement of compliance services in the creation of norms appropriate to regulating the internal organisational order of financial institutions. The need to create compliance norms relating to corporate governance in corporations in general, and financial institutions in particular, is one of those areas where it is particularly clear that they are due to various reasons simultaneously. These are:

a. legal norms,
b. recommendations derived from regulatory norms issued by administrative supervisors external to corporations,
c. the expectations expressed by organised interest groups,
d. guidelines formulated by the persons managing the corporation.[25]

---

[24] About the evolution of compliance in banking see R. Jakubowski, Rozwój funkcji compliance w polskim sektorze bankowym od 1989 r., *Monitor prawa bankowego* 11/2013, p. 58.

[25] Cf. G. S. Drori, Governed by Governance: The New Prims of Organizational Change [in] G. S. Drori, J. W. Meyer, H. Hwang, *Globalization and Organization World Society and Organizational Change*, Oxford 2006, p. 91.

Interestingly, due to the complexity of the relations in which a financial institutions corporation is involved, with different interests expressed in different norms from those entities, there is often a collision between the formal and legal requirements concerning the management of a financial institutions company, which results from the norms derived from local laws, and the expectations of the owners who are interested in the existence of a management structure that guarantees quick and direct influence on the way the financial institution conducts its business.[26]

One of the ways of responding to such conflicts is the second task of compliance services, which is to build flexible organisational structures that are compliant with the law in such a way that through their construction they facilitate an effective impact on the activity of companies. This often means the emergence of parallel matrix management structures, which, while not ignoring the formal internal links between bodies and organisational units, are imposed on them to form an independent network of powers and responsibilities.[27] A special variant of such solutions is project management, which remains even more independent of the permanent organisational structures. It is characterised by the appointment of appropriately empowered project teams for a predetermined period of time and equipping them with separate funds, the manner of spending and allocation of which are determined in advance.

The way to efficiently solve unavoidable collisions resulting from the complexity of relations arising in this way is to grant advisory, interpretation, control, and often also decision-making powers to compliance services operating within financial institutions. The tasks of compliance in such conditions are, therefore, also to create norms, which are to ensure not only compliance with norms resulting from locally binding regulations in the field of company law and financial institutions law, but also those which formulate orders which at the same time

---

[26] Cf. R. W. Hamilton, R. D. Freer, *The Law of Corporations in a Nutshell*, St. Paul 2011, p. 190.

[27] The empowerment of global financial institutions, the scope and effects of the exercise of powers held, the resulting liability, the ways of legitimizing the actual influence and the response of regulators to these phenomena see, e.g., G. R. D. Underhill, X. Zhang, Business Authority and Global Financial Governance: Challenges to Accountability and Legitimacy [in] T. Porter, K. Ronit [ed.] *The Challenges of Global Business Authority: Democratic Renewal, Stalemate, or Decay?* New York 2010, p. 117.

ensure the operation of parallel organisational structures facilitating the management of a global organisation, regardless of formal, national, local structures.[28]

The difficulty in ensuring the correctness of such rules from the point of view of local regulations lies in the sensitivity of this matter, which is related to the fact that in this area these norms often collide with the expectations of shareholders requiring, above all, efficient management of the entire institution. The most extreme examples are situations where decision-making centres are transferred from a formally existing local government to a higher level, for example a regional level. The proper structuring of corporate governance by compliance services in conditions of diverse expectations is an important and complex task, as much as it is inevitable.

A description of how project structures are constructed that subvert the typical hierarchical corporate governance system in international institutions, assumes the creation of management structures at local, regional and global levels, in which participants are selected on the basis of their usefulness for the implementation of specific projects.[29]

---

[28] More on the concept of the compliance function as a standard-setter in a global and multipolar normative environment constituting the contemporary environment of economic institutions see K. D. Wolf, A. Flohs, L. Rieth, S. Schwindenhammer, *The Role of Business in Global Governance: Corporations as Norm-Entrepreneurs*, London 2010, p. 29.

[29] Project teams are built in such a way that they are composed of members depending on the competence, nature of the project, its scope, etc. Thus, in general, in the case of global organizations conducting international projects, the project team is composed of people with different specializations working both at the local level, generally responsible for implementing the arrangements, and at the supra-local level, who coordinate these tasks and ensure consistency of their implementation in different countries. In practice, there may be different models of organizations of this type of task forces created in any configuration, which are almost always slightly different. The common feature, however, is that they largely omit formal structures of official subordination, "flatten" organizational structures for the duration of projects, operate independently of hierarchical organizational degrees, or even ownership ties, thus shortening the decision-making time, concentrating employees on tasks and facilitating their efficient implementation. There are many such project teams in each corporation at the same time—at different levels and for different parts of the business. In such a situation, it is not difficult to find cases of actions contrary to corporate governance requirements, in which the role of compliance is to create appropriate procedures ensuring, for example, the involvement of relevant decision-making bodies in making final decisions accepting decisions made by project teams. Typical examples are projects aimed at implementing new financial products. In working on such projects, the persons involved are equipped with appropriate competences representing various areas of the bank (sales, risk, finance, IT, lawyers, etc.). They work together on the parameters of

Ensuring compliance of the financial institution's operations with supervisory regulations is the third group of tasks to which the compliance services with respect to the development of compliance norms refer.[30] Due to the fact that multinational corporations manage strategic sectors of the economy that are important from the point of view of important social and economic values, such as financial security, the certainty of turnover, preventing the introduction of criminal funds into the financial system, etc., states create systemic safeguards in order to regulate the way in which corporations operate in selected areas in order to ensure respect for these values. They consist in appointing appropriately empowered administrative bodies appointed to carry out supervisory tasks, including, in particular, those authorised to issue norms for the protection of principles, interests and values important from the point of view of the state. However, one of the consequences of this state of affairs is the emergence of various areas of conflict of interest between corporations on the one hand and market regulators on the other.

In addition, multi-market financial institutions corporations are trying to relocate proven practices in some jurisdictions to other locations where they operate.[31] In response, host countries secure themselves by regulating the functioning of corporations on their own

---

such a new product, prepare appropriate plans and calculations, and set a schedule for their implementation. Ultimately, however, it is up to the management bodies of the institution to decide whether to accept the results of such a project. The advantage of creating project teams is that it enables selected employees to focus on selected project tasks. It is usually connected with shifting the importance of the tasks performed by them from the existing, everyday tasks to those of a project nature, but also shortening the paths of agreements and simultaneously taking into account in the implementation of a specific project the participation of all specialties necessary for further practical implementation of the objectives of this project. The disadvantage is the creation of a parallel, often unclear network of informal organizational links, especially when the same people participate in many projects at the same time. Organizations operating in the public space, especially financial institutions, where transparent organizational structures and clear definition of the responsibility of individuals for management is a regulatory requirement, face this type of collision on a daily basis, which in practice is resolved in favor of maintaining project team structures.

[30] M. P. Malloy, *Banking Law and Regulation*, New York 2004, p. 17.

[31] More on the stages of development of the process of globalization of legal systems and what stage a given phenomenon may be in the correlation of world regulations see M. Wolf, *Why Globalization Works*, Boston 2005, p. 97.

markets using their own normative regulatory instruments—supervisory recommendations.[32]

Efficient coping with these complexities is a requirement for compliance services. On the part of corporations, this applies not only to corporations that are international financial institutions, but also to attempts to act as regulatory arbiters by transferring decision-making centres to jurisdictions where the regulatory requirements imposed on corporations are less restrictive. In turn, the response to these attempts on the part of the regulators is to establish new regulatory mechanisms, mainly normative ones, that consist of ensuring that the international scope of supervisory regulations and sanction the international cooperation of regulators consisting of the efficient exchange of information concerning financial institutions operating in their area of competence.[33]

This can be achieved by means of several solutions. The first is the appointment of cross-border regulators with competence beyond certain jurisdictions by means of agreements concluded directly between countries. The second way is to initiate self-regulatory activities developed through agreements developed within the structures of existing international organisations. The third method is the mutual recognition of the competence of individual national regulators to issue regulatory norms with cross-border coverage.

The normative reality, as interpreted by compliance is created also by means of non-administrative methods of their impact. This applies in particular to the implementation of informal task aimed at protecting the aforementioned values carried out by the regulators in addition to their official tasks resulting from their formal mandates. Thus, the regulatory environment of a Polish financial institution, which is a part of a financial institution conducting financial activity in Europe at the same time, in particular on the London market, in the United States and on other global markets, also includes the regulations of the Polish financial institutions' supervisory authorities, but also European, British and American ones. In such a situation, the services responsible for ensuring compliance, apart from the local regulators, are not only European, British, but

---

[32] See J. R. Barth, G. Caprio Jr., R. Levine, Bank Regulation and Supervision: What Works Best? *Journal of Financial Intermediation* 13(2)/2004, p. 206.

[33] More on banking systems see C. Kosikowski, System Bankowy [in] C. Kosikowski, E. Ruśkowski [ed.] *Finanse publiczne i prawo finansowe*, Warsaw 2008, p. 204.

also indirectly American regulators, and in the long run, even those from distant jurisdictions.[34]

Regardless of whether it results from regulatory recommendations external to the corporation or by virtue of autonomous decisions taken by financial corporations, it is the task of compliance services to ensure compliance with these regulations. They ensure compliance not only because of its importance, but above all because of the specificity requiring increasing professionalisation, has been singled out in international corporations, in particular in international financial institutions, in recent times, to a group of autonomous tasks supporting their business activity. This support is expressed equally through the implementation of advisory, management and control tasks performed in connection with emerging issues relating to the adjustment of the business to the system of norms applicable to these corporations. These tasks are carried out in areas as diverse as anti-money laundering, reputation risk management or building compliance awareness within international corporations among its employees.[35]

The fourth group of tasks of compliance services consists of comprehending and ensuring the adjustment of financial institutions' activities

---

[34] In practice, compliance services in an international bank operating in an EU country must take into account the normative environment, including regulatory environment, and thus also supervisory recommendations of the local regulatory authorities, such as the country financial supervision authority, the central bank, the office of competition and consumer protection, the general inspector of financial information, the authority of personal data protection. Independently of this, compliance tasks are influenced by European regulators, including the European Banking Authority (EBA), the European Securities and Markets Authorities (ESMA), the European Insurance and Occupational Pensions Authorities (EIOPA), the European Supervisory Authorities (ESA), the European Systemic Risk Board (ESRB), the European Securities and Markets Authority (ESRB) and the European Securities and Markets Authority (EIOPA), the European Systemic Risk Board (ESRB), but also the most important regulators of major financial markets with cross-border reach, especially the UK and US, including the US Securities and Exchange Commission (SEC), the Financial Industry Regulatory Authority (FIRA), the US Federal Reserve System (FED), the Federal Deposit Insurance Corporation (FDIC), the National Credit Union Administration (NCUA), the United Kingdom's Financial Conduct Authority (FCA), the Bank of England Prudential Regulation Authority (PRA), the Royal Treasury Office (HM Tresury).

[35] On the subject of building compliance awareness within an organization as a way to ensure normative coherence and normative compliance of its conduct in the global space see R. V. Aguilera, G. Jackson, The Cross-National Diversity of Corporate Governance: Dimensions and Determinants, *Academy of Management Review* 39(4)/2014, *passim*.

to various types of soft law norms. In this case, the difficulty is all the greater because, regardless of legal norms or supervisory regulations, the proper identification of norms resulting from soft regulations is important in corporate activity.[36]

The issues arising from the practical consequences of such rules are of particular importance in the case of multinational groups, where such rules are an effective way of influencing the functioning of these companies. This is done, for example, by means of the global and international norms of conduct mentioned above, which are set by the corporations themselves.[37] These norms formulate recommendations that concern both quality and, above all, the rules of conduct that are binding on corporate employees, regardless of the jurisdiction in which the business is conducted. At the same time, in such situations there is often a collision between the need to unify the functioning of capital groups, and the regulations of local law.

In such a case, the role of compliance services in interpreting norms, which would make it possible to remove any uncertainties as to the meaning of their content, or to eliminate conflicts between the content of norms resulting from local regulations and norms contained in corporate guidelines included in the global norms of operation of a given corporation, is of crucial importance.[38] These and other related issues are settled not only with the use of well-established legal interpretative tools, but also with the use of norms contained in internal guidelines and codes of conduct.[39]

---

[36] On the subject of the role of soft law standards in banking law regulations, see R. Kaszubski, op. cit., p. 18. Also soft law in the broader context of the financial market see Z. Ofiarski, Rola soft law w regulacji rynku finansowego na przykładzie rekomendacji i wytycznych Komisji Nadzoru Finansowego [in] A. Jurkowska-Zeidler, M. Olszak [ed.] *Prawo rynku finansowego. Doktryna, instytucji, praktyka*, Warsaw 2016, p. 137 et seq.

[37] More about global, also called general, compliance standards cf. D. Pupke, *Compliance and Corporate Performance*, Hamburg 2007, pp. 112–124.

[38] A separate issue is how, regardless of the role of compliance as the guardian of compliance with global standards, the same service is subject to unification, "standardization" cf. S. Bleke, D. Hortensius, The Development of a Global Standard on Compliance Management, *Business Compliance* 2/2014, p. 316 et seq.

[39] Uniformity of norms of corporate behavior is not the only manifestation of the globalization of financial law. Another is the unification of documentation, especially for complex transactions, such as project finance, which has gone so far as to describe this phenomenon as the emergence of global contract law. See A. Golden, The Future of Financial Regulation: The Role of the Courts [in] MacNeil, O'Brien [ed.] *The Future of Financial Regulation*, Oxford 2010, p. 86.

The fifth group of tasks performed by compliance services results from issues related to the growing need for global information exchange within the corporation. One of the consequences of complex ownership structures that characterise international corporations is the need for efficient access to precise management information that enables the weffective management of global companies, such as international financial institutions. However, due to the specific nature of this information, the different regimes and degrees of protection, and issues related to the flow of information, it constitutes a complex area of issues for compliance services. This complexity results not only from the diversity of the different jurisdictions, but often also from the importance or sensitivity of the information to be protected.

In this area, the influence of regulators who are able to formulate expectations towards these entities on an ongoing basis, depending on the needs identified at the moment, is particularly strong, and thus complementing the existing regulations. However, regardless of the difficulties mentioned above, it is a necessity for the proper functioning of international corporations with complex ownership structures, including financial institutions, to ensure an uninterrupted flow of up-to-date information necessary for proper business planning. In this context, there arises an issue of particular interest concerning conflicting laws, which goes beyond the mere right of access to certain information that are justified by the interests of the owner, i.e. the right of the owner to influence decisions taken by companies belonging to a corporation but which are separate economic entities.[40]

From the perspective of the local law in a given territory, insofar as these entities are not branches but separate financial institutions operated in the form of locally registered companies, the direct authorities of an entity are usually the only bodies formally empowered to take decisions both on business plans and on their implementation. Therefore, access to information in this area and the possibility to participate in shaping decisions in these areas should only take place through actions taken in accordance with the letter and spirit defining the principles of corporate governance.

---

[40] The same problem, albeit in different manifestations, exists in many jurisdictions in principle regardless of the type of business pursued and is not limited to financial institution activities only. See D. Pupke, op.cit., p. 45.

In practice, however, these relations are shaped in a slightly different way. Naturally, especially in the case of financial institutions, this type of collision of local norms with the expectations of the owners remains a central concern of the regulators. The need for transparency in the decision-making processes, and compliance with rules related to the control of access to information, may have a direct and significant impact on the stability and security of the financial system, which these regulators are guardians.[41]

The sixth group of tasks performed by compliance services is related to ensuring the legal transmission of information and financial statements within capital groups. A special element of business strategies are the financial plans and budgets of corporations. In particular, capital plans which provide for how the financing of the activities is ensured and whether individual companies operating in a given area are adequately recapitalised, and therefore whether their establishment will have an impact on the stability of the financial system.[42] Also, in this respect, compliance norms provide for compliance services to be active in ensuring that information is provided when the circumstances arise, which raise concerns about the provision of adequate capital resources necessary for a financial institution to operate in accordance with regulatory requirements, and in a sustainable manner. While strategic and financial planning within financial institutions assumes the flow of information in the phase preceding the implementation of specific business ventures, at subsequent stages there is a need to provide information related to the settlement of the companies' activities.[43] In such situations, not only the

---

[41] Protection against outflow of information and impact on financial institution activity by market regulators see, e.g., R. Boyer, From Shareholder Value to CEO Power: The Paradox of the 1990s, *Competition and Change* 9/2005, p. 8.

[42] Here, too, a separate issue arises with regard to the accounting standards adopted in each country. While International Financial Reporting Standards (IFRS) are the predominant standard in most European countries, and Generally Accepted Accounting Principles (GAAP) in the United States, India and Japan, many countries still have national accounting policies that differ from each other and affect the ultimate values reported in financial reporting. Corporations operating in multiple markets must ensure that their financial reports comply with both local and home market regulations and the necessary standardization. See D. Tweedie, T. R. Seidenstein, Setting a Global Standard: The Case for Accounting Convergence, *New Journal for International Law and Business* 25/2005, p. 590.

[43] About reporting and the need to create model normative solutions within global financial organizations to enable effective information flow: M. Eggert, *Compliance Management in Financial Industries: A Model-Based Business Process and Reporting Perspective*, Heidelberg 2014, p. 49.

transfer of information protected by business confidentiality, but also the flow of personal data, as well as other data, including data protected by special provisions, in particular data protected by the confidentiality regulations of financial institutions, may be requested.

The activities of multinational companies in one country are also affected by the legislation of countries where other companies belonging to the same capital groups operate. This is the seventh group of tasks facing compliance services operating in corporations operating in many markets simultaneously. They must ensure that financial institutions' activities are lawful, taking into account the cross-border effectiveness of national law in corporate activities. In practice, the performance of these tasks has different foundations and takes different forms.[44] The most common of these is the introduction into the legal order of one country of norms which oblige entities operating in that country to comply with certain provisions and to ensure that the same duties are also performed by other entities in the group to which the entity belongs. In an even more extensive form, such obligations can be imposed not only on entities within the same group, but also on service providers or even customers.

This inevitable leads to conflict between norms within international economic structures, both at the theoretical level and, as a result, at the practical level.[45] Compliance services, whose tasks are to ensure that the corporation operates in accordance with the applicable norms, have an obvious difficulty in this case. They must help in resolving a given collision, taking into account the interests of the corporation, understood not only as the need to ensure the expected benefits, but above all to protect the long-term safe functioning of the institution. In the process of making such decisions, a complication is built in, which consists of the fact that compliance as a rule means compliance with both the norms of law in force in a given area, as well as with other norms, which the corporation expects to apply. In the type of situation described here, existing collisions in practice may become irreconcilable, unless the primacy of one type of norm is clearly defined over another. It is worth recalling at

---

[44] See, e.g., A. Zorska, *Korporacje transnarodowe: przemiany, oddziaływania, wyzwania*, Warsaw 2007, p. 43 et seq.

[45] C. R. O'Kelly Jr., R. B. Thompson, *Corporations and Other Business Associations: Cases and Materials*, Boston 1996, p. 160.

this point that practice has shown that it is not at all obvious that, in the opinion of corporate managers, such a primacy can always be enjoyed by the norms of a given national law.

The eighth group of tasks of compliance services operating within international financial institutions, i.e. operating on regulated markets within different legal systems, is the impact of cultural differences on the resolution of normative issues in these corporations. The essence of corporations is their international character and the cross-border scope of business.[46] As a consequence, one of the most important groups of factors influencing the complexity of compliance management in corporations is the practical impact of different legal cultures on the way in which these corporations operate. The related issues are discussed in more detail in chapter four of this book, and therefore we will only briefly discuss the issue here to maintain the completeness of the list of tasks performed by compliance services in financial institutions.

A phenomenon which is the subject of separate research is the interdependence between the regulations and traditions of different legal systems, and the resulting different legal cultures. The sources of the formation of separate legal cultures are, of course, complex and go beyond the nature and tradition of the normative regulations themselves within a given system. They are also created by such factors as historical experience, the social processes taking place in a given area, axiological conditions to which a given community refers, and even technological achievements, or economic aspirations of societies. They are also influenced by the scientific achievements of legal doctrine, jurisprudence, as well as the power of influence of other legal systems. In this context, it is particularly interesting to examine practical examples of the differences in the functioning of a corporation due to the place of business. In particular, this applies to differences in the methods of the implementation and interpretation of corporate norms depending on the jurisdiction in which it takes place.[47] International financial institutions, like few others, have to face the challenge of adapting to all the above-mentioned

---

[46] P. Molyneux, Bank Performance, Risk and Firm Financing [in] M. Aoki, K. Binmare, S. Deakin, H. Gintis [ed.] *Complexity and Institutions: Markets, Norms and Corporations*, London 2012, p. 68.

[47] This is the interpretation of norms in relation to cultural conditions in the classic sense in which Fuller proposed it, pointing out that it is a process of adapting the content of the norm to the presumed requirements and values of the social group to which it is to refer see L. L. Fuller, *Anatomia prawa*, Lublin 1968, p. 91.

cultural variables affecting the normative order, which in turn influences the way of doing business.[48]

As indicated above, compliance in financial institutions also means ensuring that their activities are in line with the recommendations of the Basel Committee on Financial Institutions Supervision regarding risk management. This is the ninth group of tasks performed by compliance services in financial institutions. The Basel Committee has published a framework document on compliance risk and compliance functions in financial institutions, with a view to clarifying the meaning of the notion of compliance risk management and, at the same time, with a view to improving solutions for financial institutions supervision and the dissemination of good practice in financial institutions. This document grants specific powers to supervisors to control the way compliance functions in financial institutions. It asserts that financial institutions supervision should have both the knowledge and disciplinary tools to effectively supervise the effectiveness of compliance policies in financial institutions. It should also be able to order the introduction of procedures relating to that policy with a view to its practical implementation. In addition, supervisors should be equipped with regulatory tools to ensure that the financial institution's board of directors can order the adoption of appropriate remedial action in the event of non-compliance.

For various reasons, the provisions of the Basel Committee's New Capital Accord are quite specific in relation to many other documents relating to the compliance function in financial institutions.[49] Some of them are listed below.

---

[48] About this the ibidem authors cited S. Mouatt, C. Adams, *Corporate and Social Transformations of Money and Banking*, Ibidem, p. 102.

[49] Szczególny charakter postanowień Nowej Umowy Kapitałowej wynika zwłaszcza z faktu, że jest to pierwszy tego rodzaju dokument, który wyraźnie wskazuje na rolę compliance w systemie zarządzania bankami, w tym zwłaszcza ich znaczenie dla właściwego określenia koniecznej dla bezpiecznego prowadzenia działalności bankowej bazy kapitałowej. Zastosowano w niej prosty model zależności – bank posiadający odpowiednie mechanizmy kontroli zgodności to bank prowadzony ostrożnie, czyli w mniejszym stopniu narażony na ewentualne skutki naruszeń obowiązujących go norm, czyli w konsekwencji bank, który potrzebuje odpowiednio niższą bazę kapitałową. Po drugie, postanowienia Komitetu Bazylejskiego stanowią pierwsze i dotychczas jedyne porozumienie międzynarodowe ustalające w tym zakresie konkretne ustalenia i nakładające na sygnatariuszy obowiązek ich wdrożenia. Po trzecie, ustalone w ramach prac tego forum postanowienia stały

This has led to the recommendation, established in line with the Basel Committee's recommendations and introduced by the transposition of its guidelines by the local regulators in their respective countries, that each financial institution should have a properly empowered financial institution employee responsible for coordinating the identification and management of compliance risk and for overseeing the activities of the compliance function as a whole.[50] The tasks directly arising from these obligations also result from the responsibility for the consistency of the financial institution's system of norms and control procedures to ensure compliance with the compliance criterion.[51]

The recommendations stemming from the Basel Committee's guidelines therefore also concern the way in which the compliance function should be placed in the financial institution's organisational structure, ensuring, on the one hand, independence and, on the other hand, easy, direct access to financial institution managers. The need to create such guarantees result from the proper placement of compliance services in the organisational structure of financial institutions is related to the importance of tasks performed by these services, i.e. compliance risk control.

Depending on the structure established within the financial institution, the organisation and functioning of the compliance norm-setting and reporting system, as well as other relations between compliance officers and the head of the compliance function may differ. The Basel

---

się de facto podstawą ustalania zobowiązań również dla podmiotów formalnie postanowieniem tym nie objętych. Tak więc regulatorzy ryków finansowych wszystkich państw rozwiniętych nakładają obecnie zobowiązania ostrożnościowe w oparciu o postanowienia Nowej Umowy Kapitałowej, która stała się wyznacznikiem minimalnych standardów w tej dziedzinie. Od tej pory powstawał szereg innych regulacji lokalnych w poszczególnych krajach, ale wszystkie one na ogół odnoszą się do postanowień bazylejskich. See S. G. Cecchetti, D. Domanski, G. von Peter, New Regulation and the New World of Global Banking, *National Institute Economic Review* 216(1)/2011, p. 30.

[50] The document even specifies that a proper mandate means in practice that it should be a bank employee at the rank of an executive director or a member of the board of directors.

[51] Differences between the competencies of the employees responsible for compliance and legal risk management within global financial institutions and in various institutions operating on global markets see R. McCormick, *Legal Risks in the Financial Markets*, Oxford 2010, p. 167.

guidelines for compliance regulations, referring, among other things, to issues such as reporting lines for compliance employees, or the names of their positions. They assume that, in order to achieve a consistent approach to compliance issues within an organisation, employees of an entity that is part of a local operating unit, i.e. separate companies within the same group or branch, may be subject to reporting to the management of that particular operating unit or branch in terms of reporting.

However, it also stipulates that such a structure is acceptable, provided that these staff members also report simultaneously to the head of compliance on issues relating to compliance responsibilities. This principle also extends to cross-border compliance structures.[52] These regulations have a practical rationale, as they de facto define the authority of compliance services and thus determine the effectiveness of the actions taken by them.[53] In fact, the Basel documents specify that in the case of large compliance units, the existence of a direct reporting path from the employees of this unit to the head of this unit is not necessary every time, unless it hinders the effective fulfilment of compliance obligations.

The scope of the duties of compliance services in financial institutions have been expanded so much that it has become a practical necessity, constituting the tenth group of tasks of compliance services, to create regulations guaranteeing that the tasks of the compliance unit are fulfilled in accordance with strictly defined compliance programmes, setting out an action plan for a certain period of time. Such programmes include reviews of financial institutions' policies and procedures, assessment of compliance risk, monitoring of the implementation of tasks deemed necessary to ensure compliance, and training of financial institution staff on compliance issues. It is a common practice to assume that compliance programmes should be formulated using a methodology to measure risks that takes into account their nature, severity and probability of their occurrence. The person responsible for all compliance risk management

---

[52] Ibidem, p. 227. More on the subject of the unifying role of the EBA in relation to the practice of functioning of risk management processes in banks in the European Union see C. Kosikowski, Nowe prawo rynku finansowego Unii Europejskiej [in] A. Jurkowska-Zeidler, M. Olszak [ed.] op. cit., p. 32.

[53] In some financial institution, the position of head of compliance is also referred to as the name of the compliance officer, while in other financial institution, the name of the compliance officer in the compliance function is referred to as the employee discharging the compliance responsibilities of the compliance function.

issues is responsible for ensuring that the established scope of the plan covers all areas of the financial institution's operational activities, and ensures a smooth flow of information, as well as coordination of tasks between the risk management units. In addition, these tasks also include creating the conditions to ensure that the relation between the compliance function and the internal audit function ensures an uninterrupted flow of information and that the activities of the compliance function are periodically controlled by the financial institution's internal audit.

Compliance is the desired state of compliance with the organisation's norms, but it is not in itself a state of security or a guarantee that the risk of violations of these norms will be eliminated. The tasks of compliance, understood as broadly, in an industry as strongly regulated as financial institutions, therefore, refer to the management of compliance risk related to the overall functioning of an effective internal control system, the establishment of which remains the responsibility of all financial institutions, and is carried out with the help of properly formulated internal norms.[54]

4 The Advisory Function of Compliance Services in Financial Institutions

The previous section presented examples of groups of tasks performed by compliance services in financial institutions in response to challenges posed to financial institutions by regulators. The presentation of the tasks of compliance services is important to illustrate the scope of the compliance norms developed in financial institutions. This section presents the functions of compliance in financial institutions. Unlike the tasks assigned to compliance services, the question of the functions they are appointed to perform in financial institutions is broader and relates to the objectives that corporate authorities set for them. Therefore, as previously indicated, the term 'tasks' refers to the issues related to the activities performed by compliance. However, the functions performed

---

[54] So Directive 2006/46/EC of the European Parliament and of the Council of 14 June 2006 amending Council Directives 78/660/EEC on the annual accounts of certain types of companies, 83/349/EEC on consolidated accounts, 86/635/EEC on the annual accounts and consolidated accounts of banks and other financial institutions and 91/674/EEC on the annual accounts and consolidated accounts of insurance undertakings (text with EEA relevance), *OJ L 224, 16.8.2006, pp. 1–7.*

by compliance services in financial institutions are understood as the role played by ensuring compliance in financial institutions among other elements that make up the whole issue related to their management. This also means that the delegation of functions is accompanied by a prior definition of objectives, the degree of achievement of which allows the quality of the functions performed to be assessed. Among the three functions performed by compliance in financial institutions: advisory, risk management and ensuring proper operation of the three lines of defence, i.e. control. This chapter deals precisely with the advisory function. Its analysis will be carried out by discussing the duties resulting from this role, as well as by indicating the importance of management information necessary for the proper performance of this function, approximation of the subject matter of training for which compliance services are also appointed, and by describing the qualifications of employees necessary to perform these functions.

It is around the hypothesis verified in this subchapter concerning the complexity of the subject matter, and the growing need to specialise in areas of knowledge related to compliance that the research described in this part of the book has been focused. Much of the information used in this subsection was the result of research based on the long-term observations of the participating author from the position of a practitioner in international financial institutions.

Each organisation, in a slightly different way, defines its own values and business priorities, and in a slightly different way defines its only relevant tasks, which are assigned to the compliance function. However, there are some typical areas of interest in the area of compliance and similar obligations for various institutions, which are imposed on compliance services in corporations. They can be divided into three main groups. The first refers to the compliance function in financial institutions, the second to the risk management function and the third to the control function. This arrangement of compliance tasks results in the persons involved in ensuring compliance in the functioning of a given institution taking full responsibility for the whole process.[55] It is up to

---

[55] Progressive professionalization of the profession of compliance officer, occurring particularly quickly in the financial sector, but also in medical and pharmaceutical corporations, manifests itself among others in attempts to unify the process of professional certification conducted on the basis of unified training courses and manuals. See D. Troklus, *Candidate Handbook, Certified Compliance and Ethics Professional, Society of Corporate Compliance and Ethics 2014*, www.compliancecertification.org (download 12 March 2019).

them to properly inform all entities operating within the financial institution of their compliance obligations and then to ensure, through the introduction of appropriate control procedures, that these obligations are respected.

Each of these consultative duties is specifically complex, as they take into account both different types of norms referred to in the same corporation, as well as different business objectives, market and social differences and—which is particularly important from the perspective of the observations contained in this book—cultural differences. The compliance activities carried out inside a financial institution, which is an international corporation, are usually precisely adjusted to local conditions.

Moreover, the advisory role of the financial institution's compliance function means that the financial institution's organisational units have a broad scope that goes far beyond actual advice. In practice, it is a collective term which includes four types of duties imposed on compliance services in addition to those included in risk management tasks. These duties are:

a. issuing opinions on existing norms, but also creating new compliance norms;
b. participation in meetings of internal committees appointed to perform advisory functions, although de facto this means in practice a direct impact on the management of the financial institution;
c. advice on the admissibility of transactions which are consulted with compliance specialists prior to entering into such transactions;
d. internal training on compliance policies offered to staff.

The advisory compliance function in financial institutions focuses on the issuing of opinions on proposed intra-financial institution normative solutions, and in this respect, it is crucial to the whole possible model of compliance solutions adopted in a given organisation. Most often, this task consists of issuing opinions on internal normative acts prepared by other substantive departments. However, in mature organisations, this process includes, in principle, all internal normative acts, regardless of their rank and scope of regulation. Indeed, there is a perception that it would be a breakthrough in this process, by highlighting only some of them, which should be subject to compliance assessment and, at the same time, leaving outside the process other regulations, for some reason considered less important. This would in fact give rise to a risk of non-compliance resulting from the possible omission of norms.

In some financial institutions, the process is even broader and covers not only the norms themselves, but also all documents, the content of which could give rise to liability towards third parties on the part of the financial institution. Such an opinion may therefore relate to the content of agreements, the content of which would impose certain obligations on the financial institution, but also marketing and information materials, the content of scripts for talks with customers, etc.

Regardless of the opinions on the documents that may carry the obligations imposed on the financial institution, its employees and third parties, the compliance services themselves often prepare drafts of internal normative acts regulating the obligation to comply with different types of normative acts that constitute reference points. These are examples of these compliance meta-norms which constitute the axis of compliance norms in a financial institution. It is they who decide what behaviour is expected of the obliged entities, and what norms contain conduct orders binding them in the context of their relationship with the financial institution in question.

The compliance advisory function is performed mainly through the participation of employees of compliance units in various types of formal committees that operate in the financial institution. Apart from the differences between the models of functioning of different financial institutions corporations manifested in a more or less collective way of making decisions, there must be certain types of committees in all financial institutions due to formal requirements. On the other hand, the role of each of them can vary. However, they are all appointed to take management decisions in relation to different areas of financial institutions activity. Their compliance representatives participate in the decision-making process, although in practice the degree of empowerment of these committees can vary and depends on their established corporate governance principles of their place in the intra-corporate hierarchy. Among the structures that make up these committees there are at least a few types that appear in a similar form in each financial institution. These are, for example, Executive Committees, whose meetings are also Management Board meetings, the core composition of which is the core of these committees. There are also Risk Management Committees, including Operational Risk Management Committees, Credit Committees, Assets and Liabilities Committees and a number of other committees such as IT Management Committees, Information Security Committees, Anti-money Laundering Committees, Human Resources Management Committees, Compensations and Benefits Committee a and Legal Risk Committees.

The existence of some of them is required by mandatory legal norms, while others are established in accordance with the organisational pragmatics binding in a given corporation. Their tasks usually remain in line with their names, and their specific scope, which stems from internally established rules of procedure, should not, as a rule, overlap. It is the responsibility of the compliance representatives in these committees to participate in their deliberations with the understanding that their decisions, recommendations and guidelines should explicitly take into account its compliance requirements. Within the framework of such participation, compliance services may contribute particularly effectively to the provision of an advisory role, as on an ongoing basis, during the work of these committees, at the conceptual stage, it gives its opinion on the compliance of decisions taken with all normative systems constituting the reference basis for the financial institution's operations.

Properly prepared management information is an essential tool for the proper functioning of financial institution management committees.[56] Such information shall, inter alia, provide data showing the effectiveness of the processes in place at the financial institution to ensure compliance of the financial institution's operations with the law, supervisory regulations and other norms. To this end, it shall include reports on the activities of the different parts of the financial institution, including the different business lines and business support functions. This type of management information, which is then the basis for the formulation of compliance opinions, includes data relating to it:

a. trends relating to the number of customer complaints;
b. the types of complaints;
c. emerging new regulatory requirements;
d. any violations of the law;
e. draft new supervisory rules and regulations.

---

[56] Ibidem, p. 71.

Advisory services are important to both the financial institutions' day-to-day operations, and also at the stage of consulting on the admissibility of concluding specific transactions. In addition to a simple analysis of credit, market, operational data, etc., carried out when assessing a proposed transaction, tests are also carried out on the likelihood of a situation of non-compliance if certain types of cooperation are undertaken. An additional, although not a secondary issue is to decide on this occasion whether there is a possibility of the damage to the reputation of the institution. A key element, preliminary to the correctness of the assessment is, first of all, to determine the rules which, from the compliance point of view, should apply when making decisions on involvement in transactions with third parties. As indicated above, such rules may apply to entities of this kind with which it is not advisable to enter into business relations, as well as to certain types of transactions, selected geographical areas, etc.

With such established and binding rules, a certain group of undesirable transactions is a priori eliminated from the compliance perspective. In this respect, there are usually general guidelines applicable to all entities actively engaged in transactions with third parties. However, there are always a number of situations in which it becomes necessary to make discretionary decisions due to the specificity of specific cases deviating from the model patterns. In addition, the adjustment of norms resulting from the observed needs of a specific financial institution operating within a larger capital group to local economic conditions, local business, local specificity of the market, and finally to local jury conditions, including those resulting from the legal culture existing in a given area, is also applied. In such a situation it is compliance services with its advisory voice that plays a role, which in principle is irreplaceable by any other services of the financial institution. It is as part of compliance that guidelines are developed to help resolve individual transactions from the point of view of the identity of the entity, in particular in the case of undesirable entities, in the case of the presence of these entities on various types of blacklists, and not only such lists, which are created inside the financial institution on the basis of experience arising from a relation, which the financial institution has with these entities, but also on the basis of completely different lists, which are created in various places in the world, that are probably created by other financial institutions, and about which the question of their legality remains open. As previously indicated, one of the criteria is where these entities are registered, operate, transact, but also on the type of transactions they make, their frequency, the type of industry in which they operate, the matching of transactions with the profile of their business, etc. The criteria are the places where they are registered, operate, carry out transactions and so on.

The group of duties performed by compliance services, which is a form of an advisory activity, is to conduct training sessions for the needs of financial institution employees, whose role is to inform others about new regulations and the ways they should be interpreted. In practice, such training sessions play a de facto quasi-promulgate role for those norms which are introduced, since they are intended to create coherent directories, and the mere inclusion of information about them in internal IT networks does not guarantee their content, especially when their programme is uniform for financial institutions operating in different places. Moreover, such training sessions, especially since they are often conducted in the form of interactive workshops, are an opportunity to conduct ad hoc consultations on all current issues in which there are decisions on how to apply the compliance norms, and in particular how to interpret them in the case of their possible ambiguity.

The proper performance of compliance advisory activity requires, first of all, properly prepared personnel. As compliance is about managing legal risks, legal education is certainly an important part of preparing for these tasks. Often, however, compliance teams consist of teams of people with different professional and educational backgrounds. Performing compliance tasks also requires a thorough knowledge of financial institutions or, more broadly, of the functioning of financial markets. Compliance, while performing advisory functions, is at the same time an element of a broader risk management system functioning within a given organisation, therefore it requires skilful use of analytical instruments, including statistical and econometric ones. As in the case of any advisory activity, it is also necessary to use soft skills useful in cooperation with employees of the entire financial institution, as well as knowledge of organisation and management. Since knowledge of compliance more and more often means the necessity to get deeper into the subject of complex financial transactions, the legal preparation itself, or knowledge of compliance norms may prove to be insufficient. The desired professional profile of people working in compliance are experts in a narrow specialisation, including financial analysis, information technology, unfair market practices, prevention of money laundering, protection of consumer rights, etc.

Compliance consulting tasks are, above all, connected with fulfilling the role of a partner for persons performing management functions within the organisation. Both the supervising regulators and, as a consequence, the financial institutions themselves recognised that the lack of strong compliance services was one of the reasons that contributed to successive financial crises.[57] Regulators therefore expect management bodies in financial institutions to take action to ensure that a compliance culture is built and maintained. Its basic element is to properly communicate the importance of being in compliance with the current normative order of financial institutions, and to explain its role, giving the right tone from the top. What is more, the emphasis on the need to respect the independence of compliance services within a financial institution does not raise any controversy at present, because only such a position can mean credible, unrestricted performance of an advisory function.

5 Compliance Assurance—Example of IP Risks

In the most developed financial markets, which have the greatest experience in building compliance structures, the traditional role of compliance services for a long time was primarily one of control. Only recently has it also started to develop into the more consultative function referred to above. As long as these services perform this function correctly, they are trusted advisors, whose actions add value to the financial institution, protect the financial institution's brand by participating in building trust in it, and by consulting employees in the event of any doubts as to whether there are any problems with the implementation of the applicable compliance norms.[58] Such an approach to compliance tasks has so far been treated as relatively peripheral, as the main emphasis has been placed on internal supervision and control. However, the most effective compliance

---

[57] Among other things, in order to avoid crises similar to the recent ones, supervision of financial markets has also been strengthened at European Union level. More on this subject see C. Kosikowski, *Prawo Unii Europejskiej w systemie polskiego prawa finansowego*, Białystok 2010, p. 113.

[58] Such views include those expressed in the debate at leval of national bar association (K. Mering and J. Moson) on the role of lawyers in finance and the subsequent article published thereon: J. Mason, Compliance – odpowiedzialny prawnik w finansach, *Radca Prawny* 3(123)/2012.

model seems to be the one that combines both proactive, advisory and reactive, control activities.

Ensuring compliance of the financial institution's operations with respect to all new processes, services and products, and at the same time monitoring compliance with applicable business norms already in place. Both functions include managing compliance risk, i.e. actively participating in determining which events in the financial institution's environment may expose them to negative consequences, and what action needs to be taken to avoid or minimise such consequences. In many compliance institutions these three functions are combined. However, while the compliance advisory function largely overlaps with the tasks focused on norm-setting, and the control function is of a follow-up nature, compliance risk management focuses on the duties of actively anticipating and responding to potential risks. Research into the risk management function of compliance is the subject of this section.

This section refers to the observation that global supervisory regulations, which are a reaction to the recent financial crisis, radically change the regulatory environment of financial institutions, which is currently undergoing fundamental transformations all over the world.[59] Public supervisory authorities carry out activities aimed at strengthening supervision of financial institutions while introducing completely new supervisory regulations relating to risk management in various spheres of financial institutions activity.[60] These are both regulations in the area of combating threats resulting from the general political situation in the world, such as financial crime, as well as prudent and in line with legal and regulatory norms in the conduct of financial institutions activities.[61] At the same time, sanctions, imposed on financial institutions and directly on members of their authorities who do not comply with

---

[59] Cf. P. R. Wood, *International Legal Risks for Banks and Corporate*, London 2014, p. 132.

[60] See M. Koetter, J. W. Kolari, L. Spierdijk, Enjoying the Quiet Life Under Deregulation? Evidence from the Adjusted Lerner Indices for US Banks, *Review of Economics and Statistics* 94(2)/2012, p. 567.

[61] On regulatory requirements relating to prudential management of the financial institution see H. Assa, Risk Management Under Prudential Policy, *Decisions in Economics and Finance* 38(2)/2015, p. 220 et seq. and F. Feretti, A European Perspective in Consumer Loans and the Role of Credit Registries: The Need to Reconcile Data Protection, Risk Management, Efficiency, Over-Indebtness, and a Better Prudential Supervision of the Financial System, *Journal of Consumer Policy* 33(1)/2010, p. 3.

their obligations are an increasing way for financial institutions to enforce compliance with these regulations.[62]

The severity of penalties does not boil down only to the amount of their financial dimension. Often high financial penalties are accompanied by other types of penalties, including periodic bans on the sale of a given product. This applies in particular to offering customers products that are more complex, and those that are riskier to buy if market conditions reverse. Penalties are also increasingly being imposed on corporate executives or other persons whose decisions may expose financial institutions to increased risk, including temporary or total prohibitions on certain professions or managerial positions.[63]

As a consequence, the importance and position of compliance services in financial institutions, when it moves towards the decision-making centre, becomes an integral part of business activity, including the part of it which concerns the management of risks associated with financial institutions activity. Moreover, as a result of this trend, members of statutory bodies are entrusted with a direct responsibility for compliance matters. The problem presented below, derives from an analysis of the types of risks related to the protection of intellectual property rights and relations with public entities, as well as the methods of managing them adopted by six international financial institutions, categorised by their types.

In order for an international financial institution, in particular an international financial institution, to function properly, it is necessary to establish a 'risk appetite' (risk appetite), i.e. an acceptable level of risk for the institution matched to the business model which the institution executes in a given market.[64] As a result of such a determination, all types of business risks are monitored, including compliance risks. In consequence, the financial results generated by a financial institution are analysed in relation to events which constitute cases of the fulfilment of such risks, the probability of which has been determined in these appetite statements.[65] For this purpose, legal risk management and compliance

---

[62] For example, JP Morgan Chase & Co., a total of $920 million, or even largest financial penalty imposed on HSBC for money laundering of $1.92 billion.

[63] See R. Patton, Trends in Regulatory Enforcement in the UK Financial Markets 2014/2015 Mid-Year Report, *Insight in Economics*, 20 October 2014.

[64] However, despite the high probability of non-compliance events occurring, the appetite for this risk is set at zero as the only one among many other categories.

[65] P. R. Wood, op. cit., London 2014, p. 67.

committees are set up within internal risk monitoring meetings, which meet with management and other key executives.[66] The task of such committees is to analyse on an ongoing basis the information obtained on potential problems that may arise in this context, as well as to monitor regulatory risks, and to take decisions on further necessary actions, including the norm-setting activities.

As compliance services become an element of risk management of activities conducted by financial institutions, they are obliged to work out solutions in a systematic way to organise the functioning of the institutions within which they operate. The risk management model is presumed to be effective when all risks to which a financial institution is exposed are clearly defined, and their management is assigned to individuals and organisations with responsibility for performing the related tasks. Taking into account the changing economic and regulatory situation, the process of risk identification and analysis is usually carried out annually, and as a result, compliance risk maps are developed. Such maps are one of the tools used by compliance services to identify areas where norms are created to ensure the financial institution's compliance policy implementation. Some of the most common risks on such maps are listed below.

The risk of non-contractual obligations in relation to possible justified claims by third parties based on identified cases of irregularities in the financial institution's activities, which is difficult to grasp due to the international scale of its activities, and at the same time deserving special attention, is widely analysed by practice.[67] Early identification of such risks is relatively difficult due to the often-differing understanding of

---

[66] On recommended practices for the involvement of board members in managing compliance risk see P. Montoya, The Role of the Board of Directors [in] F. Vincke, J. Kassum [ed.] *ICC Ethics and Compliance Training Handbook*, Paris 2013, p. 63.

[67] For the examples of non-contractual liability risks set out below, the difficulty is less in relying on the amount of compensation paid for such third-party claims. It results from the fact that international institutions operating in many markets at the same time, conducting many advertising campaigns on them, introducing and withdrawing many products, using numerous software providers etc., are exposed to a number of such violations on a daily basis. As these cases involve relatively smaller amounts, are generally disconnected and different in nature, it is difficult to collectively grasp their scale. See M. El-Bannany, A Study of Determinants of Intellectual Capital Performance in Banks: The UK Case, *Journal of Intellectual Capital* 9(3)/2008, p. 488 et seq. and T. W. Koch, S. Scott Mac Donald, *Bank Management*, Boston 2014, p. 100.

basic concepts resulting from the fact that international financial institutions, by their very nature, operate in different jurisdictions, different legal systems and different legal cultures. The risk is that non-contractual obligations arise where the assets of a financial institution that is part of an international group of financial institutions are held by a third party that is considered inappropriate or not adequately protected may result in an infringement of those rights or in an infringement of the rights of third parties. In such situations, such risks may extend not only to the financial institution whose rights have been directly affected, but also to other financial institutions that are part of the international financial institution of which they are part.

The two most common situations in which the risk of non-contractual obligations arises in practice include the following.

a. Cases of infringement by a financial institution member of the same group of rights of third parties. This applies, for example, to intellectual property rights, including trade mark rights, patents, analyses, studies, studies and documents, as well as other contractual obligations, including copyright, which may arise from contractual obligations with third parties in this matter.
b. Infringements of the ownership rights of a corporate financial institution in the event of unauthorised action by third parties against any form of exercise of this right, including in particular the possession and use of property or rights owned by the financial institution as a result of local circumstances or insufficient protection. This may be the case in any situation where there are other circumstances which give rise to a presumption that the financial institution's right of ownership is being challenged.

The difficulty of compliance tasks in a multinational corporation is that different jurisdictions differently define the nature and scope of protection of third-party rights. Although they vary from country to country, there are a number of similar rules which, irrespective of the jurisdiction, apply to values recognised as being subject to special protection regimes.[68] These include, for example, personal data, including

---

[68] On the universally accepted values in the law see A. Keay, Getting to Groups with the Shareholder Value Theory in Corporate Law, *Common Law World Review* 39(4)/2010, p. 362 et seq.

sensitive data (in this case, the specificity of local legal traditions and culture is important), personal rights (similarly, the scope of protection varies from jurisdiction to jurisdiction), human rights (individuals), good faith in business, fair competition, etc. Conversely, there are examples of infringement cases identified by various legal systems, even very distant ones, such as breaches of financial institutions secrecy, and other forms of professional and commercial confidentiality, defamation, passing off. In relation to such risks, the task of compliance consists to a large extent in developing a directory of norms, the observance of which, are imposed on the indicated addressees of norms, is to guarantee safe functioning of financial institutions in the conditions of cooperation with third parties.[69]

The risk of non-compliance arising from non-contractual obligations is, in relation to issues related to the use of intellectual property rights, not so much the question of possible regulatory sanctions as in the case of other types of non-compliance, but primarily the risk of losses to which the financial institution's result may be exposed due to the need to cover the costs of enforcing and protecting these rights. The most common cases relate to the risk that an item of intellectual property is held by unauthorised persons, or it is established that the protection under which the item is held is insufficient and there is a likelihood of infringement of an intellectual property right.[70] As a result of this state of affairs,

---

[69] M. Kozak, Compliance Programmes as a Tool of Effective Enforcement of Competition Law—A Carrot and a Stick Method? [in] T. Skoczny [ed.] *25 Years of Competition Law in Poland*, Warsaw 2015, *passim*.

[70] Issues of the same rights arising from infringements of intellectual property rights often vary considerably between jurisdictions. Listing only a few of them for Poland, the Act on Copyright and Related Rights of 4 February 1994 provides for such rights in a relatively flexible manner (Dz. U. z 2010 r. Nr 152, poz. 106), which, despite numerous changes, is still a relatively underused instrument compared to the judicial practice of other countries, which is nevertheless adapted and updated as the changes take place. Much more important are, for example, the US Federal Copyright Act 1976 or the UK Copyright, Designs and Patents Act 1988. In contrast, the French law on copyright and related rights (Loi sur le Droit d'Auteur et les Droits Voisins dans la Société de l'Information—DADVSI) of March 2006 is much more topical, as is the Russian (Part IV of the Civil Code of the Russian Federation) law of 18 December 2006 and the Kazakh (Copyright and Related Rights Act of the same year) law based on it. Laws in many other countries were drafted at about the same time, and to a much greater extent they already address copyright issues in the global space, including on the Internet. For example, these are Brazilian Copyright Act No. 9/610/98, the Hong Kong Copyright Decree of 6 July 2007 and even Act No. 32 of 2006. Emirate of Dubai amending the Earlier Copyright and Neighbouring Rights Act of 2002.

there are costs associated with this risk. Six reasons for these costs are set out below.[71] In practice, these costs may come from:

a. Impairment or reduction in the value of intellectual property constituting an asset of the financial institution, which may arise from a smaller than necessary number of licences or lower revenues from products protected by intellectual property rights, which may result from their invalidity, suspended effectiveness or unenforceability related to the challenge of this right.
b. The need to incur substantial expenses on certain markets to cover enforcement costs incurred in the exercise of the financial institution's intellectual property rights vis-à-vis third parties.
c. Additional, higher than hitherto costs of legal protection of objects covered by the provisions on intellectual property rights.
d. If the risk of infringement of intellectual property in relation to third parties by the financial institution materialises, this may include the costs of legal protection, including legal representation in the event that it is necessary to defend the financial institution's interests in court proceedings.
e. Costs resulting from a judicial or extra-judicial settlement, including any damages resulting from such settlement.
f. Other costs related to image repair in a situation where the reputation of the financial institution and its customer relations are compromised in order to minimise the negative impact of such damage on company share prices.

When assessing the risks arising from non-contractual obligations relating to the protection of intellectual property in a given country, factors that may affect their magnitude and likelihood of occurrence are usually considered. One of the groups of factors that compliance services, especially those operating in international financial institutions, must take into account is whether the financial institution is planning to develop its business in the future, and especially whether the development of this business is related to entering new markets. If so, does

---

[71] With regard to compliance costs related to infringements of intellectual property rights see K. Walsh, C. A. Enz, L. Canina, The Impact of Strategic Orientation on Intellectual Capital Investments in Customer Service Firms, *Journal of Service Research* 10(4)/2008, p. 309.

the financial institution plan to use the brands already in use on the new markets and, consequently, the guaranteed degree of protection of trademarks and the right to exclusive disposal of the goods protected by intellectual property rights on those markets.

Another group of issues concerns whether new products, services, marketing campaigns, trademarks, advertising slogans, etc., which are values protected by intellectual property rights, and whether there are intentions to develop new processes or technologies that can be the subject of patent protection, and whether their possible introduction could infringe rights under existing patents. Similarly, this group of issues includes questions relating to whether there is a financial institution's use of third-party intellectual property in new jurisdictions or in existing jurisdictions in a new way, or whether it is possible that the number of persons using it will increase significantly, and whether this happens within the framework of existing proven rights such as patents, trademarks, licences, etc.[72] The problem consists of determining if the financial institution is using the intellectual property of third parties in a new way or not. In situations of relatively frequent acquisitions of other financial institutions by international financial institutions corporations, the subject of analysis is also whether such transactions, in addition to structural transformations, also entail the inclusion of new areas of activity, i.e. new products, brands or entire intellectual property portfolios. On such occasions, compliance services must also analyse the risk that the financial institution becomes a potential target for entities earning money by registering, patenting intellectual property and suing entities infringing these rights.[73]

Corporations operating in international markets must also take into account the fact that the more local brands and other goods protected by intellectual property rights are owned by individual financial institutions, the more licensing situations may arise, and the greater is the need for third parties to use the financial institution's intellectual property.

---

[72] About the tasks of management of international corporations in relations to intellectual property rights protection see W. M. Landes, R. A. Posner, *The Economic Structure of Intellectual Property Law*, Cambridge 2003, p. 354.

[73] On the role of compliance in managing the risk of illegitimate registration of trademarks with a view to their subsequent resale to corporations under European law see M. Svensson, S. Larsson, Intellectual Property Law Compliance in Europe: Illegal File Sharing and the Law of Social Norms, *New Media and Society* 14(7)/2012, p. 1150 et seq.

The Compliance Officer in such situations also participates in deciding whether the financial institution uses, including whether it licenses or not, these rights in an appropriate manner. On the other hand, the use of global brands alone is not a sufficient way to address this risk, as fewer local brands do not always automatically mean less risk. It should be noted that this risk is also posed by local users of global brands, who operate in their respective countries. In this sense, compliance in all countries where corporate brands are used plays an important role in protecting them by participating in deciding, for example, how many global and local brand licences have been granted, and whether it corresponds to the number of de facto brand owners (suppliers, distributors, partners, sponsors, etc.). As indicated above, practice has shown that trying to limit risks by limiting the number of licences granted, for example for trademarks, does not necessarily mean that risks are reduced. The subject of analysis and the consequences of decisions in this respect is whether these licences are granted to the relevant entities, whether their scope, contractual manner of regulation and number are appropriate, and the manner of registration of licence agreements has been properly carried out.[74]

6 Reputational Risks Management

Another field of compliance analyses with respect to risks arising from the use of intellectual property rights, in connection with operations conducted by financial institutions, is the sphere of reputation risk. The global legal environment in this respect is very heterogeneous in the sense that the degree of protection of intellectual property rights in different jurisdictions is very different and these differences are to a large extent related to factors such as the legal culture expressed, among others, in a specific relation to the value of respect for the products of intellectual or artistic work.

Another factor, which, without avoiding the generalisation that is justified in this case, can be said to have an impact on the advancement of intellectual property rights protection in various countries is the degree

---

[74] This is usually done on the basis of contracts for the assignment of the right to use trademarks or other protected goods which are the subject of intellectual property with a very standardized wording, the trade mark license agreements (TMLA).

of wealth and economic development of individual countries.[75] Hence, the assessment of actual risk in this respect is carried out with the use of legal analyses conducted especially for this purpose, supplemented by the knowledge and experience of representatives of compliance services in financial institutions. It is compliance employees, acting together with marketing departments, who express the financial institution's opinion and shape its policy in this respect by examining the local legal environment and cases of intellectual property infringements occurring in a given area, but also, for example, the attitude of the entire local social, economic and, above all, legal environment (law enforcement agencies, patent and competitive administration, judiciary, enforcement systems) to the protection and use of intellectual property.[76] The analysis of compliance activities in this area proves the quality of risk management processes, but it should also be pointed out that a small number of recorded breaches may indicate a small number of such incidents, or a lack of awareness of such risks.

The reputation risk usually increases with the development of a distribution network. As part of this risk management, compliance services analyse which third parties use trademarks, brands or any other products protected by intellectual property rights. In this respect, the credibility of the licensees is usually examined up to the final beneficiary of the transaction and the final owner of the entity entering into the transaction (the so-called KYP—Know Your Partner test). It is examined for what purpose the use of goods protected by intellectual property rights takes place, what kind of operational risks the use of these goods entails, and how any resulting risks are minimised.[77] Here again, the accumulated knowledge, experience, historical data, qualitative research, as well as statistical research in cases of large-scale activities, requires efficient

---

[75] On cultural and ethical links in the context of compliance norms see M. McMillan, Difference Between Compliance, Ethics and Culture, *Risk and Compliance Journal*, 30 June 2014, http://blogs.wsj.com/riskandcompliance/2014/06/30/the-difference-between-compliance-and-ethics/ (download 3 February 2019).

[76] On the impact of differences in managing the risk of litigation resulting from different legal cultures see H. M. Kutzer, F. K. Zemans, Local Legal Culture and the Control of Litigation, *Law and Society Review* 27(3)/1993, pp. 535–557.

[77] This includes issues such as whether the TMLA is issued separately or as part of a larger contract, and whether the license agreements are concluded on standard terms that are convenient for the financial institutions in advance, or are negotiated locally on a case-by-case basis.

compliance services to correctly analyse all the variables connected with the complexities of international transactions. Although clearly, some types of entities, certain industries and certain financial products will carry a greater risk than others.

An analysis of the risks of non-compliance for intellectual property rights also takes into account additional factors such as, for example, the effectiveness of judicial redress observed in a given jurisdiction, and how the experience of legal practice in a given country in pursuing such claims is well established. The first stage of this kind of analysis is to base it on observations as to whether a given legal system, i.e. legal norms, the efficiency of the judicial and enforcement system, preparation of judges, availability of expert opinions, existing jurisprudence, elements of legal culture, etc., are conducive to the protection of intellectual property rights holders.[78] In practice, it is important for the completeness of such an analysis whether the financial institution is more likely to act as a claimant for the protection of its rights or as a defendant. Confidence in the local legal system may manifest itself in various forms, for example through the consistency of court rulings, the possibility of external influence on the whole legal system, or on individual rulings.[79]

A part of the infrastructure necessary for the effective protection of intellectual property rights, and consequently for the protection of a financial institution's interests in this area is the existence of specialised intellectual property courts, and whether they have knowledge and experienced judges, and whether the country is a signatory to the most important international treaties for the protection of intellectual property, which in practice allows the adoption that local norms are in line with them. Another group of issues is whether there are regulated possibilities of registering intellectual property through, for example, copyrights, design rights, trademarks, etc., and how to assess the effectiveness, ease and costs of enforcement of these rights, and what kind of sanctions apply in such cases (criminal or civil, whether they are severe,

---

[78] About the expanding the scope of intellectual property protection resulting from its incorporation into international law see R. Halfer, Regime Shifting: The TRIPs Agreement and New Dynamics of Intellectual Property Lawmaking, *Yale Journal of International Law* 29/2004, p. 6 et seq.

[79] So often in countries with unflagged judicial systems and in those where a dictatorship with real powers is not conducive to the building of independent judicial or enforcement institutions.

whether enforcement is quick, whether cases of infringement of these rights are also prosecuted ex officio).

The compliance services preparing internal regulations in this respect must take into account all the above mentioned factors determining the effectiveness of intellectual property protection, analysing in individual cases whether as a trademark owner, brand name financial institution is sufficiently well protected, especially in the context of whether it is more likely that the financial institution will act as a right holder or a defendant, whether a given country is known for a large number of infringements of intellectual property rights. Alignment of compliance norms with the level of protection existing in a given jurisdiction is dynamic and depends on whether changes are made to intellectual property laws in the country concerned, and whether these changes affect the level of protection, and the risk of infringements of intellectual property rights.

Therefore, as it is so important to conduct a compliance risk analysis thoroughly, it is vital that the legal competences available locally are checked. This involves examining whether there are intellectual property rights lawyers in the country concerned, who can be used to assist in cases of this kind, which is not obvious in many jurisdictions, and whether the financial institution already has an established experience of working with them.[80] Last but not least, the question of whether the financial institution employs lawyers at all in a given country, and how the above-mentioned factors may affect the knowledge of local financial institution units about the risk of infringement of intellectual property rights, and to what extent the local legal services are prepared to fulfil their reporting and control obligations in this respect. Depending on the results of this type of testing, the appropriate risk control processes, expressed in compliance procedures and other internal normative acts, can be prepared. This also applies to control processes that check whether a given entity complies with these procedures, whether employees have access to these procedures, whether each financial institution provides the required reports in this respect, or whether the legal

---

[80] Experience shows that in some central Asian countries, which were previously part of the USSR, as well as in some central African countries, the legal practice specializing in the area of intellectual property rights protection is developing slower. A useful source of practical information on the level of protection of intellectual property rights worldwide is the independent IP Watch organization (http://www.ip-watch.org).

department in a given financial institution has the right to license the use of copyrights.[81]

While participating in the management of compliance risk resulting from the use of intellectual property rights, compliance services also check the nature of the activities on the local market, and what type of intellectual property of the financial institution needs special protection, as well as what type of intellectual property belonging to third parties is used in the financial institution's operations. In practice, it boils down to a detailed examination of whether a financial institution in a given country has signed license agreements with the owners of IT software, whether the financial institution employs a team of marketing specialists, who develop their own materials, or whether the financial institution receives marketing materials from a team that prepares them centrally for a larger number of financial institutions that are members of a corporation at the regional or global level. Whether the local marketing team enters into separate agreements on the use of third parties' intellectual property rights (e.g. software, captured images, analysis, etc.) or whether it relies on regionally or globally prepared agreements.

Experience in compliance risk management indicates that the most common risks associated with infringements of intellectual property rights faced by compliance services in financial institutions occur as a result of external changes taking place in the business environment or changes carried out within a given organisation.[82] This is the case, for example, when there are changes in the nature of local activities that were not previously foreseen and were not able to be reflected in the compliance risk management procedures. The following are four typical recurring situations of non-compliance risk observed in the context of intra-organisational changes.

   a. In search of the benefits of locating part of their operations in countries where operating costs are cheaper than in large financial centres, financial institutions corporations outsource some

---

[81] Some organizations have compliance procedures in place to address this issue, as expressed in the applicable legal sections of the functional instruction manuals, where there are appropriate chapters referring to control of the risks of non-contractual intellectual property obligations.

[82] I. E. Brick, N. K. Chindambaran, Board Monitoring, Firm Risk, and External Regulation, *Journal of Regulatory Economics* 33/2008, pp. 87–116.

processes. Often, for example, the activities of call centres or debt collection departments are transferred to the territory of so-called low-cost countries. On the one hand, service centres set up specifically for this purpose are becoming places of increased use of software, while on the other hand, as indicated above, the protection of intellectual property rights in some of these countries is lower, which may result in an increased risk of infringement of licence and related rights.

b. The introduction of new financial institutions products or services often involves extensive advertising, marketing or sales activities, whether in retail or corporate financial institutions in general. Experience shows that such intensified marketing campaigns are more likely to lead to situations which may result in an increased risk of disputes related to intellectual property infringement either through the actual unauthorised use by financial institutions of certain copyright-protected creations or in the unjustified claims by third parties on such occasions that such infringements have occurred.[83]

c. Another relatively new and only little explored area in which incidents qualified as increased intellectual property rights compliance risk are recorded is the activity of financial institutions or their employees in social media. As they are by definition global and immediate in scope, any new and, in particular, ill-considered use of them creates a real risk of liability on the part of financial institutions for infringement of these rights, which can be enforced in many jurisdictions at the same time.

d. Still other risks are posed by the already mentioned earlier cooperation between financial institutions and external entities concerning the provision of certain services (advisory, marketing, advertising and media, IT, administrative, technical, etc.). Depending on who these entities are, what is the nature of the business conducted by such service providers, what are their previous experience with them, what are their corporate rules of conducting business activity, to what extent they are familiar with intellectual property

---

[83] The size of amounts relating to litigation risks varies considerably from one to another financial institution, but to illustrate the scale, it may be pointed out that in the case of London banks, the risk is high in the value of cases connected by type exceeding USD 50 million, and the risk is low in the value of cases not exceeding USD 20 million.

issues, as well as what are their own internal compliance rules, the risk in this area on the part of a financial institution may differ accordingly.

An important element of the compliance risk management function performed by financial institutions is the creation of general and partial reports analysing its compliance status. Depending on the purposes for which individual analyses and reports are created, and to whom they are addressed, these documents are prepared on the basis of different methodologies. The easiest way to present compliance reports, especially those that are addressed to people who do not deal with compliance issues in the financial institution on a daily basis is the traffic lights method (Red Amber Green—RAG). It allows for the quick identification of the weight of the reported risks by the persons to whom the reports are directed. The methodology underlying the weighing up of risks may vary considerably from one institution to another, and even if risks are identified within the same financial institutions, but it is assumed that the risk values will be tested in such a way that the risk values will eventually be defined as high, medium or low, and will be marked with the commonly understood red, yellow and green colours for traffic lights. The ways to assess which traffic lights should be assigned to particular compliance risks are sometimes different. Most often they depend on two values:

a. the exposure to the magnitude of possible material losses expected to occur in conditions of non-compliance;
b. the likelihood of such cases occurring.

In order to assess the size of possible risks, it is helpful to prioritise the cases of non-compliance according to what effect they may have. For example, they may relate to the four categories indicated below.

a. Reputation risk, where the risk is high for a limited period of time in the international media with a strong interest and a risk low, on the contrary, low interest, absence or small number of negative opinions and their appearance only in the local media.
b. Exposure to customer claims, measured, for example, by collective actions brought against a financial institution, or a large number of individual actions with an aggregate value in excess of a specified

sum of money in the case of high risk. On the other hand, low-risk situations are those in which the lawsuits filed against the financial institution were effectively dismissed, were rejected by the authorities adjudicating with the effect of res judicata, or their total value does not exceed the monetary value defined as insignificant.

c. The impact on the business continuity, which is manifested in the long-term or often recurrent inability to perform certain financial institutions activities, with a significant increase in customer complaints, in the case of high risks. The risk can be described as low in this case if the occurrence of such events only occasionally, and in a way that does not cause an increase in the number of complaints from financial institution customers.

d. Interventions of regulators, the risk is high in situations where there is a need for the involvement of financial institution authorities at the level of the financial group as a whole, and the risk is low as a result of routine controls of national post-inspection recommendations.

The classification of risk is additionally influenced by the percentage or time determined probability of occurrence of these events (for example: at least once a year, once every 2 years, once every 5 years, or within the next 12 months, within the next 2 years, etc.). The final assessment of these risks is made at the same time as the taking into account of the control exercised in the financial institution, and the ways of preventing these risks, which are carried out as a result of their actions. This is where the concepts of inherent risk and residual risk are collated, by which the risks existing before and after the introduction of appropriate mechanisms for their monitoring, minimisation and control are determined. The proper classification of risks consists of taking into account all the control factors, and only after taking them into account it is possible to measure and compare the risks arising from them.

The persons responsible for reporting compliance risks through the RAG system use four groups of sources to provide information to assist in the analysis of compliance risks:

a. Data from other internal and external reports. These include information on the number and nature of customer complaints, reports on pending court proceedings, data from databases containing information on incidents related to the materialisation of

operational risks, post-control recommendations of the team for operational risk, internal control, audit, etc.;
b. Summaries of the breaches of the rules of law, and an assessment of their gravity. For this purpose, risk prioritisation methods are used, depending on the weight given to particular types of risk by a given financial institution, and other information derived from reports on materialising risk events (including the risk of potential losses—near misses);
c. Details of any country, region or business line specific risk event reports discussed at the meetings of operational committees, risk management committees, etc.;
d. General risk assessments for a given region or business line, taking into account external (market, political, regulatory) and internal factors (e.g. whether the assessment was given in low, medium or high-risk conditions).

7 Sovereign Risks Management

When analysing and then co-managing compliance risk resulting from external factors facing a financial institution, the financial institution's relations with public entities are of particular importance. The compliance services assessing the risks associated with non-contractual obligations arising on the part of a financial institution shall take into account the examples discussed above, criteria, reports and the potential consequences of expected negative events. They shall, in particular, consider the possible risks arising from the legal, regulatory and political issues that arise in connection with the conclusion of agreements between the financial institutions and states, state-owned companies or other public entities.[84]

The process of contracting by financial institutions with public entities, including companies and agencies belonging to public authorities, may be accompanied by important legal issues and the potential

---

[84] More about the risks connected with concluding transactions with public entities resulting from the practice of using non-legal instruments of pressure and soft norms see W. Reinicke, J. M. Witte, Interdependence, Globalization and Sovereignty: The Role of Non-binding International Legal Accords [in] D. Shelton [ed.] *Commitment and Compliance: The Role of Non-binding Norms in the International Legal System*, Oxford 2000, p. 76.

compliance risks that arise from them. The following are examples of six groups of compliance risks arising from contractual relations between financial institutions and public entities, in particular when concluding such contracts in certain jurisdictions, considered to be most risky. This is truer in particular for some developing countries with a volatile and unpredictable political situation in general. These include:

a. Situations of unpredictable changes in legal norms directly or indirectly related to the financial institution's activities;
b. Cases of breaches or unilateral changes to contracts concluded with public entities in situations of changing political circumstances;
c. Invalidity of contracts as a result of political decisions by public sector bodies;
d. The introduction of foreign exchange restrictions especially concerning foreign transfers, but also credit, deposit and settlement transactions and the convertibility of the local currency;
e. Government guarantees not being honoured despite the fact that the conditions precedent included in the contracts materialised;
f. Expropriation carried out as a result of political decisions, especially when related to nationalisation.

Despite the fact that it is the task of the management of financial institutions to mitigate these risks, which compliance must take into account, the practical possibility of influencing these risks, or even of negotiating them with public entities on the other hand, is in fact limited. This is due, for example, to the fact that the terms and conditions of cooperation are often established with a real advantage of public entities that are able to influence the nature of contractual relations, e.g. by shaping the surrounding legal and regulatory conditions. In order to show a full picture of how compliance management functions in financial institutions, it is therefore necessary to identify the main legal issues and compliance risks associated with concluding agreements with countries or other public entities, and to indicate the ways in which these risks can be minimised. What is worth stressing, however, is if there is no counterparty, which is a public entity, to situations of breaches or there is no risk of a breach of contractual obligations, or other changes introduced intentionally in legal norms or supervisory regulations unfavourable for financial institutions, then compliance services in financial institutions, guided by an analysis of identified risks and expected benefits, co-decides about the possible use of the tools that can prevent or minimise the occurrence of such risks. The following are seven typical legal issues that compliance services in financial institutions take into account when concluding contracts involving states or other public entities.

    a. Contract award procedure—as a rule, the conclusion of a contract with public entities requires compliance with public procurement procedures required by the state or by a state-owned company, agency, etc., and the award of contracts by the state. This is due to the adoption of such proceedings as a general norm at present. This involves the generally declared compliance by public entities with rules on fairer competition, state aid, the transparency of procedures involving public entities and the prevention of corrupt practices. Non-compliance with the relevant rules of conduct resulting from such regulations may have undesirable consequences for the financial institution, such as exclusion from the tender process, the imposition of fines on the financial institution, the cancellation of the tender, the withdrawal from the contract if the public entity considers that there has been a breach of contract, etc. The financial institution is not obliged to comply with the provisions of the contract.[85]

    b. Since the conclusion of such contracts is usually governed by strictly defined rules of governance, for example, the public procurement procedure itself, as well as the various stages of the tendering process and the conditions under which participation in the process is possible, there is generally little scope for negotiation of their content, given the specific position of the principal. This happens even if the individual conditions seem to have little or no connection with the subject matter of the contract.[86]

---

[85] In addition, in the public tendering process, special extraterritorial legislation may also apply to anti-corruption procedures, such as the US International Corrupt Practices Act of 19 December 1977, §78dd-1 of Chapter 15 of the US Foreign Corrupt Practices Act (FCPA), which is not directly related to public procurement procedures, but is relevant to some large financial institutions doing business in many countries because it imposes additional obligations on them http://www.justice.gov/criminal-fraud/foreign-corrupt-practices-act (download 7 November 2018).

[86] For example, in the case of orders to operate in the debt instruments market, it refers to the conditions imposed on participants in a tender for their experience in similar procedures, references from other public sector principals, ratings held by recognized credit rating agencies, the provision of order execution warranties, the provision of irrevocable

c. Compliance obligations related to the management of compliance risk consist, in the context of a financial institution's participation in a public tender procedure, in the creation of conditions on the part of the financial institution in which employees are aware of the need to apply risk mitigates.
d. The prerequisite for compliance with the requirements for the tendering processes carried out by public entities is in compliance both with the norms of public procurement law in force in a given territory, as well as with the detailed regulations in force during a specific procedure.
e. The financial institution adopts its own enhanced norms for, among others, anti-corruption policies in tender procedures, independent of those generally applicable. Compliance services play a decisive role in formulating these norms, interpreting them and monitoring their practical application.
f. To this end, compliance services actively cooperate with representatives of other departments of the financial institution, including by helping to determine whether there are specific anti-corruption policies specific to a particular jurisdiction with respect to a particular public counterparty.[87]
g. In the case of the final terms and conditions being set in a tendering procedure, which deviate from those originally set, and in particular where there is doubt as to their compliance with financial institutions' internal rules in this respect, compliance services shall consider the possible 'acceptance of risk' on a case-by-case basis by obtaining the consent of the relevant stakeholders (e.g. representatives of the management body, legal department, risk, etc.).

---

relevant guarantees, the payment of specified amounts of collateral, and the execution of the order in a strictly defined manner. See J. M. Logsdon, D. J. Wood, Global Business Citizenship and Voluntary Codes of Ethical Conduct, *Journal of Business Ethics* 59(1)/2005, p. 57 et seq.

[87] This also applies to issues such as the power of representation of the entities concerned in public procurement procedures granted to individually identified persons. A particular type of complication is the cooperation with such persons who are subject to certain restrictions imposed by banks—the so-called politically exposed persons (PEP, politicians, persons sitting on the bodies of the State-owned companies etc.). See, e.g., K.-K. R. Choo, Challenges in Dealing with Politically Exposed Persons, *Trends and Issues in Crime and Criminal Justice* 386/2010, p. 53.

When financial institutions provide services of particular importance to public entities (e.g. when the financial institution is the organiser of the issue of bonds or treasury bills), the regulations of a given country may require, sometimes it can be even referred to in the constitution, with regard to the conclusion of contracts by a state administration body, local government or by other entities owned by the state or local government.[88] These rules indicate, inter alia, who is entitled to sign the contract, and what is the procedure for such signature, how this is done, whether the consent of other authorities is necessary. In addition, in certain sectors of industry of strategic importance for national security, such as defence, energy, telecommunications, norms resulting from other regulations imposing additional obligations on financial institutions may also apply.[89]

Since any instance of non-compliance in cooperation with public entities is associated with an increased degree of risk, the compliance function plays a particularly active role in this case. In such situations, it is of key importance to properly select the instruments used in order to mitigate this risk and all possible consequences of them.[90] In such cases, the most used tool is to seek internal or external legal advice. Even this issue is usually very precisely regulated by intra-corporate norms. The aim is to ensure that the opinions obtained correspond at the same time to all of the conditions listed below:

a. they are fair, based on the best legal knowledge currently available;
b. they take into account any factors which may fully reflect the current state of the law, including the state of supervisory regulation;
c. and that they are formulated by taking into account the specificities of the activities carried out with regard to both the services offered to the public body, and the way in which the financial institution itself is expected to operate in the provision of such services.

---

[88] See A. Alfonso, M. G. Arghyrou, A. Kontonikas, The Determinants of Sovereign Yield Spreads in the European Monetary Union, *European Central Bank Working Paper Series*, April 2015, https://www.ecb.europa.eu/pub/pdf/scpwps/ecbwp1781.en.pdf (download 17 February 2019).

[89] See A. Tarantino, Governance, *Risk, and Compliance Handbook: Technology, Finance, Environmental and International Guidance and Best Practices*, New Jersey 2008, p. 485 et seq.

[90] About the role of law in general as a specific management method, including risk management see M. J. Golecki, *Między pewnością a efektywnością. Marginalizm instytucjonalny wobec prawotwórczego stosowania prawa*, Warsaw 2011, p. 118.

Hence, the procedures for obtaining legal opinions provide for consulting the main legal counsel of the financial institution competent for a given jurisdiction, often with the simultaneous imposition of the obligation to cooperate with lawyers from external law firms, and authorities active in the field of legal advice (usually representatives of the academic circles writing comments and opinions of the those cooperating with these law firms as of counsels). Irrespective of receiving such an opinion, and in particular in the absence of a legal adviser employed by the financial institution, the financial institution often seeks an opinion from an external law firm competent for the jurisdiction of the state or another entity involved in the transaction, in order to obtain confirmation of the appropriate authority to enter into such a transaction.

The role of compliance in limiting a financial institution's risk related to the provision of services to public entities is also to ensure the existence of security mechanisms in the event of insolvency, but also to reduce the creditworthiness of the state or another public entity due to the occurrence of adverse political or economic events (sovereign risk). It is therefore the responsibility of the financial institution's compliance services to develop and implement specific rules of conduct for these types of cases. Interestingly, despite the experience of economic crises, in general, the constitutions and the laws of states do not contain rules on how to proceed in the event of their insolvency.[91] In principle, the same is true for companies owned by states, for which it is rare to enact special regulations for this type of circumstances. Usually, just like other legal entities, they are subject to the company law of a given jurisdiction. In the case of companies of strategic importance, whose economic situation could significantly affect the rights of financial institutions as creditors, financial institutions apply special rules of conduct, introduced by separate procedures, in the case of circumstances indicating the insolvency of these entities.

The internal rules that form part of the management of such risks, which set out how to mitigate the effects of the risk of insolvency of public entities, relate to two types of instruments.

Firstly, when asking for a legal opinion on the enforceability of a defaulted entity's obligations, it suggests considering the possibility of using first-ranking clauses to satisfy financial institution claims.

---

[91] D. Schoenmaker, *Governance of International Banking: The Financial Trilemma*, New York 2013, p. 21 et seq.

Secondly, the possibility of cross-compensation of the financial institution's claims with the claims that the state might have on the financial institution is analysed. In particular, this analysis should take into account the possibility of netting existing obligations of companies or other state-owned entities. Differences in regulation in different jurisdictions in this respect relate both to how different categories of entities are covered and to what extent they can be treated as *stationes fisci* in insolvency settlements, as well as to what types of claims in respect of a financial institution in a given jurisdiction are subject to set-off. Here, by far the most important, given the scale and value of the transaction, is to decide how local regulations treat agreements concerning debt instruments and derivative transactions.[92]

Where financial institutions execute orders for public entities, it is important, in the event of default risk materialisation, to decide on the applicable law and the courts competent to resolve disputes. Compliance services, whose duties include ensuring the conditions in which the financial institution operates in accordance with the applicable regulations, should also as a result of a dispute with public entities, implement procedures that had already been introduced at the stage of negotiating the terms of cooperation.[93]

According to financial institutions' rules on transactions with public entities, an important element that can influence the success of any proceedings, including proceedings against states and other public entities, is the possibility of obtaining a favourable determination of the applicable law and records in court. However, usually for financial institutions operating simultaneously in multiple markets and conducting multilateral international transactions, there are relatively many possibilities to

---

[92] The activities of the International Swap Dealers Association (ISDA), which issues legal opinions on the enforceability of close-out netting in relation to States and state-owned entities, are helpful in this respect. Although these opinions may not be applicable in the context of a given transaction, they are a good starting point for proper analysis. See *The Importance of Close-Out Netting*, http://www2.isda.org/search?headerSearch=1&keyword=close+out+netting (download 19 February 2019).

[93] In some jurisdictions it is not possible to determine the will of the contracting parties to the jurisdiction of another court and the law, as there is an obligation to settle only by the courts having jurisdiction over the defendant's domicile. Concerning the provisions of the court and the determination of the applicable law in the credit documentation see *Jurisdiction Clauses in Contracts*, http://www.timeshareconsumerassociation.org.uk/jurisdiction-clauses-contracts/ (download 2 April 2019).

choose the law depending on the jurisdiction of the counterparty, the place where the contractual obligations arise are performed, or the jurisdiction in which the assets of the parties to the agreement are located. The choice of law issues identified in compliance procedures are relevant for the following reasons.

a. The choice of the applicable law is relevant for determining the content of the parties' obligations by way of judicial decisions.
b. The correct choice of law may be important for the effectiveness of the enforcement of judgements given, including in particular the amount of damages awarded.
c. The reason why compliance services remain active in determining the law applicable to obligations entered into with states or other state-owned entities is that by making the conclusion of an agreement conditional upon the requirement that their agreement be governed by local legal norms, they may expose financial institutions to a real risk that any legislative changes in a given country may affect the rights and obligations of these financial institutions arising from the concluded agreements.
d. Situations where the parties to the contracts expect disputes to be settled before a particular court in certain jurisdictions may give rise to concerns about the impartiality of the relevant judicial institutions.

The above-mentioned reasons explain why the intra-financial institution compliance regulations introduced in financial institutions presuppose the application of contractual provisions which, from the point of view of global interests, mitigate risk in this respect. In practice, financial institutions negotiate that the law applicable to contracts concluded with public entities should be the law of the jurisdictions in which the corporation has the greatest experience and appropriate infrastructure, depending on the region in which the contract is to be concluded.[94] If such solutions are not achievable, consideration shall be given to whether alternative proposals from public counterparties are acceptable from the point of view of the financial institution's risk-mitigating interests.

---

[94] On the stability of judgments and the risk of cross-border disputes on the example of companies listed in the United States see B. Cheng, S. Srinivasan, G. Yu, Securities Litigation Risk for Foreign Companies Listed in the U.S., *Harvard Business School Working Paper* 13–036/2012, p. 5 et seq.

Equally important from this perspective is the question of where to settle disputes. If the contracting party does not agree with the proposal that the proceedings should take place before a court in countries with a known, credible and efficient judicial system, the solution may be an arbitration tribunal. The compliance norms presuppose that lawyers with experience in these matters, who are able to confirm the enforceability of foreign judgements or arbitration awards in a given territory are consulted on a case-by-case basis. On the other hand, if a significant part of the counterparty's assets are located outside the country, they provide for consideration to be given to the law applicable to determine the content of the agreement, and to the place of dispute settlement, in order to ensure the smooth enforcement of court decisions.

The greatest of the risks associated with transactions with public entities in the event of a dispute over the content of mutual obligations is that under international public law, as well as relevant national constitutional provisions, states and certain other public entities, their companies, agencies, institutes and representative offices and other public entities, such as local authorities, enjoy various types of immunity.

a. Firstly, it concerns the parties to judicial or other settlement proceedings. It concerns all those situations in which, in the territory of a foreign country, proceedings against these entities cannot be conducted before the courts. This applies to diplomatic missions, consular posts, permanent and intentional state missions, attachés, etc., as well as diplomats and other representatives of these countries on an equal footing with them in privileges.
b. Secondly, this relates to the enforcement of the assets of these entities. Indeed, even if, as a result of the proceedings against the state, the state-owned company, government agencies, etc., a judgement in favour of a financial institution has been issued (regardless of whether this was done in a domestic, foreign or arbitration court), there may still be restrictions that prevent the enforcement of the assets of these entities. As a result, a financial institution's economic security in a given country may be exposed to significant risks, given that the financial institution will not be able to apply for a repayment of the awarded claim from the assets of that public counterparty.

Financial institutions' compliance norms formulate recommendations for dealing with this type of risk. These include, the need to determine, already at the negotiation stage, the waiver of immunities and exclusions to the fullest extent possible, in particular with regard to the above-mentioned court, protective or enforcement proceedings. There are also cases where states, by virtue of constitutional or other constitutional provisions, exclude the waiver of immunity. In such situations, any attempt to contractually exclude immunity shall be void or, at least, ineffective under the laws of the state concerned.

The compliance norms implemented by financial institutions therefore refer in such cases to the provisions governing the mandates granted to certain entities, and in particular their ability to enter into enforceable contractual obligations.[95] In practice, it is therefore recommended that the clauses relating to the waiver of immunity should be reserved by stipulating that this is to the extent permitted by the applicable legal norms, as this includes, *inter alia*, the need to preserve the state of compliance for which the financial institution's compliance departments are responsible.[96] However, there are also slightly more favourable situations from the point of view of a financial institution dealing with this type of entity. In some states, surrendering jurisdiction is tantamount to waiving the immunity of a public body. In any case, however, in order to unambiguously confirm this information, it is necessary to obtain a local legal opinion within the jurisdiction of this type of counterparty.

A factor that may minimise the risks managed by compliance services in financial institutions is the use of the so-called stabilisation clauses. According to the constitutional principle of discounting, which is binding in many countries, the current legislative power of the state is not bound by the actions of its predecessor. As a result, state authorities may take decisions which render contracts with a financial institution unenforceable (ab initio), make them unenforceable under the applicable rules of law, or decide on the expropriation of the assets which are the subject of these contracts. Depending on their negotiating position, financial institutions usually consider stabilisation clauses in their contracts with public entities to minimise such risks. Internal compliance norms

---

[95] On the subject of cross-referencing clauses see L. Leszczyński, *Tworzenie klauzul generalnych odsyłających*, Lublin 2000, p. 17.

[96] A waiver of immunity from the framework ISDA agreement of 2002.

recommending their use usually distinguish between three types of such clauses.

 a. So-called 'freezing' clauses, the essence of which is to agree that the law applicable to the contract is the law in force at a given time (this may be both the time of the conclusion of the contract, the entry into force of the provisions set out therein, the performance of certain services agreed by the parties, etc.) and that any possible changes in the legal rules do not apply to the contract in question.
 b. 'indemnity' clauses also referred to as 'financial equilibrium' clauses. According to such provisions, the financial responsibility for the change in the conditions of performance of the contract resulting from changes in law falls on the state, in which case the provider of finance is entitled to receive appropriate compensation, in order to ensure financial equilibrium in relation to the initial calculation of the profitability of the financial instrument provided.[97]
 c. 'hybrid' clauses combine the features of freezing clauses and financial equilibrium clauses.

Another way to avoid a possible change in the law, if it is not possible to introduce stabilisation clauses, is to try to negotiate clauses in contracts concluded with public entities to open the process of renegotiation of the contract itself. It is true that such clauses provide less protection, but on the other hand they allow for more flexibility. They may provide that in the event of a change in the law, the parties not only have the right, but even the obligation, to renegotiate contracts, and that such renegotiations must be carried out in good faith in order to find a solution that will ensure the original financial equilibrium.

Typically, when introducing such clauses, if no solution is found, financial institutions reserve the right to submit the case to international arbitration or, when using economic mediation instruments, they may have recourse to experts appointed for this purpose. The financial

---

[97] Due to the noticeable usefulness of solutions developed during the introduction of stabilization clauses to the market, they are more and more often applied not only to agreements on investment financing, but also to agreements relating to investment agreements themselves, for example, concerning the implementation of long-term infrastructure projects, especially those implemented in countries with relatively high observed variability of the legal environment.

institution's internal procedures containing norms for managing compliance risk may imply that, since, as indicated above, there may be local legal norms stipulating that an agreement concluded in the past may not impose restrictions on state authorities (and the risk of such situations is compounded by the use of freezing clauses in agreements), it is necessary that the inclusion of such clauses in the agreement be preceded by a local legal opinion confirming the enforceability of any stabilisation clauses.

In addition, the procedures of a financial institution also aim to prevent the effects of the risk of changes in the law through the use of typical contract risk mitigation techniques, such as the nine indicated below.[98]

    a. Provisions concerning the right to terminate the contract with or without prior notice in the event of significant changes in the law relating to matters governed by the contract, force majeure, states of emergency, etc.
    b. Inclusion in the contract of statements containing assurances by the parties confirming the veracity of the facts taken into account when entering into the contract, statements by virtue of which a public entity gives warranty for possible legal defects relating to the subject matter of the contract and statements concerning the undertaking by the entity entering into the contract with a financial institution, *inter alia*, to the extent:

        1. actions consistent with the legal norms applicable to the content of contractual obligations, supervisory regulations concerning the subject matter of the agreement, court rulings relating to the issues covered by the agreement etc., in force on the date of conclusion of the agreement;
        2. all statutory and regulatory authorisations, as well as permits, licences, etc., remain valid.[99]

---

[98] On limiting the impact of the risk of changes in law on the content of contractual obligations see T. L. Brown, M. Potoski, Managing Contract Performance: A Transaction Costs Approach, *Journal of Policy Analysis and Management* 22(2)/2003, p. 287.

[99] The role of the warranties and representations included in the texts of contracts in the scope of their construction and liability of the providing party under the contractual terms see A. Szlęzak, H. Gardocka, *Ponownie o* representations and warranties *w umowach poddanych prawu polskiemu*, Przegląd Prawa Handlowego 2/2011, p. 31.

c. 'gross-up' clauses, i.e. those which provide for the payment of amounts due to liabilities, taking into account any difference in the value of benefits covered by the agreement due to changes in tax regulations that may take place, as well as those which allow for termination of the agreement due to changes in tax law.
d. The management of financial institutions' compliance risk in relation to contractual relations with public entities also addresses the issue of the financial institutions' compliance with international investment treaties.[100] These are agreements concluded between countries, which allow the investor to bring actions for breach of the terms and conditions of various types of investments, i.e. projects involving the provision of financing. Such actions are directed directly against states for the settlement of arbitration tribunals (one of which is the International Centre for the Settlement of Investment Disputes [ICSID]).[101] Such actions are brought on the basis of actions based on the provisions of the Treaties and are then in addition to claims for breach of contract. In principle, such international agreements are bilateral treaties. Around 2000 treaties of this kind have already been signed. Although the most well-known investment treaties such as the North Atlantic Free Trade Agreement (NAFTA) and the Energy Charter Treaty (ECT) are multilateral agreements. Despite the fact that, due to the heterogeneity of the matter, no uniform model for such a bilateral treaty has been developed so far, the role of compliance services is to ensure that the provisions of these treaties are included in agreements that provide sufficient protection for the interests of the financial institution.
e. Obligation to pay compensation to the investor and the sponsoring undertaking without delay in the event of expropriation or nationalisation of its assets. This refers to both the relatively frequent actual takeover of the investment and, as a result, often direct expropriation of the investor's assets. This is often the case where the investment has significantly lost value or the investor has control over it. Progressive expropriation or nationalisation is also possible when a large number of legal acts deprive the

---

[100] Cf. S. R. Epstein [ed.] Guilds, Economy and Society [in] *Corporations, economies et societe*, Seville 1998, p. 40 et seq.

[101] Established in 1966, the ICSID with its registered office in Washington, DC is an independent arbitration body within the World Bank.

investment of its economic value or deprive the investor of control over the investment.
f. A fair treatment clause, which is intended to oblige the state to respect the legitimate expectations of the investor. If the investor proves that, after the start of the project, the state acted contrary to its legitimate expectations (by withdrawing valid licences, introducing export quotas, etc.), this is the basis for bringing an action against the state.
g. National and most-favoured-nation clause, which assume that the host country treats the foreign investor on an equal footing as a domestic investor or as an investor from a most-favoured-nation country.
h. Ensure the payment of compensation for the loss of investment made in the event of war or civil unrest.
i. The possibility of transferring capital and profits from the host country in an easily convertible currency, more broadly referred to as a non-controlling capital clause.
j. Provisions relating to the pursuit of the above claims in a neutral territory before an impartial determining authority (usually before an international arbitration court).

As indicated above, in the course of carrying out risk management tasks, and in this case ensuring that conditions are created in advance to avoid a possible risk of placing a financial institution in a situation of non-compliance, compliance services participate in the identification of whether an appropriate international investment treaty exists in a given area and what forms of protection are available. Compliance services also remain involved in the transaction process itself, and in assisting in negotiating the most important documents, so that the treaty contains provisions beneficial for the transaction.

It is also worth mentioning here that compliance also plays an important role in the financial institution's efforts to avoid political risk resulting from its relationship with the customers of a public entity. Situations where these risks exist are contracts entered into by financial institutions with states, states' companies, government agencies, etc., where there are political conflicts of interest or situations perceived as such, which have a negative impact on financial institutions' relations with these clients. An example is the expropriation of financial institution assets by the state or by other entities on the basis of powers of attorney granted by the state. This also applies to the risks associated with the role that financial institutions can play in the sovereign debt financing process, as an organiser or advisor to the sovereign debt issuance process, treasury companies or other public entities that base the valuation of their investment credibility on sovereign ratings. In such situations, there is indeed a serious risk of acting to the detriment of investors or other financial institution customers. Then, in the internal norms of financial institutions, the mitigating factors of these risks may be the two basic ones indicated below.

a. Analysis of the transaction with the participation of both specialists in the field with relevant experience in risk measurement, including estimation of the probability of its occurrence. If deemed necessary or even justifiable, such analysis shall be carried out within the financial institution's reputational risk committee.
b. Ensuring proper communication of the specific role of the financial institution in the transaction, using the appropriate information methods to the extent permitted by law and confidentiality obligations.

In practice, the management of compliance risk does not mean that compliance risk can be completely eliminated. Not even activities related to the management of these risks directly relate to the minimisation of compliance risks. There are situations in which obtaining a legal opinion is the main element of risk management. Such an opinion submitted to the financial institutions may indicate the following legal risks resulting from the conclusion of an agreement with a counterparty.

a. A clear opinion on the enforceability of the contract cannot be obtained, or there is uncertainty about the final solvency of the entity entering into the transaction, as the local legal opinion is limited to stating that the contract is enforceable or may not be enforceable in the event of insolvency or other circumstances.
b. Local courts do not recognise foreign judgements or arbitration awards.
c. The final, non-negotiable terms proposed in the agreement are contrary to the financial institution's internal policies.

In such situations where, despite negotiations, it is not possible to limit this risk to the tolerance level set by compliance services and local lawyers, it may, however, be that the financial institution, after obtaining the consent of the financial institution's authorities, will decide to enter into a transaction or agreement on a risk acceptance basis. At the same time, it is the responsibility of the compliance services responsible for a given financial institution to inform the entities interested in the accompanying compliance risk by way of an opinion based on the analysis of significant issues that it raises, taking into account the reputation risk and the scale of the transaction.

8 THE COMPLIANCE AS CONTROL FUNCTION IN THE THREE LINES OF DEFENCE MODEL

On the basis of recommendations developed with the participation of consulting companies, which carried out reviews of the functioning of internal control structures commissioned by financial institutions, new solutions for ensuring compliance were introduced in many institutions.[102] In the course of the case-by-case analysis, situations of ineffective operation of control services were observed, among other things. As a result, a model for an internal control system based on the three lines of defence was proposed.[103] The model consists of assigning tasks related to ensuring compliance of financial institutions' operations to individual entities, defined as lines of defence against the risk of non-compliance. A new phenomenon within the three lines of defence model is the imposition of obligations to ensure that financial institution's operate in accordance with the compliance norms in all organisational units of the financial institution. These duties consist of creating within the financial institution rules for imposing compliance obligations on each entity in connection with the normal activities of these entities.

---

[102] It is also true, however, that the earliest search for the definition of the role and meaning of the internal standards of international corporations started quite a long time ago. See D. F. Vagts, The Multinational Enterprise: A New Challenge for International Law, *Harvard Law Review* 83/1969–1970, pp. 739–792.

[103] It is not, however, a non-negotiable model, which nevertheless takes place from the position of proving its ineffectiveness. See H. Davies, Banks Need to Question Their 'Three Lines of Defense', *Financial Times*, 9 July 2013. Also: *Excuse Me, How Many Lines of Defense? The New Financial Maginot Lines*, paradigmrisk.wordpress.com/2013/03/18 (download 20 November 2018).

a. The first line are business units of financial institutions (those whose employees have direct contact with customers) or business support units which are directly and primarily responsible for a given risk, the so-called risk owners.
b. The second line are the functions of financial institutions supervising a given risk, i.e. internal control units, units responsible for managing compliance risk, other units responsible for managing other types of risk and the unit of so-called financial controlling. At this level of protection there are also compliance services, which in addition to advisory duties, and those related to risk management also have control functions, which may be carried out in relation to any internal organisational unit of the financial institution. As part of this function, it is the responsibility of the compliance departments to ensure that the other departments operate in accordance with the financial institution's internal norms.
c. The third line of defence is the internal audit, the task of which is to ensure that possible risks which might not be identified by the first line of defence or by the compliance services are nevertheless ultimately identified and accompanied by appropriate corrective recommendations. The third level of protection is therefore designed to identify malfunctions in the functioning of the financial institution and to make recommendations, the implementation of which is an obligation for those entities concerned. In this respect, internal audit is an element supporting the financial institution's compliance function.[104]

In this model, the tasks assigned to each of these lines of defence are defined in the internal procedures adopted by the financial institutions, forming together related normative systems, for which the key features are consistency and completeness, in financial institutions jargon

---

[104] Although the models of the three lines of defense may differ in detail in relation to the scope of activities undertaken within their framework by individual organizational units, they are similar in substance. Possible further practical developments of this concept are a continuation of the basic model dividing the responsibility for defending against compliance risk into all financial institution's units and reserving for compliance the role of control in this respect.

compliance is also defined as tightness of controls. Therefore, they are frequently extended and tightened.[105]

The first line of defence, i.e. primary control, is carried out as part of the day-to-day business, and therefore concerns how financial institution employees comply with the procedures designed to reduce compliance risk when performing their assigned tasks. These procedures, including the normative assignment of control tasks, as well as the necessary training provided to the employees of these units and accompanying their implementation, are established and maintained in consultation with the compliance and legal services. This is intended to guarantee normative correctness that minimises the risk of non-compliance.

It is worth noting that direct control by management boards and other key executives over the functioning of financial institutions is also part of this primary control. It is therefore the responsibility of the staff performing these control functions to ensure that all activities within their area of responsibility are carried out in accordance with the financial institution's internal norms, and that the most important issues and exceptional situations are quickly identified and transferred to a higher level of competence within the financial institution's organisational structure. All the most important control tasks in financial institutions are strictly documented, taking into account the scope of roles and

---

[105] In the context of one of the more sophisticated models for managing compliance risk through three lines of defense, which operate in practice with international financial institutions, it is pointed out that the business line representatives should distinguish between them in the first line of defense:
   a. the risk owner responsible for managing the risks inherent in his activities;
   b. a risk and control manager who is an expert advising on operational risks associated with the business line within which he or she operates;
   c. the control owner responsible for the assessment, selection and management of the compliance risk control of the business.
The second line of defense in this model, in turn, provides for two main groups:
   a. risk stewards, whose tasks include defining the taxonomy related to the identified types of compliance risks, establishing formal rules in this respect and providing appropriate advisory support—this includes, inter alia, the compliance function;
   b. operational risk function managers who provide independent oversight of the operational risk activities of the institution and prepare their own reports.

responsibilities related to the implementation of business processes.[106] In principle, the exercising of the first line of defence control is not part of the compliance control function. Exceptions are processes requiring regulatory knowledge or involving a high degree of risk of illegality. These include issues relating to:

a. the disclosure of information on irregularities observed in the functioning of the financial institution;
b. the disclosure of other material information, such as that relating to the maintenance of insider lists, the disclosure of which may have a material impact on the price formation of securities.

In such situations, compliance is supervised by a compliance function, which is required to ensure that the related control activities are carried out to the highest professional norms of care.

Secondary control, the second line of defence against the risk of non-compliance, is performed by organisational units established specifically to complement the control activities carried out by the business lines and management of the financial institution under primary control. In particular, the internal control departments, under different names, monitor compliance with procedures, and analyse changing risk indicators. This is part of a secondary control, either jointly or without the participation of compliance services, which in turn may also be involved on their own will in this type of investigation. In all situations, however, the role of compliance services is to support the management in meeting their obligation to control the risk of compliance with the law. At the operational level, the internal control planning tasks described in the internal control procedures of the local compliance function staff performing second line of defence duties include the following three types of tasks.

a. First of all, to prepare and update action plans for the assessment and mitigation of the risks of noncompliance. Such plans shall be used to identify existing legislation and the risks of non-compliance with it, to determine the degree of such risks and then to take

---

[106] Cf. A document submitted for the financial institutions' consultation: *Bank for International Settlements, Consultative Document: Sound Practices for the Management and Supervision of Operational Risk*, Basel, December 2010.

regular action, including the implementation of action plans, to monitor and, as far as possible, to mitigate such risks. All this information, usually compiled in the form of structured reports, is used to support the financial institution's business activities in the process of assessing and controlling operational risk, including compliance risk. It is on the basis of these internal regulations that compliance officers are required to carry out periodic assessments of operational risk. For the purpose of obtaining complete control, this assessment is also made in relation to local compliance services. This makes it possible to determine the extent to which the activities of these services may in themselves pose an operational risk to the financial institution.

b. It is also the drawing up of annual and long-term compliance plans over several years. The purpose of such plans is to prepare the tasks for the next period, which are based on an analysis of the current and anticipated risks, taking into account the available resources necessary to achieve them. Typically, these rules provide that such plans are agreed with the business line management and reviewed by the compliance management units for their timeliness and adequacy. Although compliance plans are formally prepared once a year, exceptions to this rule are permitted in practice. According to the principle of risk assessment, compliance services may modify planned activities and even shift priorities during the year if, in accordance with a justified opinion, the degree of risk has changed.

c. On the basis of the annual compliance plan, regular monitoring and ad hoc checks shall prove necessary in order to verify the reliability of control activities and compliance with the relevant procedures. The procedures governing the operation of the second line of defence provide that this monitoring, combined with checks, may have an appropriate impact on the reliability of the indicators used and the analysis carried out by the business lines. This usually takes place after the verification of the reliability of the checks carried out, in particular by sampling. These procedures also assume that compliance services are required to conduct annual audits of key business areas.

The financial institution's third line of defence is the internal audit, which assesses whether the primary control activities are sufficient to mitigate compliance risks. In this context, it verifies the effectiveness of the secondary control activities. The audit, as a broadly established, independent function, analyses the functional control reports drawn up by the compliance departments and, if any weak points or other issues of concern are identified, may proceed to a more detailed audit of these departments.[107]

The most general conclusion is therefore that the second line of defence's compliance function relates to the control of compliance risk management by ensuring that the financial institution operates in accordance with the applicable norms. This function has five elements.

- a. Identify the norms which the institution has deemed necessary to comply with either because of their mandatory nature or because of the subjective benefit to the institution by virtue of their inclusion in the group of norms which the corporation chooses to comply with despite the fact that these norms are not mandatory.
- b. Interpretation of the obligations to which a financial institution is subject under those norms.
- c. Identification of the potential risks arising from possible non-compliance with these norms and balancing the associated risks by determining the likelihood of their occurrence and the severity of the consequences that may arise in a situation of non-compliance.
- d. Including them in the form of meta-norms applicable in a given corporation through the creation of internal regulations, in which the previously interpreted duties are included, but also the

---

[107] The question remains how to ensure compliance with the third line of defense in the face of the fact that it constitutes the final control, i.e. the question of who checks the checker. There are several ways to secure the compliance of an audit, the most common of which are:
- a. the introduction of regional control over local and global control over regional within the same function;
- b. Statutory guaranteed direct reporting of internal audit to the supervisory boards in the case of the continental corporate governance structure, or to the non-executive board members in the case of banks with authorities in common law countries;
- c. To ensure that the internal audit function is sufficiently numerous and that its structure is such that its members can maintain independent positions and peer-review of each other's activities.

Ultimately, however, the control of the correctness of internal audit in financial institutions, including compliance conditions, methodological reliability, etc., is carried out by regulators conducting audits as part of supervisory control.

addressees of these norms and risk control processes are defined, with the simultaneous assignment of responsibility for the performance of specified activities to specific organisational units.
e. Ensuring compliance with these norms by making it possible to obtain the appropriate advice on the obligations arising from these norms, followed by the establishment of adapted inspection processes.

These kinds of defined objectives for which compliance is established in financial institutions do not exhaust all the functions performed by these services in practice, while exercising control under the second line of defence. The scope of duties imposed on the compliance unit is much broader and, sometimes significantly different in individual institutions, most often includes, in addition to the performance of the aforementioned duties, control over the performance of duties related to the protection of financial institutions against the undesirable state of non-compliance, which, regardless of what they relate to in terms of subject matter, can be divided into four types. They relate to:

a. Training of staff on compliance issues, including in particular the organisation's compliance norms, and the related and properly implemented follow-up quality control consultation duties for staff questions and concerns about compliance.
b. Formulating written guidelines for employees with respect to the proper understanding of the content of compliance regulations contained in the internal regulations in force in the financial institution.
c. Preparing documents such as compliance manuals, internal codes of conduct and guidelines for existing financial institution practices, etc.[108]
d. Identifying, measuring and assessing compliance risk by the use of the selected elements of the financial institution's methodological equipment to assess other risks.

It follows from the last point that a financial institution's compliance function is required to actively identify, document and assess the

---

[108] M. Forster, T. Loughran, B. McDonald, Commonality in Codes of Ethics, *Journal of Business Ethics* 90/2009, pp. 129–139.

compliance risks associated with the financial institution's overall business. This concerns in particular issues such as the development of new products, including the development of the documentation describing the characteristics and sales of these products, other practical recommendations relating to the financial institution's operations, the financial institution's proposed involvement in new activities, new industries, new customer groups, as well as customer relations or significant changes in the nature of these relations. It is also expected that compliance departments will be represented in the new product committees of financial institutions.

Compliance quality control in a financial institution is complicated in practice, and the complexity of the issue increases with the scale and scope of a financial institution's operations. The successful implementation of this function requires taking into account the different available ways of measuring compliance risk using adequate quantitative and qualitative key performance indicators (KPIs) and using such measurements to support the qualification of the compliance risk profile.[109] The most common tools for selecting the right result indicators are modern statistical and econometric techniques that allow for the aggregation or filtering of data to signal potential compliance problems. Examples of these include observing trends in the changing number of customer complaints, non-norm financial institutions operations, high-risk transactions, etc.[110]

In order to meet these expectations, compliance services continuously assess the adequacy of the procedures and other internal regulations in force in the financial institution regarding compliance. If any inaccuracies or irregularities are identified, they shall respond to any deficiencies identified and, where necessary, make proposals for additions, updates

---

[109] In order to effectively manage the risks inherent in a given organization, specific financial institutions develop their own systems relating to key compliance risk management indicators. They are usually confidential internal documentation. However, some examples of universal, simplified and publicly accessible systems can also be found in online resources. One example of such a system, Compliance and Audit Management, can be found at: http://www.smartkpis.com/kpi/functional-areas/governance-compliance-and-risk/compliance-and-audit-management/ (download 10 September 2018).

[110] On the measurement of aggregated customer complaints see D. D. Bradlow, Private Complaints and International Organizations: A Comparative Study of the Independent Inspection Mechanisms in International Financial Institutions, *Journal of International Law* 36/2005, p. 456.

and improvements. Such control, supported by appropriate testing and subsequent reporting, means that the compliance bodies are required to carry out exhaustive and representative tests and other measurements of compliance deemed methodologically appropriate. The results of such tests and measurements should be reported to the financial institution's competent authorities in accordance with risk management procedures within the framework of the financial institution's reporting regime.[111]

Effective control of compliance risk means that the procedures are in place to ensure that any compliance deficiencies are reported on an ongoing basis by compliance services, including the reporting on compliance issues to the financial institution's management. The reports shall refer to the assessment of the likelihood of the occurrence of compliance risk for the period covered by the report, including any changes in the compliance risk profile recorded on the basis of the measurements taken for that purpose.[112] These reports summarise the weaknesses and delays identified in the application of compliance policies and the recommended corrective measures. Financial institutions' internal rules generally assume that the reporting format should correspond to the financial institution's compliance risk profile and the type of business conducted by the financial institution.[113]

Among the areas in which it is particularly important to minimise the risk of non-compliance, and which are subject to compliance meta-norms, for which compliance services in corporations, and in particular in international financial institutions, is established, there are areas of

---

[111] In case of banks operating in countries of continental law with similar principles of corporate governance, this is a management board which should receive such information on an ongoing basis, but also a supervisory board to whom compliance is required to report not only its periodically determined action plans, but also their results, including the results of ad hoc inspections and tests. In countries where the boards of directors, composed of independent members, is the principal directing body of the financial institution, compliance communicates directly to the boards of directors or through appropriate committees established at the boards (e.g. committees of compliance, audit, operational risk, etc.).

[112] On changes in the risk profile in the context of prudential requirements see A. S. Chernobai, S. T. Rachev, F. J. Fabozzi, *Operational Risk: A Guide to Basel II Capital Requirements, Models and Analysis*, New Jersey 2007, p. 22 et seq.

[113] On adjusting the risk profile to the nature of the business and variable elements of the financial institution's environment see J. Bessis, *Risk Management in Banking*, Padstow 2015, p. 263 et seq.

particular important. The selection of these areas, that are listed below does not result from a consolidated financial institutions practice, nor does it constitute a closed list, and the items are not listed in order of important. Instead, the list corresponds to the most frequently observed areas of responsibility for compliance related to the control functions due to the specific risks to which financial institutions are exposed to:

a. regulatory;
b. financial;
c. reputational.

These risks are largely related to one of the following relations:

a. relations within the structure of the financial institutions group (flow of information on customers and transactions, business planning, financial reporting, ownership and employee relations, etc.);
b. relations with individual customers of the financial institution (retail and corporate);
c. relations with third parties that are not individual customers of a financial institution operating in the public domain (public entities entering into financial relations with financial institutions, media, etc.);
d. relations with regulators.

The approach to particular types of risks described below, and thus also the areas of responsibility for compliance, differs from financial institution to financial institution. These differences may result from the profile of the business or even from the advances made in the implementation of a structured approach to determining the function of compliance in a given financial institution.[114]

---

[114] Compliance tasks are slightly different and more importance is given to relations with public entities that are bank customers in the case of investment banks than in the case of banks operating in the area of consumer finance, which in turn must build appropriate structures to protect them against the risk of money laundering by individual customers.

9 The Compliance Function Responsibilities in External Relations

In order to illustrate the degree of complexity and range of duties entrusted to compliance services within the second line of defence, we present the most common ones below. As the compliance risks relate to the four types of relations to which financial institutions are a party, the different control obligations imposed on the compliance departments, which differ in terms of substance, relate to one of these four types of relations. depending on which compliance risks they involve, they therefore relate to internal relations within the financial institution, to customer relations, as well as to relations with public entities, and with regulators with whom these relations are of a special nature.[115] The analyses presented in this subchapter are based on research that shows that the differences in the duties of compliance services, in connection with the exercise of control functions, are related precisely to which type of entities are participating in the relation with the financial institution.

The compliance function, although its primary objective is to check the state of compliance of financial institutions' activities, is performed in different ways depending on the relation in question. More specifically, depending on the type of breaches that may occur in connection with the financial institution's operations. The first sphere of control is the way in which financial institutions comply with the applicable normative conditions (legal norms, supervisory regulations, financial institutions' own internal norms) within the organisation itself. The nine types of inspections that are carried out by compliance services are described below.

Nowadays, with the global flow of information, the duty entrusted to compliance services is to ensure an adequate level of data protection, understood in the broadest sense, as all legally protected confidential information concerning, first of all, the identity of natural persons and other information held by financial institutions concerning their personal data, including sensitive, biometric, behavioural, economic and other data.[116] The second type of data subject to a special protection regime is

---

[115] On the objectives of financial market regulation see M. Lemonnier, *Europejskie modele rynków finansowych. Wybrane zagadnienia*, Warsaw 2011, p. 248 et seq.

[116] The protection of personal data is a particular challenge for international financial institution, for which reciprocal access to data granted to individual entities is a competitive advantage, inter alia, in relation to customers with reduced credit rating. See A. Powell,

information constituting financial institution secrecy, i.e. information on balances and flows on accounts, on the type, the amounts, the frequency and parties to which these transactions are carried out, and information indirectly resulting from this knowledge on the financial standing of the entities carrying out these operations.[117] The third type of information subject to protection is commercial information of a financial institution as a trading entity. The financial institution is therefore obliged to protect information of different nature in its possession with a special degree of protection.

The maximum protection of this data, and minimum access to them by unauthorised entities is the basic premise on which the classification of financial institutions as a specific type of institutions of public trust is based. Apart from considering at this point the risks related to attempts to obtain unauthorised information to which financial institutions are constantly exposed, and which are in a way an obvious element of the business environment of financial institutions, it is worth paying attention to another interesting aspect of this issue. There are numerous examples of third parties for whom the information resources held by financial institutions are of interest, given that such knowledge can result in a significant improvement in their operations. We are talking here about public institutions authorised by statute to process and analyse classified information, which use the knowledge obtained from financial institutions in practice of their preparatory activities. Only a part of such a situation is provided for in clearly defined norms of applicable law, which gives the possibility of unambiguous cooperation between financial institutions and these institutions in the provision of such information. However, many demands in this respect go beyond the powers conferred by the regulations and require prudent decisions to be made in the form of appropriate recommendations formulated by compliance services. Even more ambiguous are situations in which employees who are formally third parties of other companies in the same group have or

---

N. Mylenko, M. Miller, G. Majnoni, *Improving Credit Information, Bank Regulation and Supervision: On the Role and Design of Public Credit Registries*, Washington, DC 2004, p. 10 et seq.

[117] On banking secrecy and the flow of information within the system of financial institutions see V. Fitzgerald, Global Financial Information, Compliance Incentives and Terrorist Financing, *European Journal of Political Economy* 20(2)/2004, p. 392.

want to gain access to information of interest to them.[118] Indeed, there are arguments to show that such a flow of information within the same group confirms the existence of appropriate structures to ensure adequate control. This is how some market regulators often expect to do so, especially those who include companies at a higher level of consolidation or holding companies within the scope of their supervision. This conflict with information protection regulations is sometimes solved in favour of certain regulators, whose real range of influence, which is a phenomenon of recent years, deserves a separate analysis. In any case, however, practices concerning the protection of legally protected and particularly important information remain the subject of control by the compliance services regulated in the relevant compliance norms.

Secondly, within financial institution groups, an important issue affecting the nature of internal relations is the cross-border adjustment of all entities in the group to the increased quality of business, called global norms. The difference between these types of norms and the regulatory norms described above lies, among other things, in their source. Global norms result from a commitment to all trading participants that the corporation will implement in all jurisdictions in which it operates the highest norms of operation in force in another jurisdiction. In other words, if any of the countries have the highest norms, such as those of the law, the activities of this corporation will also be aligned in all other jurisdictions to such highest standards.[119] Compliance monitoring obligations are particularly important in this respect, as they consist not only in the identification of these norms, but also in the development of norms concerning the practice of applying these norms that have been in force since then globally, in ensuring that employees all over the world comply with them, and, in particular, in monitoring their compliance.

Thirdly, a now regularly observed phenomenon is the existence of separate units responsible for operational risk management and internal

---

[118] The scope of controls carried out by compliance in financial institutions includes a conflict between the obligation to maintain the secrecy and proper control of entities within the same capital group see K. Alexander, R. Dhumale, J. Eatwell, *Global Governance of Financial Systems: The International Regulation of Systemic Risk*, Oxford 2006, p. 134 et seq.

[119] The management of issues itself is also subject to standardization, and here too the highest standards are being set and adhered to. Cf. S. Bleker, D. Hortensius, The Development of a Global Standard on Compliance Management, *Business Compliance*, February 2014, p. 34.

control within the organisational structures of financial institutions, that function in parallel with compliance and internal audit. An element of operational risk management is its valuation.[120] This development is connected with the Basel III agreement on the New Capital Accord, which indicates that the methodology of operational risk measurement and reliability of the financial institution's internal control has a direct impact on the amount of the financial institution's required internal capitals. The risk of non-compliance, also in relation to these issues, is very important and, in the absence of clear rules, may prove rather costly through the possible need to raise capital. A financial institution cannot afford to be in a situation of non-compliance in this respect. Thus, another type of duties centre on the control activities of compliance services making it responsible for assessing whether the methodology adopted by the financial institution for the valuation of operational risk is correct and whether it is observed.

Fourthly, compliance services may also be involved in the control of business risk management, i.e. the current risk of that part of the financial institution's operations which is aimed at generating revenue. This does not only concern credit risk or so-called counterparty risk but involves a broader understanding of how risk effects how a financial institution's business activity itself is conducted. These are, therefore, issues such as whether the purpose of the business activity is to promote the stable development of the financial institution, whether the financial institution records an increase in revenues, whether it is growth based on a stable portfolio, or whether the process of selecting customers in terms of their reliability is proceeding properly.[121]

Fifthly, it is also the responsibility of the financial institution's compliance services to establish and monitor compliance in the event of abnormal situations that pose a threat to the financial institution (business continuity, disaster recovery). Such situations, although by definition specific, may occur relatively frequently in some countries or in some high-risk territories. It is important that the financial institution is

---

[120] On evaluation of operational risk see K. Alexander, R. Dhumale, J. Eatwell, op. cit., p. 201.

[121] On risk management in credit institutions, in particular through analysis of types and mechanisms of operation of collateral in financial practice and their significance for parties of financial transactions see M. Michalski, R. R. Zdzieborski, *Ustawa o niektórych zabezpieczeniach finansowych. Komentarz*, Warsaw 2005, p. 15 et seq.

prepared for them in terms of the existence and observance of properly adapted procedures ensuring the uninterrupted functioning of its core functions.[122]

Sixthly, ensuring information security is one of the most important types of duties in financial institutions (information security risk) because the risk of losing information held by a financial institution is always high. The confidential information currently available to financial institutions, in addition to the use of available filtering, analytical and matching tools, can be of considerable value to third parties vis-à-vis financial institutions, including both its competition and criminal organisations that may try to gain possession of this information. Contrary to the obligations described above, this is not a general protection of information held by financial institutions, but a specific control aimed at protecting against attempts to commit criminal activities against financial institutions. The source of these leaks of information can be people from outside the institution, as well as financial institution employees. These may be the result of intentional and unlawful action, but more often leaks are the result of ignorance, a carefree attitude, and the failure to follow the appropriate operational procedures by the financial institution's staff. The compliance officer is obliged to carry out periodic and random checks to ensure the security of information. Any breach of the mandatory financial institution's secrecy rules not only exposes the financial institution to reputational risk, but also to severe regulatory sanctions.[123]

Seventhly, large international financial institutions, like other corporations, establish their own rules for purchasing goods and services provided to them. These rules apply in particular to global procurement policies.[124] Due to the large scale often associated with procurement

---

[122] Depending on the type of operations carried out, including, for example, whether the bank provides services to consumers, whether it has a network of physical branches, whether it provides cash services and in which territories it operates, such risks may be spread differently. More on issues related to ensuring continuity of bank operations in various situations see M. Power, The Risk Management of Nothing, *Accounting, Organizations, and Society* 34(6–7)/2009, p. 851.

[123] More on information security management see D. Luthy, K. Forth, Laws and Regulations Affecting Information Management and Frameworks for Assessing Compliance, *Information Management & Computer Security* 14(2)/2006, p. 157.

[124] Mandatory contractual clauses in public procurement contracts using the example of the World Bank see S. Williams, The Debarment of Corrupt Contractors from World Bank-Financed Contracts, *Public Contract Law Journal* 36(3)/2007, p. 281 et seq.

there is the risk of fraud in relations with suppliers, therefore it is necessary to norm purchasing procedures, and ensure that they are transparent, fair and applicable regardless of the country in which they are carried out. As a result, although compliance is not normally itself part of procurement procedures, it is the responsibility of these services to establish rules for supplier relations and to check the extent to which they are respected.

The eighth type of compliance control duty is concerned with policies related to human relations internal to the institution. This includes all issues related to employment, the of shaping relations during employment, equal opportunities policies (non-discrimination),. professional development, professional advancement, relations with employee representatives, and what is called knowledge management.[125] This area is not directly regulated by compliance norms, but as in the case of many other areas described above, the norms related to this area are shaped by the norms generally binding in the organisation, in relation to which the compliance services are obliged to give their opinions, and to control their observance. Compliance services therefore help to establish rules and give opinions on the specific regulations applicable within the corporation relating to employee matters.[126] Due to the influence of court rulings on the shaping of internal regulations in this area, compliance obligations include the application of norms compliant with the law, internal guidelines for the corporation, which defines employer–employee's relations, but also to be in line with the rulings in the jurisdictions, in which the financial institutions operate.

---

[125] The differences in relation to the issue of equal treatment of workers are particularly evident in the confrontation of the constant tendency to extend employee rights and anti-discrimination guarantees in the European Union Member States and in other countries outside this area, particularly in the so-called low-cost countries. On trends in the expansion of the substantive guarantees of employees in the European Union see L. Mitrus, Równość traktowania (zakaz dyskryminacji) w zakresie zatrudnienia [in] A. Zawadzka-Łojek, R. Grzeszczak [ed.] *Prawo materialne Unii Europejskiej. Swobodny przepływ towarów, osób, usług i kapitału. Podstawy prawa konkurencji*, Warsaw 2013, p. 154.

[126] On the role of compliance in shaping internal norms relating to employee relations see L. Baccaro, V. Mele, For Lack of Anything Better? International Organizations and Global Corporate Codes, *Public Administration* 89(2)/2011, p. 460 et seq.

Ninthly, the compliance norms introduced in financial institutions create a formal framework defining the process of whistleblowing.[127] The aim is to make it easier for the employees themselves and, above all, to encourage them to actively engage in building awareness of compliance, and to create an additional source of information concerning possible irregularities for the compliance services. Therefore, it is the duty of compliance services to create such norms, which, in addition to defining the principles on which information should be provided, are intended to guarantee easy and universal access to compliance services for employees. They also define mechanisms that ensure the confidentiality of reports, that provide the possibility to report incidents of compliance breaches anonymously. This is mainly in order to ensure that a notifier does not suffer any negative consequences for their actions.[128] It should be remembered that, in general, reports under this procedure are made by subordinate of an institution, and often refer to irregularities noticed by employees in their organisational unit, or those committed by their superiors. They also establish the rules and procedures for the reporting and handling of these complaints, as well as the obligations of those employees to whom the complaints are addressed. These norms define how cooperation with compliance services is to take place, including how their control role is to be implemented, these are not only addressed to the financial institution's management. These procedures also apply to the employees who submitted a complaint, and how they should cooperation with compliance services in efficiently remedying the irregularities, which are the subject of these complaints.[129]

Compliance monitoring is also carried out in relation to the financial institution's relations with customers. As a rule, these relations focus on servicing and financing transactions and other services offered in the performance of financial institutions activities. The complexity of the

---

[127] See W. Wandeckhove, Rewarding the Whistleblower—Disgrace, Recognition or Efficiency? [in] M. Arszułowicz, W. W. Gasparski [ed.] *Whistleblowing: In Defence of Proper Action (Praxeology)*, New Brunswick 2010, p. 21.

[128] About the guarantees of protection and procedures for reporting irregularities for employees see D. D. Bradlow, op. cit., p. 477.

[129] On the subject of compliance obligations in the scope of removing irregularities in the operation of financial institutions identified by the employees themselves (the so-called self-identified issues) see P. Christmann, G. Taylor, Firm Self-Regulation Through International Certifiable Standards: Determinants of Symbolic Versus Substantive Implementation, *Journal of International Business Studies* 37/2006, p. 865.

relations that emerge today as a result of this is constantly increasing. To illustrate them, eight types of activities related to the control activities of the compliance departments are presented below.

It is the responsibility of compliance services in financial institutions to ensure that the financial institution complies with the ban on financing institutions subject to international sanctions. These prohibitions apply to certain countries, institutions, industries and types of transactions. The source of these prohibitions are sanctions in the form of embargoes, trade bans, etc., imposed by the United Nations, other international organisations, as well as by individual states.[130] The task of compliance services in this case is therefore to establish the rules of conduct, and to control compliance with these rules in relation to entities or transactions included on prohibited lists. The most important of these principles are preventive in nature and presuppose that prohibited transactions are not allowed to be financed. Others are of a follow-up nature and consist of a possible search for entities that are, but should not be, among those that are subject to international sanctions. As part of the compliance services' control duties in this respect, it is necessary to review the registers of transactions, which list the types of transactions which should not be financed by international financial institutions. These are publicly available watchlists, which, in addition to the enumeration of countries, entities and types of transactions, also contain the norms of conduct for such situations.[131] These norms are complemented and clarified by the financial institutions' own internal regulations. As with regulations in other areas, it is the responsibility of compliance to ensure that they are complied with.

A related area, but not identical to the one presented above, is the prevention of money laundering and the countering of the financing of terrorism, i.e. the prevention of funds derived from crime or undisclosed sources being put into circulation through financial institutions, and the prevention of the use of the financial system through financial institutions for the purpose of financing terrorism (Anti-money laundering

---

[130] See K. Raustiala, A.-M. Slaughter, International Law, International Relations and Compliance, *Princeton Law and Public Affairs Paper* 2/2002, p. 540.

[131] See C. E. Bannier, C. W. Hirsch, The Economic Function of Credit Rating Agencies—What Does the Watchlist Tell Us? *Journal of Banking and Finance* 34(12)/2010, p. 3040.

and combating terrorist financing).[132] Due to the dynamic complexity of money laundering worldwide, counteracting such activities has now developed into a whole branch of knowledge, which consists of identifying such threats, and taking remedial action against them. One way of preventing the use of the financial system for money laundering is to create tight procedures in financial institutions that oblige employees to take the appropriate action, including in particular as regards analysis and reporting. This includes both the reporting of suspicious events by financial institutions to the state bodies appointed to combat them, as well as the escalation of this knowledge within the financial institution's structures in order to ensure that specialised services within the financial institution take action to prevent it from being used for money laundering purposes. The financial institutions themselves, as well as compliance services within the framework of these financial institutions, together with especially established organisations that are external to financial institutions, do not only list entities suspected of money laundering (watchlists), but above all they create security procedures adjusted to the changing methods used by criminals and their organised groups.[133] It is the responsibility of the compliance departments not only to participate in the development of these procedures, but also to participate in the control of their observance.

The third type of duties performed by compliance services is the examination of individual clients' relations with public entities. Since anti-money laundering is one of the central duties of compliance services, it is worth pointing out here the customer due diligence which is necessary in the process of identifying the risk of money laundering, although it is not only useful for this purpose.[134] However, it is not a matter of estimating the credit risk involved. This is a much broader study and concerns its activities in general, previous economic experience, ownership structure and its reputation. This is related to the growing

---

[132] On practical difficulties in complying with anti-money laundering compliance obligations see A. E. Sorcher, Lost in Implementation: Financial Institutions Face Challenges Complying with Anti-money Laundering Laws, *Transactional Law* 18/2005, p. 398 et seq.

[133] More on combating money laundering in the light of European Union regulations see C. Kosikowski, *Finanse i prawo finansowe Unii Europejskiej*, Warsaw 2014, p. 75.

[134] The legal basis for such a survey is national laws to combat the marketing of criminal assets or other undisclosed sources.

expectation, formulated towards financial institutions by regulators, investors and the general public, that the activity conducted by financial institutions should also be ethical in the sense that financial institutions should not cooperate with customers whose profile and history raise doubts of a fundamental nature.[135] These expectations prompted financial institutions to introduce regulations that strictly regulate what aspects of customer characteristics should be examined, what weight should be given to them, what course of action should be taken in the situation of customer identification, with which, according to the criteria formulated towards the financial institution, cooperation should not take place.[136] Here too, as in other areas indicated earlier, there is a collision of global norms created within the corporation for their own needs with the regulations resulting from the law of a given country. These collisions concern, for example, how deep the process of studying the history and profile of a given entity can be (vetting). From the point of view of protecting the interests of the financial institution against possible risks, gathering the broadest possible knowledge of entities cooperating with the financial institution is crucial for its security, however, on the other hand, the rules in force in many jurisdictions restricting the possibility of acquiring and processing personal data do not give financial institutions sufficient freedom in this respect. The control function exercised by compliance services in this case consists of both checking compliance with the norms resulting from internal procedures, and at the same time in ensuring that financial institutions apply the legal norms applicable to them in a given jurisdiction.

The fourth group of duties relating to compliance risk control is market conduct. The assessment in this respect is given not only to corporate clients, but also to institutional clients, as well as to entities cooperating with financial institutions.[137] The latter type of entity in particular draws

---

[135] About the changes observed by major financial market actors in the role played by regulators, in particular central banks, including issues arising from the control of banking relations by defining profiles of entities with which banks should not cooperate. Cf. e.g. S. King, M. Jha, The Central Banking Revolution, *Global Economics* 2/2013, p. 11.

[136] On the inadmissibility of cooperation with terrorists and drug traffickers cf. e.g. N. W. R. Burbidge, International Anti-money Laundering and Anti-terrorist Financing: The Work of the Office of the Superintendent of Financial Institutions in Canada, *Journal of Money Laundering Control* 7(4)/2004, p. 322 et seq.

[137] See D. Vogel, The Private Regulation of Global Corporate Conduct Achievements and Limitations, *Business and Society* 49/2010, p. 71.

attention to the fact that in the case of financial institutions operating on a global scale, which conclude many global service agreements, the way trade relations are shaped can have a significant impact directly on the activities of cooperating entities as well as on the opinions about these entities. The criteria according to which the assessment of the market opinion is formulated, as well as the effects of this opinion on cooperating entities are formulated by the recommendations embedded in the internal regulations in force at these financial institutions. It is the responsibility of the compliance departments to monitor the practices of financial institutions and their customers.

The set of issues related to the building and protecting of the good image of the institution, i.e. reputation risk management, is the central area of interest of compliance services, from which the need to ensure compliance in all other areas arises. With some simplification, reputation risk management could be defined as the establishment of an open-ended catalogue that lists the areas with which a financial institution avoid involvement. It concerns which entities the financial institution does not want to cooperate with, which industry it does not support, which activities it does not practice towards clients, which employees it does not employ, in which disputes it does not manage, how it does not build relations with the media, in which industry organisations it does not get involved, which products it does not offer, etc. The creation of a compact normative system for a given organisation in relation to these issues requires not only the detailed development of individual items of this catalogue, which are instructions created by the non-compliant norms, but it also requires an attempt to ensure their application through the normative inclusion of desired patterns of behaviour for situations in which the instructions of these norms are met and, subsequently, control their observance.

Closely related to reputation risk management is the essential tool concerned with conducting communication. This issue concerns the manner and scope of any information provided concerning the financial institution. Nowadays, it is not possible to run a business effectively or even safely, especially if it takes place on a large scale, without a carefully programmed communication policy. This applies both to external communication, i.e. to entities that are not part of the structure of the capital group in which the financial institution is part, as well as internal communication, i.e. to entities that have an economic or structural relation with the financial institution and to the financial institution's employees.

Due to the importance and sensitivity of information that may enter a public domain of communication, also those rules that concern it are established, and then the control of their observance takes place in cooperation with compliance.

In periods of economic downturn on the market, resulting in an increase in the number of the financial institution's debtors failing to meet their obligations on time, it is necessary to establish rules relating to the possibility of restructuring the resulting debt. There is a tendency towards the unification of complex restructuring procedures, especially in the frequent occurring situation where several financial institutions are creditors at the same time or where the debtor has extensive interests in different jurisdictions. In such cases, the aim is to allow a debtor who has lost the ability to settle his obligations, to organise the way in which he does business, to adapt the structure of arrears to the changed possibilities of making them, etc.[138] The key challenge is to help the debtor avoid the financial institution's bankruptcy process, which usually means much higher losses for creditors than restructuring in any form. It is important that the process takes place in the most favourable form for all parties involved, and that no party suffers disproportionately more damage than others in the process. This process can take place according to a number of different models, the most popular of which are the London rules, which are applied directly, or in a form adapted to the jurisdiction of the country concerned.[139] Compliance obligations in this case include not only checking the compliance of this process with the rules of the restructuring law, but also checking compliance with other sets of rules, such as the London rules or other rules in force within the group or group of financial institutions to which the financial institution belongs.

Relations with the financial institution's environment, which are not shareholders or the media, are primarily relations with customers, including mass-served retail customers. Among them, a special group are

---

[138] On debt restructuring and reorganization in international insolvency proceedings and the role of compliance in the context of international insolvency proceedings see, e.g., S. L. Schwarz, Sovereign Debt Restructuring: A Bankruptcy Reorganization Approach, *Cornell Law Review* 85(956)/2001, p. 970 et seq.

[139] See I. Lieberman, M. Gobbo, W. P. Mako, R. L. Neyens, Recent International Experiences in the Use of Voluntary Workouts Under Destressed Conditions [in] M. Pomerleano, W. Shaw [ed.] *Corporate Restructuring: Lessons from Experience*, Washington, DC 2005, p. 63.

customers for whom collection procedures have been initiated due to non-payment or late payment. The ways in which the recovery of arrears takes place depend on this as the processes can be very different. The role of compliance services in this process is therefore important in order to ensure a way of acting that does not expose customers to unnecessary inconveniences on the one hand, while maintaining maximum effectiveness of debt collection. The most common way financial institutions avoid possible errors in this area is not only to create appropriate rules, policies or instructions, but also to create detailed scripts that prescribe the way of conducting talks with clients. Control of the correctness of debt collection processes is carried out by reviewing the correspondence sent to these customers and listening to recorded conversations between financial institution representatives and customers to check how these conversations took place (post-sales and post collection calls). In addition, any complaints from these clients (client complaints) should, as a rule, be submitted for an opinion by compliance bodies, which can thus have an insight into the process.

Compliance control activities also apply to the relations of financial institutions with public entities, which, due to their special nature and potentially high risk, are under constant supervision of these services. Below are six examples of issues contained within the responsibility of compliance function(s).

First of all, the control duties of compliance services within the system of three lines of defence include the classification of risks related to the earlier more detail discussion concerning the involvement of institutions with public entities, in particular with regard to the issue of debt instruments such as treasury bills, state bonds, self-government bonds, commercial companies owned by states or self-government units (country risk and sovereign ratings). Control in this respect is an essential activity in order to avoid engaging in cooperation involving commitments with public entities with which the financial institution does not wish to be associated for reputational reasons.[140] However, as in the case of the classification of individual customers, it is not a matter of credit risk assessment. For this purpose, other entities within the financial institution are usually established. In this case, it is a matter of assessing the risks arising from the mere fact of engaging in cooperation with public sector entities

---

[140]Cf. G. W. Downs, M. A. Jones, Reputation, Compliance and International Law, *The Journal of Legal Studies* 31/2002, p. 97.

and, in the case of global financial institutions, from acting in favour of the interests of individual countries. This is an area in which it is necessary to involve compliance services in the development of norms in financial institutions operating in the international area to help assess political and macroeconomic risks.[141] This assessment takes the form of ratings or classifications given to public entities, as well as ratings given by credit rating agencies. Unlike the latter, however, these assessments are not generally publicly available.[142] They usually remain at the exclusive internal disposal of financial institutions. However, there are many ethical aspects to their attribution. Especially in the context of allegations of attempts to influence and negative perception of the ratings given by financial institutions to other entities. The strict enforcement of the rules applicable to financial institutions in this area, and ensuring this process is correctly controlled are necessary to make the classifications credible.

Secondly, the need for compliance norms also arises even in areas such as physical security risk and security travel advice. Financial institutions are institutions that, for obvious reasons, are exposed to direct attacks. This issue is particularly important in the case of the frequent threats that arise in some jurisdictions, which should be considered complex from a security point of view. In general, separate services are responsible for the physical security in financial institutions. However, their task is mainly to develop safeguards in the form of procedures to be followed in the event of such a risk. Obligations of compliance in this case consist of supplementing the issue of risk management with norms relating to recommended behaviours, methods of establishing contact practices with local police or law enforcement agencies, the level of insurance against similar events.

Thirdly, in most countries, bribery is penalised, but the severity of the punishment, as well as the details of the regulations that define what bribery is can vary greatly. The degree of social acceptance of such activities also varies greatly from country to country. Anti-bribery actions are therefore very often developed by compliance services and are at

---

[141] On political risk in financial institutions' activities see J. Madura, *International Financial Management*, Stamford 2015, p. 495 et seq.

[142] This includes the rankings of organizations such as Transparency International. On the use and abuse of such rankings by other financial institutions see S. Andersson, P. M. Heywood, The Politics of Perception: Use and Abuse of Transparency International's Approach to Measuring Corruption, *Political Studies* 57(4)/2009, p. 748.

the centre of a set of control responsibilities aimed at harmonising their approach to this type of issue.[143] The expectation of external opinions towards the financial institutions, but also towards the employees themselves, is that these regulations should be equal to the highest norms.

Fourthly, another area of compliance obligations is the control of corporate rules of conduct in relation to environmental issues. It is clear that this is a global sustainability issue, and only if it is dealt with in such a broad sense can it have the desired effect.[144] Corporations in general, including financial institutions, are attributed responsibility for contributing to the destruction of the environment.[145] Financial institutions not only through their activities, but also by supporting the activities of other companies that comply with environmental law and those that introduce their own intra-corporate norms for sustainable development, can contribute to the promotion of environmental activities on the one hand and, on the other hand, protect themselves from the risk of non-compliance in this area.[146]

Fifthly, the issue of compliance with legal norms and supervisory regulations and guidelines on financial matters, including, in particular, those relating to public law financial obligations, in the case of financial institutions is clear. It covers a wide range of issues as the type and quality of reporting, the application of the appropriate accounting norms, international settlements, including within the same capital group, issues of transparency of tax settlements, especially in the context of optimisation of tax structures and flows within the same corporation, etc. In the

---

[143] J. G. Lambsdorf, *Causes and Consequences of Corruption: What Do We Know from a Cross-Section of Countries* [in] S. Rose-Ackerman [ed.] *Handbook of the Economics of Corruption*, Northampton 2006, p. 20.

[144] T. Dyllick, K. Hockerts, *Sustainability at the Millennium: Globalization, Competitiveness & Public Trust*, *Business Strategy and the Environment* 11(2)/2002, pp. 130–141.

[145] S. Macleod, D. Lewis, *Transnational Corporations: Power, Influence and Responsibility Global Social Policy* 4/2004, p. 80 et seq., and also, for example, articles and monographs devoted to this subject: T. R. Piper, Odnaleziony cel: przywództwo, etyka i odpowiedzialność przedsiębiorstw [in] L. V. Ryan, J. Sójka [ed.] *Etyka biznesu: z klasyki współczesnej myśli amerykańskiej*, Poznań 1997; M. Żemigała, *Społeczna odpowiedzialność przedsiębiorstwa*, Cracow 2007; also D. Walczak-Duraj, *Ład Etyczny w gospodarce rynkowej*, Łódź 2002 i W. Gasparski, A. Lewicka-Strzałecka, B. Rok, G. Szulczewski, *Etyka biznesu w zastosowaniach praktycznych: inicjatywy, programy, kodeksy, PAN*, Warsaw 2002.

[146] A. Kolk, op. cit., pp. 1–15.

case of doubts caused by the uncertain application of these compliance regulations, it is compliance function that performs the control duties. As a result, norms are created, which are in their nature universal, so that they are applied more widely, going beyond the territory of one country, and become part of the rules applicable to the whole financial institution.[147] This is also in line with the expectations of regulators, investors, the public and customers.

Sixthly, financial institutions operating in the global financial market have their own established policies for the financial sector (financial sector policies), which relate to relations with other financial institutions. These policies are based on assumptions, policies and instructions to other financial institutions, insurance companies, investment funds, hedge funds, securitisation and other financial institutions to determine how to deal with these entities, the types of transactions that are permitted, the amount of exposure limits set for each type of transaction and for transactions with individual entities.[148] Practice confirms that the risk of non-compliance with these policies is high.[149] Compliance services are usually directly involved both in the development of these policies, and in monitoring their compliance, as well as in issuing opinions on unclear situations in which there might be a risk of a financial institution considering of entering into transactions with other financial institution, in a manner or to a scale that does not justify such involvement.[150]

As a rule, the management of the relation with regulators is the responsibility of compliance services. In the event that these relations

---

[147] On the unification of financial standards in international companies see D. Masciandaro, Politicians and Financial Supervision Unification Outside the Central Bank: Why Do They Do It? *Journal of Financial Stability* 5(2)/2009, p. 130 et seq.

[148] On basic principles of conduct of banks in international transactions with other financial institutions see J. Gitman, R. Juchau, J. Flanagan, *Principles of Managerial Finance*, Pearson 2011, p. 435 et seq.

[149] Irregularities detected by supervisors in relations between banks and other financial institutions may pose a significant threat to the stability of the financial system as a whole. Hence the importance of anticipatory compliance services for controlling and regulating these issues see D. W. Arner, *Financial Stability, Economic Growth, and the Role of Law*, Cambridge 2007, p. 51.

[150] Restrictions on the involvement of banks in their relations with other financial institutions may result from various reasons. As a result, they are subject to internal compliance regulations. See G. Ercel, Globalization and International Financial Environment, *Bank of International Settlements Review* 79/2000, p. 4.

are conducted by other organisational units in financial institutions, it is compliance services, who are obligated to control the propriety of this relation. The three types of situations in which such controls take place are listed below.

The first, an important area of compliance obligations is cooperation in the providing of information to auditors in situations of control carried out in a financial institution by regulators or in cooperation with regulators. This subject becomes particularly complicated when extraordinary audit situations arise, which do not fit into the normal audits carried out by auditors appointed for that purpose or by auditors authorised by law to carry out such inspections. In normal situations, the role of compliance services is limited to establishing the rules of conduct of employees towards auditors, providing guidance in the event of requests for information that go beyond normal practice, knowing how to communicate with the auditors, and monitoring compliance with the recommendations that were in practice. However, there are more and more audits which are not usual, for which it is necessary to develop binding rules of pragmatics, which, on the one hand, enables and even facilitates their execution, on the other hand, secures the interests of the financial institution, and ensures compliance with the obligations imposed on it under the mandatory legal norms. One example of such audits is a review carried out by representatives of the internal audit function within the same group, but who are not employees of the controlled financial institution. A similar situation occurs when the audit is carried out by employees of the same function (e.g. working in a legal department, compliance, risk, etc.) but who are employed in another financial institution belonging to the same group.

Formally, in both situations, the auditors do not have the authority to carry out control activities, especially those that would involve access to confidential data, including personal data. Another, slightly more complex, situation is where the audit is carried out by representatives of the regulatory authorities from another country, in connection with a broader audit carried out in the home country of the holding company.[151] The authorisation to conduct such an audit in a financial institution, which is not conducted in a branch of a credit institution, and

---

[151] More about the audits carried out by regulators see J. R. Fichtner, The Recent International Growth of Mandatory Audit Committee Requirements, *International Journal of Disclosure and Governance* 7/2010, p. 237 et seq.

in a commercial company registered in the host country, requires special caution, and may also lead to complicated relations with the local regulator in the event that the terms of such an audit conducted in its territory have not been precisely defined beforehand. It is the responsibility of the compliance department to control the propriety of this process.

The second area remaining under the control of the compliance services are the obligations imposed on financial institutions by supervisory authorities with regard to its clients (regulatory duties to clients). What we are not discussing here the kind of obligations that financial institutions impose on themselves in order to ensure customer satisfaction with the quality of the products and services offered, but the obligations imposed on financial institutions by regulators. It is noteworthy that these are not regulatory obligations, but only those relating to customer relations, usually, but not exclusively regulated by contractual provisions.[152] The trend observed recently in this area is that most often this type of supervisory recommendations is of a follow-up nature in so far as it is the result of previously detected irregularities in the activities of a specific financial institution. As a result of this type of anomalies, a need arises for the regulator to carry out subject (so-called thematic) studies of a much wider scale, covering more than one financial institution. What is more, it is correct to constantly increase the scope of such checking activities also in other countries, using the increasingly better international cooperation between different regulators. A further step, if the magnitude of the observed irregularities is confirmed, is to impose severe penalties on financial institutions, including high-value fines, and obligations not to apply the defective practices to customers, as well as to pay them damages.[153]

Within this area, the responsibility of compliance departments goes far beyond formulating good practices that are designed to build customer confidence and control. It is a matter of creating compliant normative recommendations, the aim of which is to prevent huge financial losses

---

[152] Obligations imposed by regulators on banks in contractual provisions with customers see R. Inderst, Retail Finance: Thoughts on Reshaping Regulation and Consumer Protection After the Financial Crisis, *European Business Organization Law Review* 10(3)/2009, p. 457.

[153] J. Bischof, H. Daske, F. Elfers, L. Hail, A Tale of Two Regulators: Risk Disclosures, Liquidity, and Enforcement in the Banking Sector, *University of Pennsylvania Law Papers* 5/2015, p. 20.

resulting from irregularities in the actions of financial institutions vis-à-vis their own customers. However, almost the same risk of these irregularities appears also after they are detected by regulators and they impose penalties on institutions.[154] This risk always occurs when the regulations in force are not precise and complete enough, or when there are incidents of non-compliance with them.

From the perspective of transnational operations conducted by global corporations, the obligation imposed on compliance services is to set norms for the control of compliance with regulations in relation to cross-border activity of financial institutions (regulatory norms vs. cross border activities) is becoming more and more important. It is often observed that regulatory authorities expect international corporations, including financial institutions, to have supervisory norms extended to other jurisdictions. Although formally not covered by the jurisdiction of these regulators, they remain the space in which they operate, and this activity may have an impact on home markets. One, but not the only reason why such expectations arise is the willingness to force financial institutions to operate in compliance with regulatory requirements regardless of the place where these regulations were issued, and to prevent the evasion of these requirements by transferring all or part of this activity to territories not covered by these regulations.[155]

The compliance function also applies to breaches of financial institution norms. Such cases are referred to as 'compliance incidents', and contrary to their name, they may concern both small and serious situations and as such, depending on their seriousness, in addition to the fact that they are the subject of intra-group reporting, they may also create obligations on the part of the financial institution to inform the supervisory authorities about them.[156] Depending on local regulatory obligations, financial institutions, both in the case of regulations in this respect and in the absence thereof, establish rules for reporting incidents of compliance. These rules set out, among other things, the definitions

---

[154] Criticizing the ineffectiveness of regulators' penalties for detected irregularities see J. A. Allison, Market Discipline Beats Regulatory Discipline, *Cato Journal* 34/2014, p. 345.

[155] On cross-border compliance obligations to comply with regulatory requirements see J. G. Sutinen, K. Kuperan, A Socio-Economic Theory of Regulatory Compliance, *International Journal of Social Economics* 26(1/2/3)/1999, pp. 174–193.

[156] See A. Lawrence, M. Minutti-Meza, D. Vyas, Is Operational Control Risk Informative of Financial Reporting Risk? *Rotman School of Management Working Paper* 6/2014, p. 29.

of compliance incidents, the prerequisites for mandatory compliance reports including information about these violations, the applicable reporting procedures, etc. The rules also define the requirements for the preparation of compliance reports. The internal rules on incidents of non-compliance generally also indicate the methodologically structured ways of establishing corrective programmes to address and prevent future occurrences (lessons learned).[157]

10 COMPLIANCE FUNCTION AND CORPORATE GOVERNANCE

It was the regulatory authorities that supervised the international financial institutions that initially noticed that the norm understanding of risk in financial institutions focusing on liquidity and credit risks were proving to be insufficient.[158] Analyses conducted by these regulators contributed to the preparation of recommendations, both at the global and national levels, which extended the obligation to manage risk to areas that had been omitted so far.[159] They indicate that financial institutions should first of all have effective control mechanisms in place to protect the institutions against the risk of penalties being imposed on them by regulatory authorities in connection with non-compliance, exposure of these institutions to financial losses resulting from imprudent conduct of business and other risks, including the reputation risks described above. It is therefore a type of risk that may affect a financial institution as a result of its failure to comply with the applicable legal norms and norms applied.

Therefore, the source of penalties imposed on financial institutions may be the legislation of each of the countries in which they operate, supervisory regulations in force there, intra-financial institution international regulations, as well as norms developed in the practice of market processes established by market participants. In the course of the

---

[157] Cf. F. Partnoy, J. Eisinger, What Is Inside American Banks? *America's Banks* 1/2008, p. 3 et seq.

[158] M. Cihak, A. Demirguc-Kunt, M. S. M. Peria, A. Mohseni-Cheraghlou, Bank Regulation and Supervision Around the World: A Crisis Update, *World Bank Policy Research Working Paper* 1/2012, p. 6286.

[159] Cf. A. Milne, Bank Capital Regulation as an Incentive Mechanism: Implications for Portfolio Choice, *Journal of Banking and Finance* 26(1)/2001, pp. 1–23.

observations, it was also noted that the risk of maladjustment also applies to the rules of honesty, reliability, transparency and thus to concepts derived from the world of values.[160] The financial institution's reputation is closely linked, and more specifically it is built on the basis of the conviction of market participants that the financial institution's activities are conducted in compliance with the law and internal rules of conduct adopted by the financial institution, and on the basis of ethical norms accepted by the market.[161]

The recommendations resulting from these analyses indicate that adjusting the activity of financial institutions to the required norms helps them to achieve and maintain a good reputation, and thus to meet the expectations of the business environment, i.e. customers, investors-shareholders and employees.[162] The result of these analyses is supervisory recommendations, according to which it is expected that all the above-mentioned elements should comprise the compliance obligations existing in the financial institutions. In addition, it was also noted that the proper functioning of the compliance services in the financial institutions requires their proper allocation in organisational structures, appropriate empowerment and the necessary independence to be guaranteed. Based on observations of financial institutions practice in this respect, they are the subject of analyses described in this subsection.

The expectations expressed by regulators, which transfer broader public expectations, underline that the chances of the effective implementation of compliance policies depend on the involvement of financial institution authorities in the process. In line with this approach, the most effective builders of a proper corporate culture with regard to fairness norms are those financial institutions in which boards of directors and management make the process more credible through their personal commitment. In view of the scale of operations carried out by global financial institutions corporations and the multitude of challenges faced

---

[160] The importance of ethical issues in building appropriate conditions for business development in compliance conditions see A. B. Carroll, A. K. Buchholtz, *Business and Society: Ethics, Sustainability, and Stakeholder Management*, Stamford 2015, p. 175.

[161] See C. Brummer, Why Soft Law Dominates International Finance—And Not Trade, *Journal of International Economic Law* 13(3)/2010, p. 228 et seq.

[162] K. Wulf, *From Codes of Conduct to Ethics and Compliance Programs: Recent Developments in the United States*, Berliner Arbeiten zur Erziehungs- und Kulturwissenschaft, t. 57, Berlin 2011, p. 202.

by the authorities of these institutions, such an expectation is in fact a considerable complication, but at the same time testifies to the importance that regulators attach to the issue of compliance.[163] However, in addition to the authorities themselves, this also applies to all other financial institution employees as it should also be seen as an integral part of their activities. The overriding guideline in this respect is that financial institutions should apply the highest norms in their operations and try to comply with both the 'letter and spirit' of the norms that apply to them.[164] Indeed, the possible lack of financial institution involvement in this area ignores the supervisory recommendations and ignores the opinions voiced by the public about financial institutions' behaviour, and the impact that this has on their shareholders, customers, employees and markets. As a result, it also leads to an unfavourable opinion and damage to the reputation of such a financial institution, even if the law is not broken. One of the important elements ensuring the prevention of adverse effects of non-compliance is the location of compliance services in the organisational structures of financial institutions, so they can effectively perform the tasks entrusted to them. At the same time, the organisational structure in the consideration of this work is held to be the entire system of internal regulations that define the service relations between statutory authorities, and all organisational units, as well as the scope of other service relations between these units within the financial institution.

It is true that there is no uniformly binding universally agreed model determining the place of compliance function in the organisational structures of the financial institution. At the same time, an appropriately high position of compliance function, with strong competences assigned, contributes to the proper protection of the compliance risk. An appropriate organisational structure ensuring the efficient operation of compliance services in financial corporation's is regulated by internal normative acts defining the hierarchy of positions within the financial institution itself, the scope of authorisations, corporate governance rules, the right to issue internal normative acts and to carry out controls. There is a widespread

---

[163] About the importance given by corporate authorities to compliance issues, the so-called "tone from the top" see O. Boiral, The Certification of Corporate Conduct: Issues and Prospects, *International Labour Review* 142(3)/2003, p. 322.

[164] B. P. Volkman, The Global Convergence of Bank Regulation and Standards for Compliance, *Banking Law Journal* 115/1998, p. 550 et seq.

perception among financial institutions that it is important that compliance services are sufficiently placed in the hierarchy of the company so that they are not subordinate to too many people in the organisation, as reporting to the service could limit the independence of control activities, and force them to refrain from interfering in certain areas of the financial institution's activities.

Therefore, when referring to the location of compliance services in the organisational structures of control functions in financial institutions, two aspects should be taken into account:

a. the compliance obligations imposed on financial institutions by regulators as well as the compliance obligations imposed on financial institutions as a result of public pressure from the group; and
b. assigning responsibility for the performance of these duties to the different entities within their organisational structure.[165]

As an example, according to the Basel Committee's recommendations, which are of key importance for subsequent national regulations, the verification of the practical implementation of compliance recommendations should fall within the responsibility of the specialised persons designated to carry out compliance tasks in all these areas. However, in practice it is also expected that it should form part of the guidelines applicable to all employees in a given corporation, often referred to as the culture of a given organisation. At the same time, the New Capital Accord's recommendations assume that financial institutions become more effective in managing compliance risk if they separate compliance units. The term is used to refer to organisational units within the organisational structures of financial institutions, regardless of their form, to which tasks related to the management of compliance risk have been entrusted.

It is true that there are no detailed recommendations on how financial institutions should organise their compliance function, and what compliance risk management tasks they should prioritise for these functions. The very lack of detailed regulations in this respect can also be regarded

---

[165] The organizational structures introduced in different corporations are not uniform and differ significantly from each other, they are also subject to constant changes. These changes in complex international structures are usually the result of both new regulations and other factors, including business needs (new development plans, reductions, ownership changes, introduction of new products, or even just the departure of key employees, etc.).

as an appropriate approach, as it is conducive to adapting the organisational structure to current regulatory needs, local corporate governance practices, the profile and size of the business, etc. However, it is important that they are set in a manner consistent with the financial institution's other structures and with the financial institution's own risk management strategy. Some financial institutions integrate their compliance function into the organisational structure of their operational risk unit, as there is a particularly close link between compliance risk and certain aspects of compliance risk in their activities.

Other financial institutions, on the other hand, separate compliance and operational risk units, but put in place procedures requiring the close cooperation between the two units on all compliance risk management issues. As a result, there are numerous differences between financial institutions regarding the location of compliance function within their organisational structures. Very large international financial institutions also establish compliance management functions at the regional and global level. In smaller financial institutions, compliance function staff are usually located in smaller but also separate business units. In some financial institutions, however, there are separate entities established exclusively to serve specific specialised areas within the sphere of compliance tasks such as data protection and prevention of money laundering and terrorist financing.

There is no single model for locating compliance in the organisational structure of financial institutions, there are not even uniform practices applied by financial institutions in this respect. Like many other compliance issues, such as the tasks they perform, the scope and rank of their internal regulations, etc., the position of compliance units among other services in financial institutions is often the result of ad hoc needs currently prevailing in these financial institutions, rather than of concepts developed as a result of in-depth analyses in this area. However, among these separate models one can distinguish a few of the following usually observed characteristic features in relation to the location of compliance services in the organisational structures of financial institutions.

a. Compliance services may be located under the direct authority of the management of the financial institutions or their chairpersons.
b. Compliance services may have the right to refer such information directly to the financial institution's supervisory authorities with regard to irregularities identified.

c. There is a guaranteed separation between the compliance units and the independent internal audit function of the financial institutions.
d. Compliance may be a completely separate entity or form part of larger organisational units (departments, divisions). Most often in conjunction with the legal department, the internal control department, the operational risk department mentioned above or simply with the large risk department responsible for managing all other risks.

The latter model of consolidating into a single risk management function all entities responsible for different risks, including compliance risks, and thus separating this entity from the legal function is a relatively new and criticised trend.[166] In such a model, within the combined risk department, in addition to compliance, the tasks of the entity include tasks related to the management of credit risk, operational risk, as well as other types of risk, such as data security and fraud prevention. On the other hand, due to other tasks and a traditionally autonomous position, it does not include, for example, a finance department, whose tasks usually include all tax matters. In this respect, however, compliance can be exercised as a control function.

As indicated above, the Basel Committee's guidelines on compliance management require financial institutions, in order to ensure compliance with the norms of compliance, to create the conditions under which their statutory bodies will recognise and express the particular importance of ethical principles, including integrity, in the conduct of the organisation they manage. Compliance with applicable laws, supervisory regulations, as well as internal normative acts and norms should

---

[166] B. W. Heineman, *Don't Divorce the GC and Compliance Officer*, the Harvard Law School Forum on Corporate Governance and Financial Regulation and Harvard Kenedy School of Government, December 2010, www.law.harvard.edu/corpgov (download 15 March 2019); B. W. Heineman, Can the Marriage of the GC and Chief Compliance Officer Last? *Corporate Counsel*, 30 March 2012, Law.com (download 15 March 2019); D. Boheme, When Compliance and Legal Don't See Eye to Eye, *Corporate Counsel*, 8 May 2014, www.compliancestrategists.com/csblog/2014/05/11/ (download 20 October 2018). Also: M. W. Peregrine, The Increasingly Problematic Coordination of 'Legal' and 'Compliance': New Pressures on the Board: Best Practices for Resolving Tasks, *Bloomberg Law*, 3 September 2014, www.Bloomberg_Law/law/compliance (download 20 October 2018).

be seen as a key element necessary to create such conditions.[167] As with other risk categories, the financial institution's authorities, including the supervisory board, are responsible for ensuring that an appropriate compliance risk management approach is in place at the financial institution. The board directors should therefore supervise the implementation of this approach, including ensuring that compliance issues are effectively and efficiently resolved by the management board supported by the compliance function. According to the Basel Committee's guidelines, the

---

[167] The particular position of the Basel Committee's guidelines is due in particular to their transnational scope and the optional nature of the guidelines. Contrary to the recommendations issued by national regulators of the markets in which individual banks operate, the Basel Committee does not have the power to bind banks. It only sets out a framework within which it is possible to structure their risk management and subsequent capital adequacy activities in an optimal way. Other regulators operating within their own jurisdictions issue regulations whose application becomes an obligation for institutions operating in a given area. Although the scope of these regulations is not always exclusively local, it is rather due to the fact that some regulators have the possibility to influence banking groups due to the fact that the seat of these banks is located in the territory subject to their cognition. It is essential, however, that these individual regulators refer in their regulations to the recommendations made within the framework of the Basel Committee's work. In practice, although international banks cannot formally assume that some regulators are more important, the importance of the recommendations of some of them, due to the scope of their impact, the possibility of influencing large areas of business activity or, for example, their influence on the elements necessary for this activity that are particularly important for the banks' operations (access to foreign exchange markets, capital requirements, imposing additional obligations with respect to maintaining reserves at an appropriate level, etc.), plays a de facto leading role. Thus, for example, recommendations issued by the FED—Federal Reserve System, FRB—Board of Governance of the Federal Reserve System, FDIC—Federal Deposit Insurance Corporation, FinRA—Financial Industry Regulatory Authority, NASD—National Association of Securities Dealers, SEC—US Securities and Exchange Commission, NYSPD—New York State Banking Department, OCC—Office of the Comptroller of the Currency, FISMA—European Commission Directorate-General for Financial Stability, Financial Services and Capital Markets Union, ECB—European Central Bank, EBA—European Banking Authority, PRA—Prudential Regulation Authority, FCA—Financial Crime Authority and other regulators operating on American, European Union or London markets are, on the one hand, important from the point of view of compliance activity, the task of which is to ensure their observance. On the other hand, however, with regard to the definition and positioning of compliance obligations, it often develops and gives substance to the ideas developed by the Basel Committee. See K. L. Young, Transnational Regulatory Capture? An Empirical Examination of the Transnational Lobbying of the Basel Committee on Banking Supervision, *Review of International Political Economy* 19(4)/2012, p. 670.

board should have the power to delegate these tasks to one of the board committees (e.g. the audit committee).

There is an assumption that in order to meet the conditions for recognising that compliance services have an independent position in a financial institution, i.e. one that is considered necessary to enable it to perform the tasks entrusted to it, the four interdependent elements presented below must exist.[168]

   a. The compliance function should have formal status within the financial institution, i.e. it should be formally separated in the organisational structure.
   b. A senior official should be appointed at group level in an international financial institution, together with a head of compliance in each of the individual financial institutions in the group with overall responsibility for coordinating the management of compliance.
   c. The staff of the compliance function, including in particular the head of the compliance function, should not occupy positions where there is a risk of possible conflicts of interest between their compliance responsibilities, and any other duties that might be imposed on them.
   d. Employees of the compliance function should have free access to the information and other staff of the financial institution whose assistance is necessary for them to carry out the duties to which they are subject.

The concept of independence as an attribute for the proper performance of compliance obligations does not mean that the compliance function should not cooperate closely with the management and other employees of different organisational units of the financial institution. Indeed, cooperation within the established business relation between the compliance function and other business units is essential to identify and manage compliance risk at an early stage. Usually knowledge about possible irregularities manifested in the lack of respect for compliance norms first appears in a place other than the compliance unit, and only then it is transferred to it. Many of the elements considered necessary

---

[168] See D. A. DeMott, The Crucial But (Potentially) Precarious Position of the Chief Compliance Officer, *Brooklyn Journal of Corporate, Financial and Commercial Law* 8/2013, p. 60 et seq.

for the attributes of compliance services in a financial institution should be treated as safeguards to ensure the effective functioning of the compliance function, irrespective of the very close cooperation between the compliance function and other organisational units. The manner in which these safeguards are implemented depends to a large extent on the specific obligations imposed on that entity within the financial institution.[169]

Following the recommendations of the Basel Committee, financial institutions shall appoint a member of the board of directors or executive director responsible for the overall coordination of the identification and management of compliance risk, and for overseeing the activities of the entire compliance function within the segregated compliance function. Employees of a unit which is located in the organisational structure of a financial institution operating in the form of a company registered in a given country or part of a local branch may be subject to reporting to the management of that organisational unit, which reports to the management of that company or to the management of the branch.[170] Practical observations confirm that the effectiveness of the organisation of the compliance norm-setting system in the financial institution, and reporting irregularities in compliance with these norms, but also other tasks performed by compliance services, as well as functional relations between employees performing compliance tasks and managers of these units, depend on the manner in which these units have been located in the financial institutions, what kind of duties have been entrusted to them and how the work of these units is organised.

In terms of reporting, compliance employees are first and foremost report to the head of the compliance unit on issues relating to compliance obligations. Depending on the organisational structure, in some financial institutions, the position of head of compliance is referred to as a 'compliance officer', while in others it simply refers to every

---

[169] These protections are implemented using all available tools to ensure their effectiveness on the basis of the results of research in the field of management theory. The introduction of procedures and other internal regulations at different levels of the hierarchy would not be sufficiently effective in so many organizations as multinational corporations if it were not accompanied by simultaneous training, information campaigns and incentive systems and evaluation of employees in this area.

[170] U. C. H. Valey, *Multinational Corporations in Political Environments: Ethics, Values and Strategies*, New York 2001, p. 69 et seq.

employee of the compliance function who performs compliance duties. In very large institutions, where compliance departments are numerous, employees of the compliance unit are organised into separate support teams, whose task is to deal with particular areas. These units are then divided into teams dealing with compliance with legal norms, financial control, counterparty risk management, etc. The units are then divided into teams dealing with compliance with legal norms, financial control, counterparty risk management, etc. In such cases, a separate reporting path from the staff of these teams to the head of compliance is not considered necessary. However, it is stressed that these entities should work closely with the head of the compliance function so that it can carry out its responsibilities effectively.

Restrictions on the full independence of compliance services include the fact that their activities are subject to assessment by internal audit in financial institutions. The assessment of the probability of the occurrence of the circumstances of non-compliance, including in particular the risk of breaching the financial institution's internal compliance norms should be included in the methodology used by the internal audit unit to assess the remaining risks related to the financial institution's operations. The audit programme in place at a financial institution should therefore include an examination of the adequacy of the measures taken, the effectiveness of the controls carried out and, in particular, the application of corrective procedures in cases of breaches of the norms established within the organisation by the financial institution's compliance function.

To a large extent, as in the case of other reviews carried out by a internal audit unit, such a programme should include the testing of control mechanisms applied by compliance services considered by it to be appropriate to the level of risk estimated in the financial institution. This principle implies that the compliance function and the audit function within the financial institution structure should be kept separate so that the activities of the compliance function can be subject to independent scrutiny. For this reason, financial institutions also have a formal normative framework, that were formulated to provide terms of reference documents in such a way that tasks such as risk assessment and control activities are shared between the two entities.

This separation, as formulated in the financial institution's compliance policies, also establishes the rules under which the audit unit informs the head of compliance of any audit findings resulting from its reviews of compliance issues carried out by the compliance function. In the case of cross-border institutions, the structure is by its very nature much more complex, but the rules governing the relation between the two entities are similar. In fact, financial institutions comply with the provisions of the separate legal orders in which they operate, but they retain the authority and structure of compliance units that are adapted to local legal and regulatory requirements.

The division of the UK's most powerful financial supervisory authority to date, the FSA—the Financial Services Authority—into two separate authorities the Financial Conduct Authority (FCA) and the Prudential Regulatory Authority (PRA) has been directly and immediately reflected in the organisational structures of the compliance departments in multiple financial institutions.[171] This division was thus reflected in the creation of departments within the financial institutions, in particular those operating in the City of London and listed on the London Stock Exchange, designated to manage two separate compliance areas.

Just as the UK supervisory authority regulating the largest financial market, London, individual financial institutions have, in many cases, divided their hitherto uniform internal compliance units, particularly at regional and supra-regional levels, in accordance with the recommendations of the regulator there. Following the example of the FSA, regulators in other countries have started to set similar requirements. This will mean that this part of the compliance services dealing with the management of the risk of non-compliance with criminal law norms concerning finance (financial crime compliance) will be a separate unit from the services dealing with the management of the risk of non-compliance with supervisory regulations (regulatory compliance).

When analysing how tasks were assigned to the two separate units performing compliance tasks within a single structure, it is necessary to return to the original assumption that the primary compliance function remains compliance risk management. It is therefore to ensure that the applicable laws and supervisory regulations are adequately reflected in precisely formulated internal normative acts and that these norms are properly applied. The measure of such adequacy is the effectiveness of the financial institution's compliance regime or, in other words,

---

[171] The major British banks have adjusted their compliance structure to the organizational changes introduced at the regulators' level. See P. O. Mülbert, Corporate Governance of Banks After the Financial Crisis—Theory, Evidence, Reforms, *European Corporate Governance Law* 130(4)/2010, p. 12 et seq.

the effectiveness of reducing compliance breaches. This is based on the general assumption that the basis for the system of preventing the occurrence of non-compliance risk is an approach based on methods of identifying and anticipating risks and implementing mechanisms for their removal or minimisation, which have been established by management theory.[172] In addition to the overall management of the compliance risk of the institution as a whole, there are areas for which compliance services have a particular responsibility. They are:

a. the fight against money laundering and terrorist financing;
b. the resolving of conflicts of interest;
c. the establishing of binding norms of conduct in customer relations;
d. the defining ethical business conduct;
e. the protection of personal data;
f. outsourcing;
g. the protecting of financial institutions secrecy;
h. the prevention of fraudulent financial transactions.

If the regulatory compliance unit is separated in the structure, it is important to ensure that there are mechanisms for their close and permanent cooperation with other units responsible for risk control. Certain elements of the compliance assurance system are implemented by compliance separated in the organisational structures of the services, which

---

[172] The question of to what extent some regulations may be more relevant than others remains separate. It can be assumed that the materiality of regulations is determined by the following factors:
  a. cross-border nature;
  b. a reference to the holding company, worded in such a way that the regulatory requirements include obligations on all the entities in the financial group;
  c. a reference to those activities that are an essential part of the financial institution's overall business model (e.g. restrictions on US operations due to temporary suspension of the license as a penalty for non-compliance with compliance have severe consequences for the penalized bank);
  d. the recognition by the financial institution of certain regulations as important for reasons specific to the organization (e.g. environmental regulations, fair trading rules, safety of working conditions, etc.), which may be classified as important for the expectations of shareholders, customers or the public and thus elevated to supra-local obligations, irrespective of specific, and often less restrictive, obligations under the relevant laws of the jurisdiction concerned.

support compliance, especially in the identification of these risks. The operational risk management unit shall focus on managing the risk of operational losses resulting from failed internal risk control processes of the institution or from external events that may affect it. Unlike the internal audit unit, however, it performs periodic checks on the functioning of the institution as a whole, but it is not competent to manage risk in any of the financial institution's areas of activity.[173]

On the other hand, in the case a division that results in a separate financial institution unit responsible for the managing the risk of regulatory and criminal compliance, it is worth looking at the main sphere of responsibilities of such a unit. First of all, there is a difference between the well-established anti-money laundering task, and the much more broadly understood new compliance unit's task of preventing financial crime. It is also worth taking a look at the differences that emerge from here. While, anti-money laundering (AML) concerns the area most often taken together with the prevention of terrorist financing, the financial crime prevention (FCP) covers the prevention of financial fraud in all its forms.[174]

The scope of responsibility of compliance units always depends on the model adopted in a given institution, but while most often counteracting money laundering is one of the key compliance tasks, counteracting fraud in many countries is still an area outside of compliance services. In practice, the difference is that fraud prevention deals with the detection primary crimes, e.g. the fraudulent use of credit from financial institutions or unauthorised use of funds on the client's account, while money laundering prevention focuses on detecting and reporting to law enforcement agencies cases of using a financial institution to legalise funds derived from crime, i.e. creating the impression that they come from lawful activity.

In order to identify the specificities of compliance units identified to manage the risk of non-compliance with financial crime legislation

---

[173] As for example, in the Basel Committee on Banking Supervision document, *Internal Audit in Banks and the Supervisor's Relationship with Auditors: A Survey* of August 2002, http://www.bis.org/publ/bcbs92.pdf (download 19 July 2018).

[174] These adjusting organizational changes, although already introduced in banks, have not yet covered many institutions. For example, the world's largest UK organization of corporate compliance specialists, the International Compliance Association, issues qualification certificates to applicant institutions that still cover both areas together.

that focuses on fraud prevention, it is helpful to employ concepts that not always are clearly defined in law, such as high-risk clients.[175] The adoption of such a definition is a consequence of the increased prudence shown by institutions towards certain customers, on the basis of risk assessment that associates them with money laundering or terrorist financing.[176] In other words, high-risk customers are those financial institution customers who, on the basis of an analysis of their known business profile, may be suspected of being involved in transactions to market and legalise funds derived from crime or from undisclosed sources to finance different types of criminal activity. Some institutions, including the European Union, have imposed an obligation on every financial institution of the Member States to implement a customer risk assessment model based on identified plausible factors. These are:

a. country of residence;
b. the type of business activity carried out;
c. the presence on the watch lists of persons suspected of terrorist activity.

By taking this risk assessment into account European financial institutions, classify their clients, such as those who constitute a higher (high) risk group, and who are subject to specific measures, including enhanced monitoring of all their transactions, in particular by the financial institution in question.[177]

---

[175] The Basel Committee on Banking Supervision also refers to the issue of banks' relations with high-risk customers and their obligations towards the classification of customers in this category, in the document *Customer Due Diligence for Banks*, October 2001, http://www.bis.org/publ/bcbs85.htm (download 13 February 2019).

[176] M. T. Biegelman, J. T. Bartow, *Executive Roadmap to Fraud Prevention and Internal Control: Creating of Culture of Compliance*, New Jersey 2012, p. 47.

[177] This means that it is determined whether account transactions are carried out in accordance with the knowledge of the client's business and do not involve the financial institution in illegal or unethical activities consisting not only in the financing of drugs or terrorism, but also other activities that the financial institution deems inappropriate from its perspective, such as cooperation with certain countries, institutions or industries like the military industry.

11 Compliance Risk Management and Legal Risk Management

Regardless of compliance risk management, which consists of ensuring compliance with the entire normative order applicable to a given financial institution, a special function is created in many institutions, whose task is to ensure the management of legal risks in the broad sense of the term. Therefore, in addition to the three types of risks indicated earlier—regulatory, financial and reputation risks, in the management of which compliance services participate, the following are classified as types of legal risks. They concern all types of events whose negative consequences are classified as legal risks other than compliance risks. In this case, the criteria for distinguishing them are based on the source of these risks.[178] In this sense, compliance risk is not included in the group of legal risks.[179] In terms of subject matter, legal risks are divided into four types that are indicated below.

- a. Legislative and regulatory risks—including any negative consequences of the conducted activity resulting from changes in the external normative environment.[180]
- b. Contractual risks—consisting of the occurrence of adverse effects of erroneous, incomplete or inconsistent contract provisions. In particular in reference to the normative environment. Or inconsistency with the interest of financial institutions, provisions resulting from agreements or other documents regulating the legal situation of the parties to financial institutions' transactions.

---

[178] R. Robson, A New Look at Benefit Corporations: Game Theory and Game Changer, *American Business Law Journal* 52/2015, p. 501 et seq.

[179] The division used here is not, of course, the only possible one, but only the one used most frequently by the large international financial institutions. Such systematization of legal risks derives from the common law, where a large part of financial centers is located.

[180] The complexity of issues related to the management of legislative and regulatory risk is due to at least three factors:
  a. multiple simultaneous changes;
  b. the diversity and heterogeneity of sources of change in the various markets;
  c. difficulties in assessing the impact of ongoing changes on financial institutions' performance.

c. Dispute risks—settlement, securing and enforcement proceedings resulting from or assertion by the parties of claims which have not been satisfied in the course of the normal execution of the transaction, or activities of bodies appointed to this end, acting in order to secure legally protected public interests.
d. Non-contractual risks—any other legal risks not mentioned in the previous points, including mainly those related to possible infringements of property rights, including intellectual property rights.

In order to ensure the management of legal risks, separate organisational units are created by financial institutions within the structures of legal departments, which at the same time remain outside the structures of compliance services.[181] The separation of structures in financial institutions responsible for this area is a relatively new phenomenon that is the result of a broadening in the understanding of legal functions in financial institutions. Despite the fact that these services are located outside the compliance structures, and in fact deal with all types of legal risk and not only with the risk of non-compliance, in practice, the success of their activities is determined by their close cooperation with the compliance services.[182]

The fact that the structure of compliance services, both in public regulatory offices and in financial institutions, is similarly constructed, results from the fact that in both types of compliance institutions operates within the financial system, which enforces a similar approach, with both existing to ensure compliance with applicable normative regulations, good industry practices, rules of ethics, etc. The different structures they employ are the result of the tasks for which each type of

---

[181] D. A. DeMott, Stages of Scandal and the Roles of General Counsel, *Wisconsin Law Review* 13/2012, p. 490 et seq.

[182] Lack of compliance is only one of the types of legal risks, it refers in principle only to the norms currently in force and remains the domain of compliance services, while the tasks of legal departments traditionally focused on advisory tasks supporting business activity. In view of this division, entities specializing in a broadly defined management of all legal risks, including the identification of those elements of the business activity which may expose corporations to new types of risks and anticipating the effects of potential unpreparedness for these risks, are relatively new creations, whose importance in the complex global financial environment is constantly growing.

institution is established, and therefore in the scope of norms to which the organisation has to be adapted.[183]

The growing importance and gradual extension of the responsibility for compliance functions is therefore in practice often associated with the need to create the appropriate structures in financial institutions, equip them with appropriate competences, and ensure that these institutions provide them with sufficient resources to perform the tasks entrusted to them. As a consequence, despite the effects of financial crisis and the necessary budget savings in financial institutions, in the area of compliance, as a rule, an increase in expenditure and the number of employees has been observed. Regardless of the strengthening of the composition of compliance management units in financial institutions, information technology is becoming increasingly important in monitoring compliance.[184] Because of the increasing number of obligations concerning the monitoring and reporting of non-compliance situations, and the increasing amount of information that is collected, processed and analysed, is precisely why the use of technology is becoming more necessary. Adapted to the needs and reporting obligations, IT systems allow for the preparation of ready-made reports, which allow compliance specialists to analyse and draw conclusions, replacing, in this case, a large number of the people who would have collected and verified the necessary data. As always when humans are replaced by technology there is less chance of human error. The use of information technology therefore makes it possible to create an integrated, more effective compliance function.

The community of compliance specialists is integrated through compliance associations where their members are persons professionally involved in compliance, including, inter alia, money laundering and the fight against financial crime.[185] This applies especially to the financial sector, i.e. people working in financial institutions, brokerage houses, investment fund companies, insurance institutions and law firms.

---

[183] R. C. Bird, P. A. Borochin, J. D. Knopf, The Role of the Chief Legal Officer in Corporate Governance, *Journal of Corporate Finance* 34/2015, p. 5.

[184] N. Stanley, Clearly, and Quite Righty, Data Loss Is Now a Legal Issue and IT Professionals Need to Be Aware of Their Responsibilities, *A White Paper by Bloor Research*, March 2009, https://www.qualys.com/docs/EU_Compliance.pdf (download 11 March 2019).

[185] An example of the scope of activities of that a local compliance association can be found e.g. on the following site: http://compliancepolska.pl.

These associations, as well as other institutions of this type, aim to broaden knowledge about compliance in the financial sector, develop contacts with regulators, and promote education and integration of the compliance environment.[186] These associations also represent their member institutions with the relevant supervisory authorities. The main objective of these associations is to develop the financial markets in an ethical and harmonised way.

---

[186] This type of associations also publishes their own bulletins, organize regular trainings and large compliance conferences, whose subject matter, depending on the needs arising in a given period, concern such different issues as new regulations and technologies and their impact on the compliance functions and anti-money laundering in its own financial institutions.

CHAPTER 4

The Scope of Compliance Norms in Financial Institutions

1 Introduction

The purpose of the fourth chapter is to show the relation between compliance norms and the other factors influencing their content.

The issue addressed in the first subsection to reference these norms to other, external norms in relation to their impact on compliance norms in financial institutions. This applies to rulebooks such as those of the Basel Committee, but also to the general principles of the US and the EU legislation. This subchapter also refers to the complications that result from the need to create compliance norms that are compliant with supervisory regulations, extra-legal normative systems and with many different normative systems at the same time. The second subchapter focuses on cases of irregularities detected in financial institutions, which have had a wide impact both on the content of compliance norms and on the overall approach to compliance in financial institutions, even if the cases of irregularities were not directly related to these financial institutions. The analysis of these cases is important to clarify the material scope of many compliance regulations.

Subsections three and four focus on the role played by compliance norms, i.e. ensuring that financial institutions act in compliance with mandatory regulations as well as with the regulations that voluntarily have been recognised by financial institutions corporations as binding. Subchapter three focuses on compliance with the law, while subchapter four deals with compliance with intra-corporate norms. Subchapter five organises individual types of compliance norms, taking into account the criterion of the scope of norms. At the same time, it presents a conceptual apparatus containing definitions for particular types of compliance norms created by financial institutions.

The analysis presented in this chapter relates to the extraterritorial impact of certain regulations, and the results of investigations concerning financial institutions, and their impact on the content of the subsequent compliance norms created by these financial institutions. The verification of these observations carried out in this part of the analysis was based, among other things, on the impact of the remedial actions taken by financial institutions on irregularities, the aim of which was not only to prevent these infringements, but also to introduce normative collaterals, the aim of which is to prevent similar situations in the future. The conclusion drawn from these observations was that normalisation processes are similar. They are a response to legislative, regulatory and administrative actions wherever these actions are carried out, and models of norm-setting procedures and norms themselves show similarities.

The description of the phenomena presented here is the result of research and observations concerning matters that have taken place in financial institutions all over the world over the last several years. Comments relating to the conceptual apparatus, definitions and material scope of various types of compliance norms are the result of comparative research conducted on internal documents of various global financial institutions.[1]

2 Extraterritorial Normative Systems as the Reference Points for Compliance Norms

When characterising what compliance is, and above all how compliance norms are structured, it should be first noted that the notion of compliance itself must always be referred to something else.

The expression 'compliance risk', for example in the Basel documents, is defined as the risk of sanctions imposed by regulatory authorities, the risk of material financial loss or the risk of loss of good repute to

---

[1] Among the examined bank documents (taking into account the fact that the research was conducted in a different available access) there are the following materials HSBC Holdings Plc., JPMorgan Chase & Co., Citigroup Inc., Bank of America Corp., Barclays Plc., Royal Bank of Scotland Group Plc., and The Goldman Sachs Group Inc.

which a financial institution is exposed as a result of its failure to comply with applicable laws, norms of conduct and other internal regulations applicable to its business.[2] However, within the meaning of the Basel Committee's guidelines, the relevant laws and norms address some of these issues, such as compliance with good practice regarding certain types of market behaviour, management of conflicts of interest, fair treatment of clients, including the provision of the appropriate level of information, and advice needed to take their respective financial decisions.[3]

Therefore, compliance at a financial institution is usually related to a set of desirable patterns of behaviour relating to both employees and cooperating entities, which have been considered important to ensure the economic success of a given corporation, and sometimes simply to ensure its existence. In contrary, the risk of non-compliance is the risk, determined by the degree of probability, of the occurrence of instances of behaviour contrary to best practices deemed necessary and appropriate. Compliance is characterised by the fact that it refers to patterns of conduct resulting from various types of norms: legal, regulatory, moral, cultural, and other specific created in the process of deciding how a particular economic entity, a financial institution defines itself.[4] Since such a set of references is unique in the case of each corporation, compliance in each of the surveyed organisations is therefore in relation to an exclusive, autonomous axiological normative system.

---

[2] See Basel Committee on Banking Supervision, *Compliance Function in Banks*, April 2005, https://www.knf.gov.pl/Images/Zgodnosc%20i%20funkcja%20zapewnienia%20zgodnosci%20w%20bankach_tcm75-25055.pdf, p. 9 et seq. (download 25 March 2019).

[3] Among these other financial issues relating to bank customers are also issues relating to tax evasion, money laundering and the financing of terrorism. The document also provides a warning by stating that a bank that is knowingly engaged in transactions aimed at avoiding 'regulatory or financial' reporting obligations by the client, evading tax liability or facilitating illegal transactions, is exposed to a 'serious risk of non-compliance' (*"significant compliance risk"*). M. Ojo, Basel II and the Capital Requirements Directive: Responding to the 2008/09 Financial Crisis, *IGI Global* 18/2009, p. 12.

[4] The Basel Committee's guidelines indicate that laws, regulations and compliance standards have different sources, including primary legislation, rules and standards issued by legislative and supervisory authorities, market rules, codes of practice issued by professional associations and internal codes of conduct for bank employees. The document also stresses that these non-legal norms refer to more broadly understood rules of conduct set out in accepted standards of integrity and codes of ethics. R. Ayadi, E. Arbak, W. P. De Groen, Implementing Basel III in Europe: Diagnosis and Avenues for Improvement, *Centre for European Policy Studies* 275/2012, p. 10.

In light of these definitions discussed above a financial institution will usually position itself in a certain relation to external norms, for example to legal norms or regulatory guidelines, and at the same time to internal, differently stated internal norms that are considered important.[5]

Among the external norms referred to for compliance norms, reference should be made in particular to the Basel Committee's Guidance Group, whose very specific set of norms we have already mentioned above. These norms result from three consecutive sets of recommendations issued by the Basel Committee on Financial institutions Supervision, the Capital Accords, published in 1988, 2004 and 2010.[6] These were the result of a consensus among the world's major financial institutions, who came to the conclusion that improved coordinated cooperation that is based on harmonised guidelines is necessary to preserve the security of the global financial system.[7] As a result, these

---

[5] While mechanisms to ensure compliance with corporate norms may appear less complex due to the uniform nature of these norms, compliance with laws and supervisory regulations is particularly difficult for global organizations given the amount of regulation that international financial institutions must take into account at the same time. This applies not only to the varying degrees of importance of corporate-level rules of continental law in relation to corporate activities, norms arising from precedent-setting court judgements in common law jurisdictions, but also, for example, from the different types of norms issued by regulators. Compliance services monitor changes in this respect at both local and global levels, where specialized units are set up to prepare so-called legislative and regulatory trackers, compiling information on this issue from multiple sources simultaneously. These sources include all types of legislative alerts usually prepared by law firms and trade associations, participation in various forums, discussions and conferences, as well as "ordinary" sources such as the legal press and the online available legal databases.

[6] In practice, the individual capital agreements are referred to as Basel I, Basel II and Basel III, respectively.

[7] The source of the Basel regulations dates back to 1974 and is linked to the collapse of the German bank Bankhaus Herstatt AG as a result of losses incurred as a result of its speculative activity in the foreign exchange market. This event also caused unprecedented problems for many other financial institutions that were counterparties to the bankrupt bank, and consequently for the currency market turbulence. In response to these developments, the Governors of the G10 central banks set up a permanent committee, the Basel Committee on Banking Regulation and Supervisory Procedures, under the auspices of the Bank for International Settlements. Over time, this institution has been renamed the Basel Committee on Banking Supervision, which has become a forum for ongoing cooperation between the countries concerned in the field of banking supervision. Since then, one of the Committee's areas of activity has been the development of minimum standards for prudential standards for banks. The parallel objective of its activities was to develop a set of principles complementing the gaps in the banking supervision system and to promote

financial institutions agreed on the content of agreements containing a number of provisions relating to internal procedures.[8] In the first place, these agreements concern the stable and prudent management of financial institutions, first of all with regard to their capital adequacy, i.e. the adjustment of the size and manner of allocation of liabilities to the nature of the business. Importantly, the first introductory points also refer to the issue of compliance as a key factor necessary for the safe and stable conduct of financial institutions operations.[9]

The specificity of the Basel Capital Accords lies, inter alia, in the fact that they are neither legal acts nor international agreements under public law and are therefore in principle not binding either on states or on private entities, including financial institutions operating in those states. In practice, however, regardless of whether individual countries decide to transpose their provisions into their own national legal systems, both individual financial institutions and national regulators use their guidelines because of the systemic benefits resulting from their implementation.[10] Recently, in the European Union, the Basel guidelines have been

---

such international standards of risk management in banks as to ensure that problems similar to those that were the original cause of the Committee's establishment are avoided in the future. In 2009, the Committee was enlarged to include 17 new member states and is now composed of representatives of 27 countries. These countries are represented on the Committee by the delegates of their central banks or banking supervisors.

[8] R. M. Lastra, Risk-Based Capital Requirements and Their Impact Upon the Banking Industry: Basel II and CAD III, *Journal of Financial Regulation and Compliance* 12(3)/2004, p. 230.

[9] The provisions of the Introduction to the Second Capital Accord authorize, inter alia, the Basel Committee on Banking Supervision, as part of the continuous improvement of banking supervision arrangements and the dissemination of good practices in banking institutions, to publish guidelines on compliance risk and the implementation of compliance functions in banks. The objective is to ensure that banking supervisors know that an effective compliance policy is in place, that procedures are established, and that management takes appropriate corrective action when non-compliance is identified. The document also states that "compliance policy starts at the top" and will be most effective in a corporate culture that emphasizes standards of integrity and honesty, where boards set examples to others. A bank should apply high standards of business conduct and always strive to respect both the spirit and the letter of the law. M. El Kharbili, S. Stein, I. Markovic, E. Pulvermüller, *Towards a Framework for Semantic Business Process Compliance Management*, Osnabrueck 2008, p. 9 et seq.

[10] See M. Stefański, Nowe regulacje dotyczące wymagań kapitałowych wobec banków, *Materiały i Studia NBP* 12(212)/2006, p. 9 et seq.

transposed into European legislation by means of directives, regulations and implementing acts of the relevant EU bodies (currently part of the CRD IV—Capital Requirements Directive).[11]

Basel I was published in 1988 and was the result of the first agreement reached following the Committee's work on minimum capital requirements for financial institutions. The agreement focused primarily on credit risk, and on how to determine the minimum capital that could be considered adequate for a financial institution in view of its credit risk.[12] A significant novelty of this work was the reference of the required amount of capital necessary to conduct financial institutions activity to the value of risk-weighted assets. Over time, as further observations related to the behaviour of individual financial institutions were made, a number of new issues were added to the scope of Basel I in 1996, in particular concerning specific capital requirements for market risk. Here, too, these regulations have been followed up by the introduction of mechanisms by many institutions to ensure the effectiveness of the compliance approach. Subsequent versions of the Capital Accord, i.e. Basel II and Basel III, were created in response to new major crises on the international financial markets caused by the financial bankruptcy of Barings Bank in 1995 as a result of failed speculative transactions carried out by an employee of the Singapore branch of the financial institution and Lehman Brothers at the end of 2008.[13] The subsequent versions

---

[11] The implementation of Basel III in the EU Member States takes place through the CRD IV package, which consists of the directive (CRD—Capital Requirements Directive), which replaces the provisions of Directive 2006/48/EC relating to the taking up and pursuit of the business of credit institutions and Directive 2006/49/EC on the capital adequacy of investment firms and credit institutions and the regulation (CRR—Capital Requirements Regulation), which entered into force on 1 January 2014. Further specification of the prudential standards of the CRD IV package takes place in the so-called third level acts, i.e. acts issued in the form of binding technical standards (BTS), non-binding guidelines prepared by the European Banking Authority (EBA), which will be in force on a self-discipline basis (comply or explain). See A. Jurkowska-Zeidler, Nowe europejskie ramy ochrony stabilności wewnętrznego rynku finansowego [in] A. Dobaczewska, E. Juchniewicz, T. Sowiński [ed.] *System finansów publicznych. Prawo finansowe wobec wyzwań XXI wieku*, Warsaw 2010, p. 195 et seq.

[12] See J. B. Caouette, E. I. Altman, P. Narayanan, *Managing Credit Risk: The Next Great Financial Challenge*, New York 1998, p. 23.

[13] The intention of the so-called New Capital Accord, also commonly referred to as Basel II, was to strengthen the security and stability of the international banking system and to improve the manner in which the bank's capital requirements were determined depending

of this inter-banking agreement, by key players in the financial markets, supplement and modify the previous provisions. They refer to the following areas:

a. capital requirements;
b. risk management parameters;
c. the quality of the processes involved;
d. market discipline, i.e. the ways and scope of disclosing data related to the risk profile taken by financial institutions in connection with their transactions;
e. the introduction of risk mitigation measures;
f. the imposing of requirements for the corporate governance of financial institutions.

These are universal norms, developed jointly on the basis of previous costly experience. These norms are therefore essential for the stability of the global financial system as a whole. The compliance mechanisms introduced internally in financial institutions for this purpose play an essential role in this process.[14]

---

on the level of risk incurred and the size of its operations, as well as to take fuller account of new innovative financial instruments based on three pillars when determining capital adequacy. The first pillar concerns minimum capital requirements, which are calculated as the sum of capital requirements for credit, operational and market risk incurred by the bank using an improved method based on an appropriate classification of exposures. The second pillar concerns qualitative requirements related to internal processes of effective and safe risk management and mitigation. The third pillar concerns so-called market discipline, i.e. banks' obligations to disclose risk related information. The Basel III objectives, on the other hand, are primarily: increasing banks' capital requirements both in quantitative and qualitative terms, introducing capital protection mechanisms, introducing counter-cyclical capital buffer solutions (equipping financial supervisors with tools to temporarily increase banks' capital requirements when, in the opinion of supervisors, excessive credit growth in the banking sector leads to significant systemic risks), limiting leverage, introducing new standards limiting short- and long-term liquidity risk and further specifying rules related to corporate governance and risk management in general. A. J. McNeil, R. Frey, P. Embrechts, *Quantitative Risk Management: Concepts, Techniques and Tools*, Princeton 2015, p. 42.

[14] See Basel Committee on Banking Supervision, *Compliance and Compliance Functions in Banks*, April 2005, https://www.knf.gov.pl/Images/Zgodnosc%20i%20funkcja%20zapewnienia%20zgodnosci%20w%20bankach_tcm75-25055.pdf, p. 13 et seq. (download 4 February 2019).

While analysing supervisory norms and regulations which are a reference point for the compliance regulations in financial institutions, it should be noted that there are also those which, although issued in other countries, have an impact on the activity of financial institutions in other countries. This type of impact is referred to as extraterritorial or transboundary (extraterritorial, cross-border effect).[15] Seven examples of this extraterritorial application of the national laws of some countries are given below.[16]

Firstly, the application of norms arising from national laws outside national borders often makes use of the interdependencies existing within international groups. In practice, this is usually done in such a way that the element ensuring the implementation of these norms is the threat of administrative, tax or other sanctions against a given entity for non-compliance with certain norms by other entities of the same capital group with its registered office in other countries.[17]

Secondly, the extraterritorial application of national norms also takes place in situations where the requirements for transactions concern only one party to the transaction established in the country where the requirement applies, but may also apply indirectly to the other, foreign party to the transaction. An example of this type of regulation is the EMIR regulation and the FATCA and Dodd-Frank Acts that we describe below.[18]

Thirdly, a common phenomenon that should be taken into account when analysing the complexity of cross-border dimension is the fact that the courts in a given country may prescribe the application of national

---

[15] See J. K. Levitt, Bottom-Up Lawmaking: The Private Origins of Transnational Law, *Global Legal Studies Journal* 15/2008, p. 50 et seq. and J. E. Stiglitz, Regulating Multinational Corporations Towards Principles of Cross-Border Legal Frameworks in a Globalized World Balancing Rights with Responsibilities, *American International Law Review* 23/2007, p. 467 et seq.

[16] See also P. R. Wood, Op. cit., p. 132.

[17] An example is the US Act of 18 November 2010 on tax compliance of foreign account holders, described in more detail below (Foreign Account Tax Compliance Act—FATCA), https://www.irs.gov/Businesses/Corporations/Foreign-Account-Tax-Compliance-Act-FATCA (download 22 April 2019).

[18] *EMIR, i.e. European Market Infrastructure Regulation of 4 July 2012 on OTC derivatives and Dodd-Frank Wall Street Reform and Consumer Protection Act adopted by the American Congress on 15 July 2010.* See T. Aron, N. Lalone, C. Jackson, EMIR: An Overview of the New Framework, *Journal of Investment Compliance* 14(2)/2013, p. 57 et seq.

law, regardless of which law has been chosen by the parties or even determined by the conflict-of-law rules.[19]

Fourthly, in addition to the previous point, the submission of disputes with a contracting party to the courts of another country may lead to the application, also in the substantive sphere, of the provisions in force in that country.[20]

Fifthly, in addition, in the case of acquisitions of shareholdings in financial institutions or shares in entities controlling a financial institution, it may be necessary to apply restrictions on the direct or indirect acquisition of shares in financial institutions in the country where the financial institution is established, even if the transaction is concluded under the laws of another country, between entities from other countries, and concerns shares in an entity which is established in the territory of another country.[21] Similar restrictions may also apply to other categories of regulated entities.

Sixthly, extraterritorial rules also sometimes apply to consumer protection when a customer habitually resident in a country where such rules apply enters into a transaction with a foreign trader governed by the law of another country.[22]

Seventhly, similar rules also apply to some of the labour laws of the country in question, which apply even if a contract of employment has been concluded with a foreign employer and is governed by the law of another country.[23]

For financial institutions operating in the European Union, the reference system is EU law, especially that part of the entire EU acquis which relates to financial markets.[24] In practice, we are talking about virtually

---

[19] Such a practice may turn out to be highly unfavourable in financial institutions' relations with their customers. This may be exemplified by situations occurring in practice where, as a result of such decisions, when the parties were obliged to apply the provisions of the laws specifying the manner of calculating maximum interest.

[20] The growing protection of consumer interests manifests in multiple provisions of laws relating to that on the countries' levels.

[21] Similarly referred to in the local banking laws provisions in numerous countries.

[22] See art. 6 Regulation (EC) No 593/2008 of the European Parliament and of the Council of 17 June 2008 on the law applicable to contractual obligations (Rome I), *OJ L* 177, 4 July 2008, pp. 6–16.

[23] See art. 8 Ibidem.

[24] More on the specific role of financial security regulations and prudential requirements adopted in the European Union in response to financial crises, which are a solid reference

all international financial institutions corporations, and certainly all those that offer corporate financial institutions services, financing of international trade and servicing of equity debt instruments for international corporations and other financial institutions operating in the space of the international corporation.[25]

An example is the European Market Infrastructure Regulation of the European Parliament and of the Council (EMIR).[26] The Regulation itself, as well as other regulations and implementing acts based on it, impose a number of obligations on financial institutions and non-financial entities related to the conclusion and clearing of over the counter (OTC) derivatives and the reporting of derivative transactions.[27] The regulation entered into force on the 16th of August 2012, but most of the reference provisions and implementing acts gradually came into force later. As the EMIR Regulation has direct effect in all EU Member States, financial institutions' compliance services are under an obligation to quickly adapt their compliance activities to comply with the requirements of the Regulation.

---

for compliance standards. See A. M. Jurkowska-Zeidler, *Bezpieczeństwo rynku finansowego w świetle prawa Uni Europejskiej*, Warsaw 2008, p. 198 et seq. On the same subject in. The context of the EU regulations. See C. Kosikowski, Nowe prawo runku finansowego Unii Europejskiej [in] A. Jurkowska-Zeidler, M. Olszak [ed.] *Prawo rynku finansowego. Doktryna, instytucje, praktyka*, Warsaw 2016, p. 27.

[25] See J. K. Levitt, The dynamics of International Trade Finance: The Arrangement on Officially Supported Export Credits, *Harvard International Law Journal* 45/2008, p. 65 et seq.

[26] Regulation (EU) No 648/2012 of the European Parliament and of the Council of 4 July 2012 on OTC derivatives, central counterparties and trade repositories. Text with EEA relevance, *OJ L* 201, 27 July 2012, pp. 1–59 and Commission Delegated Regulation (EU) No 148/2013 of 19 December 2012 supplementing Regulation (EU) No 648/2012 of the European Parliament and of the Council on OTC derivatives, central counterparties and trade repositories with regard to regulatory technical standards on the minimum details of the data to be reported to trade repositories. Text with EEA relevance, *OJ L* 52, 23 February 2013, pp. 1–10.

[27] OTC transactions are transactions concluded on the over-the-counter (OTC) market. It is a securities market where transactions take place directly between market participants and therefore without the intermediation of a third party, typically a on stock exchange. On the OTC markets, share prices are set between the parties, for each transaction separately. The over-the-counter market enables companies to raise capital more quickly and without having to meet the high requirements of stock exchanges. As OTC markets are characterised by a higher level of risk and in many countries the possibility to invest in OTC markets is limited to specialised entities and investors with relevant experience, such as investment banks. OTC markets are regulated and supervised in most countries.

4 THE SCOPE OF COMPLIANCE NORMS IN FINANCIAL INSTITUTIONS 173

As the EMIR Regulation aims primarily at increasing transparency and reducing systemic risks in the derivatives market, in particular in the OTC market, and is therefore in principle in line with the tasks imposed on compliance in financial institutions, the compliance norms introduced within institutions transpose EMIR obligations into the specificities of each financial institution. In the EMIR Regulation itself, the following two basic obligations for market participants serve this purpose.

a. Obligation to report derivative transactions to so-called trade repositories. The reporting obligation, which entered into force on the 12th of February 2014, falls on both parties to the transaction. However, the parties may agree that this obligation will be performed by one of the parties on behalf of both parties, or by a third party. In practice, in relations between financial institutions and their clients, the obligation to report on behalf of both parties is most often assumed by financial institutions.[28]
b. the obligation to clear certain types of derivative transactions through Central Clearing Counterparties (CCPs). The central clearing of transactions is where two opposite transactions between CCPs and each party are concluded in place of one transaction between two parties (so a CCP is the seller to each buyer and the buyer to each seller). The central clearing obligation applies to standardised derivative transactions and depends on the allocation of entities intending to enter into a transaction to one of the categories introduced by the EMIR Regulation.[29]

---

[28] The repositories of the OTC transactions usually are established at the country depositories of securities.

[29] These categories are:

a. FC (financial counterparts)—financial institutions;
b. NFCs (non-financial counterparts)—non-financial institutions;
c. NFC+ (non-financial counterparty plus)—non-financial institutions whose average exposure to derivatives exceeds the threshold set out in the EMIR Regulation during 30 working days.

Only certain types of derivatives concluded between each other are subject to central clearing obligations:

a. a counterparty of FC and another counterparty of FC;
b. counterparty to FC and counterparty to NFC+;
c. between two NFC+ counterparties.

The US system occupies a special place among national legal systems due to the cross-border coverage of certain provisions relating to financial markets. There are multiple regulations and two examples of such provisions are presented below:

a. obligations imposed on financial institutions related to tax liabilities of clients of such institutions, based on the US Act of the 18th of November 2010 on compliance with tax obligations by holders of foreign accounts (FATCA)[30];
b. obligations imposed on financial institutions related to the strengthening of transaction transparency and stability of financial markets—an example is the Dodd-Frank Act of the 15th of July 2010 on Wall Street Reform and Consumer Protection.[31]

The FATCA is an example of a legal act which is a reference point for norms created by compliance services in financial institutions all over the world. The process of its implementation has been spread over several years. The main objective of the FATCA is to increase US government tax revenue by making it more difficult for US citizens and other US tax payers to conceal foreign property and income from US tax authorities.[32] This objective is to be achieved through agreements between the US

---

[30] *FATCA—Foreign Account Tax Compliance Act* Adopted by the US Congress as part of a wider law on the creation of instruments to promote employment growth (H.R.2847—Hiring Incentives to Restore Employment Act—*HIRE*), *public law 111-147* of 18 March 2010, https://www.congress.gov/bill/111th-congress/house-bill/2847 and http://www.gpo.gov/fdsys/pkg/PLAW-111publ147/pdf/PLAW-111publ147.pdf (download 5 June 2019).

[31] H.R.4173—Dodd-Frank Wall Street Reform and Consumer Protection Act—(*an act to promote the financial stability of the United States by improving accountability and transparency in the financial system, to end "too big to fail", to protect the American taxpayer by ending bailouts, to protect consumers from abusive financial services practices, and for other purposes*), https://www.congress.gov/bill/111th-congress/house-bill/4173 (download 5 June 2019).

[32] The responsibility of banks for cases of tax evasion by their customers, measured by the amount of penalties granted, leaves no doubt as to the necessity of a strong involvement of compliance services in the control over the correctness of their operations in this field as well. An example is Credit Suisse, which in May 2014 was found guilty of facilitating the use by American citizens of products that allow them to avoid paying taxes, as a result of which it had to pay a $2.6 billion fine to the US tax authorities. Cf. S. C. Morse, Tax Compliance and Norm Formation Under High-Penalty Regimes, *Connecticut Law Review* 44(3)/2012, p. 679 et seq.

Internal Revenue Service (IRS) and foreign financial institutions (FFI), under which these institutions are obliged to provide the IRS with information on financial operations of US clients of these institutions. Although such agreements are in theory voluntary, in practice they are forced upon financial institutions by a number of mechanisms put in place by the FATCA, in particular the retention by the IRS of 30% of any payment channelled from US sources (or related to the sale of US securities) to a financial institution not party to such an agreement. Moreover, on the basis of agreements concluded with the IRS, financial institutions are obliged to collect for the benefit of the IRS a tax on payments made to those financial institutions that evade such an agreement (non-compliant FFIs), as well as to some American entities evading their disclosure obligations towards the IRS in respect of financial assets held abroad.

Attention should be drawn to the very broad understanding of the term 'the US person', this including not only US citizens and residents and US companies, but also, for example, foreign companies in which more than 10% of shares or stocks are held by US entities.[33] In preparing financial institutions around the world to comply with the requirements of the FATCA has been and remains a complex logistical and procedural task. For obvious reasons, compliance financial institutions are involved in the process of such preparation. This preparatory work entails:

a. the preparation of the appropriate regulations, followed by the processes and practices that identify all customers who are subject to US tax;
b. the designation of those entities in the information systems and databases of the financial institutions;
c. appropriate notification of those entities to the US tax authorities;
d. the settlement of accounts;
e. the making of payments resulting from the obligations laid down in this Act.

---

[33] See R. Eccleston, F. Gray, Foreign Accounts Tax Compliance Act and American Leadership in the Campaign Against International Tax Evasion: Revolution or False Dawn?, *Global Policy* 5(3)/2014, p. 225 et seq., J. Heiberg, FATCA: Toward a Multilateral Automatic Information Reporting Regime, *Washington and Lee Law Review* 69/2012, p. 1698 et seq. and also D. Singh, *Banking Regulation of UK and US Financial Markets*, Hempshire 2007, p. 69.

The sources of compliance norms in financial institutions all over the world are, therefore, directly related to the regulations of a foreign state specified in this act, to which these financial institutions have to adapt.

The Dodd-Frank Act is another example of this type of regulation, which is a direct reference point for financial institutions compliance norms. It emerged as a response to the financial crisis that started in the United States in 2007 as part of the so-called G20 coordinated efforts to increase the stability and transparency of financial markets. The scope of the Dodd-Frank regulation is wide and includes:

a. the reorganisation of US institutions responsible for supervision of financial markets;
b. provisions to enable financial institutions in financial difficulties to fail and be wound up in an orderly manner which limits systemic risks;
c. rules on mortgage lending for housing purposes, with a view to reducing the irresponsible lending of mortgage loans to persons who raise reasonable doubts as to their ability to repay;
d. provisions relating to the strengthening of consumer protection in financial markets[34];
e. rules on the entering into, clearing and reporting of derivative transactions with a view to enhancing the stability and transparency of the market in those instruments.

The most important aspect of this legislation from the point of view of global financial markets is the last of the above-mentioned areas of the Dodd-Frank regulation, as it has a direct impact on the international derivatives market. In this respect, the Dodd-Frank Act is the US equivalent of the EMIR Regulation and the regulation of the derivatives market in the Dodd-Frank Act is largely similar to those contained in the EMIR regulation. Like the EMIR, the Dodd-Frank Act regulates the conclusion, clearing and reporting of derivative transactions, as well as the reduction of related risks, in particular systemic risks. However, there are differences between the two regulations:

---

[34] More on current trends in consumer protection in financial markets in connection with global development trends in the economy. See K. Ward, F. Neumann, Consumer in 2050. The Rise of the EM Middle Class, *Global Economics*, October 2012, p. 20 et seq., D. Freeman, The Role of Consumption of Modern Durables in Economic Development, *Economic Development and Cultural Change* 19(1)/2011, p. 24 et seq.

a. material scope—the regulations define the classes of derivatives in a different way;
b. personal scope—the regulations categorise in a different way entities which are subject to regulatory obligations (for example, the Dodd-Frank Act does not make affiliation to any of the categories conditional on a given entity exceeding a fixed volume of transactions threshold), although they do so on the basis of a similar concept of division into financial and non-financial entities;
c. reporting obligation—unlike the EMIR, the Dodd-Frank Act imposes this obligation on one party to the transaction and does not require reporting of exchange-listed instruments but provides for the obligation to be reported in real time.

3 Compliance Norms and Other Normative Systems

Compliance norms are referred to in various normative systems, and are considered important by a given corporation, mainly due to its own economic interest. These include in particular the legal systems of the jurisdictions in which these corporations operate. The essence of the compliance norms, however, is that apart from the legal regulations, they also refer to the catalogue of norms extended by norms fulfilling other functions than the legal regulations of a given country. Usually, compliance norms in a corporation can be described as institutional reaction to the imposition of obligations to perform certain tasks, resulting from legal regulations, and at the same time from other obligations recognised as important by the corporation and resulting from other types of norms. Below are listed the six types of the most common normative orders from which the directives referring to compliance norms may derive.

The first, most frequent example is the list of norms of a given legal system enriched with regulatory and supervisory norms issued by the authorised market regulators. Leaving aside the analysis conducted in this book the issue of the often criticised cases of non-compliance by these bodies outside the framework of regulatory intervention permitted by law, i.e. whether, in fact, in every case and whether, to any extent, these bodies are entitled to such actions, it should be noted that it is these regulatory norms, in combination with legal norms, that constitute the most basic normative reference system, compliance with which is the compliance obligation most frequently declared by corporations. In addition, such a declaration of compliance not only does not raise objections but can even be considered correct and expected.

The second and, in the opinion of the author, much more controversial reference is the situation, shown in several examples above, in which the legal system of a given jurisdiction, is enriched with legal rules that originate from other jurisdictions. This usually occurs when a corporation's compliance system is defined as a set of legal norms applicable in a jurisdiction in which some part of the corporation's activity is carried out and is extended by legal norms belonging to another legal system—usually the one in which its authorities have their seat. Therefore, the financial institution determines that its declared compliance policy will be based on compliance with the law of a given country, but also with the legal norms of its home country. If we want to rationalise this kind of approach, we could probably assume that such an understanding of compliance policy does not raise much controversy when a given corporation decides to act both in accordance with the laws of one country and at the same time with others. In practice, this an obvious source of complication in the event of any divergences in the way in which the same issues may arise in the application of legal norms from different systems.[35] Therefore, in such a situation it may occur and in practice it is not uncommon for a situation which cannot be easily eliminated—contradictions of regulations and, as a consequence, inconsistencies of the entire normative system to which the compliance of a given corporation refers. An additional complication occurs in the face of a possible attempt to ensure the compliance of corporate activity with norms derived both from the provisions of continental law and from the common law system, in which norms must also be read from precedents that make up its essence normative legacy.

The third normative system that constitute a reference for corporate compliance norms are the legal systems of the jurisdictions in which these corporations conduct their activities supplemented by axiological references, i.e. a catalogue of values set by them.[36] The catalogue

---

[35] Moreover, in rare cases of conflicting regulations that may have a direct impact on the costs of banking activities, such as where differently defined systemic risks incurred by banks in different jurisdictions are associated with different core capital requirements and capital adequacy ratios, there is usually a tendency to determine the choice of more favourable regulatory environment and thus the arbitrage of regulatory regimes. See R. Lindsey, Capital Adequacy Standards, *Journal of Financial regulations and Compliance* 4(3)/1996, p. 209.

[36] An interesting voice in the discussion on the extent to which the establishment of private values catalogues by corporations is the fulfilment of an axiological deficit and on the difference between democratic legitimacy in relation to the undemocratic performance of functions by entrepreneurs, i.e. the difference between governance (German Regierung)

includes not so much every value important for the whole legal system, but only those that were considered crucial for identity identification, bearing the value of individualisation, distinction, and thus subjectively important for a given corporation.[37] The compliance norms formulated in such a situation will therefore include all those directive statements which require the entities to which they are addressed to follow a procedure that is adapted both to the norms resulting from legal regulations and from other axiologically shaped models of conduct.

As in the case described above, the fourth, uncontroversial set of norms, they do not constitute a compact, uniform system, and consist of internal norms of a binding nature. This refers to all kinds of norms, rules describing 'corporate culture', etc. These are norms of a slightly different nature than norms based on values. Therefore, these are rules of conduct based on a certain pattern, a certain desirable pragmatics, although in contrast to values, rather lacking solid ethical justifications. What is interesting, although we are talking about norms created within the corporation, in practice they are not only binding for its employees.[38] Their very wording also results in obligations imposed on other entities to behave in a specific way, most often with regard to customers and service providers, sometimes also with regard to other beneficiaries of financing, including entities receiving support in the form of financing from these financial institutions. A typical example is sponsorship agreements in which the financed entity undertakes to comply with the rules of the sponsoring financial institution's norms.

The fifth supplement to the legal system, which is a reference for compliance norms in financial institutions, is introduced in corporations within the framework of which these financial institutions operate in accordance with corporate governance rules. In this case, we are talking not so much about generally applicable regulations resulting from

---

and management (German Verwaltung). See Z. Bauman, *Szanse etyki w zglobalizowanym świecie*, Cracow 2007, pp. 239–282.

[37] This identity identification by reference to concrete values is also indicated by F. Tönnies as a basic feature distinguishing the community from the enterprise, in addition to the very purpose of unification. F. Tönnies, *Community and Society: Gemeinschaft and Geselschaft*, Michigan 1957, pp. 223–231.

[38] The relationship between corporate standards and ethical standards and the programs implemented in companies to promote value among employees and the benefits of this. See e.g. B. Rok, Kręgosłup moralny firmy, *Thinktank* 18/2013, p. 56.

the provisions of law in force in a given jurisdiction, but about the rules adopted in a specific capital group, characteristic only for it and recommended for the application of principles, directional guidelines concerning the arrangement of relations between statutory or appointed regardless of the wording of the statutes of committees and other bodies supporting the operation of the financial institution. This is particularly relevant for financial institutions corporations operating in jurisdictions with different corporate governance models, where there is a need for harmonised rules that can be applied to all group entities.[39]

Similarly, the legal system supplemented by a catalogue of tasks and business objectives defined by the company in its mission statements may also become the basis for the compliance norms it creates. These form a separate sixth set of, directional guidelines, that indicate the economic plans and define the target model of operation in relation to customers, employees and shareholders. In cases where a financial institution has such specific guidelines, and this is usually the case because such a definition of a financial institution's 'mission' can be a useful marketing tool by the way, the whole set of rules of conduct included in the normative compliance system to be applied to employees, co-workers and customers is based on such formulated objectives, in more precise accordance with such formulated objectives remains consistent.

In reality, however, compliance norms are usually based on normative references containing elements of all of these models indicated above.

The norms of compliance refer to the legal regulations in force in a given jurisdiction, with which compliance is the duty of each institution, but also to regulatory recommendations, legal regulations from other international jurisdictions, the norms of conduct adopted by the capital group, principles of corporate governance, etc. The norms of compliance apply to all the jurisdictions in which compliance is the duty of each institution to act. The difference in their content, depending on the corporation, depends both on what these references are, as well as what weight each corporation assigns to each of the selected elements. Interestingly, the interpenetration and interaction between norms of different types and the law-forming effect of such

---

[39] Przykładem jest choćby nieznana w spółkach funkcjonujących w jurysdykcjach kształtowanych pod wpływem niemieckiej myśli prawniczej instytucja rady dyrektorów z członkami posiadających i nieposiadających kompetencje zarządcze (*executive* i *non-executive directors* w ramach jednej *board of directors*).

interpenetration of norms may be the subject of separate theoretical and legal considerations. However, it is enough to point out that, just like every organised population, corporation strives to develop only the right norms.

Regardless of the form and conditions in which norms are developed within a corporation, they may over time become legal norms, which is often the case. Before this happens, however, it is specified that, until then, they take the form of rules—"pre-legal" rules.[40] Apart from the considerations contained in this book, there is an observation described in the institutional theory of law, which assumes the dual nature of any norms placed simultaneously in thought and reality.[41] At this point it is worth pointing out the theory of autopoieticism resulting from the performative function of normative statements, which, similarly to other legal systems and subsystems, can also be applied to norms created within corporations.[42] The theory of social systems based on the claim that performativity is one of the basic principles supporting the existence of the social system refers directly to the performative function of cultural and philosophical texts. It is precisely this modern handling without the 'myth of the beginning' that justifies social systems, and the reference to performativity that has led to the formulation of a thesis of the so-called autopoietic character of social systems. Autopoieticism is in this case the ability to self-renew and self-control social systems, and within them normative systems as statements containing sets of meanings and symbols of a directive character that create social relations and precisely thanks to the performative function of normative statements replacing the reality of physical systems in them.[43] In this sense, such autopoietic normative systems may create intra-corporate compliance norms.

In order to discuss further how they arise, evolve, what they refer to and what role are played by the internal normative systems built in

---

[40] The importance of dynamics of rules, standards and discretion in prelegal social groups more: R. A. Posner, *The Problems of Jurisprudence*, Harvard 2000, p. 42.

[41] N. MacCormick, O. Weinberger, *An Institutional Theory of Law. New Approaches to Legal Positivism*, Dodrecht 2010, p. 37 et seq.

[42] See M. J. W. van Twist, L. Schaap, Introduction to Autopoiesis Theory and Autopoietic Steering [in] R. J. In t' Veld, L. Schaap, C. J. A. M. Termeer, M. J. W. van Twist, *Autopoiesis and Configuration Theory: New Approaches to Societal Steering*, Rotterdam 1991, p. 129 et seq.

[43] M. Zirk-Sadowski, *Wprowadzenie do filozofii prawa*, Warsaw 2011, p. 111.

corporations, it is worth returning to the classic dispute between Ronald Dworkin and Herbert Hart, which resulted in a criticism of the recognition rules. In Dworkin's practical theory there are no two types of rules, one of which are social rules, confirmed by the practice of a common way of proceeding, and the other are normative rules. According to this theory, the law can be applied in such a way that, on the one hand, it is possible to agree on a legitimate social practice, and to consider a rule of conduct as legitimate, while at the same time disagreeing on its specific content proposed in a specific context. In contrast, positivism referring to practical content does not identify such a distinction. When we apply this to corporate norms originating in different normative orders, one could say that the recognition rule, if it is reduced to the role of a test identifying legal rules, is too simple.

Hart's thesis that in every society, here respectively in the community, populations that have their own normative system, a certain rule (the recognition rule), which defines the obligation to recognise as law any other pre-legal, primary rule, turns out to be unsustainable. According to it, in each social group which is connected by a common normative system, in this case such an artificially united group is a community functioning within a defined corporation, there is a normative test, which is enough to distinguish binding corporate rules from other rules, which remain outside this order of rules. Referring further to Dworkin in his criticism of the principle of recognition, it is necessary to go far beyond the limits of legal norms in order to examine whether a norm is in force. The result is an extension of the boundaries of the notion of norm and a blurring of the boundaries of law and morality.[44]

When analysing non-legal references to intra-corporate compliance norms, it is worth quoting Eugen Ehrlich's thesis, who, while formulating the claims of the school of free law, stated that not all law is included in codes and laws created by the state. A large part of the law is spontaneously created by the society itself in the form of property relations, family and marriage, inheritance orders, etc. People have many legal relations with each other without touching the courts or referring to the content of the law. This thesis divides legal material in society into three layers:

---

[44] M. Zirk-Sadowski, Ibidem, p. 166.

a. social law, which is the primary layer of society;
b. legal law, which is the creation of lawyers;
c. state law, the centralistic law of the public authorities.[45]

Eugen Ehrlich created two important theories for the Sociology of law:

a. the theory of living law—living law realistically functions in the behaviour of social groups and communities, influencing the way it is applied to the whole of the ever-changing legal reality, in which social law is transformed in response to legal and state law;
b. the theory of free law—the creative role of a judge in jurisprudence, undermines the principle that a judge is only a statute.[46]

Of particularly important from the perspective presented here is the first theory, which compares the existing normative order to the realistically functioning patterns of behaviour existing in a given community, which in a specific case may be a corporation.

This concept of the living law goes in a similar direction as considering the so-called omnipresent law (*Ubiquitus Lex*, Ubiquitous Law).[47] This concept is based on understanding the law by abstracting it from the lawmaking power of the state, while at the same time establishing the conditions for communicating the content of legal norms directly between entities that may have norm-making powers. Analyses carried out in the current of the ubiquitous law are only partially informed by methodological considerations, because to a large extent they also refer to the regulating content contained in the norms.[48] These studies argue that the description of the right is to a large extent imprinted by the assumption that the state alone has exclusive competence to determine what is a right and that there is in practice an exclusive right transferred

---

[45] E. Erlich, *Fundamental Principles of the Sociology of Law*, New Brunswick 2002, p. 39 et seq.

[46] Ibidem, p. 192.

[47] On contemporary European concepts for interpreting omnipresent law. See M. Hertogh, A 'European' Conception of Legal Consciousness. Rediscovering Eugen Ehrlich, *Journal of Law and Society* 31(4)/2004, p. 456.

[48] See K. Shields, A. Perry-Kessaris, Rewriting the Centricity of the State in Pursuit of Global Justice [ed.] *Socio-Legal Approaches to International Economic Law: Text, Context, Subtext*, New York 2013, p. 235 et seq.

to the legal personnel and most often exercised in an authoritative manner as to whether the community has to apply certain norms.[49] The criticism of such a traditional approach that identifies the state as the only entity empowered to identify the law results from the statement that the law created by experts is so detached from the original content of norms resulting from communication between entities that at the same time it tears apart the networks of mutual social obligations resulting from this communication.

The counter-proposal of the Ubiquitous Law school of thoughts suggests the use of a new methodology for identifying norms in law theory, which is not based on rigid epistemological or normative assumptions, but rather on 'self-reflection, mutual understanding and criticism', in order to make acceptable differences with respect to a common basis. Ubiquitous Law is therefore directed towards determining the possibility of determining universal objectivity, both in relation to the very existence of norms (what is and what is not the norm) and in relation to their content. However, this arrangement alone does not exclude or radically disqualify questions about the diversity of sources of law or its validity.[50] As it was emphasised earlier, compliance norms, even if only because of the meaning of the term itself, are primarily intended to ensure that the institution operates in accordance with the entire normative order applicable to the activities of this institution. Analysing the relation between compliance norms and other norms, or rather the entire normative systems to which it refers, to some extent there is an identification of the opposition of formalism and realism. As a result of this, considerations on formalism and realism, but also on their mutual opposition remain empty—the very concept of omnipresent law is about opposing formalism—realism and recognition that the sources of norms should be sought in a broader context of all social processes.[51]

---

[49] Cf. M. Velverde, The Ethics of Diversity: Local Law and the Negotiations of Urban Norms, *Law and Social Inquiry* 33(4)/2008, p. 895.

[50] E. Melissaris writes about what the law is not omnipresent that the ubiquitous law concept is neither a suppressed and closed theory of diversity nor a radically undefined question about the relationship of the right to integrity. See E. Melissaris, *Ubiquitous Law: Legal Theory and the Space for Legal Pluralism*, Ashgate 2009, p. 80 et seq.

[51] About the emptiness of neo-formalism in legal theory. See B. Z. Tamanaha, *Beyond the Formalist-Realist Divide. The Role of Politics in Judging*, Oxford 2010, p. 159.

The content of compliance norms varies depending on the type of business conducted by the corporation. To identify the characteristic of compliance norms of a given industry, and then a given institution from their sources, it is necessary to indicate the main types of compliance norms.

a. Compliance norms that ensure compliance with the legislation in force in the field. While the compliance norms, which prescribe the type of behaviour resulting from generally binding provisions of law, are only a reinforcement of obligations concerning all entities and, as a rule, they are neither necessary nor individualising, those based on the provisions of law in force in a given area constitute an important regulating element determining which business model a given corporation wishes to adopt within the framework of the legal framework specified by law.
b. Compliance norms ensuring compliance with regulations issued by the administrative supervisory authorities applicable to the type of institution in question. It refers to both those supervisory regulations that:

   (1) are binding due to their binding force (regulations, orders, resolutions, etc.);
   (2) are formally non-binding, but de facto in practice they oblige them to take specific actions through the general power of influence of the body (recommendations, recommendations, etc.).[52]

c. customary norms adopted for internal compliance, expressed not only by the principles of corporate governance but also in everything that is defined by the concept of organisational culture of the organisation concerned. It is precisely these exclusive norms for a particular organisation, usually resulting from the integration of many norms derived from different legal and corporate cultural traditions, often accumulated over many years of operation.
d. Ethical norms introduced into the compliance order based on values established by a given corporation. It is worth noting here that these values do not have to be interpreted from some more widely

---

[52] See K. Gordon, Rules for the Global Economy: Synergies Between Voluntary and Binding Approaches, *Organisation for Economic Cooperation and Development Working Paper* 1999/2000, p. 11 et seq.

accepted axiological system, but rather from a set of concepts considered important for determining the success factors of a given corporation. In this context, it might even be appropriate to recognise that these are not, in fact, values par excellence, but rather requests that indicate the desired set of concepts, practices, etc., to which behaviour, in their activities, the addressees of these norms should adhere.
e. Compliance norms relating to expectations derived from entities external to the corporation that attempt, with varying degrees of effect, to influence the way in which they function both as a whole and the approach to which they are guided in making individual decisions. Such entities are in particular organised groups of shareholders activists, non-governmental organisations, the media, as well as other entities operating in the economic turnover, including even competitive entities.

Therefore, the individualising, financial institution-specific compliance norms refer to relevant legal regulations, supervisory regulations and norms coming from various sources. They are created both by legislators and other authorised legislators and supervisors, as well as by established market conventions, codes of ethics created by industry associations, etc., and other internal normative regulations of the financial institution applicable to its employees. For the reasons set out above, due to their objectives and sources, they may be broader in scope than the provisions of applicable law and impose higher norms of honesty and ethics.

4 COMPLIANCE NORMS AND IRREGULARITIES IN FINANCIAL INSTITUTIONS

The aforementioned document 'The compliance function in financial institutions' adopted by the Basel Committee in 2003 became the first attempt to formally define the definitions and tasks related to this area of a financial institution's activity. The key issue for indicating the issues that should be covered by compliance regulations is to determine why it was decided to emphasise the importance of the need for financial institutions to adapt to detected irregularities, i.e. compliance, among others. A guideline for answering such a question is the observation that irregularities occurring in the activity of financial institutions uncover deficiencies in the existing regulations and allow for the identification of areas that require better regulation, more adapted to changing circumstances. The examples presented in this section illustrate these cases of irregularities, which then became the basis for reflection on the need to create compliance norms in subsequent areas. The division of legal risks that can materialise in practice, presented here is a reference to the content of subsequent compliance norms.

Supervisory institutions around the world have recognised that the traditional understanding of risk in financial institutions activities, including credit risk, counterparty risk, liquidity risk, etc., has proved to be insufficient, too narrow. This has given rise to supervisory recommendations in various countries, imposing an obligation to manage risk also in areas that have so far been overlooked. One example is the recommendation that financial institutions put in place mechanisms to identify and mitigate operational risks and, importantly from the point of view of this work, compliance risks. A practical way of reducing such risks is the standardisation activities carried out by the compliance services as a result of controls. They help to identify and mitigate the identified compliance and related reputational risks, the occurrence of which can have both financial and non-financial consequences that can have a serious impact on financial institutions' activities.

The dynamic business environment forces regular reviews of existing compliance regulations in the company in order to supplement and adapt them to the changing normative environment, but also because the scope of the subject matter, which includes compliance norms, it is becoming wider and wider. In practice, during reviews it is often established that certain areas of financial institutions activity are not covered by regulations at all, or that the existing procedures do not regulate all aspects of its activity. Experience has also shown that even if, as a matter of principle, the employees of financial institution have been properly prepared and are fully aware of how to act in specific difficult situations, the lack of the appropriate provisions in the internal regulations still may expose the financial institution to a risk that result in irregularities. Then, employees may refer to the lack of sufficiently clearly formulated regulations indicating the correct manner of behaviour.

In order to clearly formulate the scope of the subject matter of compliance norms, it is worth pointing out the cases in which compliance risk has recently materialised in some financial institutions. In all these situations, financial institutions had compliance services, which were obliged to create, and update regulations aimed at avoiding similar problems. In none of these cases has the day-to-day compliance activities or compliance norms proved to be sufficiently effective.

One such example of risks is the likelihood of losing or reducing the scope of cross-border financial institutions licences. To a lesser extent, this applies to operations carried out in the countries of the European Economic Area, and in particular in the European Union, where specific rules are applied in this respect, the purpose of which is to facilitate the conduct of activities directed from one country to another. However, this is a real and often materialising risk in the case of global operations conducted by financial institutions. Depending on the nature of their activities and the products they offer, local requirements for the scope of the licence rights shall apply to such transactions carried out by financial institutions operating in several different markets at the same time.[53] The term licence used here also refers to licences and means the right, obtained by a decision of a competent public administration body, to conduct the financial institutions' activities specified therein, to the extent, in the manner and place specified by it.

Thus, national financial supervisors often grant separate licences for individual branches and establishments of the financial institution and for the products and services that can be marketed within them. The lack of appropriate licences, or the failure to comply with the terms and conditions of those licences may therefore have adverse legal and regulatory consequences, ranging from fines to the restriction or even withdrawal of the licence. In order to mitigate this risk, financial institutions formulate in their internal compliance regulations a number of obligations that are imposed on employees of particular financial institution services and create a framework for taking possible control actions.

Compliance obligations may include, for example, an order addressed to a financial institution to analyse the legal status, and to identify the scope of permitted operations under a licence, the obtaining of prior

---

[53] F. Snyder, Governing Economic Globalization: Global Legal Pluralism and European Law, *European Law Journal* 5/1999, p. 334.

approval from local legal and compliance services, prior to entering into cross-border transactions. Under these conditions, on the basis of the procedures established in these norms, any circumstances likely to affect the nature and scope of the activities carried out under cross-border licences shall be examined in consultation with these services. Wrong analyses being the basis for issuing erroneous opinions or undertaking by activities contrary to the authorisation resulting from the licence, or that are contrary to the opinion obtained as to the content of this licence, are examples of errors in the advisory, management or compliance control functions.

Another type of risk that often materialises is the dynamics surrounding legislative changes, in relation to which compliance norms are created, the aim of which is to prepare institutions for these changes.[54]

For example, the number of legislative changes concerning the area of treasury transactions in global markets transactions in treasury financial institutions is high. This can contribute to the risk of non-implementation in a timely or insufficiently appropriate manner to new rules. In order to limit this risk, the compliance norms provide the following five control measures:

First, the formal process of monitoring mainstream legislative developments by leading financial markets in all types of financial institutions activities should involve specialised lawyers, whose task is to provide periodic reports on the key developments in this area. Where appropriate, consultations and lobbying activities should also be undertaken directly or through industry associations. Due to the need to adapt to changing regulations, business strategy and planning also require ongoing adjustments.

To demonstrate the scope and quantity of the above issue, here is a list only the most recent attempts to regulate global financial institutions: Financial institutions Union regulations, the so-called benchmark regulation, the Capital Requirements Directive, the Data Protection Regulation, the Regulation on financial market abuse, the MiFID regulation (discussed above), the Money Market Funds Regulation, the Mortgage Credit Directive, the revised Payment Services Directive, the Directive on financial institution repair and resolution, the Directive on

---

[54]W. Rogowski, *Nowe koncepcje i regulacje rynku finansowego*, Warsaw 2014, p. 50.

securities issues and trading, the EMIR, the Single Euro Payments Area Regulation, etc.[55]

Secondly, due to the serious risk of non-compliance with the requirements of US law, with respect to Chapter VII of the Dodd-Frank Act on transactions involving the conversion of large amounts of money on global markets (swaps), financial institutions have begun to develop

---

[55] The regulations quoted here are accordingly:

a. Directive 2014/65/EU of the European Parliament and of the Council of 15 May 2014 on markets in financial instruments and amending Directive 2002/92/EC and Directive 2011/61/EU Text with EEA relevance, OJ L 173, 12 June 2014, pp. 349–496;
b. Opinion of the European Economic and Social Committee on the Proposal for a Regulation of the European Parliament and of the Council on Money Market Funds COM(2013) 615 final—2013/0306 (COD), OJ C 170, 5 June 2014, pp. 50–54;
c. Directive 2014/17/EU of the European Parliament and of the Council of 4 February 2014 on credit agreements for consumers relating to residential immovable property and amending Directives 2008/48/EC and 2013/36/EU and Regulation (EU) No 1093/2010 Text with EEA relevance, OJ L 60, 28 February 2014, pp. 34–85;
d. Directive (EU) 2015/2366 of the European Parliament and of the Council of 25 November 2015 on payment services in the internal market, amending Directives 2002/65/EC, 2009/110/EC and 2013/36/EU and Regulation (EU) No 1093/2010, and repealing Directive 2007/64/EC (Text with EEA relevance), OJ L 337, 23 December 2015, pp. 35–127;
e. Directive 2014/59/EU of the European Parliament and of the Council of 15 May 2014 establishing a framework for the recovery and resolution of credit institutions and investment firms and amending Council Directive 82/891/EEC, and Directives 2001/24/EC, 2002/47/EC, 2004/25/EC, 2005/56/EC, 2007/36/EC, 2011/35/EU, 2012/30/EU and 2013/36/EU, and Regulations (EU) No 1093/2010 and (EU) No 648/2012, of the European Parliament and of the Council Text with EEA relevance, OJ L 173, 12 June 2014, pp. 190–348;
f. Directive 2004/109/EC of the European Parliament and of the Council of 15 December 2004 on the harmonization of transparency requirements in relation to information about issuers whose securities are admitted to trading on a regulated market and amending Directive 2001/34/EC, OJ L 390, 31 December 2004, pp. 38–57;
g. Regulation (EU) No 648/2012 of the European Parliament and of the Council of 4 July 2012 on OTC derivatives, central counterparties and trade repositories Text with EEA relevance, OJ L 201, 27 July 2012, pp. 1–59;
h. Regulation (EU) No 260/2012 of the European Parliament and of the Council of 14 March 2012 establishing technical and business requirements for credit transfers and direct debits in euro and amending Regulation (EC) No 924/2009 Text with EEA relevance, OJ L 94, 30 March 2012, pp. 22–37.

compliance regulations setting out how to monitor and implement these regulations in the main financial institutions' centres. At the same time, the same regulations prohibit smaller organisational units of local financial institutions and financial institution branches from engaging in swap transactions. The compliance regulations of most large financial institutions contained in the internal compliance norms have therefore been updated to ensure compliance with these recommendations. According to these norms, the managing directors of the global financial institutions area of any entity involved in such transactions are required to confirm that the entity they manage complies with those norms that require them not to engage in swap transactions. It also follows from the same norms that financial institutions should implement a process of local controls by designated business risk managers to ensure that individual smaller entities comply with the ban on swap transactions.[56]

Thirdly, when discussing the subject matter of compliance norms, which is shaped as a result of events observed in practice that reveal deficiencies in the existing state of adjustment of business organisations to the external normative environment, among many other issues, situations of deficiencies or even outdated documentation existing in financial institutions are revealed. The aim of the compliance norms is to create a framework not only for the financial institution's activities to simply comply with the applicable normative environment, but also for this adaptation to be carried out in a coherent manner, improving the financial institutions' activities in a multijurisdictional and multicultural normative space.

To illustrate this problem with a practical example, it is worth pointing out the frequent problem of templates of documents used by global financial institutions, which should be agreed with lawyers and inspected. In practice, some document templates are outdated, incomplete or erroneous. Obviously, defective documents used at the customer contact stage

---

[56] The obligations under the Dodd-Frank Act do not only apply to swap transactions. They also imply, for example, obligations deriving from the so-called Volcker Rule. They concern financial operations on global markets and relate to certain transaction bans linked with hedge funds and private equity, which are referred to as 'covered funds'. In connection with regulations in this area, banks usually set up various types of steering committees for derivative transactions, including commodity options on their own account (proprietary trading). J. Vinãls, C. Pazarbasioglu, J. Surti, A. Narain, M. Erbenova, J. T. S. Chow, *Creating a Safer Financial System: Will the Volcker, Vickers, and Liikanen Structural Measures Help?*, Washington 2013, p. 7 et seq.

mechanically expose financial institutions to multiple legal risks. They do not reflect the changes taking place in the law and other regulations in force in the financial institution, or even do not take into account the evolution of doctrine views, interpretations developed, emerging jurisprudence lines, or the observed practice of their application, and finally they do not sufficiently protect the interests of the parties. In order to mitigate this risk, financial institutions undertake actions resulting from internal normative acts, which require the documentation to be adjusted to the requirements of the normative environment on an ongoing basis.

Fourthly, these internal compliance norms in financial institutions therefore require the preparation and agreement with those responsible for the financial institution's area of activity, including, in particular, financial institutions activities in global markets, of action plans laying down an obligation to prepare or update all existing document templates. The same norms also apply to the obligation, once these templates have been developed, for risk managers to carry out day-to-day checks to ensure that the documentation provided to contractors complies with the templates developed in this way. In those types of financial institutions which operate on global markets, and where documentation based on templates is not used, if only due to the nature of the transactions to which it relates, then these norms specify the requirements for the preparation of separate documentation, taking into account the current state of legal knowledge and practice, so that the documentation meets the conditions referred to above.

Incidentally, it should be pointed out that there is a real and often occurring risk that a lack of proper communication with properly prepared legal services on this issue may lead to the incorrect identification of contractual risk and, consequently, to its insufficient limitation. In order to limit this risk, measures are taken, including control measures with regard to non-norm, i.e. separately prepared documentation, the parameters of which should be agreed, on the one hand, with the persons responsible for the management of individual business lines and, on the other hand, with the legal and compliance services.

In addition, internal procedures detailing this obligation require legal services to consult with those responsible for the type of financial institutions in question as well as other possible measures to mitigate this risk, including the establishing the obligation for business risk managers to carry out ongoing controls to ensure that separate, non-norm documentation is in line with the established parameters.

Fifthly, in some jurisdictions, the document templates developed by the global financial institutions area may prove invalid or ineffective. In order to mitigate this risk, a number of practical steps are being taken, not only in the form of mandates for the control of existing documentation, but also in the form of a system-wide implementation of norms that force the financial institution's services to take appropriate security and adjustment measures. These norms show that in order for the scope of potential problematic issues related to the templates of local documentation used by global financial institutions to be fully understood, it is necessary to take stock of the legal situation, and then prepare a list of documents relevant to the market in question, which are necessary to ensure the validity of the documentation at hand and the effectiveness of transactions.

An example of the necessary adjustment actions resulting from compliance norms aimed at ensuring compliance is to take into account the complications related to the applicable competition law. Competition law can, of course, be infringed in a number of ways, mainly through the adoption of commercial practices that abuse a financial institution's dominant market position in a given market or through the disclosure or provision of confidential information to competitors, or simply for internal reasons, i.e. the ineffectiveness of the controls carried out by competition authorities.

Nevertheless, there has been an increase in the number of enforcement proceedings in the financial sector, particularly in the UK, the USA, but also in Brazil and the Asian markets, for example. A high percentage of these court cases were won against financial institutions for damages, mainly as a result of collective actions brought as a result of a breach of competition law.[57] This is a consequence of the actions of regulators, who clearly indicate in their recommendation's irregularities in the functioning of financial institutions, while at the same time applying additional methods of influencing financial institutions' approach to these issues by publishing observations and assessments to which financial institutions are subjected in this respect from entities with which financial institutions cooperate.

In order to limit this risk, the compliance norms in financial institutions provide for various security measures to be taken. The scope of

[57] O. Wyman, Conduct Risk Management in the Asia Pacific Region. Improving Relationship, Returns and Regulation, *Asia Pacific Finance and Risk Series* 1/2014, p. 11.

these activities varies from one institution to another, but usually risk management committees exist in various forms at financial institutions, which define the scope of work on globally binding norms to limit competition risk. In practice, the norms introduced in this respect oblige the legal services in financial institutions to cooperate with the persons managing global operations to ensure adequate project resources have been provided, and that plans have been established for the implementation of activities within the framework of projects dedicated to this purpose.[58]

The implementation of such norms consists of a series of necessary preparations to ensure consistency of action in all countries where the financial institution operates. This refers to:

a. the provision of compulsory training for all workers, regardless of their current place of work. These are often conducted remotely via e-learning, as well as other activities, including individual training, the interpretation of internal manuals of conduct applicable in the organisation, the adjustment and updating of other internal regulations already in force, for example concerning contacts with competitors, the control and limitation of employee participation in industry organisations, and any ongoing activities consisting in assessing and controlling the associated risks.
b. creating compliance norms to address the specificities of action in higher-risk countries. This particular type of risk usually stems from a threat to the stable and safe conduct of financial institutions business, political, social, economic situation, etc. The development of appropriate norms in this respect, that take into account these specificities, entails the identification and assessment of risks to the financial institution's activities in all countries in order to better understand the types and degrees of risk.
c. the adoption of detailed procedures in case of unannounced inspections by supervisory authorities (ex-raid).

Another type of risk of financial institutions activity, which is the subject of regulations of compliance norms created as a result of emerging

---

[58] The involvement of lawyers in project management in global corporate transactions and the involvement of lawyers and compliance services in resolving issues related to the financing of projects by banks. See J. Dewar, *International Project Finance. Law and Practice*, Oxford 2011, p. 21 et seq.

legal regulations in this respect, is the improper sale of offered products and services (misselling).[59] In particular, those elements of the directive which consist of insufficient information to customers about the risks associated with the use of those products, about additional obligations imposed on customers or about the total price of those products, including any additional costs associated with those products.[60] It is often pointed out that this risk is related to allegations of the mismatch of products, sales processes and documentation used, with the needs and capabilities of customers who become their buyers.[61] Another reason is also the failure to provide sufficient and complete information on all the parameters of these products, as well as the inadequacy of the accompanying sales advice, which result in complaints to regulators and suits against financial institutions before the courts.[62]

---

[59] Misselling is also defined as offering financial products in a manner that is misleading or offering products that are not suited to the financial capabilities (affordability), needs (suitability) or risk profile (appropriateness) of customers.

[60] In the UK market, the amount of penalties and compensations paid by banks offering insurance products to customers, whose nominal purpose was to secure repayment of credits taken out by customers in the event of circumstances preventing such repayment (Payment Protection Insurance—PPI), has been spectacular. In practice, however, these products were so linked to the loans themselves that it was not possible to obtain loans without purchasing insurance products at the same time, the customers were not informed about their nature and price, and regardless of this, their design was so misaligned with the actual needs of customers that, due to their mass nature, in many tens of thousands of cases the subject of insurance were events that could not take place in practice. This is the case, for example, with the sale of products that insure against loss of job credit to people of retirement age. The total amount of disbursements of British banks on this account exceeded GBP 16.6 billion.

[61] The obligation to provide full information is now increasingly reflected in national law and in a wider range of banking products. Cf. on the information obligations imposed on banks for the sale of consumer credit.: Z. Ofiarski, *Ustawa o kredycie konsumenckim. Komentarz*, Warsaw 2014, p. 138 et seq.

[62] Regulatory supervisors alone are increasingly using the instruments at their disposal, such as, for example, the obligation for banks to implement resolution plans. Regardless of this, the regulators themselves, depending on the jurisdiction, impose penalties or seek redress before the courts. For example, the Financial Conduct Authority has introduced an obligation to control interest rate swaps sold to clients defined as non-professionals according to FCA criteria, as opposed to professional clients. Failure to meet the requirements within a set time limit will result in high penalties. The amount of penalties paid so far in the UK for this alone exceeded GBP 365 million. See J. Salmon, Shocking Tactics at the Heart of Lloyds Scandal: Whistleblower Opens Up Over Interest Rate Swaps, *This Is Money* 15 September 2014, www.thisismoney.co.uk (download 2 February 2019).

In order to mitigate such risks, intra-financial institution compliance norms provide for appropriate hedging measures to be taken by financial institutions. These include the obligation to ensure that legal opinions on the products offered are presented together with other information materials at each stage of the relation between the financial institution and the professional customer. A usual recommendation is that lawyers and compliance function representatives should also be represented in all key committees responsible for financial institution management. These norms also provide that the sales processes for financial institutions products should be reviewed on a regular basis.

A separate group of external legal environment risk factors influencing the shape of internal compliance norms in financial institutions are administrative and litigious proceedings between financial institutions and other external entities, including first of all competent supervisory authorities, referred to as dispute risk.[63] The term is so broad that it covers not only court disputes, but also all administrative and extra-judicial proceedings at all stages:

a. from the initial investigations of financial institutions (investigations);
b. by means of litigations pending before the dispute settlement authorities;
c. up to enforcement proceedings.[64]

The compliance norms, i.e. those which by definition are to create internal normative conditions that ensure the functioning of the corporation in a manner adapted to the external normative environment, must therefore take into account all such situations. The obvious complication of this task stems from the fact that global corporations operate in a multi-jurisdictional environment, with different legal systems, redress procedures, legal cultures and even, which cannot be underestimated in practice, widely differing political circumstances, where the independence and incapacity of administrative or judicial power is often graded according to the existing political guarantees.[65]

---

[63] See J. Gregory, *Counterparty Credit Risk and Credit Value Adjustment: A Continuing Challenge*, Chichester 2012, p. 220 et seq.

[64] N. Gennaioli, A. Martin, S. Rossi, Sovereign Default, Domestic Banks, and Financial Institutions, *The Journal of Finance* 69(2)/2014, p. 840.

[65] See E. Blankendurg, Civil Litigation Rates as Indicators for Legal Cultures [in] D. Nelken [ed.], *Comparing Legal Cultures*, Brookfield 1997, p. 41.

One interesting example of such a controversial situation in which many corporations, especially financial institutions, have recently found themselves in, is a situation in which they have had to make a strong impact on the internal compliance procedures introduced in response to the deferred prosecutorial agreement (DPA), concluded between financial institutions and the US supervisory authorities acting with the support of the US Department of Justice.

Depending on each of the case, the terms of an agreement signed by financial institutions within the DPA may be violated if the financial institution:

First, it will not comply with the obligations stemming from the remedial action imposed on it, the purpose of which is to remedy any irregularities which are the subject of a prosecution as if the financial institution had refused to cooperate with those authorities and to inform them of any irregularities observed which create the likelihood of similar situations occurring in the future.

Second, once the conditional agreement is signed and the financial institution will violate US federal or state criminal law, which it has committed itself to comply with under an agreement with that prosecutor.

Third, it will make a public statement contrary to the evidenced facts set out in the materials on which the agreement is based.

Fourth, in the cases known so far, the procedure ensuring the implementation of such an agreement assumes the appointment of a person to act as a controller (monitor) to monitor the financial institution's compliance with the provisions of the agreements concluded.[66] The task of such an official is to monitor the financial institution's compliance with the concluded agreement on an ongoing basis, in particular with regard to the implementation of compliance processes ensuring the avoidance in the future of irregularities which are the cause of the investigation underlying the concluded agreement. Periodic reports prepared by the monitor in this respect shall be submitted to the supervisory authorities. What is interesting, the person performing this function is equipped with appropriate tools ensuring the service of tasks addressed to an entity employing tens, and sometimes hundreds of thousands of employees. These are usually very numerous teams, and their structure, as well as the way and pace of work are the subject of an exclusive decision of the monitor.

---

[66] See E. Blankendurg, Civil Litigation Rates as Indicators for Legal Cultures [in] D. Nelken [ed.], *Comparing Legal Cultures*, Brookfield 1997, p. 41.

In order to adapt the functioning of the financial institution to the specific regulatory situation it finds itself in as a result of an agreement to suspend prosecution proceedings, compatible normative acts are adopted which, with a view to reducing the risk of non-compliance, prescribe between the control activities undertaken in order to reduce the risk of non-compliance:

Firstly, the competent services responsible for contacts with the monitor in cooperation with the legal and compliance services worked on formulating general principles of supervision over the implementation of the most important legal and compliance obligations in accordance with the agreement concluded. This is usually linked to corporate-wide coordination and communication activities to ensure that employees are aware of these commitments. The communication addressed to the financial institution's employees itself concerns the financial institution's current obligations, including the requirements of US criminal law.

Secondly, the legal departments and services responsible for contacts with the monitor were required to make adjustments in order to improve cooperation with the monitoring team. They should also be obliged to prepare opinions on particular versions of periodic reports prepared by the monitor, especially if these reports contain critical recommendations.

Events that have had a significant impact on the current form of compliance rules are proceedings against a group of major financial institutions, following investigations by the UK Financial Conduct Authority (FCA) in conjunction with regulators in other jurisdictions into speculation on the foreign exchange markets.

The procedure followed by the UK regulators may seem pretty similar. In the initial phase, the FCA informs selected financial institutions of its preliminary evidence that shows in detail they have committed serious foreign exchange market failures which, in the Authority's view, could potentially be classified as financial crimes.[67] At the same time, the European (often together with Swiss) competition authorities investigate any potential anti-competitive behaviour, including in particular

---

[67] Class actions against several banks are brought before US courts on behalf of persons who have been party to foreign exchange transactions at the rate published by WM/Reuters. The allegations against banks relate to price collusion in order to manipulate the exchange rate published by WM/Reuters and thus violate U.S. antitrust law.

suspicions of tacit collusion agreements on foreign exchange markets in connection with the same activities of these financial institutions.[68]

In order to respond in a short time to the investigation conducted by the FCA and other regulators in many financial institutions, the process of comprehensive internal controls concerning the manner of concluding currency transactions, regulated in internal compliance regulations, was initiated. Due to the scale of the project and the need to conduct an impartial review, reputable external law firms are involved in this process. With the support of these law firms, a monitoring plan is prepared and then presented to the supervisory authorities and before entering the implementation phase. The plan provides for the review of documentation, listening to recordings from direct communication devices (mainly recordings from telephone conversations, as currency transactions are most often made by this means), the analysis of other relevant data and evidence that may have an impact on further findings, as well as the hearing of witnesses.

A widely publicised matter which resulted in financial institutions introducing measures that comprehensively overhauled compliance regulations was the Madoff case. Some financial institutions and their subsidiaries outside the United States provided custody and administrative services to several funds not registered in the United States whose assets were invested in Madoff Securities.[69] The Fund, its investors and the trustee of Madoff Securities have brought legal action against a number of companies, including these financial institutions entities in the USA, Ireland, Luxembourg and other countries. Some lawsuits, including class actions brought before US courts, accuse financial institutions that they knew or should have known of fraud committed by Madoff Securities

---

[68] At a number of times, both the European Commission and some national competition authorities of EU Member States have assessed the market behavior of some banks as being in breach of European competition rules. Similar information was provided, for example, by the Swiss Competition Commission, which reported on an ongoing investigation into potential anti-competitive behavior in currency markets without identifying the institutions that were under surveillance of the authority. In practice, questions to banks from competition authorities about currency speculation have been arriving relatively slowly.

[69] The case concerns mainly entities incorporated in the United States, the United Kingdom, Luxembourg, the British Virgin Islands, the Cayman Islands, Bermuda, the Channel Islands, Italy, Switzerland and Austria and other related entities. See B. J. Richardson, *Fiduciary Law and Responsible Investing: In Nature's Trust*, New York 2013, p. 279 et seq.

and yet participated in the sale of its securities, thereby violating an obligation to act in the interests of investors.[70]

In this multi-threaded proceeding, there are various factors that may affect the final determination and financial consequences for the financial institutions involved in the proceedings relating to Madoff Securities. Among these circumstances are the facts related to the deliberate misrepresentation of the financial institutions themselves, the multiplicity of jurisdictions in which proceedings are being conducted and the number of plaintiffs and defendants in these cases. Therefore, although it is not possible at this stage to make a reliable estimate of the total amount of liabilities arising from all the pending cases, it can only be presumed to be significant. However, financial institutions are of the opinion that they have arguments that will help them to defend themselves against claims. The arguments put forward by the financial institutions centre on the fact that financial institutions have introduced a number of compatible internal norms aimed at preventing similar situations in the future by imposing obligations on employees to carry out an even more in-depth examination of the funds whose units are offered to customers, better analysis of the risks involved and to provide full information to customers in this respect will be of importance.

Another group of spectacular proceedings against the global financial institutions concerns allegations relating to the setting of the LIBOR, EURIBOR and other reference interest rates between financial institutions on the inter-banking institution market.[71]

---

[70] For example, in two of the larger number of cases against banks, HSBC Institutional Trust Services (Ireland) Limited (HTIE) concluded a settlement agreement in November and December 2012 in relation to claims brought by investors of Thema International Fund Plc against HTIE, which were brought before the Supreme Court in Ireland. In April 2013, HTIE successfully dismissed an action for EUR 25 million (USD 38 million) brought before a Milan court by a shareholder of Thema against HTIE and other entities. However, since then, several other settlements have been made for several hundred million dollars, including tens of millions of dollars of litigation costs. See http://webcache.googleusercontent.com/search?q=cache:B5MPMoboLOcJ:www.hsbc.com/~/media/hsbc-com/newsroomassets/2011/pdf/110607-exhibit-a-stipulation-and-agreement-of-partial_settlement%3Fla%3Den-gb+&cd=2&hl=pl&ct=clnk&gl=pl&client=safari (download 15 December 2018).

[71] In principle, these are investigations carried out by the regulatory authorities of the United States, the United Kingdom, Canada, the European Union and some Asian countries. In these countries, including the United Kingdom, the United States, other EU countries, Switzerland, Hong Kong, Thailand, South Korea, investigations and inspections

In view of the fact that some financial institutions are participants in the fixing, they are called upon by the competent regulatory authorities to provide information on the pricing methodology for selected types of transactions and to cooperate with these authorities in their investigations. As a result of inspections already carried out in relation to alleged manipulation in some countries, reports on these inspections are systematically transmitted to these authorities. However, financial institutions are preparing for both individual and collective actions, especially in cases of manipulation of LIBOR rates for the US dollar.[72] Already, some of the participants of the fixing have been sued in the US courts in actions for manipulation of LIBOR rates for the US dollar brought by natural persons. In these cases, both individual and collective actions have been filed, most of which have been transferred to the Federal Court for the

---

are conducted by both regulatory and competition authorities, as well as by enforcement authorities in order to secure execution of potential fines, both in connection with the alleged manipulation of LIBOR and EURIBOR rates, but also in connection with other interest rates, including the exchange rate by the participants of the fixing. Fixing is understood as the exchange trading system based on the single price of the day as a result of which prices of financial instruments are determined. In this case, it concerned the establishment of uniform daily exchange rates at the interest rates binding on interbank rounds, i.e. prices at which banks are willing to borrow currencies from each other. The effects of such pricing apply to all market participants, including those not connected with the interbank market, since the level of all interest rates, and thus even the interest rate on individual loans, depends directly on the cost of raising money for the bank. Irregularities in this respect took different forms and consisted in allowing price collusion, as a result of which the victims were numerous groups of people. See P. Ashton, B. Christophers, On Arbitration, Arbitrage and Arbitrariness in Financial Markets and Their Governance: Unpacking LIBOR and the LIBOR Scandal, *Economy and Society* 44(2)/2015, p. 188 et seq.

[72] Regardless of the pending litigation cases before the courts, financial penalties were imposed on banks charged with manipulating LIBOR rates. So far, the total amount of penalties imposed on this account by American and British regulators has exceeded USD 3 billion, of which the FCA itself has punished banks with USD 532 million. Among these amounts are the USD 290 million fine for Barclays Bank and the USD 218 million fine for Lloyds Bank. For related similar manipulations on Forex platforms on which currency trading takes place, the British regulator imposed a penalty of USD 233 million on UBS, USD 225 million on Citibank, USD 222 million on JP Morgan, USD 217 million on RBS and USD 216 million on HSBC. The American regulator, on the other hand, on Citibank and JP Morgan for USD 310 million each, on RBS and UBS for USD 290 million each and on HSBC for USD 275 million. See e.g. http://www.cnbc.com/2014/03/11/forex-manipulation-how-it-worked.html (download 4 October 2019); E. Talley, S. Strimling, The World's Most Important Number: How a Web of Skewed Incentives, Broken Hierarchies and Compliance Cultures Conspired to Undermine LIBOR, *Financial Services Institute of Australasia Journal JASSA* 2/2013, p. 50.

South District of New York and merged for the purpose of the pre-trial proceedings. The lawsuits contain allegations against financial institutions and other fixing participants under US law, including antitrust law, racketeering law, the Future Market Act and other state laws.[73]

In March 2013, the US Federal Court, before which a joint LIBOR manipulation proceeding against the US dollar was pending, issued an order in six of the oldest cases dismissing in its entirety the action for breach of federal and state antitrust law, racketeering and the related allegation of unjust enrichment. The Court identified and forwarded for further proceedings some of the claims for breach of the Act on the futures market, which it considered justified under the applicable provisions of law. Some of the plaintiffs appealed against the order to the Federal Court of Appeal for the Second State of New York County. The Court of Appeal dismissed the appeals as unfounded and rejected the petition filed by the plaintiffs to reconsider the case.

The remaining part of entities acting as the plaintiff party filed with the Regional Court supplemented lawsuits containing additional allegations, in response to which the defendants filed a motion to dismiss the claim in its entirety. The District Court set a deadline for the oral presentation of the grounds for the motion to dismiss the claims and suspended the proceedings in the other cases conducted under the combined proceedings. As in the Madoff case, in this case too, in parallel with the defence before the courts, financial institutions have acted by introducing appropriate compliance rules to prevent similar irregularities in the future.

A similar case, with even more complex implications in terms of the cross-border coverage of regulators' rules and the serious complications they create for financial institutions, was related to the collective actions brought in US courts for the manipulation of the TIBOR for the Euro to

---

[73] The case of liability for manipulation of LIBOR has recently taken on a new dimension, as it increasingly affects individuals, not only institutions, and in addition to disciplinary liability, penalties are also imposed. In August 2015 Tom Hayes was the first person to be sentenced during a trial in the United Kingdom on LIBOR manipulation penalties. He was proved guilty of eight charges and sentenced to 14 years' imprisonment. In November 2015, the first judgment in the United States was passed on the manipulation of the LIBOR exchange rate, in which the Manhattan Court found two London traders, Anthony Allen and Anthony Conti, guilty. See D. Hou, D. Skeie, LIBOR: Origins, Economics, Crisis, Scandal, and Reform, *Federal Reserve Bank of New York Staff Reports*, Staff Report Nr 667/03/2014 p. 120 et seq.

Yen exchange rates (European fixing). Several UK and US financial institutions participating in the fixing were sued in collective actions brought in the United States on behalf of individuals and entities that invested in futures and options on the euro-yen exchange rate. Although some financial institutions are not members of the Japanese Banking Association, which sets the TIBOR for European and the LIBOR for the Japanese yen, they were accused of manipulating these rates and thus violating US antitrust law, the Future Market Act and New York State law.[74]

This example shows how far-reaching the consequences, also in this literal geographical sense, are the questionable actions taken by financial institution employees, even at a relatively lower level. This has resulted in further tightening procedures in many financial institutions, in particular equipping employees with knowledge of how to skilfully shape relations with competitive financial institutions, and in particular with respect to pricing issues that may affect a wider range of global financial market players.

Similar consequences were caused by class actions filed in the US courts for damages based on suspicion of manipulation of the EURIBOR by some financial institutions against the EURIBOR established in the inter-banking market. Some financial institutions, together with other fixing participants, were sued in class actions brought in the United States on behalf of persons who carried out transactions on futures contracts and other financial instruments at the fixed EURIBOR. Also, in these lawsuits, the financial institutions are accused of manipulating the EURIBOR and thus violating the US antitrust law. Admittedly, on the basis of the information currently available, it would be difficult to predict the results of the proceedings initiated and their long-term effects on financial institutions, and even their duration. However, on the basis of the conclusions drawn from these proceedings, financial institutions introduce compliance rules governing the relation between financial institutions in matters related to the setting of currency prices, taking

---

[74] Moreover, price manipulation, which consists in unfair practices that can affect the prices quoted on financial exchanges, does not concern only currencies. They also apply to so-called commodities, i.e. other goods valued and traded on these markets. For example, Barclays Bank was fined USD 330 million for proven manipulation of electricity prices and USD 26 million for manipulation of gold prices. See R. McCormick, The 'Conduct Crisis': Will Banks Ever Get It Right?, *Business Law International* 16(2)/2015, p. 110 et seq.; G. Giroux, *Accounting Fraud: Maneuvering and Manipulation Past and Present*, New York 2014, p. 60 et seq.

into account the positions expressed by the European Commission during the preparation of this process.

A similar issue which gave rise to further work at financial institutions to supplement existing compliance rules was the so-called "Skilled Person's report" developed by the UK Financial Crime Authority (FCA). Under Section 166 of the Financial Services and Markets Act (FSMA), the FSMA required financial institutions to appoint skilled persons to assess and report on their previous reviews of three reference interest rates. The preliminary reports presented by the auditors show that the financial institutions' review of the LIBOR GBP, JPY and USD pricing process was so reliable and detailed as to identify in advance potential harmful behaviour of employees. The report does not indicate that the independent auditors appointed for this purpose have identified serious deficiencies in financial institution reviews. In particular, in order to ensure that any irregularities detected are sufficiently significant to make it impossible to identify certain irregularities. Nevertheless, as a result of the audit, several recommendations were issued in order to increase the overall level of credibility of the processes carried out in the financial institutions.

The cycle of interest rate fixing proceedings also covered the investigation carried out by the European Commission concerning the setting of the EURIBOR on the European inter-banking market. As a result, on the 4th of December 2013 the European Commission announced a decision to impose financial penalties on eight financial institutions for participating in illegal price agreements on derivatives denominated in the Euro and the Japanese Yen. Despite the fact that only a few entities were among the institutions concerned and penalised as a result of this investigation, the European Commission also informed the other institutions active on this market and requested that they adjust procedures in connection with this investigation. This applies in particular to euro-denominated derivatives. The European Commission has informed these financial institutions that it is considering opening a further investigation against them, which will be carried out in accordance with the procedure foreseen for price cartel proceedings. At present, there is a high degree of uncertainty as to the direction in which these proceedings will be conducted, their duration and expected results, including the potential level of penalties imposed. At this point it is worth mentioning that the specificity of these proceedings consists, include, the fact that, as work progresses and new facts, data and circumstances are disclosed, these penalties may be systematically increased.[75] The risks that financial institutions have to take into account in such a situation are significant and, in each case, one of the defence strategies is to carry out adjustments taking into account the findings and guidance disclosed by the European Commission in the course of the proceedings. As part of this alignment exercise, an intra-financial institution compliance framework is being prepared, further specifying the permitted behaviour of financial institution staff responsible for cooperation with other financial institutions in matters relating to the determination of fixings.

A case belonging to the group of consumer financial institution customer relations cases is the UK proceedings concerning irregularities in the sale of certain types of derivatives offered to the public. These investigations resulted in reports from the Financial Conduct Authority (FCA, the successor of the former Financial Services Authority) on the sale of interest rate protection products (IRP). At this point, it is worth pointing out that these reports relate both to the sale of these products to individual customers and to small and medium-sized enterprises, which are increasingly being put on an equal footing with consumers due to a similar lack of sufficient expertise in relation to financial products. As a result, financial institutions were required to take the following two adjustments.

[75] The total amount of penalties imposed on Citibank by the FCA (Financial Conduct Authority) and CFTC (The U.S. Commodity Futures Trading Commission) on 12 November 2014 by the decision of the British, American and Swiss regulators for applying illegal currency fixing practices amounted to $668 million, while the amount for JP Morgan was $662 million, while for RBS and HSBC it was $634 million and $618 million, respectively. UBS Bank was also fined by FINMA (Swiss Financial Market Supervisory Authority) and the total amount of penalties for this bank is exactly $800 million. Earlier, other banks also received financial penalties from CFTC for manipulating the reference exchange rates: on 28 July 2014 Lloyds Bank—in the amount of $105 million, on 29 October 2013 Rabobank—in the amount of $475 million, on 6 July 2013 RBS—in the amount of $325 million, on 19 December 2012 UBS—in the amount of $700 million, on 27 June 2012—in the amount of $200 million. As Aitan Goelman stated, 'The setting of reference rates was not just one more opportunity to increase profits for banks. Countless individuals and companies around the world, acting with confidence in these rates, have determined the financial value of contracts, believing in the integrity of those who have set them.' G. Tchetvertakov, *In a Co-Ordinated Blitz, Regulators Bombard Top Banks for Systemic Collusion in the Forex Market*, www.forexmagnates.com/ (download 22 February 2019).

a. Offering appropriate compensation to 'non-professional' customers (non-qualified customers) to whom these relatively complex structured instruments were sold, which were allegedly incorrectly sold precisely because of the complexity of their structure.[76]
b. Review sales transactions of other IRP-like products to non-professional customers. The obligation imposed on financial institutions included the task of carrying out a review covering the last 12 years.

In line with UK financial supervision requirements, financial institutions have appointed independent auditors to review and report on the adjustment measures they have agreed to take. For each of the larger financial institutions, it is estimated that the number of retail financial institutions transactions classified under MiFID is measured in thousands and has been carried out by thousands of entities, while the value of sales of IRP products at the base rate was tens of billions of dollars, as well as the estimated value of loans granted on the basis of base rates set in relation to the value of these products.[77] In view of this scale, financial institutions are forced to propose adapted methodologies and procedures for reviewing the sales processes for these products and, where necessary, to offer compensation to customers already at this stage of payment, as agreed with the financial supervisory authority. Already on the basis of the pilot case reviews carried out, after testing the methodology and procedures, the first summary reports of the reviews carried out were issued, together with conclusions on the operation of the pilot audits carried out by UK financial institutions.[78]

---

[76] See more broadly on unfair practices in financial market financial markets with clients who are not professional trading participants. E. Rutkowska-Tomaszewska, *Nadzór nad rynkiem finansowym a nieuczciwe praktyki rynkowe banków wobec konsumentów – zakres, potrzeba i możliwości podejmowanych działań*, http://www.bibliotekacyfrowa.pl/Content/38956/010.pdf (download 18 August 2018).

[77] More on current trends in corporate law with regard to investor interests. See G. Ferrani, E. Wymeersch, *Investor Protection in Europe: Corporate Law Making, The MiFID and Beyond*, Oxford Scholarship Online 2009, http://econpapers.repec.org/bookchap/oxpobooks/9780199202911.htm (download 11 April 2019); Developing Our Approach to Implementing Mifid II Conduct of Business and Organizational Requirements, *Financial Conduct Authority Discussion Paper* Nr 3 (DP15/3), March 2015 passim.

[78] A comprehensive UK market study conducted by the FCA in 2012 concluded that a total of 25% of investment advice provided to clients was debatable, of which 15% were not sufficiently covered by advisers. See D. O'Loughlin, A. Wassall, HSBC Estimates GBP 96m Bill for Investment Advice Mis-Selling, *FT Adviser*, 24 February 2014.

This was followed by the approval of the revised methodology with adapted procedures and the initiation of major reviews. On the basis of the results of the pilot versions of the reviews and the guidance issued by the FCA, it was already possible to make a preliminary estimate of the amount of the liabilities of individual financial institutions after some of the major reviews had been carried out.[79]

The amount of compensation paid to financial institution customers depends on the individual circumstances of each case, especially when taking into account issues such as this:

a. whether the client was classified as non-professional according to the criteria indicated;
b. whether, in the particular case, it is established that the financial institution has not complied with the relevant sales norms, the nature of the compensation offered if, as a result of the irregularity in the sale, the customer has suffered losses (for example, some customers receive all the compensation in cash, while some customers receive all the compensation in part and an alternative product will be offered);
c. what was the amount of losses incurred by the customer directly resulting from inappropriate sales norms.

Although financial institutions have largely completed all the tests to determine whether a customer falls into the non-professional category, a large proportion of all the customers in this category are still in one of the stages of the reviews referred to above. This usually means that sales are assessed for compliance with the compliance norms already in place at the financial institutions and arrangements are made for the proposed amount of compensation. Due to the large scale of the proposed offer, some customers' cases were not examined at all, despite the fact that the financial institutions systematically tried to reach them and sent them compensation offers. Regardless of this, customers continue to report a number of complaints that have gone directly to financial institutions or to the Financial Ombudsperson. Several actions have also been brought in relation to this case, although most proceedings at an early stage have been suspended pending the results of financial institution

---

[79]The amount of these obligations, including customer indemnification and financial penalties imposed on banks, exceeds GBP 7 billion.

reviews, which may provide relevant evidence. As in other cases, financial institutions are cooperating with external law firms, which in this case act as independent auditors, who monitor financial institutions' responses to claims for losses incurred.[80] As a result, also in the case of these anomalies, further tightening of compliance norms in financial institutions.

The area in which numerous and serious deficiencies in the activities of financial institutions have emerged, which have resulted in a number of adjustments, including the adoption of appropriate compliance norms, has turned out to be the offering of certain mortgage products to retail customers.[81] In particular, the issue and sale of mortgage-backed securities by Fannie Mae and Freddie Mac. The case, due to both its scope and the size of assets offered on the markets, aroused both understandable interest from the media and regulatory authorities. In September 2011, the US Federal Housing Finance Agency (FHFA) filed a lawsuit against 17 selected financial institutions and a group of financial institution employees responsible for the underwriting and issuing of certain types of Mortgage Based Securities (MBS) to Fannie Mae and Freddie Mac from 2005 to 2007. The FHFA alleged that these financial institutions provided false and misleading information, and deliberately omitted

---

[80] So in art. 166 of *Financial Services and Markets Act 2000—FSMA*, http://www.legislation.gov.uk/ukpga/2000/8/section/166 (download 3 January 2018).

[81] The amicable settlement of this case with customers affected by irregularities in the sale of these products in 2005–2007 cost different banks depending on the degree of their involvement, the scale of their operations and the amount of losses incurred by customers in huge amounts. For Deutsche Bank, for example, this was a $1.9 billion fine paid to the US Federal Housing Finance Agency in December 2013. Earlier, in November 2013, Bank JP Morgan Chase paid the American regulators a record amount of USD 13 billion, while on the same days it agreed to pay out USD 4.5 billion at the same time on the basis of an agreement concluded with pension funds and other institutional investors in connection with the sale of these products. In the same way, the sums paid out amounted to USD 16 billion, which were paid by the Bank of America as a result of a settlement following a class action brought against it. USD 7 billion was paid in a similar case by Citigroup, USD 1.25 billion by Morgan Stanley and USD 885 million by Bank UBS, and the total amount of penalties imposed on other banks in connection with the practice of selling these products amounted to over USD 8.5 billion. See R. H. Brescia, Tainted Loans: The Value of a Mass Torts Approach in Subprime Mortgage Litigation, *University of Cincinnati Law Review* 78/2009, p. 6 et seq.; J. Ackermann, The Subprime Crisis and Its Consequences. Regulation and the Financial Crisis of 2007–08: Review and Analysis, *Journal of Financial Stability* 4(4)/2008, p. 230 et seq.; G. Gorton, The Subprime Panic, *European Financial Management* 15(1)/2009, p. 20.

material facts which could have an impact on both the valuation and the decisions on whether or not to buy these securities in the sales notes. In addition, the allegations also concerned the lack of due diligence when preparing these products for sale and the misrepresentation of the quality of the underlying mortgage products.[82]

In its action, the FHFA sought the cancellation of the transaction and compensation. Claims made against individual institutions differed depending on the scale and nature of irregularities detected in individual financial institutions.[83] While some financial institutions were found to be fraudulent during the process, other financial institutions were not charged with such far-reaching allegations. The original amount in the lawsuit corresponding to the value of the subject matter of the dispute is measured in billions of dollars, whereas the nominal amount currently demanded is approximately 1/3 of the total amount. This is due to the fact that more than 2/3 of the disputed value has been repaid so far. Interestingly, no losses have so far been recorded in respect of these bonds. The presiding judge instructed the defendants in the first lawsuit, who commenced further proceedings before the Federal Court for the South District of New York to respond to the lawsuit. Individual financial institutions, adopting different defence strategies, applied for the dismissal of the action, but all of them were rejected. Nor has it resulted in the use in these cases of a theoretically available legal instrument consisting of an appeal against a court's decision. In all such situations, the actions were dismissed. At the same time, the court of first instance set deadlines for financial institutions to provide evidence in this case.

A detailed analysis of the available evidence is currently underway in all the financial institutions involved in this proceeding. At the same time, settlement negotiations are being conducted both with the

---

[82] The total amount of financial penalties imposed on banks and other financial institutions, including brokers offering mortgage-backed investment products on properties, the "subprime mortgage" segment, by September 2014 by the SEC amounted to USD 35.9 billion, www.sec.gov/spotlight/ent-actions-fc.shtml (download 4 January 2019).

[83] For example, Bank Morgan Stanley—one of the world's largest investment banks—has been fined USD 3.2 billion for misleading customers and investors when selling subprime mortgage bonds without simultaneously providing a full assessment of the risks associated with these instruments that should have been held by the bank. Bank Morgan Stanley did not grant risky loans itself, but only bought them from other financial institutions and distributed mortgage-based bonds. See *Money.pl/wiadomości_bankowe/swiatowy_kryzys* z 12 February 2016 r. (dowload 23 March 2019).

regulatory authority and with customers.[84] During the settlement procedure with the participation of appointed experts, the evidence is to be analysed in terms of facts, circumstances and consequences of actions taken by financial institutions. Once the analysis of the evidence submitted by the parties has been completed, a further part of the investigation will be initiated on the basis of the collected evidence, but without the parties' participation. It shall include statements by credit rating agencies and persons involved in the conclusion of credit agreements. The procedure provides that, as a result of this examination, the FHFA will communicate to the financial institutions the results of the risk assessment undertaken by the financial institutions together with a position on the quality of their risk management. If the procedure to reach an agreement on a possible settlement fails, a date for the hearing is set, and thus to initiate the normal procedure. Financial institutions have already taken a number of far-reaching self-regulatory measures for all similar products and their distribution channels at an early stage, some of which have put in place procedures to ban the sale of such products in the future.

Another example of issues is the Statement of Objections received by a group of financial institutions in July 2013 from the European Commission in connection with an investigation into alleged anti-competitive activities by several participants in the credit derivatives market between 2006 and 2009. The Statement of Objections contains the preliminary views of the European Commission and, while not prejudging the final outcome of the investigation, it may have serious consequences in terms of financial penalties imposed on these financial institutions. In anticipation of the possible consequences, individual financial institutions responded to the European Commission's concerns.

The case became much more complicated by the fact that, following proceedings initiated by the European Commission, these financial

---

[84] In the case of some banks, settlement negotiations did not yield the result expected by the banks. Examples include the Bank of America Bank with a fine of USD 17 billion and JP Morgan Chase with a fine of USD 13 billion, both banks selling mortgage loan bonds "using their customers' naivety'". The risk backed securities had a higher yield than deposits, which made them more attractive to customers. J. Rakoff, a federal judge adjudicating the case, stated that the penalty was imposed at such a high level primarily because of "false and reckless credit activity, which created conditions conducive to the development of the financial crisis in 2008". See *financemagnates.com* 25 August 2014 r. (download 5 February 2019).

institutions were sued in class actions brought before the federal courts of New York and Chicago. The lawsuits accuse the defendant financial institutions, but also other market participants, including the ISDA and other financial institutions, of violating federal antitrust law by means of a collusive supply-side curtailment that hindered access to information on the criteria determining transaction prices and credit risk. As a result, according to the claimants, new participants were blocked from entering this market, which, according to the allegations made, was aimed at artificially inflating the price on the American market. The plaintiffs in this case are persons who have acquired or sold securities in the United States to the defendants.

A similar case, which significantly affected the financial market and influenced the issuance of many new compliance regulations within the institutions concerned, was the FSA investigation concluded with a skilled person's report into Prudential Plc and AIG Group Limited. The report presented the role of these institutions in the unjustified, in the opinion of the supervisory authorities, interruption of the issue of pre-emptive rights of Prudential enabling the simultaneous acquisition of AIG Group Limited. The FSA expressed concern about the procedures and controls applied by the entities participating in the process and, as an accusation of particular importance, expressed doubts as to the reliability of their cooperation with the FSA.[85]

In a first phase, the financial institutions under investigation were required to provide the independent auditor with all identified documents deemed essential for the audit, this was followed by a series of explanatory interviews with key personnel. As usual in this type of procedure, after these steps, the financial institutions had the opportunity to familiarise themselves with the first versions of the prepared reports and respond to the initial version of the reports, which resulted in the final content of the document being submitted to the FCA. As a result of the investigation, the FCA expressed the view that financial institutions' actions in the case under investigation diverged significantly from the norms required of financiers, and that there was a cultural difference in expectations regarding financial institutions' open and proactive

---

[85] The report results from the FSA's notification to HSBC, JP Morgan Cazenove, Credit Suisse Securities (Europe) Limited and Prudential Plc of the obligation to prepare a "Skilled Persons Report" pursuant to Article 166 of the Financial Services and Markets Act (FSMA).

cooperation with the UK Listing Authority (UKLA).[86] As a result, a number of meetings were held between the UKLA and the audited financial institutions to discuss the implemented recommendations and conclusions, and in particular to present the internal regulations introduced by the financial institutions on how to prevent situations, irregularities in the handling of securities issues, occurring again, and thus undermining the expectations of stock exchange investors from the way such operations are carried out.[87]

Another area of the financial institution's activity, in which the detection of irregularities has resulted in the production of detailed compliance rules, is the offering securities lending. For years it has been one of the most popular services offered to institutional clients. Not infrequently, as these services are not normally part of the typical range of activities of financial institutions, this is done by specialised intermediaries operating under agency-like agreements, which lay down strict guidelines on the range of proposed bids set by the financial institutions, which are then agreed with the customers. Due to the value of volumes, the frequency of such transactions and the multitude of parties involved in offering them, in practice it is important to determine precisely the amounts of settlements resulting from mutual obligations. On the other hand, the algorithm of distribution of securities transaction fees between financial institutions and their agents is usually one of the modules of IT systems used in the area of securities lending in financial institutions.[88] As a result of such calculations carried out within these systems, the results achieved by individual intermediaries are classified. This, in turn,

---

[86] In March 2013, Prudential Assurance Company Limited was fined £16 million (USD 24 million). Prudential Plc received a fine of GBP 14 million (USD 21 million). The banks, on the other hand, received letters from UKLA, in which the FCA's concerns resulting from the auditor's report were presented.

[87] This was a very well-known, but not the only, case of violation of bank investors' confidence as a result of irregularities in the securities issue process. Another well-known case is that of Hypo Group Alpe—Adria Bank (now HETA Asset Resolution AG) against Bayern LB, which acquired a majority stake in the Hypo Group. See R. Cotarcea, *Banking Debacle Worth Billions, CEE Legal Matters. In-Depth Analysis of the News and Newsmakers that Shape Europe's Emerging Legal Markets*, vol. 2 April 2015, p. 25.

[88] Cf. T. Mellor, M. Rogers Jr., *An Introduction to Legal Risks and Structuring Cross-Border Lending Transaction, The International Comparative Legal Guide to: Lending & Secured Finance 2014. A Practical Cross-Border Insight into Lending and Secured Finance*, London 2104, p. 15 et seq.

helps securities traders to identify the right investment opportunities for each client. As a result of such arrangements traders change the conditions in about 50–60% of transactions. Most of these changes are due to the misalignment of customers' investment opportunities, their income, or because they do not meet the transaction conditions (this concerns the lender's requirements for collateral for repayment of liabilities, inappropriate form of transaction, etc.).

Currently, in principle, all these actions are covered by recommendations resulting from the compliance norms, which prescribe the conduct with regard to the legitimate interest of the client, understood in this case as a good analysis of real needs and investment opportunities and adjusting them to the profile of this client expressed in his willingness to take risks. However, the data necessary to make an appropriate classification, are received from these systems by the risk takers. There are cases where systemic errors, such as the exclusion of the night-time data calculation system, may mean that some clients have been harmed by not receiving an allocation of their investment opportunities in securities. In other words, the resources allocated to them could have worked and, as a result of technological errors, they did not work.

In order to find out the real scale of the phenomenon, a review covering the period from 2008 to the present has analysed millions of transactions in several of the most important London financial institutions. Fees alone for securities lending alone totalled well over GBP 2 billion. External law firms acting as investigating auditors were again involved in this process. The task entrusted to them is to issue an opinion and to certify the correctness of internal analyses carried out previously within the framework of internal financial institutions as to the legal consequences, and possible damages suffered by clients due to irregularities in the process of qualifying investment opportunities of clients who should have benefited from the securities lending offer.[89]

As a result of the work of lawyers operating both within the structures of the financial institutions themselves, as well as lawyers employed by the UK regulator and investigative auditors themselves, the financial institutions were offered a series of remedial actions concerning the classification of customers at the stage of selling these products and the

---

[89] Cf. L. Sasso, *Capital Structure and Corporate Governance. The Role of Hybrid Financial Instruments*, New York 2013, p. 140.

mechanisms for controlling the functioning of IT systems. These actions were reflected in the compliance norms prepared for this purpose, on the basis of which not only were the employees of relevant services in the financial institution obliged to carry out additional regular diagnostic checks of financial institutions IT systems, but also the change management processes were analysed. In connection with the identified claims of customers who have been unsuccessful so far, these norms also include a methodology established together with the FCA to calculate the compensation scheme for injured customers. Since the identification of the case, a number of consultations have been held with this regulator, which in effect gave its consent to initiate a process of communication with affected customers on the means of settling their claims.

Another event affecting the compliance regulations in financial institutions in recent times is a wave of collective actions concerning irregularities in underwriting of shares conducted by some financial institutions in the United States. A large number of financial institutions, in particular financial institutions and insurers, have been sued in these actions brought over the last five years before several different state courts and the Federal Court in the United States. These lawsuits accuse them of violating US federal securities law by making false statements about, among other things, financial stability, internal security and the business practices of securities issuers.[90] The participation of the majority of the financial institutions concerned in these proceedings results from the underwriting of debt and equity securities of issuers provided by these financial institutions, which were financed on the basis of loans secured by mortgages on real estate made available to them in order to secure their real estate. The specificity of this type of construction lies in the fact that the underwriters, i.e. the financial institutions mentioned here, are exempted from liability for damages for improper performance of obligations resulting from their role in the securities issue process, except for those cases in which lawsuits were brought against insolvent issuers.[91]

---

[90] This relates to numerous such issuers as Ambac, Countrywide, Lehman Brothers, Wells Fargo, Indymac, Citigroup, Wachovia, AIG, ING, BNP Paribas, General Electric, Kosmos Energy, Metlife and Overseas Shipping.

[91] According to the SIFMA Underwriting Agreement signed by the sub-issuers in the US, the underwriter is fully indemnified against any liability in respect of the securities it underwrites unless the issuer goes bankrupt.

Therefore, if financial bankruptcy proceedings of securities issuers have been initiated, entities which may have suffered damage as a result of such proceedings, regardless of their participation in financial bankruptcy proceedings, may claim compensation from underwriters' financial institutions in separate proceedings.[92] This was also the situation in these cases, where collective actions have been brought against these financial institutions. As a result of these suits, a number of pre-trial conciliation proceedings were initiated, concerning only those issuers who were insolvent and for whom it was highly probable that the financial bankruptcy conditions would be met, and consequently that compensation disputes would be won. The amounts of compensation claimed, including in this case, are estimated to be billions of dollars. As a result of these calculations and the likelihood of a possible loss of disputes, in view of the large amounts requested by the claimants, some of the companies withdrew from the reconciliation proceedings originally opened in connection with the class actions.

Here, too, the mechanism for the subsequent alignment of the internal financial institutions' norms originally in force when these institutions entered into transactions as underwriters of securities was also in place. Soon afterwards, these rules were also generally extended to the way financial institutions behaved in the situation of valuing the credibility of counterparties, and, which is particularly important, to the creation of internal structures and control mechanisms in this area.

In many financial markets, the collapse of Lehman Brothers, which was considered to be a model of stable management, has had a broad resonance. The reaction to this event was multidimensional and changed the behaviour of many other financial institutions. This impact resulted from the wide area of operations of the failed financial institution and the cooperation between the financial institution and other large financial corporations existing in many markets.[93]

---

[92] In practice, in the case of actually pending bankruptcy proceedings, this instrument is so strong that in some of the claims against Ambac, IndyMac, GE, MBIA, Countrywide, Citigroup, Wachovia, BNP Paribas, Wells Fargo and HSBC, these claims ended in an agreement which became a safer solution for these institutions than taking the risk of entering into court proceedings, the outcome of which, from the formal point of view, could in all probability prove to be unfavourable to them.

[93] One example of the numerous negative consequences for many other financial institutions that have emerged from the collapse of Lehman Brothers was the need to compensate

Since the beginning of 2009, several class actions have been brought before the Southern District of New York Financial Bankruptcy Court on behalf of investors in Lehman Brothers' mini-bonds against many financial institutions, their subsidiaries, but also against their employees. These companies were mainly accused of selling, and previously also of mispricing, the so-called Lehman Brothers mini-bonds:

a. without taking into account the possible risks to investors;
b. without proper communication of the risk;
c. the lack of simultaneous and recommended purchase of collateral with the highest AAA rating for mini-bonds;
d. ignorance or, more specifically, the lack of mechanisms to analyse information on Lehman Brothers' previous financial problems before the financial institution filed for financial bankruptcy;
e. no action was taken to protect investors' interests.

It was also an aggravating circumstance for the defendants that these actions were not taken even after Lehman Brothers declared financial bankruptcy. The defendant financial institutions defended themselves, using the available legal means, justifying the motions to dismiss the action with the impossibility of anticipating in advance the consequences of the financial bankruptcy of Lehman Brothers. This did not, however, protect them either from the increased checks carried out by the regulators or from the disastrous effects on their reputation in the minds of the general public. This was due in particular to the universality of this product resulting from its availability in terms of its price

---

for their involvement in the servicing of so-called minibonds. This structure consisted in the fact that numerous financial institutions acted as trustees for several Lehman Brothers' bills of exchange programs, acting as representatives for companies within their own structures in other markets, outside the USA, including in particular Hong Kong and other Asian countries. However, this did not automatically mean that these institutions were also distributors of mini-bonds. The corporate services provided to Lehman Brothers consisted in providing extensive on-site services for these issues, including the provision of expert advisory services to the issuer, inclusive of the secondment of its employees to senior management positions at Lehman Brothers. Other companies from the same banking groups, on the other hand, acted as depositories of the credit derivatives underlying the bonds. After the collapse of Lehman Brothers as a result of investor concern about the value of the promissory notes held, the whole matter gained wide publicity and became the subject of analyses and, with time, investigations by regulators.

and its wide distribution. In the few years following the collapse of the Lehman Brothers, demonstrations by mini-bonds holders have occurred frequently in Hong Kong.[94] Until now, they have been periodically increasing in strength and are particularly violent. Often, as a result of the actions of specific groups of activists, they are targeted at specific financial institutions. The case is still pending before many courts. It was not until March 2011 that the first conditional settlement agreement between several trust financial institutions, Price Waterhouse Coopers as receiver and Lehman Brothers, was announced with regard to collateral for mini-bonds in the Hong Kong market. Although the settlement did not complete the US collective redress proceedings, it compensated part of the losses incurred by the holders of the mini-bonds, and the plaintiff agreed to the settlement procedure.

Financial institutions involved in the issue of Lehman Brothers mini-bonds have signed agreements on the allocation of court costs and have established a fund for the payment of liability costs established within the framework of ongoing proceedings. These financial institutions also participate in mediation proceedings in order to analyse the possibility of settling all or at least some of the claims brought against them. However, no settlement procedure has yet been closed.

This case, like all the cases described above, is an example of proceedings against financial institutions resulted in the development of a number of compliance norms. The scheme of conduct of financial institutions in such cases remains similar. Those responsible for managing compliance risk in the identified areas saw the need to develop norms governing the behaviour of financial institutions to prevent similar irregularities from arising in the future.[95] However, in addition to the control activities carried out by regulatory bodies or investigating financial institutions, the financial institutions themselves carried out their own analyses and generally recognised the need to develop their own normative regulations after in light of the findings of the research.

The criticism to which the compliance services were subject in the course of these proceedings consisted primarily in their reactivity, the fact that the actions carried out were of a follow-up nature and attempts

---

[94] M. C. S. Wong, *The Risk of Investment Products. From Product Innovation to Rik Compliance*, Singapore 2011, p. 41 et seq.

[95] See O. Wyman, Streamlining Risk, Compliance and Internal Audit. Less Is More, *Asia Pacific Finance and Risk Series* 2/2015, s. 8.

to settle the irregularities were made after they had been detected. The defence against such accusations consists, of course, in pointing out that even the most efficient compliance services cannot guarantee that there will be no violations in financial institutions. However, the existence of written norms makes it possible to oblige employees of these organisations to behave in a specific way and to prevent at least some undesirable activities, and to take appropriate disciplinary action, even of a legal nature, in the event of their occurrence.

Thanks to the existing compliance programmes, members of the authorities of financial institutions have additional tools to control the activities of their own organisations, as well as to defend themselves against civil, criminal and administrative liability of these institutions and their employees. Considering the usual scope of tasks of compliance services, it is they who are most often responsible for contact with regulatory supervisors.[96] In many institutions, they are not only responsible for creating, but also for implementing compliance norms, issuing opinions on new financial institutions products, opening new business lines or entering new markets. However, the duties of compliance services include, first of all, the creation of regulations allowing for the identification, measurement and assessment of compliance risk and its monitoring, testing and reporting of noticed irregularities, as well as the provision of advice and training in this area.

5 Norms Ensuring Compliance with the Law

Compliance in this book is understood as a principle of operation adopted by corporations, and in particular by financial institutions, consisting in adapting their operations to orders resulting from mandatory norms and to those norms whose observance results from the obligation assumed by these corporations to recognise them as binding in relation to it.

According to such a division, two basic groups of norms can be distinguished: local laws and other norms recognised by corporations as binding. According to the terminology used in multinational corporations, the local law is considered to be the law of one specific country in which

---

[96] For a comparison of the location of the compliance function in banks operating in different jurisdictions and the scope of its responsibilities, see Legal and Regulatory Risk Note. A risk management briefing putting the key issues at the top of the agenda, *Allen and Overy Report*, London 2014, p. 24 et seq.

the corporation's company operates, not local law. The presentation of the characteristics of norms created by corporations in order to ensure compliance with legal norms is the subject of this subchapter.

The studies described in this part of the work were based on the analysis of several particularly important aspects of these compliance norms. They refer to the importance of this type of compliance norms to ensure the correct operation of the corporation, the specific requirements in practice for financial institutions, the obligation to comply with economic sanctions, and the complications associated with ensuring compliance with the law in the conditions of transferring part of the business to other jurisdictions (outsourcing).[97] It also presents issues related to the characteristics of norms ensuring compliance with the law in relation to personal data protection issues and presents elements of a model procedure for the creation of compliance norms ensuring compliance with the law.

The notion of ensuring compliance with legal norms, which is a postulate formulated especially for large multinational companies, in contrast to the broader notion of compliance, firstly began to appear in the United States in the 1990s on the wave of criticism of economic crimes detected in corporations at that time. The US Supreme Court held at the time that each company should take action to ensure that internal policies are established and that processes are in place to ensure compliance with the law. At the same time, it was pointed out that the desired effect of these steps was to create conditions for its bodies and employees to act in accordance with the law, while at the same time protecting the interests of the company itself against liability to regulators and dissatisfied customers. It has been recognised that the most important thing is that such rules should be consistent in all organisational structures of the corporation and at all levels.[98] The procedures should clearly define the responsibilities and competences of the authorities and staff. In particular, the board of executives is required to ensure that all processes in the financial institution are supervised and managed in such a way that they can be controlled and managed on an ongoing basis.

---

[97] More on practical legal issues faced by banks outsourcing part of their operations. See M. Olszak, *Outsourcing w działalności bankowej*, Warsaw 2006, p. 36.

[98] On building corporate governance and the resulting complications in the context of global economic processes. See D. A. Krueger, The Governance and Corporation of Business Regulation [in] D. A. Krueger [ed.] *The Business Corporation and Productive Justice*, Nashville 1997, p. 75.

In addition, it is also necessary to establish mechanisms to ensure that existing procedures are reviewed periodically, and that any risks that may arise are identified and eliminated. These procedures should also provide for the provision of appropriate training for employees, which should not only supplement their knowledge of the norms applicable to the corporation, but also build awareness of the importance of acting in accordance with the applicable norms. The task of this type of training is to try to eliminate situations in which both legal regulations or internal norms would be insufficiently clear.

The concept of compliance became widespread outside the United States when, as a result of acquisitions and mergers through branch and subsidiary structures, capital groups operating in various markets began to play an increasingly important role in the international economy. The introduction of uniform procedures in all companies belonging to the organisational structure of these corporations has become necessary in order to provide a framework for similar functioning.[99]

Currently, compliance services are being established in an increasing number of corporations, regardless of whether they are companies operating in the regulated area or not. Compliance specialists currently also employed in industrial manufacturing companies, pharmaceuticals, food manufacturers, transport companies, etc. Wherever there is a risk of the violation of the applicable norms in a given sector, the issues for which compliance is responsible take on particular importance. All these corporations are creating increasingly well-established mechanisms to ensure that their internal processes are organised and properly regulated, and the responsibility for their implementation, enforcement and control of their implementation is clearly defined.

When analysing the areas of compliance of financial institutions' legal provisions that have recently become particularly topical, given the observed international political tensions, it is clear that issues relating to compliance with the ban on financing transactions with entities subject to all types of sanctions has come to the foreground. Global financial institutions protect themselves against compliance risks in this respect by implementing the internal norms that make up their 'sanctions policies' applicable to all companies within the group. These policies lay down uniform global norms to ensure the proper management of the

---

[99] W. Frąckowiak, *Fuzje i przejęcia*, Warsaw 2009, p. 131 et seq.

sanctioning of risk that arises for financial institutions each time they fail to comply with the mandatory provisions in this respect. The aim of these policies is to ensure that compliance with the rules on sanctions applies both to all corporate entities and individual employees of those entities in the areas where the corporations operate.

Failure to comply with the norms resulting from the regulations contained in these policies exposes corporations to disciplinary action taken by regulators, administrative fines, civil or criminal liability, but also to public criticism, i.e. to reputation losses.[100] According to the content of obligations resulting from these procedures, failure by employees to comply with them usually results in disciplinary consequences, often including the termination of their employment contract. However, if employees fail to comply with the internal rules of the sanctions policies, this may also lead to an infringement of the laws and, depending on the sanctions concerned, may have serious consequences for them personally, including fines and imprisonment.[101]

It is worth pointing out what sanctions resulting from different nature of public-law provisions are at present and what is their connection with the activities of financial institutions. Indeed, sanctions are the most effective, although not effective enough, policy tool pursued by states and international organisations, such as the UN or the EU, which aim to counter potential threats to the security of these entities.[102] Sometimes they are simply, and come in the form of consequences of non-compliance with specific prohibitions, a way of bringing the activities of other entities

---

[100] For example, the French Bank BNP Paribas was fined USD 8.83 billion in July 2014 by the US Department of Justice's Attorney General for breaching sanctions against Iran, Cuba and Sudan. Earlier, in 2012, Bank Standard Chartered agreed to pay a fine of USD 340 million on charges of concealing "billions of pounds" worth of transactions to support terrorist activity and drug trafficking.

[101] "Global Sanctions Policies" of financial institutions are published in internal procedures relating, for example, to global risk management compliance procedures.

[102] Responsibility for compliance with sanctions in EU countries is regulated by Directive (EU) 2015/849 of the European Parliament and of the Council of 20 May 2015 on the prevention of the use of the financial system for the purposes of money laundering or terrorist financing, amending Regulation (EU) No 648/2012 of the European Parliament and of the Council, and repealing Directive 2005/60/EC of the European Parliament and of the Council and Commission Directive 2006/70/EC (Text with EEA relevance), *OJ L* 141, 5 June 2015, pp. 73–117, https://eur-lex.europa.eu/legal-content/EN/TXT/?uri=CELEX:32015L0849 (download 6 May 2019).

into line with norms generally recognised by the international community.[103] Although international sanctioning regimes of different types differ in their content, principles and restrictions, as well as in the subject matter and frequency of enforcement activities from those imposed unilaterally by individual states, they generally fall into one of two categories:

a. Sanctions against a country are intended to restrict financial and commercial cooperation with the country concerned, its administrative authorities, public agencies or entities with a bearing on the country.
b. Sanctions against specific activities - these include, inter alia, terrorism, drug trafficking, international organised crime, proliferation of specific types of weapons, etc.

Restrictions and obligations under the norms contained in the sanctions policies may relate to the following issues.

Firstly, they can specify a list of sanctioned countries.

a. In such a case, the policy prohibits the provision of services to individual customers whose place of residence or business registration or principal place of business (most frequently Iran, North Korea, Syria or Sudan), or imposes restrictions on customers from countries such as Cuba, Belarus, Russia or Burma.[104]
b. Also bans business cooperation with Iran, North Korea and Syria, in all currencies, and imposes restrictions on certain areas of business cooperation with Sudan, Cuba and Burma.
c. Imposes restrictions on transactions with customers who have indirect contact with Iran, North Korea, Syria or Sudan.

---

[103] It is worth taking this opportunity to draw attention to the question of the legitimacy of this type of regulation and the strengthening of its effectiveness in terms of recognition of the legitimacy and correctness of its implementation. ("*Individuals consider legitimacy not only in terms of substantive outcomes, but moreover in procedural fairness.*")—E. F. Gerding, *Bubbles, Law and Financial Regulation*, New York 2014, p. 215. On the rightness and distinction of this concept from the concept of good in justice. See J. Rowls, *Teoria sprawiedliwości*, Warsaw 2013, p. 635 et seq.

[104] These and other examples have been identified in policies relating to the obligation to comply with international sanctions created within the framework of different financial institutions and which are subject to successive amendments.

Secondly, they may indicate the course of action to be followed in the event of possible evasion of the prohibitions in force. For example, when credit requests, the opening of an account, attempts to conceal or change identity or other personal information are recognised, they require immediate in-depth scrutiny and reporting each time that the above customer activities appear to be related to circumventing or avoiding sanctions prohibitions.

Thirdly, they may require additional checks on the personal data of new customers. This means that before allowing new customers to trade, even if a financial institution account has already been opened for them, additional checks of the personal data of those customers or their trading counterparties are required if there is any doubt about the nature of those entities or their transactions.

Fourthly, they may also require an extensive audit of the personal data of all customers. In such a case, the scope of information subject to control is extended to include requirements for the control of other data, including the actual address of the customer and related parties, or even the place where the services are provided by them.

Fifthly, carrying out transactional controls, which extends the range of types of transactions to be checked in real time and, in any case, an annual transaction risk assessment is introduced to identify the types of transactions to be checked.

Sixthly, it is also possible to inspect employees and external service providers. In such a situation, an obligation is introduced to inspect employees and partners of the financial institution itself, including entities providing services to the financial institution before starting employment or business cooperation.

In global financial institutions, the so-called sanctioning policy usually takes effect immediately on all the activities carried out by each of the entities that make up the group. At the same time, in accordance with the provisions of this policy, analysis is conducted to identify any gaps in the existing mechanisms of compliance with the sanctions obligations to date, in order to assess their compliance with the requirements of the new policy. Such analysis is usually coordinated by teams led by members of financial crime compliance (FCC) teams. Such analysis is intended to identify the requirements of the national regulatory authorities. This provides compliance services with information on the various aspects of the sanctioning policy at national level, as well as on cases of operational restrictions, meaning that in extreme cases it may be necessary to temporarily grant an entity's consent to deviate from the policy provisions.

Until the analysis of the gaps in the internal sanctioning procedures is completed and the results of these analyses are developed and discussed, usually at the highest decision-making level of the corporation, there can be no question of a possible deviation from the provisions of such a policy. The process of adapting internal procedures usually proceeds in the following way: if, as a result of this analysis, gaps in existing procedures are identified in all entities of the financial institution or in many areas of business activity, adjustment measures are taken at a global level. In such a situation, the procedure for applying for individual waivers shall not apply. Where a group entity is dependent on central IT systems enabling it to perform its duties under sanctioning regulations or on the introduction of new global security control solutions, the licensing procedure is carried out on a global level. Subsequently, communication on policy waiver decisions shall be addressed to all members of such a global financial institutions group. However, this can only happen once the gap analysis to provide information on which permits are to be global, which multi-stakeholder and which relate to specific entities or only to certain areas of activity has been completed.

The implementation of sanctioning policies is the responsibility of the managing directors at the global level of particular areas of financial institution's activity, and of other members of management performing functions of significant importance for the financial institution. Their task is to ensure that the financial institution complies with the following two conditions.

  a. The group's internal procedures should be aligned with global sanctioning policies. Moreover, on the basis of strictly defined procedures, they should be updated periodically, as well as each time when circumstances necessitating such updates occur, i.e. in practice, most often when further sanctions are introduced.[105] Where new procedures require special technological improvements to information systems, they are required to ensure that the process of

---

[105] Depending on the level of detail of the internal procedures, these may be of a general nature and may include common rules of procedure for all the group's entities, as well as more detailed guidelines for specific entities and obligations to carry out specific actions in the event of specific situations. In some banks, for example, these are functional instruction manuals (in the absence of a better translation, "functional" in this case means what it means for specific functions), business procedures manuals, and desk instruction manuals.

updating these procedures, which for operational reasons may take longer, is carried out.[106]

b. Introduce procedures to ensure that all employees who may come into contact with customers are informed of their obligations and responsibilities in relation to possible non-performance, including emerging new rules of conduct towards customers linked to sanctioned countries, as well as the need to report suspicions about transactions by customers that may be related to possible attempts to avoid sanctions.[107]

In connection with the performance of duties related to ensuring compliance of the financial institution's operations with legal norms, various types of risks related to the globalisation of operations carried out by international financial institutions corporations arise. For organisations operating globally, one of the advantages that they can offer customers is a unified offer available at the same high quality in different markets. Achieving uniform quality of service is possible thanks to the concentration of knowledge accumulated by specialised employees in service centres serving multiple locations at the same time. An additional benefit, in view of the subject matter of the present study, which is outside the scope of the present analysis, is the possibility of increasing cost-effectiveness achieved through this concentration.

The risks associated with the frequent outsourcing of a financial institution's activities usually fall into one of the following four groups, which are then described in more detail below.

a. Activities that cannot be outsourced under national regulations. These are usually the activities of financial institutions which are reserved for the exclusive competence of financial institutions, as opposed to other actual activities related only to financial institutions activity, but which do not constitute such activity (examples of such actual activities provided to financial institutions include debt collection, maintenance and maintenance of IT equipment, or development and production of printed matter and information materials).

---

[106] In most financial institutions, updates are required at least every 6 months.

[107] Such adaptation work consists, for example, in the introduction of a specific type of client designation in automated databases, filters to capture specific entities or types of transactions, or connecting transactions that may be linked.

b. Financial institution management, including in particular all activities directly related to business risk assessment, cannot be outsourced outside the formal structure of the financial institution. However, it is often difficult in practice to clearly identify which activities can be considered as part of the decision-making process.
c. Centralised service centres shall operate on the basis of uniform procedures for all serviced entities in the group, which may be inconsistent with the rules applicable to individual financial institutions locally.
d. The control over the way service centre staff operate is inherently weaker than the control that financial institutions can exercise directly over their staff.

The model of operation that financial institutions employs for using service centres usually consists in outsourcing a part of support functions to such service centres, which constitute separate entities rendering services simultaneously to many financial institutions belonging to the same group, in relation to particular financial institutions. This organisation of services stems from the fact that a growing number of processes are global in nature and that the management of their services seeks to harmonise their management process.

The first associated risk is therefore connected with the implementation of such unified processes in the entities. In practice, however, they are managed on a separate basis, and local financial institution boards have only indirect and limited supervision in this respect. As a result of the creation of such structures, more and more global processes, regulated by separate procedures, are being implemented and managed autonomously by these global service centres on a day-to-day basis. Those procedures may therefore be common to several centres and relate to the services they provide in a uniform manner for the same or even only similar activities carried out by separate entities.

As a result, another risk arises here, due to the specific nature of the financial institution's operations in different countries, and thus in countries where there may be different scope of sanctioning duties. Moreover, a similar risk arises from the case of decisions concerning the business aspects of the local operations of individual financial institutions as part of process improvement initiatives taken by the management of the region in which the service centre operates.

Another observed practice that may give rise to compliance risk is that, in accordance with the procedures in force in this respect, decisions to grant consent to carry out a transaction that goes beyond the strict criteria for financial institutions operating within the group to make their own decisions are sometimes transferred from the local level for consideration and possible acceptance by compliance staff at the group level. In this case, the risk of non-compliance arises from the fact that, under the laws in force in many countries, the exclusive competence to manage the financial institution rests with the internal bodies set up for this purpose. The outsourcing of any functions related to financial institution management, including asset and liability management, creditworthiness assessment, credit risk analysis and the management of any other risks outside the financial institution's internal bodies is also often not allowed at all.

Therefore, when deciding to outsource, financial institutions should make sure that the outsourcing will not have a negative impact on locally binding legal regulations, as well as on the financial institution's stable management and internal control system. The risk related to different aspects of financial institution management and internal control system in the context of outsourcing may take different forms depending on the degree of supervision over employees providing global service centres to financial institutions.[108]

As indicated above, financial institutions may as a result of outsourcing have limited control over the work of individual centres. These issues are often questioned by regulators in the case of financial institution inspections. The audits carried out by the regulators draw attention to the actual place where decisions are taken, and to ensuring that their content is not influenced outside the structure of the financial institution's internal bodies. In the event that risk management practices are challenged by the regulator, financial institutions are subject to a general audit on compliance with regulatory requirements, and since regulators have recently adopted a more conservative approach to local governance models and the required independence of financial institutions, this becomes one of the issues frequently raised in these audits with regard to these financial institutions. These issues are particularly likely to be brought to the attention of regulators when analysing the management

---

[108] This is similarly regulated in the banking laws of many EU member countries.

of global processes, for which regional or even global committees operating outside the country remain the centre of decision-making.

A side issue, but no less important, arises in connection with outsourcing when it becomes a possible tax risk when determining the fixed place of business of a given entity. According to similarly worded tax regulations in different jurisdictions, it is the place where management decisions are made, of which risk management decisions are the most important in the case of financial institutions activities, which determine the tax jurisdiction.

Another type of risk arising in connection with the outsourcing by financial institutions of their activities is the one related to the protection of personal data. According to the law concerning financial institutions of many countries in the field of outsourcing, the cooperation of the financial institution with external providers, including other entities from the same group, whose purpose is to provide services to clients, entails the obligation to collect the necessary information about these entities' organisational structure, financial results and ways of securing data containing elements of financial institutions secrecy. However, in the case of European financial institutions, prior regulatory approval is also required for suppliers outside the European Economic Area.[109] In each case, one of the regulatory requirements is a direct, contractually regulated relation between the service provider and the financial institution shaped in such a way that it indicates an express prohibition on subcontracting part of the activities of service providers. It is in this context that there are cases where certain services provided centrally to all entities of the same financial institutions group at global or even regional level are transferred to other entities without prior notification to the financial institution concerned. Especially when the timing of the provision of these services is so short as to make it impossible to obtain prior regulatory approval. As a result, this leads to breaches of regulatory requirements and, as a consequence, to the nullity of concluded contracts and the imposition of penalties by regulatory authorities.[110]

---

[109] A. Grünbichler, P. Darlap, Integration of UE Financial Markets Supervision: Harmonization or Unification? *Journal of Financial Regulation and Compliance* 12(1)/ 2004, p. 59 et seq.

[110] This raises the issue of whether, in the absence of consent to the conclusion of an outsourcing agreement for a financial institution, such as services related to banking activities, or in the absence of such an agreement, the disclosure of personal data is unlawful and constitutes a breach of both the rules on the protection of bank secrecy and on the protection of personal data.

Moreover, in practice, it appears that some global service centres are not interested in concluding intra-group service agreements (IGSA) directly with individual financial institutions, which are required in order to obtain the regulatory authority's consent prior to starting cooperation with a given provider. This situation may have different sources, but most often these are hidden in the tax policy, which ensures transparency and at the same time tax optimisation in case global service centres conclude agreements only with the entity representing the corporation at the highest level of consolidation, and not directly with individual business partners.

Other practical problems can often be a source of risk of non-compliance. Hence, compliance representatives in financial institutions, while performing advisory and control functions, must simultaneously analyse the functioning of the existing processes in terms of technical and operational aspects. For example, the tasks performed due to the current complexity of the IT management departments' structure, which makes it difficult to obtain information on which and to which systems the data is transmitted, who administers the individual systems, and who can potentially have access to the data stored in them. This applies both to customer personal data and employee data. The more extensive the organisational structure of individual financial institutions, the greater such difficulties. In order to solve such problems, initiatives can be taken to include information sharing clauses in the documentation. Such clauses may turn out to be good solutions from the point of view of the proper shaping of contractual relations, including, in particular, transparency for those concerned.

On the other hand, however, it is objectively difficult for financial institutions to obtain appropriate approvals from all interested customers within a definite period of time. Therefore, due to the fact that the infrastructure of IT systems is becoming more and more complex and the number of global processes resulting from initiatives concerning specific IT improvements is constantly growing, compliance services must bear in mind the possibility of the associated risks, and therefore plan properly and determine the ways of managing such risks in the internal norms they create.[111]

---

[111] An example of the most common ways to manage this risk is to strictly define the so-called levels of access for bank employees to information of different kinds by directly defining it in the relevant internal procedures, as well as to contractually guarantee adequate protection of such data in the event of authorized access by third parties in relation to the provision of outsourcing services to the financial institution. Cf. A. Martin, T. M. Lakshmi, V. P. Vankatesan, An Information Delivery Model for Banking Business, *International Journal of Information Management* 34(2)/2014, p. 139.

Letting financial institutions' monitor transactions serves as one example of an area where internal compliance norms must be developed to ensure compliance with national rules. In the case of examining the nature of transactions carried out by customers through financial institutions due to the possibility of committing significant errors resulting from the scale of their operations, the financial institutions are subject to so-called transaction monitoring optimisation (TMO). Due to the importance of these tasks, they become key projects in the initiatives setting global norms, as mentioned earlier in this book. These tasks consist primarily in carrying out an initial analysis of personal data contained in the systems and databases used by the IT financial institutions. At the same time, information is being analysed on potential limitations existing in legal regulations, which could affect the analytical work carried out.

The model, built on the basis of similar examples, of an intra-institutional procedure, created in connection with the data security in the outsourcing processes, assumes the analysis of the existing state of data management quality and predicts that such analysis takes place in the three stages described below.[112]

The first stage involves the anonymisation of data, and ensuring that the different types of transactions are appropriately marked in such a way as to ensure, on the one hand, that the identity of entities cannot be determined if this information has been illegally acquired and, on the other hand, that an unambiguous and easily distinguishable matching of entities carrying out certain types of transactions is possible.[113] In addition to the creation of appropriate norms in this area, the task of compliance services is also to carry out checks, as a result of which reports containing examples of various types of errors, consisting in assigning incorrect markings to specific types of transactions, are created.

---

[112] The procedural model presented here has the character of an author's reconstruction model, reproduced from normative practice observed in financial institutions, and is therefore not a normative model. Therefore, it does not constitute a formal representative model in the strict sense of the term. See T. Gospodarek, *Modelowanie w naukach o zarządzaniu oparte na metodzie programów badawczych*, *Monografie i opracowania Uniwersytetu Ekonomicznego we Wrocławiu* 189/2009, p. 61.

[113] This is made possible by assigning the right codes to the right transactions.

Stage two is to develop recommendations for improvements in the segmentation and grouping of data contained in customer databases. This will include ways to obtain information to analyse the data in available IT systems to find the most effective solutions, resulting in a proposal for appropriate data segmentation that will facilitate the monitoring of transactions.

The third stage is to develop recommendations for establishing precise criteria for each type of data identified within the second stage of work—for a specific type of transactions carried out by customers of a specific type. The aim is to create a kind of mechanism to warn against the likelihood of attempts to carry out illegal activities, and to avoid erroneous acceptance of such transactions by the financial institution. The result of this stage of work is usually a report containing recommended criteria for each separate type of data.

At this point, it is worth noting the specificity of the compliance norms arising from or in connection with the applicable national regulations. The task of these norms, as in the example above, is to ensure that the obligations incumbent upon financial institution employees are tightly and unambiguously defined, regardless of the jurisdictions in which they operate and the legal and regulatory reality in which they operate.

6 Norms Ensuring Compliance with Corporate Guidelines

Another function of compliance norms is to ensure compliance of a financial institution's operations with the internal guidelines of varying degrees of importance recognised by corporations as sufficiently important that they are defined as binding for all companies operating within the entire financial institutions group. It would seem that the lack of such defined and, as a result, codified corporate norms expressed in the form of principles and rules of conduct may in practice give rise to serious risks to the uniformity of operation of entire financial institutions groups and may expose them to numerous legal, organisational and business consequences. Compliance programmes institutions being exposed to a range of risks, from unfavourable opinions about their activities, through to falling share prices caused by uncertainty about the correctness of existing control processes, or dissatisfaction with the corporate authorities' approach to ensuring the correctness and transparency of investors' actions, etc.[114] In practice, these consequences can go even further and consist of the imposition of financial penalties, but also in the cancellation of agreements already concluded and the withdrawal of licences to conduct financial institutions activities.[115] Compliance norms to ensure compliance expressed in internal normative acts such as rules and procedures of varying degrees also have another task. They ensure the flow of harmonised information and perpetuate desirable behavioural patterns by establishing rules for joint action for all actors operating in different locations.

A description of the analysis of compliance norms aimed at ensuring compliance of financial institutions corporations' operations through their corporate guidelines is the subject of this subchapter. This section presents the results of a study of the London financial institutions' practices over the last few years.[116] The issues examined in this section relate to the process of norm unification in corporations, the monitoring of compliance with these norms, factors that ensure the effectiveness of compliance norms, including their global effectiveness, and to cooperation with other specialised services co-responsible for compliance control in financial institutions.

An organisation's compliance policy and procedures consist of policies and procedures at a global level to reduce compliance risk, defined as the risk of non-compliance with applicable laws and regulations governing business operations in certain countries or territories in which operations

---

[114] See B. Gong, *Understanding Institutional Shareholder Activism: A Comparative Study of the UK and China*, New York 2014, p. 46 et seq.; L. Canibano, E. De las Heras, Enforcement in the European Union. A Comparative Survey: Spain and the UK [in] G. Frattini [ed] *Improving Business Reporting: New Rules, New Opportunities, New Trends*, Milano 2007, p. 202; and I. G. MacNeil, Risk Control Strategies: An Assessment in the Context of the Credit Crisis [in] I. G. MacNeil, J. O'Brien [ed.] *The Future of Financial Regulation*, Portland 2010, p. 154.

[115] On financial penalties imposed on the banking sector for fraudulent behavior in operations carried out by banks in their own name and on their own behalf. See e.g. R. Wandhoefer, *Transaction Banking and the Impact of the Regulatory Change*, New York 2014, p. 249 et seq.

[116] The practice investigated concerns five London banks: HSBC Holdings Plc., Lloyds Banking Group Plc., Standard Chartered Plc., Barclays Plc. and Royal Bank of Scotland Group Plc.

are carried out.[117] It may also be regulations in force outside the country or territory, whose extraterritorial scope is reflected in local legal regulations. Therefore, the employees responsible for monitoring compliance norms should in practice be aware of all policies related to the areas of the financial institution's operations and the procedures in force within the corporate framework. This task itself is generally both important and difficult due to the usually complex system of relations between the entities in a financial institutions group and their legal and regulatory environment.

Regardless of the different nature of the difficulties, the area of compliance regulated by the norms in force within the corporation, regardless of the place of business activity belongs to:

a. procedures for dealing with customer complaints;
b. rules against bribery;
c. the policy of not financing business activities related to the arms industry and arms trade.

Such compliance procedures apply both to persons working in the compliance area, and to all other employees of the financial institutions group whose actions may be a source of compliance risk.

The approach to risk management compliance in financial institutions is fundamentally different from that of other types of risk management. Traditionally, in financial institutions, the management of credit risk or market risk involves weighing up risks, seeking compromises between the risk identified and the expected return that may result from taking action despite the risk of the client defaulting or an unfavourable market situation. Compliance risk falls into a completely different risk category in the sense that it is difficult for regulated institutions to accept that they can act fraudulently at all and, in principle, it is not accepted in practice for a financial institution to accept the materialisation of compliance risk as part of its approach to the different risk categories.[118]

---

[117] See. N. King, *Governance, Risk, and Compliance Handbook*, Birmingham 2012, p. 415.

[118] Recent discussions within banking institutions have raised the question of whether a zero risk appetite approach to compliance risk makes any sense at all, given the obvious fact that breaches do occur and that, despite the implementation of increasingly restrictive

The compliance approach of many financial groups has recently been updated in such a way that, in accordance with the content of intra-corporate norms, but also with the intention accompanying the creation of its records, maintaining good reputation is a value of paramount importance. Interestingly, strengthening the compliance function has become a priority despite the widespread market trend to cut costs in order to increase profits in this way. Not exposing financial institutions to reputation damage by strengthening compliance mechanisms is currently the dominant trend in the financial industry.[119]

The importance of compliance norms in practice may be demonstrated by the fact that although the legal regulations in force in some countries, on the basis of which the norms have been created, may have limited force in other countries or not be in force at all, the norms are also introduced there. The justification for introducing, by means of internal normative acts, the same rules allowing corporations to operate in a uniform manner is often of a negative nature, referring to the need to prevent the risk of conducting market practices that violate the behavioural patterns desired within a given corporation.[120] Since financial institutions groups usually operate, directly or through correspondent financial institutions, in international markets, their reputation is assessed according to global norms. It is therefore necessary to create a unified image of the financial institution as a predictable player with recognised and predictable rules of conduct both internally and vis-à-vis external partners, regardless of possible differences in the legal environment in different jurisdictions.

The previous lack of unified compliance regulations in financial institutions, which resulted in serious reputational damage in the recent period, included:

---

control mechanisms, it is difficult to assume that they could be excluded completely. However, it has not yet been decided to change this approach and to specify in the formal bank documents to be disclosed to regulators that the bank would be prepared to accept the risk of non-compliance to a certain extent.

[119] See L. Hobe, *The Changing Landscape of the Financial Services*, *International Journal of Trade, Economics and Finance*, 6(2)/2015, p. 146 et seq.

[120] See L. Thévenoz, R. Bahar, *Conflicts of Interest: Corporate Governance and Financial Markets*, Aalphen an den Rijn 2007, p. 119 et seq.

a. transactions related to misconduct in advice and trading;
b. insider trading;
c. market collusion relating to currency prices (cartel foreign exchange fixing) and interest rates (cartel interest rate fixing);
d. deriving hidden profits from the sale of financial institutions products by the agency (hidden commissions).

The process of unifying some of the compliance norms, consisting in the implementation of similar norms, especially in European financial institutions, is to a large extent the result of harmonisation of compliance norms in preparations for the implementation of the CRD IV Directive relating to the most important issues of financial institutions management.[121]

For example, Article 91 of the Directive defines the Management Authority by indicating the attributes that its members should possess. An important novelty is that among these attributes, in addition to strictly professional qualifications, references to other characteristics are also made. In particular, the members of the management bodies should be of good repute at the same time as possessing sufficient knowledge, skills and experience to perform the duties assigned to them. In addition, it draws attention to the need for a collegiate collection of appropriate qualifications among the members of the management body as a whole. Indeed, it is understood that the composition of the management body assessed as a whole should reflect a wide range of experience and expertise. The members of that body should be qualified in particular as regards knowledge of matters relating to the conduct of financial institutions business, including the regulatory requirements designed to ensure the prudent and sound management of a financial institution.

Other requirements relating to the way financial institutions are managed relate to ensuring that the commitment to the institution with all members of the management body devoting sufficient time

---

[121] To a similar extent, this issue was also addressed in the US by the Dodd-Frank Act. See E. D. Herlihy, L. S. Makow, *A Federal Reserve Wake-Up Call to Directors of Financial Institutions*, Harvard 7 June 2014, www.blogs.law.harvard.edu (download 16 February 2019). Also: *The Future of Global Banking. Bank Governance Leadership Network View Points*, December 2014, www.tapestrynetwork.com (download 16 February 2019) as well as: J. O'Kelley III, Insights from Conversations with U.S. Banking Regulators: Implications for Bank Directors, *Global Leadership* 09/2014, p. 203.

to performing their functions within the institution. These types of regulations, although they give the impression of being unnecessary (because they are obvious) and imprecise, are primarily an expression of the intentions of supervisory authorities who formulated these guidelines as a result of earlier observations of irregularities taking place in financial institutions. Similarly, the obligation for financial institutions to establish control mechanisms so that the number of directorships that one member of the board of directors can perform simultaneously takes into account the individual circumstances and the nature, scale and complexity of the institution's activities. Where those circumstances are relevant in view of the size, organisational structure and the nature, scope and complexity of the activities of the institution, the members of its management body may no longer perform, from 1 July 2014, more than one executive director function including a maximum of two non-executive directorships or four non-executive directorships at the same time.[122]

For the purposes of Article 91(3) of the Directive, members of the statutory bodies of financial institutions with executive or non-executive powers on the boards of directors of companies operating under common law, as well as members of the boards of directors and supervisory boards of financial institutions incorporated under continental law, are considered in practice as directors. Irrespective of the legal environment in which the financial institution operates, this applies both to all those functions carried out within the same group and to those carried out within the institutions covered by the same institutional protection regime, provided that the conditions laid down in Article 113(7) of Regulation (EU) No 575/2013 of the European Parliament and of the Council or to undertakings (including non-financial entities) in which the financial institutions institution has a qualifying holding are fulfilled.[123]

---

[122] This does not apply if they are members of the governing bodies of banks and, by virtue of their function, represent a member state.

[123] Regulation (EU) No 575/2013 of the European Parliament and of the Council of 26 June 2013 on prudential requirements for credit institutions and investment firms and amending Regulation (EU) No 648/2012 Text with EEA relevance, *OJ L* 176, 27 June 2013, pp. 1–337, https://eur-lex.europa.eu/legal-content/EN/TXT/?uri=CELEX:32013R0575 (download 6 June 2019).

The requirement of adequate involvement in the activity of financial institutions is therefore implemented by limiting the possibility of working for many organisations at the same time. It is assumed that the guarantee of proper supervision over the correctness of financial institutions' operations is to allow such activities for several organisations at the same time only in exceptional situations. Competent authorities may allow a member of the management body to perform an additional non-executive director (supervisory board member) function. However, it is necessary in such a case to introduce the principle of informing the European Financial institutions Authority of such authorisations on a regular basis.

Another group of requirements mentioned above concerns qualifications and professional experience gathered by members of the financial institution's governing bodies. As previously indicated, it is important that these requirements apply both to individual members and collectively to bodies considered as a whole, in which the relevant knowledge, skills and experience necessary to ensure a full understanding of the specific activities of financial institutions, including in particular the associated risks, notably compliance and legal risks, should be pooled together.

The guidelines set out in the Directive even concern the way in which members of the financial institution's governing bodies exercise their management.[124] Individual members of the management body are expected to act honestly and ethically, with independence of judgement, in order to be able to properly assess and, if necessary, challenge the decisions of their senior management in order to effectively supervise and monitor the decision-making process of financial institution staff. The indication in the Directive that financial institutions should devote adequate organisational and financial resources to carrying out these duties concerns in practice, both the proper selection and continuous training of members of the financial institution's bodies, and the creation of an adapted organisational framework to ensure the creation of internal regulations defining these issues. The charters of association, regulations and codes of conduct, which are often in force in financial institutions,

---

[124] More on the responsibilities of members of bank governing bodies. See J. Gliniecka, *Publiczne prawo bankowe*, Warsaw 2013, p. 177.

regulate these issues in this way with regard to internal relations within financial institutions.[125]

Norms ensuring compliance with corporate guidelines also regulate issues related to the conduct of inspections, reviews and monitoring of compliance norms by financial institutions and their employees. In order to ensure that employees of the various departments of a financial institution, as well as the compliance departments themselves, act in accordance with the applicable laws and group compliance rules, various analyses and controls are carried out at all times within these institutions. The frequency and detailed guidelines on how to carry them out determine the need for regular monitoring and periodic reviews. Taking into account the existing needs and available resources, it is advisable to adapt the planned activities to the assessment of the main risk areas. However, review and control policies often indicate that independent analysis of a business activity by compliance does not relieve management of its supervisory responsibility towards its employees. It is up to them to ensure that financial institutions operate in accordance with the principles of the compliance policy in the first instance.

Monitoring carried out by compliance staff takes place through frequent contact with the other employees of the financial institutions, including those working in sales and business support. This contact takes place through visits to branches and operational departments of the financial institution. This allows the compliance services staff to gain practical awareness of the rules and methods for conducting business in specific areas of the financial institution, as well as the way in which the persons managing these areas perform their duties. As part of such regular contacts, compliance officers are required to monitor all sensitive areas of the financial institution's business in order to identify potential compliance issues with the law and corporate guidelines.

In practice, a complete picture is obtained by using the sum of available information, including internal audit reports, previous reports on non-compliance, statistics on complaints and fraud and other management information. The areas subject to such monitoring vary depending on the type of activity of the financial institution. They also often differ in other respects depending on the nature of the regulatory regime and

---

[125] The deadline for the European Banking Authority to issue the guidelines referred to here is 31 December 2015. Meanwhile, the Member States were obliged to implement this directive by 31 December 2013.

the internal control system previously in place. Despite these differences, compliance officers are obliged to analyse the following issues during the monitoring process.[126]

   a. Known weaknesses in the procedures in place to control the correct functioning of the financial institution—an example may be the inappropriate division of duties between departments operating in direct contact with customers (front office) and units operating in the financial institution's back-office.
   b. Customer complaints - the number of such complaints, the reasons for their referral, the amount of compensation paid as a result of complaints, possible information concerning specific sellers, branches where irregularities in the sale of products may occur, the time needed to deal with complaints, etc.
   c. Cases of customer withdrawals from concluded transactions, which may indicate aggressive selling methods, often resulting in inappropriate product selection or fictitious transactions.
   d. Situations where certain sellers or branches have a disproportionate sales performance compared to other sales, in which case it is necessary to examine how they achieve them and whether they are subject to appropriate supervision by the responsible supervisors.
   e. Likelihood of conflicts of interest—this may be the case where a financial institution is simultaneously the issuer of units in its investment funds and, on the other hand, sells such financial products offered by other institutions. In such situations, compliance procedures involve checking whether the sale of these products is in fact the execution of orders on terms that are most favourable to the client (best execution).
   f. Know your customer (KYC) process is also the subject of the study, which should be carried out in accordance with both the applicable regulations and the anti-money laundering rules in force in the organisation concerned.

[126] It is not a complete list, but only an example of the tasks performed by compliance within the framework of monitoring activities. They vary in scope and scope from one institution to another, and depending on the profile of the bank's business, the recommendations made by regulators, the legal environment, the expectations of bank authorities, etc., may include different spaces and may differ in the methodology used and the depth of research carried out.

g. Moreover, such controls should also take into account the latest methods of preventing money laundering arising from the work of the various centres specialising in this field, such as government offices as well as those used in other entities belonging to the same organisation.
h. Very effective customer and transaction controls, which is a key element of any counter-terrorist financing programmes and attempts to disregard sanctions imposed on certain entities that restrict the ability to execute transactions on their behalf, should also be examined.
i. Control of the effectiveness of compliance norms also means conducting research into the implementation of newly introduced rules and even business practices until they are rooted in the organisation.
j. Examination of the ways of keeping custody accounts, reflected in the quality of investment results, frequency and suitability of transactions.
k. Controls of transactions in own securities by the financial institution's employees (proprietors trading)—in such situations, irregularities may be disclosed when persons achieving profits disproportionately high in relation to the market that there may be a reasonable suspicion that such transactions were carried out with knowledge unavailable to other trading participants.
l. Controls on potential other irregularities—in practice, they also cover e.g. dormant accounts and other instruments related to the handling of trading transactions that can be used to conceal delays in booking profit, transfers of profits between accounts, changes in charges for booking profit, delays or the avoidance of certain types of settlements.

The frequency and scope of checks depends on:

a. the nature of the financial institutions' activities under scrutiny;
b. the degree of regulatory risk associated with the area analysed;
c. the adequacy of the control and supervision system put in place at the financial institution by its management;
d. actions previously taken by internal audit.

Hence the expectation that employees working in compliance are aware of significant changes in the law, and that they observe trends and events that affect the effectiveness of compliance norms.[127]

This applies in particular to the twelve issues identified below.[128]

a. The emergence of new legislation on financial institutions activities, including extraterritorial provisions.
b. Both the most recent and frequently occurring changes in the management of the financial institution, its organisational structure, business processes, internal procedures and IT systems.
c. Other new business ventures that have not been introduced without prior consultation of the compliance function.
d. Newly employed financial institution employees without the necessary permits and other relevant documents.
e. New sales targets or incentive schemes that may affect the impartiality of information provided to customers about the products offered by the financial institution.
f. New information systems or software.
g. Increased number of financial institutions operations, which could potentially lead to problems with the execution of transactions, settlements or reconciliations of account balances.
h. Increase in the number of sales staff which may necessitate an increase in the quantity and content of training offered to staff and an increase in the intensity of supervision.
i. Reductions of significant number of workers, in particular those of a collective redundancy nature which may result in backlogs in the day-to-day execution of tasks or non-compliance with the control procedures in force.

---

[127] Cf. D. Cowan, Legal Consciousness: Some Observations, *Modern Law Review* 67(6)/2004, p. 928 et seq.

[128] Knowledge in the areas mentioned here is not only helpful but also necessary. The areas themselves, however, are not listed in a catalogue, and their calculation here is only an example of the extent of the matter in which knowledge may affect the quality of performance of tasks by the compliance functions. All these issues have an impact on the environment in which the compliance function operates.

j. High management turnover, which may indicate that the financial institution is in an unstable situation threatening their safe conduct.
k. Changes in local and international organisational structures resulting in changes in the reporting lines.
l. Mergers of two or more different business areas as a result of changes in the organisational structure.

When developing norms to ensure compliance with corporate guidelines, compliance services usually review all relevant reports prepared by internal and external auditors and regulators. In those areas of the financial institution's business where compliance problems existed, the services monitor the remedial actions until they are fully implemented. This applies both to problems identified by compliance employees and by employees of other organisational units of the financial institution.[129] Usually, in order to rely on the results of the control work of other employees, compliance function employees make a prior examination as to whether the persons responsible for the control system in question perform their duties properly. The result of this type of research is usually the creation of compliance norms regulating the proper way of performing control duties in accordance with the model expected by the corporation.

The audits carried out by the compliance services described here are an essential element in the implementation of international, and in the case of companies with a global reach, global compliance assurance models.[130] These global full compliance models are implemented in the same way across all compliance services, regardless of the jurisdiction in which they operate. Their aim is to increase the probability of the early detection of potential irregularities and to improve the proactive (and therefore pre-emptive) management of the risk of noncompliance, as opposed to the subsequent management of the risk of non-compliance in the same way everywhere. In this respect, the need to cooperate with internal audit and legal services within the financial institution is particularly evident.

---

[129] This may include reviewing sales documentation in relation to the requirements of customer identification programs or ensuring the suitability of products offered to customers.

[130] See C. Chinkin, Normative Development in International Legal System, *International and Comparative Law Quarterly* 38/1989, p. 850 et seq.

The compliance and internal audit policies developed within global financial institutions organisations, expressed in internal regulations, should complement each other, and take into account the specificity of the organisation in question. Compliance and internal audit services complement each other to a large extent, creating a mechanism for controlling the correctness of financial institutions' operations based on close cooperation and effectively communicated tasks. The compliance and internal audit complement each other not only in the scope of controls, but also in terms of correcting existing irregularities and determining properly functioning processes. Therefore, cooperation between the two services is designed to avoid the duplication of responsibilities, and to make the best use of the information and resources available to them.

The procedures operating within large financial institutions with extensive organisational structures assume that each local internal audit department should select a person whose duties should include staying in constant contact with regional and global compliance services. In such a situation, compliance service employees are obliged to support internal audit through additional verification activities, but also through regular, ongoing supervision over the compliance of the institution's operations with the norms adopted in the corporation. Four of these tasks are listed below.

a. Assessing the existing level of compliance risk on the basis of arrangements between compliance services and the competent internal audit department, which are designed to enable an examination of those areas of compliance risk that have been identified as significant. Typically, in large international organisations, the unit responsible for an internal audit is not only allocated geographically, but also according to the type of services offered and groups of clients. There may be separate specialised auditing units in each country dealing exclusively with certain types of offers, for example, some credit products for corporate customers, some deposit products for corporate customers and some other products for private customers.

b. Agreeing with local internal audit services on areas of corporate risk of noncompliance that are relevant prior to the planned audit, in particular with regard to new products or services, as well as new procedures and other relevant compliance issues.

c. Making available to local internal audit departments appropriate reports on reviews and monitoring previously carried out by compliance.
   d. Provide internal audit units with information on planned or already initiated inspections by regulatory bodies of administrations and provide copies of the reports drawn up by these regulators following inspections.

The internal compliance procedures of individual financial institutions provide that the cooperation between the audit and the compliance function is also based on the fact that the internal audit function should support compliance function staff through the following actions.

   a. It should include in its audit plans, normally established yearly and then in the relevant reports, an examination of the key compliance requirements of each local financial institution.
   b. It should make available and discuss with compliance personnel audit reports, and in particular those parts thereof, which address the issue of observed irregularities in compliance processes.
   c. Before proceeding with an audit of compliance services, which should also take place and which generally take into account internal financial institutions procedures, the internal audit should consult with the management of the appropriate level within this unit. Before commencing a local compliance audit, the scope of the audit is agreed with the relevant global compliance manager.

In practice, in order to reduce the degree of overlap between compliance reviews and audits, and to increase the effectiveness of each of these studies, internal procedures shall take into account the situation in which compliance may propose to rely on the results of internal audit work. It is in such situations that the scope of this work should be agreed with the local compliance services when compliance plans are being prepared or periodically updated.

The internal audit should then address any identified compliance issues in its own reports and other official documents.[131] It should be

---

[131] These are co-called *internal audit guidance letters*.

borne in mind, however, that some compliance issues are so complex, and require such specialist knowledge that only specialised compliance personnel are able to identify them. The responsibility for deciding whether a given audit point is related to the area of compliance does not fall within the scope of internal audit duties.[132] On the other hand, however, most situations in which an audit detects irregularities can be interpreted as entailing some form of risk of non-compliance with intra-corporate norms and requiring action to ensure repairing actions.

As in the case of the above-mentioned relation between the tasks of compliance services and internal audit, there is also cooperation between compliance services and separate legal services in financial institutions, regulated by internal compliance procedures. However, while the former results to a large extent from the control function performed by compliance, the latter refers to consultative and norm-setting functions undertaken by compliance. If the financial institution employs lawyers, it is up to them to first deal with all compliance issues, the resolution of which requires a legal opinion. Sometimes lawyers employed in financial institutions also seek external legal advice. All opinions drawn up by internal or external lawyers, i.e. in practice opinions drawn up by qualified lawyers, i.e. equivalents of legal advisers or attorneys with respect to significant compliance issues, constitute an important source of decisions in the area of compliance.

Compliance procedures provide that any instances of non-compliance that may result in actions being brought against a financial institution or financial institution employee acting on its behalf, and even the risk of such actions, should be promptly consulted with the relevant legal department. This also applies to any events occurring as a result of the above circumstances. In view of the scale and breadth of the activities of financial institutions, these procedures usually lay down thresholds of amounts relating to the value of the litigation over which actions are considered to be significant. There is an obligation to deal specifically with such actions, to report on the risk of their occurrence, and to

---

[132] Definition of audit issues related to compliance responsibilities in the internal audit policy of one of the London banks: "Information contained in the audit report which carries a direct risk of non-compliance and indicates the need for consultation or support by the compliance function prior to taking action to mitigate the above risk".

undertake appropriate consultations.[133] Such procedures prescribing a harmonised approach to legal compliance issues is important because it allows for consistency of action in cases where, in the absence of a structured approach, the risk of obtaining different, and even more contradictory, legal opinions would increase.

The support of compliance by legal services at the earliest possible stage of proceedings or preparatory acts is of particular importance for international organisations operating in different jurisdictions, in the case of cross-border proceedings. This also applies to the involvement of legal services in various types of external and internal investigations, including administrative proceedings involving the provision of information to regulatory authorities that are necessary to carry out factual and formal investigations. In the event of pending litigation, financial institutions shall exercise their right to respond to the allegations made and to provide an adequate statement of reasons therefore. This also applies to the use of other available legal remedies. However, the rules on the applicability of the selected types of legal protection tools may differ from one jurisdiction to another. Since this is a complex cross-border issue, financial institutions' compliance norms provide for detailed guidance to be requested from the legal department before starting an investigation into potential breaches that give rise to a situation of non-compliance.

7 Types of Internal Corporate Acts Containing Compliance Norms

Regardless of the previously proposed approach to compliance norms, it is also worth paying attention to the hierarchical relations between them. One of the obvious reasons for the heterogeneity of the types of regulations applied by international financial institutions is the fact that they are in fact complex corporations operating in different jurisdictions and are created under conditions resulting from different normative traditions. In the first part of the introduction to this book, four main types of compliance norms created in financial institutions were distinguished

---

[133] These values are different in various banks. However, they usually exceed USD 1.5 million (or the equivalent in other currencies). All criminal lawsuits against banks and administrative proceedings involving regulators who take action in relation to irregularities detected and threatened by fines imposed by regulators are usually also granted the status of material cases.

due to the criteria of the legal and regulatory environment and their place in the hierarchy. These are principles, rules, recommendations and guidelines. They concern above all those types of compliance norms which carry interpretative guidelines necessary to ensure uniform application of compliance norms within the whole corporation, regardless of local differences. The criteria for separating these types also relate to the importance of the issues to be addressed, their scope and the objectives for which they are designed.

The eleven most common types of acts containing compliance norms are listed below. Their selection differs from financial institution to financial institution, as it depends on the nature of their operations and the place of these documents in the hierarchy of internal normative acts. Examining the characteristics of compliance norms presented earlier, that result both from the tasks and functions performed by compliance services in financial institutions and from other factors, including irregularities detected in financial institutions, a description of the most frequently used normative acts containing compliance norms in financial institutions is presented here. Among the presented normative acts, it should be noted that the names of some of them coincide with the previously presented types of norms. An additional necessary proviso also applies to the fact that, despite the partial terminological similarity of some used names of normative acts with certain types of norms, not all of these acts contain only these types of norms, and not all of them contain only normative statements in their content. Some of them, apart from norms, also contain other types of statements.

Importantly, there is no one universal, commonly used directory of types of documents in which legal norms are formulated. These types vary from jurisdiction to jurisdiction, not least because of different terminological traditions. They also differ within the same jurisdictions, and often financial institutions in the same country have documents containing similar norms relating to the same subject matter in a different way. This presentation is therefore a generalisation, the purpose of which is to indicate the common features of the different types of documents.

'Standards'—although they may include other types of statements in addition to norms, normative acts called standards, may be considered as one of the most important elements of normative compliance systems in financial institutions. This is due to the nature of their directional indications of proceedings, which, without being limited in their material scope or geographical area of application, are aimed at unifying regardless of the differences that exist locally in individual jurisdictions. For this reason, they can be considered the most general normative acts within financial institutions corporations, containing directive expressions, indicating certain types of attitudes and best practices as appropriate.[134] The characteristic feature of the norms is the fact that they belong to a given corporation in the sense that, regardless of differences resulting from local legal normative obligations, they formulate models of conduct to which all entities belonging to a given organisation are obliged to behave. Therefore, if the norm adopted by a financial institution is to maintain an eight-hour working day, unless local legislation provides for a shorter day, then in none of the financial institutions in a given group can the working day be longer, even if national legislation does not address these issues at all, and market practice even allows for a much longer daily working time.[135] Similarly, if the norm adopted by the corporation is the implementation of environmental assumptions consisting, for example, in not participating in the financing of energy projects which would result in the emission of greenhouse gases into the atmosphere, the composition of which would be more than 550 mg of CO_2 per cubic metre, then none of the financial institutions comprising it would finance the modernisation of the CHP plant, as a result of which 700 mg of CO_2 per cubic metre would remain the amount of the gas emitted into the atmosphere, even though a more modern plant of this type would be built as a result of such financing, and the existing carbon dioxide emissions would be significantly reduced.

'Principles' are both the type of norms and the name of normative acts used in corporations that contain generally expressed patterns of behaviour that are built on the basis of valuation assessments originally carried out by the managers of corporations, indicating selected attitudes as beneficial from the point of view of long-term economic objectives. The term in this case will be both general normative statements of a directional nature, as well as documents containing such statements, whose task is to determine not only specific types of behaviour, but also the way of approaching certain types of situations, even if they are not

---

[134] The concept of 'directive expression' has been attributed here to the meaning of the conventional verbal act of influencing people's behavior. See K. Opałek, *Z teorii dyrektyw i norm*, Warsaw 1974, p. 152 et seq.

[135] See J. J. Kirton, M. J. Trebilcock, *Hard Choices, Soft Law: Voluntary Standards in Global Trade, Environment and Social Governance*, Toronto 2004, p. 121.

regulated in detail, to all employees of particular financial institutions belonging to the corporation. The principles also constitute a field of axiological reference for all norm-setting activities undertaken by corporations in the sense that any internal normative acts created by financial institutions organisations should be consistent with them. Moreover, the formulation of certain principles by corporations may in some cases require normative actions to be taken in order to fulfil their specific instructions. The principles within the corporate compliance norms system are binding. They take precedence over other norms and act as a reference for all actions that should be taken.

'Rules'—as in the case of principles, rules are the type of compliance norms referred to by this name, but also the type of acts containing norms-rules, which determine the desired specific type of behaviour in such a way that the addressees are indicated the way to proceed in cases which are most often described in detail, in a casuistic manner. Only the possibility of fulfilling the obligation imposed on them or violating it in a situation different from the one indicated, shall be left to them. In practice, most often the rules serve to unify the understanding of certain desirable types of behaviour, or to order a specific manner of fulfilling obligations arising from the provisions of law, supervisory regulations, decisions of administrative bodies or adjudicating entities.

'Policies' are documents that formulate harmonised guidelines for the required course of action, in varying degrees of detail, on a particular subject matter. Although the term is widely used in the regulatory practice of corporations, it does not have the same meaning in different organisations. On the contrary, depending on the type of business conducted by a given financial institution, the regulatory tradition prevailing in a given area and the subject matter of regulation, policies may differ greatly in practice between themselves. Policies are one of those types of normative acts in which, apart from compliance norms, there are most often other types of statements. Policies may include normative regulations introduced within a given corporation, or parts of its entities, which contain guidelines both directly related to compliance issues and do not contain such references at all, and which are only a set of rules of conduct in matters belonging to a given type of issues. For example, a credit policy or a liquidity management policy may be implemented in a financial institution. Each of them will determine the obligations to carry out certain types of economic analytics, statistical calculations, or the obligation to take certain actions as a result of the fulfilment of the forecasts based on the probability calculations on which decisions are based, the stress tests under stress conditions as well as the reporting obligations. Some of these regulations may certainly be considered as compliance norms, while others may become the basis for issuing such norms.

'Strategies' (strategies) are acts which usually do not only contain compliance norms, but also other types of statements, including, for example, planning norms. They are documents based on generally defined economic objectives, containing long-term plans for proceeding, containing in their content provisions either directly defining a course of action appropriate from the point of view of the financial institution's interests, or even allowing for its universal interpretation. Contrary to the common understanding of the term, in practice corporate strategies are a useful tool for shaping the attitudes of employees, especially considering the declared need for the corporation to conduct its business in accordance with the adopted strategy. They are also an instrument applicable to external entities, in particular to customers and market regulators, who are offered a reading of the financial institution's operations in the spirit of the declared strategy. If, for example, a financial institution adopts a 'fair play strategy' document, the content of which declares a plan to reconstruct all the financial products on offer, irrespective of to which customers are being directed, in such a way that their design and sales method are clear and equally sensitive to the interests of both parties, then even if it is of a general nature, it certainly forms part of the financial institution's overall compliance system and is central to the financial institution.[136]

'Codes of conduct' are normative acts existing in financial institutions, but also in other international business organisations for a relatively long time, containing norms that are sets of rules of conduct the systematise the distributed norms of compliance within the same corporation, whose task is to group, prioritise and unify them regardless of the countries in which business is conducted, but also to introduce interpretative rules that facilitate uniform understanding of the resulting orders. To a large extent, apart from the normative function, the content of these documents is also used by corporations in order to convey to external entities, such as market regulators or the public opinion, a declaration of how to

---

[136] "Fair play strategies", "Treat customer fairly strategies" and other documents with similar names have recently been adopted by most international banks.

act in relations with customers and employees. The codes of conduct therefore impose, for example, an obligation on employees to immediately report cases of internal fraud (internal frauds) observed in the financial institution, specifying how this should be done, what guarantees are in place to protect employees making such reports, and what must happen as a result of the financial institution becoming aware of such information. Therefore, these are not only rules that define the obligations of employees, but also declarations of active reaction by financial institutions to any irregularities that may occur.

'Manuals', including global manuals to be used universally by all those working in a given corporation, regardless of jurisdiction and the role played by individual organisational units, are, contrary to the name, documents, also often in the form of normative acts, which, like the above-mentioned codes of conduct, perform unifying tasks. They are often referred to as functional manuals, i.e. a set of rules that imposing on employees the obligation to perform tasks related to their functions. Therefore, a separate regulation is created by functional manuals for employees responsible for risk management in the financial institution, other ones referring to employees of the finance department, while others refer to internal audit employees, etc. Due to the diversity of tasks and the specific nature of operations, manuals for legal and compliance departments are also separate. They contain not only a large part of their content of the calculation of very basic duties associated with functionally divided parts of financial institutions, but also because they are intended to be used as a daily 'handholding' assistance for employees.

'Instructions' are normative acts containing norms addressed to financial institution employees, which are rules of conduct in relation to strictly and usually narrowly defined matters. In particular, in the case of procedures issued in the form of instructions, they prescribe the performance of certain activities in connection with a specific financial institution's product or service. For example, the specific instructions for the sale of investment products specify how the information is to be provided to clients on the actual costs to the client and the nature of the risks associated with the purchase of certain types of products. Similarly, instructions may cover what kind of information should be received from customers if they express an interest in purchasing such products. The clarification of such obligations on the part of employees and the subsequent detailed handling of this information in the instructions is intended to avoid offering customers products that are not suitable for their needs and, consequently, to avoid the risk of offering customers products that are unnecessary and create unnecessary costs for them. This example illustrates the typical preventive role played by compliance norms, whose task is to create conditions in financial institutions to ensure the implementation of the publicly declared compliance approach.

'Recommendations' are normative acts containing in their content, apart from other types of statements, such as opt-outs, also compliance norms, formulated most often as a result of control activities, which require actions to be taken, as a result of which the state of compliance with applicable laws or supervisory regulations is restored. Recommendations are therefore issued retrospectively and most often refer to detected irregularities in the observance of obligations related to the proper performance of financial institutions activities or to perceived deficiencies in the proper interpretation of the content of the norms in force in the financial institution. At least part of the content of the audit recommendations is of a regulatory nature and contains statements of a directive nature.

'Guidelines' are normative acts containing guidelines for employees on how to deal with a specific group of issues, or even one problem. The purpose of guidelines is to ensure a legal, but also in the corporation's interests, uniform approach to the selected issue. For example, the employees of international financial institutions receive guidelines on the approach to personal data protection, the observance of which is intended to ensure a consistent understanding of the complications involved, but above all the same level of data protection in all the jurisdictions in which the financial institution operates. Therefore, the guidelines indicate a desirable model of conduct, determined as a result of the interpretation adopted by corporations and the recommended method of application of applicable laws or supervisory regulations.

'Rules' are normative acts containing intra-financial institutions norms regulating selected groups of issues which determine the correct course of action usually related to corporate governance structures separated within a given company (regulations of management boards, supervisory boards, directors' boards, regulations of risk management committees, etc.). The rules of procedure may also address specific groups of issues relevant to the internal functioning of these organisations. These are, for example, regulations relating to employee issues related to the performance of compliance tasks (regulations on bonuses for attitudes supporting compliance activities, etc.).

Apart from the examples of different types of acts containing different types of compliance norms due to their tasks, there are also simple attempts to classify these norms into primary, derived and secondary norms according to the criterion of the location of their sources. According to this division, the primary norms for compliance norms will be those derived from legal and deontological sources. Therefore, these will be constitutional norms, norms of international law, statutory, legal executive norms, but also ethical and customary norms.[137] Derivative norms will be, in such a division, norms relating to binding statutory, regulatory and contractual recommendations. Secondary norms, on the other hand, are orders of conduct whose task is to shape the way of doing business and to recommend activities that adjust to primary or derived norms.

It is a division resulting from the norms adopted for the application, whose shaping competence lies inside or outside the organisation. According to such a division, the compliance norms in force in the financial institution, but based directly on statutory provisions, are norms derived from primary sources occurring in environment of the financial institution. Theoretically, this division makes it possible to determine the criterion of importance, purpose limitation, functional and organisational cohesion, and allows for a formalised division of activities undertaken by the compliance function. According to this division, the following types of norms are included in the outer zone.[138]

a. Material norms—sources of universally binding law regulating the activity of financial institutions, aimed at the effect of activities undertaken by financial institutions, the measure of which is the confrontation of the legal situation of entities outside the financial institution with common legal norms and the existence of a direct link between the financial institution's behaviour and the results of such activities.

b. Formal norms—sources of universally binding law regulating the manner of performing financial institutions activities, relating to the obligations of financial institutions. Formal norms are

---

[137] See S. K. Mandal, *Ethics in Business and Corporate Governance*, New Delhi 2010, p. 62 et seq.

[138] Originally, this division for insurance corporations may also apply to banking compliance norms. See M. Olszak, *Bankowe normy ostrożnościowe*, Białystok 2011, p. 72.

directives answering the questions of how to act and to which market players is it directed. However, there is no need for third parties to be adversely affected by actions that are not in line with formal norms. An example of this could be a deviation from the prudential supervision rules or the policy on the protection of classified information.

c. Industry norms are all kinds of rules, recommendations or guidelines of codes of conduct and ethics, customs, codified rules and good practices. The negative effects of non-compliance with these norms may aggravate the situation of external parties directly or indirectly through negative assessments of financial institutions in terms of morals, good practices, etc., even when such actions do not cause any damage. These are activities that may have a negative impact on a financial institution in the long term, influencing their evaluation by the market and stakeholders such as customers, shareholders, employees, consumer and business organisations and the general public.

The external sphere is the source of norms, non-compliance with which can have the most pronounced, most acute and direct consequences for the institution concerned. This is due not only to the validity of these norms, but also to the possibility of a direct comparison of the effects of each financial institution's activities against the norms that all market players are obliged to comply with.

According to this classification, the division of the internal zone is that organisational and operational norms require the taking of actions in accordance with the statute of the institution, organisational regulations of individual bodies, principles of competence division, post-inspection recommendations issued by the audit, long-term development strategies of financial institutions, etc. Therefore, the compliance norms described in this chapter are those whose observance is intended to lead to compliance with the guidelines formulated by the corporation. Another type of norms that perform a similar function, however, are compliance norms, which can be defined as special ones, aimed at defining obligations relating to activities aimed at implementing recommendations to reduce the risk of financial institutions, concerning the non-disclosure of data, the protection of information, prudence, the prevention of crime in the organisation, contingency plans, an appropriate approach to the issue of debt collection, etc.

Regardless of which of the divisions may prove useful for the proper qualification of particular types of compliance norms, attempts to create a formal framework for their unification within multinational corporations are equally considered necessary for the efficient management of these corporations, and difficult due to both their different legal environment and their significant impact on their understanding in these countries due to their cultural legal differences.[139]

---

[139] These eight banking groups are: HSBC Holdings Plc., Citigroup Inc., ING Groep NV, Societe Generale SA, BNP Paribas SA, Barclays Plc., Royal Bank of Scotland Group Plc. and Credit Agricole SA.

CHAPTER 5

The Impact of Cultural Differences on Compliance Norms

1 Introduction

The aim of this chapter is to analyse the impact of cultural differences on the creation, application and interpretation of compliance norms, and on the practical ways to eliminate the difficulties in building uniform compliance normative systems for international financial institutions. The results of the research conducted in the writing of this book confirm the hypothesis that different cultural conditions have an impact not only on the manner of regulation within the corporation, but also on the assessment of legal risks, and even on the selection of issues covered by the compliance regulations. The aim of this chapter is also to present the results of detailed research that compared the differences and identified the similarities between differences in legal cultures within the financial institutions.

The first subchapter analyses the impact of cultural differences expressed in law and supervisory regulations on the way compliance issues are regulated in international financial institutions. These differences in turn influence the selection of both the manner and the subject matter of the issues to be regulated by the financial institutions. This section also presents trends concern the unifying of the rules for creating compliance norms. The analysis was carried out by examining the cultural specificities of selected jurisdictions.

Subchapter two focuses on the difficulties associated with the practicalities of uniformly applying compliance norms in different cultural conditions. In the third subchapter, difficulties with the interpretation of compliance norms resulting from cultural differences are analysed. First of all, it examines the different content of legal and supervisory norms and regulations issued in culturally different jurisdictions. Secondly, it identifies that the origins of these difficulties lie in the culturally rooted different understandings of the same concepts. Thirdly, it examines the issues related to the applicability of creative interpretations of compliance norms. By 'creative interpretation' it is meant there a need to clarify the content of norms using terms that include legal concepts, open, vague or requiring a restrictive or broadening interpretation.

The analyses presented in this chapter are the result of research carried out by comparing the methods of creating and applying compliance norms issued by global financial institutions operating simultaneously in many markets in different cultural conditions. The research covered compliance norms functioning in eight financial institutions groups, each of which operates on at least three continents.

2 The Influence of Cultural Legal Differences on the Methods of Regulation

Financial institutions operate internationally either through branches or in the form of subsidiaries of which they are the owners. The legal or regulatory requirements for financial institutions may differ from one legal order to another. This may depend on the type of business conducted by these financial institutions or on the legal form in which the activity is conducted in a given area. Obviously, financial institutions that have chosen to operate in a particular country are obliged to comply with the legal and regulatory requirements of that jurisdiction.[1]

There may also be special requirements for branches of foreign financial institutions in certain jurisdictions with respect to the creation of conditions ensuring that their activities take into account specific compliance requirements. In particular, local branches of international financial institutions shall ensure that compliance responsibilities in their area rest with individuals with knowledge of local compliance, legal and economic

---

[1] B. Maurer, International Political Economy as a Cultural Practice: The Metaphysics of Capital Mobility [in] R. W. Perry, B. Maurer [ed.] *Globalization Under Construction: Governmentality, Law and Identity*, Minneapolis 2003, p. 72 et seq.

conditions and that they are supervised by the head of compliance in cooperation with the other financial institutions business units responsible for managing the risks associated with their activities.

Despite the universal approach of regulators and lawmakers to issues related to the functioning of the financial sector, legal traditions and cultures still have a significant impact on both the way norms are developed, and how they are interpreted. The rapid economic development of recent years, which includes international contacts between civil law countries companies, including financial institutions, makes it possible to adapt to the best practices in world norms, either because of the requirements set by their owners, or because of the need to adapt to the expectations of employees and partners have to prove they implement these best practices.

One of such pattern, which allows for an attempt to reduce the risk to the business, strengthen its competitiveness and its market position, as well as facilitating contacts with other participants of global financial markets, which results in the improvement of the company's image and the trust of customers, is precisely the building of a strong compliance position. Following the observed international trends, new areas of compliance development are becoming more and more visible. The actions of compliance units that were so far addressed mainly to boards of directors and a small circle of top management of financial institutions, are increasingly also addressed to the owners—shareholders of these financial institutions. Such a change is a natural development of compliance, the aim of which is to ensure full compliance of the financial institution's operations with applicable laws and supervisory regulations. Increased transparency of financial institutions' operations in this respect is also an additional source of data useful for a more complete analysis of the environment in which the financial institution operates.

It is now accepted practice in financial institutions to consider that the compliance risk occurs on its own, alongside other subcategories of legal risks in financial institutions, in addition to the risk of incurring financial loss due to defective contractual provisions, the risk of litigation, the risk of misinterpretation, legislative risk and regulatory risk.

Compliance, as a relatively new area of analysis conducted as part of financial institutions activity, can be classified as a mechanism that supports the internal control systems in financial institutions. In accordance with such an approach, compliance analysis can be seen as consisting of verifying the non-conflicting and consistency of regulations resulting from internal corporate norms adopted and applied in financial institutions, with generally applicable regulations and norms created by financial institutions supervision.[2] Therefore, compliance in such an approach is primarily a verification of the degree of implementation of the universally applicable legal norms addressed to financial institutions in their internal regulations. The cultural determinant which influences the way compliance norms are being created, which like many other norms, is still to a large extent, going through a period of political and economic transformations. Although a significant period of time has passed since the beginning of the changes, which resulted in the adaptation of the existing legal order to the needs of complex economic relations, this task still remains one of the overriding determinants of the way regulations are created at various levels. As much as local specificities determine the overall corporate culture of any financial institution, they also impact the compliance function itself. They influence the corporate governance organisational structures, the shape of the internal policies and procedures, the business processes, and even the ways the company communicates with its clients. The variety of culturally determined compliance models is as rich as the number of financial institutions. Therefore, as thorough comparison of those differences lays outside of the scope of this book, this chapter's purpose is rather to point out the existence of this phenomenon than to propose the exact analysis of it.

Perhaps, for many reasons, the United States is the most important jurisdiction from the point of view of shaping norms of compliance, due to its global economic position. Respect for the law, and in principle all norms established on the basis of equity, is considered in the US legal culture as a superior, constitutive value in relation to any community. A notable feature of the American approach to compliance issues is also the interpreting of the content of norms from the entire legal environment, typical especially for common law, and so it is not limited only to the content of legal regulations applicable to financial institutions, but also derived from judicial trends, regulatory changes and the evolving legal doctrine.[3]

---

[2] On the regulatory role of banking supervision, see A. Jurkowska-Zeidler, Status prawny Komisji Nadzoru Bankowego jako organu administracji publicznej w świetle wyroku Trybunału Konstytucyjnego z dnia 15 czerwca 2011 roku, *Gdańskie Studia Prawnicze* XXVIII/2012, p. 144.

[3] E. M. Fogel, A. M. Geier, Strangers in the House, Rethinking Sarbanes-Oxley and the Independent Board of Directors, *Deleware Journal of Corporate Law* 32/2007, pp. 33–72.

How compliance is defined in practice in financial institutions in the American legal reality can be defined as a combination of the control function with advisory activity in the scope of defining and interpreting norms.[4] However, compliance tasks also include broadly understood preventive actions, anticipating the risk of possible threats resulting from the failure to adapt the business to the legal requirements of the environment. In addition, compliance also includes remedial actions in the event of detection of such irregularities. Compliance support is provided in various forms to financial institutions within the framework of which this function operates in the course of ongoing legal proceedings, as well as building structures within the organisation and, which is particularly important from the point of view of this research, the creation of internal norms, both material and procedural, the existence of which determines the achievement of compliance. Therefore, it is a whole range of issues affecting the legal liability and the image of the financial institution.

Observation of the practice of compliance units in financial institutions leads to the impression that internal procedural norms play a special role among the norms created by the compliance function in American conditions. The task of these procedures is to ensure an uninterrupted flow of information to the management of the institution on the conclusions resulting from the conducted compliance studies, monitoring the implementation of corrective actions in this area and providing support in making decisions on the allocation of sufficient resources to ensure the efficient operation of compliance mechanisms. The result of this is to enable knowledge-based decision-making. First of all, compliance obligations in financial institutions operating on the American market are currently closely related to legal risk management. In addition, they are performed by highly professional personnel as compliance units usually work with a high degree of autonomy, and the staff requirement is a thorough understanding of the functioning of the whole entity. Compliance specialists often have an in-depth knowledge not only of law, but also finance, process management, IT as well as other skills, especially communication, due to the need for frequent cooperation with other financial institution employees, regulators, media, customers, etc.

[4] R. Aggarwal, V. Azofra, F. Lopez, Differences in Governance Practices Between US and Foreign Firms: Measurement, Causes and Consequences, *Review of Financial Studies* 23(3)/2010, pp. 3131–3169.

Recently, it has become a practical necessity, especially in the American market, to regulate transparently, through compliance norms, such issues as the responsibility of individual persons for the tasks assigned to them, establishing efficient reporting processes, defining norms related to the circulation of documents, as well as, for example, establishing procedures for how to proceed in some cases of imposing penalties on financial institutions for failure to comply with the above obligations. All these tasks, which vary slightly from one US financial institution to another, are only intended to reduce the risk of illegal activity and, in the event of such a risk materialising, to ensure the appropriate procedures are followed in such an event. Equally important for the completeness of the normative characteristics of compliance activities in financial institutions in the United States is the emphasis on the importance in this process of the corporate values system, with which all internal norms of a given corporation should comply. This applies both to key documents such as internal policies, but also, for example, to the principle of professional ethics, to which both the management and all employees are obliged to adhere, who, depending on their place in the organisational structure of the company, are responsible for various elements of implementation of the compliance policy recommendations.

To a large extent nowadays in the United States, especially in large corporations, it has become established that the successful implementation of a compliance system requires that particular tasks be tailored to the needs of a particular organisation and to be undertaken in a timely manner. In many cases, the pressure brought by both regulators and the public opinion has made the management of financial institutions, their employees and their co-workers aware that an efficient compliance system is an indispensable element of modern business.[5]

The most common compliance model in US corporations is therefore to focus on ensuring the implementation of applicable laws, supervisory regulations, rules and norms, which are filled in with precisely formulated norms containing instructions and a description of the desired shape of internal processes, as well as to ensure their proper implementation and compliance in practice.[6] In addition to overall compliance

---

[5] On the requirements for compliance functions in financial institutions in the US cg. P. Moles, R. Parrino, D. S. Kidwel, *Corporate Finance*, Glasgow 2011, p. 26.

[6] S. Oded, *Corporate Compliance*, Cheltenham 2013, p. 143.

risk management within institutions, particular importance is attached in the United States to some of the identified areas to which compliance functions are associated. Such an area is, in particular, the prevention of money laundering, prevention of terrorist financing, avoidance of conflicts of interest, observance of the principles of customer service with the utmost care and respect for their interests. These areas also include the principles of ethical conduct in business, the protection of personal data, ensuring control over the quality of outsourced activities performed for the benefit of the financial institution and the principles defining the individual aspects of the protection of financial institutions secrecy, or the prevention of financial manipulation.

The most developed financial market, apart from the United States, which is worth noting due to the importance of compliance is the United Kingdom. The British legal culture, which has been shaped by many factors over the centuries including that of its imperial past, is evidenced particularly clearly in the special importance attached to the preservation of often very casuistically formulated detailed procedures.[7] It is precisely the need to build a uniform understanding of the interests of a British company by employees working for them from very different places that has traditionally resulted in the practical necessity to create precise regulations that minimise the risk of misunderstanding of the tasks set. This approach to norm-setting issues is distinctly different from the approach known from the practice of continental law, in which further norms are added to the existing system and contain clear references to it. The creation of internal normative acts in British financial institutions follows such a pattern and is based on a practical approach to the issues described, using examples and plain English.

A good example of the UK approach to compliance norms is the establishment of internal corporate grievance procedures. What is characteristic of this case is the creation of precise procedures for the clarification of facts and mediation aimed at removing any ambiguities, in order to avoid any misunderstanding which could lead, as a consequence, to legal disputes considered particularly harmful from the point of view of the reputation risk. Such procedures assume the primacy of the methods established within the corporation for establishing facts and deciding on

---

[7] I. Maher, Limitations on Community Regulation in the UK: Legal Culture and Multi-Level Governance, *Journal of European Public Policy* 3(4)/1996, p. 577 et seq.

the possible liability for the infringements of employee rights, but also good practices in the relation between the employer and the employee. Moreover, they describe in detail the different stages of the procedure in case studies of such complaints, and their basic assumption is that such complaint procedures should take precedence over the regulations in force in a given country.

Therefore, in situations where employees may complain about irregularities in relations with the employer, especially if, in the employer's opinion, such irregularities could lead to legal proceedings, it is expected that superiors, acting in accordance with the relevant norms of compliance, will conduct an intra-corporate employee complaint procedure.[8] The rationale for this assumption is not only the need to maintain uniformity of conduct throughout the corporation, but also the claim that such conduct ensures a more impartial and discreet handling of the case, which often turns out to be more advantageous for the employee but is always more advantageous for the corporation itself.[9]

Another norm-setting tradition is that of the financial corporations of France. This is not only because, unlike in British common law, the French legal environment is characterised by a strong interrelation of norms expressed in hierarchically structured legal acts of different levels, and the accompanying expectation that the internal norms governing the functioning of corporations should refer to this order.[10] Possible discrepancies between corporate norms and the letter and spirit of public law create situations of normative conflict, which should always be resolved in favour of the latter.[11] The extensive competences of financial

---

[8] D. W. Ewing, *Justice on the Job: Resolving Grievances in the Nonunion Workplace*, Harvard 1989, p. 312.

[9] L. B. Bingham, D. R. Chachere, Theoretical and Empirical Research on the Grievance Procedure and Arbitration: A Critical Review [in] A. E. Eaton, J. H. Keefe [ed.] *Employment Dispute Resolution and Worker Rights*, Champaign 1999, p. 137.

[10] This is not an isolated approach—the same is true for corporations operating in other jurisdictions of the continental cultural circle of Europe, such as the Netherlands and Germany. See E. Blankenburg, The Infrastructure of Legal Culture in Holland and West Germany, *Law and Society Review* 28(4)/1994, p. 790 et seq. Cf. also: J. L. Gibson, G. A. Caldeira, The Legal Cultures of Europe, *Law and Society Review* 30(1)/1997, p. 60.

[11] More on this subject: J. Bell, *French Legal Cultures*, Cambridge 2001, p. 50 et seq.; J.-L. Halperin, F. Audren, La culture juridique francaise: Entre mythes et realite, *Broche*, 28 November 2013 *passim*.

institutions and broader financial supervision, including control over the functioning of the compliance risk management system, have been simultaneously entrusted to several administrative bodies equipped, inter alia, with the prerogatives to apply the sanctions provided for by law.[12] In addition, the high level of unionisation of financial institutions in France, compared with the United States and the United Kingdom, is reflected in a more pro-worker approach to issues related to the imposition of possible additional obligations on employees.[13]

The norm-setting activities of corporations in France also take into account to a greater extent the social expectations resulting from the extra-corporate reality formulated by the institutionalised forms of associations of employees, customers and other stakeholder groups.[14]

The different way that regulations are formulated in varying financial institutions is the product not only of cultural legal differences, but also of the different ways in which compliance risk is assessed. These estimates are made primarily by using qualitative methods, in which risk management is based on continuous measurement. Such measurements assume that the risks associated with financial institutions operations, including compliance risk, as well as other operational risks, should be estimated using two basic parameters—the probability of occurrence and the weighting of effects. Analysis of the probability of occurrence of a possible undesirable future event is measured as a percentage based on expert predictions (best guess) and based on historical observations determined on the basis of recorded past events. The expected effects are assigned a weighting measured by the potential amount of losses that the financial institution could incur if an undesirable event were to occur.

Next, the key question for this type of analysis refers to the culturally determined differences of acceptable risk. If a high level of risk is

---

[12] Cf. L. Góral, *Zintegrowany model publicznoprawnych instytucji ochrony rynku bankowego we Francji i Polsce*, Warsaw 2011, p. 98, also E. Bouretz, J.-L. Emery, Autorite des marches financiers et Commission bancaire: Pouvoirs de sanctio et recours, *La Revue Banques* 702/2008, p. 50 et seq.; P.-E. Partsch, *Droi bancaire et financier europeen*, Paris 2009, p. 105.

[13] A. Garapon, French Legal Culture and the Shock of "Globalization" [in] D. Nelken, J. Feest [ed.] *Legal Culture, Diversity and Globalization*, Social and Legal Studies 4/1995, p. 493.

[14] See J. Pelisse, From Negotiation to Implementation: A Study of Reduction of Working Time in France, *Time and Society* 13(2/3)/2004, p. 226.

not acceptable, then mechanisms must be put in place to limit it, reducing the probability level and the seriousness of the consequences of the occurrence of this risk.[15] The type of risk mitigation measurement depends on the size of the risk appetite, i.e. the level of acceptable risk in the business.

Therefore, when analysing the impact of cultural differences on the way of creating compliance norms, one should pay attention not only to the traditions of legal cultures appropriate for different regions, but also to the readiness to take the risk of non-compliance with the normative environment, which is appropriate for each corporation separately, or to incur reputation losses. For international financial institutions operating in multiple markets at the same time, the geographical division of jurisdictions due to the different national legal systems and, in particular, the likelihood of an infringement of the applicable rules, becomes the key to making decisions that take into account the complexity of the issue.[16] Due to the fact, there are multiple stakeholders having impact on the shape of compliance in the financial institutions. That impact may be strongly differing depending on a jurisdiction. If assumed the main stakeholders fall into one of the five groups, namely: shareholders, clients, employees, regulators and activist NGO's, then the content of the compliance norms as well as the way they are created, implemented and interpreted can often be the result of their expectations. It is impossible to analyse this impact in detail in this text as there are thousands of varieties implemented in practice of the financial institution. However, for the purpose of illustration, in a very big simplification, it can be observed that the shareholders expectations differ in various jurisdiction towards the corporate governance structure; the clients' expectations are mostly reflected in the quality of the products' offer and clarity of communication; the employees' relations—in the management style and the CSR actions; the regulators'—in the stability and the market conduct; and the NGO's—in transparency and responsiveness.

Different legal traditions and cultures that influence the norm-setting process in general also influence the way compliance norms that are created in the following different ways:

---

[15] Cf. M. Faure, *Tort Law and Economics*, Cheltenham 2009, p. 444.
[16] J. H. Bracey, *Exploring Law and Culture*, Long Grove 2006, p. 121 et seq.

a. identifying the areas to be regulated;
b. considering whether existing regulations relating to the market in which a financial institution operates are complete or whether they require additional subsidiary regulation by corporate norms;
c. assessing how a regulation should be achieved (for example, how prescriptive compliance norms should be, what form they should take, what type of internal normative acts are most appropriate to regulate a given issue);
d. align compliance norms with how best to ensure that these norms are applied (for example, how they should be promulgated, published, informed, and how others should be educated about their content, but also, for example, how and if so, whether or not to sanction their application should be regulated);
e. determine how norms should be interpreted and how any differences in their meaning and application remedied (for example, which interpretative principles are most appropriate to interpret their content as intended by their respective corporations.[17] This will be discussed further below, where it will be argued that in the case of corporate compliance norms, the principles of system interpretation are more important than linguistic interpretation, and about whether and to what extent authentic interpretations are used).

Observations concerning the influence of cultural legal differences on the way compliance norms are created in the conditions of international corporations operating on many markets at the same time relate indirectly to the issues of law defragmentation in intercultural conditions, conclusions on reflexive law and responsive law, as well as to the concept of fuzzy norms. In a special way, the issue of creating compliance norms so as to ensure their effective application in the case of international structures is connected with the issue of using soft law for this purpose, and how it is influenced by intercultural conditions.[18] For this purpose,

---

[17] See R. Michaels, J. Pauwelyn, Conflict of Norms or Conflict of Laws? Different Techniques in the Fragmentation of International Law [in] T. Broude, Y. Shany [ed.] *Multi-Sourced Equivalent Norms in International Law*, Oxford 2011, p. 40.

[18] See L. Benton, *Law and Colonial Cultures*, Cambridge: Cambridge University Press 2002, p. 32 et seq.

the aforementioned codes of ethics, various international and global norms, etc., are created within the corporation.[19] On the one hand, they take into account the cultural specificity of individual areas, but on the other hand, they contribute to building something that is sometimes referred to using the misused concept of 'corporate culture'. The influence of legal cultures is also important when it is necessary to mitigate the inevitable collisions with local regulations, which consist on the one hand in the need to unify the way in which these corporations operate in different markets for their own interests, but on the other hand meet the demands expressed by their leading regulators.[20]

Different legal traditions and cultures may relate to a completely different understanding of the following issues:

a. corporate governance;
b. the approach to the need to ensure that the financial institution operates in a transparent and anti-corruption manner;
c. ensuring an efficient flow of information on customers and employees;
d. attitudes towards corporate social responsibility.[21]

An analysis of cultural differences in relation to the importance they have for the creation of corporate compliance norms is largely based on the adoption of generalisations. Generalisations in the analysis of cultural differences, not only in relation to the analysis of legal norms, despite their obvious drawbacks, facilitate this analysis and perform three different functions indicated below.

Firstly, of all, they may constitute a reference point for the assumptions and interpretations adopted, as corruption activities will be

---

[19] E. J. Rudolph, *The Board Must Take the Lead in Establishing a Corporate Culture of Ethics and Compliance*, 1 July 2014, www.Corporatecomplianceinsights.com (download 14 March 2019).

[20] Difficulties in harmonizing internal corporate norms are also due to many other reasons. See e.g. G. Bierbrauer, *Toward an Understanding of Legal Culture: Variations in Individualism and Collectivism*, Law and Society Review 2(2)/1994, pp. 243–264.

[21] Interestingly, these issues are currently of interest to shareholders, but also to the media and other entities external to companies, to the extent that banking institutions include information about them in their annual reports alongside financial reports.

understood differently in the Nordic countries of Europe, and differently in other countries.[22]

Secondly, they make it easier to anticipate certain behaviour, and therefore help to formulate corporate norms properly and in accordance with their purpose, especially in the interpretation and application of these norms.

Thirdly, they also help to build self-awareness both among those professionally appointed to apply these norms (in this case it refers to financial institution management boards, lawyers, compliance staff), but in fact also among all other addressees of these norms.[23]

The impact of cultural legal differences on individual compliance tasks concerns many areas regulated by internal corporate norms, including compliance meta-norms regulating the issues of compliance risk assessment and norms created within financial institutions relating to policies and procedures. Compliance risk assessment is usually carried out in a formalised form in corporations. It is discussed by various levels of committees, described in their analyses, subjected to stress tests, properly measured, recorded in compliance reports, etc. This is because all elements that may have an impact on the size, likelihood of occurrence or impact on a financial institution's financial performance, which involve a significant compliance risk, must be recorded and measured.

Moreover, compliance risk, as one of the aspects of operational risk, should be assessed from a business point of view, according to the operational risk assessment methodology adopted by the corporation. The documentation of the operational risk assessment may often contain insufficient information to apply the risk analysis of non-compliance management. For this reason, a separate methodology for assessing the risk of non-compliance is usually drawn up. At the same time, on the other hand, it is the responsibility of compliance services to ensure that the assessment of non-compliance risk is consistent with the relevant elements of assessment, control and regular monitoring of operational risk.

---

[22] Comments on the meaning of certain concepts rooted in European legal culture, see A. Sulikowski, Z zagadnień teorii i filozofii prawa. W poszukiwaniu podstaw prawa, *Acta Universitatis Wratislaviensis* 2878/2006, p. 235 et seq.

[23] See R. Cotterell, The Concept of Legal Culture [in] D. Nelken [ed.] *Comparing Legal Cultures*, Brookfield 1997, p. 15.

Ensuring that compliance norms are harmonised despite differences involves the establishing of consistent principles for the use of tools such as the compliance reports mentioned above. These principles presuppose that it is necessary to identify all locally applicable rules which may create obstacles and therefore create a significant risk of non-compliance.[24] They are then recorded in these compliance reports or in other similar documents. In such situations, it is the duty of compliance staff to ensure that the documents for the types of financial institutions they handle are consistent with the current state of affairs. These updated documents are then submitted to the appropriate global compliance structures, which, thanks to the collection of such aggregate information, are able to make a comprehensive assessment as to whether or not the entire financial institutions group operates under compliance conditions. These documents shall also contain information allowing the internal audit to carry out a control including an assessment of significant compliance risks.

Creating and updating these documents, including compliance reports, is an important part of employees' compliance responsibilities, although these responsibilities extend beyond that.[25] This involves supporting individual business lines in financial institutions in matters relating to compliance with laws and regulations, taking into account local circumstances (including cultural, differences and conditions), which is done through the direct involvement in the development of compliance norms, control activities, monitoring, reporting, etc.[26]

In practice, compliance officers are responsible for assessing the compliance risk in relation to the financial institutions area supported by them, assigned to them, with specific business and cultural characteristics. As part of this assessment, all risks whose management has been entrusted to compliance services are identified, and assessed in order to plan appropriate measures to prevent or mitigate their occurrence.

---

[24] Apart from the subject of this study, there are other, existing in practice, supra-regional factors influencing the unification of bank operations in different jurisdictions. One such factor is the supervisory role of the European Central Bank in relation to the financial stability of banks operating in the European Union. See more on this subject M. Fedorowicz, Op. cit., p. 379 et seq.

[25] Cf. T. M. J. Moellers, Sources of Law in the European Securities Regulation—Effective Regulation, Soft Law and Legal Taxonomy from Lamfalussy to de Larosiere, *European Business Organisation Law Review* 3(11)/2010, p. 379.

[26] P. R. Wood, op.cit., p. 97.

In line with the procedures established at financial institutions, such compliance risk assessments are documented and regularly reviewed to ensure that the risks identified are complete and their rating remains valid.

In practice, risk assessment is reviewed every time there is a need to do so, e.g. in the case of poor results of external audits, negative results of compliance reviews, unfavourable assessments resulting from internal audit reports, or external audit firms. These assessments are detailed enough to identify areas requiring a specific approach without difficulty and to address issues that require particular attention. An example is compliance with the provisions on money laundering prevention.

Importantly, the centre of these uniformity processes is the introduction of regularity despite the differences that exist. The point is that such actions should not be one-off. There are areas which, either because of the economic interest of the financial institutions or because of the recommendations of the regulators, require special care and a structured approach. These include customer service diligence, with special attention being paid to high-risk customers (including politically exposed financial institution customers, politically exposed persons (PEPs) and monitoring of suspicious transactions.

Within international financial institutions groups, it is assumed that each financial institution's activity should be described in detail in manuals and procedures in order to ensure effective management of compliance risk despite the differences in legal cultures in the different markets. The responsibility for the application of compliance norms introduced by corporations and for the practical management of instructions, procedures and other forms of compliance norms rests with the management of financial institutions. In practice, this means both ensuring that they are adhered to and that these norms are easily accessible by employees and that employees are properly trained in their content and are aware of the requirements they face. On the other hand, it is the responsibility of local compliance staff who know the cultural and market specificity of a given area to provide the financial institution management with appropriate control mechanisms in order to ensure that these norms are maintained in compliance with the applicable regulations. Here, too, appropriate verification takes place periodically, for example in the framework of regular examinations, monitoring or reviews.

The conduct of business and compliance requirements shall, as far as possible, be systemically integrated into coherent sets of procedures that can be applied in day-to-day work.[27] Although the concept of a single set of procedures is a recommended solution, due to practical conditions, decisions are also made which recommend the creation of separate procedures in relation to individual compliance issues. Compliance employees are also obliged to ensure that the management boards of financial institutions are informed on time about the necessary updates of compliance norms, both in connection with changes in the operations of financial institutions and in legal regulations constituting the legislative environment of their operations.

3 Difficulties in the Application of Compliance Norms Due to Cultural Differences

The complexity in analysing compliance norms in multinational companies, including financial institutions, also lies in the fact that cultural differences play a special role not only in their creation, but also in the approach to the application of these norms. The same concepts may have completely different meanings in different legal cultures, as in different cultures in general. It is therefore equally important to use the right concepts, taking into account the cultural context when applying them.[28] It is equally important to use guidelines for the application of these norms in order to partially eliminate cultural differences for 'common sense' principles.[29] This term, although apparently not a legal term, is widely used in the practice of interpreting norms created within international corporations.[30] The application of uniform rules based on a common understanding of certain concepts for financial institutions,

---

[27] There are also exceptions, which include areas where certain compliance procedures are not part of everyday activities, such as private transactions in securities by bank employees.

[28] On the cultural differences in understanding of the changes in law due to the frequent withdrawal of countries from their traditional role and the fact that global business organizations take over the field in this respect, see A. C. Aman, *The Democracy Deficit: Taming Globalization Through Law Reform*, New York 2004, p. 139 et seq.

[29] See J. Winczorek, Systems Theory and Puzzles of Legal Culture, *Archiwum Filozofii Prawa i Filozofii Społecznej* 1(4)/2012, p. 106.

[30] In the interpretative practice of corporate standards containing recommendations for specific actions, the term "common sense test" is even used to determine the assessment to which such recommendations should be subjected in a given legal environment.

irrespective of cultural differences, proves to be the simplest but helpful interpretative guide.

An illustration of such rules is the well-known 'too - to handle' warnings (too hot to handle, too good to be true, etc.), which are addressed to employees. However, as is anecdotal, such an interpretation rule has not become a pejorative term for financial institutions too big to fail, which is making a huge career in the press. The condition for their effectiveness, however, is the existence of proper control mechanisms also regulated by the compliance norms.[31] In this section there are presented the difficulties in applying the norms of compliance due to cultural differences are presented their individual types, as well as the ways to norm their application regardless of cultural differences.

When describing the impact of legal cultures on the application of compliance norms in practice, it is worth looking at the difficulties that were discussed above concerning those differences which should be taken into account when formulating these norms.[32] Seven types of issues are listed below.

Compliance recommendations relate also to corporate governance, including the organisational structure within the individual companies within the group. Often in companies operating in common law jurisdictions there is one board of directors, as the general body of a financial institution, where the members may have managerial powers or not. They therefore perform a variety of functions, including sitting on the committees attached to these Boards. There are also differences in the understanding of the responsibilities of persons performing similar functions within different local structures in relation to regional and regional in relation to global ones.

A clear example illustrating the difficulties in uniform application of the same compliance norms depending on cultural conditions is the whole area related to the prevention of corruption. Paid protection, i.e. the acceptance of unauthorised benefits in exchange for the performance

---

[31] See S. Schelo, *Bank Failing or Likely to Fail. Restoring Confidence. The Changing European Banking Landscape*, London 2014, p. 23.

[32] A separate but indirectly related issue outside the scope of this study is the consideration of the different functions that the law performs depending on the cultural legal traditions. In particular on the communication function, including the function of programming and coding social attitudes through legal rules in the examined cultural conditions. See N. Luhmann, *Law as a Social System*, Oxford 2004, p. 173 et seq.

of certain services or their performance in a specific manner in accordance with the wishes of the provider of such benefits, can be considered a criminal act even if none of the parties is a public entity. This is always the case when it is to the detriment of other entities, including to the detriment of shareholders or other market participants. However, the understanding of the same concepts may be completely different in this case, so it is important to make clear recommendations as to what benefits cannot be accepted in a specific situation, and what benefits can and should be accepted.

Similarly, compliance norms regulating the transfer of information between entities belonging to the same capital group to which a given financial institution belongs are understood and applied in a different way within the corporation. Especially if they are entities or at least the representatives of these entities sitting on bodies at a higher decision-making level in the organisational structure. These issues also concern the provision of customer information, which is a particularly sensitive issue for financial institutions, as well as the modalities of cooperation with these customers.[33]

Another area in which the application of intra-corporate norms may vary in the same financial institutions group from place to place due to cultural legal differences is the relation with investors, the media, suppliers and generally with third parties. An example of this is the media, who are usually regarded as important public partners, deserving reliable and complete information on the issues important to the institution. This is the case in markets where democratic institutions based on the rule of law are firmly established. However, this is not the case in countries whose political system is characterised by a democratic deficit and the transparent conveying of information to the public is not a generally accepted norm.

As in the case of media relations, often the attitude towards market regulators also depends on the maturity of democratic institutions in a given country, and on whether there is a tradition of open cooperation between private sector companies and public administration. In mature jurisdictions, these relations are usually partnership-based, consultative, or even allow lobbying activities conducted in accordance with the applicable

---

[33] On cultural differences in the understanding of what is and may not be lawful, see e.g. S. S. Silbey, Legal Culture and Cultures of Legality [in] J. R. Hall, L. Grindstaff, M. Ch. Lo [ed.] *Handbook of Cultural Sociology*, London and New York 2010, p. 472.

laws. In the developing countries, meanwhile, these relations are petty and not being subject of the jointly established a regulatory reality.

A very different element, depending on the tradition and legal maturity of individual jurisdictions, is the approach to the norms contained in regulations shaping the relations between employees and employers. In modern managed global corporations, there is a tendency to broaden the interpretation of norms relating to guarantees of workers' rights, and even to involve workers in the consultation process on issues related to the further development of the company. At the same time, many other corporations, including those operating in international markets, continue to experience outrageous practices of over-exploitation of workers, enforcing absolute obedience, depriving them of their rights, or even restricting their freedom by, for example, taking passports away.[34] And all of this is allegedly in accordance with the provisions of the internal norms in force in these corporations.[35]

Cultural differences can also be reflected in the application of a number of other recommendations resulting from corporate compliance norms. An example of this is the attitude to norms defining recommendations relating to corporate social responsibility (CSR) tasks, and how these norms shape the impact that such activities have on the company's image.[36] Such normative regulations defining the activities of financial institutions in this area constitute a model of reference for desired behaviours to the recommended internalisation of values in the addressees of norms and building acceptance of normative obligations created by the financial institution, whose actions are considered worthy of imitation.[37]

---

[34] Taking away passports from employees as a guarantee of loyalty is still common practice in some developing countries-based service centers of financial institutions and other international corporations.

[35] On the limitation of labour and wider human rights by corporations engaged in global trade, see M. B. Likosky, *The Silicon Empire. Law, Culture and Commerce*, London 2005, p. 185 et seq.

[36] S. Shanahan, S. Khagram, Dynamics of Corporate Responsibility [in] G. S. Drori, J. W. Meyer, H. Hwang [ed.] *Globalization and Organization: World Society and Organizational Change*, Oxford 2006, p. 196 et seq.

[37] On increasing corporate social responsibility in the context of the role of corporations as 'global private authorities' shaping, by means of normative instruments, the general pro-social attitudes as expected by them, see R. Shamir, Corporate Social Responsibility [in] B. de Sousa Santos, C. A. Rodriguez-Garavito [ed.] *Law and Globalization from Below*, Cambridge 2005, p. 92.

Therefore, despite the different cultural sources from which they may originate, attitudes are promoted among employees, which contribute to building a uniformly positive image of a financial institution which conducts such a socially responsible activity.[38]

The complexities associated with the interpretation of norms in multicultural corporations have also been recognised by the Basel Committee with regard to financial institutions that choose to operate in many countries with different legal systems. It points out that, in any event, there should be procedures to identify and assess the likelihood of the occurrence of compliance risks, including, in particular, the risk to the reputation of the financial institution as a result of non-compliance with, or equally frequent misinterpretation of, these norms. This may be the case if the financial institution offers such products or decides to do business in some of those areas which would not be allowed in the financial institution's home country. In spite of this, financial institutions groups seeking to harmonise their offers sometimes decide to introduce such offers on markets where this is not acceptable. Uniformity of the offer is sometimes ensured by the creation of interpretations of the compliance norms from which the possibility of carrying out such activities arises. In general, such practices occur when competence to interpret the content of compliance norms is transferred from the local to the regional or higher level. However, the interpretation of compliance norms should be treated as the basic area of compliance risk management within the financial institution.

In general, only a part of strictly defined, specific compliance tasks, which, moreover, usually only cover activities indirectly related to financial institutions activity, may be outsourced, i.e. in the situation described above, to a supra-local level. In such cases, however, entities performing these activities on behalf of the financial institution should be subject to appropriate supervision by local compliance services. Therefore, all responsibility for maintaining full compliance, including avoiding misunderstandings about the interpretation of compliance norms at the financial institution, remains with the central axis of the financial institution's management in a multicultural environment.

---

[38] About the role of compliance in building internal cohesion of companies through employee involvement in CSR activities, see R. Hurley, X. Gong, A. Waqar, Understanding the Loss of Trust in Large Banks, *International Journal of Bank Marketing* 32(5)/2014, p. 350.

The authorities of financial institutions operating in many countries, in order to ensure uniform application of compliance norms, create procedures aimed at ensuring that persons responsible for the compliance area are appointed to the positions in the financial institutions. Those persons in the financial institutions structure should be able to report directly to management on any instances of doubt as to the misapplication of these norms. Below are the eight situations that most frequently require such a consultation.

a. The planned introduction of new products or services or changes to the previously described appetite for risk of a given financial institution or a proposed change in its target customer base.
b. Planned changes in the corporate or management structure of a given financial institution.
c. The planned implementation of a new or amended legal or regulatory requirements.
d. Planned other changes, which may have an indirect impact on the interpretation of compliance norms, such as outsourcing, when third parties are to perform activities related to the financial institution's operations for the benefit of the financial institution.
e. Emerging risk of regulatory breaches or situations where regulatory authorities have negatively assessed a specific type of financial institution activity.
f. Internal or external audit reports shall indicate any regulatory problems arising in connection with the financial institution's activities.
g. There is an increased number of customer complaints related to the liquidation of certain products or activities by a financial institution, which may indicate non-compliance with certain laws or intra-corporate norms by employees.
h. The need for corrective actions or issues related to reputation risk resulting from supervisory recommendations or directly from legal regulations.

The compliance officers are required to draw up annual plans and reports on the assessment of the risk of non-compliance usually refer in these reports to issues related to the observed application of compliance norms. These annual plans include the tasks proposed for the monitoring and control of compliance norms, together with proposed guidelines and procedures, and take into account the planned training session for all financial institution employees in the field of these norms. The content of these reports and plans is usually agreed with financial institution management. In practice, compliance tasks also include the provision of sufficient resources, including budgetary, human, technological and training resources, necessary to carry out the tasks provided for in the action plans to ensure the uniform application of compliance norms.

As indicated above, it is a complex task under different legal traditions and cultures. The internal procedures relating to the principles of compliance, do not only require the submission of periodic reports on the implementation of the plans. These plans should also include information on the division of responsibilities to ensure the uniform application of the compliance norms, as expressed in the description of the responsibilities of the management and other employees to whom responsibilities related to these issues have been delegated.[39]

4 Differences in the Interpretation of Compliance Norms

For a corporation operating simultaneously in many markets, when it is faced with the conflicting laws from different jurisdictions, it is particularly interesting in selecting the rules of interpretation that allow it to determine their content, which should be applied in the specifically analysed situation. If an irreconcilable contradiction arises from the content of these norms, and it is not possible to establish a common non-contradictory content for these norms, then a decision needs to be made which of these norms should be complied with.[40] In other words, which of these norms prevails and is applied in the practice of corporate activity? This section presents examples of the complications resulting from cultural conflicts between laws and supervisory regulations, and

---

[39] Quote from the internal procedure for ensuring the uniform application of compliance norms in one of the international financial institutions: "The role of compliance is to support management in fulfilling the above responsibilities. This involves pro-active support in identifying, assessing and evaluating risks including compliance risk, monitoring, reporting and certification, as well as promoting a corporate culture based on compliance with uniformly understood laws and optimising relations with regulators."

[40] On the role of culture creating power of decisions on the validity of the law, see B. Maurer, The Cultural Power of Law? Conjunctive Reading, *Law and Society Review* 38/2004, p. 843 et seq.

also presents the examples of complications resulting from the different interpretations of the same concepts. It further discusses the issue of the application of a creative interpretation to cases where there are discrepancies between the meanings interpreted from norms, i.e. the different understanding of which can be derived from the cultural differences that occur in multinational financial institutions corporations.

Multinational corporations operating simultaneously in numerous jurisdictions are confronted with conflicts between laws and supervisory regulations in various configurations.[41] The most typical is one in which, from the point of view of the management of the entire capital group, it is desirable to introduce internal norms or to order the application of existing norms which are contrary to the legal norms in force in one or more jurisdictions in which the activities of the corporation are carried out. As a result, lawyers, practitioners and persons responsible for the compliance area, whose task is to ensure that the corporation remains in compliance with the entire normative order, carry out a number of actions aimed at removing the collisions. In such a situation, it is a matter of resolving the above-mentioned conflict of laws in such a way that the content of the various norms can be read through the instruments available for interpretation rules, which would make it possible to remove these conflicts of interest.

In this context, we contend that it is worthwhile to look at this difficulty from the point of view of the choice of interpretative rules, or more precisely their relevance. Despite the different content of the conflicting norms, by referring to the available rules of interpretation, it is possible to determine such uniform content that would allow the corporation to remain in compliance with the normative order in force in a given area, and at the same time meet the expectations of the corporate authorities.

On the other hand, however, not all interpretative rules can equally apply in such situations. Unlike when the content of a norm is simply not unambiguous and other references must be made in order to derive a meaning free of ambiguity, in the case of collisions between several norms, especially those belonging to different orders, not all of these references may prove equally appropriate.

---

[41] Large multinational corporations, adapting their activities to local conditions, change these conditions at the same time, being at the same time considered as a more important influence agents on the shape of what is currently the global economic turnover than politicians or structures of international political organizations. See A. Mickleth, A. Wooldridoe, *The Company: A Short History of a Revolutionary Idea*, Washington 2005, p. 159 et seq.

Reflecting on the tasks of compliance services, which are co-responsible for managing one of the main risks of doing business in financial institutions corporations, it should be pointed out that its key role, but also a particularly complex challenge, manifests itself in ensuring the compliance of these corporations with all the norms applicable to them, including in such a situation in which there is a conflict between the norms in force simultaneously. Then, the decision on how to read the content of these norms, or to reject the application of certain norms, in a situation of a collision which cannot be otherwise removed, acquires decisive importance for the direction of the corporation's operations.

Once again, the issue of the complexity of these tasks arises because of the fact that, by definition, financial institutions conduct complex activities within different jurisdictions, and therefore under different understandings of the content of the same, the same or similar norms. These unavoidable collisions may result not only from differences between the norms in force in different jurisdictions, compliance with which is the assumption of the business activity conducted by financial institutions corporations. These conflicts can also, and in practice often do so, result from differences in the way these norms are interpreted, and more specifically from a different understanding of the concepts to which the norms refer.[42] Therefore, the role of selecting the appropriate rules for interpreting these concepts is important in the compliance activity in financial institutions. The very selection of interpretative rules, in view of the multitude of legal systems in which the corporation operates, is based on the criteria set by corporations, the most important of which is the criterion of practical utility. The aim is to adopt the rules for interpreting the norms according to which potential contradictions or gaps originating in cultural differences will be eliminated, and thus this type of interpretation will result in the cohesion of the normative framework of corporations' operations. Therefore, it is worthwhile looking at the most frequently used rules of interpretation, precisely because of the utility criterion described here in relation to financial institutions operating in different legal cultures.[43]

---

[42] On the differences in interpretation of similar legal norms in various jurisdictions, see W. Twining, Social Science and Diffusion of Law, *Journal of Society and Law* 32(2)/2005, p. 210 et seq.

[43] On the subject of contradictions in practice of interpretation of norms by social institutions, including commercial ones due to cultural differences, see P. Ewick, The Structure of Legality: The Cultural Contradictions of Social Institutions [in] R. A. Kagan, M. Krygier, K. Wiston [ed.] *Legality and Community*, Berkeley 2002, pp. 149–155.

The use of grammatical rules, based on the analysis of the content of a norm resulting from the linguistic meaning of normative expression, is relatively limited. The difficulty with grammatical rules of interpretation is due both to the multitude of languages in which norms can be expressed, and the fact that the meaning of expressions used in norms is often linked to their conventional content, which in turn is closely related to the cultural context, given by the norm-making activities in the specific conditions of a given jurisdiction. In addition, this conventional meaning may be compounded by difficulties arising from the multiplicity of languages themselves. Problems in properly understanding the meaning of the expressions that make up the content of the norm stems from the fact that it is often impossible to attribute the same meaning to seemingly the same concepts because the assumption of the identity of expressions is burdened with an error resulting from the assumption that translation means faithful rendering of the whole content contained in the denominated concept.[44] However, that is not the case as complications that arise from translation manifest themselves not only in the case of complex concepts, related to definitions developed by doctrine and jurisprudence practice (what is understood as a 'bribe' in some countries may not mean exactly the same in the others), but even in the understanding of modal rulers, such as 'should', 'must', 'has an obligation', 'is obliged', etc., the precise translation of which requires reference to the legal cultural context.[45]

Another possible solution to the issue is to examine the functional interpretation rules that apply to norms. Functional rules may be applied in the interpretation of norms of divergent meaning coming from different legal systems, however, the difficulty in this case is that in order to be able to interpret correctly using these rules, it is necessary to know in the first place the function that these norms should serve. This difficulty stems from the fact that the aims for which the conflicting norms in question were created may be either difficult to read or unclear and, although legible, may remain in a similar contradiction to the norms themselves, the resolution of which by reading these original functions was supposed to be helpful. It is not uncommon for a situation in which, in an attempt to remove a contradiction arising from the reading of

---

[44] More on the linguistic aspect of the law, see J. Jabłońska-Bonca, *Wprowadzenie do Prawa. Introduction to Law*, Warsaw 2012, p. 28.

[45] Cf. L. Rosen, *Law as Culture*, Princeton 2006, p. 76.

norms, it appears that the functions to be fulfilled by those norms are quite different and, in this context, recourse to functional rules does not help to establish effectively a uniform content for those norms.

The same is true for purpose-specific rules, the application of which in theory can and should be the most appropriate. In such a case it is necessary to clearly communicate the goal, i.e. the desired effect to be achieved by the individual financial institutions belonging to the corporation. Such communication is intended to bring about a situation which removes contradictions and introduces a unified interpretation of the same rule in different jurisdictions. However, the systemic interpretation rules are less applicable. The system itself, as a point of reference for their interpretation, treats them differently, in such a way that it would be the whole set of all internal and external rules applicable in all the jurisdictions in which a financial institution operates and applicable to that financial institution.

In conditions where there is a divergence in the understanding of norms resulting from the cultural complications described here, and from the highly volatile financial institutions legal environment, interpretations made in order to remove inconsistencies are often of a creative nature. When analysing such an effect, it is worth referring to the phenomenon of creative interpretation described in the literature, which is carried out on the basis of national law. In relation to the theory of constitutive interpretation applied by courts, there are four situations in which the interpretation of courts may be of a creative nature. These are: the interpretation of legal terms, the interpretation of open notions, expansive and restrictive interpretation and the interpretation of vague, unclear or other notions whose meaning gives rise to justified doubts.[46] In the case of resolving conflicts of law in the terms of a corporation operating in several jurisdictions at the same time, although this is not the case, similar functions can be seen in the course of their interpretation. In this case, a creative interpretation may be used precisely when the interpretation concerns norms that come from culturally different legal systems. The interpretation of the meaning of conflicting norms in this case is made from the point of view of the economic interest derived from the overall business of the financial institution concerned.

---

[46] See L. Morawski, *Główne problemy...*, p. 271.

The complex normative reality in which the corporation operates requires first of all that the financial institution itself, i.e. in practice the compliance services responsible for compliance, undertake the task of defining an appropriate, uniform understanding of the content resulting from various, potentially conflicting norms, already at the level of understanding legal terms. It is not just a matter of particularly complicated terms, it also applies to very common terms. In the case of norms stemming from different legal, regulatory and jurisprudential cultures, reference is made to terms as often used, such as the term 'norm' or 'norm': 'data protection', 'financial institutions secrecy', 'third party', 'action against an employer's decision' or even as obvious as it would seem: 'supervisory board' or 'law'. (sic!), require an interpretative effort to remove the collision situation.

In this context, a relatively difficult challenge is to make interpretations, open concepts, i.e. those whose meaning is not fully defined and should be derived from the wider current normative legal context, but also from the social, axiological, etc.[47] In view of the fact that this context may differ significantly in each jurisdiction in which a corporation operates, it may therefore be particularly difficult to read open concepts. In this case, a narrowing interpretation, and especially its creative and constitutive character, proves helpful. Taking into account the economic interest of a given corporation and matching it with the scope of terms used in the norms, it is possible to achieve a significantly alignment content of norms formulated in different legal systems.

Norms governing the activities of financial institutions in international conditions are not a ready-made, clearly defined and consistent set of concepts that define the sphere of entities by legislators, as presented by Austin in relation to the law in general, or recognised by them through a test of origin, as defined in Hart's concept as a recognition rule. These norms are a dynamically changing fact of interpretation, in the face of which the search for some uniform established semantics does not make sense. In such an interpretative approach, the task of

---

[47] On the role of social norms referred to in communication between regulators and regulated entities, including how useful they are in enhancing the effectiveness of communication and how much reference to these norms facilitates the interpretation of the content of legal norms today, see S. Martin, 98% of HBR Readers Love This Article. Businesses Are Just Beginning to Understand the Power of Social Norms, *Harvard Business Review* October 2012, p. 23.

compliance practitioners is to search for the most appropriate, removing contradictions, understanding norms and values in the context of cultural conditions.[48] This addition of cultural contexts in the interpretation of different and changing norms over time can be compared to the Dworkins' comparison of the constitution of law as a joint novel-building through generations of authors who have added subsequent chapters to the text.[49]

---

[48] It is precisely the establishment of this cultural context that becomes crucial in the process of every reading of legal norms, especially in the confrontation of these norms with the social tasks they perform. T.W. Aldorno writes that the inclusion of the objective spirit of the epoch in the concept of culture from the very beginning points to an administrative point of view which, from the perspective of the people above the hierarchy, has the task of collecting, dividing, evaluating and organizing. T. W. Aldorno, Culture and Administration [in] J. M. Bernstein [ed.] *The Culture Industry: Selected Essays on Mass Culture by Theodor W. Aldorno*, London 1991, p. 93.

[49] M. Zirk-Sadowski, *Wprowadzenie...*, p. 170 et seq.

CHAPTER 6

Organising Postulates—A Proposal for a Model Approach

1 Introduction

The sixth chapter of the book is based on detailed research, conducted at leading international financial institutions. This order does not reflect the hierarchy of norms existing in any of these institutions. However, it is the result of analyses and collection of conclusions drawn from them, taking into account the mutual relations between compliance norms. These relations result from the dependencies described in this chapter concerning in particular: the differences in the classification of individual norms carried out on the basis of the criteria is set out in subchapter 1, while the different directive power of individual types of norms and their interdependence of the subject matter is analysed in subchapter 2. The issue presented in the first subchapter concerns the possibility of establishing a mutual relation between compliance norms from a static perspective, and thus due to their position in the hierarchy of norms. The second subchapter focuses on the interdependence of these norms with regard to the area of regulation, so it concerns the mutual relation of these norms from a dynamic perspective.

The classifications and mutual relations between compliance norms presented in this part of the book are a generalisation that is proposed on the basis of good practices that have been developed by leading financial institutions. The starting point of the proposed order is the definition of the necessary minimum regulatory content constituting *iunctim* between the different types of norms irrespective of the legal, regulatory, economic and cultural conditions in which they are created. The third subchapter, which is a summary of the research conducted for this book, refers to the most important aspects of the proposal to apply these legislative techniques, which allows for the flexible adaptation of the process of creating compliance norms to changing environmental conditions.

The observations in this chapter refer to the statement that the compliance norms form interconnected teams which, despite the differences in the types of financial institutions activity and the conditions in which they operate, may be proposed as a model arrangement reflecting the nature of the relations between them. The research that formed the basis for the analyses presented in this chapter consisted of comparing the content and manner of regulation of issues related to compliance risk management, included in the existing compliance norms in financial institutions conducting global operations.[1]

2 Hierarchy of Norms—Conclusions
DE LEGE FERENDA

Regardless of the reflection on the difficulties related to the meaning of the compliance norms in force in corporations resulting from cultural differences, a question arises whether on the basis of previous observations it is possible to determine what should be the hierarchical relation of these norms to each other. Is it possible to design a norms system that is structured on the basis of the relation of individual norms to others? Can rules, ethical norms, global corporate norms, even if not written down, take precedence over norms resulting from applicable laws, or vice versa? There are relatively clear reasons and objectives for which the established compliance norms differ in rank. So, it is quite easy to determine what is the purpose of policymaking, what is the procedure, what is the purpose of the manual, what are the rules and why are there instructions. The characteristics of these documents and the differences between them were the subject of the analysis contained in the fifth subchapter of Chapter 4 of this book.

[1] The following banks have been analyzed: HSBC Holdings Plc., Citigroup Inc., Bank of America Corp., Banco Santander SA, ING Groep NV, Lloyds Banking Group Plc., Societe Generale SA, Standard Chartered Plc., BNP Paribas SA, Barclays Plc., Royal Bank of Scotland Group Plc., and Credit Agricole SA.

If it is assumed that a hierarchy of normative consensual statements should rank all the statements addressed to a particular community—usually associated with a given organisation—a request or authorization for a particular behaviour. Then a model of mutual outcome of these norms from the point of view of their importance and degree of detail should be proposed. In so far as those norms are inscribed in the economic objective of the organisation, the social, political, environmental, etc., context, expressed in the conviction that it is possible to impose on the addressees of those norms a particular pattern of conduct expressed in the organisation, the injunction, prohibition or power to do so inscribed in them becomes a norm of conduct belonging to that system. In the case of the compliance norms described here, both the legitimacy and the expectation of adjustment to a specific pattern of behaviour are formulated by a given economic organisation, i.e. a financial institutions corporation, functioning in the conditions of a given social group. Due to the narrow reference of these norms to the indicated organisation, they are specific social norms. Contrary to other norms that are formulated or supported by relatively broad social groups and addressed to members of these groups at the same time, compliance norms are described through a broader social context only indirectly. On the other hand, they are directly determined by the axiomatic and economic context of a given organisation.[2]

In order to draw wider conclusions as to the proposed static relation of outcome, the source of which lies in the hierarchical ranking of norms, it should be assumed that any norm belonging to the internal compliance system, in order to be considered as such and to have the desired effect, must, like other social norms, contain three necessary elements.

a. The identification of the addressees and thus of the entities to whom the norm requires, prohibits or permits certain behaviour. A special element in the comparison with other social norms relating to a broad community, in the case of compliance norms, is the designation of addressees in relation to other entities that do not

---

[2] See M. Hashmi, A Methodology for Extracting Legal Norms from Regulatory Documents, *IEE Papers* 9/2015, p. 41 et seq.; A. Newman, E. Posner, Transnational Feedback, Soft Law, and Preferences in Global Financial Regulation, *Review of International Political Economy* 11/2015, p. 5 et seq.

belong exclusively to the community narrowed down by the framework of a given corporation. The addressees of compliance norms of a given organisation are primarily the employees, but they may also be customers, cooperating entities and shareholders of this corporation. Distinguishing, the circle of entities to which the norms are addressed is not assigned to a single jurisdiction but is always valid in the legal systems in which the organisation currently operates.
b. The determination of the desired norm of conduct to be followed by those addressees. This is the focal point in the consideration of compliance norms. These norms, usually created on the basis of Anglo-Saxon formulas and, like them, characterised by a large casuistry, are a firm order, and less often an unequivocal right, to perform a specific action or refrain from action, the aim of which is to lead to the formation of a strictly defined model of behaviour.
c. The defining of the circumstances which determine compliance, i.e. the circumstances in which the addressees are to act in a particular way. On the one hand, these are dictated by the fact that countries from the Anglo-Saxon legal culture are often the place where these norms are created, and on the other hand, these norms are to reach their recipients, addressees from geographically and culturally diverse places, and therefore detailed descriptions of these circumstances makes it easier to avoid possible differences in their interpretation.[3]

Compliance norms, being sui generis norms of conduct, show a significant similarity to other legal norms in this respect, in which they constitute a form of implementation of binding legal regulations within a given corporation. They are used to identify behaviour which is considered to be dependent on the will of the actor and which are feasible. At the same time, it is worth paying attention to their relation to other, also non-legal references, especially to the values set by the corporation, which are considered to be conducive to the achievement of the set business objectives. Due to the different weights assigned to individual values, there may

---

[3] More about the concept of culture in law in the context of differences in the interpretation of norms, the causes of which derive from cultural differences, see W. H. Sewell Jr., The Concept of Culture [in] V. E. Bonnell, A. H. Hunt, R. Biernacki [ed.] *Beyond the Cultural Turn*, Berkeley 1999, p. 35.

also be different means of achieving the expected results. Therefore, the hierarchy of these norms should be different, and the relation between norms of different place in this hierarchy should show a clear relation.

Applying the methodology used for analysing norm types in the general theory of norms, it should be assumed that the individual components of the norm allow for the identification of the tools with which the norm writer can determine the desired patterns of behaviour for its addressee. However, the very division of norms into those expressing duty (orders and prohibitions) and those granting rights (including competences) does not resolve the issue of the importance of a given norm, as it can only be determined jointly by placing it in relation to other norms, as well as by comparing it to the above-mentioned business objectives. The place in the hierarchy of compliance norms is not defined by the mere determination of different ways of sanctioning non-compliance with the guideline, which the norm defines, although in combination with the previously indicated elements it is an important determinant. The attempt to describe the place in the hierarchy of individual norms should therefore always be complemented by a discussion of the type to which the norm belongs, and what distinguishes it due to the specific function that a given type performs in the compliance system of a given corporation.[4]

It is helpful in an attempt to make a hierarchical order of compliance norms by using the classic, division into norms-rules and norms-principles for the analysis of the ways of determining the duties and rights of the addressees of these norms.

According to this criterion, the norm-rule can be defined as those binding internal norms within the compliance system of a given corporation, which in this system occupy a superior position, directing towards other norms and perform the function of setting the framework for all actions that should be taken. Therefore, the principles are the guidelines contained in the financial institution's regulatory policy, which impose on all entities in the group the obligation to cooperate openly with regulatory authorities in all matters in which they request it from the financial institution. As it is emphasised in the general theory of norms, it is not possible to derive from the norms—principles of a clearly defined manner

---

[4]See I. Okhmatovskiy, R. J. David, Setting Your Own Standards: Internal Corporate Governance Codes as a Response to Institutional Pressure, *Organisation Science* 23(1)/2011, p. 156.

of desired behaviour, however, they are clearly normative in character and have binding force in relation to the indicated group of addressees. In this case, these are primarily the financial institution's authorities, which are obliged to ensure the appropriate conditions for the implementation of the principle described here. In the indicated example, norms-principles provide conditions for the creation of a specific hierarchy of normative acts in a given corporation, allowing for the implementation of the postulate contained in this norms-principle.

On the other hand, self-regulatory rules determine the desired behaviour in such a way that the addressees are in fact only able to fulfil the obligation imposed on them or to breach it in a situation other than the one indicated. Norms-regulations of compliance as well as norms-regulations of law cannot be violated only to a certain extent. The norm-reference in the conditions illustrated in the previous example is therefore the norm requiring a financial institution, which is part of a larger corporation, to send a report to the local regulator on a detected transaction which is suspected of being an attempt to market measures for the financing of terrorism. Such a compliance norm, introduced into the internal compliance system through a simple transposition of a legal norm resulting from the regulations in force in, may or may not be fully complied with. In the absence of the timely execution of an order under this norm, a financial institution which is obliged to send certain information to the regulator.

The division of norms into strong and weak norms, which is also derived from the category of concepts relevant to the general theory of norms, may be helpful in the ranking of compliance norms.[5] It is, in fact, as is the case with other legal norms, too much of a simplification, because there is, in fact, an uninterrupted sequence of different types of norms with different powers inscribed in them.[6] Thus, in

---

[5] See T. Doyle, Cleaning up Anti-money Laundering Strategies: Current FATF Tactics Needlessly Violate International Law, *Houston Journal of International Law* 24/2002, p. 288 et seq.; Y. M. Isa, Z. M. Sanusi, M. N. Haniff, P. A. Barnes, Money Laundering Risk: From the Bankers' and Regulators Perspectives, *Procedia Economics and Finance* 28/2014, p. 7 et seq.; M. Bergström, K. Svedberg Helgesson, U. Mörth, A New Role for For-Profit Actors? The Case of Anti-money Laundering and Risk Management, *Journal of Common Market Studies* 49(5)/2011, p. 143.

[6] See L. Bélanger, K. Fontaine-Skronski, 'Legalization' in International Relations: A Conceptual Analysis, *Social Science Information* 51(2)/2012, p. 240 et seq.; K. Irwin, C. Horne, A Normative Explanation of Antisocial Punishment, *Social Science Research* 42(2)/2013, p. 562.

the intra-corporate system of compliance norms, there may exist indications of specific behaviours barely meeting the condition of being a norm through the poor indication of the manner of behaviour constituting only its proposals, up to such norms, which through the categorically of the directive orders contained therein are actually considered as inviolable norms, i.e. those whose violation cannot be justified by any circumstances. Therefore, these are unconditionally binding compliance norms, i.e. in other words, norms against which it is not possible to waive their validity.

As in the analysis of legal norms from the general position of the theory of norms, also the imperative and directive power of sanctioning compliance norms, manifested in the manner of responding to their violation, is relativised first of all to the axiological function performed by them, derived from the conviction of the persons influencing the determination of value judgments in a given institution, as to what degree of protection for specific goods the institution wants to provide.[7] The directive power, and thus also the position in the hierarchy of compliance norms will depend on the location of the given norm depending on the values to which the norm refers.[8] The designation of this item of a given norm is henceforth necessary for its correct reading by the entities to which it is addressed. It depends on the extent to which the behavioural pattern indicated in the norm is expected, desirable or necessary to perform its axiological function.

Regardless of the location of the compliance norm in the system of a given organisation, for a clear reading of the meaning of this norm it is also important that the description of the desired behaviour included in the indicated pattern is also unambiguous and capacious enough to ensure that in typical conditions of a given corporation, the addressee of the norm is sure what the pattern of conduct should be, what is the

---

[7] See L. K. Trevino, N. A. Den Nieuwenboer, G. E. Kreiner, D. G. Bishop, Legitimating the Legitimate: A Grounded Theory Study of Legitimacy Work Among Ethics and Compliance Officers, *Organizational Behavior and Human Decision Process* 123(2)/2014, p. 187 et seq.; P. Eberl, D. Geiger, M. S. Asslaender, Repairing Trust in an Organization After Integrity Violations: The Ambivalence of Organizational Rule Adjustments, *Organization Studies* 36(9)/2015, p. 1205 et seq.

[8] M. Perezts, S. Picard, Compliance or Comfort Zone? The Work of Embedded Ethics in Performing Regulations, *Journal of Business Ethics* 4/2014, p. 2 et seq.

weight of the norm in relation to other norms and what is its sanctioning power.[9] The addressee should therefore be able to understand what expectations that norm places on him, what action is required, what behaviour is correct to meet the indications of that norm and to assess whether his behaviour sufficiently fully meets that norm or whether there are conditions for considering that there has been a breach of that norm. As in the case of legal norms, according to the accepted observations about them in the general theory of norms, there is a situation when the addressee of the norm behaved in a manner contrary to the specified in the norm, or did not take the required action, or admittedly attempted the required action, but did not fully meet the requirements of the norm, and thus, there was not a full implementation of the norm in relation to its provisions.

The template of actions contained in compliance norms, regardless of their position in the hierarchy, must contain the potential ability to direct and give the desired characteristics to actions to be taken by the addressees of these norms and enable their evaluation. This, in turn, may result in the imperative function triggering sanctions. The mode of operation defined by the norm, which has such content-related properties, whose characteristic is the repetitiveness of the actions undertaken, performs one more function, defined in theory as a regulatory or designating function, it concerns both norms-principles and norms-rules. It is usually a more comprehensive concept in the case of norm-principles than in the case of norm-rules, although both have this regulatory function.

Regardless of the community to which the directive refers, it is true that the more a model of conduct becomes the norm, the more it shapes order in that community and the stronger, the more imperative it becomes a means of perpetuating that order. This also applies to the compelling role of compliance norms play in relation to the above described community associated with each of the corporations. The

---

[9] Among the features determining the state of formally understood certainty of the normative system, the following are most frequently mentioned: clarity, openness, determinability, recognizability, accessibility, calculability, predictability, continuity, stability, durability, concentration, codification, positivism, promulgation, reliability, non-contradiction, cohesion, system transparency, etc. See, e.g., J. Potrzeszcz, *Bezpieczeństwo prawne z perspektywy filozofii prawa*, Lublin 2013, p. 276. The analysis of the extent to which the norms created by corporations, which affect a wider community, correspond to these characteristics, could be considered separately.

tools that organise the social activity of the members of the community, i.e. patterns of behaviour, in their strong form becoming norms, can be ranked due to their power of influence, starting with the weakest, i.e. the least compelling, in the least fulfilling the functions of norms, as it is emphasised, not related to any special reflection on the necessity of their application, i.e. the clear experience of duty, the expectation of sanctions, all the way to the strongest, the most compelling and the most unambiguous in terms of content, related to the strong experience of duty, specific action, as well as to the sense of the inevitability of the sanction.

Obligatory indications binding within the corporation, according to the order understood in this way, should be considered as compliance norms. They are located closer to the end of the continuum of norms described here, which is characterised by relatively strong norms. However, not all of them will be located in the same place. The place of these compliance norms, which are the ordering instruments in the aforementioned continuum, depends on many complex processes taking place within a given organisation. They can be influenced, but this happens only to a limited extent.

It is also sometimes the case that compliance regulations binding within a corporation remain only indications, models of action or directional directives, declarations of expected attitudes and it is difficult to determine unequivocally that they have obtained the status of norms. Such a state of affairs may result from imperfections in the internal regulations introduced by a given corporation. It is not true that models of operation which fully and to the maximum extent fulfil all the functions of norms are at the same time the most effective regulatory mechanisms. They often have a more effective impact on the internal order in the corporation. It is sometimes the case that seemingly weaker statements, which are proposals for behaviour that are supported by an appropriate non-sanctioning mechanism of persuasion, can have a more effective impact and lead to the intended results. Nevertheless, due to the effectiveness achieved in shaping corporate activity, they should be included in the entire internal system of compliance norms.[10]

---

[10] Considerations on the effectiveness of compliance standards in relation to axiological justifications, see M. Romanowski, op. cit., p. 82 et seq.

3 The Interdependence of Compliance Norms Due to Their Content

When attempting to develop a hypothesis concerning the interdependence of compliance norms in a corporation, it should be pointed out that they should flow from one another, and that they are also the subject of regulation.[11] Activities aimed at bringing the activities of a financial institution into line with the applicable norms may not only cover individualised matters designed to ensure the normal performance of the financial institution's obligations. They must also take into account the effect of non-legislative normative systems, and their impact on the content of compliance regulations. These issues, as well as other external references, are discussed in the first two parts of this section. The last part contains references to the minimum content of the compliance norms.

As an example of multiple references appropriate for compliance norms in financial institutions, we can discuss tax settlements. Financial institutions are often in the position of being taxpayers, obliged by virtue of various tax regulations. Compliance norms specify the behaviour of persons responsible for tax settlements in financial institutions, referring to the content of legal regulations, supervisory regulations, administrative decisions, judgments of adjudicating bodies, achievements of doctrine, current jurisprudence, but also to the expectations of the public expressed by the media and socially recognised ethical norms. At the same time, compliance norms should be precise and refer to the financial institution's proprietary arrangements with respect to the subject matter, dates and persons responsible for these settlements.[12] The role played by compliance norms can be divided into two stages of their operation: the initial stage covers the process of adjusting the corporation's operations to the whole of its external normative environment, and the secondary stage, in which all activities aimed at maintaining the state of compliance achieved as a result of the first stage, during changes in the norms themselves, as well as during the financial institution's development in a given economic reality are performed.

---

[11] Cf. S. Kaźmierczyk, Dynamiczne ujęcie normy prawnej, *Acta Universitatis Wratislaviensis* 44(244)/1978, p. 9 et seq.

[12] Among other things, on the ethical aspects of tax compliance in corporate activities, see B. Torgler, *Tax Compliance and Tax Morale: A Theoretical and Empirical Analysis*, Cheltenham 2007, p. 104.

Corporate compliance is affected by multiple normative systems at the same time. National law, which remains the central reference point for building a compliance space, is not the only normative system through which the behaviour of addressees of compliance norms is controlled. A similar function, in addition to legal requirements, is fulfilled by the economic objectives, ethics, commercial customs and other collective norms adopted within the institution. The desired pattern of behaviour shaped by all the norms that regulate the behaviour of their addressees within an organisation can be called its ethos. Therefore, also in the context of compliance norms, ethos is a pattern of behaviour shaped by a complex system of relations between different normative systems influencing the operation of a given corporation. In order to fully describe this ethos, as well as the entire normative system that affects it and the values underlying it, there is a need to look at it through the key interrelations that affect it. The most important of these are the relations between the regulations that shape the operation of a given organisation and the adopted as binding rules of ethics, i.e. a network of constantly changing interdependent relations of the entire axiological normative system.

In one of the types of descriptions defining the relation between law and morality in the general theory of norms, there are three types of relations that can also be used to indicate references within the corporate compliance system between norms whose purpose is to ensure compliance with the applicable law and ethical principles considered mandatory in a given organisation. These relations are:

a. the subject matter;
b. validation;
c. functional.[13]

While, according to the general theory of norms, the scope of the regulation of legal and moral norms do not completely intersect, and therefore there are types of behaviour which regulate exclusively morality and are not governed by the law, as well as those which are regulated solely by the law and not by morality, there is also a sphere of behaviour in which the scope of regulation by the law and by morality overlap, it

---

[13] More on the subject, validation and functional relationship between norms and values, and more broadly between law and morality, see L. Morawski, *Wstęp do Prawoznawstwa*, Toruń 2006, p. 44.

would not be possible to make such a distinction in the system of norms of compliance because the system is complete. This means that whatever the nature of the norm and whatever the normative order it is derived from, it is de facto binding and, moreover, in principle only indirectly affects its validity. Therefore, it is worth noting the validation and functional relations occurring within the normative compliance system, regardless of the attempt to describe the subject relations considered in this part.

Validation relations refer to the issue of how non-compliance with moral norms affects the very existence of legal norms. Different positions were presented from the perspective of supporters of legal positivism from those indicated by supporters of the non-positivistic approach, including in particular representatives of the school of law of nature. At present, in each of these concepts, verified by observations of contemporary phenomena in the law which, among other things, are the result of globalisation processes causing the interpenetration of various normative orders, an appropriate correction had to take place.[14] It is not, therefore, the case today within the democratic legal order of views expressed in such a way that, even if legal norms are deprived of the attributes of legitimacy derived from a socially accepted moral conviction, or if they should be considered unfair on the basis of such beliefs, this does not affect their validity, provided that these norms have been properly established and have not been abolished. There are also no views which require the search for a basis derived from the moral order for each legal norm. This convergence of views on the relation between law and morality is visible in the conditions of the internal compliance system in corporations, in which, while it is still possible to identify the source of a given compliance norm, it certainly cannot be considered to have an impact on its validity.

This is not the case for the functional relation between law and morality, which refers to the way in which moral norms influence the content of legal norms, and vice versa, i.e. how law can shape the content of a community's shared moral beliefs. These considerations are related to the internal normative system of the corporation in a much clearer way allow to observe the dynamics of mutual relations. Especially in the context of an uninterrupted sequence of changes taking place both in the

---

[14] See L. C. Backer, *Harmonizing Law in the Era of Globalization: Convergence, Divergence and Resistance*, Durham 2007, p. 10 et seq.

legal space with which the corporation's internal normative order should be in harmony, and in the field of beliefs and ethical assessments, which, following social changes, are subject to gradual transformations.[15] As in the case of the assessment of the impact of morality on law in the theory of norms, according to which law is, in principle, a system open to moral values, it can also be stated in the analysis of compliance norms within institutions that the principles of ethics, the values referred to in the activities of a corporation and the wider moral principles applicable within a given social space strongly influence the order in which a given compliance system is regulated. In the case of legal norms, basing legal systems on the positivist thesis of separation of law and morality means that a legal norm does not lose its validity even if it is contrary to moral norms. Similarly, when introducing regulations based on the will to ensure compliance with the law, corporations do not share the conviction that moral principles must also be taken into account in this process. However, when introducing compliance norms within a corporation, there is a conviction that their effectiveness depends to a large extent on whether they are universally accepted.[16] It is their acceptance that will be connected with whether the compliance system is based on the values that are accepted in a given corporation, and at the same time considered to be of business use.

Compliance norms are created and function within the corporate space in specific references. They are:

a. the economic strategies of corporate governance;
b. stakeholder expectations;
c. regulatory trends;
d. changing public opinion;
e. worldviews appropriate to the communities in which they operate.

Their relevance is entirely related to the conditions both within and around the corporation. From the ontological point of view, compliance norms exist in this environment both in the sense of remaining in the normative consciousness of their addressees, as well as through the

---

[15] D. Awrey, W. Blair, D. Kershaw, Between Law and Markets: Is There a Role for Culture and Ethics in Financial Regulation?, *Delaware Journal of Corporate Law* 38/2013, p. 191.

[16] W. H. Shaw, V. Barry, *Moral Issues in Business*, Boston 2014, p. 221.

practice of actions taken in order to make them effective. Another issue is that the relation between the existence of a compliance norm in the consciousness of the addressees and its application is not always close and direct. This practice of actions aimed at ensuring their application does not need to be determined solely by the content remaining in the awareness of the addressees. For a simple illustration of this situation, it can be pointed out that the very conviction of the addressees of the norm, even if it is to be widely shared, that the indicated pattern of behaviour is a compliance norm, in each specific situation does not automatically entail a state of compliance at the level of fulfilling the disposition of this norm. The behaviour of the persons to whom the norm is addressed does not always comply with the norm.

Therefore, it can be pointed out that there are differences in both the impact and function between such models of conduct, which are given as examples of good practice, but which do not yet become norms of compliance, and more explicit statements of a directive character, prescribing a specific course of conduct. The difference in such situations lies, among other things, in the degree to which these statements perform an axiological function, and their reference to the values considered important in a given corporation. These statements, which have a directive function and the aim of which is to ensure that the characteristics of a certain behaviour are fulfilled, to a large extent fulfil this function, create conditions for ensuring compliance and communicate an unambiguously strong duty. At the same time, they fulfil the regulatory function of compliance norms to varying degrees, depending on the closeness of its relation to specific values.

Therefore, such good practices as role models may be both axiologically strongly involved and almost neutral, thus becoming a much weaker duty in such circumstances, as they are not based on an accepted value added order. In any case, however, such recommendations should have sufficiently distinctive characteristics, and an understandable description of the desired behaviour, and thus fulfil the regulatory function, and be clear in order to constitute an appropriate normative model of conduct.[17]

For the analysis of the subject matter of these interdependencies that occur between compliance norms, the content of these norms is

---

[17] Cf. D. D. Bobek, A. M. Hageman, C. F. Kelliher, Analyzing the Role of Social Norms in Tax Compliance Behavior, *Journal of Business Ethics* 115/2013, p. 453 et seq.

important, i.e. the statement contained in an unambiguous linguistic message that articulates in its content an indication of the manner of desired behaviour. The content of the compliance norms may have a complex structure and not be closed only in the pattern of assumed behaviours to achieve the business goals. Although compliance norms refer to multiple normative systems, in order to fulfil a regulatory function, i.e. to define a desired pattern of behaviour, they should contain the minimum regulatory content, i.e. the necessary information to enable them to be observed. As in the analysis of static relations between norms, also in functional relations, the information contained in the content of compliance norms defines the following elements:

a. the conditions under which they should be implemented,
b. the addressees of those norms,
c. a description of the desired action.

As regards the determination of the conditions in which a given behaviour should be performed, i.e. the determination of the conditions for the performance of the obligation or, less frequently, the indication of the circumstances in which the right is granted, this is a normatively relevant situation in which a specific action is to take place. An example is compliance norms with a relatively wide range of impacts: 'if you are an employee of a financial institution x....', 'representing an entity seeking to provide services to a corporation y...', 'as a client who is a financial institution that concludes treasury transactions with a financial institution on international markets ...' and norms with a much more limited scope of influence: 'if you are an employee of the compliance department obliged to report suspicious transactions ...', 'as a lawyer authorised to represent a law firm hired to draw up credit documentation to support a y project financed by a financial institution x...', etc.

The determining of the addressees of compliance norms consists of indicating which persons have the appropriate subjectivity enabling effective implementation of a given normative indication, by fulfilling the postulate of specific behaviours. These addressees of compliance norms may be considered normatively relevant provided that they are clearly defined and have an implied ability to implement the recommendations to which the content of the analysed norms in the part indicating the expected behaviours refers. Such definitions of entities are: 'the "board", "head of compliance department", "service provider", "endowed foundation"', etc.

The disposition of compliance norms is the part of their content in which the characteristics that make up the characteristics of the action that realises the desired pattern of behaviour are defined, i.e. the normatively relevant characteristics of the action are specified.

4   Flexible Norm-Setting Approach to Assure Compliance Adjustment to Changing Environment

The rules of constructing the legal system that are relevant to the general theory of norms form a normative concept of sources of law, the elements of which may be applied to analyse the optimal methods for the methodological unification of norms of compliance where there are differences resulting from different legal cultures.[18] The basic function of the normative concept of the sources of law of a particular system is to be able to decide which norms belong to a given legal system, and which remain outside that system. Similarly, using this concept in the conditions of a normative system of compliance within a corporation, it is possible to decide which norms belong to this system and which do not.

Within the normative concept of sources of law, two types of rules can be distinguished.

   a. The first type are validation rules, i.e. a set of rules which orders the addressee of a norm to consider some facts as lawmaking facts, and thus which gives the authorisation to mark certain behaviours as entitled to give normative value to specific patterns of behaviour.
   b. The second are rules of interpretation, i.e. those which require linking with legal facts of the existence of certain legal norms. It is they who clarify any doubts that may arise in this respect.

Both types of rules may apply directly to compliance norms in the compliance system, in particular the one in force in one corporation operating in many markets.

It is interesting to refer norm-setting activities within the compliance system to three types of rules relating to legislative activities:

---

[18] Observations on legal cultures, in the specific context of the mandate to create norms and the differences in the way they are created in relation to legal cultures, cf. S. S. Silbey, op. cit., p. 470.

a. to constitutive rules;
b. to the technical rules;
c. to the rules of conduct.

The constitutive rules, classified as the rules of legal system construction, determine the entities equipped with normative competences, as well as the form and procedure in which these norms may be established. Technical directives indicate what to do if someone has accepted the purpose. Part of the scope of the technical directive is the acceptance of an objective or state of affairs which, from the user's point of view, is available, leaving the addressee of a norm to make a choice. Norms of conduct are norms of this kind, which require the establishment of further normative implementing acts specifying the appropriate way to proceed in order to establish the norms.[19] Each of these rules and all of these rules together, regardless of their degree of awareness, also apply to compliance norms.

An important factor for the effective introduction of compliance norms in the context of culturally anchored differences resulting from different legal conditions is the creation of appropriate interactive competences on the part of the addressees. Interaction competence is a set of skills needed to correctly read the contents of norms in their respective contexts. Each interaction, that is expressed in behaviour in accordance with the indications of a given norm, that occur between the norm-setter and the addressee of the norm requires both that the addressee of the norm knows the expected pattern of behaviour, respects its binding character, but also that it is able to understand the meaning of actions meeting the recommendations of the norm. Therefore, it is about the expected social communication competence of the addressees. In the case of the compliance norms of competence it is referred to in two vectors:

a. to the context resulting from the environment specific to the territory;
b. to the expectations of corporations formulated using the content of this norm.

---

[19] N. M. Korkunow, *General Theory of Law*, Boston 2000, p. 41; J. D. Wallace, *Ethical Norms, Particular Cases*, Cornell 1996, p. 96.

Interactional competence in relation to compliance norms understood in this way is much more than just knowledge of the meaning of words used in the language of a given norm, it is also more than understanding expectations as to the desired patterns of behaviour. Such competence is also the knowledge of a whole set of cultural codes used to communicate in specific circumstances, the correct reading of which serves to interpret clearly the context in which the communication process of a given norm takes place.[20]

Interactional competence is therefore the ability to read out a significant similarity, defined as an idiosyncratically relation between the behavioural pattern resulting from a given norm and the action aimed at achieving that norm. The deriving by the addressees from compliance norms of appropriate interactive competences appropriate for given conditions is one of the necessary measures taken by corporations operating on many markets at the same time in order to ensure the effectiveness of the impact of these norms. It is the relation between the action pattern contained in the norm and actions performed in accordance with these norms that is the basis for assessing the effectiveness of compliance norms. A given model of action is therefore implemented idiosyncratically in relation to the orders of a norm, provided that the addressees of the norm, who has interactive competence, recognises which model of action should be implemented in a given case.

It can be assumed, therefore, that the model of operation only then becomes an effectively binding norm in a given space, when it meets the requirements, which not only result from their source context, defined by the corporation-creator, but also from the proper reading of this norm. It is only when these conditions are met that a given pattern of action makes it a readable, properly delineated norm. Thus, just as not every pattern of action becomes a norm, not every norm has a chance to become a compliance norm, which can be considered as properly formulated in a given cultural context. It is also worth mentioning briefly the implications of an incorrect cultural recognition for the scope of application of a given compliance norm.

There can be no question of a correctly formulated compliance norm, when the ordered model of behaviour meets the requirements set for norms, however, due to cultural mismatches that result in the

---

[20] A. Piotrowski, O pojęciu kompetencji interaktywnej [in] A. Schaff [ed.] *Zagadnienia Socio- i Psycholingwistyki*, Warsaw 1980, p. 107.

failure to read it properly, it will only be understood by a narrow group of recipients, or it will even only refer to an individually defined recipient. In such conditions, it can become at most a micro-social norm or even an individual one. A given design of the prescribed behaviour, although it meets the conditions for becoming the norm, due to the limited range resulting from cultural reasons, becomes effective only in relation to a narrow group of addressees, it binds only this small community. Such a mistake in the process of creating compliance norms can be avoided by ensuring an appropriate level of knowledge of the cultural context of the place.[21]

There are examples in which role models that are culturally limited norms have no chance of becoming effective norms in relation to a wider audience, even if such a role model is considered justified or even necessary by the corporation that creates such norms. These are norms whose observance leads to a state of affairs that are not considered in a given social context to be consistent with valued values. Such corporate malpractice in establishing compliance norms refers to incomprehensible values that are not regarded as values in general or even considered as ant values in a given territory and social environment. The same observation applies also to similar normative actions missed due to moral mismatch, i.e. theoretically those whose defectiveness is much less pronounced.

Examples of this kind, although they do not refer to some particularly isolated groups, which, in the face of globalisation and the unification of knowledge and social experiences, are by necessity becoming less and less likely, show how important it is to take into account the specificity of experiences and values attributed to the community operating in a given place. The difficulty of the task facing a corporation building its own normative system lies in the natural pursuit of consistency of the recommendations given for application. If such a situation occurs, the above described communication deficiencies, then it will result in a lack of understanding of the content of such norms. There are also other reasons for cultural mismatches that are related to, for example,

---

[21] On the avoidance of errors in the creation of norms through knowledge of cultural legal conditions, see C. W. Bame-Aldred, J. B. Cullen, K. D. Martin, K. P. Parboteeah, National Culture and Firm-Level Tax Evasion, *Journal of Business Research* 66(3)/2013, p. 390 et seq.; F. P. Ramos, International and Supranational Law in Translation: From Multilingual Lawmaking to Adjudication, *The Translator* 20(3)/2014, p. 313.

disturbances in the processes of normative socialisation, i.e. learning how to function properly in the social order, i.e. the processes of learning and using certain norms. All these factors should be taken into account in the construction of compliance norms.

In order to ensure that the behavioural patterns introduced in a corporation are not only certain ideal models of operation, and that the directives only define the direction of these behaviours, but that they become effective compliance norms, it is necessary to meet an additional requirement. This is the fact that a model of behaviour of the axiological function, is defined by the norm, i.e. a potential possibility of its recognition by the obliged entity as a way of achieving the goal set by the corporation, because it has a value-adjusted value. It is recognised as an action that is expected by the corporation to fulfil a specific obligation. In such a model, the behaviour in accordance with the model that should be followed is this one:

a. which the norm-setting corporation expects;
b. which is considered desirable and appropriate by the addressees themselves.

In such a context, the compliance of a given norm with its axiological function is confirmed by the uncontroversial and permanent conviction of the addressees of the norm that the specified values can be protected by behaviours in accordance with the design of the given norm. The effectiveness of this norm is then manifested in practice in the community to which the norm is addressed. Another sign of recognition of the effectiveness of compliance norms in a given area are the reactions of other entities operating there, i.e. business partners, customers, regulators, media, etc. These positive reactions, i.e. those expected by the corporation, will occur when the behaviour is considered to be in accordance with the normative formula. The attempt to assess the effectiveness of the matching compliance norms to the cultural context is therefore the positive or negative social reactions of the environment accompanying corporate activities. In a given social environment that can be distinguished due to cultural specificity, the meaning of a normative message in circumstances where it takes the form of a linguistic statement, becomes an adjusted compliance norm assuming that it fulfils an axiological function related to a locally accepted value system. This reference is supplemented by a simple imperative function that prescribes behaviour and a regulatory function that determines by means of content the description of the desired characteristics of such behaviour.[22]

The main objective of establishing common compliance norms for the whole corporation, regardless of where it operates, is to ensure its uniform functioning in the area of desired behaviours reduced to minimum expectations. In other words, in the model approach, the task of compliance norms is to ensure that all entities acting on behalf of the corporation apply the norms and principles at the level not lower than those deemed necessary. The purpose of the implementation of compliance norms results from:

a. objectives relating to the intra-corporate norms themselves;
b. objectives of the entire strategy adopted in the organisation (policy, mission, vision, etc., depending on the terminology adopted by the corporation) of compliance;
c. the objectives imposed by other regulatory norms;
d. other overarching objectives, the achievement of which is determined by law, the will of the regulator and other stakeholders.

The ability of the compliance staff determines the effectiveness of the task of creating internal legislative plans relating to compliance norms, which with minimum economic outlays should include the achievement of the objectives of primary and derived norms, while at the same time constituting an important pillar of the ownership and management policy in a given organisation.

In the implementation of this task, the basic function is to guarantee the effective impact of compliance norms not only by ensuring their correct formulation, but also by building mechanisms for testing their effectiveness. This consists of examining how the addressees of the compliance norms comply with norms designed to reduce the risk of non-compliance.[23] Such investigations obligate staff carrying

---

[22] Cf. L. G. Zucker, The Role in Institutionalization in Cultural Persistence [in] W. W. Powell, P. J. DiMaggio [ed.] *The New Institutionalism in Organizational Analysis*, Chicago 2012, p. 83 et seq.; S. Pejovich, *Economic Analysis of Institutions and Systems*, Dordrecht 2012, p. 39.

[23] On testing and monitoring the effectiveness of compliance in corporations, see L. T. Ly, S. Rinderle-Ma, D. Knuplesch, P. Dadam, Monitoring Business Process Compliance Using Compliance Rule Graphs, *Lecture Notes of Computer Science* 7044/2011, pp. 82–99.

out supervisory tasks to ensure that compliance with applicable norms relating to all activities within their sphere of responsibility remains at the expected level. The results of this research are documented, monitored and collected in appropriate IT systems, and the procedures regulating it assume taking into account the definitions and responsibilities related to the supervision of business processes in accordance with the applicable compliance norms. Such investigations are usually not part of the tasks of compliance services, with the exception of processes requiring regulatory knowledge or involving a high risk of non-compliance. These include disclosure of information about irregularities or other material inside information about corporate companies that may affect the value of their shares.[24] The compliance services in the model provide:

a. Preparation of test plans for the establishment of compliance norms based on a prior assessment of the risk of non-compliance. These plans are based on:

   (1) the identification of the applicable laws,
   (2) the identification of applicable supervisory regulations,
   (3) the identification of changing case law,
   (4) current legal literature,
   (5) market practices.

They also include an assessment of compliance risk, that takes into account the degree of residual and inherent risks.[25] They then refer to the obligation to take regular steps to ensure that these risks are monitored and mitigated. In practice, these plans also have a wider use, for example in the assessment of controls in the area of operational risk, which is closely linked to compliance risk. The testing plans for norm-setting activities also provide for periodic operational risk assessment in order to determine to what extent their tasks, and more specifically their inadequate performance, can in itself constitute an operational risk for the financial institution.

---

[24] See R. W. McGee, Applying Utilitarian Ethics and Rights Theory to the Regulation of Insider Trading in Transition Economies, *Fayetteville State University* 4/2014, p. 11.

[25] P. Hopkin, *Fundamentals of Risk Management: Understanding, Evaluating and Implementing*, London 2014, p. 17 et seq.

b. Carrying out, on the basis of compliance plans, regular, cyclical monitoring and ad hoc quality assessment controls of norm-setting activities ensuring the state of compliance and reliability of observance of the procedures in force in this respect. The assumption is that the monitoring of the planned process of creating compliance norms ensures appropriate discipline of the conducted analysis of the degree of implementation and adequacy of compliance norms.

In addition to the compliance norms applicable to financial institutions operating in different jurisdictions, there are also globally applicable norms to mitigate corporate compliance risks. These different levels of global compliance norms are intended to reduce both the risks arising from non-compliance with the relevant regulations governing business activities in a given country or territory. They may also refer to provisions in force outside the country or territory whose extraterritorial scope is reflected in local legislation.[26]

The four most common types of corporate policies belong to the areas regulated by the intra-corporate compliance norms, which are unified in financial institutions so that they are uniform in all the jurisdictions in which they operate, regardless of the content of local regulations.

a. Customer complaints policies—to ensure that the highest possible norm of customer service is uniformly applied in all countries where financial institution customers may need to settle their cases with a financial institution.
b. Extraordinary business offer policies—regulate in particular issues related to the acceptance by financial institution employees of property benefits related to their activities.
c. Funding policies for military equipment—in many financial institutions, this is an area which is subject to detailed norm-setting in order to avoid the possible risk of such situations in which the financing by a financial institution of this type of transaction in one territory could damage the image of the entire capital group in the face of a negative assessment of the transaction by the public or the authorities of any country.

---

[26] Similarly, in *Compliance Regulation Drafting Manual* of one of the corporations, a document classified as 'confidential'.

d. Fiduciary risk management policies—regulating fiduciary liability in transactions on global markets that are inherently cross-border in nature.[27]

The above international compliance norms mention procedures applicable to entire financial institutions groups that impose specific behavioural obligations both for persons working in the compliance area and for all other employees of the corporation whose actions may be a source of compliance risk. Individual corporations implement in practice a number of other policies aimed at harmonising compliance norms across all jurisdictions. Although their subject matter varies according to the type of business pursued, the geographical coverage of the financial institutions and other factors, the four policies listed above are those that are always present in all global corporations, including financial institutions operating on such a scale.

When analysing model solutions relating to the issue of creating compliance norms, it is worth recalling that, unlike in the case of credit risk, market risk and other types of risk management, which traditionally constitute the central axis of financial institutions operations, compliance risk belongs to a completely specific category.

The separation of this area of financial institution's risk management consists, among other things, of the fundamental disagreement by international financial institutions on the assumption of compliance risk.[28] The management of these risks is usually carried out on a global level, not least because relying only on national rules might not be sufficient, as in some countries' legislation regulating the same issues may have a different content, limited power and also may not even be in force at all. As a consequence, limiting the compliance obligation to local national rules could lead to market practices that violate the declared financial institution rules.

---

[27] More on importance of risks associated with lack of understanding of common fiduciary principles regardless the jurisdictions' specificities, see T. Frankel, Towards Universal Fiduciary Principles, *Boston University School of Law Working Paper* 9/2012, passim. On fiduciary liability in transactions on bank custody accounts, see P. B. Szymala, *Ryzyko prawne w działalności banków*, Poznań 2006, p. 34.

[28] Criticizing the failure to agree to discuss the necessary acceptance of compliance risks and the ineffectiveness of the approach of a proliferation of global compliance standards instead of active risk management and the necessary simplifications see more broadly, see PwC Report, Let's Make a Difference: Managing Compliance and Operational Risk in the New Environment, *PwC FS Viewpoint* 2013, p. 5 et seq.

The compliance norms developed today by international financial institutions are intended to provide the authorities of these corporations with appropriate instruments to manage the risk of non-compliance in meeting their obligation to conduct their business in accordance with regulations and internally set objectives. These norms therefore support financial institutions corporations' authorities in identifying and assessing compliance risks, monitoring them, creating a reporting framework and promoting their own 'corporate culture', that are based on compliance with laws and supervisory regulations issued by administrative regulators, which is established on a case-by-case basis in each financial institution. The most common types of internal compliance acts fulfilling these functions are those related to particular issues covered by the scope of compliance, described earlier.

a. Global standards;
b. Codes of ethics;
c. Codes of conduct;
d. Best practice principles;
e. Codes of compliance;
f. Conflicts of interests' rules;
g. Ethical principles for the sale of the financial institutions' products, etc.[29]

The model approach to compliance norms, notwithstanding the observations indicated earlier in this book, should also take into account the general directives of legislative technique, which, due to their content, are not only significant in terms of content, but also of technical and ordering significance. We are talking here both about directives that are fundamental to the quality of the norms being drawn up, relating to the clarity, legibility, comprehensibility, consistency, non-conflict ability and completeness of the normative text and about the way in which normative provisions are written, organised and systematised. In this context, it is particularly useful to take a structured approach to all those norm-setting directives which indicate how to formulate, mark and systematise into collections individual directive statements having the character of normative acts, as well as how to change the content of those

---

[29] All the names proposed in this book usually have their translations in the internal normative acts currently used by financial institutions in the world.

statements, how to include them and eliminate them from the normative systems of individual corporations.

Statements that order certain behaviours are compliance norms, provided that the model of action described in them fulfils simultaneously and to a due degree the functions described above, making it a tool for shaping order consistent with the direct or indirect interest of this corporation. In the case of compliance norms, it can be assumed that this is done only through acts of communication, which take the form of linguistic expressions, provided that they are properly adjusted to socially determined cultural contexts. In practice, their application is complemented by the necessary processes for monitoring compliance with these norms and by the different powers of sanctions provided for infringements. Compliance norms, being neither a requirement that imposes a model of conduct, nor an experience accompanying such a requirement, nor the language used for communicating them, are the very meaning, the sense of expression that is formulated within these norms. Similar to legal norms, they are therefore the meaning of normative messages provided by corporations, which is related to many normative systems at the same time.

When stating that the compliance norms regulate the course of activities aimed at achieving the objectives set by corporations, it should be understood both as the fact that activities are carried out in accordance with these norms, shaped by the will of the authorities of these institutions, as well as the fact that in their description the specific content of the model of conduct itself is set out. The first meaning of such a statement refers to the impact of a particular norm. The frequency of behaviours consistent with the formula contained in the norm allows to assess the behavioural effectiveness of this norm, the degree of its regulating influence. In developing compliance norms, observations in this area are of key importance. The observed effectiveness of compliance norms refers not only to the fact of performing activities compliant with it, but also to the occurrence of expected consequences of these activities, regardless of whether they are indicated directly by the norm or can only be interpreted from its content.[30]

[30] On this subject, e.g. C. L. Israels, *Corporate Practice*, New York 1974, p. 232 et seq. and some newer works L. Suarez-Villa, *Corporate Power, Oligopolies, and the Crisis of the State*, New York 2015, p. 339 et seq.; R. V. Turcan, S. Marinova, M. B. Rana, Empirical Studies on Legitimation Strategies: A Case for International Business Research Extension

This book reveals the need for further detailed research relating to the new phenomena of the norm-setting activities by entities other than publicly legitimated right-makers. In addition other possible subjects of further research, there is a need to analyse the impact of such norms on the evolving social and economic reality as a result of the complexity of global connections, and also to systemic changes, or even systemic redefinitions, which are taking place as a result of their presence in the legal normative space.[31]

[in] L. Tihanyi, T. M. Devinney, T. Pedersen [ed.] *Institutional Theory in International Business*, London 2012, p. 427.

[31] For more on the influence of contemporary globalization processes on defining the principles of law and more broadly, on understanding the role of law, see, for example, W. Scheuerman, Globalization and a Fate of Law [in] D. Dyzenhaus [ed.] *Recrafting the Rule of Law: The Limits of Legal Order*, New York 1999, p. 245 et seq.; J. R. C. Kuntz, D. Elenkov, A. Nabirukhina, Characterizing Ethical Cases: A Cross-Cultural Investigation of Individual Differences, Organizational Climate, and Leadership on Ethical Decision-Making, *Journal of Business Ethics* 13(2)/2013, p. 318.

Summary

The text summarises theoretical legal research into the compliance norms produced by international corporations and is based on examples from the financial institutions sector. The methodology applied during the research combined a critical analysis of the legal, economic, financial and management literature as well as authentic financial institutions documentation related to the compliance norms. This was supplemented by the engaged observations of the author, who for over a dozen years had been responsible for legal and compliance matters in international financial institutions. The research relates to compliance norms that have been created by international financial institutions since the beginning of the twenty-first century.

The starting point for the research was the growing trend for international corporations and financial institutions in particular of creating norms that regulate their business activities. It has been demonstrated within this book how the substance and the scope of these norms exceeds the subject of external norms compliance. Compliance norms in financial institutions nowadays are not only extensive autonomic axiological-normative systems to assure legal and compliant way of operating by the financial institutions, but also supporting tools to achieve desired perception and economic goals.

The text describes the importance of groups of norms created by corporations in parallel to the public systems of norms for the general coherence of the entire normative system. It has also been an opportunity to systemise and to present the tasks, the role and the structure of compliance units in financial institutions. Thanks to this, it was possible to list and to describe compliance norms created in financial institutions. The international operations of the major financial groups and, by definition, the global reach of their operations made it necessary to look at the cultural legal differences that have impact on the creation, application and interpretation of compliance norms in the particular local franchises of the financial institutions. As a result of the comparative studies, the text presents systemised and terminologically ordered conclusions relating to financial institutions compliance norms.

There are various approaches to compliance obligations that depend on the specificities of particular corporations that result from different legal and cultural environments, the expectations of stakeholders, the short-term and long-term political agendas of states as well as the decisions of the regulators responsible for the stability of the financial system. None of these approaches dominates the other, none of them may be correct. All of them however are reactive in the sense that they are responses to their own problems or fines. Or in some cases, they are responses to the problems and fines of their competitors. Nevertheless, their common feature is their growing importance to the complex multipolar and ubiquitous normative reality of contemporary societies.

Legal Acts

Regulation (EC) No. 2560/2001 of the European Parliament and of the Council of 19 December 2001 on cross-border payments in euro, *OJ L* 344, 28 December 2001, pp. 13–16 (no longer in force), https://eur-lex.europa.eu/legal-content/EN/TXT/?uri=uriserv:OJ.L_.2001.344.01.0013.01.ENG&toc=OJ:L:2001:344:TC (download 7 July 2019).

Regulation (EC) No. 1781/2006 of the European Parliament and of the Council of 15 November 2006 on information on the payer accompanying transfers of funds (Text with EEA relevance), *OJ L* 345, 8 December 2006, pp. 1–9 (no longer in force), https://eur-lex.europa.eu/legal-content/EN/TXT/?qid=1559920717930&uri=CELEX:32006R1781 (download 7 July 2019).

Regulation (EC) No. 861/2007 of the European Parliament and of the Council of 11 July 2007 establishing a European Small Claims Procedure, *OJ L* 199, 31 July 2007, pp. 1–22, https://eur-lex.europa.eu/legal-content/EN/TXT/?qid=1559921150803&uri=CELEX:32007R0861 (download 7 July 2019).

Regulation (EC) No. 1060/2009 of the European Parliament and of the Council of 16 September 2009 on credit rating agencies (Text with EEA relevance), *OJ L* 302, 17 November 2009, pp. 1–31, https://eur-lex.europa.eu/legal-content/EN/TXT/?qid=1559921295079&uri=CELEX:32009R1060 (download 7 July 2019).

Regulation (EC) No. 924/2009 of the European Parliament and of the Council of 16 September 2009 on cross-border payments in the Community and repealing Regulation (EC) No. 2560/2001 (Text with EEA relevance), *OJ L*

© The Editor(s) (if applicable) and The Author(s), under exclusive license to Springer Nature Switzerland AG 2019
T. Braun, *Compliance Norms in Financial Institutions*,
https://doi.org/10.1007/978-3-030-24966-3

266, 9 October 2009, pp. 11–18, https://eur-lex.europa.eu/legal-content/EN/TXT/?qid=1559921415226&uri=CELEX:32009R0924 (download 7 July 2019).

Regulation (EU) No. 1092/2010 of the European Parliament and of the Council of 24 November 2010 on European Union macro-prudential oversight of the financial system and establishing a European Systemic Risk Board, *OJ L* 331, 15 December 2010, pp. 1–11, https://eur-lex.europa.eu/legal-content/EN/TXT/?qid=1559921522433&uri=CELEX:32010R1092 (download 7 July 2019).

Council Regulation (EU) No. 1096/2010 of 17 November 2010 conferring specific tasks upon the European Central Bank concerning the functioning of the European Systemic Risk Board, *OJ L* 331, 15 December 2010, pp. 162–164, https://eur-lex.europa.eu/legal-content/EN/TXT/?qid=1559921655610&uri=CELEX:32010R1096 (download 7 July 2019).

Regulation (EU) No. 1093/2010 of the European Parliament and of the Council of 24 November 2010 establishing a European Supervisory Authority (European Banking Authority), amending Decision No. 716/2009/EC and repealing Commission Decision 2009/78/EC, *OJ L* 331, 15 December 2010, pp. 12–47, https://eur-lex.europa.eu/legal-content/EN/TXT/?qid=1559921816523&uri=CELEX:32010R1093 (download 7 July 2019).

Regulation (EU) No. 1094/2010 of the European Parliament and of the Council of 24 November 2010 establishing a European Supervisory Authority (European Insurance and Occupational Pensions Authority), amending Decision No. 716/2009/EC and repealing Commission Decision 2009/79/EC, *OJ L* 331, 15 December 2010, pp. 48–83, https://eur-lex.europa.eu/legal-content/EN/TXT/?qid=1559921916667&uri=CELEX:32010R1094 (download 7 July 2019).

Regulation (EU) No. 1095/2010 of the European Parliament and of the Council of 24 November 2010 establishing a European Supervisory Authority (European Securities and Markets Authority), amending Decision No. 716/2009/EC and repealing Commission Decision 2009/77/EC, *OJ L* 331, 15 December 2010, pp. 84–119, https://eur-lex.europa.eu/legal-content/EN/TXT/?qid=1559922020503&uri=CELEX:32010R1095 (download 7 July 2019).

Regulation (EU) No. 260/2012 of the European Parliament and of the Council of 14 March 2012 establishing technical and business requirements for credit transfers and direct debits in euro and amending Regulation (EC) No. 924/2009 Text with EEA relevance, *OJ L* 94, 30 March 2012, pp. 22–37, https://eur-lex.europa.eu/legal-content/EN/TXT/?qid=1559922104561&uri=CELEX:32012R0260 (download 7 July 2019).

Regulation (EU) No. 648/2012 of the European Parliament and of the Council of 4 July 2012 on OTC derivatives, central counterparties and trade repositories Text with EEA relevance (European Market Infrastructure Regulation [EMIR]), *OJ L* 201, 27 July 2012, pp. 1–59, https://eur-lex.europa.eu/legal-content/EN/TXT/?qid=1559922203172&uri=CELEX:32012R0648 (download 7 July 2019).

Commission Delegated Regulation (EU) No. 148/2013 of 19 December 2012 supplementing Regulation (EU) No. 648/2012 of the European Parliament and of the Council on OTC derivatives, central counterparties and trade repositories with regard to regulatory technical standards on the minimum details of the data to be reported to trade repositories Text with EEA relevance, *OJ L* 52, 23 February 2013, pp. 1–10, https://eur-lex.europa.eu/legal-content/EN/TXT/?qid=1559922399703&uri=CELEX:32013R0148 (download 7 July 2019).

Regulation (EU) No. 575/2013 of the European Parliament and of the Council of 26 June 2013 on prudential requirements for credit institutions and investment firms and amending Regulation (EU) No. 648/2012 Text with EEA relevance, *OJ L* 176, 27 June 2013, pp. 1–337, https://eur-lex.europa.eu/legal-content/EN/TXT/?qid=1559922522082&uri=CELEX:32013R0575 (download 7 July 2019).

Regulation (EU) No. 1022/2013 of the European Parliament and of the Council of 22 October 2013 amending Regulation (EU) No. 1093/2010 establishing a European Supervisory Authority (European Banking Authority) as regards the conferral of specific tasks on the European Central Bank pursuant to Council Regulation (EU) No. 1024/2013, *OJ L* 287, 29 October 2013, pp. 5–14, https://eur-lex.europa.eu/legal-content/EN/TXT/?qid=1559922621530&uri=CELEX:32013R1022 (download 7 July 2019).

Council Regulation (EU) No. 1024/2013 of 15 October 2013 conferring specific tasks on the European Central Bank concerning policies relating to the prudential supervision of credit institutions, *OJ L* 287, 29 October 2013, pp. 63–89, https://eur-lex.europa.eu/legal-content/EN/TXT/?qid=1559922749563&uri=CELEX:32013R1024 (download 7 July 2019).

Regulation (EU) No. 468/2014 of the European Central Bank of 16 April 2014 establishing the framework for cooperation within the Single Supervisory Mechanism between the European Central Bank and national competent authorities and with national designated authorities (SSM Framework Regulation) (ECB/2014/17), *OJ L* 141, 14 May 2014, pp. 1–50, https://eur-lex.europa.eu/legal-content/EN/TXT/?qid=1559922893807&uri=CELEX:32014R0468 (download 7 July 2019).

Regulation (EU) No. 575/2013 of the European Parliament and of the Council of 26 June 2013 on prudential requirements for credit institutions and investment firms and amending Regulation (EU) No. 648/2012 Text with EEA relevance, *OJ L* 176, 27 June 2013, pp. 1–337, https://eur-lex.europa.eu/legal-content/EN/TXT/?qid=1559922978746&uri=CELEX:32013R0575 (download 7 July 2019).

Council Implementing Regulation (EU) No. 790/2014 of 22 July 2014 implementing Article 2(3) of Regulation (EC) No. 2580/2001 on specific restrictive measures directed against certain persons and entities with a view to combatting terrorism, and repealing Implementing Regulation (EU) No. 125/2014, *OJ L* 217, 23 July 2014, pp. 1–4 (no longer in force), https://eur-lex.europa.eu/legal-content/EN/TXT/?qid=1559923092666&uri=CELEX:32014R0790 (download 7 July 2019).

Council Directive 93/22/EEC of 10 May 1993 on investment services in the securities field *OJ L* 141, 11 June 1993, pp. 27–46 (no longer in force), https://eur-lex.europa.eu/legal-content/EN/TXT/?uri=celex%3A31993L0022 (download 7 July 2019).

Directive 2000/12/EC of the European Parliament and of the Council of 20 March 2000 relating to the taking up and pursuit of the business of credit institutions, *OJ L* 126, 26 May 2000, pp. 1–59 (no longer in force), https://eur-lex.europa.eu/legal-content/EN/TXT/?uri=CELEX%3A32000L0012 (download 7 July 2019).

Directive 2002/87/EC of the European Parliament and of the Council of 16 December 2002 on the supplementary supervision of credit institutions, insurance undertakings and investment firms in a financial conglomerate and amending Council Directives 73/239/EEC, 79/267/EEC, 92/49/EEC, 92/96/EEC, 93/6/EEC and 93/22/EEC, and Directives 98/78/EC and 2000/12/EC of the European Parliament and of the Council, *OJ L* 35, 11 February 2003, pp. 1–27, https://eur-lex.europa.eu/legal-content/EN/TXT/?qid=1559923761647&uri=CELEX:32002L0087 (download 7 July 2019).

Directive 2002/92/EC of the European Parliament and of the Council of 9 December 2002 on insurance mediation, *OJ L* 9, 15 January 2003, pp. 3–10 (no longer in force), https://eur-lex.europa.eu/legal-content/EN/ALL/?uri=CELEX%3A32002L0092 (download 7 July 2019).

Directive 2004/39/EC of the European Parliament and of the Council of 21 April 2004 on markets in financial instruments amending Council Directives 85/611/EEC and 93/6/EEC and Directive 2000/12/EC of the European Parliament and of the Council and repealing Council Directive 93/22/EEC (Markets in Financial Instruments Directive [MiFID]), *OJ L* 145, 30 April 2004, pp. 1–44 (no longer in force), https://eur-lex.europa.eu/legal-content/EN/TXT/?uri=celex%3A32004L0039 (download 7 July 2019).

Directive 2005/1/EC of the European Parliament and of the Council of 9 March 2005 amending Council Directives 73/239/EEC, 85/611/EEC, 91/675/EEC, 92/49/EEC and 93/6/EEC and Directives 94/19/EC, 98/78/EC, 2000/12/EC, 2001/34/EC, 2002/83/EC and 2002/87/EC in order to establish a new organizational structure for financial services committees (Text with EEA relevance), *OJ L* 79, 24 March 2005, pp. 9–17, https://eur-lex.europa.eu/legal-content/EN/TXT/?uri=CELEX%3A32005L0001 (download 7 July 2019).

Directive 2005/60/EC of the European Parliament and of the Council of 26 October 2005 on the prevention of the use of the financial system for the purpose of money laundering and terrorist financing (Text with EEA relevance), *OJ L* 309, 25 November 2005, pp. 15–36 (no longer in force), https://eur-lex.europa.eu/legal-content/EN/TXT/?uri=CELEX%3A32005L0060 (download 7 July 2019).

Directive 2006/48/EC of the European Parliament and of the Council of 14 June 2006 relating to the taking up and pursuit of the business of credit institutions (recast) (Text with EEA relevance), *OJ L* 177, 30 June 2006, pp. 1–200 (no longer in force), https://eur-lex.europa.eu/legal-content/EN/TXT/?uri=CELEX%3A32006L0048 (download 7 July 2019).

Directive 2006/49/EC of the European Parliament and of the Council of 14 June 2006 on the capital adequacy of investment firms and credit institutions (recast), *OJ L* 177, 30 June 2006, pp. 201–255 (no longer in force), https://eur-lex.europa.eu/legal-content/EN/TXT/?uri=CELEX:32006L0049 (download 7 July 2019).

Directive 2007/64/EC of the European Parliament and of the Council of 13 November 2007 on payment services in the internal market amending Directives 97/7/EC, 2002/65/EC, 2005/60/EC and 2006/48/EC and repealing Directive 97/5/EC (Text with EEA relevance), *OJ L* 319, 5 December 2007, pp. 1–36 (no longer in force), https://eur-lex.europa.eu/legal-content/en/ALL/?uri=CELEX%3A32007L0064 (download 7 July 2019).

Directive 2008/48/EC of the European Parliament and of the Council of 23 April 2008 on credit agreements for consumers and repealing Council Directive 87/102/EEC, *OJ L* 133, 22 May 2008, pp. 66–92, https://eur-lex.europa.eu/legal-content/EN/ALL/?uri=celex:32008L0048 (download 7 July 2019).

Directive 2009/22/EC of the European Parliament and of the Council of 23 April 2009 on injunctions for the protection of consumers' interests (Codified version) Text with EEA relevance, *OJ L* 110, 1 May 2009, pp. 30–36, https://eur-lex.europa.eu/legal-content/EN/TXT/?uri=uriserv:OJ.L_.2009.110.01.0030.01.ENG (download 7 July 2019).

Directive 2009/65/EC of the European Parliament and of the Council of 13 July 2009 on the coordination of laws, regulations and administrative provisions relating to undertakings for collective investment in transferable securities (UCITS) (Text with EEA relevance), OJ L 302, 17 November 2009, pp. 32–96, https://eur-lex.europa.eu/legal-content/EN/ALL/?uri=CELEX%3A32009L0065 (download 7 July 2019).

Directive 2009/110/EC of the European Parliament and of the Council of 16 September 2009 on the taking up, pursuit and prudential supervision of the business of electronic money institutions amending Directives 2005/60/EC and 2006/48/EC and repealing Directive 2000/46/EC (Text with EEA relevance), OJ L 267, 10 October 2009, pp. 7–17, https://eur-lex.europa.eu/legal-content/EN/TXT/?uri=CELEX%3A32009L0110 (download 7 July 2019).

Directive 2011/89/EU of the European Parliament and of the Council of 16 November 2011 amending Directives 98/78/EC, 2002/87/EC, 2006/48/EC and 2009/138/EC as regards the supplementary supervision of financial entities in a financial conglomerate Text with EEA relevance, OJ L 326, 8 December 2011, pp. 113–141, https://eur-lex.europa.eu/legal-content/GA/TXT/?uri=CELEX:32011L0089 (download 7 July 2019).

Directive 2013/36/EU of the European Parliament and of the Council of 26 June 2013 on access to the activity of credit institutions and the prudential supervision of credit institutions and investment firms, amending Directive 2002/87/EC and repealing Directives 2006/48/EC and 2006/49/EC Text with EEA relevance, OJ L 176, 27 June 2013, pp. 338–436, https://eur-lex.europa.eu/legal-content/EN/TXT/?uri=celex%3A32013L0036 (download 7 July 2019).

Directive (EU) 2015/2366 of the European Parliament and of the Council of 25 November 2015 on payment services in the internal market, amending Directives 2002/65/EC, 2009/110/EC and 2013/36/EU and Regulation (EU) No. 1093/2010, and repealing Directive 2007/64/EC (Text with EEA relevance), OJ L 337, 23 December 2015, pp. 35–127, https://eur-lex.europa.eu/legal-content/en/TXT/?uri=CELEX:32015L2366 (download 7 July 2019).

Directive 2014/65/EU of the European Parliament and of the Council of 15 May 2014 on markets in financial instruments and amending Directive 2002/92/EC and Directive 2011/61/EU Text with EEA relevance, OJ L 173, 12 June 2014, pp. 349–496, https://eur-lex.europa.eu/legal-content/EN/TXT/?uri=celex%3A32014L0065 (download 7 July 2019).

Directive (EU) 2015/849 of the European Parliament and of the Council of 20 May 2015 on the prevention of the use of the financial system for the purposes of money laundering or terrorist financing, amending Regulation (EU) No. 648/2012 of the European Parliament and of the Council, and repealing

Directive 2005/60/EC of the European Parliament and of the Council and Commission Directive 2006/70/EC (Text with EEA relevance), *OJ L* 141, 5 June 2015, pp. 73–117, https://eur-lex.europa.eu/legal-content/EN/TXT/?uri=celex%3A32015L0849 (download 7 July 2019).

2001/150/EC: Decision of the European Central Bank of 10 November 2000 on the publication of certain legal acts and instruments of the European Central Bank (ECB/2000/12), *OJ L* 55, 24 February 2001, pp. 68–80, https://eur-lex.europa.eu/legal-content/EN/TXT/?qid=1559926590920&uri=CELEX:32000D0012(01) (download 7 July 2019).

2014/541/EU: Decision of the European Central Bank of 29 July 2014 on measures relating to targeted longer-term refinancing operations (ECB/2014/34), *OJ L* 258, 29 August 2014, pp. 11–28, with later amendment (ECB/2015/5), https://www.ecb.europa.eu/ecb/legal/pdf/oj_jol_2014_258_r_0006_en_txt.pdf (download 7 July 2019).

2011/C 140/10: Decision of the European Systemic Risk Board of 25 March 2011 adopting the Code of Conduct of the European Systemic Risk Board (ESRB/2011/3), *OJ C* 140, 11 May 2011, pp. 18–19, https://www.esrb.europa.eu/pub/pdf/CoC_en.pdf (download 7 July 2019).

2011/C 302/04: Decision of the European Systemic Risk Board of 21 September 2011 on the provision and collection of information for the macro-prudential oversight of the financial system within the Union (ESRB/2011/6), *OJ C* 302, 13 October 2011, pp. 3–11, https://www.esrb.europa.eu/shared/pdf/110921_decision_collection_information.en.pdf?9b66ebe5b3e5c122f69b1ae889558b8b (download 7 July 2019).

Guideline of the ECB of 7 April 2006 on the Eurosystem's provision of reserve management services in euro to central banks and countries located outside the euro area and to international organizations (ECB/2006/4), *OJ L* 107, 20 April 2006, pp. 54–57, with later amendment ECB/2013/14, https://www.ecb.europa.eu/ecb/legal/pdf/l_10720060420en00540057.pdf (download 7 July 2019).

Guideline of the European Central Bank of 20 June 2008 on the management of the foreign reserve assets of the European Central Bank by the national central banks and the legal documentation for operations involving such assets (recast) (ECB/2008/5), *OJ L* 192, 19 July 2008, pp. 63–83, https://eur-lex.europa.eu/legal-content/EN/TXT/?qid=1559928637129&uri=CELEX:32008O0005 (download 7 July 2019).

Guideline (EU) 2015/510 of the European Central Bank of 19 December 2014 on the implementation of the Eurosystem monetary policy framework (ECB/2014/60), *OJ L* 91, 2 April 2015, pp. 3–135, with later amendments EBC/2015/20, EBC/2015/27, EBC/2015/34, https://eur-lex.europa.eu/

legal-content/EN/TXT/?qid=1559928802068&uri=CELEX:32014O0060 (download 7 July 2019).

2014/304/EU: Guideline of the European Central Bank of 20 February 2014 on domestic asset and liability management operation by the national central banks (ECB/2014/9), *OJ L* 159, 28 May 2014, pp. 56–65, with later amendments, https://eur-lex.europa.eu/legal-content/EN/TXT/?uri=CELEX%3A32014O0009 (download 7 July 2019).

Guideline (EU) 2016/65 of the European Central Bank of 18 November 2015 on the valuation haircuts applied in the implementation of the Eurosystem monetary policy framework (ECB/2015/35), *OJ L* 14, 21 January 2016, pp. 30–35, https://eur-lex.europa.eu/legal-content/EN/TXT/?qid=1559929777191&uri=CELEX:32015O0035 (download 7 July 2019).

Other Documents

Bank of America 2014 Annual Reports & Proxy Statements, http://investor.bankofamerica.com/phoenix.zhtml?c=71595&p=irol-reportsannual#fbid=Fea1Pkdph3P (download 12 October 2015).

Bank of New York Mellon 2014 Annual Report and Proxy, https://www.bnymellon.com/us/en/investor-relations/annual-report-proxy.jsp (download 12 October 2015).

BNP Paribas Registration Documents & Annual Financial Reports 2014, https://invest.bnpparibas.com/en/registration-documents-annual-financial-reports (download 12 October 2015).

Citigroup 2014 Annual Report, https://www.citigroup.com/citi/investor/quarterly/2015/annual-report/ (download 12 October 2015).

Connecting Customers to Opportunities for 150 Years, HSBC Holdings plc Annual Report 2014, http://www.londonstockexchange.com/exchange/news/market-news/market-news-detail/12289521.html (download 12 October 2015).

Consultative Document: Sound Practices for the Management and Supervision of Operational Risk, Basel, "Bank for International Settlements Papers", December 2010, http://www.bis.org/publ/bcbs183.pdf (download 12 October 2015).

Credit Agricole S.A. Financial Results 2014, http://www.credit-agricole.com/en/Investor-and-shareholder/Financial-reporting/Credit-Agricole-S.A.-financial-results (download 12 October 2015).

Developing Our Approach to Implementing MiFID II Conduct of Business and Organizational Requirements, "Financial Conduct Authority Discussion Paper", Nr 3 (DP15/3), March 2015.

Driving Investment, Trade and the Creation of Wealth Across Asia, Africa and the Middle East—Standard Chartered Bank 2014 Annual Report, https://www.sc.com/annual-report/2014/ (download 12 October 2015).
Evolving Banking Regulation: Is the End in Sight, KPMG 2014 EMA Edition.
Goldman Sachs Group Inc., http://www.annualreports.com/Company/goldman-sachs-group-inc (download 12 October 2015).
K. Gordon, *Rules for the Global Economy: Synergies Between Voluntary and Binding Approaches*, "Organisation for Economic Cooperation and Development Working Paper", 1999/2000.
Heart of the Financial District for over 300 Years Barclays Plc. 2014 Annual Report, https://www.home.barclays (download 12 October 2015).
HSBC Holdings plc., Report of the Directors: Corporate Governance 2013.
ING Groep NV Annual Report 2014, http://www.ing.com/About-us/Annual-Reporting-Suite/Annual-Reports-archive.htm (download 12 October 2015).
JPMorgan Chase & Co. Annual Report and Proxy Statement 2014, http://investor.shareholder.com/jpmorganchase/annual.cfm (download 12 October 2015).
Jurisdiction Clauses in Contracts, http://www.timeshareconsumerassociation.org.uk/jurisdiction-clauses-contracts/ (download 2 September 2015).
Legal & Regulatory Risk Note: A Risk Management Briefing Putting the Key Issues at the Top of the Agenda, A&O Edition, London 2014.
Let's Make a Difference: Managing Compliance and Operational Risk in the New Environment, Report, "PwC FS Viewpoint", 2013.
Lloyds Banking Group plc Company Results 2014, http://www.lloydsbankinggroup.com/investors/financial-performance/lloyds-banking-group/ (download 12 October 2015).
Raport zespołu pod przewodnictwem Erkki Liikanena 2 października 2012 pod auspicjami Komisji Europejskiej zawierający projekt reformy strukturalnej w bankowości pt., "Final Report High-Level Expert Group on Reforming the Structure of the EU Banking Sector", http://ec.europa.eu/internal_market/bank/docs/high-level_expert_group/report_en.pdf (download 10 November 2015).
RBS Annual Report and Accounts 2014—Earning Our Customer's Trust, http://investors.rbs.com/~/media/Files/R/RBS-IR/2014-reports/annual-report-2014.pdf (download 12 October 2015).
Société Générale SA Registration Document 2014, http://www.societegenerale.com/sites/default/files/societegeneraleddr2014en_0.pdf (download 12 October 2015).
The Importance of Close-Out Netting, http://www2.isda.org/search?headerSearch=1&keyword=close+out+netting (download 17 November 2015).
We Want to Help People and Business Prosper—Banco Santander SA Annual Report 2014, http://www.santanderannualreport.com/2014/pdf/en/annual-report.pdf (download 12 October 2015).

Bibliography

A. Aarnio, R. Alexy, A. Pecznik, W. Rabinowicz, J. Woleński, *On Coherence Theory of Law*, Lund 1998.

J. Ackermann, The Subprime Crisis and Its Consequences: Regulation and the Financial Crisis of 2007–08: Review and Analysis, *Journal of Financial Stability* 4(4)/2008.

R. Aggarwal, V. Azofra, F. Lopez, Differences in governance Practices Between US and Foreign Firms: Measurement, Causes and Consequences, *Review of Financial Studies* 23(3)/2010.

R. V. Aguilera, G. Jackson, The Cross-National Diversity of Corporate Governance: Dimensions and Determinants, *Academy of Management Review* 39(4)/October 2014.

T. W. Aldorno, Culture and Administration [in] J. M. Bernstein [ed.] *The Culture Industry: Selected Essays on Mass Culture by Theodor W. Aldorno*, London 1991.

K. Alexander, R. Dhumale, J. Eatwell, *Global Governance of Financial Systems: The International Regulation of Systemic Risk*, Oxford 2006.

A. Alfonso, M. G. Arghyrou, A. Kontonikas, The Determinants of Sovereign Yield Spreads in the European Monetary Union, *European Central Bank Working Paper* Series, April 2015.

J. A. Allison, Market Discipline Beats Regulatory Discipline, *Cato Journal* 34/2014.

A. C. Aman, *The Democracy Deficit: Taming Globalization Through Law Reform*, New York 2004.

A. Amaya, Justification, Coherence, and Epistemic Responsibility in Legal Fact-Finding, *Journal of Social Epistemology* 5/2008.

S. Andersson, P. M. Heywood, The Politics of Perception: Use and Abuse of Transparency International's Approach to Measuring Corruption, *Political Studies* 57(4)/2009.
T. Aron, N. Lalone, C. Jackson, EMIR: An Overview of the New Framework, *Journal of Investment Compliance* 14(2)/2013.
D. W. Arner, *Financial Stability, Economic Growth, and the Role of Law*, Cambridge 2007.
P. Ashton, B. Christophers, On Arbitration, Arbitrage and Arbitrariness In financial Markets and Their Governance: Unpacking LIBOR and the LIBOR Scandal, *Economy and Society* 44(2)/2015.
H. Assa, Risk Management Under Prudential Policy, *Decisions in Economics and Finance* 38(2)/2015.
M. S. Asslaender, J. Curbach, Corporate or Government Duties? Corporate Citizenship from a Governmental Perspective, *Business and Society* 5/2015.
D. Awrey, W. Blair, D. Kershaw, Between Law and Markets: Is There a Role for Culture and Ethics in Financial Regulation? *Delaware Journal of Corporate Law* 38/2013.
R. Ayadi, E. Arbak, W. P. De Groen, Implementing Basel III in Europe: Diagnosis and Avenues for Improvement, *Centre for European Policy Studies*.
L. Baccaro, V. Mele, For Lack Of Anything Better? International Organizations and Global Corporate Codes, *Public Administration* 89(2)/2011.
L. C. Backer, Global Panopticism: Surveillance Lawmaking by Corporations, States, and Other Entities, *Global Legal Studies* 101/2008.
L. C. Backer, *Harmonizing Law in the Era of Globalization: Convergence, Divergence and Resistance*, Durham 2007.
L. C. Backer, Multinational Corporations as Objects and Sources of Transnational Regulation, *International & Compliance Law* 499/2008.
I. Baczewska-Ciupak, *Przywództwo organizacyjne w kontekście aksjologicznych i moralnych wyzwań przyszłości*, Lublin 2013.
M. Bączyk, E. Fojcik-Mastalska, L. Góral, J. Pisuliński, W. Pyzioł, *Prawo bankowe. Komentarz*, Warsaw 2003.
J. Bakan, *The Corporation: The Pathological Pursuit of Profit and Power*, New York 2004.
A. Baker, The New Political Economy of the Macroprudential Ideational Shift, *New Political Economy* 1(18)/2013.
C. W. Bame-Aldred, J. B. Cullen, K. D. Martin, K. P. Parboteeah, National Culture and Firm-Level Tax Evasion, *Journal of Business Research* 66(3)/2013.
C. E. Bannier, C. W. Hirsch, The Economic Function of Credit Rating Agencies—What Does the Watchlist Tell Us? *Journal of Banking and Finance* 34(12)/2010.
C. A. Barlett, S. Ghoshal, Matrix Management: Not a Structure, a Frame of Mind, *Harvard Business Review* 60(4)/1990.

J. R. Barth, G. Caprio Jr., R. Levine, Bank Regulation and Supervision: What Works Best? *Journal of Financial Intermediation* 13(2)/2004.
C. L. Basri, J. E. Murphy, G. J. Wallance, *Corporate Compliance: Caremark and the Globalization of Good Corporate Conduct*, New York 1998.
A. Bator, Integracja i globalizacja z perspektywy filozofii prawa [in] J. Stelmach [ed.] *Filozofia prawa wobec globalizmu*, Kraków 2003.
A. Bator, W. Gromski, A. Kozak, S. Kaźmierczyk, Z. Pulka, *Wprowadzenie do nauk prawnych. Leksykon tematyczny*, Warsaw 2012.
Z. Bauman, *Szanse etyki w zglobalizowanym świecie*, Kraków 2007.
L. Bélanger, K. Fontaine-Skronski, 'Legalization' in International Relations: A Conceptual Analysis, *Social Science Information* 51(2)/2012.
J. Bell, *French Legal Cultures*, Cambridge 2001.
L. Benton, *Law and Colonial Cultures*, Cambridge 2002.
M. Bergström, K. Svedberg Helgesson, U. Mörth, A New Role for For-Profit Actors? The Case of Anti-money Laundering and Risk Management, *Journal of Common Market Studies* 49(5)/2011.
J. Bessis, *Risk Management in Banking*, Padstow 2015.
C. Bicchieri, *The Grammar of Society: The Nature and Dynamics of the Social Norms*, Cambridge 2006.
M. T. Biegelman, J. T. Bartow, *Executive Roadmap to Fraud Prevention and Internal Control: Creating of Culture of Compliance*, Hoboken, NJ 2012.
G. Bierbrauer, Toward an Understanding of Legal Culture: Variations in Individualism and Collectivism, *Law and Society Review*, Oxford 1994.
L. B. Bingham, D. R. Chachere, Theoretical and Empirical Research on the Grievance Procedure and Arbitration: A Critical Review [in] A. E. Eaton, J. H. Keefe [ed.] *Employment Dispute Resolution and Worker Rights*, Champaign 1999.
R. C. Bird, P. A. Borochin, J. D. Knopf, The Role of the Chief Legal Officer in Corporate Governance, *Journal of Corporate Finance* 34/2015.
J. Bischof, H. Daske, F. Elfers, L. Hail, A Tale of Two Regulators: Risk Disclosures, Liquidity, and Enforcement in the Banking Sector, *University of Pennsylvania Law Papers* 5/2015.
S. Blake, D. Hortensius, The Development of a Global Standard on Compliance Management, *Business Compliance* 2/2014.
E. Blankenburg, Civil Litigation Rates as Indicators for Legal Cultures [in] D. Nelken [ed.] *Comparing Legal Cultures*, Brookfield 1997.
E. Blankenburg, The Infrastructure of legal culture in Holland and West Germany, *Law and Society Review* 28(4)/1994.
M. Błachut, W. Gromski, J. Kaczor, *Technika prawodawcza*, Warsaw 2008.
S. Bleker, D. Hortensius, The Development of a Global Standard on Compliance Management, *Business Compliance*, February 2014.
D. D. Bobek, A. M. Hageman, C. F. Kelliher, Analyzing the Role of Social Norms in Tax Compliance Behavior, *Journal of Business Ethics* 115/2013.

D. Boheme, *When Compliance and Legal Don't See Eye to Eye, Corporate Counsel*, 8 May 2014, www.compliancestrategists.com/csblog/2014/05/11/.
O. Boiral, The Certification of Corporate Conduct: Issues And Prospects, *International Labour Review* 142(3)/2003.
S. Bottomley, *The Constitutional Corporation: Rethinking Corporate Governance*, Applied Legal Philosophy, London 2007.
E. Bouretz, J.-L. Emery, Autorite des marches financiers et Commission bancaire: Pouvoirs de sanctions et recours, *La Revue Banques* 702/2008.
R. Boyer, From Shareholder Value to CEO Power: The Paradox of the 1990s, *Competition and Change* 9/2005.
J. H. Bracey, *Exploring Law and Culture*, Long Grove 2006.
D. D. Bradlow, Private Complaints and International Organizations: A Comparative Study of the Independent Inspection Mechanisms in International Financial Institutions, *Journal of International Law* January 2005.
R. H. Brescia, Tainted Loans: The Value of a Mass Torts Approach in Subprime Mortgage Litigation, *University of Cincinnati Law Review* 78/2009.
I. E. Brick, N. K. Chindambaran, Board Monitoring, Firm Risk, and External Regulation, *Journal of Regulatory Economics* 33/2008.
T. L. Brown, M. Potoski, Managing Contract Performance: A Transaction Costs Approach, *Journal of Policy Analysis and Management* 22(2)/2003.
B. Brożek, Legal Interpretation and Coherence [in] M. Araszkiewicz, J. Savelka [ed.] *Coherence: Insights from Philosophy, Jurisprudence and Artificial Intelligence*, Law and Philosophy Library 107, Springer 2013.
C. Brummer, Why Soft Law Dominates International Finance—And Not Trade, *Journal of International Economic Law* 13(3)/2010.
R. P. Buckley, *International Financial System: Policy and Regulation*, Alphen aan den Rijn 2008.
N. W. R. Burbidge, International Anti-money Laundering and Anti-terrorist Financing: The Work of the Office of the Superintendent of Financial Institutions in Canada, *Journal of Money Laundering Control* 7(4)/2004.
L. Canibano, E. De las Heras, Enforcement in the European Union. A Comparative Survey: Spain and the UK [in] G. Frattini [ed.] *Improving Business Reporting: New Rules, New Opportunities, New Trends*, Milano 2007.
J. B. Caouette, E. I. Altman, P. Narayanan, *Managing Credit Risk: The Next Great Financial Challenge*, New York 1998.
A. B. Carroll, A. K. Buchholtz, *Business and Society: Ethics, Sustainability, and Stakeholder Management*, Stamford 2015.
S. G. Cecchetti, D. Domanski, G. von Peter, New Regulation and the New World of Global Banking, *National Institute Economic Review* 216(1)/2011.
B. Cheng, S. Srinivasan, G. Yu, Securities Litigation Risk for Foreign Companies Listed in the U.S., *Harvard Business School Working Paper* 13-036/2012.
A. S. Chernobai, S. T. Rachev, F. J. Fabozzi, *Operational Risk: A Guide to Basel II Capital Requirements, Models and Analysis*, Hoboken, NJ 2007.

C. Chinkin, Normative Development in International Legal System, *International and Comparative Law Quarterly* 38/1989.

K.-K. R. Choo, Challenges in Dealing with politically Exposed Persons, *Trends and Issues in Crime and Criminal Justice* 386/ 2010.

P. Christmann, G. Taylor, Firm Self-Regulation Through International Certifiable Standards: Determinants of Symbolic Versus Substantive Implementation, *Journal of International Business Studies* 37/2006.

M. Cihak, A. Demirguc-Kunt, M. S. M. Peria, A. Mohseni-Cheraghlou, Bank Regulation and Supervision Around the World: A Crisis Update, *World Bank Policy Research Working Paper* 1/2012.

D. I. Clelant, W. R. King, *The Cultural Ambience of Matrix Organization*, Hoboken 2008 (download 6 October 2015).

S. Conway, M. E. Conway, *Essentials of Enterprise Compliance*, Hoboken, NJ 2008.

R. Cotarcea, *Banking Debacle Worth Billions*, CEE Legal Matters: In-Depth Analysis of the News and Newsmakers That Shape Europe's Emerging Legal Markets tom 2 April 2015.

R. Cotterell, The Concept of Legal Culture [in] D. Nelken, *Comparing Legal Cultures*, Brookfield 1997.

D. Covan, Legal Consciousness: Some Observations, *Modern Law Review* 67(6)/2004.

H. Cronqvist, R. Fahlenbrach, Large Shareholders and Corporate Policies, *The Review of Financial Studies* 22(10)/2009.

H. Davies, *Banks* Need to Question Their 'Three Lines of Defense', *Financial Times*, 9 July 2013

D. A. DeMott, The Crucial but (Potentially) Precarious Position of the Chief Compliance Officer, *Brooklyn Journal of Corporate, Financial and Commercial Law* 8/2013.

D. A. DeMott, Stages of Scandal and the Roles of General Counsel, *Wisconsin Law Review* 13/2012.

B. Dennis, *Criminal Compliance*, Baden-Baden 2011.

C. Derber, *Corporation Nation: How Corporations Are Taking over Our Lives and What We Can Do About It*, New York 1998.

J. Dewar, *International Project Finance. Law and Practice*, Oxford 2011.

S. Dinah [ed.] *Commitment and Compliance: The Role of Non-binding Norms in the International Legal System*, Oxford 2000.

E. M. Dodd, R. J. Baker, *Cases and Materials on Corporations*, New York 2000.

G. W. Downs, M. A. Jones, Reputation, Compliance and International Law, *The Journal of Legal Studies* 31/2002.

T. Doyle, Cleaning Up Anti-money Laundering Strategies: Current FATF Tactics Needlessly Violate International Law, *Houston Journal of International Law* 24/2002.

J. N. Drabek [ed.] *Norms and the Law*, Cambridge 2006.

G. S. Drori, Governed by Governance: The New Prism of Organizational Change [in] G. S. Drori, J. W. Meyer, H. Hwang [ed.] *Globalization and Organization World Society and Organizational Change*, Oxford 2006.

J. N. Druckman, The Implications of Framing Effects for Citizen Competence, *Political Behavior* 23(3)/2001.

A. Drwiłło, D. Maśniak, *Leksykon prawa finansowego*, Warsaw 2015.

R. Dworkin, *Biorąc prawa poważnie*, Warsaw 1998.

T. Dyllick, K. Hockerts, Sustainability at the Millennium: Globalization, Competitiveness & Public Trust, *Business Strategy and the Environment* 11(2)/2002.

P. Eberl, D. Geiger, M. S. Asslaender, Repairing Trust in an Organization After Integrity Violations: The Ambivalence of Organizational Rule Adjustments, *Organization Studies* 36(9)/2015.

R. Eccleston, F. Gray, Foreign Accounts Tax Compliance Act and American Leadership in the Campaign against International Tax Evasion: Revolution or False Dawn? *Global Policy* 5(3)/2014.

M. Eggert, *Compliance Management in Financial Industries: A Model-Based Business Process and Reporting Perspective*, Heidelberg 2014.

S. Ehrlich, *Oblicza pluralizmów*, Warsaw 1985.

S. Ehrlich, *Wiążące wzory zachowań. Rzecz o wielości systemów i norm*, Warsaw 1995.

M. El-Bannany, A Study of Determinants of Intellectual Capital Performance in Banks: The UK Case, *Journal of Intellectual Capital* 9(3)/2008.

M. El Kharbili, S. Stein, I. Markovic, E. Pulvermüller, *Towards a Framework for Semantic Business Process Compliance Management*, Osnabrueck 2008.

H. Elffers, P. Verboon, *Managing and Maintaining Compliance*, The Hague 2006.

S. R. Epstein [ed.] Guilds, Economy and Society [in] *Corporations, economies et societe*, Seville 1998.

G. Ercel, Globalization and International Financial Environment, *Bank of International Settlements Review* 79/2000.

E. Erlich, *Fundamental Principles of the Sociology of Law*, Brunswick, NJ 2002.

Ethics and Compliance Risk Management: Improving Business Performance and Fostering a Strong Ethical Culture Through a Sustainable Process, LRN Publications, New York 2007.

P. Ewick, The Structure of Legality: The Cultural Contradictions of Social Institutions [in] R. A. Kagan, M. Krygier, K. Wiston [ed.] *Legality and Community*, Berkeley 2002.

D. W. Ewing, *Justice on the Job: Resolving Grievances in the Nonunion Workplace*, Harvard 1989.

M. Fairfax, Rhetoric of Corporate Law: The Impact of Stakeholder Rhetoric on Corporate Norms, *Journal of Corporate Law* 675/2005–2006.

M. Faure, *Tort Law and Economics*, Cheltenham 2009.
M. Fedorowicz, *Nadzór nad rynkiem finansowym w Unii Europejskiej*, Warsaw 2013.
F. Feretti, A European Perspective in Consumer Loans and the Role of Credit Registries: The Need to Reconcile Data Protection, Risk Management, Efficiency, Over-Indebtness, and a Better Prudential Supervision of the Financial System, *Journal of Consumer Policy* 33(1)/2010.
G. Ferrani, E.Wymeersch, *Investor Protection in Europe: Corporate Law Making, The MiFID and Beyond*, Oxford Scholarship Online 2009, http://econpapers.repec.org/bookchap/oxpobooks/9780199202911.htm.
J. R. Fichtner, The Recent International Growth of Mandatory Audit Committee Requirements, *International Journal of Disclosure and Governance* 7/2010.
V. Fitzgerald, Global Financial Information, Compliance Incentives and Terrorist Financing, *European Journal of Political Economy* 20(2)/2004.
E. M. Fogel, A. M. Geier, Strangers in the House, Rethinking Sarbanes-Oxley and the Independent Board of Directors, *Delaware Journal of Corporate Law* 32/2007.
M. Forster, T. Loughran, B. McDonald, Commonality in Codes of Ethics, *Journal of Business Ethics* 90/2009.
T. Frankel, Towards Universal Fiduciary Principles, *Boston University School of Law Working Paper* 9/2012.
W. Frąckowiak, *Fuzje i przejęcia*, Warsaw 2009.
W. C. Frederick, *Values, Nature, and Culture in the American Corporation*, Oxford 1995.
D. Freeman, The Role of Consumption of Modern Durables in Economic Development, *Economic Development and Cultural Change* 19(1)/2011.
L. L. Fuller, *Moralność prawa*, Warsaw 1978.
J. Galli, *Plemienna korporacja*, Warsaw 2013.
A. Garapon, French Legal Culture and the Shock of "Globalization" [in] D. Nelken, J. Feest [ed.] *Legal Culture, Diversity and Globalization, "Social and Legal Studies"*, Thousand Oaks 1995.
W. Gasparski [ed.] *Etyka biznesu w zastosowaniach praktycznych: inicjatywy, programy, kodeksy*, Warsaw 2002.
W. Gasparski, A. Lewicka-Strzałecka, B. Rok, G. Szulczewski, Etyka biznesu w zastosowaniach praktycznych, *Inicjatywy, programy, kodeksy, IFiS PAN*, Warsaw 2002.
N. Gennaioli, A. Martin, S. Rossi, *Sovereign* Default, Domestic Banks, and Financial Institutions, *The Journal of Finance* 69(2)/2014.
E. F. Gerding, *Bubbles, Law and Financial Regulation*, New York 2014.
M. Gibbins, A. Richardson, J. Waterhouse, The Management of Corporate Financial Disclosure: Opportunism, Ritualism, Polices and Processes, *Journal of Accounting Research* 1/1990.

L. Gibson, G. A. Caldeira, The legal cultures of Europe, *Law and Society Review* 30(1)/1997.
G. Giroux, *Accounting Fraud: Maneuvering and Manipulation Past and Present*, New York 2014.
J. Gitman, R. Juchau, J. Flanagan, *Principles of Managerial Finance*, Pearson 2011.
J. Gliniecka, *Publiczne prawo bankowe*, Warsaw 2013.
D. Golden, The Future of Financial Regulation: The Role of the Courts [in] I. MacNeil, J. O'Brien [ed.] *The Future of Financial Regulation*, Oxford 2010.
B. Gong, *Understanding Institutional Shareholder Activism: A Comparative Study of the UK and China*, New York 2014.
L. Góral, *Zintegrowany model publicznoprawnych instytucji ochrony rynku bankowego we Francji i Polsce*, Warsaw 2011.
G. Gorton, The Subprime Panic, *European Financial Management* 15(1)/2009.
T. Gospodarek, Modelowanie w naukach o zarządzaniu oparte na metodzie programów badawczych, *Monografie i opracowania Uniwersytetu Ekonomicznego we Wrocławiu* 189/2009.
J. R. Gottlieb, *The Matrix Management Organization Reloaded*, London 2006.
J. Gregory, *Counterparty Credit Risk and Credit Value Adjustment: A Continuing Challenge*, Chichester 2012.
W. Gromski, *Autonomia i instrumentalny charakter prawa*, Wrocław 2000.
A. Grünbichler, P. Darlap, Integration of UE Financial Markets Supervision: Harmonization or Unification? *Journal of Financial Regulation and Compliance* 12(1)/2004.
T. Guzman, T. Meyer, International Soft Law, *The Journal of Legal Analysis— UC Berkeley Public Law Research Paper* 2(1)/2011.
R. Gwiazdowski, *A nie mówiłem? Dlaczego nastąpił kryzys i jak najszybciej z niego wyjść*, Prohibita 2012.
U. C. V. Haley, *Multinational Corporations in Political Environments: Ethics, Values and Strategies*, Knoxville 2001.
R. Halfer, Regime Shifting: The TRIPs Agreement and New Dynamics of Intellectual Property Lawmaking, *Yale Journal of International Law* 29/2004.
T. C. Halliday, B. G. Carruthers, The Recursivity of Law: Global Norm Making and National Lawmaking in the Globalization of Corporate Insolvency Regimes, *American Journal of Sociology* 112(4)/2007.
J.-L. Halperin, F. Audren, *La culture juridique francaise: Entre mythes et realite*, Broche 2013.
R. W. Hamilton, R. D. Freer, *The Law of Corporations in a Nutshell*, St. Paul 2011.
S. O. Hansson, *The Structure of Values and Norms*, Cambridge 2004.
H. L. A. Hart, *Pojęcie prawa*, Warsaw 1998.

M. Hashmi, A Methodology for Extracting Legal Norms from Regulatory Documents, *IEE Papers* 9/2015.
J. Heckman, S. Navarro-Losano, Using Matching, Instrumental Variables, and Control Functions to Estimate Economic Choice Models, *The Review of Economics and Statistics* 86(1)/2004.
J. Heiberg, FATCA: Toward a Multilateral Automatic Information Reporting Regime, *Washington and Lee Law Review* 69/2012.
B. W. Heineman, Can the Marriage of the GC and Chief Compliance Officer Last? *Corporate Counsel*, 30 March 2012, Law.com.
B. W. Heineman, Don't Divorce the GC and Compliance Officer, The Harvard Law School Forum on Corporate Governance and Financial Regulation and Harvard Kennedy School of Government, December 2010, www.law.harvard.edu/corpgov.
E. D. Herlihy, L. S. Makow, *A Federal Reserve Wake-Up Call to Directors of Financial Institutions*, Harvard 7 June 2014, www.blogs.law.harvard.edu.
M. Hertogh, A 'European' Conception of Legal Consciousness. Rediscovering Eugen Ehrlich' *Journal of Law and Society* 31(4)/2004.
W. Heyderbrand, Globalization and the Rule of Law at the End of the 20th Century [in] A. Febbraio, D. Nelken, V. Olgiati [ed.] *Social Process and Patterns of Legal Control*, "European Yearbook of Sociology of Law", No. 25/2000 (2001).
G. Hilary, *Regulations Through Social Norms*, London 2014.
L. Hobe, The Changing Landscape of the Financial Services, *International Journal of Trade, Economics and Finance* 6(2)/2015.
I. Hobson, Jr., *The Unseen World of Transnational Corporations' Powers*, New York 2004.
G. Hofstede, B. Neuijen, d. D. Ohayv, G. Sanders, Measuring Organizational Cultures: A. Qualitative and Quantitative Study Across Twenty Cases, *Administrative Science Quarterly* 35(2)/1990.
F. den Hond, F. G. A. de Bakker, Ideologically Motivated Activism: How Activists Groups Influence Corporate Social Change Activities, *Academy of Management*, 32(3)/2007.
P. Hopkin, *Fundamentals of Risk Management: Understanding, Evaluating and Implementing*, London 2014.
D. Hou, D. Skeie, LIBOR: Origins, Economics, Crisis, Scandal, and Reform, *Federal Reserve Bank of New York Staff Reports*, Staff Report No. 667/03/2014.
J. F. Houston, C. Lin, Y. Ma, *Regulatory Arbitrage and International Bank Flows*, Hong Kong 2012.
N. Hsieh, Does Global Business Have Responsibility to Promote Just Institutions? *Business Ethics Quarterly* 19/2009.

E. Huepkes, Compliance, Compensation, Corporate Governance [in] M. Roth [ed.] *Close-up on Compliance Recht, Moral und Risken—Nahaufnahmen zu Compliance Management und Governance—Fragen*, Zürich 2009.

R. Hurley, X. Gong, A. Waqar, Understanding the Loss of Trust in Large Banks, *International Journal of Bank Marketing* 32(5)/2014.

B. M. Hutter, *Compliance: Regulation and Environment*, Oxford 1997.

R. Inderst, Retail Finance: Thoughts on Reshaping Regulation and Consumer Protection After the Financial Crisis, *European Business Organization Law Review* 10(3)/2009.

K. Irwin, C. Horne, A Normative Explanation of Antisocial Punishment, *Social Science Research* 42(2)/2013.

Y. M. Isa, Z. M. Sanusi, M. N. Haniff, P. A. Barnes, Money Laundering Risk: From the Bankers' and Regulators Perspectives, *Procedia Economics and Finance* 28/2014.

C. L. Israels, *Corporate Practice*, New York 1974.

J. Jabłońska-Bonca, O partnerskiej komunikacji prawników i biznesmenów, *Studia Iuridica* 40/2002.

J. Jabłońska-Bonca, Soft justice w "państwie sieciowym" [in] S. L. Stadniczenko, H. Duszka-Jakimko [ed.] *Alternatywne formy rozwiązywania sporów w teorii i w praktyce. Wybrane zagadnienia*, Opole 2008.

J. Jabłońska-Bonca, *Wprowadzenie do Prawa. Introduction to Law*, Warsaw 2012.

A. M. Jurkowska-Zeidler, *Bezpieczeństwo rynku finansowego w świetle prawa Unii Europejskiej*, Warsaw 2008.

A. Jurkowska-Zeidler, Nowa Globalna Architektura Finansowa, *Gdańskie Studia Prawnicze* tom XXV/2011.

A. Jurkowska-Zeidler, Nowe europejskie ramy ochrony stabilności wewnętrznego rynku finansowego [in] A. Dobaczewska, E. Juchniewicz, T. Sowiński [ed.] *System finansów publicznych. Prawo finansowe wobec wyzwań XXI wieku*, Warsaw 2010.

A. Jurkowska-Zeidler, Status prawny Komisji Nadzoru Bankowego jako organu administracji publicznej w świetle wyroku Trybunału Konstytucyjnego z dnia 15 czerwca 2011 roku, *Gdańskie Studia Prawnicze* tom XXVIII/2012.

R. Kaszubski, *Funkcjonalne źródła prawa bankowego publicznego*, Warsaw 2006.

S. Kaźmierczyk, Dynamiczne ujęcie normy prawnej, *Acta Universitatis Wratislaviensis* 44(244)/1978.

S. Kaźmierczyk, O tożsamości prawa w związku z jego jakością, *Acta Universitatis Lodziensis. Folia Iuridica* 74/2015.

S. Kaźmierczyk, O trzech aspektach jakości prawa, *Studia z Polityki Publicznej* 1(5)/2015.

A. Keay, Getting to Groups with the Shareholder Value Theory in Corporate Law, *Common Law World Review* 39(4)/2010.

N. King, *Governance, Risk, and Compliance Handbook*, Birmingham 2012.

S. King, M. Jha, The Central Banking Revolution, *Global Economics* 2/2013.

J. J. Kirton, M. J. Trebilcock, *Hard Choices, Soft Law: Voluntary Standards in Global Trade, Environment and Social Governance*, Toronto 2004.

J. M. Kline, TNC Codes and National Sovereignty: Deciding When TNCs Should Engage in Political Activity, *Transnational Corporations* 14(3)/2005.

T. W. Koch, S. Scott Mac Donald, *Bank Management*, Boston 2014.

M. Koetter, J. W. Kolari, L. Spierdijk, Enjoying the Quiet Life Under Deregulation? Evidence from the Adjusted Lerner Indices for US Banks, *Review of Economics and Statistics* 94(2)/2012.

A. Kolk, Sustainability, Accountability and Corporate Governance: Exploring Multinationals' Reporting Practices, *Business Strategy and the Environment* 17/2008.

M. Kordela, *Zasady prawa. Studium teoretycznoprawne*, Poznań 2012.

N. M. Korkunow, *General Theory of Law*, Boston 2000.

C. Kosikowski, *Finanse i prawo finansowe Unii Europejskiej*, Warsaw 2014.

C. Kosikowski, Nowe prawo runku finansowego Unii Europejskiej [in] A. Jurkowska-Zeidler, M. Olszak [ed.] *Prawo rynku finansowego. Doktryna, instytucje, praktyka*, Warsaw 2015.

C. Kosikowski, *Prawo Unii Europejskiej w systemie polskiego prawa finansowego*, Białystok 2010.

C. Kosikowski, Samodzielny byt prawa finansowego jako działu prawa i problem jego autonomiczności [in] C. Kosikowski [ed.] *System Prawa Finansowego* tom I, Warsaw 2010.

C. Kosikowski, System Bankowy [in] C. Kosikowski, E. Ruśkowski [ed.] *Finanse publiczne i prawo finansowe*, Warsaw 2008.

C. Kosikowski, J. Matuszewski, Geneza i ewolucja oraz stan obecny i przewidywana przyszłość prawa finansowego [in] C. Kosikowski [ed.] *System Prawa Finansowego* tom I, Warsaw 2010.

M. Kozak, Compliance Programmes as a Tool of Effective Enforcement of Competition Law—A Carrot and a Stick Method? [in] T. Skoczny [ed.] *25 Years of Competition Law in Poland*, Warsaw 2015.

D. A. Krueger, *The Governance and Corporation of Business Regulation* [in] D. A. Krueger [ed.] *The Business Corporation and Productive Justice*, Nashville 1997.

J. Kuciński, W. J. Wołpiuk, *Zasady ustroju politycznego państwa w konstytucji Rzeczypospolitej Polskiej z 1997 roku*, Warsaw 2012.

J. R. C. Kuntz, D. Elenkov, A. Nabirukhina, Characterizing Ethical Cases: A Cross-Cultural Investigation of Individual Differences, Organizational Climate, and Leadership on Ethical Decision-Making, *Journal of Business Ethics* 13(2)/2013.

H. M. Kutzer, F. K. Zemans, Local Legal Culture and the Control of Litigation, *Law and Society Review* 27(3)/1993.

J. G. Lambsdorf, Causes and Consequences of Corruption: What Do We Know from a Cross-Section of Countries [in] S. Rose-Ackerman [ed.] *Handbook of the Economics of Corruption*, Northampton 2006.

W. M. Landes, R. A. Posner, *The Economic Structure of Intellectual Property Law*, Cambridge 2003.

W. Lang, J. Wróblewski, *Współczesna filozofia i teoria prawa w USA*, Warsaw 1986.

E. W. Larson, D. H. Gobeli, Matrix Management: Contradictions and Insights, *California Management Review* 29/1987.

R. M. Lastra, Risk-Based Capital Requirements and Their Impact Upon the Banking Industry: Basel II and CAD III, *Journal of Financial Regulation and Compliance* 12(3)/2004.

A. Lawrence, M. Minutti-Meza, D. Vyas, Is Operational Control Risk Informative of Financial Reporting Risk? *Rotman School of Management Working Paper* 6/2014.

M. Lemonnier, *Europejskie modele rynków finansowych. Wybrane zagadnienia*, Warsaw 2011.

L. Leszczyński, *Tworzenie klauzul generalnych odsyłających*, Lublin 2000.

J. K. Levit, Bottom-Up Lawmaking: The private Origins of Transnational Law, *Global Legal Studies Journal* 15/2008.

J. K. Levit, The Dynamics of International Trade Finance: The Arrangement on Officially Supported Export Credits, *Harvard International Law Journal* 45/2008.

N. D. Lewis, *Law and Governance*, London 2001.

I. Lieberman, M. Gobbo, W. P. Mako, R. L. Neyens, Recent International Experiences in the Use of Voluntary Workouts Under Destressed Conditions [in] M. Pomerleano,W. Shaw [ed.] *Corporate Restructuring: Lessons from Experience*, Washington 2005.

M. B. Likosky, *The Silicon Empire: Law, Culture and Commerce*, London 2005.

K. Llewellyn, *The Common Law Tradition: Deciding Appeals*, Boston 1960.

J. M. Logsdon, D. J. Wood, Global Business Citizenship and Voluntary Codes of Ethical Conduct, *Journal of Business Ethics* 59(1)/2005.

W. D. Loppit, The Neoliberal Era and the Financial Crisis in the Light of Social Structure Accumulation Theory, *Review of Radical Political Economics* 46(2)/2014.

I. Love, Corporate Governance and Performance Around the World, What Do We Know and What We Don't, *The World Bank Observer*, 2010.

N. Luhmann, *Law as a Social System*, Oxford 2004.

D. Luthy, K. Forth, Laws and Regulations Affecting Information Management and Frameworks for Assessing Compliance, *Information Management & Computer Security* 14(2)/2006.

L. T. Ly, S. Rinderle-Ma, D. Knuplesch, P. Dadam, Monitoring Business Process Compliance Using Compliance Rule Graphs, *Lecture Notes of Computer Science* 7044/2011.

I. MacCormick, O. Weinberger, *An Institutional Theory of Law. New Approaches to Legal Positivism*, Dordrecht 2010.
I. G. MacNeil, Risk Control Strategies: An Assessment in the Context of the Credit Crisis [in] I. G. MacNeil, J. O'Brien [ed.] *The Future of Financial Regulation*, Portland 2010.
J. Madura, *International Financial Management*, Stamford 2015.
I. Maher, Limitations on Community Regulation in the UK: Legal Culture and Multi-level Governance, *Journal of European Public Policy* 3(4)/1996.s
B. Makowicz, *Compliance w przedsiębiorstwie*, Warsaw 2011.
M. P. Malloy, *Banking Law and Regulation*, New York 2004.
S. K. Mandal, *Ethics in Business and Corporate Governance*, New Delhi 2010.
R. Markfort, Verantwortung der Gschaeftsleitung fuer Compliance, *Risk, Fraud and Compliance. Praevention und Aufdeckung durch Compliance-Organisationen* 4/2004.
A. Marmor, *Interpretation and Legal Theory*, Oxford 2005.
A. Martin, T. M. Lakshmi, V. P. Vankatesan, An Information Delivery Model for Banking Business, *International Journal of Information Management* 34(2)/2014.
S. Martin, 98% of HBR Readers Love This Article: Businesses Are Just Beginning to Understand the Power of Social Norms, *Harvard Business Review*, October 2012.
D. Masciandaro, Politicians and Financial Supervision Unification Outside the Central Bank: Why Do They Do It? *Journal of Financial Stability* 5(2)/2009.
J. Mason, Compliance – odpowiedzialny prawnik w finansach, *Radca Prawny* Nr 123, Marzec 2012.
B. Maurer, The Cultural Power of Law? Conjunctive Reading, *Law and Society Review* 38/2004.
B. Maurer, International Political Economy as a Cultural Practice: The Metaphysics of Capital Mobility [in] R. W. Perry, B. Maurer [ed.] *Globalization Under Construction: Governmentality, Law and Identity*, Minneapolis 2003.
R. McCormick, The 'Conduct Crisis': Will Banks Ever Get It Right? *Business Law International* 16(2)/2015.
R. McCormick, *Legal Risks in the Financial Markets*, Oxford 2010.
R. W. McGee, Applying Utilitarian Ethics and Rights Theory to the Regulation of Insider Trading in Transition Economies, *Fayetteville State University* 4/2014.
M. McMillan, Difference Between Compliance, Ethics and Culture, *Risk and Compliance Journal* 30 June 2014, http://blogs.wsj.com/riskandcompliance/2014/06/30/the-difference-between-compliance-and-ethics/.

A. J. McNeil, R. Frey, P. Embrechts, *Quantitative Risk Management: Concepts, Techniques and Tools*, Princeton 2015.
A. J. Meese, N. B. Oman, Hobby Lobby, Corporate Law, and the Theory of the Firm, *Harvard Law Review* 127/2014.
E. Melissaris, *Ubiquitous Law: Legal Theory and the Space for Legal Pluralism*, Ashgate 2009.
T. Mellor, M. Rogers Jr., *An Introduction to Legal Risks and Structuring Cross-Border Lending Transaction, The International Comparative Legal Guide to: Lending & Secured Finance 2014. A Practical Cross-Border Insight into Lending and Secured Finance*, London 2014.
R. Michaels, J. Pauwelyn, Conflict of Norms or Conflict of Laws? Different Techniques in the Fragmentation of International Law [in] T. Broude, Y. Shany [ed.] *Multi-sourced Equivalent Norms in International Law*, Oxford 2011.
M. Michalski, R. R. Zdzieborski, *Ustawa o niektórych zabezpieczeniach finansowych. Komentarz*, Warsaw 2005.
A. Mickleth, A. Wooldridoe, *The Company: A Short History of a Revolutionary Idea*, Washington 2005.
A. Milne, Bank Capital Regulation as an Incentive Mechanism: Implications for Portfolio Choice, *Journal of Banking and Finance* 26(1)/2001.
B. Minton, A. Sanders, P. E. Strahan, *Securitization by Banks and Finance Companies: Efficient Financial Contracting or Regulatory Arbitrage?* Columbus 2004.
L. E. Mitchell, *Understanding Norms*, Toronto 1999.
L. Mitrus, Równość traktowania (zakaz dyskryminacji) w zakresie zatrudnienia [in] A. Zawadzka-Łojek, R. Grzeszczak [ed.] *Prawo materialne Unii Europejskiej. Swobodny przepływ towarów, osób, usług i kapitału. Podstawy prawa konkurencji*, Warsaw 2013.
T. M. J. Moellers, Sources of Law in the European Securities Regulation— Effective Regulation, Soft Law and Legal Taxonomy from Lamfalussy to de Larosiere, *European Business Organisation Law Review* 3(11)/2010.
L. Moerel, *Binding Corporate Rules: Corporate Self-Regulation of Global Data Transfers*, London 2012.
P. Moles, R. Parrino, D. S. Kidwel, *Corporate Finance*, Glasgow 2011
P. Molyneux, Bank Performance, Risk and Firm Financing [in] M. Aoki, K. Binmare, S. Deakin, H. Gintis [ed.] *Complexity and Institutions: Markets, Norms and Corporations*, London 2012.
P. Montoya, The Role of the Board of Directors [in] F. Vincke, J. Kassum [ed.] *ICC Ethics and Compliance Training Handbook*, Paris 2013.
L. Morawski, *Główne problemy współczesnej filozofii prawa. Prawo w toku przemian*, Warsaw 2005.
L. Morawski, *Wstęp do prawoznawstwa*, Toruń 2006.

S. C. Morse, Tax Compliance and Norm Formation Under High-Penalty Regimes, *Connecticut Law Review* 44(3)/2012.
S. Mouatt, C. Adams, Corporate and Social Transformations of Money and Banking [in] M. Aoki, K. Binmare, S. Deakin, H. Gintis [ed.] *Complexity and Institutions: Markets, "Norms and Corporations"*, London 2012.
P. Muchlinski, *Corporations in International Law*, Oxford 2009, http://opil.ouplaw.com/view/10.1093/law:epil/9780199231690/law-9780199231690-e1513?rs-key=35hRr8&result=1&prd=EPIL (download 5 September 2015).
P. Muchlinski, *Multinational Enterprises and the Law*, Oxford 2007.
P. O. Mülbert, Corporate Governance of Banks After the Financial Crisis—Theory, Evidence, Reforms, *European Corporate Governance Law* 130(4)/2010.
J. E. Murphy, G. J. Wallance, *Corporate Compliance: How to Be a Good Citizen Corporation Through Self-Policing*, New York 1996.
A. Newman, E. Posner, Transnational Feedback, Soft Law, and Preferences in Global Financial Regulation, *Review of International Political Economy* 11/2015.
S. Oded, *Corporate Compliance*, Cheltenham 2013.
Z. Ofiarski, Rola soft law w regulacji rynku finansowego na przykładzie rekomendacji i wytycznych Komisji Nadzoru Finansowego [in] A. Jurkowska-Zeidler, M. Olszak [ed.] *Prawo rynku finansowego. Doktryna, instytucji, praktyka*, Warsaw 2016.
Z. Ofiarski, *Ustawa o kredycie konsumenckim. Komentarz*, Warsaw 2014.
Z. Ofiarski, Źródła prawa finansowego i problemy legislacji finansowej [in] C. Kosikowski [ed.] *System Prawa Finansowego* tom I, Warsaw 2010.
M. Ojo, Basel II and the Capital Requirements Directive: Responding to the 2008/09 Financial Crisis, *IGI Global* 18/2009.
C. R. O'Kelly Jr., R. B. Thompson, *Corporations and Other Business Associations: Cases and Materials*, Boston 1996.
J. O'Kelley III, Insights from Conversations with U.S. Banking Regulators: Implications for Bank Directors, *Global Leadership*, 9/2014.
I. Okhmatovskiy, R. J. David, Setting Your Own Standards: Internal Corporate Governance Codes as a Response to Institutional Pressure, *Organisation Science* 23(1)/2011.
M. Olszak, *Bankowe normy ostrożnościowe*, Białystok 2011.
M. Olszak, *Outsourcing w działalności bankowej*, Warsaw 2006.
D. O'Loughlin, A. Wassall, HSBC Estimates GBP 96m Bill for Investment Advice Mis-Selling, *FT Adviser*, 24 February 2014.
K. Opałek, *Z teorii dyrektyw i norm*, Warsaw 1974.
D. T. Ostas, The Law and Ethics of K Street: Lobbying, the First Amendment and the Duty to Create Just Laws, *Business Ethics Quarterly* 17(1)/January 2007.

K. Pałecki, *Prawoznawstwo zarys wykładu*, Warsaw 2003.
K. Pałecki, Uwagi o dobrym prawie – wprowadzenie do dyskusji [in] P. Mochnarzewski, A. Kociołek-Pęksa *Dobre prawo, złe prawo – w kręgu myśli Gustawa Radbrucha*, Warsaw 2009.
C. Parker, V. L. Nielsen, *Explaining Compliance: Business Responses to Regulations*, Northampton 2011.
F. Partnoy, J. Eisinger, What Is Inside American Banks? *Americas Banks* 1/2008.
P.-E. Partsch, *Droi bancaire et financier europeen*, Paris 2009.
R. Patton, Trends in Regulatory Enforcement in the UK Financial Markets 2014/15 Mid-Year Report, *Insight in Economics*, 20 October 2014.
S. Pejovich, *Economic Analysis of Institutions and Systems*, Dodrecht 2012.
J. Pelisse, From Negotiation to Implementation: A Study of Reduction of Working Time in France, *Time and Society* 13(2–3)/2004.
M. W. Peregrine, The Increasingly Problematic Coordination of 'Legal' and 'Compliance': New Pressures on the Board; Best Practices for Resolving Tasks, *Bloomberg Law*, 3 September 2014. www.Bloomberg_Law/law/compliance.
M. Perezts, S. Picard, Compliance or Comfort Zone? The Work of Embedded Ethics in Performing Regulations, *Journal of Business Ethics* 4/2014.
T. Pietrzykowski, *Intuicja prawnicza*, Warsaw 2012.
A. Piotrowski, O pojęciu kompetencji interaktywnej [in] A. Schaff [ed.] *Zagadnienia Socio- i Psycholingwistyki*, Warsaw 1980.
T. R. Piper, Odnaleziony cel: przywództwo, etyka i odpowiedzialność przedsiębiorstw [in] L. V. Ryan, J. Sójka [ed.] *Etyka biznesu: z klasyki współczesnej myśli amerykańskiej*, Poznań 1997.
R. A. Posner, *The Problems of Jurisprudence*, Harvard 2000.
A. Powell, N. Mylenko, M. Miller, G. Majnoni, *Improving Credit Information, Bank Regulation and Supervision: On the Role and Design of Public Credit Registries*, Washington 2004.
M. Power, The Risk Management of Nothing, *Accounting, Organizations, and Society* 34(6–7)/2009.
F. P. Ramos, International and Supranational Law in Translation: From Multilingual Lawmaking to Adjudication, *The Translator* 20(3)/2014.
K. Raustiala, A.-M. Slaughter, International Law, International Relations and Compliance, *Princeton Law and Public Affairs Paper* 2/2002.
J. Rawls, *Liberalizm polityczny*, Warsaw 1998.
J. Rawls, *Teoria sprawiedliwości*, Warsaw 2013.
K. K. Reed, A Look at Firm—Regulator Exchanges: Friendly Enough or Too Friendly, *Business and Society* 48(2)/2009.
W. Reinicke, J. M. Witte, Interdependence, Globalization and Sovereignty: The Role of Non-binding International Legal Accords [in] D. Shelton [ed.] *Commitment and Compliance: The Role of Non-binding Norms in the International Legal System*, Oxford 2003.

B. J. Richardson, *Fiduciary Law and Responsible Investing: In Nature's Trust*, New York 2013.
B. Roach, *Corporate Power in Global Economy*, Medford 2007.
R. Robson, A New Look at Benefit Corporations: Game Theory and Game Changer, *American Business Law Journal* 52/2015.
B. Rok, Kręgosłup moralny firmy, *Thinktank* 18/2013.
W. Rogowski [ed.] *Nowe koncepcje i regulacje rynku finansowego*, Warsaw 2014.
M. Romanowski, Wpływ compliance na skuteczność prawa gospodarczego [in] T. Giaro [ed.] *Skuteczność prawa, "Konferencje naukowe WPiA UW"*, Warsaw 2010.
L. Rosen, *Law as Culture*, Princeton University Press 2006.
M. Roth, *Close Up on Compliance: Recht, Moral und Risken: Nahaufnahmen zu Compliance management und Governance- Fragen*, Zuerich 2009.
E. J. Rudolph, *The Board Must Take the Lead in Establishing a Corporate Culture of Ethics and Compliance*, 1 July 2014, www.Corporatecomplianceinsights.com.
R. D. Russel, C. J. Russel, An Examination of the Effects of Organizational Norms, Organizational Structure and Environment Uncertainty on Entrepreneurial Strategy, *Journal of Management* 18/1992.
E. Rutkowska-Tomaszewska, *Nadzór nad rynkiem finansowym a nieuczciwe praktyki rynkowe banków wobec konsumentów – zakres, potrzeba i możliwości podejmowanych działań*, http://www.bibliotekacyfrowa.pl/Content/38956/010.pdf.
E. Rutkowska-Tomaszewska, *Ochrona prawna klienta na rynku usług bankowych*, Warsaw 2013.
M. Safjan, The Universalization of Legal Interpretation [in] J. Jemielniak, P. Mikłaszewicz [ed.] *Interpretation of Law in the Global World: From Particularism to a Universal Approach*, Berlin 2010.
M. Safjan, *Wyzwania dla państwa prawa*, Warsaw 2007.
J. Salmon, Shocking Tactics at the Heart of Lloyds Scandal: Whistleblower Opens Up over Interest Rate Swaps, *This Is Money*, 15 September 2014, www.thisismoney.co.uk.
P. Sarnecki [ed.] *Konstytucjonalizacja zasad i instytucji ustrojowych*, Warsaw 1997.
L. Sasso, *Capital Structure and Corporate Governance: The Role of Hybrid Financial Instruments*, New York 2013.
S. Schelo, *Bank Failing or Likely to Fail: Restoring Confidence—The Changing European Banking Landscape*, London 2014.
A. G. Scherer, G. Palazzo, Toward a Political Conception of Corporate Responsibility: Business and Society Seen from a Habermasian Perspective, *Academic Management Review* 32(4)/2007.
W. Scheuerman, Globalization and a Fate of Law [in] D. Dyzenhaus [ed.] *Recrafting the Rule of Law: The Limits of Legal Order*, New York 1999.

D. Schoenmaker, *Governance of International Banking: The Financial Trilemma*, New York 2013.
B. Scholtens, Cultural Values and International Differences in Business Ethics, *Journal of Business Ethics* 75(3)/2007.
P. A. Schott, G. T. Schwartz, *Bank Compliance*, Washington 1989.
S. L. Schwarcz, Sovereign Debt Restructuring: A Bankruptcy Reorganization Approach, *Cornell Law Review* 85(956)/2001.
D. Sciulli, *Corporate Power in Civil Society: An Application of Societal Constitutionalism*, New York 2001.
I. Seidl-Hohenveldern, *Corporations In and Under International Law*, Cambridge 1987.
W. H. Sewell Jr., The Concept of Culture [in] V. E. Bonnell, A. H. Hunt, R. Biernacki [ed.] *Beyond the Cultural Turn*, Berkeley 1999.
A. K. Shah, *Regulatory Arbitrage Through Financial Innovation*, University of Essex, Colchester 2007.
G. C. Shaffer, M. A. Pollack, Hard vs. Soft Law: Alternatives, Complements and Antagonists in International Governance, *Minnesota Law Review* 94/2010.
R. Shamir, Corporate Social Responsibility [in] B. de Sousa Santos, C. A. Rodriguez-Garavito [ed.] *Law and Globalization from Below*, Cambridge 2005.
S. Shanahan, S. Khagram, Dynamics of Corporate Responsibility [in] G. S. Drori, J. W. Meyer, H. Hwang [ed.] *Globalization and Organization: World Society and Organizational Change*, Oxford 2006.
W. H. Shaw, V. Barry, *Moral Issues in Business*, Boston 2014.
D. Shelton, *Commitment and Compliance: The Role of Non-binding Norms in the International Legal System*, New York 2000.
K. Shields, A. Perry-Kessaris, Rewriting the Centricity of the State in Pursuit of Global Justice [in] *Socio-Legal Approaches to International Economic Law: Text, Context, Subtext*, New York 2013.
D. Singh, *Banking Regulation of UK and US Financial Markets*, Hempshire 2007.
W. T. Singleton, *Compliance and Excellence*, Baltimore 1979.
S. S. Silbey, Legal Culture and Cultures of Legality [in] J. R. Hall, L. Grindstaff, M. Ch. Lo [ed.] *Handbook of Cultural Sociology*, London and New York 2010.
G. Skąpska, J. Stelmach, Współczesne problemy i modele legitymizacji prawa, *Colloquia Communia* 41–42/1988–1989.
T. A. Smith, The Efficient Norm for Corporate Law: A Neotraditional Interpretation of Fiduciary Duty, *Michigan Law Review* 98(1)/1999.
F. Snyder, Governing Economic Globalization: Global Legal Pluralism and European Law, *European Law Journal* 5/1999.

A. E. Sorcher, Lost in Implementation: Financial Institutions Face Challenges Complying with Anti-money Laundering Laws, *Transactional Law* 18/2005.
B. De Sousa Santos, *Towards a New Legal Common Sense: Law, Globalization, and Emancipation*, London 2002.
S. L. Stadniczenko, H. Duszka-Jakimko [ed.] *Alternatywne formy rozwiązywania sporów w teorii i w praktyce. Wybrane zagadnienia*, Opole 2008.
R. Stammler, Gospodarka i prawo [in] M. Szyszkowska, *Europejska filozofia prawa*, Warsaw 1995.
N. Stanley, Clearly, and Quite Righty, Data Loss Is Now a Legal Issue and IT Professionals Need to Be Aware of Their Responsibilities, *A White Paper by Bloor Research*, March 2009, https://www.qualys.com/docs/EU_Compliance.pdf.
T. Stawecki, Prawo i zaufanie. Refleksja czasu kryzysu [in] J. Oniszczuk [ed.] *Normalność i kryzys – jedność czy różnorodność. Refleksje filozoficzno-prawne i ekonomiczno-społeczne w ujęciu aksjologicznym*, Warsaw 2010.
T. Stawecki, P. Winczorek, *Wstęp do prawoznawstwa*, Warsaw 2003.
M. Steinberg, *Governance, Risks Management, and Compliance: It Can't Happen to Us Avoiding Corporate Disaster While Driving Success*, New Jersey 2011.
M. Stefański, Nowe regulacje dotyczące wymagań kapitałowych wobec banków, *Materiały i Studia NBP* 12(212)/2006.
J. Stelmach, Integracja i globalizacja z perspektywy filozofii prawa [in] J. Stelmach, A. Bator, S. Kaźmierczyk, A. Kozak [ed.] *Filozofia prawa wobec globalizmu*, Kraków 2003.
J. Stelmach, Law and economics jako teoria polityki prawa [in] M. Soniewicka [ed.] *Analiza ekonomiczna w zastosowaniach prawniczych*, Warsaw 2007.
J. Stelmach, R. Sarkowicz, *Filozofia prawa XIX i XX wieku*, Kraków 1999.
J. E. Stiglitz, Multinational Corporations: Balancing Rights and Responsibilities, *Proceedings of the American Society of International Law* 101/2007.
J. E. Stiglitz, Regulating Multinational Corporations Towards Principles of Cross-Border Legal Frameworks in a Globalized World Balancing Rights with Responsibilities, *American International Law Review* 23/2007.
J. G. Sutinen, K. Kuperan, A Socio-Economic Theory of Regulatory Compliance, *International Journal of Social Economics* 26(1/2/3)/1999.
A. Sulikowski, Z zagadnień teorii i filozofii prawa. W poszukiwaniu podstaw prawa, *Acta Universitatis Wratislaviensis* 2878/2006.
M. Svensson, S. Larsson, Intellectual Property Law Compliance in Europe: Illegal File Sharing and the Law of Social Norms, *New Media and Society* 14(7)/2012.
E. T. Swanson, *Let's Twist Again: A High-Frequency Event-Study Analysis of Operation Twist and Its Implications for Quantitative Easing*, San Francisco 2011.

A. Szlęzak, H. Gardocka, *Ponownie o* representations and warranties *w umowach poddanych prawu polskiemu*, Przegląd Prawa Handlowego Luty 2011, s. 31 i n.
P. B. Szymala, *Ryzyko prawne w działalności banków*, Poznań 2006.
E. Talley, S. Strimling, The World's Most Important Number: How a Web of Skewed Incentives, Broken Hierarchies and Compliance Cultures Conspired to Undermine LIBOR, *Financial Services Institute of Australasia Journal JASSA* 2/2013.
B. Z. Tamanaha, *Beyond the Formalist-Realist Divide: The Role of Politics in Judging*, Oxford 2010.
A. Tarantino, *Governance, Risk, and Compliance Handbook: Technology, Finance, Environmental and International Guidance and Best Practices*, New Jersey 2008.
G. Tchetvertakov, *In a Co-ordinated Blitz, Regulators Bombard Top Banks for Systemic Collusion in the Forex Market*, November 2014, www.forexmagnates.com/.
L. Thévenoz, R. Bahar, *Conflicts of Interest: Corporate Governance and Financial Markets*, Alphen aan den Rijn 2007.
B. Torgler, *Tax Compliance and Tax Morale: A Theoretical and Empirical Analysis*, Cheltenham 2007.
F. Tönnies, *Community and Society: Gemeinschaft and Geselschaft*, Ch. P. Loomis [ed.] Michigan 1957.
L. K. Trevino, N. A. Den Nieuwenboer, G. E. Kreiner, D. G. Bishop, Legitimating the Legitimate: A Grounded Theory Study of Legitimacy Work Among Ethics and Compliance Officers, *Organizational Behavior and Human Decision Process* 123(2)/2014.
D. Troklus, *Candidate Handbook, Certified Compliance and Ethics Professional*, Society of Corporate Compliance and Ethics, 2014, www.compliancecertification.org.
R. V. Turcan, S. Marinova, M. B. Rana, Empirical Studies on Legitimation Strategies: A Case for International Business Research Extension [in] L. Tihanyi, T. M. Devinney, T. Pedersen [ed.] *Institutional Theory in International Business*, London 2012.
M. J. W. van Twist, L. Schaap, Introduction to Autopoiesis theory and Autopoietic Steering [in] R. J. In t' Veld, L. Schaap, C. J. A. M. Termeer, M. J. W. van Twist [ed.] *Autopoiesis and Configuration Theory: New Approaches to Societal Steering*, Rotterdam 1991.
D. Tweedie, T. R. Seidenstein, Setting a Global Standard: The Case for Accounting Convergence, *New Journal for International Law and Business* 25/2005.
W. Twining, Diffusion of Law: A Global Perspective, *The Journal of Legal Pluralism and Unofficial Law* 36(49)/2004.
W. Twining, *General Jurisprudence: Understanding Law from a Global Perspective*, Cambridge 2008.

W. Twining, *Globalization and Legal Theory*, Cambridge 2000.
W. Twining, Social Science and Diffusion of Law, *Journal of Society and Law* 2(32)/2005.
G. R. D. Underhil, X. Zhang, Business Authority and Global Financial Governance: Challenges to Accountability and Legitimacy [in] T. Porter, K. Ronit [ed.] *The Challenges of Global Business Authority: Democratic Renewal, Stalemate, or Decay?* New York 2010.
D. F. Vagts, The Multinational Enterprise: A New Challenge for International Law, *Harvard Law Review* 83/1969–1970.
U. C. H. Valey, *Multinational Corporations in Political Environments: Ethics, Values and Strategies*, New York 2001.
M. Velverde, The Ethics of Diversity: Local Law and the Negotiations of Urban Norms, *Law and Social Inquiry* 33(4)/2008.
J. Vinãls, C. Pazarbasioglu, J. Surti, A. Narain, M. Erbenova, J. T. S. Chow, *Creating a Safer Financial System: Will the Volcker, Vickers, and Liikanen Structural Measures Help?* Washington 2013.
D. Vogel, The Private Regulation of Global Corporate Conduct Achievements and Limitations, *Business & Society* 49/2010.
B. P. Volkman, The Global Convergence of Bank Regulation and Standards for Compliance, *Banking Law Journal* 115/1998.
K. Walsh, C. A. Enz, L. Canina, The Impact of strategic Orientation on Intellectual Capital Investments in Customer Service Firms, *Journal of Service Research* 10(4)/2008.
J. D. Wallace, *Ethical Norms, Particular Cases*, Cornell 1996.
W. Wandeckhove, Rewarding the Whistleblower—Disgrace, Recognition or Efficiency? [in] M. Arszułowicz, W. W. Gasparski [ed.] *Whistleblowing: In Defense of Proper Action (Praxeology)*, New Brunswick 2010.
R. Wandhoefer, *Transaction Banking and the Impact of the Regulatory Change*, New York 2014.
K. Ward, F. Neumann, Consumer in 2050: The Rise Od the EM Middle Class, *Global Economics*, October 2012
G. R. Weaver, L. K. Trevino, Compliance and Values Oriented Ethics Programs: Influences on Employees' Attitudes and Behavior, *Business Ethics Quarterly* 9(2)/1999.
J. Wieland, Corporate Governance, Values Management, and Standards: A European Perspective, *Business Society* 1/2005.
S. Williams, The Debarment of Corrupt Contractors from World Bank-Financed Contracts, *Public Contract Law Journal* 36(3)/2007.
J. Winczorek, Pluralizm prawny wczoraj i dziś [in] K. Dobrzeniecki, D. Bunikowski [ed.] *Pluralizm prawny. Tradycje, transformacje, wyzwania*, Toruń 2010.
J. Winczorek, Systems Theory and Puzzles of Legal Culture, *Archiwum Filozofii Prawa i Filozofii Społecznej* 1(4)/2012.

D. A. Wirth, Commentary: Compliance with Non-binding Norms of Trade and Finance [in] D. Shelton [ed.] *Commitment and Compliance: The Role of Non-binding Norms in the International Legal System*, Oxford 2003.

M. J. Whincop, *Corporate Governance in Government Corporations, Law Ethics and Governance*, Burlington 2005.

G. Włodarczyk, *Norma ISO 19600 – próba standaryzacji zarządzania ryzykiem braku zgodności (compliance) – zagadnienia wstępne*, Warsaw 11 September 2014, http://compliancemifid.wordpress.com/ (download 9 October 2015).

R. C. Wolf, *Trade, Aid and Arbitrate: The Globalization of Western Law*, Oxford 2004.

M. Wolf, *Why Globalization Works*, Boston 2005.

K. D. Wolf, A. Flohs, L. Rieth, S. Schwindenhammer, *The Role of Business in Global Governance: Corporations as Norm-Entrepreneurs*, London 2010.

M. C. S. Wong, *The Risk of Investment Products: From Product Innovation to Risk Compliance*, Singapore 2011.

P. R. Wood, *International Legal Risk for Banks and Corporate*, London 2014.

S. Wronkowska, *Podstawowe pojęcia prawa i prawoznawstwa*, Poznań 2005.

S. Wronkowska, Z. Ziembiński, *Zarys teorii prawa*, Poznań 2001.

S. Wronkowska, M. Zieliński, *Komentarz do zasad techniki prawodawczej z dnia 20 czerwca 2002 r.*, Warsaw 2004.

K. Wulf, *From Codes of Conduct to Ethics and Compliance Programs: Recent Developments in the United States, Berliner Arbeiten zur Erziehungs- und Kulturwissenschaft*, Berlin 2011.

O. Wyman, Conduct Risk Management in the Asia Pacific Region: Improving Relationship, Returns and Regulation, *Asia Pacific Finance and Risk Series* 1/2014.

O. Wyman, Streamlining Risk, Compliance and Internal Audit: Less Is More, *Asia Pacific Finance and Risk Series* 2/2015.

K. L. Young, Transnational Regulatory Capture? An Empirical Examination of the Transnational Lobbying of the Basel Committee on Banking Supervision, *Review of International Political Economy* 19(4)/2012.

M. Zieliński, *Wykładnia Prawa. Zasady, reguły, wskazówki*, Warsaw 2012.

Z. Ziembinski, *Historical Interpretation vs. Adaptive Interpretation* [in] A. Zeidler-Janiszewska [ed.] *Epistemology and History*, Poznan 1994.

Z. Ziembiński, *Wstęp do aksjologii dla prawników*, Warsaw 1990.

M. Zirk-Sadowski, *Wprowadzenie do filozofii prawa*, Warsaw 2011.

A. Zorska, *Korporacje transnarodowe: przemiany, oddziaływania, wyzwania*, Warsaw 2007.

L. G. Zucker, The Role in Institutionalization in Cultural Persistence [in] W. W. Powell, P. J. DiMaggio [ed.] *The New Institutionalism in Organizational Analysis*, Chicago 2012.

M. Żemigała, *Społeczna odpowiedzialność przedsiębiorstwa*, Kraków 2007.

Index

A
acceptance of risk, 103
adequacy, 119, 122, 150, 153, 154, 167–169, 178, 240, 307
adequate control, 127
administrative decisions, 4, 294
advisory function, 54, 77, 78, 80, 84, 85
analytical instruments, 83
anti-corruption, 102, 103, 268
anti-money laundering, 68, 133, 156, 161, 239
applicable law, 5, 47, 48, 106, 107, 126, 186, 295
arbitrage, 30, 48, 178, 201
arbitration, 108, 110, 112–114, 201
assignment of responsibility, 121
associations, 23, 30, 35, 36, 72, 160, 161, 165, 166, 186, 189, 265
audits, 5, 77, 100, 116, 119, 120, 123, 128, 141, 149, 151, 153, 156, 204, 206, 211, 223, 227, 238, 240, 242–245, 251, 252, 254, 270, 271, 277
authorisations, 111, 237
autopoietic normative systems, 181
axiological environment, 7
axiological function, 291, 298, 304
axiological references, 33, 178

B
Basel Committee, 43, 56, 57, 74, 75, 147, 149, 150, 152, 156, 157, 163, 165–167, 169, 186, 276
behavioural patterns, 44, 232, 234, 304
behaviours, 9, 11, 46, 138, 275, 291, 299, 300, 304, 305, 310
blacklists, 82
bonuses, 14, 48, 252
breaches, 89, 93, 100, 101, 125, 131, 143, 153, 155, 228, 233, 246, 277
budgets, 71
business continuity, 21, 99, 128
business institutions, 1, 3, 9, 48
business planning, 56, 70, 124

C

capital groups, 9, 69, 71, 72, 220
capital requirements, 21, 150, 167–169, 178
claim, 108, 181, 202, 215, 264
classified documents, 23, 55
codes of conduct, 251
coherence, 25, 29–31, 33, 45, 68
collisions, 46, 48, 49, 64, 72, 134, 268, 279, 280
common law, 7, 27, 120, 158, 166, 178, 236, 260, 264, 273
communication processes, 37
compensation, 7, 87, 106, 110, 112, 113, 206, 207, 209, 214, 215, 239
competition, 41, 68, 89, 102, 129, 193, 194, 198, 199, 201
complaints, 81, 99, 122, 131, 137, 195, 207, 233, 238, 239, 264, 277, 307
compliance, 1–27, 29–31, 36, 40, 42, 43, 46–48, 51, 53–105, 107–109, 111–156, 158–161, 163–170, 172–182, 184–194, 196–199, 201–205, 207, 208, 211–214, 217–221, 223, 225, 227, 229–235, 237–247, 249–255, 257–280, 283–310
Compliance, 49
compliance assurance, 84
compliance awareness, 68
compliance committees, 86
compliance management, 69, 73, 101, 119, 127, 148, 149, 160, 269
compliance monitoring, 127, 131
compliance norms, 1–3, 5–15, 17–19, 21–27, 29, 36, 43, 46, 49, 53–56, 60, 62, 63, 66, 71, 77, 79, 80, 83, 84, 93, 95, 108, 109, 115, 121, 127, 130, 131, 138, 151, 153, 163, 164, 166, 173, 176–182, 184–189, 191–194, 196, 207, 208, 213, 214, 217–219, 230–235, 238, 240–242, 246, 247, 249, 250, 252–255, 257, 258, 260, 262, 263, 266–268, 270–278, 285–295, 297–310
compliance programmes, 76
compliance reports, 98, 144, 269, 270
compliance risk, 25, 53, 54, 74–77, 85, 87, 95–98, 100, 103, 111, 112, 114–117, 119–123, 134, 146–148, 150–152, 154, 158, 164, 165, 167, 188, 217, 218, 227, 232, 233, 243, 259, 262, 265, 269–271, 276, 278, 286, 306, 308
compliance structures, 76, 84, 159, 270
compliance unit, 76, 121, 151, 152, 155, 156
conduct, 1–3, 5, 6, 8, 11, 12, 31, 40, 41, 47, 58, 59, 68, 69, 80, 83, 85, 95, 102, 105, 119, 121, 132, 134, 139–141, 144–146, 149, 155, 165, 167, 168, 178–180, 182, 188, 194, 199, 206, 213, 217, 225, 231, 234, 235, 237, 238, 242, 248–254, 263, 264, 266, 271, 280, 287, 288, 291, 292, 298, 301, 309, 310
conduct procedures, 40
confidential information, 44, 125, 129, 193
confidentiality, 8, 9, 16, 47, 72, 89, 114, 131
conflicting laws, 70, 278
conformity, 1, 2

consistency, 3, 15, 25, 29–31, 33, 34, 65, 75, 94, 116, 194, 246, 259, 303, 309
Consistency, 30
constitutional provisions, 108, 109
consultative function, 84
consumer protection, 68, 171, 176
contracting party, 108, 171
contractual obligations, 88, 101, 107, 109, 111, 171
contractual relations, 101, 112, 229
controls, 5, 99, 117, 127, 141, 146, 153, 187, 191–193, 199, 211, 223, 238, 240, 243, 306, 307
convergence, 44, 296
corporate executives, 86
corporate governance, 3, 7, 15, 30, 47, 55, 58, 63, 65, 70, 80, 120, 123, 144, 146, 148, 160, 169, 179, 180, 185, 219, 252, 260, 266, 268, 273, 297
corporate practice, 7, 46
corporations, 1–6, 8–21, 24, 26, 29, 30, 35, 36, 38–51, 55, 62–73, 78–81, 88, 91, 96, 107, 115, 120, 123, 127, 129, 130, 134, 139, 143, 145–147, 152, 159, 163, 165, 172, 177–183, 185, 186, 196, 197, 215, 218–221, 224, 225, 229, 231–234, 242, 243, 246–255, 257, 262–269, 271, 272, 274–276, 278–280, 282, 283, 286–305, 307–310
Corporations, 39
corrective measures, 123
counterparty risk, 128, 153, 187
court rulings, 94, 111, 130
credit risks, 19, 128, 133, 137, 144, 149, 168, 187, 211, 227, 233, 308

crime, 132, 156, 157, 222, 254
crises, 43, 60, 61, 84, 105, 168, 171
cross-border effectiveness, 56, 72
cultural context, 272, 281, 284, 302–304
cultural differences, 7, 26, 42, 44, 73, 79, 257, 258, 266, 268, 272–274, 279, 280, 286, 288
customer claims, 98
customer relations, 90, 122, 125, 142, 155, 205
customers, 6, 8, 19, 37, 40, 43, 45, 46, 54, 58, 59, 62, 72, 80, 86, 99, 113, 116, 124, 125, 128, 131, 134–137, 140, 142, 143, 145, 146, 155, 157, 165, 171, 174, 175, 179, 180, 195, 200, 205–210, 212, 213, 219, 222, 223, 225, 229–231, 239, 241–243, 250, 251, 254, 259, 261, 265, 268, 271, 274, 288, 304, 307

D

damages, 18, 90, 107, 142, 193, 203, 213, 214
data protection, 16, 46, 68, 125, 148, 219, 252, 283
debt instruments, 102, 106, 137, 172
decision-making process, 80, 226, 237
defence, 78, 104, 115–121, 125, 137, 202, 205, 209, 218
deficiencies, 11, 61, 122, 123, 187, 191, 204, 208, 252, 303
delays, 123, 240
deontological codes, 12, 44
derivatives, 58, 170, 172, 173, 176, 177, 190, 204, 205, 210, 216
derivative transactions, 173, 191

discriminatory practices, 19
disputes, 35, 97, 106–108, 135, 171, 196, 215, 263
division of competences, 47

E

economic efficiency, 18
economic environment, 6, 25
education, 83, 161
effectiveness of compliance norms, 232, 302, 310
embargoes, 132
employees, 1, 2, 6, 8, 14–16, 18, 19, 25, 35, 37, 40, 43, 45, 46, 48, 54, 55, 62, 65, 68, 69, 75, 76, 78, 80, 83, 84, 93, 95, 97, 103, 116, 117, 121, 126, 127, 129–131, 133, 135, 139, 141, 145–147, 151, 152, 160, 165, 179, 180, 186–188, 197, 198, 200, 203, 204, 208, 214, 216, 218–221, 223, 225, 227, 229, 231, 233, 238, 240–243, 249–252, 254, 259, 261–266, 268, 270–273, 275–278, 288, 307, 308
empowerment, 45, 64, 80, 145
energy, 4, 45, 104, 248
enforceability, 105, 106, 108, 111, 114
enforcement, 89, 90, 93, 94, 107–109, 138, 156, 159, 193, 196, 201, 220, 222
ethical dilemmas, 22
ethical justifications, 179
ethics, 8, 12, 44, 55, 159, 165, 186, 254, 262, 268, 295, 297, 309
exchange of information, 44, 67
expropriation, 109, 112, 113

F

financial crime, 58, 85, 154, 156, 160, 223
financial crisis, 85, 160, 176, 210
financial equilibrium, 110
financial industry, 13, 24, 26, 30, 63, 234
financial institutions, 1–14, 16–19, 21–23, 25, 26, 29, 37, 39, 42, 43, 46, 53–61, 63, 64, 66–68, 70–80, 82–93, 96–107, 109, 110, 112–118, 120–132, 134, 136–145, 147–149, 151–161, 163, 164, 166–176, 179, 186–194, 196–238, 240, 241, 243–247, 249–254, 257–266, 269–280, 282, 283, 285–287, 294, 307–309
financial instrument, 110
financial products, 59, 65, 94, 195, 205, 239, 250
financial reporting, 71, 124
financial security, 66, 171
force majeure, 111
foreign jurisdictions, 20
formalism, 184
freezing clauses, 110, 111

G

globalisation, 22, 225, 303
good faith, 89, 110
governance practices, 8, 148, 261
government agencies, 108, 113
green papers, 23
guarantees, 30, 54, 64, 75, 101, 103, 130, 131, 196, 251, 275
guidelines, 5, 6, 8, 15, 20, 23, 37, 59, 63, 69, 75, 76, 81, 82, 121, 130, 139, 147, 149, 150, 165–168,

180, 212, 224, 231, 232, 236–238, 242, 247, 249, 252, 254, 272, 277, 289

H
hedge funds, 140, 191
high-risk territories, 128
holding companies, 127
human error, 160

I
identification, 48, 60, 61, 69, 75, 87, 98, 113, 127, 134, 152, 156, 159, 179, 184, 187, 192, 194, 214, 218, 242, 287, 289, 306
illegality, 118
immunity, 108, 109
impartiality, 107, 241
indemnity, 110
independence of compliance, 84
individual rulings, 94
informal organisational subordination, 14
informal structures, 14
infringement, 32, 88–90, 95, 97, 221, 266
inherent risk, 99
insolvency, 19, 105, 106, 114, 136
inspection processes, 121
institutions of public trust, 126
instructions, 6, 135, 137, 140, 249, 251, 262, 271, 286
insurance companies, 45, 140
intellectual property, 86, 88–97, 159
intellectual property rights, 86, 88–97, 159
internal company statutes, 14
internal control, 77, 100, 115, 116, 118, 127, 149, 227, 239, 259

internal hierarchy, 3
internal normative acts, 1, 5, 35, 79, 80, 95, 146, 149, 154, 192, 232, 234, 247, 249, 263, 267, 309
internal norms, 77, 125, 166, 179, 220, 261, 262, 264, 275
internal procedures, 111, 116, 134, 167, 192, 221, 224, 229, 241, 244, 278
international corporations, 30, 44, 68, 143, 172
internationalisation, 25, 37, 44
international law firms, 23
international transactions, 106
international treaties, 94
interpretation, 13, 22, 49–51, 56, 64, 73, 194, 250, 252, 257, 258, 267, 269, 273, 275–283, 288, 300
intra-corporate norms, 17, 21, 46, 47, 104, 139, 163, 234, 245, 274, 277, 305
invalidity of contracts, 101
investigation, 44, 118, 197, 199, 204, 210, 211, 246
investment funds, 140, 239
IP risks, 84
irregularities, 1, 8, 10, 11, 60, 87, 118, 122, 131, 142, 143, 148, 151, 152, 163, 164, 186, 187, 193, 197, 202, 204, 205, 208, 209, 212–214, 217, 218, 236, 239, 240, 242–247, 251, 252, 261, 264, 306

J
judgments, 107, 108, 114, 166, 291, 294
judicial decisions, 107
judicial institutions, 107
judicial redress, 94

K
KYP, 93

L
legal cultures, 1, 3, 6, 7, 9, 13, 26, 27, 59, 61, 73, 82, 88, 92–94, 196, 197, 257, 260, 263, 264, 266, 268, 269, 271–273, 280, 288, 300
legal orders, 48, 154
legal provisions, 12, 31, 220
legislation, 10, 11, 16, 72, 102, 118, 144, 156, 163, 165, 168, 176, 185, 208, 241, 248, 307, 308
legislative technique, 25, 30, 31, 34, 309
legislators, 4
liabilities, 18, 112, 167, 200, 207, 213
licenses, 91, 92
lobbying, 8, 150, 189, 274
local law, 15, 22, 69, 70, 218
losses, 18, 89, 98, 100, 136, 142, 144, 156, 166, 207–209, 217, 221, 265, 266

M
Management Board, 80
management decisions, 15, 47, 80, 228
management information, 70, 78, 81, 238
managerial positions, 86
manuals, 6, 35, 78, 96, 121, 194, 224, 251, 271
marketing campaigns, 91, 97
marketing materials, 96
market regulators, 8, 23, 54, 55, 60, 66, 71, 127, 177, 250, 274
matrix management structures, 64
measurements, 122, 123, 265

media, 62, 97, 98, 124, 135, 136, 186, 200, 208, 261, 268, 274, 294, 304
mediation instruments, 110
meta-norms, 4, 80, 120, 123, 269
mitigation techniques, 111
money laundering, 17, 58, 83, 86, 124, 132–134, 148, 155–157, 160, 165, 221, 240, 263, 271
monopoly, 38
morality, 12, 182, 295, 296
moral order, 296
multinational companies, 72, 219, 272

N
nationalisation, 101, 112
national security, 104
New Capital, 74, 128, 147, 168
NGOs, 8
non-compliance, 17, 53, 74, 80, 89, 96, 115, 117, 120, 121, 128, 139, 143, 144, 146, 153–156, 159, 160, 165, 167, 198, 227, 232, 234, 242, 245, 246, 266, 269, 276, 289, 305, 307, 309
non-contractual obligations, 87–90, 100
non-contradiction, 20, 30–32, 292
non-financial institutions, 3
normative environment, 1, 4, 22, 29, 30, 42, 65, 68, 158, 187, 191, 192, 196, 266, 294
normative order, 20, 25, 58, 74, 84, 158, 183, 184, 279, 296, 297
normative rules, 182
normative systems, 6, 10, 26, 36, 37, 45, 48, 81, 116, 163, 164, 177, 181, 184, 257, 294, 295, 299, 310
norm-makers, 9

INDEX   353

norms, 1–15, 17, 19, 20, 22, 24–27, 29–37, 39–54, 56, 57, 59, 61–69, 71–73, 75, 77, 79–83, 85, 87, 89, 91, 94, 100, 101, 103, 104, 107, 109, 111, 114, 116–118, 120, 121, 125–127, 130–132, 134, 135, 138, 139, 141, 143–145, 149, 152–155, 159, 160, 163–166, 169, 170, 174, 177–189, 191–194, 196, 200, 207, 208, 211, 214, 215, 217–222, 225, 229–235, 242, 243, 246–254, 258–264, 266–269, 271–273, 275–296, 298–305, 307–311
Norms, 45
norm-setters, 31
norm-setting, 2, 8, 35, 41, 43–45, 75, 85, 87, 164, 245, 249, 263–266, 300, 304, 306, 307, 309, 311

O

omnipresent law, 183, 184
operational risk, 100, 117, 119, 123, 127, 128, 148, 149, 156, 269, 306, 308
optimization, 41, 229
organisational structures, 18, 53, 54, 58, 64, 65, 128, 145–148, 154, 155, 242, 243, 260
ownership structure, 21, 39, 133

P

patents, 88, 91
penalties, 18, 86, 142–144, 174, 195, 201, 202, 204, 205, 207–210, 228, 232, 262
permits, 111, 224, 241, 287

personal data, 16, 46, 68, 72, 88, 125, 134, 141, 155, 219, 223, 228–230, 252, 263
pluralistic legal theories, 24
policies, 6, 35, 44, 71, 74, 76, 79, 103, 114, 123, 129, 130, 137, 140, 145, 153, 219–222, 224, 232, 238, 243, 249, 260, 262, 269, 307, 308
practitioners, 24, 25, 49, 279, 284
principles, 2, 5, 6, 14, 27, 30, 32, 34, 40, 47, 55, 66, 70, 80, 123, 131, 132, 140, 149, 163, 166, 180, 181, 185, 198, 222, 231, 238, 247, 249, 254, 263, 267, 270, 272, 278, 289, 292, 295, 297, 305, 308, 309, 311
privileges, 108
procedures, 60, 65, 74–76, 79, 95, 96, 102, 103, 105–107, 111, 117–119, 122, 123, 129–131, 133, 136–138, 144, 148, 152, 153, 164, 167, 187, 189, 194, 196, 197, 203, 204, 206, 210, 211, 219–221, 224–227, 232, 233, 239, 241, 243–245, 251, 260–263, 269, 271, 272, 276, 277, 306–308
profitability, 110
prudential norms, 12
public entities, 54, 86, 100–110, 112, 114, 124, 125, 133, 137
public procurement, 102, 103, 129

R

RAG system, 99
recognition rule, 182, 283
recommendations, 2, 5, 6, 22, 31–33, 43, 51, 55–57, 59, 63,

67–69, 74, 75, 81, 99, 100, 109, 115, 116, 122, 126, 135, 141, 142, 144–147, 150, 152, 154, 166, 180, 185, 187, 191, 198, 204, 212, 213, 231, 239, 247, 252–254, 262, 271–275, 277, 298, 299, 301, 303
regulated sectors, 4
regulations, 1, 3–7, 10–14, 18–20, 23, 25, 26, 30, 31, 34–36, 40, 43–46, 48, 51, 53, 55–59, 61, 62, 64–73, 76, 79, 81, 83, 85, 95, 101–107, 111, 112, 119–122, 125, 126, 129, 130, 132–135, 138–140, 143, 144, 146–150, 152, 154, 155, 159, 161, 163–166, 168, 170–172, 174–180, 185–192, 194, 199, 211, 212, 214, 217, 218, 220, 221, 224, 225, 227, 228, 230–232, 234, 236, 237, 239, 243, 246, 249, 252, 254, 257–260, 262–265, 267, 268, 270–272, 275, 277–279, 288, 290, 293–295, 297, 306, 307, 309
Regulations, 34
regulators, 4, 6, 15, 20–22, 41, 48, 56, 58, 63, 64, 67, 68, 70, 71, 75, 77, 84, 99, 120, 124, 125, 127, 134, 140–145, 147, 150, 154, 161, 166, 167, 193, 195, 198, 199, 201, 202, 205, 208, 216, 219, 221, 227, 234, 239, 242, 244, 246, 259, 261, 262, 266, 268, 271, 278, 283, 304, 309
regulatory environment, 4, 6, 15, 29, 48, 56, 58, 62, 67, 68, 85, 178, 233, 247
regulatory norms, 127, 143, 177
regulatory pressures, 8
regulatory processes, 43

reliability, 119, 120, 128, 145, 211, 292, 307
remuneration, 14
renegotiations, 110
repayment, 108, 195, 213
reporting, 9, 14, 15, 47, 71, 75, 76, 95, 99, 120, 123, 131, 133, 139, 143, 147, 152, 156, 160, 165, 172, 173, 176, 177, 218, 223, 242, 250, 262, 270, 278, 309
reporting lines, 14, 15, 76, 242
reporting regime, 123
reports, 23, 57, 71, 76, 81, 95, 98–100, 117, 119, 120, 123, 131, 144, 152, 160, 173, 189, 197, 198, 201, 204–207, 211, 212, 225, 230, 231, 238, 242, 244, 245, 251, 268, 270, 271, 277, 278, 290, 299
reputation risk, 19, 68, 92, 93, 98, 115, 135, 263, 277
residual risk, 99
reviews, 5, 76, 115, 153, 187, 204, 206, 207, 238, 244, 271
risk acceptance, 115
risk management, 4, 15, 43, 51, 54, 68, 74–76, 78, 79, 83, 85–87, 93, 96, 98, 100, 104, 113, 114, 116, 120, 122, 123, 127–129, 135, 138, 147–150, 153, 154, 156, 158, 167, 169, 194, 210, 218, 221, 227, 228, 233, 251, 252, 261, 263, 265, 276, 286, 308
rule of law, 30, 274
rules, 1, 2, 5, 6, 12, 13, 16, 31–35, 37, 40, 43, 44, 47, 48, 50, 51, 55, 56, 65, 69, 71, 81, 82, 88, 97, 100, 102–106, 109, 110, 115, 117, 119, 123, 128–132, 134, 136–141, 143, 145, 146, 153, 155, 159, 165, 166, 169,

171, 176, 178–182, 188, 189, 198, 199, 202–204, 212, 215, 219, 221, 224–226, 228, 230, 231, 233, 234, 238–240, 246, 247, 249–252, 254, 257, 262, 266, 270, 272, 273, 278–282, 286, 289, 290, 292, 295, 300, 301, 308, 309
rules of conduct, 69, 105, 165, 250

S

safety, 60, 155
sanctioned countries, 19, 222, 225
sanctions, 4, 17, 18, 67, 85, 89, 94, 129, 132, 164, 170, 219–225, 240, 265, 267, 292, 293, 310
scoring models, 46
secrecy, 16, 46, 89, 126, 127, 129, 155, 228, 263, 283
self-regulations, 4, 43
self-restriction, 11
settlement, 18, 71, 90, 101, 108, 112, 159, 175, 196, 200, 208–210, 217
shareholders, 1, 6, 43, 54, 62, 65, 136, 145, 146, 155, 180, 186, 254, 259, 266, 268, 274, 288
social expectations, 10, 11, 62, 265
social media, 97
social networking, 37
sovereign debt, 114
sovereign ratings, 114, 137
sovereign risks, 100
sponsoring, 112, 179
stabilization clauses, 109, 110
stakeholders, 6, 20, 62, 103, 254, 266, 305
standards, 12, 35, 38, 40–43, 58, 69, 71, 115, 127, 131, 140, 165–169, 172, 179, 181, 247, 272, 293, 308, 309

state authorities, 109, 111
state-owned companies, 100
statutory authorities, 1, 146
strategies, 6, 41, 71, 205, 209, 250, 254, 297
subsidiaries, 21, 47, 199, 216, 258
supervisory authorities, 1, 4, 55, 56, 60, 67, 85, 142, 143, 148, 161, 165, 185, 194, 196, 197, 199, 211, 236
suspicious events, 133
systemically important financial institutions, 60

T

tax avoidance, 17
tax liabilities, 18, 174
tax obligations, 18, 174
tax transparency, 17, 18
technology, 30, 83, 160
telecommunications, 104
tendering procedure, 103
tender process, 102
terrorism, 132, 157, 165, 222, 290
theory of management, 24
theory of norms, 1, 2, 4, 7, 27, 289–292, 295, 297, 300
think-tanks, 8
three lines of defence, 115
trade guilds, 11, 38
trademarks, 91–94
trading platforms, 37
traditional legislators, 35, 43
traffic lights method, 98
transactions, 11, 18, 19, 23, 38, 44, 53, 69, 79, 82, 83, 91, 94, 100, 101, 106, 108, 122, 124, 126, 128, 131, 132, 140, 155, 157, 158, 165, 168–170, 172, 173, 176, 177, 188–194, 198, 199, 201, 203, 206, 212, 213, 215,

220–223, 225, 230, 231, 235, 239–241, 271, 272, 299, 308
treasury bills, 104, 137

U
ubiquitous law, 183, 184

V
validity, 19, 50, 184, 193, 254, 278, 291, 296, 297

values, 12, 30, 33, 42, 43, 66, 67, 71, 73, 78, 88, 91, 98, 145, 178, 179, 185, 246, 262, 275, 284, 288, 291, 295, 297, 298, 303, 304
value system, 25, 304
violation, 9, 212, 220, 291

W
warranty, 111
watchlists, 132, 133
weaknesses, 123, 239

Printed in Great Britain
by Amazon